The Vets

THE VETS

STEPHEN LEATHER

ISIS
LARGE PRINT
Oxford

Copyright © Stephen Leather, 1993

First published in Great Britain 1993
by
Hodder & Stoughton
A division of Hodder Headline PLC

Published in Large Print 2009 by ISIS Publishing Ltd.,
7 Centremead, Osney Mead, Oxford OX2 0ES
by arrangement with
Hodder & Stoughton
An Hachette Livre UK Company

British Library Cataloguing in Publication Data
Leather, Stephen.
    The vets [text (large print)].
    1. Bank robberies - - China - - Hong Kong - -
    Fiction.
    2. Vietnam War, 1961–1975 - - Veterans - - Fiction.
    3. Hong Kong (China) - - Fiction.
    4. Suspense fiction.
    5. Large type books.
    I. Title
    823.9'14–dc22

ISBN 978–0–7531–8296–3 (hb)
ISBN 978–0–7531–8297–0 (pb)

Printed and bound in Great Britain by
T. J. International Ltd., Padstow, Cornwall

For In-Hei

As he levelled the helicopter off at 3,000 feet above the choppy South China Sea, the pilot marvelled as he always did at the way it managed to stay in the air. The cyclic control stick twitched in his right hand, the collective pitch control lever vibrated in his left, and his feet made small adjustments to the directional control pedals as he headed out to the waiting ship some six miles away in the Gulf of Tonkin. All four of his limbs were needed to keep the helicopter in the air, though he had been flying for so long that he was no longer aware of them as individual movements. He was part of the machine: his nerves and tendons ran from the rotor blades throbbing above his head to the skids below him. He could feel the blades cutting through the night air and the tail rotor fighting against the torque the blades produced, and when he swung the helicopter to the left to make a course correction it was flesh and blood that turned and not metal; he saw only the sea and the sky, not the Plexiglas windows. He scanned his instrument panel, taking in the information from the myriad dials and gauges without reading them in the same way that his skin recorded the chill in the air and his nose picked up the smell of the fuel that had slopped over the fuel tank filler while they were preparing the helicopter at a Special Forces airfield outside Da Nang.

The pilot was alone in the cockpit and the second set of controls in front of the co-pilot's seat moved as if guided by ghostly hands and feet, mirroring his own actions. During his year-long tour of duty with 1st Cav he'd never flown solo on a mission, but Air America did things differently and he hadn't been surprised when he'd been told that he'd be flying alone.

He clicked the microphone trigger switch on his cyclic control stick and identified himself to the target ship which was still some two miles away, bobbing in the sea like a toy boat. He had no problems communicating with the ship on the prearranged VHF frequency and he decreased power to the 1,100 shp Lycoming T53-L-11 turboshaft engine as he made his approach.

It was dusk and there was enough light to see by, but just to be on the safe side he thumbed the switch on the collective pitch control lever which turned on the searchlight mounted under the front of the Huey to give him a better view of the deck of the ship as it bucked and tossed in the waves. A guy with a torch in either hand guided him down until he was hovering just six feet above the heaving deck and then the pilot chose his moment, cut the power and dropped, pulling back the cyclic and dropping the collective at the last moment to cushion the impact as best he could. The guy drew his hand across his throat telling the pilot to cut his engine but he'd already done it and slammed on the rotor brake. More men rushed forward to tie the

Huey down as the pilot removed his flight helmet and put it on the co-pilot's seat.

A man with a blond crew cut, wearing civilian clothes, appeared from somewhere, took the pilot by the upper arm, and guided him below deck to a tiny steel-lined cabin containing a folding bunk and a wooden chair on which was a green file and a plastic mapcase.

"That's your flight plan," said the man. "Anything else you want?" He hadn't introduced himself, nor did he ask to see any identification from the pilot.

"Just water," said the pilot.

He sat down on the bed and studied the maps and papers. A few minutes later the man with the crew cut came back with a glass of water which he handed to the pilot without a word before leaving and closing the door behind him. The pilot took a mouthful of the cold water and then placed the glass on the floor. He looked at the solid gold Rolex on his wrist. It was just before eight o'clock, and according to the flight plan he was due to take off at 2200 hours. The course he was to fly was marked on the map in red, north-west up to the coast near Quang Tri, then due west across Vietnam to the border with Laos. He was to follow the border up twenty klicks and then cut into Laos towards a town which was marked as Muang Xepon. There were no details as to how he was to find the LZ but that was nothing unusual. When you flew for Air America almost everything was on a need-to-know basis. That would explain the missing co-pilot. Presumably one of the passengers would be sitting in the co-pilot's station to help guide him in. The flight would be 275 klicks, 550 klicks there and back, and he'd be carrying four passengers and a small cargo. The standard Huey had a range of about 540 klicks with its 200-gallon capacity but the UH-1E had been fitted with extra fuel tanks and it now had a range closer to 700 klicks. The pilot would have preferred to have refuelled at a Special Forces camp closer to the border but whoever had planned the mission obviously didn't want the chopper on the ground between the ship and its final destination. The take-off would be tricky, but once they'd burned off a few gallons they'd have no problems. It would be a milk run. After the drop in Laos they'd be returning to the ship. The pilot took off his leather shoulder holster and slid out his .25 calibre handgun, checked that it was fully loaded and that the safety was on and put it on the chair. He read through the papers, rechecked the maps, and then lay down on the bunk and stared up at the ceiling, relaxed but not asleep. He pictured an ice cube in his mind, a square block which he allowed gradually to melt until nothing remained but a pool of water which slowly evaporated. His breathing slowed and his pulse rate dropped and his mind was empty. He stayed that way until a sharp knock on the door announced that it was time to go.

The man with the crew cut took him back to the Huey where the restraining ropes were being untied. The pilot carried out his pre-flight checks then strapped himself in to the high-backed armoured seat before checking the positions of the circuit breakers

4

and switches. Satisfied, he looked back over his shoulder to see if there was any sign of his passengers.

Four men were walking towards the Huey. All were dressed in tiger-stripe fatigues and bush hats and had camouflage streaks of green and brown across their faces which blended so well into the material of their uniforms that he couldn't see where skin ended and material began. They walked two abreast, the men in front carrying rifles at the ready, the two behind with their weapons shouldered as they manhandled a heavy metal chest between them. As they got closer the pilot could see the weapons they were carrying. One of the men in front, the thinner of the two, carried a Commando submachine-gun, a variation of the standard M16 infantry rifle, and the man on his right held a Kalashnikov AK-47, the Soviet assault rifle which had become the weapon of choice of the Viet Cong. The pilot wasn't surprised to see the AK-47 in the hands of a Special Forces soldier. They tended to use whatever gear they were comfortable with, and there were obvious advantages of operating with VC equipment in enemy territory. The man who was carrying his end of the chest with his left hand had an M16 slung over his shoulder and what looked to be a sawn-off shotgun hanging from his belt. His companion on the other end of the chest had an M16 and a radio on his back. Apart from the weaponry, there was little to tell the four men apart: all were lean and wiry, all were clean-shaven with no hair showing under the floppy bush hats and all moved with a fluid grace that brought to mind images of lions on the prowl.

The man with the Commando walked around the Huey and pulled himself into the co-pilot's seat and nodded as the pilot handed him a flight helmet. The other three manhandled the chest through the doorway, grunting as they slid it along the metal floor. They climbed in and pulled the sliding door shut behind them.

The pilot pushed in the igniter circuit breaker and prepared to start the turbine. Before he squeezed the trigger switch he became aware of a knocking sound coming from somewhere within the Huey, a tapping that he felt rather than heard. It was like Morse code. Dit-dit-dit daa. Dit-dit-dit daa. Three short taps and a long one. The Morse code signal for V, and also the first notes of Beethoven's Fifth Symphony, being repeated over and over again. He twisted around but he couldn't see where it was coming from. He shrugged and settled back in his seat. As he gave his instruments a quick visual scan he saw that the noise was coming from the man in the co-pilot's seat. His right hand held the Commando barrel up between his legs while his left hand was against the bulkhead. He was tapping, three times with the tips of his fingers, the fourth with the flat of his hand. A sign of nerves, Doherty reckoned, but once he started the T53 turboshaft engine the tapping sounds were lost.

The pilot waited for the exhaust-gas temperature gauge to settle into the green before opening the throttle. He pulled on the collective, increasing the power to the whirling blades and lifting the Huey off the deck before nudging it forward with a push on the cyclic. The Huey was sluggish, loaded down as it was with the extra fuel, and the pilot took it up slowly to 3,000 feet. It was a cloudless night and a full moon hung in the sky and the pilot could see clear to the horizon.

Forty minutes later they flew over a narrow strip of beach and above the jungle which shone blackly in the moonlight. The pilot took the Huey up another thousand feet. The thinner air meant he'd burn fuel up faster but they had plenty in reserve. He followed the course on the map he'd been given, climbing way above the mountain ranges where VC snipers were prone to take pot-shots at passing helicopters, no matter how high they were. There was no indication of where Vietnam ended and Laos began but the pilot knew that two hours after leaving the ship he'd crossed over whatever border existed. The knife-edged ridges far below were no different from the mountain ranges in the west of Vietnam and he knew that the Viet Cong criss-crossed the border as if it didn't exist. The map meant nothing, in the air or on the ground.

The pilot felt a touch on his arm and turned to see the man in the co-pilot's seat mouthing to him. He reached over and showed him how to operate the microphone trigger switch on the cyclic.

"Can you take it down?" he said, the voice crackling in the pilot's ear.

"Sure," he said, dropping the collective pitch and nosing the Huey down with the cyclic. He levelled off a thousand feet or so above the jungle while the passenger peered out of the window.

"What are you looking for?" asked the pilot.

"A river," said the man. "A river shaped like a heart. It's within fifteen klicks of that range." He pointed to a steep rocky outcrop which speared through the jungle like an accusing finger.

"It's not on the map," said the pilot.

The man ignored him and kept looking out of the side window. "Lower," he said.

The pilot eased the Huey down until it was about 200 feet above the treetops.

"There she is," said the man, pointing.

"Got it," said the pilot, turning the Huey towards the thin ribbon of water. It did look like an oddly stretched heart, as if the river had lost its sense of direction for a few miles and almost turned in a circle before realising its mistake.

"Go as low as you can," said the passenger. "There's a clearing about one klick from the base of the heart."

As the pilot guided the Huey down he saw a light flash on the ground, then another.

"See the lights?" said the passenger.

"I see them," replied the pilot.

"Land between them."

The pilot put the Huey in a hover about ten feet above the thick grass of the clearing while he checked for obstructions as best he could. Seeing none, he reduced the power and put the skids softly on the ground. There was no sign of whoever had been holding the flashlights that had guided them in.

The passenger clicked the intercom on. "We'll be gone for about five minutes, not much longer. Keep the blades turning in case we have to leave in a hurry."

The passenger pulled off his flight helmet. He left it on the floor as he climbed out of the Huey. His hair was blond, cut close to his skull, and it gleamed in the moonlight. The pilot felt the Huey shudder as the cargo door was opened and he turned to watch the men haul the chest out. The four men moved cautiously towards the treeline as the rotor blades beat the air above their heads. They bent down like grunts always did, fearful that the blades would take off their heads, even though there was more than enough room. You'd have to be a basketball player leaping in the air to stand a chance of being hit by the main rotor. The tail rotor was a different matter; the pilot had seen two grunts killed by running the wrong way when leaving a Huey. The rotor was a fraction of the size of the one on top but it was the perfect height for taking off a man's head.

The four men disappeared into the undergrowth leaving the pilot feeling suddenly alone. He shivered and leant back in his seat, filling his mind with the melting ice cube. If there was a VC out in the jungle with his name on a bullet there was nothing he could do about it. He blocked out thoughts of what might be and concentrated on the cold, wet ice.

A firefly sparked to his left, a red dot that glowed briefly and then was gone. Ice. Melting ice. Another spark, then another. He ignored them. A fourth appeared but this didn't disappear, it moved in a straight line, blinking on and off. The pilot realised with a jolt that it wasn't a flying insect but a light in the far distance, the blinking effect caused by it passing behind trees. He killed the lights on his instrument panel and widened his eyes, trying to calculate the distance between him and the lights as they came down the hill. One klick? Maybe two? Maybe closer. He swung around and looked anxiously at the vegetation at the edge of the clearing. There was no sign of the men. He put his hand on the butt of the gun in his shoulder holster, the metal warm to the touch. He could fire a warning shot, but that was just as likely to attract the attention of whoever was on the hillside as it was to bring the Special Forces guys back. But he had no other way of getting in touch with them, they hadn't told him the frequency their radio operated on. He took his hand off the gun and rubbed his face. The lights were getting closer. There were three of them. As he watched, the lights disappeared one by one.

The rule was that the pilot stayed with the slick, but he couldn't face sitting in the Huey waiting for whoever it was to arrive. He had to do something. He had to warn them and get the hell out. He peered up the hillside. No more lights. He could picture them moving in the darkness, crouching low with AK-47s in their hands, black pyjamas and wide, conical hats. He shuddered.

He slapped the cyclic stick in frustration and swore before climbing down from the Huey and running towards the area where he'd last seen the men take the chest. He hated the jungle with a vengeance. The only time he felt comfortable with it was when he was looking down on it from a great height. Long, scratchy things clawed at his shirt as if they were alive, and damp fronds wrapped themselves around his face as if they wanted to squeeze the life out of him. Something squelched under his foot but it was too dark to see what it was. He stopped and listened but all he could hear was the whup-whup of the Huey behind him. He pushed on through the undergrowth, feeling his way with his gloved hands in front of his face. He heard water only seconds before he splashed into a stream which came up to his knees. It was slow-moving and no danger but it was uncomfortable. He thought of leeches and river snakes and waded through quickly, slipping once on a wet rock.

In the distance he saw a yellowish glow and he moved towards it, praying that it was the Special Forces team and not another group of Viet Cong. He slowed down as he came closer to the light, and peered around a massive tree trunk around which wound thick vines, like varicose veins on an old woman's leg. He saw the young man with the Commando and was just about to shout to attract his attention when something stopped him. The Commando was levelled at a group of what the pilot guessed were Laotian mercenaries, dark-skinned men with high cheekbones and narrow eyes, some with AK-47s, others with wicked-looking machetes. There were about a dozen, some of them little more than children carrying weapons that were almost as big as they were. The three other Special Forces men were facing the mercenaries, spaced so that they couldn't be cut down with one burst of automatic fire.

In between the two groups were three hemp sacks lined up on the ground next to a small campfire which was clearly the source of the glow he had seen when he entered the jungle. One of the Laotians was kneeling by the middle sack and cutting a small hole in it with a curved knife. He dug the blade into the sack and it came out with white powder on the end. He carefully carried it over to the man with the Commando, one hand held under the knife to catch any spillage. The American licked his finger, scraped it along the white-powdered blade, and licked the tip. He nodded to the other Special Forces men, a white smile breaking through the painted face.

The pilot couldn't take his eyes off the scene that was being played out in front of him, even though he knew the danger from the men on the hill was growing by the minute. The Laotian sheathed his knife and walked over to the chest standing about six feet or so in front of the two men who'd carried it. They stepped back, their guns in the ready position, as the mercenary leaned down to open it. Two more of the mercenaries moved forward to stand either side of him. From where he was standing behind the tree, the pilot couldn't see what was in the chest. He slowly went down on all fours and crept along the damp jungle floor, moving slowly and taking great care where he put his hands, until he reached a tree with thick, rubbery leaves. He hugged its trunk and peered around. He now was looking at the backs of the Laotians, and through their legs he could see inside the open chest. Blocks of metal gleamed in the light of the flickering fire. The mercenary who had opened the sack bent down and picked up one of the blocks. He had to use both hands, and even from thirty feet away the pilot knew it could only be gold. He knew he was seeing something more than a simple "need-to-know" CIA operation. The Special Forces men were about to swap the gold for drugs and the Huey was to fly the drugs back to the ship. The pilot was confused. He'd heard of Air America planes being used to ferry drugs around for the Thai drug barons as a way of getting them to help in the fight against the VC, but what he was seeing was something different. The Americans were paying for the drugs, with gold; it wasn't a case of doing a favour for the Laotians or supplying them with cash or arms. This was a straightforward drug deal he was witnessing.

For the first time he became aware of another group of Laotians standing further behind and to the right of the mercenaries on the edge of the circle of warm light cast by the fire. The group was composed of women and very small children. One of the women held a baby in her arms and she was making small shushing noises to keep it from crying. Whereas the men were dressed in khaki combat fatigues, the women and children wore brightly coloured clothes made from red, green, yellow and blue striped material, the girls in skirts, the small boys in leggings. The women had their hair tied back and were wearing strips of cloth wound around their heads like badly tied turbans.

The pilot wanted to shout a warning to the Americans, to tell them that they had to go, but he was unsure how they'd react to him being there. The decision was made for him when the American with the Commando fired at the three Laotians standing by the chest, cutting them down before they had a chance to raise their weapons. The three other Americans fired almost immediately afterwards and bullets ripped through the foliage near where the pilot was standing. Those mercenaries who weren't killed outright were screaming in pain, flowers of blood spreading across their fatigues. The women and children made as if to move forward to help their men but one of the women, old with shrivelled skin and no teeth, shouted to them and waved them back. The pilot reached for the automatic pistol in his shoulder holster but didn't draw it out. What could he do? Shoot the Americans? Plead with them to stop the slaughter? Tell them he'd report them when they got back to the ship? None of the choices was viable. He let the butt slide from his sweating fingers. The women and children turned and ran, stumbling and tripping in their panic. The four Americans fired together, raking the Laotians with a hail of bullets, the individual weapons making separate identifiable sounds but the end result was the same: women and children falling to the ground and dying.

A gasp escaped involuntarily from the pilot's mouth and he tasted bitter vomit at the back of his throat. His ears were hurting from the sound of the guns and even when the firing stopped they were still ringing, making it hard to think. The humid night air was thick with the smell of cordite and hot metal. The two men who'd carried the chest from the Huey ran over to it and closed the lid. The guy with the Commando shouted something and one of the men went to the dead Laotian with the knife and kicked him over on to his back, searching the ground until he found the gold bar he'd picked up before he died. The bar was returned to the chest and the lid lowered. As two of the men lifted the chest, one of them looked in the pilot's direction. He pointed and the pilot flinched as if he'd been fired at. While watching the massacre he'd stepped away from the tree without realising it and now he could clearly be seen in the firelight. His feet felt as if they were rooted to the ground. The man with the Commando stepped forward, walking slowly with the barrel of his gun lowered. He stopped when he was about thirty feet away from the pilot, his face in darkness because the fire was behind him. The pilot couldn't see his face but he could feel the man's eyes boring into him. He could hear the blood pounding through his veins and feel the sweat clinging to his forehead. He knew he had never been so close to death and that everything depended on how he reacted. He dropped his hands to his sides and gave a half shrug as if nothing mattered. The man with the Commando stood stock still, his feet planted shoulder width apart, his left side slightly closer to the pilot than his right, the perfect shooting position. The barrel of the gun was still pointed at the ground. The pilot widened his smile. He knew that his face was clearly visible in the firelight, that they could see his every expression.

The man's upper body appeared to relax as if he'd come to a decision and the pilot let out a sigh of relief. He was about to step forward when the Commando swung. The pilot dived without thinking, throwing himself to his left and rolling on the ground before scrambling away into the undergrowth. He didn't look back so he didn't see the muzzle flashes but he felt the air crack as bullets passed within inches of his head. He ran by instinct, dodging trees before they loomed out of the darkness, avoiding vines on the ground without seeing them, jumping the stream without getting wet, as if his subconscious mind had recorded every step of his journey through the jungle and was now replaying it in reverse because it knew that if it made one wrong move he'd be dead. His breath came in ragged bursts and his arms pumped up and down as he ran, his eyes wide with fear, his muscles screaming in agony as his feet pounded on the jungle floor.

He burst out of the jungle into the clearing and ran headlong towards the Huey, throwing himself into the pilot's seat and pulling on the collective before he'd even sat down. The turbine whined and the blades speeded up until they were a blurred circle above his head. Relieved of the weight of its four passengers and cargo it soared almost vertically out of the clearing. From the corner of his eye he saw the four Special Forces men tear out of the undergrowth and point their guns at him. Red dots streamed past the Huey and up into the night and he heard a series of bangs behind him, thuds of metal against metal. He waggled his directional pedals frantically, jerking the slick from left to right to make himself less of a target, all the time increasing the power to the rotors to give it extra lift.

It was only when the altimeter showed 2,000 feet that he relaxed. He put the Huey into a hover while he considered his next move. He pushed the right pedal and nudged the cyclic to the right and pointed the nose of the Huey east, towards Vietnam. A thousand thoughts crowded into his head, all seeking attention, but they were dulled by the conflicting emotions he felt: horror at what he'd seen, guilt for not doing anything to stop it, anger at the men behind the massacre, terror at being hunted, fear of what would happen to him when he got back to the ship. If he got back. He took deep breaths and tried to focus his thoughts, to bring some sort of order to his bewildered mind. When it happened it happened suddenly, without him knowing, the way water freezes, turning from liquid to solid so quickly that there is no borderline between the two states. One moment he was in total confusion, the next he knew with perfect clarity what he would do.

He pushed the cyclic to the left and pressed the left foot pedal, swinging the Huey round and losing height because he didn't increase power, until the helicopter was pointing in the opposite direction, due west. He hovered for a moment, steadying his breathing, concentrating on the block of ice in his mind, feeling the helicopter react to the small, almost imperceptible, movements of his hands and feet, absorbing the data from the instruments. He sighed, a deep mournful emptying of his lungs, then pulled on the collective and pushed the cyclic forward. The turbine roared and the

Huey jumped forward as if eager to go. Within minutes the pilot had the Huey up to its maximum speed of 138 mph, flying low and level, just above the treetops, as the ice block slowly melted to cool, clear water.

The rain had caught Paris by surprise and many of those walking down the Champs-Elysées on pre-Christmas shopping trips were shivering damply as they looked in the store windows. The weather forecast had been for a mild day, sunny even, and the Parisians were accustomed to taking the forecasters at their word. Anthony Chung trusted no one's judgment other than his own, however, and he'd worn his black mohair coat after scrutinising the steely grey morning sky from the window of his penthouse flat in Rue de Sèvres. He wore a slightly smug expression as he walked out of the Charles de Gaulle Etoile Métro station and into the fierce rain-spotted wind that blew up the thoroughfare from Place de la Concorde.

He walked by shops packed with some of the best names in European fashion: Guy Laroche, Louis Vuitton, Christian Dior, Nina Ricci; but above them, atop the centuries-old buildings, were the signs of the new economic masters of the world: Toshiba, NEC, and Ricoh. Even in France, one of the most chauvinistic of countries, the Japanese displayed their dominance. Chung looked around for evidence of America's encroachment on to the Parisian scene. To his left he saw a McDonald's outlet and less than a hundred yards further down a Burger King and garish posters promoting *Le Whopper*, *Les Frites*, and *Le Milk Shake*.

There was a message there somewhere, thought Chung as he walked down towards Fouquet's, on the corner where Avenue George V met the Champs-Elysées. He looked at his watch. It was eleven-thirty. The watch, a gold Cartier, had been a present from his father almost ten years earlier on the day he'd graduated from the Sorbonne. Thoughts of his father crowded into his mind and he pushed them away, concentrating instead on the American he was to meet. Colonel Joel Tyler. An ex-colonel, if the truth be told, but Tyler was a man who insisted on using the title and, bearing in mind the business he was in, it was understandable.

Chung crossed the busy Champs-Elysées looking left and right because he knew that the Parisians paid little heed to the colour of the traffic lights or the location of pedestrians. The traffic was heavier than normal as shoppers poured in from the suburbs to buy last-minute Christmas presents for their families and friends. It would be even busier at night, Chung knew, when the millions of tiny white lights would come alive in the leaf-bare chestnut trees of the avenue and the sidewalks would be packed with sightseers and lovers. He pushed open the doors to the café, nodded at a white-coated waiter and went over to a table. He shrugged off his coat and draped it over one of the wicker and cane chairs, looking at his watch again. Five minutes to go. He placed a copy of the *International Herald Tribune* on the table and then sat down, smoothing the creases on the trousers of his 2,000 dollar suit. He ordered a hot chocolate from a grey-haired waiter and smiled at the man's look of professional disdain. Chung never failed to be amused by the cultured arrogance of French waiters, or by the raised eyebrows when they heard his fluency in their language. The bottom half of the windows were obscured with thick red velvet curtains on brass rods so he couldn't see out into the street. Fouquet's was not the sort of place where you went to rubberneck like a tourist; everyone knew that the power was inside, not outside on the pavements looking in. Each time the door opened Chung would look up, but he cursed himself for doing so, for appearing to be over-eager. He looked at his watch again. The American was five minutes late and Chung tut-tutted under his breath. Punctuality was not a gift or an ability inherited from one's parents, it was something that had to be worked at. Chung always made it a point to be on time for appointments; to do otherwise, his father had always said, was to be discourteous to the person you were to meet. Chung picked up the paper and idly read the headlines, but there was nothing in its American-orientated news that interested him and he threw it back down on the table. When he looked up again it was into a pair of cold blue eyes that rapidly crinkled into a smile. The face that looked down on Chung was thin, almost skeletal, and with its prominent hooked nose it reminded him of a leathery-skinned bird. A hawk maybe. Yes, Chung decided, there was a lot of the hawk about Colonel Joel Tyler. Chung had the man's photograph in the inside pocket of his coat, but there was no need to check it against the original, there could be no mistaking the short-cropped steel grey hair, the beak-like nose or the small white scar over the right eyebrow. He pushed back the chair and got to his feet. Chung was tall for a Chinese, a fraction under six feet, but he had to look up to meet Tyler's gaze as they shook hands. He felt Tyler's eyes move quickly over his body, taking in the suit, the watch, the shoes, putting together a snap mental assessment, and the grip tightened as if he was checking his strength. Chung held Tyler's gaze and his grip, matching them like for like until the American grinned, relaxed his handshake and then withdrew his hand.

"Mr Chung," he said quietly.

"Colonel Tyler, thank you for coming," said Chung, and waved him to a chair. A waiter appeared at his side while Tyler wound his wiry frame into the chair opposite Chung. Tyler ordered a black coffee, in English.

"Your room is comfortable?" Chung asked.

"It's fine. I always like the George V," Tyler replied. "Though, on balance, I think I prefer the Hotel Crillon or the Lancaster."

Chung smiled and sipped at his chocolate. The waiter returned with Tyler's coffee. The American dropped in two lumps of sugar and slowly stirred it. A steel Rolex Submariner appeared from under the cuff of his shirt. Tyler was wearing a brown checked sports jacket, a dark brown wool shirt and black slacks, not too expensive, not too flashy, and Chung realised it was camouflage, as much of a way of keeping out of sight in the city as the green fatigues the soldier had worn in the jungles of South-East Asia. Tyler watched Chung as he stirred, through eyes which rarely blinked. Chung knew he had the American's undivided attention. "Everything is on schedule?" Chung asked.

Tyler nodded. "I leave for the States tomorrow, and I should be in Thailand in early April to assemble the team."

"You have the men picked out already?"

"Some. Not all. But there won't be any problems. I'll do the final selection myself in Vietnam. My immediate concern is the helicopter and the armaments."

"I thought you already had the helicopter?"

"The helicopter, yes. But I've spoken to a technical expert who tells me that it's going to need more work than I'd anticipated."

Chung frowned. "How much work?"

Tyler lifted his coffee cup. "A new engine and gearbox. Minimum." He drank two deep mouthfuls while Chung took in the news.

"That doesn't sound good," said Chung.

"Actually it's not a problem. I've a contact in the Philippines who can put me in touch with a supplier. The Philippine military has more than eighty Bell 205A-1s and UH-1Hs and the corruption there has to be seen to be believed. I'll have no problem buying the parts."

Chung didn't bother asking how much it would cost. He had paid half a million dollars into a Swiss bank account to cover all expenses. He took a thin, white envelope from his jacket and handed it to the American.

"Here is the name and address of a man in Bangkok who will arrange to have the helicopter shipped to Hong Kong. All you have to do is tell him where it is. He'll do the rest. He'll have it put in a container and shipped over. It'll take two weeks at most. He'll arrange payments to the Customs officials at both ends." Tyler smiled at the way Chung said "payments". Both men knew that they were talking about bribes. He put the envelope, unopened, into his jacket pocket. "Also in there are the details of a contact in Hong Kong, the man who will arrange for your weapons," Chung continued. "His name is Michael Wong and he's the leader of one of Hong Kong's smaller triads. Get in touch with him once you've arrived." He took out a leather-bound notebook and a slim gold pen and slid them over the table to Tyler. "It would save time if you gave me a list of your main requirements now. It is possible to buy anything in Hong Kong, but some things take longer than others."

Chung drank the rest of his chocolate while Tyler wrote with firm, clear strokes. When Tyler finished he snapped the notebook shut and handed it back. "I think that just about covers it," said Chung. "Does anything else come to mind? I will be uncontactable for the next five months."

"I realise that," said Tyler. "No, I think everything is under control." He unwound himself out of the chair and waited for Chung to get to his feet. They shook hands firmly. "So, the next time we meet will be in Hong Kong," said Tyler.

"And we'll both be considerably richer," said Chung. The two men laughed and then Chung watched as the American left. He sat down and automatically smoothed the creases from his trousers again. The waiter hovered at his shoulder and Chung ordered another hot chocolate, in French. While he waited for it to arrive he opened the notebook and studied the American's list.

Barton Lewis drove his car on autopilot as he headed south on Interstate 95, towards Washington. He stayed in the inside lane and barely noticed the traffic which streamed by him. His hands tightened on the steering wheel as some of the doctor's words played over and over in his head. They were words which he could barely pronounce, but they spelled out a death sentence. Words like fiberoptic gastroscopy, endoscopic biopsies, gastric carcinoma. Words that meant cancer. Two tumours, the doctor had said, one in the stomach, one in the pancreas. It wasn't what Lewis had expected when he'd gone to the clinic to complain about stomach pains and an uncharacteristic loss of appetite. At worst he'd expected to be told it was an ulcer. Cancer meant rapid weight loss, half-dead skeletons in hospital beds plugged into drip feeds, children with bald heads and sunken eyes. Cancer didn't apply to an overweight black man who used to tuck away three Big Macs at one sitting and still went back for apple pie. Hell, he'd been putting weight on, not losing it.

A blue Pontiac came rushing at him from a slip road and Lewis slowed to let it in front. He was in no rush.

24

The pancreatic tumour was inoperable, the doctor had said. No chemotherapy. No radiation therapy. Just increasing pain and eventual death.

Lewis wiped the back of his hand across his forehead. God, he wanted his wife so much. He still thought of her as his wife, even though the divorce had been finalised over a year ago and she was now living in Boston with a computer programmer in his four-bedroom town house. He wanted her with him, wanted to put his head on her shoulder and have her caress the back of his neck and have her tell him that everything was going to be okay.

That was one of the reasons the marriage had gone sour, she'd told him. She said that he depended on her too much, that at times it was as if she were mother to two children. She said she couldn't cope with the restless nights, his bad dreams, the temper tantrums, the flashbacks. She'd said she'd met somebody else and that was the end of it. The court gave her half the apartment, half the car, and all of Victor. Now he was alone. Alone and dying. A horn sounded behind him and he looked in his rearview mirror. A truck was sitting on his tail, and he saw that his speed had dropped to forty mph. He accelerated away from it.

Lewis had been having irregular stomach pains for more than a year but had been putting it down to too much junk food after his wife had left him. He hadn't bothered cooking for himself — hell, he hadn't known how to, he'd just snacked at McDonald's or Burger King or Kentucky Fried Chicken — and when his stomach had felt bad he'd taken a slug of

Pepto-Bismol. He should have gone to the clinic earlier, even though the doctor had said it would have made little difference.

Lewis had asked how long he had left and the doctor hadn't pulled his punches. Probably six months. Possibly a year. Eighteen months absolute maximum. The doctor had prescribed painkillers for the intermittent pain but warned that they wouldn't be effective for long. Eventually he'd have to be hospitalised. The doctor had suggested he get his affairs in order, spend time with his family and friends, make his peace. Treat the death sentence as an opportunity to put his life in order.

He reached the Capitol and managed to find a parking space on Constitution Avenue between a shiny black Cadillac and a white Dodge. Lewis had visited the Vietnam War Memorial once before, in June of 1991, when he'd been in Washington for the Desert Storm celebrations. He'd visited it but hadn't managed to get close to the wall because it was obliterated by tourists in T-shirts and shorts clicking away with cameras and chattering inanely.

Spend time with your family and friends, the doctor had said. The only family he had now was Victor, and that was only on one weekend in four. And the best friends he had were dead. That's why he'd driven from Baltimore to Washington. To spend time with them. Just like the doctor ordered. As he locked the door to his Saab two men and a girl jogged by, talking and laughing as they ran. They were followed by a middle-aged man, balding and with unsteady, flabby legs, whose training shoes slapped on the ground with an irregular rhythm. His running vest was wet with sweat and his shorts were too tight around the tops of his legs and his breath was coming hard and fast. He was wearing a Sony Walkman with bright yellow headphones and his eyes had the glazed look of a tortured animal. Lewis stopped to watch the man wobble past. They were probably about the same age, he thought. What the hell was he keeping fit for? Why was he bothering? It didn't matter how many press-ups you did or how much you ran. When you died, you died. The cancer grows and kills you, the heart goes into spasm, the blood vessels burst, the body dies. Lewis wanted to call after the man, to tell him that he was wasting his time, that he should take it easy and enjoy what little life he had left.

He didn't. He walked across the grass towards the memorial. He could see that there were far fewer visitors gathered around the slabs than there had been on his last visit. He went first to the bronze sculpture at the side of the memorial, three life-size grunts, war-weary and carrying their weapons as if they'd marched a long way. One of the three figures was black, and it looked uncannily like Lewis had done when he was in Nam: short, curly hair, squarish face, medium build, an M16 in his left hand, a towel slung around his neck to soak up perspiration. Yeah, thought Lewis. That was then. Now he'd put on another twenty-eight pounds, most of it around his waist, and the taut neck muscles had become flabby, giving him the jowls of an old bloodhound. The hair was longer, but greying at the temples and not as curly. It was tired, like the rest of him. But it was nothing compared to what the cancer would eventually do to his body, he was sure of that. He shuddered and turned away from the evocative sculpture.

To the left of the cobbled path which led down to the memorial were a number of metal lecterns containing bound volumes protected from the weather by perspex shields. He flicked through one of the volumes with his left hand and took a leaflet on cancer which the doctor had given him and a pen from the inside pocket of his sports jacket. There were six names he wanted, all of them childhood pals from Baltimore, kids he'd grown up with, played games with, stolen cars with, back in the days when he thought stealing was a game and that he was too smart to get caught.

The book was an alphabetical list of all those whose names were carved into the black marble, along with details of the city they came from, their rank, unit, and date of birth. The six weren't the only friends that Lewis had lost in Vietnam, but they were the ones he missed the most because they were part of his childhood, a time when he had truly been happy despite the poverty and deprivation of Baltimore. He carefully wrote down the slab and line numbers of the six names, then walked along the path to the memorial. The slabs were all the same width but they started small and grew deeper as he walked until they were taller than he was. The blocks of marble had been set into the side of a hillock so it appeared that he was looking at a solid cliff face of names. The lettering was brutal in its simplicity. Just names, nothing else. No details, no descriptions, no attempt to chronicle the horror of the individual deaths. It was simply a roll-call of the dead.

At the base of the wall were small American flags hanging limply in the still air. Next to one was a floppy camouflage hat, faded by exposure to the sun and rain. There were wreaths, too, from parents and wives and children, and one from a high school in Chicago.

There were no tourists that Lewis could see, though he wasn't alone. A middle-aged black woman in a cheap coat and thick stockings stood at the far left wiping her eyes with a red handkerchief, a black plastic handbag looped over one arm. A hefty guy in his forties with a bushy beard and thick prescription lenses stood staring at the wall, his arms folded tightly across his chest, rocking backwards and forwards on his heels. The man slowly turned his head until he was looking directly at Lewis. Even through the distorting lenses Lewis felt the cold eyes bore right through him. Lewis nodded but there was no reaction from the man and eventually Lewis had to look away. It was like looking at a dead man.

He found the first name at about the level of his knee, two-thirds along the memorial. James E. Colby. Not that anyone other than his mother had ever called him James. On the streets he'd been Cherry, because he'd never managed to lose his virginity while he was in Baltimore. Tall, lanky with bad skin, he was a bit on the slow side but played a mean game of basketball and was never short of friends. He'd died six weeks after arriving in Vietnam, crushed by an American tank driven by a nineteen-year-old guy from Albany who was high on his first ever joint. Cherry hadn't even had time to get laid. Lewis reached up and ran his fingers over the individual letters that made up the boy's name. James E. Colby. Forever a virgin. Lewis still owed him five dollars, he suddenly remembered.

He heard a scratching sound to his left and he looked over to see a woman standing on tiptoe with a piece of paper held against the wall. In her other hand was a pencil and she was making small brushing movements with it to take an impression of the name below it as if she were making a brass rubbing of a medieval church decoration. The woman was well dressed and a gold bracelet jangled and glinted with the movements of her hand.

One by one, Lewis located the six names and paid homage to them, touching the marble and filling his mind with thoughts of his friends. Overhead he heard the whup-whup of helicopter blades and for a wild moment he flashed back to a muddy pick-up zone in Nam, hovering twenty feet above the ground because the pilot didn't want to put the Huey down in the mud, throwing down a ladder to pick up a reconnaissance team who'd been out in the jungle for six days and nights. He looked up and saw that the slick was a civilian model, blue and white, circling overhead. Full of sightseers, maybe. He couldn't think of any other reason for its flight pattern.

He spent more than an hour at the wall, saying goodbye to the friends he'd lost. In some crazy way it made him feel easier, knowing that guys he'd grown up with were dead and that he'd be joining them. It wasn't that he was religious — but there was a feeling of security knowing that he wasn't alone, that others had died and that it was just part of the process of life. You're born, you live, you die. Seeing the names made him feel less frightened. They'd been through it already, and they'd died suddenly with no chance to prepare themselves. Lewis decided that he would take advantage of the opportunity the diagnosis had given him. He'd prepare himself. He'd do some of the things he'd always promised that he'd do when he had the time. Now he'd make the time. He had a few thousand dollars in a savings account, and he knew that his two mechanics could take care of the business, which wasn't exactly booming, what with the recession and all. He wouldn't wait until the cancer got so bad that he couldn't take care of himself, though. That he was sure of. He'd live life to the full until he couldn't go on, and then he'd end it himself. He had no intention of wasting away in a hospital bed.

Dick Marks slammed the door of the black Wrangler Jeep and heard the sound reverberate around the hill like half a dozen gunshots. There was no need to be quiet because Eric Horvitz would hear him coming through the forest anyway. Besides, it was better to give Horvitz advance warning of his approach. He wasn't the sort of man to creep up on. Not if you wanted a friendly conversation with him.

He slung his small nylon haversack over one shoulder, stepped away from the Jeep and began to climb, watching where he put his feet and taking care not to grab any branches before checking that they weren't home to a snake or spider or anything else that might bite him. Marks was not comfortable in the great outdoors. Never had been, never would be. Still, he was being well paid for his trouble, and for the risk. Eric Horvitz was a man who had to be treated with kid gloves. He had already served two prison terms, one for assault and one for manslaughter, and if it wasn't for his war record and the clutch of medals that he was entitled to wear he'd have still been doing time in some maximum security institution. That was why Horvitz had moved to the woods. He was safer there, less likely to fly off the handle and use the skills which the US Army had given him, skills which made him such a success during his three tours in Nam and which were such a liability in peacetime. It was only after six visits to the camp deep in the woods that Horvitz had come to accept Marks, not as a friend but at least as a non-threatening visitor.

The first time Horvitz had refused to speak to Marks though he'd at least listened to his speech about the US-Indochina Reconciliation Project and how it had initiated a programme to send veterans with Post-Traumatic Stress Disorder back to Vietnam. Horvitz hadn't replied to any of the questions that Marks had asked and eventually he'd simply wandered off into the trees. On his second visit Horvitz had sat down while Marks had talked, and he'd offered him a joint of the sweetest dope he'd had in a long time. When Marks had asked where he got the dope, Horvitz had smiled and admitted to growing it himself. It was the first time he'd spoken to Marks.

On subsequent visits Horvitz had gradually opened up to the point of spending several hours talking, reminiscing about his days in Vietnam and explaining how he managed to live all alone in the wilds. It was like winning the confidence of a wild animal, taking it step by step, making no sudden movements or pushing it too hard, talking softly and smiling a lot. Marks was the only outsider Horvitz had spoken to during the three years he had been living rough. There were other Vietnam veterans in the woods, but they rarely encroached into each other's territory. They were there to be alone, not to form support groups. Almost all were like Horvitz, trained to be killers and now superfluous. They had given everything for their country and when they had needed something in return, their country had failed them. Horvitz and the rest needed to be debriefed, to be eased back into society, but instead they had been treated like lepers, unwanted reminders of the war that America lost. That was something that Marks had touched on in his later conversations: how Horvitz now felt about his country. In the abstract, Horvitz was as patriotic an American as you'd ever meet: he'd been prepared to die for his country during the war, and would still lay down his life for the flag. It was his feelings for the people of America that had changed. Now he felt nothing but resentment, bordering on hostility, for those who had treated him so badly on his return. They'd spat at him and called him Baby Killer. Young girls had refused to serve him in supermarkets. Waiters had sneered and spilled soup on him. College kids had taunted him and scratched "Murderer" on his car.

Horvitz had been back in America only two weeks when he was drawn into his first fight. He got into an argument with two redneck mechanics about whether or not the United States should have been in Vietnam in the first place. They had been old enough to escape the draft and told Horvitz that anyone stupid enough to fight another man's war deserved everything they got. He'd tried to walk away but they'd pushed him and taunted him and eventually he'd snapped and put them both in hospital for the best part of a month. Horvitz was lucky: he came up before a sympathetic judge who'd served in the Korean War and he let him walk free on condition that he sought psychiatric help. Horvitz didn't, and before the year was out he was behind bars on an assault charge.

According to the file on the back seat of the Jeep, Horvitz must have been holding himself back to merit only a charge of simple assault. Eric Horvitz was a man who had been trained to kill in a thousand different ways, and had used most of them during his three tours of duty with the Long Range Reconnaissance Patrols and later with Special Forces teams. Even the stilted military language of the citations in the file couldn't conceal the horrors that Horvitz had been through, or the fact that he was a very, very dangerous man. After his release from prison Horvitz did go and see a psychiatrist but it didn't appear to have done him any good because he kept on getting into trouble, usually following arguments over the Vietnam War. He was back in prison in the early eighties after killing a man with a pool cue in a bar in Cleveland after they'd called him a baby killer. This time Horvitz's war record didn't help and he only escaped a murder charge because the guy he'd hit had had a heart condition and Horvitz's lawyer managed to produce a doctor who told the court that the blow to the chest wouldn't normally have resulted in death.

Horvitz was released in the summer of 1991, just in time for the celebrations of America's victory in the Gulf. He'd gone down to New York to see the parade to welcome back the veterans of Desert Storm, men and women who had seen less than one hundred hours of combat in a conflict where there had been more injuries playing sports than there had been from enemy fire. He'd been sickened by the sight of the cheering, waving crowds and the way the parading troops revelled in the adulation, heads held high and chests out, heroes one and all. That hadn't been in the file, the details had come out during Marks's later conversations with Horvitz. Horvitz had vividly described the marching bands, the ticker tape, the children sitting on parents' shoulders waving flags, and the displays of military hardware. And he'd recalled the Vietnam vets he'd seen at the back of the crowds: guys in wheelchairs, guys with limbs missing, guys with blank looks in their eyes. He'd felt red-hot anger rise in his throat then, he'd wanted to lash out, to kill indiscriminately, to pick up an M16 and blow away as many of the rosy-cheeked heroes as he could. He'd wanted to rip them apart with his bare hands, to tear out their hearts and eat the warm flesh. He'd wanted to kill so much that he could taste it, and he'd seen his hatred reflected in the faraway eyes of the other Vietnam vets who'd waited silently for the parade to pass as each of them recalled the way they'd been treated when they returned home, not as heroes but as the vanquished, an embarrassment that America could well do without. The baby killers. That was the moment when Horvitz decided that he could no longer live as a normal member of so-called civilised society, and that he faced only two possible futures: to spend the rest of his life behind bars, or to live alone in the wilderness. Four days later he was living rough in a Canadian forest with a rucksack of supplies and survival goods.

Marks looked at his compass and peered through the trees. It was a chilly morning but he'd worked up a sweat walking uphill and the backs of his legs ached. He knew he was within a few hundred yards of Horvitz's camp but he had no way of pinpointing it exactly; every tree seemed just like its neighbour and the view was unchanging no matter which way he looked. He wasn't lost, because he knew that if he kept going south-east he'd eventually hit the road, but there was a world of difference between not being lost and knowing where you were. Horvitz had told Marks how after being in the jungle for a few days his sense of smell had intensified to the extent where he could smell GIs a mile away and could pick out the individual scents of urine, sweat, tobacco and toothpaste. Marks stopped and sniffed the forest air, taking in small breaths and closing his eyes as he tried to interpret what his nose was telling him. All he could smell was vegetation, smelled it so strongly that it actually seemed to smell green. He tipped his head back and breathed again. Nothing. He opened his eyes and saw Horvitz standing in front of him, an easy smile on his bearded face. It wasn't the same face that was in the file he'd been given. In the black and white photograph an eager, bright-eyed teenager smiled with perfect teeth into a future that held nothing but promise, he had a slight cleft in his chin, his short, blondish hair was neatly combed back from a high forehead, his skin was smooth and blemish-free: a face that could be found in any one of a thousand high school yearbooks along with the forecast "most likely to succeed" or "most popular". The face that looked back at Marks was moustached and bearded, the facial hair greying in places and unkempt. The teeth were still white and even but the skin was dry and leathery and the lips had grown thinner and seemed to have a cruel edge to them, even when he smiled. The eyes had lost their sparkle, too. They were cold and distant.

"Morning, Dick," said Horvitz in his laconic West Virginian accent. "Long time, no see."

"Jesus, Eric. How the hell did you creep up on me like that?"

"Wasn't creeping. That's the way I move."

"I didn't hear a thing."

"Next time I'll cough or something." Horvitz raised one eyebrow to show that he was joking.

"Thanks, I'd appreciate it," said Marks.

"You eaten?"

Marks shook his head. "No. Not yet."

"I've a rabbit stew cooking," said Horvitz, and turned away.

He threaded his way through the trees and, as always, Marks marvelled at the way in which Horvitz seemed to glide silently through the undergrowth. He didn't appear to take special care where he put his feet but he never cracked a twig under his boots and branches never snagged his clothes the way they seemed to grab hold of Marks. It wasn't as if Horvitz was a small man, either. He was taller than Marks, and Marks was only half an inch under six feet. Horvitz was lean but not stringy; his figure belonged more to a quarterback than a basketball player, and Marks could see that three years in the wilderness hadn't hurt him at all. He'd only known Horvitz for about six months, but he doubted that he'd lost weight living rough. If anything it had probably toughened him up. The first time Marks had met Horvitz he'd been surprised by the man's height because, according to the file, Horvitz had spent nine months on attachment to the Tunnel Rats at Cu Chi, the Vietnamese stronghold which included a network of tunnels which ran all the way from Saigon to the Cambodian border. The Tunnel Rats were as a rule Puerto Ricans or Hispanics — small, wiry men who could move through the narrow, claustrophobic passages as easily as their Vietnamese enemy. Marks couldn't imagine Horvitz crawling through the tunnels, he seemed too big, his legs would be too long for him to turn quickly, his head would be for ever banging on the roof. The Tunnel Rats fought a war like no other — deep underground, in the dark, never knowing what danger the darkness held, moving by touch towards an enemy they couldn't see. They were all volunteers. Had to be, because there was no way a man could be forced to go underground to fight. Most soldiers couldn't cope with the darkness and heat, never mind the booby traps and the Viet Cong. Horvitz must have had a reason for wanting to go underground. A death wish, perhaps. The Tunnel Rats had an unofficial motto: *Non Gratum Anus Rodentum*. Not worth a rat's ass. Maybe that was how Horvitz had felt, that his life wasn't worth living and that going down into the tunnels would be a way of proving it, one way or another.

The only weapon Horvitz was carrying was a large Bowie knife in a leather sheath which was fixed to the belt in the small of his back. Despite living alone in the forest, Horvitz hadn't wanted to take a gun or rifle with him when he'd turned his back on society. Marks had once asked him why but Horvitz hadn't answered, in fact he hadn't said anything for a few minutes and his eyes had seemed to glaze over. Marks had understood intuitively that Horvitz was afraid that if he had a gun in his hands he'd end up putting the barrel in his mouth and pulling the trigger and dimming the memories by ending it all.

Horvitz took him to a secluded clearing where a pot of stew simmered over an open fire. As Horvitz spooned out the food on to enamel plates, Marks raised the subject of Vietnam and whether or not Horvitz had had any thoughts of going back. He had been trying to persuade the vet over several months to take up his offer of a free trip to Vietnam along with other former soldiers. At first Horvitz had rejected the idea out of hand, but during his more recent visits Marks had got the impression that he was gradually coming around to the idea.

Horvitz wiped his greasy lips with the back of his hand. "Who else will be there?" he asked.

"Guys like yourself, guys who lost something in Nam. The trip is only for vets, and for their families; you won't be with any tourists, don't worry on that score."

"And who'll be taking us around?"

"We'll be responsible for you until you get to Bangkok, and then you'll be taken care of by the Vietnamese government while you're in Vietnam. They'll take you around Saigon, up to the Iron Triangle, a full tour. You'll get to meet former VC, talk with them."

Horvitz threw a rabbit bone into the fire and watched it sizzle and crack. "I'm not sure that I want to speak with any VC, Dick. I'm not sure I've got anything to say to them."

"No one is forcing you to go, Eric. Hell, no one can force you to do anything, you know that. But do you want to spend the rest of your life like this? Living rough?"

Horvitz shrugged. "I chose it," he said.

"Sure, you chose it. But I figure you chose it because you didn't like the alternative. I figure you're here because you're frightened about what might happen if you live among other people. Am I right?"

Horvitz looked at him with dead eyes, unblinking. "Maybe," he said.

"So our programme could maybe help you come to terms with your anger. It might help you lay the ghosts. And you'll be doing it with others like yourself, guys you can relate to."

"You wanna smoke?" Horvitz asked.

"Sure," said Marks, somewhat surprised by the abrupt change of subject.

Horvitz got to his feet in a smooth, flowing motion and walked over to a shelter made from branches and reeds at the edge of the clearing which was so cunningly designed that from fifty feet it was practically invisible. He went inside and came out with a large joint. Marks had no idea how Horvitz managed to grow his own marijuana out in the Canadian wilderness, but he had to admit it was damn good shit. Horvitz lit the reefer with a flaming branch from the fire, took a deep pull, and then handed it to Marks as he exhaled. The two men continued to exchange the joint and after his fourth lungful Marks began to feel a little light-headed. The two men sat in silence, enjoying the dope. Marks always felt as if he got a better hit when smoking outdoors, or maybe it was just that Horvitz was growing a better strain of marijuana plant.

"When is the next trip?" asked Horvitz eventually.

"Couple of weeks," said Marks. "They're going quite regularly these days, though. If you miss that one, I can get you on another. And like I told you before, I can put anything you want into storage while you're away."

"Haven't got much here," said Horvitz. "One rucksack full of stuff, the rest I got from the forest."

"Whatever," said Marks. "I can take care of it for you, and if you decide you want to come back here afterwards, I'll drive you."

Horvitz ran his hand through his rough beard. "I haven't any money at all, you know that?"

"It won't cost a thing, Eric. Everything's paid for, and we'll give you money to spend. Not much, but enough to get by." He sensed that Horvitz had finally decided to go.

"I haven't got a passport," said Horvitz. "I threw my old one away once I crossed the border. It'd be out of date, anyway."

Marks reached for his haversack and opened it. "I've got the papers right here," he said. "I'll pick up a copy of your birth certificate for you." He took a Polaroid camera out of the haversack. "And I can take photographs right here."

"Hell, Dick. Did you know I'd say yes?"

Marks grinned. "I'd love to say that was so, Eric, but I've had this with me for the last three visits. Does that mean you'll go?"

Horvitz got to his feet and scraped the remains of his stew into the fire where it sizzled and spluttered. He looked over at Marks and nodded. "Shit, okay. What the fuck have I got to lose, hey?"

Marks helped Horvitz fill in the application form and took half a dozen Polaroid shots of him, then said goodbye and walked back to his car. The walk back was easier because most of the route was downhill, but it took him longer to cover the distance because of the dope he'd smoked. He eventually emerged from the trees a couple of hundred yards to the rear of the Jeep.

He opened the passenger door, threw the haversack into the back, and climbed in.

"How did it go?" asked the man with the military-looking haircut sitting in the driver's seat.

"Perfect," said Marks. "He's agreed. I'll get the passport fixed up and I've arranged to pick him up here in ten days to get some new clothes, a suitcase, stuff like that."

The man nodded and handed over a bulging, white envelope. "Here's another 5,000," he said. "I'll give you the rest when Horvitz is on the plane."

Marks took the money as the man started the Jeep and drove down the road. He didn't know why the man he knew as Joel Tyler was so keen to see Eric Horvitz back in Vietnam, but the amount of money he was paying was more than enough to stifle his curiosity.

It was getting hot in the boiler room, really hot, which was just the way Dan Lehman liked it. When the atmosphere heated up the adrenaline flowed, everyone worked that much harder and they could all feed off each other's excitement. It was a buzz that almost came close to the rush he got from cocaine. Almost. He took a pull from his can of Diet Coke and leant back in his black leather swivel chair and surveyed the room. There were two ranks of desks facing each other across the room, ten on each side, linked at one end by two long tables so that a huge U shape was created which filled most of the floor space. Each of the desks had two telephones and a console on which flashing lights indicated calls coming in and steady red lights showed which lines were in use.

All the desks were manned: mostly by men but in two of the positions were women, an unemployed actress who Lehman had once seen in a dental floss commercial and a middle-aged woman who reminded him of his mother. The men were a mixed bag, young thrusting guys in their twenties who worked standing up, pumping their fists in the air as they talked, middle-aged guys in staid suits who polished their spectacles between calls, and one old man in his sixties, a former mutual fund salesman who spoke with a marked stammer when he was on the phone but who had no speech problems when he chatted with the guys in the room. Each of the desks also had a red plastic covered pitch book, a Rolodex, a yellow order pad and a glass pot of pens and pencils. As the orders were taken over the phone they were placed on a metal spike and periodically a stocky, square-jawed man with a thick moustache walked around pulling the slips off the spikes and carrying them to his desk where he jotted down the details, marked them up on a white board on the wall behind him, and then dropped the papers into a large white bucket.

The board showed the value of the orders taken so far that month. Lehman was in second place with 280,000 dollars. In the lead was the man with the stammer who had grossed 340,000 dollars. The stammer helped. It made his clients feel sorry for him and a few minutes into the pitch they'd usually be finishing his sentences for him. It was a hell of a technique and Lehman had nothing but admiration for the man. The wall to the left of the board was all glass but the blinds were drawn and the only illumination came from the fluorescent lights mounted in the ceiling.

Two lights were flashing on the console but Lehman made no move to lift his receiver, figuring that he'd leave it up to one of the other slammers to do it. He'd just sold 25,000 dollars' worth of shares in a non-existent oil and gas drilling company to a schoolteacher in San Francisco and he reckoned he deserved a couple of minutes to himself. He took another mouthful of Coke and put his feet up on his desk. Max Cilento stood up and with a black felt-tipped pen marked up the new figures. Gordon Dillman, the man with the stammer, had sold another 40,000 dollars and his lead had widened. Cilento turned around from the white board and grinned at Lehman. Lehman pulled a face and took his feet off the desk and began to flick through the reference cards which contained the details of all his clients.

Cilento sat down and dumped the sales slips into the bucket and then checked the tape on the cassette deck on the table. Wires from the deck snaked along the floor and up the walls to four speakers mounted in the top corners of the boiler room from where the sounds of a busy brokering operation blared out: ringing telephones, dealers shouting share prices, secretaries typing. The sound effects helped keep the adrenaline levels of the slammers up but more importantly helped convince the suckers they were dealing with a busy, and successful, firm.

Lehman raised his arms above his head and stretched like someone deprived of exercise for too long. He looked like a man who would be good at sports. He was a little over six feet tall and lean, clean-shaven and with dark brown hair which was just a shade too long to be neat and which he was always brushing out of his eyes. His eyebrows were bushy and Mephistophelian which made him appear vaguely sinister when he smiled and positively evil when he was angry. As he went through his cards his brow furrowed, giving him the look of one in pain or deeply troubled. In fact he was completely at ease; the look of anguish was his normal expression.

"You're lagging behind, Dan," said Cilento. Cilento, who ran the boiler room operation for his brother, a Los Angeles-made-man, put a hand on Lehman's shoulder. He squeezed and Lehman could feel the power in the large, sausage-like fingers. "Don't let Dillman get away from you. Your reputation is at stake."

Lehman looked up at Cilento. They were about the same age, but Lehman had been in the boiler room business for a hell of a lot longer than Cilento. Cilento was only in charge because his brother carried weight in the mob. Lehman had signed up three months earlier after investigators from the Orange County District Attorney's office had closed down his last workplace. Lehman hadn't been in the office at the time so he'd been able to find another base pretty quickly. A week or so after he'd joined Cilento's operation he'd discovered that it was connected to the mob but he'd figured that so long as the cash kept coming through he'd grin and bear it. The only drawback had been Cilento himself, who seemed to think that slammers needed constant goading if they were to perform. The white board had been his idea, as had been the idea of taking away the chair of the worst-performing salesman so that he or she had to work standing up. Cilento could be brutal, verbally and physically, but Lehman was certain that it was the brutality of a bully who wasn't sure of himself. He'd seen him reduce a young woman to tears because he reckoned she wasn't producing enough, and he'd slapped around a former accountant who'd answered back when Cilento had cursed him out for not following the sales pitch to the letter. Cilento usually left Lehman alone because he was consistently one of the operation's top three producers.

"Yeah, whatever you say, Max," said Lehman, with no warmth in his voice.

"Maybe you should develop a stammer, like Dillman," said Cilento, the grip tightening. Lehman looked at the hand on his shoulder. It was big and wide, the nails neatly clipped, the flesh soft and white. Each finger wore a large, gold ring and the four rings had the collective appearance of a knuckleduster. Cilento wouldn't have to hit hard to do a lot of damage.

"Diff'rent strokes," said Lehman. "I always find that my boyish charm pays off."

Cilento nodded and released his grip. "Just keep it up, Danny boy," he said, slipping the sales orders off Lehman's spike and taking them back to his table. Cilento had a glass-panelled office in the far corner of the room but he rarely used it, preferring instead to be with the salesmen.

The young man in an LA Lakers sweatshirt who'd been standing up for the last three days and who'd probably be out of a job by the end of the week, put his hand over the mouthpiece of his phone and called out, "Conrad Morgan?"

"That's me," shouted Dillman. In the boiler room, no one used their real name with the punters. Lehman finished his Diet Coke and he lobbed the can through the air towards a wastepaper-basket. It smacked into the rim and then slipped in with a clatter. One of the young slammers clapped his hands and yelled "Two points!" and Lehman stood up to take a bow. He needed a caffeine boost, he decided, and went over to the small kitchenette where the coffee machine was and poured himself a styrofoam cup of black coffee. Dillman finished his call and came up to put a croissant in the microwave. As he waited for it to heat up he asked Lehman how he was getting on.

"Doing okay," said Lehman. "I think Cilento is trying to work up a grudge match between the two of us."

"He's a charmer, isn't he?" said Dillman. "If it wasn't for his brother I doubt that they'd let him within a mile of an operation like this." Dillman folded his arms across his chest and leaned against the storage cupboard where the men kept their tea and coffee supplies. With his tweed suit and wool tie Dillman looked more like a small-town schoolteacher than the first-rate slammer that he was.

"Yeah. He wants me to copy your stammer."

Dillman laughed and ran his hand across his balding head. "Well, Dan, it's never f-f-f-failed m-m-m-me."

The microwave dinged and Dillman took out his croissant. "Well, back to the grind," he said.

Lehman sipped his hot coffee and surveyed the room. Cilento had a telephone receiver pressed against his ear as he flicked through the lines, listening in on the salesmen's conversations to check that they were following the sales pitches. One of the younger slammers was working his way through a list of mineral-right holders that Cilento had bought from the Department of the Interior's Bureau of Land Management, knowing that investors who'd dabbled in minerals once could usually be persuaded to invest again. Another was reading the *Wall Street Journal* and circling comments which he could use when talking to his clients. Another amateur, thought Lehman. Any slammer worth his salt should have read the *Journal*, the *Financial Times* and scanned the financial wire services before he even sat down at his desk.

Lehman felt no guilt about taking money from punters. In his opinion all he was doing was taking advantage of their greed. Most of the time he was simply telling them something they already wanted to hear: that there was a quick, simple way to riches that didn't involve hard work or taking risks. If they believed that, well, as far as Lehman was concerned, they deserved everything they got. It wasn't that he was totally amoral. Lehman would never do anything to harm a child or lie to a nun, but he regarded practically everyone else in the world as fair game. There were times when he pictured himself as a sleek shark carving through shoals of small, silver fish, twisting and turning and swallowing them whole. If the small fish weren't fast enough or smart enough to get the hell out of the way, then they deserved to be eaten. That was the way of things. The law of the jungle. Just as the shark feels no remorse for the prey it rips apart, so Lehman never worried about the people he took money from. With one exception. He would never, under any circumstances, defraud a fellow Vietnam veteran. Whenever he was delivering his sales pitch he'd check the mark out to make sure that he hadn't done a tour of duty in Nam, and if he had, Lehman would gently steer him away, making sure that Cilento wasn't listening in on the line. Lehman himself wasn't exactly sure why he was like that, though he knew it had something to do with the camaraderie he felt with the men he'd fought with, the fact that he'd been to the edge with them, the fact that he'd come back totally unscathed when so many of his friends had come back in body bags or with limbs missing. "Lucky" Lehman they'd called him in Nam, because of the number of times bullets had cracked by him and mortars had exploded into craters only yards away from his helicopter. The nickname had been appropriate, but it came loaded with bitterness, too, because most of the time the bullets and the shrapnel that missed him ended up causing the death of others. Mortar shells would miss him but instead blow apart grunts that had just left his Huey. Tracers would go zipping past the Plexiglas window of his Huey only to rip through the helicopter behind him. Lehman had been lucky, of that there was no doubt, but those around him often didn't share in his good fortune, and after a while he began to regard the "lucky" tag as a curse. If he'd bothered to speak to a psychologist about how he felt when he'd returned to the States he'd probably have identified him as suffering from a bad case of survivor's guilt, but Lehman never felt the need to talk over how he felt with anyone. He was totally self-contained emotionally and unwilling to share his feelings with anyone, which is why he was pushing himself so hard in the boiler room. He had two failed marriages behind him and two ex-wives who were both chasing him for alimony payments. He earned big bucks pushing non-existent investments, but he spent big, too.

Dillman flicked a switch on his console and called out, "Call on line six for Michael Glenn."

"That's me," said Lehman, lobbing his empty coffee cup into the waste-paper bin.

"Name's Komer. Rob Komer. From Albany."

Lehman sat down at his desk and pulled out Komer's reference card. Michael Glenn was the name he used for oil and gas investments, in particular non-existent oil-wells in Texas. Lehman had obtained Komer's name from a junk mail shot offering free investment advice and according to the details on the card he had about 185,000 dollars to invest. Three days earlier Lehman, or Michael Glenn, had persuaded him to part with 125,000 dollars, though the cheque hadn't arrived yet.

Lehman switched on to the line. "Rob, how's it going?"

"Fine, Michael, just fine. Though I'm starting to have second thoughts about Lone Star Oil and Assets."

"I'm sorry to hear that, Rob. You were lucky to get in on the ground floor on that one. We're turning investors away now. I can't tell you how enthusiastic the response has been to that company. You made a real good decision there. I reckon you're showing a profit of almost 15,000 dollars already. That's more than ten per cent, and your cheque hasn't even been cashed yet. You did send the cheque, didn't you, Rob? I'd hate for you to have missed out on this."

"Oh yeah, I sent the cheque as soon as I was off the phone to you. It should be with you today. But I gotta tell you, Michael, I'm starting to wonder if I've done the right thing."

"I don't think there's any doubt on that score. I could sell your interest today for 15,000 dollars more than you paid, though you'd have to pay two sets of dealing costs. You'd show a small profit, but Rob, Lone Star Oil and Assets is going to keep going up, I can assure you. If I were you, I'd stick along for the ride.

The 15,000 dollars you've made so far is nothing to the profits you'll be able to make. Doesn't it make sense to take a bigger profit than a smaller one?"

"I suppose so," said Komer hesitantly. Lehman could hear another voice in the distance, as if someone was standing next to Komer, then the line went quiet as if he'd put his hand over the receiver.

When Komer's voice came back on the line, he sounded less hesitant. "The thing is, Michael, my wife thinks that I shouldn't be putting all my eggs in one basket, investment-wise. She thinks I should spread my money around."

"Rob, I don't know how much your wife knows about financial markets, but I know that my wife always leaves decisions on that score up to me. Wives are always on the conservative side, you know that. They're not as good as we are at taking risks, they prefer to play it safe. But Rob, we both know that there's a time for playing safe, and a time when you've just got to go for the big one. It's a judgment call, and in my opinion you've called this one just right. Tell your wife you've already made 15,000 dollars profit and that there's more to come. She should be proud of you, Rob."

"Yeah, I told her that," said Komer. "But she'd rather sell now and spread the money around. She says I should have used some of the money to pay off the mortgage on our house, what with interest rates being so high and all."

Lehman shook his head. God save me from interfering wives, he thought. Damn the woman. He heard Komer's muffled voice arguing with his wife but the man's hand was over the receiver again and he couldn't make out what was being said. He could guess, though.

The next voice he heard on the line was a woman's. "Hello, Mr Glenn. This is Tracey Komer, Rob's wife."

"Yes, Tracey. I guess Rob has told you how well he's done with his oil investment. He's showing a real good profit after just three days. You guys should be celebrating."

"Well, naturally I'm pleased that the investment has gone up, but I personally feel that we'd be safer if we had the money in the bank rather than in more speculative investments."

"I could understand that if you were showing a loss, but that's not the case, is it? You've already made 15,000 dollars and as I told your husband, there are investors queuing up to buy into this company. We're having to turn them away. Your husband was lucky to get in when he did."

"That's good, Mr Glenn. You shouldn't have any problem in selling our interests to another investor then. Could you do that for us, please?"

"I could, Tracey, of course I could. But I'd sincerely recommend that you hold on to the investment, I really would. I'm sure it'll continue to appreciate."

"I'm sure it will, but that money represents almost all of the inheritance my husband received from his late father's estate. I don't know if he told you, but he's in a wheelchair and he can't work. We need that money, it's all we have." Lehman heard Komer's voice protesting in the background. "He has to know, Rob," he overheard Tracey say. "Sometimes you're just too stubborn. Too proud." To Lehman, she said, "Mr Glenn, we just want our money back."

"Believe me, Tracey, that money is as safe as if it were in the bank. In fact, the way some of our Californian banks are going, it's probably safer in Texas."

"That's probably right, but we need to have that money where we can get it at short notice. We need a totally risk-free investment, Mr Glenn. Rob has other problems, too, problems that mean he can't work. He hasn't been able to work since he came back from Vietnam."

Lehman went cold. "Vietnam?" he said.

"He stepped on a mine, Mr Glenn. He's lucky to be alive."

"He didn't tell me," said Lehman.

"He doesn't like people to know that he's handicapped, Mr Glenn. He's a proud man." Her hand covered the receiver again and Lehman heard a muffled argument.

"Mrs Komer?" he called. "Mrs Komer? Are you there?"

"I'm here, Mr Glenn. I was just talking to my husband."

"Can I speak with him please, Mrs Komer?"

"We've already made up our minds, Mr Glenn. We just want our money back."

"I understand that. But could I please speak to your husband."

"I don't think that's a good idea, Mr Glenn," she said coldly. "I think you've said more than enough to him already."

Her voice was firm but polite, and Lehman could tell that she was not a woman who could be talked into, or out of, anything. She'd make a damn good slammer. "Mrs Komer, I promise I won't talk him into anything. I was in Vietnam, too. I'd just like a word with him, that's all."

"Well . . ."

"Please, Mrs Komer."

She agreed, reluctantly, and handed the telephone to her husband.

"Michael, I'm sorry about this," Komer began to say, but Lehman cut him off.

"Rob, why the hell didn't you tell me you were in Nam?"

"It's not something I volunteer, you know. I'm not exactly proud of what happened to me. And I don't want to be treated like some sort of cripple. The fact that I'm in a wheelchair shouldn't make any difference to the way I get treated. I mean, I know it does, but at least on the phone no one can tell that I've got wheels instead of legs."

"Shit, man. I wish you'd told me. When were you in country?"

"'67, '68," said Komer. "I got hurt on April Fool's Day, 1968. Khe Sanh. Like Tracey said, I stepped on a mine. We were on Route 9, to the west of Ca Lu."

"Marines, huh?"

"Yeah, I was with the 2nd Battalion, 1st Marines. You were at Khe Sanh?"

"Not in '68. But I was there in 1970. I was a chopper pilot."

"Yeah? Chopper saved my life. If the Dustoff pilot hadn't got me out of there as quick as he did, I wouldn't be around now. I mean, sometimes I think that it might have been better if . . ."

Lehman heard Komer's wife interrupt and then Komer saying, "Yeah, yeah, I know, I know," to her. "Tracey doesn't like it when I talk like that," he explained to Lehman.

"I can understand why," said Lehman. "Look, Rob, you didn't tell me you were a vet. If you had it would've put a different complexion on my advice to you, investment-wise."

"I don't follow."

"The investment advice I gave you was based on the assumption that you were working, that you didn't have any health problems, that medical bills wouldn't be on the cards. I'll be honest, if I'd known that you were disabled, I wouldn't have suggested that you go into oil, I really wouldn't. Your wife is right, a man in your position would be better paying off his mortgage and leaving the rest in the bank."

"Yeah? Hell, where does that leave me, then?"

"Well, like I said, we haven't got your cheque yet. Why don't you just call your bank right now and get them to cancel your cheque?"

"But what about the 15,000 dollar profit we made?"

"Let me be honest, Rob, the dealing costs will just about swallow up all of that, and there'll be a delay in getting the money to you. Far better we simply call it off right now. Just cancel the cheque, okay?"

"Okay, Michael, I'll do that."

"If you need any more advice about investing, go along to your local VA office. They'll be able to steer you in the right direction. And Rob, take care of your wife, you hear? She's got a good head on her shoulders. She knows what she's doing."

"You're not telling me anything I didn't already know," said Komer. "Thanks, Michael, I really appreciate it."

When Lehman cut the line he looked up and saw Cilento watching him, the receiver of his own phone pressed against his ear. Cilento was glaring at him under bushy eyebrows, his other hand clenching and unclenching on the table. He slammed down the receiver and stood up so violently that his chair fell over.

"Lehman! My office," he yelled and stormed into his glass cubicle where he paced up and down, powerful arms swinging at his side. Most of the slammers were too engrossed in their own sales pitches to notice what was going on, but Dillman watched Lehman with concern in his eyes.

"Shut the fucking door, you two-faced son-of-a-bitch," cursed Cilento as Lehman arrived.

Lehman did as he was told, but he kept facing Cilento as he closed the door. The man wasn't the type you'd turn your back on at the best of times.

"I can't fucking well believe what I just heard," ranted Cilento, pacing up and down in front of his desk. His face was red and a vein was pulsing in his temple and his eyes were filled with hatred. "How much was that sucker in for?"

Lehman shrugged. "One two five K, I guess."

Cilento clenched his fists and slammed them against his sides. "Is he one of your own clients, or was he one of my leads?"

Lehman knew that there was no point in lying because Cilento kept records of all the leads he supplied to the slammers. They got a smaller commission for in-house leads than if they used their own initiative to find someone to dance with. "He was one of yours, Max."

Cilento stopped pacing and walked up to Lehman, thrusting his head forward on his bull neck so that he was only inches away from Lehman's face. His breath smelt of stale onions and tobacco. "So let me get this fucking straight, Mr Good Fucking Samaritan. I give you a lead which is good for 125,000 dollars, and you go and tell him to cancel his cheque because his investment is a touch risky. That'd be about it, would it? Or did I miss something? Well, Mr Wonderful, did I fucking well miss something, or what?"

Lehman could see flecks of spittle on Cilento's moustache as he glared up at him. Cilento was a good three inches shorter than Lehman and he appeared even shorter because of the way he was pushing his head forward, but his lack of height made him no less intimidating. Cilento was well used to using his anger as a weapon and defeating bigger opponents by the sheer force of his personality, but he was also capable of brutal violence so Lehman looked him straight in the eye, waiting for any sign that he was about to strike.

"That's pretty much what happened, Max," he said quietly. He had no intention of explaining himself to Cilento. His feelings about vets and his responsibility to them was not something he could share with anyone, certainly not a muscle-bound, ranting thug who wouldn't have been out of place in a boxing ring.

"And how do you think I'm going to explain to my fucking brother that I'm short 125,000 dollars?" Cilento shouted. He waved a gold-ringed fist under Lehman's nose, pushed him back with his other hand, flat against his chest. He pulled back his fist and grunted, but before he could land the punch Lehman drew his knee up sharply and thrust it into Cilento's groin. Cilento yelled and bent double and both of his hands instinctively went down between his legs as if they'd be able to massage away the pain. His head was level with Lehman's chest and he was too close for Lehman to punch him so he used his elbow instead, banging it hard against Cilento's temple and knocking him cold. Cilento slumped to the ground, his hands still clapped against his groin, blood trickling down his chin because he'd bitten his tongue when Lehman hit him.

"I've always wanted to do that," said a voice at the doorway.

Lehman looked up to see Dillman standing there. He hadn't heard the door open, but Dillman had hold of the handle, the upper part of his body leaning in as if he was afraid to put his feet on Cilento's carpet. Lehman rubbed his right elbow. "Be my guest," he laughed.

"Nah, I'd never hit a man when he's down. Not even a piece of shit like Cilento." He peered down at the body. "He's not dead, is he?" As if in answer Cilento rolled on to his side and drew his legs up to his stomach. "Nope, he's not dead," said Dillman. "Never mind, better luck next time. What are you going to do, Dan?"

Lehman ran his hand over his face and rubbed his cheek thoughtfully. "I guess now would be a bad time to ask him for a raise, huh?"

Dillman laughed and slipped inside the door, closing it behind him. The upper section of Cilento's cubicle was glass, the lower was aluminium panelling so the slammers outside couldn't see Cilento's body on the floor. "Seriously, Dan, you've got a mess of trouble here, you know that. Cilento's brother isn't going to let you get away with this. It's a matter of honour. It doesn't matter what a shit Max is, you attack him, you attack the family."

"What if I were to say I was sorry?" asked Dan, grinning.

"I doubt it would do any good."

"What if I were to say I was really sorry?"

Dillman laughed. "It's good to see you've still got your sense of humour, Dan. But I doubt that you'll be laughing when Mario Cilento gets hold of you."

"Yeah, you're right. I guess now's as good a time as any to move on."

"Why was he having a go at you?"

Lehman didn't want to tell Dillman how he'd let Komer off the hook so he just said, "Money. He reckoned I wasn't trying hard enough."

"Hell, Dan, you're doing better than anyone else out there. His brother must be putting him under pressure. You know that Mario has been using this operation to launder mob money?"

"No, I didn't," Lehman answered. So long as his commission cheque arrived each month, Lehman hadn't given any thought to the workings of the boiler room.

"Just remember that Cilento is connected. It won't be enough to get out of Los Angeles, or even Orange County. You're only going to be safe if you leave the States, for a while at least. Cilento'll move heaven and earth to get even."

Lehman was beginning to realise what a hole he'd dug for himself. He'd reacted instinctively to Cilento's threatened attack and hadn't given any thought to the consequences. If he'd avoided hitting Cilento he could perhaps have worked out some sort of deal, taken a lower commission on the next few hits, promised to make good the deficit. Lehman always preferred to talk his way out of trouble whenever possible. He'd seen more than enough violence in Vietnam to last him a lifetime and knew that it rarely solved anything. But Cilento had given him no room for manoeuvre and he hadn't been prepared to take a punch in the mouth just to keep his job. Lehman wasn't a man given to losing his temper, but he wasn't the type to back away from a fight, either. And besides, it had sure felt good when his knee had connected with Cilento's private parts. "Thanks for the advice, Gordon."

Cilento groaned on the floor but his eyes were still closed tight. Lehman stepped over him and began sorting through the unopened envelopes on Cilento's desk. He found one postmarked Albany and tore it open. Inside was Rob Komer's cheque for 125,000 dollars. Lehman tore it up into small pieces and dropped them over Cilento's head. He could see that Dillman was dying to ask what he was doing but Lehman just shook his hand and left the office without saying another word. One or two of the slammers looked up as he picked up his Rolodex and the few personal possessions he had in his desk drawer, but they were all too busy on the phone to say anything to him.

In the underground car park far below the boiler room, Lehman threw his Rolodex on to the back seat of his Porsche and drove out into the bright LA sunshine. He took a pair of Ray-Bans from his glove compartment and slipped them on. He reckoned he had about fifteen minutes until Cilento had recovered enough to call his brother, and maybe half an hour after that before they'd be able to get some heavies around to his apartment. Lehman looked at the Mickey Mouse watch on his wrist. The roads were relatively clear and he'd be able to get home within ten minutes, giving him just enough time to throw a few clothes into a suitcase and grab the cash hidden under the bedroom carpet. The apartment, like the furniture, the electrical equipment and the car, were all leased. He dismissed the idea of driving out to the airport because he was sure that Cilento would have that covered. He'd drop off the car, hire something less conspicuous from Hertz, and drive to San Francisco. From there he'd catch a Greyhound and head east, to Chicago maybe. And in a couple of days he'd catch a plane out to Asia. He'd been thinking of taking a trip to the Far East for some time, ever since he saw a newspaper advert that had intrigued him. A travel agency based in Chicago was offering to take Vietnam War veterans back to Vietnam, partly as a holiday and partly to help them come to terms with what had happened out there.

The idea appealed to Lehman: Vietnam had long been an itch that he'd felt incapable of scratching, a source of memories and ghosts that kept coming back to haunt him more than twenty years after he'd taken the Freedom Bird back to the world. Now was the perfect time to go back. As he waited at a red light the irony of it suddenly made him smile. The way things were going, Vietnam was just about the safest place on Earth he could be just then.

The mission was straightforward. The team of hand-picked mercenaries had to fight their way through tough jungle terrain, seize a powerful speedboat and fight their way upriver to a canyon held by rebel forces. Once they'd reached the canyon they were to dump the boat and shoot it out on foot until they arrived at an enemy camp where five hostages were being held in a fortified three-storey block. The mercenaries were to release all the hostages, shoot their way out of the camp and seize a plane at the nearby airport which they would fly to safety. It was straightforward, but if they were to succeed they would need a hell of a lot of luck. Luck, and skill, and quarters.

Jonathan Pimlott had yet to see anyone get through the entire video game for less than three dollars and it usually took him about four, but he was getting better, no doubt about it. The canyon stage was the worst, he kept running out of ammunition before reaching the far end and enemy forces ripped him apart while he was helpless. The electronic images had no mercy. There was no possibility of surrender. It was kill or be killed.

There was no one on the video game when Pimlott and his girlfriend arrived at the arcade so he told her to stand in front of it while he got change. Pimlott had loved video arcades ever since he'd first been taken into one by his father when he was just six years old. Now he spent almost all of his spare cash on the machines and often visited one of his favourite arcades before morning lectures. He was a second-year law student and he always rebutted claims that he was addicted to the games by arguing that he needed something to counterbalance all the reading he had to do. He seemed to spend half his life with his nose buried in law books, and that couldn't be healthy, could it? He didn't have time to waste playing football or tennis or any of the pursuits that the university's jocks devoted themselves to. He barely had enough time to satisfy Suzanne, though at least she appeared to share his enthusiasm for arcades. He had only been going out with the pretty blonde for three weeks so he wasn't sure yet if she was faking it. Most of his former girlfriends had pretended to enjoy his daily visits to the arcades but had soon begun nagging him to go see a movie or a ball game instead once they realised that it wasn't a temporary fad.

He hoped that Suzanne wouldn't go the same way. She had the cutest butt and the best legs and, swear to God, she loved to play Nintendo while they were in bed. That had been a first, a definite first.

The change booth was squashed between an air-hockey table and a bright red motorcycle mounted in front of a video screen. Kid's stuff, Pimlott reckoned. He opened his wallet and took out a ten dollar bill.

The guy in the glass-sided cubicle was sitting back in his chair reading a copy of *True Detective*, a photograph of a buxom blonde in a black bikini wielding a large knife on the cover. He had unkempt light brown hair and a beard that seemed to be the result of neglect rather than an attempt to cultivate facial hair. It grew high up his cheeks and obscured most of his face, giving him the look of an emaciated Old English sheepdog. He was wearing wrap-around black sunglasses so Pimlott couldn't tell if he'd seen him or not, so he coughed quietly. The man slowly turned a page of the magazine and continued to read.

"Hey, buddy, any chance of some change here?" said Pimlott.

The man lifted his head to look at Pimlott and Pimlott could see himself reflected in both lenses. He waved the banknote and his two reflections waved it back.

"Back for more punishment, College Boy?" said the man, putting the magazine in his lap.

"Yeah," said Pimlott, impatiently.

"You must have put, what, fifty bucks in so far this week? Am I right, or what?"

Pimlott felt that his ability on the machine was being questioned and his cheeks reddened.

"Hey man, just give me change, okay?" He thrust the ten dollar bill through the semicircular hole in the glass.

"You want the whole ten bucks in quarters, College Boy?" asked the man, grinning. It wasn't a pleasant smile, it was loaded with sarcasm and bitterness and Pimlott knew that the eyes behind the dark lenses had no humour in them.

"Yeah. I'd like it all in quarters," answered Pimlott. "Please."

The guy sighed and leant forward to take the banknote. He put it in a drawer and pushed across two piles of quarters. "Think that'll be enough?" he asked.

"What do you mean?" said Pimlott.

The man leaned back in his chair and put his feet on the shelf so that Pimlott was looking at the soles of a pair of old brown cowboy boots with silver tips. "Seems to me that the way you're going, that'll only last you ten minutes or so. Maybe you ought to save yourself a trip and give me another twenty bucks or so." He sniggered and reached up to pinch his nostrils as if stifling a sneeze.

"Hey man, what's your problem?" said Pimlott, irritated. He couldn't understand why the man was picking on him. It couldn't have been personal. He didn't recognise the guy. In fact he wouldn't have been able to describe any of the men who manned the change booth; he was usually too busy to get back to the game and wherever possible he used the automatic change-giving machines. The dark glasses and beard made it difficult to assess his age; he could have been anywhere between thirty and forty. He was about five nine, five ten, though the way he slouched in the chair could have been deceptive. He was skinny and his shoulders sloped sharply away from his long neck. He was wearing a black sweatshirt that appeared to be a size too big for him, and faded blue jeans that were ripped at the knees. There was a large American eagle on the sweat-shirt and underneath it in white lettering it said "POWMIA. You Are Not Forgotten". Pimlott wondered what the initials stood for. He ran various combinations quickly through his mind and rapidly came to the conclusion that it meant "Prisoners of War — Missing in Action" and that the man was probably a Vietnam vet. Great, thought Pimlott. Just what I need. A vet with a grudge.

"Hey, I'm not the one with the problem, College Boy," the man sneered. "You're the one who's blowing all Daddy's money on a game he can't handle."

The comment struck home and Pimlott felt his cheeks blush. His father was picking up the tab for his education, and was paying his living expenses, too. It wasn't that he didn't want to work, it was just that the economy was so stretched that part-time jobs just weren't available, and it was only Ivy Leaguers who managed to get high-paying vacation jobs with legal firms. The best he could find last vacation had been serving drinks in a downtown bar and he'd hated that so much that he quit after the first week. Hell, he was training to be a lawyer, not a cocktail waiter. He'd pay his father back once he was qualified and had a job, and besides, he needed most of his free time to study. You didn't get to be a lawyer without putting in the hours with the books.

"Think you can do better?" Pimlott asked.

The man snorted. "I'm damn sure I can," he laughed.

"Wanna put money on it?"

"You mean your daddy's money, College Boy?"

"It doesn't matter whose money it is, does it? Do you want to put your money where your mouth is?"

The man took his cowboy boots off the shelf. "Fifty bucks," he said quietly.

"Fifty bucks?" repeated Pimlott. He didn't want to embarrass himself by taking his wallet out but he was pretty sure that was about all he had.

"Too rich for your blood, College Boy? Yeah, I thought it might be. Why don't you go and ask Daddy for a raise and come back and see me."

"I've got the money," said Pimlott, angrily. "I'll take you on."

The man laughed, throwing his head back. "Take me on?" he said. "Take me on? This isn't going to be a competition, College Boy. It's going to be a walkover. I could beat you one-handed." He stood up and turned his back on Pimlott to put his magazine on a table at the rear of the booth.

"Oh yeah?" said Pimlott.

"Yeah," said the man, turning around and holding up his left arm. For the first time Pimlott noticed that the man's left hand was missing. In its place was a steel claw made from three interlocking metal curves. The man grinned and made the pieces click together. Pimlott frowned, trying to work out how he'd managed to do that. The claw must be connected to the tendons in what remained of his arm, he realised.

"Oh come on, man," said Pimlott.

The man thrust his neck forward. "You backing out, College Boy?" he spat. "Cos if you're backing out, I want the fifty bucks."

"But this isn't fair," said Pimlott.

The man peered at Pimlott through the dark lenses. "You implying something by that, College Boy? Are you implying that maybe I'm not up to it? That the fact I'm short a hand makes me less of a man than you? Is that what you're saying, College Boy?"

Pimlott felt his cheeks go even redder and he shook his head. "No, it's cool. You wanna play, I'll play."

The man smiled and clicked his claw again. It sounded like some huge insect. "Good," he said. "That's real good." He used the claw to put a "Closed" sign over the hole in the window and locked the door behind him. Pimlott followed him to the video machine where Suzanne was waiting anxiously. He badly wanted to check to see how much cash he had in his wallet but didn't dare risk it.

On the screen in front of them pictures of enemy soldiers flashed up, followed by brief descriptions of their weapons and the terrain that lay ahead. Then the screen cleared and a series of initials and numbers flashed up and began scrolling. The numbers on the left represented the ranking of the players who'd been on the machine that day, the score was in the middle, and to the right were the initials of the players. The results scrolled up to the top to show the top ten players since the video game had been switched off. Pimlott's initials, JRP, were in third place, alongside his all-time record score. Suzanne's were in eighth place. First and second place were taken by someone with the initials LC and both scores were about 100,000 ahead of Pimlott's. Pimlott had never seen LC in action, but the initials regularly headed the rankings and the guy was obviously an expert. He placed his pile of quarters next to his gun and began feeding them into the machine.

The vet tapped the glass screen with his claw and Pimlott looked up, startled.

"Maybe I should introduce myself," he said, grinning evilly. "The name's Carmody. Larry Carmody."

Pimlott looked at the man's leering face and at the initials on the screen. "Oh fuck," he said. His stomach churned as he realised that there was no way he could even hope to match the man's score.

"Are you ready, College Boy?" goaded Carmody, holding the barrel of the machine-gun with his claw and caressing the trigger with his other hand.

"Ready when you are," replied Pimlott, trying to sound confident as he put the remainder of his quarters in a pile on top of the machine. Then he had second thoughts and handed them to Suzanne and asked her to feed them into the slot when necessary.

"How about you pressing the start button, little lady?" said Carmody, hunching over the gun.

Pimlott nodded at her and she hit the button. A swarthy colonel appeared on screen to deliver his briefing and Suzanne stabbed at the "two-player" button to go straight to the game. Pimlott began spraying the screen with bullets and letting fly with grenades, his eyes wide as he breathed heavily through his nose. Suzanne put her hand on his shoulder but he shrugged it away.

Carmody's technique was more measured and economical. He fired in short bursts of three or four bullets, used his grenades only when faced with a group of enemy soldiers or heavy armour, and when he wasn't firing he centred his sights on the middle of the screen. His score quickly moved ahead of Pimlott's.

"Come on, College Boy, you're not trying," Carmody hissed.

Pimlott ignored him and lobbed a grenade at a lone sniper. He had the satisfaction of seeing the soldier explode in a cloud of blood but then four heavily armed men leapt out of a tree and when he tried to throw another grenade he discovered he was out, he'd used them all up. He tried frantically to swing around the machine-gun but he wasn't fast enough and took several hits before he mowed them down.

"Bad move, College Boy," sniggered Carmody, taking out a large snake curled around the lower branch of a tree before it could strike.

"Take it easy, Jonathan," whispered Suzanne but he didn't appear to hear her. Most of his ammunition had gone now. She glanced over at Carmody's score. He was already 80,000 ahead of her boyfriend and had plenty of ammunition and grenades and was showing no body damage at all. Suzanne could see that Pimlott was starting to panic, firing almost randomly instead of picking his targets and when they cleared the first section it was clear that he didn't have much time left. She fed the rest of the quarters into the machine and saw the credits flick up. As she did so, Pimlott lost another life and she heard him curse under his breath. Carmody sniggered and sent a grenade spinning through the air to destroy a tank and then picked off two soldiers with machetes as they stepped from behind a tree with evil grins of intent on their comic-book faces.

They came to the end of the jungle stage and Pimlott wiped his forehead with the back of his hand. His score was low, much lower than he'd usually achieved at this stage of the game. The way it was going, he'd be lucky to get through the river section. He stole a glance at Carmody's score. It was more than 100,000 ahead and he'd only taken a couple of hits. He had stacks of ammunition and six grenades left.

The words disappeared from the screen and they were cruising along the river. He destroyed the floating log just as a waterlogged soldier came from underneath it and he was aiming in the sky even before two helicopters came swooping out of the clouds. A boat bristling with armed soldiers came out of a tributary and he sprayed it with bullets, killing them all.

"Yes!" said Suzanne, slapping the machine with her hand. Pimlott ignored her and picked off a soldier crouching by a rock. Two more appeared on the left of the screen and he fired but as he did a helicopter roared down from the clouds and let fly a guided missile which sped towards him. He tried to bring his gun to bear on the fast-moving target but before he could pull the trigger the screen went red and yellow and then a skull and crossbones appeared. Game Over. Pimlott swallowed and tasted blood. He'd been biting the inside of his mouth without realising. Suzanne slipped her arm through his and squeezed but the show of affection didn't make him feel any better. He hated losing, and he hated even more losing to a man like Carmody. The vet was still shooting and his score was already higher than Pimlott's personal best.

"It's only a game," Suzanne whispered.

"I know," Pimlott replied. It might only be a game but he'd bet fifty bucks on the result and he wasn't sure that he actually had the money in his wallet.

Carmody seemed to get bored with playing on his own and he stepped away from the machine while soldiers were still shooting at him.

74

"Well, College Boy, time to pay up," he said, clicking his claw. "Fifty big ones." He held the claw out for the money and opened it. Pimlott stared at the three metal prongs. Carmody seemed to revel in his discomfort and clicked the claw impatiently. "Come on, it's only Daddy's money, after all."

"What gives with this College Boy thing? And why all the digs about my father?"

Carmody sneered at the youngster. "Because all my life I've seen guys like you, rich kids, who don't even have to wipe their own noses. Rich kids with rich fathers, who don't know what life is about, who think they own the world because they can pay for it. Well, College Boy, you're nothing, you never will be. Whenever you come up against someone like me you'll get knocked right down." He gestured towards the video machine with his claw. "See this?" he said. "You use your daddy's money to play this fucking game, shooting at helicopters, blowing away soldiers, playing at being a man. You ever really shot a man, College Boy? Ever killed anyone? Of course you haven't. How old are you? Eighteen? Nineteen? Just a kid."

Carmody's voice was becoming louder and more strident, and some of the children playing in the arcade stopped and looked across to see what was happening.

"Well let me tell you, College Boy, when I was nineteen I was doing that for real. I was shooting real bullets at real people, and when my friends were hit they died, they didn't just put in another handful of Daddy's quarters and hit the 'restart' button. They came home in body bags. Tell me, College Boy, where was your father when I was blowing people away in Vietnam? What did your old man do during the war? I bet he wasn't caught up in the draft, was he? I'll bet he sat in some nice, safe college somewhere studying to be a high-powered lawyer or rich fucking doctor. Am I right?"

Pimlott said nothing. He looked down at the floor, afraid to look at the man's face, afraid of how his reflection would appear in the lenses of the sunglasses.

"I don't think you're being fair," said Suzanne.

Her support just made Pimlott feel even more ashamed. The vet had been right. His father hadn't fought in the war, he'd been in medical school. "Look, I don't want any trouble," Pimlott said quietly.

Carmody sneered. "You couldn't handle trouble, College Boy," he said. "Not the sort of trouble I'd give you anyway." He held out his claw. "Fifty bucks," he said.

"What is your problem?" asked Suzanne, her hands on her hips.

"No problem," he said. "But it seems to me that you're wasted on the college boy here. Seems to me that you'd be a hell of a lot happier with a real man. A man who could give you what you want. What's he give you, lover? Stimulating conversation? Witty repartee? A quick grope in the back seat of his daddy's car? You know what you'd get from me, lover? Do you want me to tell you what I could do for you?"

Suzanne looked down at the floor, hugging herself tighter. She wanted to attack, to strike out, verbally if not physically, at the angry stranger who seemed to be

76

able to look right through her, but she knew that, intelligent and quick-witted as she was, she was no match for him. She wasn't used to hurting people, but he clearly was.

"Well?" pressed Carmody, unwilling to accept her silence. "Do you, lover?"

She shook her head, small, jerky movements. "No," she said quietly.

"Hey, man, leave her alone," said Pimlott, but his voice was shaking so much that it contained no threat. It was a plea, and Carmody looked at him with open contempt. He clicked his claw. Pimlott reached into his back pocket and took out his wallet. He opened it and flicked through the bills inside, conscious that the vet was looking at the two credit cards it contained. The cards were in his father's name.

Pimlott extracted the notes and quickly counted them. Most of them were one dollar bills, and there were a couple of fives and a ten. Thirty-eight dollars. That was all he had. Suzanne read the confusion on his face and she began going through the pockets of her skirt and her blouse. She found a five dollar bill and two singles and she gave them to Pimlott with trembling hands.

Pimlott recounted the notes and then bit his lower lip, mentally cursing himself for being such a fool, for not checking beforehand that he had enough cash to cover the bet.

"The money, College Boy," said Carmody.

"I've only got forty-five dollars," said Pimlott, his voice little more than a whisper.

"I can't hear you, College Boy," said Carmody.

"I said I've only got forty-five bucks," said Pimlott, louder this time. "I'm five dollars short."

Carmody nodded and began to move his jaw as if he was chewing gum. He reached up and scratched his beard with his claw. It made a rasping sound that reminded Pimlott of a blade being sharpened. "Well, isn't that a fucking pity," said Carmody.

"I can get the five dollars," said Pimlott, holding out the notes. One dropped to the floor and he knelt down to retrieve it, groping around with his free hand until he found it because he didn't want to take his eyes off the man's face, fearful of what he might do while he wasn't looking. He straightened up and handed over the bills. Carmody took them effortlessly with his claw and poked them into the breast pocket of his shirt.

"I don't trust you, College Boy," said Carmody. "I think you might not come back. I think you're a chip off your old man's block. I think you're a coward. I think you'd rather run away than fight."

A crowd of ten or twelve people had gathered around, openly staring at the argument. Pimlott looked around the curious faces, hoping to see someone who would take his side, but all he saw were teenagers who didn't want to get involved. They had been brought up on a diet of violent television shows and space invader video games and now they wanted to see blood on the floor. His blood. He couldn't believe that the man would actually get physical in front of so many witnesses, but each time he tried to get by his way was blocked, and the vet began making poking gestures with his claw, threatening to hit him in the face. Pimlott felt tears of helplessness and shame sting his eyes. "Just let me go," he whined. He felt Suzanne's grip loosen and when he turned to look at her she'd gone. Part of him hoped that she'd gone for help, but at the back of his mind was the thought that she'd abandoned him. "I just want to go home," he said. "Please."

Carmody shook his head firmly. "You owe me five dollars, College Boy. If you haven't got it, I want you to leave something as security."

"What? What do you want?"

Carmody pushed his sunglasses further up his nose with his good hand. "Your watch," he said, nodding at the boy's wrist.

"My watch?" said Pimlott. It had been a gift from his father, a reward for getting into law school. "Come on, man. It's worth over 500 bucks."

"The money, College Boy. Or the watch."

Pimlott scanned the crowd again but no one made a move to help him. Over the vet's shoulder he could see the entrance to the arcade.

Carmody smiled and clicked his claw. "The watch," he repeated.

Pimlott began to tremble and his bladder felt as if it was about to empty. He reached across to his watch with his right hand but as his fingers touched the metal he seemed to explode into action, kicking out with his right leg, flailing with his hands and screaming like a stuck pig.

Carmody stepped back, feinted a punch with his left hand and then slammed the metal claw into Pimlott's temple, flooring him instantly. The metal prongs tore into the flesh and blood trickled down his cheek as he fell to the floor. The crowd gasped and moved back but not too far, shocked by the violence but still entranced by it. Carmody glared at them as if daring them to intervene. When no one said anything he bent down and slipped the watch off the boy's wrist.

When Pimlott regained consciousness, a paramedic was holding something soft against his temple and telling him to lie still. Above him he could make out two uniformed police officers talking to the owner of the arcade, a stocky, balding man with rolled-up sleeves and chunky gold bracelets. Pimlott's vision blurred and he felt as if he was going to throw up so he closed his eyes.

"Yeah, his name was Carmody," he heard the owner tell the police. "Larry Carmody. He was a vet with a king-size chip on his shoulder, a real attitude. Shouldn't be hard to track down, one of his fucking arms was missing. Which one? The left, I think. He was living in some flophouse downtown, I've got his address somewhere in the office. Yeah, seems to be about 3,000 dollars missing, but I won't know until I've checked the books. Yeah, cash. This is a cash business, right? Of course it was cash. What do you think he'd take, pizza? Cleared out the fucking safe and took the change float, too. A social security number? What do you think I'm running here, fucking IBM?"

It seemed to Anthony Chung that only someone with a particularly British sense of humour could have given the name "Nineteen 97" to a bar frequented by Hong Kong's beautiful people. There was nothing the average Hong Konger had to celebrate about the date when the British colony was due to be handed back to its true owners, but the bar cum disco was nevertheless packed with young exuberant expatriates and affluent Chinese, dancing themselves senseless to the driving beat of the latest Canto-pop hits.

Chung leant on the bar and surveyed the dancers as he sipped a brandy on the rocks. A girl with shoulder-length wavy brown hair and too much green eye-shadow smiled at him but he ignored her. Two young Americans, tall and thin enough to be basketball players, moved to each side of him and tried to attract the attention of one of the barmaids. Chung eased himself out from between them and went to stand by a pillar. It was Saturday night, Nineteen 97's busiest time. Most Hong Kongers worked a five and a half day week and Friday night was always more subdued because a high proportion of the bar's clientele had to be in the office Saturday morning. There were several American ships in port, too, and it didn't take long for the navy boys to find their way to Gweilo Alley, the narrow thoroughfare which contained Nineteen 97 and more than a dozen other bars and chic restaurants. There was a garbage disposal depot at the end of the road, built at the insistence of Chinese bureaucrats shortly after the Lan Kwai Fong district reached the pinnacle of its popularity. Chung thought that demonstrated a particularly Chinese sense of humour.

The small dance floor was the showcase for some of Hong Kong's prettiest girls, Chinese and Caucasian. Two long-haired Eurasian girls, one in a tight-fitting white dress, the other in black, danced together, their eyes only for each other. Chung watched the two basketball players try to split them up and fail, walking dejectedly back to the bar to nurse their beers. They'd been wasting their time. One of the girls was a lesbian, often featured in the showbiz pages of the Chinese gossip magazines on the arm of her latest lover. She was an actress in an afternoon historical soap opera and she had the reputation of picking up pretty shop assistants in high-class boutiques, seducing them, keeping them as close companions for about a month, and then dropping them. Chung didn't recognise the other girl, the one in black, but whoever she was she clearly wasn't wearing any underwear under her low-cut dress. The pop record was replaced by a slow ballad and the two girls moved together into a clinch, arms around each other. The actress reached up to stroke the other girl's hair, and gradually moved her head around until their lips were together and they kissed passionately.

Chung dragged his eyes away. He scanned the faces of the rest of the dancers but didn't see the girl he was looking for. It was the second Saturday night he'd gone in search of Debbie Fielding. He knew what she looked like because she was regularly featured in the *Hong Kong Tatler*, usually between her mother and father, holding a glass of champagne with a napkin and a fixed smile on her face. He was in no rush. There was a limited number of places where the daughter of the chairman of one of the biggest banks in Hong Kong would go to enjoy herself on a Saturday night. He'd find her sooner rather than later.

"Nice jacket," said a voice to his right. He turned to see the girl with wavy brown hair. She smiled and put her head on one side, showing white, even teeth. She was pretty and full-figured, her black halter top barely concealing her large breasts which she aimed at his chest like a gunslinger taking aim. She stroked the pale tan material. "Armani?" she asked.

Chung nodded.

"My favourite designer," she said. "My name's Sandy."

"Anthony," he said, raising his glass. "Anthony Chung."

"Do you want to dance?" she asked. Chung was surprised by her forwardness. He knew that many Caucasian women were attracted to his lithe physique and good looks, his dark brown eyes and high cheekbones, but they usually waited for him to make the first move because they weren't sure how to handle a Chinese.

"I'm not much of a dancer," he said. In fact he was an excellent dancer — ballroom, Latin American and modern — but he didn't have time to waste on the girl, attractive as she was.

She rubbed her breasts against the front of his jacket and looked up at him. For the first time he saw how glazed her eyes were and smelt the gin on her breath. She raised her eyebrows, trying to look cute but actually looking as if she were about to pass out. "Will you take me home?" she asked. He felt her hand move down the front of his trousers and squeeze him.

He looked at her levelly. "I can't," he said. "I'm waiting for my boyfriend."

The hand stopped moving. She took a step back, confused, then she smiled. "I could make you forget your boyfriend," she said, running her right hand down the side of her breast.

"I'm sure you could, but he gets very jealous," he said.

She shrugged, turned on her heels, and went over to one of the navy boys. Within thirty seconds she was rubbing herself up against him and squeezing him between the legs.

Chung placed his half-finished drink on a table and left the bar, his ears ringing from the loud music. In the street outside a young man with slicked-back hair was throwing up in the gutter, much to the amusement of his friends, who laughed like public schoolboys and slapped each other on the back. Two Chinese boys, barely out of their teens, giggled and walked down a flight of steps into one of the gay bars that were to be found in Lan Kwai Fong. Homosexuality had been illegal in Hong Kong until 1991, but the authorities never prosecuted. In fact, even before 1991 it wasn't unusual to see government officials and lawyers dancing with Chinese men in some of the more discreet up-market bars that served the gay community.

A dark green Mercedes sounded its horn and edged past the youth in the gutter and turned on to the main road towards the central business district. An English couple, he in a tuxedo and she in a glittering gown and pearls, walked arm-in-arm into a French restaurant. It was a hot and humid night and Chung felt sweat trickle down the middle of his back. He took off his jacket and held it over his arm as he walked to the California bar along the road. It was the fifth he'd been in that night.

A pretty brunette sitting on a stool behind a wooden lectern smiled at him and asked if he had a membership card. When he admitted that he didn't she took a hefty entrance fee from him and waved him in with another smile.

The volume of the music was lower than in Nineteen 97 but the clientele was similar, young men and women dressed in expensive designer clothes, partying as if there were no tomorrow, trying to squeeze as much enjoyment out of the place as they could in the little time they had left. Chung knew that most of them reckoned that under Chinese rule the good times would soon be over. The frantic excitement of the Lan Kwai Fong revellers reminded Chung of nothing so much as the band playing as the *Titanic* went down.

Two executives of one of the more successful Chinese stockbroking firms were drinking a bottle of champagne at a table. Chung had done business with them in the past and they waved him over. They offered him a glass but he said no, he was there to meet someone. They presented him with new business cards listing their recently opened offices in Singapore, Taipei, Jakarta and Bangkok. Like most of the colony's local brokerage firms, they were preparing for the day when the world's investment community would regard

Hong Kong as just another inefficient Chinese bureaucratic nightmare rather than a freewheeling tax haven and manufacturing centre. When that happened the downgrading would be rapid and severe, and investment money would shift dramatically away from the local stock market and into the other little dragons in the region. The ever resourceful Hong Kong Chinese stockbrokers would make money either way. Chung wished them well and went back to the bar where he ordered himself a brandy and ice.

The dance floor in the California was bigger than that in Nineteen 97 and less crowded, giving the dancers more room to move. They were taking full advantage of it — a cosmopolitan mix of Chinese, Caucasian and Eurasian. Lan Kwai Fong was one of the few places in Hong Kong where all the races truly mixed on a social level, where the only qualifications for acceptance were a wallet full of money and the desire to have a good time.

Chung had sipped about half of his drink when he saw her coming out of the Ladies. The photographs in the *Tatler* didn't do her justice. Debbie Fielding was about five foot six, slim in a boyish way, with fair skin and straight blonde hair that reached just past her shoulders. From across the room Chung couldn't tell the colour of her eyes but he guessed they'd be blue or green. She had a slight upturn to her nose and a sprinkling of freckles and her cheeks were flushed as if she weren't used to alcohol. Her lips were full but she didn't appear to have any make-up on. He put her age at about nineteen, maybe twenty. She was wearing a simple off-the-shoulder pale blue dress which looked like silk and which ended just above the knee. She had good legs which were accentuated by very high heels.

She was walking alongside a short, plump girl with close-cropped brown hair and they were laughing at something. Debbie put both her hands up to cover her mouth and her eyes widened. Her nails were painted a vivid red and she had a bracelet of deep red stones which were probably rubies. Her laugh was high-pitched, like a little girl being teased by her father.

The two of them went over to a table where two girls and a young man with long hair and wire-rimmed spectacles were drinking brightly coloured cocktails through straws. Chung studied the group over the top of his drink. She'd looked older in the pictures, and less vulnerable. Though the adult dress and the high heels were obviously her own, she still looked like a schoolgirl dressed up in her mother's clothes. Chung wondered if Debbie Fielding was a virgin.

The man got up from the table and reached out his hand to the plump girl. She took it and he led her to the dance floor and swung her into a lazy jive. Debbie looked at the thin silver watch on her wrist and put a hand over her mouth to stifle a yawn. One of the girls leaned over and said something to her but she shook her head. The other girls sipped their drinks through their straws and then stood up and went over to the dance floor together, leaving Debbie alone at the table.

Chung walked over to her table, his glass in his left hand.

"Hi," he said. "Mind if I join you?"

She looked up, frowning. He saw her eyes weigh him up, checking out his Armani jacket, the white linen shirt, the black wool trousers, the Bally loafers, and the Cartier watch, then she looked at his face. She smiled, and he knew that he'd passed muster.

"Sure," she said. "But I'm just going."

"Husband waiting at home for you?" he asked, sitting down and straightening the creases of his trousers.

She laughed. "Hardly," she said, fluttering her left hand in front of his face so that he could see she wasn't wearing a ring. "I have a junk party tomorrow, and I've got to be at Queen's Pier at nine o'clock."

"But it's not as if you need any beauty sleep," he said, raising his glass to her.

"Why thank you, kind sir," she said.

"Anthony," he said. "Anthony Chung."

"Debbie," she replied. "Debbie Fielding." She extended her hand and he shook it. Her skin was warm and dry and there was no strength in her grip.

"Can I buy you a drink?" he asked.

She shook her head. "No, really. I must be going." She stood up and waved goodbye to her friends on the dance floor. They waved back and she blew a goodbye kiss to the plump girl.

"Can I give you a lift?" asked Chung, getting to his feet.

"I have a car," said Debbie, picking up her handbag.

"How about a race, then?" he asked.

She stopped dead. "I'm sorry?" she said.

"A race," repeated Chung. "How about a race?"

"A race?"

"A race home. If I can't give you a lift, the least you can do is give me a race."

She grinned, thought about it, and then nodded. "Okay, Anthony Chung. You've got your race. But I warn you, I've got a Jaguar XJS."

"Nice car," said Chung. "I'll meet you outside in five minutes. That okay with you?"

"Fine."

"So where are we going?" She told him the address of her house on the Peak which Chung knew was her parents' house. "I'll see you outside, then," he said.

When Chung went out to get his car, Debbie asked one of the waiters to arrange to have her Jaguar brought over. While she waited she lit a cigarette.

"Smoking?" said a voice. It was her friend, May. "I thought you'd given up."

"It's the only one I've had today," said Debbie.

"Who was the Chinese guy?"

"Anthony Chung. I've never met him before tonight."

"Seems cute," said May.

"Very," agreed Debbie.

"And you let him get away?"

"We're about to have a race, actually," said Debbie.

"You're what?" exclaimed May.

"A race. You know, brum-brum, first one past the chequered flag is the winner."

A waiter came up and told Debbie her car was outside. "Gotta go, kiddo," said Debbie and kissed May on the cheek.

"Be careful," May said, but Debbie was already gone.

Debbie slid into the driver's seat and slipped off her high heels. She turned the ignition key. The Jaguar's engine purred and she stroked its gear stick absent-mindedly as she waited for Chung to arrive. She heard his car before she saw it — a deep-throated roar that seemed to vibrate up through her seat. She looked over her shoulder as he drew up next to her Jaguar. His window slid down smoothly and he smiled across at her.

"Tell me that's not a Ferrari F40," she said.

Chung raised an eyebrow. "Okay, it's not a Ferrari F40," he said.

"Four-valve V8 engine, 478 brake horsepower at 7,000 rpm, Weber Marelli fuel injection system, carbon fibre and Kevlar body." She rattled off the statistics like a Ferrari salesman.

"That's the one," he said. "But you forgot the twin turbos." He gunned the accelerator. She could hear the whistle of the turbo and the clatter of the cams and saw that several heads turned to stare at the lipstick red car and its good-looking driver.

"That is one terrific car," said Debbie, enviously.

"And fast," said Chung.

Debbie slowly pushed her foot down on the clutch and put the Jaguar in first gear. "So tell me, Anthony..." she said, but roared off before she finished the sentence, leaving him fumbling for his own gear stick.

"Bitch!" he shouted, surprised by her sudden departure. He put the Ferrari into first and spun the rear wheels on the cobbled road as he accelerated after her. He had to brake to avoid a red and grey taxi which pulled out in front of him, and by the time he reached Arbuthnot Road she was out of sight. It was just after midnight so there was little traffic about. He ran a red light and headed up Robinson Road, towards Shan Teng, the Peak. She lived on Findlay Road and he was pretty sure she'd head up the narrow, winding Old Peak Road where he'd find it difficult to overtake.

He roared up Robinson Road, the noise of the engine behind his shoulder blades almost deafening him. The F40 didn't come with a stereo system because when the car was in full flight you couldn't hear anything above the jet engine whistle of the turbos and the whir of pumps and motors that fed the 2,936 cc of greedy piston space. The Pirelli P Zero tyres gripped the road like a limpet as he cornered, and as he entered Old Peak Road he saw the rear lights of her Jaguar about a hundred yards ahead. In its early climb up the Peak the road was a respectable size, but after it intersected with Tregunter Path it became treacherously narrow so Chung pushed his foot down on the accelerator and moved the tall, thin gear lever quickly through the kink in the gate from first to second, a manoeuvre which had taken quite a bit of getting used to. The Ferrari kicked and the turbines whistled and he hit seventy mph, still in second gear. The car seemed to hug the ground even tighter as it followed the curves and bends of the road, passing the Ladies' Recreation Club on his left, and he smiled as he saw how quickly he was gaining on her. He wasn't surprised; the F40 was a racing car made street legal while the XJS was a luxury executive car, albeit a stylish one. It was like putting an Olympic sprinter up against a weekend jogger.

He eased off the accelerator but he still gained on Debbie and he had to brake sharply to avoid hitting her rear bumper. She accelerated and for a second it looked as if she were going to lose control as the back wheels slid to the left but then they gripped and she increased the gap between them. Chung had wanted to make more of a race of it, but he realised that she wasn't a particularly good driver and if he pushed her too hard it would end in disaster. He could see that she wasn't even wearing her seat belt whereas he was firmly strapped into his bucket seat by the Ferrari's six-point racing harness. He decided to end it as quickly as possible.

He nudged the F40 to within ten feet of the back of the Jaguar, checked that there was nothing coming in the opposite direction, then flicked the car to the side and forward, feeling the end slide, corrected for it and pushed the accelerator to the floor. The Jaguar dissolved into a blur on his left and then disappeared behind him. The road narrowed and bent to the left and right and he flicked the steering wheel to stay in his lane. A yellow and cream-coloured minibus flashed towards him and then was gone, leaving an image in his mind of an old driver, mouth wide open and chin forward as the Ferrari zipped by, missing it by inches.

He eased back on the accelerator and went into third gear, hearing the guttural roar of the eight cylinders relax as the speedometer touched ninety mph. He was nowhere near testing the car's performance, and he knew it. The F40 could do nought to ninety mph in less than seven seconds on a straight run and its top speed was close to 200 mph. Put wings on it and it'd fly. He wanted to get so far ahead of Debbie that she'd give up and drive home at a sensible speed. He kept looking at the rearview mirror but he was alone on the road. The Ferrari flashed over the tunnel where the Peak tram clawed its way to the top of the highest point of Hong Kong Island and on to Barker Road, the lights of Kowloon away to his left. He put the Ferrari into a tight turn and swung into Findlay Road, scanning the numbers as they whizzed by until he saw the Fielding residence. He began braking but the F40 was still more than 200 feet past it when it came to rest. He turned the car round and stopped in front of the gates to the Fielding house, keeping the engine running at a high rpm to stop the plugs from fouling while he waited for Debbie.

It was a full thirty seconds before she turned into Findlay Road. Her brakes squealed as she stopped the XJS in front of Chung's car. He got out and walked over, putting his hand on the roof of the Jaguar and leaning down as she lowered the window.

"Congratulations," she said. She was smiling, but there was a hard edge to her smile as if she weren't used to losing.

"It's a fast car," he said. "I'll let you drive it some time."

Her smile brightened. "I'd like that," she said.

"But first, we've got to decide on the prize."

"The prize?"

"For winning the race." He tapped his fingers on the roof of the Jaguar.

"I didn't know we were racing for a prize," she said.

"Oh sure," said Chung. "I won a date with you."

"A date with me?" she said, flustered. "What would I have got if I'd won?" Chung grinned. "Don't tell me," she said. "A date with you."

"Good job I won, huh?" smiled Chung. "How about next Saturday? I'll pick you up here at eight."

Debbie thought about it for a moment or two, then nodded. "Okay. But one condition."

"Sure." He already knew what it was.

"You bring the Ferrari."

"Deal," he said. "Till next Saturday, then." He took his hand off the roof of her car and waved once. "Bye," he said.

Debbie drove the car up the drive towards the house. She had been sure that Anthony Chung would try to kiss her and was vaguely disappointed that he hadn't. She'd been annoyed that he had so easily beaten her, but she realised that there was little she could have done against a Ferrari. He hadn't gloated, either, like so many men would have done. No, a date with him wouldn't be a trial. In fact, she was already looking forward to it.

She parked the Jaguar next to her mother's black convertible Saab and switched off the engine. She stroked the steering wheel and wondered what it would be like to drive Chung's Ferrari. She jerked herself out of her daydream, locked the car and went into the house through the connecting door at the rear of the garage.

There were lights on in the lounge and Debbie pushed open the door. Her mother was sitting on the low leather sofa in front of the fireplace, a drink in her hands and a faraway look in her eyes. The fireplace was only lit during the winter months but it made a perfect focal point for the room. On top was a line of printed invitations, some embossed, most with gold around the edges. Anne and William Fielding received a constant stream of invitations to cocktail parties, dinners and junk trips. From where she stood by the door, Debbie could see her mother's face reflected in the large gilt-framed mirror above the white marble fireplace. She looked sad and lost, like a little girl who'd mislaid her parents.

"Hi, Mum," said Debbie.

Anne Fielding jerked as if wakening from a dream and the clear liquid in her glass slopped over the side and down her hand. "Shit," she said. She pulled a handkerchief from the pocket of her beige Chanel dress and wiped her hand, shaking her head as if annoyed at her loss of control. The dress was one of her favourites. It showed off what she thought was her best feature — her long, shapely legs — though it was her green eyes and long lashes that men usually found most appealing. Debbie had always been grateful that she'd inherited her mother's hair, eyes and legs, though she felt cheated when it came to her figure. At forty-five, Anne Fielding had curves that would do credit to a lingerie model, firm breasts that turned the heads of men half her age and hips that were only an inch or so wider than when she was a teenager and before she'd given birth. She knew how good she looked, too, and enjoyed showing herself off. The reason she liked the Chanel so much was because it emphasised her cleavage, though she'd never have admitted it.

Debbie's first thought had been that her mother had been waiting up for her, but she clearly had something on her mind. She walked into the room and sat down on the grey sofa. "Are you okay, Mum?" she asked, concern in her voice. It wasn't unusual to find her mother sitting alone in the lounge with a drink late at night, but this was different. She looked as if she were about to burst into tears.

Anne Fielding rubbed her nose with the wet handkerchief. Debbie could smell the gin. "It's stupid really," said Anne. "It's nothing."

"Is it Dad?" Relations between her mother and father had been cool since before she'd left to go to university in Britain. But when she'd got back nine months earlier with an upper second-class degree in Communications Studies she'd sensed that the twenty-four-year marriage had taken a turn for the worse and the double bed in the master bedroom had been replaced by two singles.

Anne smiled thinly and shook her head. "No, it's not your father." She sniffed and dabbed at her eyes. "It's Sally Remnick. She's leaving Hong Kong." She brushed a lock of blonde hair from her face.

"For good?" Sally was just about Anne's best friend and confidante, as well as her regular tennis partner at the Ladies' Recreation Club.

Anne nodded. "She and Michael are being transferred to Singapore. Their bank is relocating its head office." She threw the handkerchief on to the coffee table. "It's not fair!" she said. "It's not bloody well fair!" She picked up the glass and took a big swallow of her gin and tonic.

Over the past year at least a dozen of Anne Fielding's close friends had left the colony, and Debbie knew that her mother was feeling increasingly isolated.

"I'm sorry, Mum," she said helplessly, knowing there was nothing she could say that would make it better.

"Everybody's leaving," said Anne. "The rats are deserting the sinking ship and soon I'll be the only one left." Her hands were shaking. Debbie took the glass from her hands and placed it on the table next to the discarded handkerchief.

"They're not rats, they're just being sensible," said Debbie. "They're moving because they're worried about what'll happen after 1997, you know that. Everyone's doing it, all the companies are moving to Singapore or Thailand. You mustn't take it personally, Mum."

Anne shook her head. "Oh, I know that. But they're my friends, my last real friends in this godforsaken city. You don't know how alone I feel, Debbie."

"But doesn't Dad . . ."

"Ha!" snorted Anne. "Your father's only concern is the bank and his blessed racehorses. You know that."

Debbie nodded and took her mother's hands in her own. They felt hot and she could feel them trembling. "I know, Mum. But you know how much the bank means to him. He has to safeguard its future after 1997."

"And what about me, Debbie? What about my future? He's fifty-eight years old and he's got to retire at sixty, come what may. He has the bank for two years at most, he's got the rest of his life with me. Where do you think his priorities should lie?" She pulled her right hand away and reached for the glass again.

"Please, Mum, don't drink so much," pleaded Debbie.

Anne watched her daughter over the top of her glass as she drank. She drained the gin and tonic and slowly put the glass back on the table.

"I don't think I can take much more, Debbie," said Anne quietly. "This place is going to the dogs. The crime rate's up, the Hong Kong Chinese hate us, the mainland Chinese just want us to get the hell out, all the good people are leaving. Somebody spat at me while I was shopping yesterday."

"What?"

"Somebody spat at me. Down my back. I didn't realise until I got home. They'd spat all down the back of my jacket. I tell you, Debbie, they hate us for what we've done to them. You can see it in their eyes. It's going to get worse, too, as 1997 approaches. It's a pressure cooker just waiting to explode. And I don't want to be here when it happens."

"Please, Mum, you're over-reacting, you really are. You're just upset because Sally's going, that's all. You'll feel better tomorrow, I know you will."

Anne wiped her eyes with the back of her hand. "I suppose so," she sighed. She stood up and smoothed the material of the dress around her thighs.

"Where were you tonight?" asked Debbie.

"Dinner at the Mandarin with Chase Manhattan," she said.

"Dressed to kill?"

Anne's smile brightened. "You know these Americans. Once they get into their fifties they drop wife number one and get themselves a trophy wife. I wanted them to see that your father already has one."

"You look stunning," said Debbie.

"Yeah, your mother can still cut a dash when she tries," said Anne.

"I hope I look half as good as you when I'm your age," sighed Debbie.

Anne raised a warning eyebrow. "Don't push it, kid," she said. "You've cheered me up, no need to overdo it."

Debbie laughed and hugged her. There was the briefest flush of resentment when she felt her mother's soft breasts press against her own flat-chest but she suppressed it and kissed her mother on the cheek. "Goodnight, Mum," she said.

Anne broke away and bent down to pick up the glass. On her way to the kitchen she stopped and put her hand to her forehead. "Oh, I forgot to tell you, that policeman called. What's his name? Neil?"

"Oh, hell."

"Three times."

Debbie pulled a face.

"Why don't you put the poor lad out of his misery?" said Anne. "Just tell him you're not interested."

"He's thirty-four years old, Mum. He's hardly a lad."

"That may be, but he's acting like a lovelorn teenager," said Anne.

"It's worse than that," said Debbie. "He wants to get engaged."

"That'll please your father no end," said Anne, arching one eyebrow.

"Oh, don't tell him, Mum. Please. Neil's just being stupid."

"For a policeman, he doesn't seem to have much in the way of common sense." She looked at Debbie, suddenly serious. "Don't lead him on, Debbie. It's not fair to him, and it could be embarrassing for you."

"And for Dad," said Debbie.

Anne nodded. "He'd hit the roof," she said. "You're not serious about him, are you?"

Debbie shook her head emphatically. "I went out with him a few times, that's all, Mum. He just thought it was more serious than it was. He's nice, but, you know . . ." She shrugged.

"Yeah," said Anne. "I know." She turned and went into the kitchen, her high heels clicking on the shiny wood floor. "Goodnight, God bless," she called over her shoulder. "And don't forget we're on the junk tomorrow."

"Goodnight, Mum," Debbie replied, and scampered upstairs to her room. She was in the bathroom brushing her teeth when her mother tiptoed back into the lounge to pour herself another gin and tonic.

There were ten men on the tour, and two women, and they met for the first time in Bangkok before flying on to Ho Chi Minh City. The men were a mixed bunch, but that was pretty much to be expected because the only thing they had in common was that at some point they'd served in Vietnam. It was obvious to Dan Lehman, though, that they had different memories of their time in Indochina. There was a balding overweight life insurance salesman from Seattle who'd brought his wife and who was pretty vague about what he'd actually done during his tour of duty. Lehman had a gut feeling that the only action he'd seen had been in the bars and brothels of downtown Saigon. His wife had the worn-out look of a woman who'd heard too many of his, probably fictional, war stories and she'd quickly teamed up with the other woman in the party, a perky, slim blonde who seemed to be a good deal older than her husband, Pete Cummings, a grunt who'd served during the last year of the war. He hadn't been injured but several times he'd referred to friends he'd lost and Lehman reckoned he had a bad case of survivor's guilt.

One thing had hit Lehman as soon as the group had assembled at the Indra Regent Hotel in Bangkok and been introduced by the tour group leader, a big-boned Australian girl with a bad case of sunburn, and that was that there was only one black guy on the trip. Statistically there was something wrong with that, because a disproportionate number of black Americans, and brown, and yellow, had served and died in Vietnam. The percentage of blacks in the army during the war was about the same as in the States — about twelve per cent. But blacks made up twenty per cent of combat troops and accounted for almost a quarter of casualties. Yet only three per cent of officers weren't white. Lehman wondered immediately why there was only one black in the group. His first thought was that it was a question of money. Most of the non-whites who'd served had been poor, with little or no prospects, so maybe they just didn't have the money to relive memories which weren't all that pleasant in the first place. But then he realised there was probably more to it than that. Maybe it was because they'd been used to hardships all their lives and the Nam was just another load of shit they had to go through, like street gangs, probation and prison, and once they'd done their tour they just moved on. More than once Lehman had been told by black grunts he was dropping into a hot LZ that it was nothing compared to the Bronx on a Saturday night. Guys like Cummings, though, were pulled away from loving homes, small towns full of friends and memories, and thrown into hostile jungles with a back-breaking pack and a loaded gun. The lives they went back to would never seem the same again and the mental scars took that much longer to heal. But it seemed too trite, Lehman thought, to suggest that blacks were more able than whites to come to terms with what had happened during the war. Maybe the answer was even simpler. Maybe they just didn't want to hang around with a bunch of white vets reliving old times, times when the whites got the medals and promotions and the blacks got the bullets and the latrine duty.

The black guy on the trip, Barton Lewis, had been a crew chief with the 1st Cav and now worked as a mechanic in Baltimore, a city Lehman had visited occasionally but never liked. He was affable and easy-going and usually when the group had travelled *en masse* Lehman had found himself sitting next to him. He was a good talker, not full of the gung-ho bullshit that poured forth from the salesman from Seattle, but made careful observations about the people and places they passed through, told jokes that didn't have a sarcastic edge to them and stories which more often than not had himself as the fall guy. He had a ready laugh but sometimes it seemed to Lehman that it was a little forced and there were times when Lewis lapsed into long silences. Then his forehead would be creased with worry lines and his eyes narrowed as if he had a headache. Lehman wasn't sure why Lewis had come on the trip. He'd discussed his theory about why blacks didn't seem to want to return to Vietnam and Lewis had agreed but hadn't been forthcoming about his own reasons and Lehman hadn't pressed him.

Another guy whom Lehman got on with well was a computer programmer from Cleveland, a big, beefy, bearded man called Joe Stebbings who swore blind that he remembered Lehman lifting him off a hill near Khe Sanh. Lehman didn't remember and when Stebbings described the operation it sounded like any one of a hundred. That was something else Lehman had quickly noticed about the group — the preponderance of facial hair. Stebbings wasn't alone in hiding his face behind a bushy beard and moustache. Cummings didn't have a beard, but Lehman guessed that was because his wife insisted that he stayed clean-shaven, and Lewis didn't have one either. But of the ten men in the group, half of them had beards, and not just neat trim ones, or closely clipped moustaches; the beards worn by the vets were big and bushy as if they were trying to lose themselves behind a mass of hair. Lehman noticed, too, that the ones with beards also tended to be the ones who wore sunglasses even inside the hotel, as if they didn't want to be looked in the eye.

Two were from Atlanta: Lorne Henderson and Arnold Speed, and Lehman had rarely met two such laid-back characters, even among the airheads of southern California. It was as if the war had taken every bit of aggression out of them and left them placid, almost docile. Henderson carried a Nikon camera and Speed was never without a Sony camcorder and they spent hours wandering around with wide eyes, taking pictures of each other.

Another guy with a beard was Eric Horvitz. On the rare occasions he removed his sunglasses, Lehman could see that he had the thousand-yard stare, eyes that looked right through you even when he was smiling, dead eyes that had seen too much at too young an age. Lehman had had a beer with Horvitz in Bangkok and there had been a conversation, of sorts, made difficult by the fact that Horvitz preferred to keep his answers monosyllabic. To Lehman it felt as if Horvitz wasn't used to the company of other human beings; it was almost as if he resented them intruding into his world. Lehman had told him that he flew choppers, but when he asked Horvitz what he'd done in Nam the man just looked at him coldly and said, "I was just there, that's all." He didn't say it viciously or nastily, just in the same matter-of-fact way that he answered all of Lehman's probing, the way an adult would deal with questions from a child who was too young to understand why the sky is blue or why dogs wag their tails when they're happy. There was a tension about Horvitz, but it wasn't that he was highly strung, it was the tension of a leopard stalking a herd of antelope. He appeared relaxed, almost nonchalant, but every movement seemed to have a purpose and each time Horvitz entered a room, people would check where he was and what he was doing: like prey knowing that the predator was around but uncertain what to do about it, anxious not to draw attention to themselves. If Lehman had been asked to sum up Horvitz in one word, that word would have been "dangerous".

Dangerous was also the description that could be applied to another bearded member of the group, the youngest, a guy from New Jersey called Larry Carmody with a hook for a hand and a major chip on his shoulder. Carmody seemed to be a mass of tension. He was argumentative and garrulous and he annoyed the hell out of Lehman. Apparently he had been a helicopter doorgunner and when he found out that Lehman was a pilot he tried to befriend him, slapping him on the back and wanting to talk about "the good old days". The good old days, it turned out, were the times when Carmody had been flying low over the rice paddies of Vietnam shooting water buffalo and the occasional farmer, shooting them and laughing about it. If it hadn't been for losing his hand, Carmody would probably have really enjoyed his war and would have been as happy to go back as the salesman from Seattle.

The last member of the group was, like Lehman, close-shaven, and was almost certainly the oldest. Lehman would have guessed that the man was in his fifties, tall and lean with short grey hair. He was almost as reticent as Horvitz, but that seemed to be because he was more interested in watching and learning than in giving his opinions. He seemed intelligent and thoughtful, and had alert eyes, keen and watchful like a hawk on the wing. He was a pilot, he told Lehman, and had come on the tour to see at ground level the country he used to fly over thousands of feet in the air. He didn't say as much, but Lehman got the impression that he also wanted to see the sort of people he'd been dropping bombs and napalm on all those years ago. His name was Joel Tyler.

The tour had started with a twenty-four-hour stopover in Bangkok. The Australian girl who had handled the Thai end of the trip had arranged a get-together in the hotel coffee shop and given them a briefing on what to expect when they got to Ho Chi Minh City and afterwards Lehman, Lewis, and Tyler had gone out for a quiet beer. The salesman from Seattle had wanted to take them to the red light area but the three had refused, saying they were all jet-lagged and wanted an early night.

Lehman had heard horror stories about the airports in Vietnam, how petty bureaucracy and red tape meant delays of several hours and a myriad of forms to be stamped, but it turned out to be even quicker than when he flew into the States. The standard of English was better, too.

Immigration consisted of a quick look at his visa and a pleasant smile, and Customs was nothing more than two signatures on his three forms and a few questions about currency from a pretty girl in a green uniform with a peaked cap perched on the top of her head and huge shoulder boards that made her hips look all the more slight. The girl caught him by surprise; he expected them all to be plain and drab as befitted a communist regime, but she was young and very pretty with purple eye-liner and pink-varnished nails that would have done credit to a Las Vegas showgirl. She waved him through without even checking his luggage and wished him a pleasant stay, which is more than had ever happened to him when he arrived at Los Angeles. Twenty minutes after their Thai Airways Airbus A300 had landed they were all out of the Customs hall and in the main reception area, where it first hit home that they really were in a Third World country. The heat was wet and stifling, worse even than it had been in Bangkok, and the crowd formed an almost impenetrable wall. There were so many people there that Lehman couldn't believe for a minute that they were all there to meet arrivals. Most of those waiting were poorly dressed, and many looked the worse for wear, a sign of a bad diet and lousy health care. The faces were smiling, though, and there were flashes of gold teeth. Every second mouth seemed to have a cigarette in it. There was chatter, too, and laughter, as if the airport were a good place to hang out if you didn't have a job or anything else to do on a hot April afternoon.

Tyler appeared at Lehman's shoulder. He was wearing gold-framed sunglasses and looked for all the world like a CIA agent searching for a contact. Both men were towing Samsonite suitcases and had shoulder bags bearing the name of the company that had arranged the tour and they scanned the crowds looking for their tour guides. A small Vietnamese woman in a white blouse and a black skirt spotted their bags and waved a small cardboard sign bearing the name of their travel company. Her name was Judy, she said, and she welcomed them all to Vietnam. At first glance and from a distance she looked like a schoolgirl, barely five feet tall with shoulder-length black hair and a slim, boyish figure, but when Lehman got up close he could see that she was older, probably in her mid-forties. She shepherded them into a minibus and introduced the driver, a man called Hung.

"Well Hung?" laughed the salesman from Seattle. He clapped the man hard on the shoulder and looked round to make sure that everyone got the joke.

Judy gave them a guided tour as Hung drove the bus through the streets to their hotel. The roads were packed with motorcycles and mopeds which buzzed in and out of the crowds of cyclists. The bicycles all seemed ancient, and few had working brakes. Many of the bikes carried passengers, often wives hanging on to their husbands' waists or small children sitting on the crossbar and hanging on to the handlebars with their little hands. There were young girls with floppy hats to protect them from the sun and evening gloves stretching up to their elbows, wearing the traditional *ao dais* silk blouse slit up the sides.

The cyclos were still around, Lehman noticed, the three-wheeled pedal-powered taxis that carried one passenger, two at a pinch. Sitting in a cyclo was one of the best ways to see Saigon, Lehman knew, half sitting, half lying, with nothing in front of you but your feet as the driver powered his way through the traffic. It was like being in the front of a sled. Or a helicopter on an attack run.

There were some new cars around, mostly Japanese models, but the trucks all seemed to have been around for decades. Lehman could see none of the big-finned American cars that he remembered from his days in Saigon, and there were none of the yellow and blue Renault taxis that used to rattle around. In fact, he couldn't see taxis anywhere.

Most of the life of Saigon seemed to be lived on the streets, much as when Lehman had last been there more than twenty years earlier. But the city now was a shell of its former self. Lehman had half expected to find it in war-torn ruins like some Asian version of Beirut, but the damage was a result of neglect rather than explosives. The very fabric of the buildings appeared to be falling apart: paintwork was peeling, plaster crumbling, wood rotting, and little or nothing was being done to hold back the creeping decay.

"Look what they've done to this fucking place," sneered the salesman from Seattle. "Look where communism gets you. Right?"

"Right," agreed Carmody from the back of the bus.

Henderson was clicking away with his Nikon and Speed was filming him taking photographs. Tyler was sitting next to Horvitz. He was talking quietly, with Horvitz nodding occasionally.

The shops they drove past were almost all open to the sidewalk, without windows or doors, and most had men and women sprawled idly on old leather chairs, fanning themselves with pieces of cardboard or sitting in the breeze of an electric fan. There were shops selling food, second-hand tools, cheap clothes and shoes. There were unexpected shops too, selling Japanese colour televisions, stereo systems and brightly coloured refrigerators. Lehman even saw one shop which seemed to sell nothing but electric guitars. The best-maintained buildings seemed to be those belonging to the banks. On the sidewalks were a plethora of small businesses, food stalls selling noodle soup or French bread sandwiches, wooden cases on stools full of Vietnamese and American cigarettes, and bicycle-repairers squatting on the kerb with the patient gaze of vultures, waiting for tyres to burst or chains to break.

The bus pulled up in front of their hotel and as the group climbed out of the air-conditioned interior and into the stifling heat five Vietnamese men in turquoise sailor suits and berets with white pom-poms began unloading their cases. They had been booked into the Saigon Floating Hotel which was moored at Me Linh Square and the owners had insisted on continuing the nautical theme through to the staff uniforms.

"Hotel used to be in Australia, at Great Barrier Reef," Judy explained as they strolled along a covered walkway towards reception, the sailors following behind, pushing the bags on a large trolley. "They tow it here to Ho Chi Minh City. Now it is the best hotel in Vietnam."

According to the itinerary they'd all been given in the States, the first few days were to be spent at Vung Tau, a beach resort some 75 kilometres to the south of Ho Chi Minh City. Lehman had flown to Vung Tau during the war. The US Army had a big camp there and it had been the place where the CIA had trained Vietnamese commando teams.

After Judy left, Lehman asked if anyone fancied a walk around town before dinner. Tyler agreed, as did Horvitz, Lewis, Cummings and his wife, and Henderson and Speed, and they all arranged to meet an hour later in the lobby after they'd showered and changed.

Lehman was down first, followed by Peter and Janet Cummings. Horvitz and Tyler came down in the lift together, still deep in conversation. Lehman wondered what the former pilot and the man with dead eyes had to talk about.

Lewis was the last to arrive and he appeared out of breath, apologising profusely and wearing a shirt that would have done credit to a Hawaiian beach barbecue, a swirl of reds, blues and purples on which were superimposed swaying palm trees and windsurfers.

Lehman put on his sunglasses. "Hell, Bart. I didn't realise we were dressing for dinner," he said.

The black man laughed and punched him on the shoulder.

"Let's go," he said.

They walked out of the hotel and turned along Ton Duc Thong Street, the Saigon River on their left. Cyclo drivers kept ringing their bells and touting for business but Tyler waved them away. A group of bare-chested boys and girls — though it was difficult to tell them apart they were so young — ran across the road and then danced around them, chanting, "*Lien Xo! Lien Xo!*"

"What are they saying?" Janet Cummings asked.

"They're calling us Russians," Tyler explained. "I suppose most of the Caucasians they meet are from Russia, technical experts and advisers. It's only recently that Westerners have been allowed in."

"And we probably all look alike to them," said Lewis.

"Bart, the only black Russian I know is a godforsaken drink," said Lehman and they all laughed.

The kids continued to call out "*Lien Xo!*" in their singsong voices and passers-by smiled at the group. The smiles seemed good natured, and Lehman got the feeling that the people of Saigon were glad to see visitors from America in their country once more.

The children had singled out Tyler as the leader of the group, probably because he looked to be the oldest, and one of the girls took his hand, singing "*Lien Xo*" over and over again.

Tyler looked down at her and smiled. "*Chung toi khong phai la nguoi Lien Xo*," he said.

The girl looked astonished, her eyes wide and her mouth open.

A boy, bolder than the rest, stood in front of him, his chin up defiantly. "*Ong la nguoi gi?*" he asked.

"*Chung toi la nguoi My*," answered Tyler.

The girl slipped her hand out of Tyler's and began jumping up and down on the spot, holding out her hands.

"Yeah, American! American!" she shouted with glee. "Give me dollar, give me dollar."

Tyler grinned sheepishly at the rest of the group. "I guess it was a mistake saying we were from the States, huh?" he said. They wandered to the end of the road and then swung right, along Ben Chuong Duong Street, ignoring the calls of the cyclo drivers. Most of the talk was about the Saigon they used to know and how it had changed. All were surprised at the total lack of military presence. They had expected to see NVA troops and tanks at every corner with machine-gun posts outside important buildings, but there were none. Saigon was not a city under occupation with communism being forced down its throat by force. The city had gone into a catastrophic decline under the Hanoi-based regime, that was clear, but the people were always smiling and laughing and seemed to be making the best of a bad job, like refugees in the aftermath of an earthquake, knowing that things were bad, really bad, but they wouldn't be bad for ever.

Alongside the road were a line of men in their forties and fifties sitting by collections of tools and engineering parts which had been carefully cleaned and oiled and placed on squares of old blankets. Some of the men were missing limbs and Lehman realised that they were almost certainly war veterans, though it was impossible to tell from which side, north or south. From the smiles and nods, most of which showed missing teeth, he guessed they were from the South. Their wares were heartbreakingly meagre, a few screwdrivers, sets of spanners, batteries, old flashlights, cogs and wheels that had been wirebrushed clean, bicycle chains and spark plugs. The men waved their arms across their makeshift stalls, appealing for the group to buy something, but there was nothing there that any of them could possibly want.

The air was split with the crackle of small arms fire, close by and rapid. To Lehman it was as if everything that happened in the few seconds after the rapid series of bangs took place in slow motion, but it was only hours afterwards, as he lay in his room in the Floating Hotel, that he was able to put it all into perspective and realised that they had all acted differently and that the way they had reacted gave an insight into their characters in a way that hundreds of hours on a psychiatrist's couch could never have achieved.

Lehman himself jumped when he heard the sound of shots, his head shrinking into his shoulders as he ducked involuntarily, a flinch that he couldn't control.

114

But he made no other movement because every other time he'd come under fire, and there had been many, there was nothing he could do but continue to fly his helicopter and any panic or jerking on the controls could lead to a crash.

Peter Cummings seemed to go into shock when he heard the shots: his head whipped around as he looked for the source of the shots and then he rushed to a wall where he crouched down as if hugging it for protection. His eyes were wide with panic and he shuffled along the wall trying to find a more secure place to hide. His wife dashed over and held him, resting her chin on the top of his head, whispering to him.

Henderson and Speed both flinched and jumped back. Of the two, Speed seemed to be more in control, and he reached over and took Henderson by the arm, shouting to him that it was okay, it was just firecrackers going off outside a shop across the road. Henderson seemed to have gone into shock; his whole body trembled like he had a fever and it only subsided when Speed put his arms around him and hugged him, pretty much as Janet Cummings held her husband.

Bart Lewis dropped to the ground and kept low, obviously scared but none the less alert. It was a reaction Lehman had seen time and time again in combat from grunts who were frightened out of their wits but who knew that the only way to survive was to identify the danger and either defeat it or move away from it, that cowering got you nowhere and that action, any sort of action, was better than just staying put and being shot at. Lehman could tell that if an officer yelled at Lewis to attack, or to dig in, or to pull back, he'd obey immediately. He might not want to, but he'd do it, whereas Cummings would be paralysed with fear and Henderson would have just run, eaten up by fear and panic.

Horvitz was the first to react, of that Lehman was sure. He'd been standing just in front and to the left of Lehman when the shots cracked and it almost seemed as if the man had started to move before the sounds, so fast had he been. Horvitz leapt to the left, and it wasn't a startled reaction but a controlled, disciplined movement — a low dive to the ground where he rolled over his shoulder past a startled Vietnamese hawker. Horvitz's hand moved out to grab a screwdriver from the blanket next to the hawker and as he continued to roll he brought up the tool into a throwing position. At first Lehman had thought the dive had been random, but the move took Horvitz behind the rear wing of a battered white Lada and when he was in a kneeling position with the screwdriver ready to be thrown he was the only one who had found himself effective cover. But that wasn't what had impressed Lehman. It was the way that Horvitz didn't appear to be the least bit scared. There was no sign of exertion, no panting or heaving chest. He was totally calm and prepared for whatever might come next. When he saw the group of onlookers watching the firecrackers explode across the road there was no sign of relief on his face; he just stood upright, walked back over to the hawker and placed the screwdriver back on the blanket. Lewis was grinning sheepishly as he got to his feet and rubbed the dirt off his hands, but there was no embarrassment at all on Horvitz's face.

The reaction that most intrigued Lehman was that of Tyler. While everyone else was moving and scrambling to identify the threat, Tyler seemed to react almost lazily. He stood exactly where he was, hands on his hips and slowly turned his head towards the noise, then smiled when he saw the firecrackers popping and the hand-painted sign above the building which proclaimed "Japanese Manufactures Welcome Vietnamese People to Exhibition of Sewing Machines".

It was as if Tyler had heard the cracks, identified them immediately as fireworks and not gunfire, and reacted accordingly. He looked around at the vets in their various positions and shrugged. Across the road the crowd applauded a small Japanese gentleman who cut a yellow ribbon with a big pair of scissors and they all went inside, still clapping.

As he lay on his bed in the hotel, his hands behind his head, Lehman wondered how a former pilot could be so calm when most of the experienced grunts reacted so badly. And why a man whose war was supposedly fought thousands of feet above the rice fields of Vietnam should be fluent in Vietnamese.

Senior Inspector Neil Coleman carried his burning hot plastic cup of machine coffee over to his desk and put it down next to the telephone. He dropped down into his chair and surveyed the office which he shared with two other policemen, both Chinese. The desks were standard issue, grey metal with a drawer full of files on the left side and three drawers on the right, all with locks which could be opened with a paperclip. Being the senior of the three, Coleman's desk was on its own by the window where he could look down on the bustling streets below. His colleagues, Tommy Yip and Kenneth Hui, sat facing each other to the left of the room, their desks touching so they could answer each other's phones. On the right of the office was a line of green metal filing cabinets filled to capacity. The overspill was piled high on a table behind Yip's desk. Coleman had requisitioned extra filing cabinets but there was a staff shortage in the supplies department, he'd been told, and it was taking months rather than weeks to process equipment requests. It seemed that every department in the Royal Hong Kong Police Force was losing people and finding it next to impossible to fill its vacancies. It wasn't a brain drain, it was a people drain. Secretaries, clerks, drivers — they were all rushing to emigrate if they had relatives abroad, or moving to better paid jobs so that they stood a chance of buying a passport if they hadn't. The police didn't pay well, and there was the ever present worry about what would happen when the Chinese took over in 1997. Some feared that they would be regarded as "contaminated" by the new rulers, others feared that promotion would go only to reliable cadres and true communists. Either way, few were eager to take the risk and those who could go were leaving like fleas jumping off a drowning dog.

Yip and Hui were both speaking on their telephones, using Cantonese. When he'd joined the force eight years earlier Coleman had gone through the force's intensive Cantonese course but he'd spent most of his time since in Arsenal Street headquarters and he was now rusty to say the least. For all he knew Yip and Hui were talking to each other on their phones. He'd only been working with them for about six months and he didn't trust them at all. They were forever talking to each other in Chinese and sometimes they'd look over at him when they thought he wasn't looking, as if to check whether or not he was trying to eavesdrop. They'd both tested him early on, speaking directly to him in Cantonese to see if he'd understood, and seemed happy when they discovered the limits of his comprehension of their language. Of the two he liked Tommy Yip better — at least he went to the police social club occasionally and drank a couple of bottles of Heineken with Coleman. So far as he could tell, Hui never drank, never socialised, and had no life outside the force. Hui's English was good, too, so good that Coleman was sure that he'd have no trouble getting a much better paid job in the private sector if he wanted. But he appeared to be quite happy with his job and, on the one occasion Coleman had brought up the subject, he'd expressed no interest in leaving Hong Kong. Coleman suspected that he was a spy. It was general knowledge among the expatriate officers that Beijing was sending agents to join the force in the run-up to 1997 so they'd get the inside track on what was happening and who they could trust once they took over. Late at night, in the social club or in the bars of Wan Chai, they'd compare notes on who they thought

119

was working for the mainland and Coleman always had Hui at the top of his list.

Above the filing cabinets was a graph showing the number of cases being dealt with by the Stolen Vehicles Group. There were two lines on the chart: a thick red line showed the number of cases of stolen cars, a blue line below showed the number of cars the group had recovered. The two lines were drawing inexorably apart.

Hong Kong's stolen car problem stemmed from its proximity to China, where there was always a shortage of vehicles. Each year up to 10,000 were stolen and only about two-thirds were recovered. Of the rest, most ended up in mainland China. As China's foreign currency shortage worsened, so grew its appetite for stolen Hong Kong cars. The triads had got the business so well organised that they would steal on order if the price was right. A cadre in Beijing or Shanghai could choose the make, model and probably the colour of the car he wanted, and within the month the triads would deliver it to his door. Most cadres wanted a top-of-the-line Mercedes, but the car most commonly smuggled into China was the humble Toyota because it was so easily converted to left-hand drive. Hong Kong followed Britain's lead and used right-hand-drive cars which would stick out in China so they were usually converted before being smuggled across to the mainland.

The original Stolen Vehicles Unit had been absorbed into Criminal Investigations Department as a cost-saving measure, but as the number of cars being stolen continued to rise, the problem was turned over to the

Serious Crimes Group, with Interpol becoming responsible for liaising with their opposite numbers in China, Malaysia and Thailand, which also benefited from the trade. Eventually Serious Crimes Group found they couldn't cope with the workload and so a new Stolen Vehicles Unit was formed, with about half the manpower it originally had. Coleman had been seconded to it, despite his protests that he wanted to stay with anti-triad investigations. He was curtly informed that chasing stolen cars was anti-triad work, and there had been no further argument.

A middle-aged woman police constable clumped in and dropped a stack of files into his in-tray. She nodded a good morning to him and waved to Hui and Yip as she went out. Coleman flipped his thumb across the new arrivals. Thirty-four. "Terrific," he said to himself.

Hui put down his phone and stood up. Coleman motioned at the pile of files but Hui shrugged. "I have to go to Lok Ma Chau border checkpoint, remember?" said Hui. "We're taking delivery of twenty Toyotas at midday."

Coleman had forgotten. "Yeah, enjoy your trip."

Hui laughed and lit a cigarette. He held the packet out to Coleman who shook his head. "I'm trying to give up," said Coleman.

"I forgot," said Hui.

Coleman doubted that Hui forgot anything. In fact, in all probability he went home at night and wrote down every single thing that had happened to him that day in the minutest detail. Yip put down his phone and said something to Hui in Cantonese. They laughed together and Hui went out.

The return of the twenty Toyotas was the result of two months of hard negotiations between the British and Chinese authorities and represented less than one per cent of the cars that they believed had been smuggled into China over the past year. The procedure was first to establish which cars had been really stolen and which had been mislaid by their owners or borrowed by Hong Kong's many joyriders and road-racers. Once they were sure a car had been stolen Coleman's office sent the details upstairs to Interpol. The staff officer there, a superintendent, waited until he had a list of 500 or so before he passed on the details of the cars, including chassis numbers and engine numbers, to his opposites in other Asian countries. In China he dealt with the Public Security Bureau through their Gung On Kuk office in Beijing.

It was then a case of the Beijing Interpol office persuading the police to investigate. It was a slow, tortuous process. The PSB had its own criminals to deal with and its men were less than happy at spending their time returning the cars of what they saw as Hong Kong fat cats. The fact that so many high-ranking Chinese officials and their families ended up as recipients of the stolen cars didn't exactly help Coleman's investigations.

Coleman sipped his hot coffee and glared at the files. He wanted a cigarette, badly, but he'd promised himself that this time he really would give up. He'd given up at least six times before but never managed more than two weeks before lighting up. This time he was determined to quit. A good chunk of that determination had come from Debbie Fielding. She'd been trying to give up, too, and he'd promised to help. Even though he hadn't seen her for almost two weeks he wanted to set her a good example. Thoughts of Debbie gradually replaced his urge to smoke, though both left him with a nagging ache in his guts, a longing that kept his mind off his work.

He'd met Debbie at one of the Lan Kwai Fong nightclubs, seen her dancing with a girlfriend, bought her a drink and, he thought, got on really well with her. The one drink led to others and they left together. She could barely stand and he'd had to help her to her car. A Jaguar XJS, of all things, a car the cadres would kill for in Beijing. She'd insisted that she could drive but he'd poured her into the passenger seat and taken her home. At least he'd tried to get her home. Halfway up the Peak her hand had begun to wander into his lap and she'd giggled and stroked him until he thought he'd burst. She'd persuaded him to turn off the road into a secluded side-street and practically leapt over the gear lever to his side of the car. Not that Coleman had needed much persuasion. It was cramped and their lovemaking had been quick and urgent. She hadn't even given him time to remove his trousers.

Afterwards she'd said that she was sober enough to drive the rest of the way home and she'd dropped him off on the main road so that he could catch a taxi back to Wan Chai where he rented a small flat on the twenty-third floor of a cockroach-infested residential tower block.

Coleman had called her the following day, and the day after that, and they'd gone out five or six times. At the end of each date she'd ended up making love to him in the passenger seat of the Jaguar, hard and fast like a wild animal. He'd fallen for her in a big way but she wouldn't see him more than once a week, she wouldn't go back with him to his flat and she wouldn't take him home to meet her parents. Now she seemed to be avoiding him and wouldn't even return his phone calls.

He thought back to their last date, more than two weeks earlier. They'd eaten at a Thai restaurant and caught a movie at Ocean Centre in Tsim Sha Tsui. She'd offered to drive him home with a sly smile and he thought she'd go up to his apartment for the first time but instead she'd insisted they make love in the car, parked in the car park under his building. The car park was well lit and regularly used but she said she didn't care. She'd been wearing a black dress, cut low at the front, and she'd unzipped him and mounted him in one smooth movement because she wasn't wearing underwear. She allowed him to slip the dress down over her shoulders so that he could kiss her breasts but when he'd tried to take off his shirt she'd told him that they didn't have enough time. She wouldn't kiss him while they were making love, either, as if she didn't want intimacy, just the use of his body. Thinking about the way she'd ridden him made him hard under the desk and he shook his head. He wanted to call her the same way that he wanted to draw on a cigarette, but he'd called yesterday and left a message with one of the family's Filipina maids. He'd give her until the afternoon, at least.

All the vets seemed to grow more relaxed during their stay at the beach resort of Vung Tau, as if they finally sensed that Vietnam was no longer the threat it used to be, and that the smiling Vietnamese were smiling because they were glad to see tourists, not because they were planning to put ground glass in their beer or a bomb under their Jeep.

Hung and Judy drove them back to Ho Chi Minh City and booked them all back into the Floating Hotel. Judy then shepherded them on a series of tourist trips around the city: tours of pagodas and temples, a visit to an army surplus market that was still doing a healthy trade in US equipment and clothing, a look around the zoo — which was in as much of a sad decline as the city itself — a children's amusement park, and an orchid farm.

Lehman found himself enjoying the city, despite its obvious poverty. The people they met were friendly and helpful and he could see that they were keen to get back on equal terms with the West. He made a mental note to look at the possibilities of some sort of Vietnamese venture capital fund. Not a real one, naturally, but a scam to fleece investors. He was convinced it would pull in the suckers like flies to jam.

Even Carmody appeared to relax. At first he'd done nothing but pick faults and arguments, calling the hotel staff "gooks" behind their backs and making fun of the cyclo drivers because of their cheap clothes and bad teeth. But as the days went by he became less sarcastic and bitter and began to take a real interest in what Judy was showing them.

Gradually, though, the sights that Judy took them to became more political. She took them to the Military Museum and showed them its collection of NVA equipment used to defeat the South. Then she took them to the Museum of the Revolution which celebrated the communist struggle for power. Inside the white neoclassical building were huge gilded ballrooms which had been converted to exhibition rooms containing Viet Cong weapons and photographs of what the Vietnamese called "The Liberation of Saigon". She showed them equipment the VC had used to conceal papers and weapons — a hawker's display of cigarettes with a secret compartment underneath, a boat with a false bottom in which guns and explosives could be hidden, a sewing machine with space underneath in which a bomb could be concealed. It was terrorist equipment yet Judy didn't treat it as such; instead she proudly demonstrated it to the Americans and cited it as an example of Vietnamese ingenuity in the face of US oppression.

Lehman heard Tyler talking to Carmody at the back of the group. "She doesn't seem to realise that most of this stuff was used in Saigon, for booby traps and sneak attacks," he whispered. "It wasn't used in the war, it was urban terrorism. What use would a sewing machine be in the jungle, for God's sake?"

Lehman didn't turn around but he agreed with Tyler's sentiments. Judy seemed to take great pride in the things she was showing them, without acknowledging that it was equipment which the VC had used to take the fight behind the lines, to the shops, bars and cinemas of the city.

She went on to show them maps and photographs of the fall of Saigon but there was no mention of the thousands killed by the North Vietnamese forces in the months that followed "Liberation" or of the hundreds of thousands who were sent off to the re-education camps.

Lehman got the feeling that Judy had been breaking them in gently, that she had done all the tourist stuff first to put them at their ease before starting to push the government line. Sure enough, the following day Judy and Hung took the group to the Museum of American War Crimes. When she first told them where they were going they thought she was joking, unable to believe that the Vietnamese could be so aggressively untactful about naming an exhibit. But no, she was serious. They got off the bus and were each handed a leaflet headed "Some Pictures of US Imperialists' Aggressive War Crimes in Vietnam". It was badly written but the grainy photographs spoke for themselves — bodies at My Lai, US soldiers posing in front of dismembered bodies, setting fire to huts, and horrific pictures of victims of phosphorous bombs and napalm. Carmody flicked through his brochure and, as Judy watched, screwed it up and dropped it on to the floor. Horvitz glanced at his and then pushed it into the back pocket of his jeans.

In the yard in front of the museum was a collection of US artillery and armoured vehicles, including a 175mm Howitzer, an M48 tank and, behind it, an M41. Judy took them slowly around the equipment, each of which had a small information sign in Vietnamese and English. It was the first museum they'd visited where signs were in English, and as he read the one in front of the Howitzer he could see why that was. "The US imperialists mostly used this Howitzer in their numerous criminal acts in the Iron Triangle area," it said.

Horvitz snorted as he read the sign. "Most of the criminal acts I remember in the Iron Triangle were on their side," he said to Lehman. He had tied his long hair back in a ponytail and it swung from side to side as he shook his head. "This is shit, man," he said.

"It's their view of what happened," said Speed, appearing behind Horvitz and Lehman. "They're entitled to their viewpoint." He stepped to the side and began filming the tanks. Tyler was looking at the M48 but he moved away when he heard the whirr of Speed's camcorder. He came over and stood by Lehman.

"Bit one-sided, wouldn't you say?" Tyler asked.

"It's the type of propaganda they pushed all the way through the war," Lehman said, unable to keep the bitterness out of his voice. "I didn't expect to find them still calling us imperialists."

"You read this?" Tyler said, brandishing the leaflet. He opened it and read aloud. "The war against

128

Vietnam had caused lasting sting to the US conscience thus sparkling — yeah, *sparkling* — off widespread antiwar movements in US walks of life. We — Vietnamese people — are sincerely grateful to world peoples, including progressive Americans, for their precious support of our just struggle for Independence, Freedom and Happiness."

Lehman shook his head sadly. "Independence, Freedom and Happiness," he repeated. "Can't say I've seen much of that here."

"Have you seen what's over there?" asked Tyler, pointing over Lehman's shoulder.

Lehman swung round and his eyes widened as he saw the tadpole-shaped helicopter squatting among a clump of bushes.

"A Huey," said Lehman.

The two men walked over and stood in front of the helicopter. The paintwork was peeling as if it was suffering from some incurable skin disease and Lehman could see through the Plexiglas that most of the electronics inside had been stripped out. Most of the structure was intact, though, and there was an M60 machine-gun mounted in the doorway on the left.

Lehman reached over and stroked the bulbous nose of the helicopter as if he was petting a horse.

"Think it'd still fly?" Tyler asked.

Lehman grinned. "I shouldn't think so," he said. "It's probably rusted away inside."

"The panels look good. And the rivets seem okay," said Tyler, walking around the Huey.

"Yeah, but it's been out in the open for God knows how long. The turbine will be fucked and the gearbox will probably have seized up." He stuck his head inside the cabin. "And a lot of the electrics have been pulled out. No, it'll never fly again."

"Brings back memories, though?"

"Yeah, it does that." He went over and tried the door to the pilot's station but it had been padlocked. He shaded his eyes and pressed his face against the Plexiglas. Inside he could see the metal frame seats and their webbing covers. A headset was lying on the pilot's seat, still plugged into its socket in the roof.

"How many flights did you make?" asked Tyler.

"Nine hundred and sixty three," replied Lehman without hesitation. "A total of 2,146 hours in the air."

"All in the Huey?"

"Most of it." He pushed himself away from the window and looked at Tyler. "You ever flown in one?"

Tyler shrugged. "I prefer something a bit faster," he said, which Lehman recognised as just another evasion, even though it came with a friendly smile. Tyler was wearing his sunglasses so Lehman couldn't see his eyes.

"You weren't a pilot, were you?" Lehman asked. He could see his own reflection in the black lenses.

"I can fly," said Tyler quietly.

"That's not what I asked."

Tyler nodded slowly. "I know it isn't." He smiled and continued walking again. "How do you feel about what happened here, in Nam?" he asked.

Lehman watched Tyler walk away and slowly followed, looking at the ground. "I think we were here for the right reasons," said Lehman. "I think it was a war worth fighting. And I think from what we've seen of the place in the last couple of days that it would have been better for everybody if we had stayed."

"What do you think we were fighting for?" Tyler asked.

Lehman thought for a while. "It might sound corny, but I think we were fighting for freedom. It's like it says on JFK's tomb — we shall pay any price, bear any burden, meet any hardship, support any friend, oppose any foe, in order to ensure the survival and success of liberty. I really felt like that back then. I know the regime here was as corrupt as hell, but it had to be better than what they've got now. Saigon used to be buzzing. It was a vibrant, lively city. The whole country could be as rich as hell — it's got great land, great natural resources — and yet look at it. It's Third World. It's pitiful. And it's the communists who've done it. Yeah, I was happy to fight for that."

"You volunteered?"

Lehman nodded. "Yeah. And that's what made it all the worse when I went back to the States and found that no one cared. Or worse, that they thought I was a fascist child killer who'd had no right to be there in the first place."

"It hurt," said Tyler.

"Damn right it hurt. I was out here fighting for something I believed in."

"Something you still believe in?"

Lehman thought for a while. "Now I just believe in myself," he said eventually. "Myself and the guys I fought with. Guys like Lewis and Horvitz. Everything else is shit."

The black lenses stared impassively at Lehman for a full ten seconds, and Lehman felt like a laboratory specimen being studied under a microscope.

"Can you still fly?" Tyler asked.

"Sure."

"When was the last time you flew a helicopter?"

"I worked as a pilot for an air taxi firm up until a few years ago. And I still fly now and then, just to keep my licence up to date, you know. Why? Are you looking for a helicopter pilot?"

"Maybe," said Tyler softly. "Maybe I am. Come on, let's catch up with the rest of them."

They walked by the salesman from Seattle, who was sitting astride the turret of the M48 tank with a big grin on his face as his wife snapped away with a small Japanese camera. The barrel was sticking between his thighs like some huge phallus and he patted it and wiggled his eyebrows suggestively at Lehman.

"How about having this between your legs, Dan?" he laughed.

"Yeah, right," said Lehman, biting back the retort that one big prick deserves another because, much as he disliked the man's over-the-top bonhomie, he wasn't worth picking a fight with.

Lehman and Tyler walked up to Horvitz who was studying a selection of American mines, shells and bullets in glass cases. He was bending down to look at a claymore mine, about the size of a brick that had been bent into a curve. He pointed at the words imprinted on the convex side of the grey metal block. "Front Towards Enemy," he read out to the two men. "We didn't exactly send our best and brightest, did we?" he asked, his voice loaded with bitter irony. "I'm always surprised that they didn't write 'bullets come out here' on the barrels of our M16s."

Lehman laughed. "Or 'this way up' on the tops of our Hueys," he said.

Judy led the group into the museum proper, a series of single-storey buildings where the walls were lined with black and white photographs and exhibits.

She stopped them as they passed over the threshold of the first room and asked them to gather around a small glass-fronted display case which had been mounted on the wall. It contained a small cluster of medals and a small plaque from a US infantry sergeant which read: "To the people of a United Vietnam. I was wrong. I am sorry."

"This soldier admit that what he did was wrong," said Judy. "He very brave. He true American hero. Only a brave man can admit that he was wrong." She looked around the group for signs of agreement, and found it from Henderson, Speed and Cummings, who all nodded. There was a metallic clicking noise from behind Lehman and he turned to see Carmody opening and closing his steel claw. There was a Purple Heart in the case and Lehman knew that Carmody would have received the same decoration, at the very least, for his injury. He smiled in sympathy at Carmody but received no response because Carmody was staring stonily at the tour guide. Tyler, too, had a look of contempt on his face and Lehman wondered how many decorations he had received, and for what. Whereas Carmody looked the type to treat his medals with contempt — though not to the extent of sending them to the Vietnamese — he could tell that Tyler was a man who would wear them on his chest with pride.

Horvitz sighed and shook his head and walked away while Judy rattled off statistics about the war: the number of Americans who fought in Vietnam, the cost to America, the number of civilians killed, the number of Vietnamese civilians who died.

"Do you believe this crap?" Horvitz asked, nodding at a series of photographs on the wall. They detailed a series of amputations which had been carried out on a VC prisoner in a bid to make him talk. First his feet were amputated, then his legs below the knee, then finally above the knee, operations which the museum said were totally unnecessary because the man only had superficial wounds. After each operation he was given time to recover, questioned, and then sent back under the surgeon's knife. He was a hero, said the sign under the photograph of the man with stumps where his legs should have been. And another sign carried a list of all the operations and the dates.

"Do you believe it?" asked Horvitz, looking at Lehman with his dead eyes.

"Maybe," said Lehman. "I was just a pilot. I didn't see much of what went on at ground level."

"Yeah, well I was on the ground, and I never saw stuff like this. I saw killings and I saw firefights but I never saw no torture. Not like this. Not from

Americans. I know the South Vietnamese did it to the VC, and the Koreans were a mad bunch, but we never did stuff like this."

"My Lai happened," said Lehman. "You can't deny that. We killed more than 500 people there, most of them women and children and old folks."

"It was a war," said Horvitz. "I'm not trying to excuse it, but it was a war."

Horvitz continued to stare at the photograph of the man with no legs, running his hand through his unkempt beard. The facial hair made it difficult for Lehman to assess his companion's age; it could have been anywhere between thirty-five and fifty, though the well-muscled body suggested he was still in his thirties.

"I had a friend once, in Nam," said Horvitz, his voice almost a whisper. "Name of Wills. Billy Wills. His dad had named him William Wills, can you believe that? He was nineteen, a couple of years younger than me. We were in the Lurps, the Long Range Reconnaissance Patrols. He was a mad bastard. Totally without fear, you know? Always wanted to go point, always fretting when we were laid up at base camp, always first off the helicopter and last one back on. He'd volunteer for anything, just so long as it got him out in the field. He was so gung-ho. Good guy to be out with, though, because he was careful, too. And he had a gift for spotting booby traps, ambushes, stuff like that. We were together for about six months, part of a five-man team, long range recon, nothing too heavy. Had a few close calls but we knew what we were doing, clean in and clean out, hardly any kills to speak of. Just doing our job, you know? We weren't sent out to cause trouble, just to draw maps, identify VC trails, spot NVA activity, and get back to base without anyone knowing we were there." Horvitz didn't look at Lehman as he spoke, and Lehman felt for all the world like a priest hearing confession from a Catholic who'd stayed away from the confessional box for too long.

"They sent us into the Iron Triangle. Dropped us by Huey thirty klicks from where they wanted us so that no one would know we were there and the deal was that we walked in and walked out, no Dustoff unless we were in deep, deep shit. Total radio silence. We moved by night, holed up during the day. The whole mission should have taken us eight days, and that's a hell of a time in the jungle. A hell of a time."

He shook himself suddenly as if waking from a dream and, without looking at Lehman, began slowly to walk along the display of pictures. Lehman wasn't sure if he'd finished talking so he walked with him. Judy, followed by the rest of the group, left the case of unwanted medals and began to relate the story of the amputee in a shrill voice.

"There was hardly any moon, but the starlight was all that we needed. We were three days out when the weather changed, low cloud cover and the air so wet that we got soaked just sitting still. The clouds blocked out all light, everything, couldn't even see the luminous dials on the compass. We kept close, so close we could touch the man in front of us, stopping whenever we wanted to take a bearing and using a flashlight inside a rucksack so that we could read the compass. Out in the jungle, they can come from anywhere, and it's full of sounds, sounds that could be insects or small animals or a squad of NVA ready to blow you to kingdom come. You can't see where you're stepping, whether there's going to be a foot trap or a wire stretched across the trail to a hand grenade or a mine that's going to take your foot off, not nice and clean like the surgeons did to that VC but jagged and ripped and the pain so bad you want to die. Have you seen a guy step on a mine, Dan? Not the big ones, not the anti-tank jobs that blow a man to pieces so small that there's nothing to put in the body bag afterwards, I mean the ones that are aimed at grunts. They just blow off a foot, maybe a whole leg. You still die, unless a Dustoff gets you to a field hospital within a few minutes. And it's not a good way to die."

"There's no good way to die," said Lehman, quietly.

Horvitz turned to look at him. He smiled at Lehman, a cruel, ironic baring of the teeth.

"There's good ways, Dan, and there's bad ways. I've seen both. And I've been responsible for both. You don't want . . ." He shook his head and fell silent. It wasn't as if he were overcome with emotion — there was no sadness or regret in his voice. It was as if he couldn't be bothered explaining himself to Lehman. The two men stood side by side and looked at a series of photographs of B-52 bombers dropping swarms of bombs on Hanoi. BUFFs, they'd called them during the war, Lehman remembered with a smile. Big Ugly Fat Fuckers. They usually carried more than one hundred 500 pound bombs packed with high explosive.

The VC and NVA called them "the Whispering Death" because the first they knew of a B-52 raid was the whistle of the bombs.

"Billy had been on point for three hours and in the dark that's a hell of a long time," Horvitz continued. "He was starting to slow so we gave him the drag and I went point. A minute out there feels like a year. An hour is like a lifetime. Everything just stops, stops dead. You don't know if your next step is going to be your last, if a bullet is going to slam into your chest or if you're going to hear the little click that means you've trodden on a mine and that you've got half a second before you see the yellow flash and about a second before the pain rips through you. You want to just stop and curl up under a bush but you have to keep on going, you have to keep on taking the next step, the one that could be your last. I've never felt so close to death, Dan. Never. And you know something?" He turned to look at Lehman again. "I've never felt so alive."

Lehman nodded, not sure what he should say. He tried to hold Horvitz's gaze but he couldn't, the man's eyes seemed to bore right through into his soul and their intensity was almost painful. Lehman looked away. Horvitz snorted quietly as if acknowledging Lehman's weakness.

"The clouds kept opening and closing. Sometimes we could see strips of sky like ripped material, and then there would be enough starlight for us to move at normal speed, but then just as quickly the clouds would close and we'd be back to feeling our way through the jungle. When there was starlight we'd open up our

138

formation, and then we'd bunch together in the darkness, keeping close enough to touch. I don't know if it was my fault for moving too quickly or if it was Billy's for not moving quickly enough, but the sky clouded over and we lost him. He couldn't have been more than twenty steps from me and we lost him. Maybe the VC crept up on him, maybe they were lying in wait and I just walked right by them, I still don't know. I mean, if I walked by them, why didn't they just open up and kill us all?" The question was rhetorical because he didn't give Lehman a chance to answer, he just kept right on talking in his dull monotone voice. "Maybe there were only a couple of them and they knew they'd be outgunned. Maybe if he'd have been point and I'd have been covering the rear then I'd be dead and he'd be here now telling it to you."

Judy and the group came closer and Horvitz moved away as if they were magnets of the same polarity. They stood in front of more photographs, a record of the My Lai massacre.

"I don't know how long it was before we realised he was missing. Could have been just a few yards, could have been a hundred. First we knew about it was when he screamed. Screamed like I'd never heard a man scream before. They kept him screaming for hours, moving him around so that we could never catch up with them. They must have gagged him while they moved him because his screams would come from one direction, then nothing for fifteen minutes or so, and then the screaming would start again somewhere else. We went out of our minds, Dan. He was my best friend

139

and they killed him by inches. We found him the following day. Not because we were particularly good at tracking, but because they wanted us to find him. They'd laid him out in a clearing. You want to know what they did to him, Dan? Do you want to know?"

Lehman said nothing. He didn't want to know what had happened to Billy Wills, he didn't want to share any of the hellish secrets that had resulted in Eric Horvitz having the eyes of a corpse. But he felt that if he listened to Horvitz, then maybe it would help him, and he was clearly a man who needed help.

"His body was covered in cuts, some of them small, some of them deep, none of them lethal. Hundreds of them. That's not what killed him, though. They were what had made him scream. They'd disembowelled him. And they'd cut off his prick. Either would have killed him, but it would have taken some time. Lots of blood. Lots of pain. You'd have thought that that would have been enough, wouldn't you? They'd tortured him, and they'd killed him. But it wasn't enough, they wanted to teach us a lesson. They wanted to scare us. They spread his intestines all around his body, yards and yards of it. You'd never believe how long your guts are, not until you've seen them laid out. They shoved his prick in his mouth. We didn't look too closely in case we found that he'd still been alive when they did that. Then they cut off his head. Not one clean cut, but lots of small cuts, like they'd sawn it off. Then they put the head in the body cavity. They went to all that trouble, Dan. It takes a particularly perverse sort of mind to do that. A particularly nasty mind. So why don't I see any indication of that on the walls here? Why do we just have all this anti-American crap?"

"It's like Speed said outside. It's their view. It's not the truth, it's just their version of it."

"Remember Hue? February 1968, when we finally cleared out the VC. They moved in during the Tet Offensive, January 31, and it took us until February 25 to retake it. We discovered almost 3,000 bodies in mass graves. A lot of them had been buried alive, almost all of them had been mutilated. Heads chopped off, and worse. Much, much worse. When the VC moved in they had death lists, names of bureaucrats, teachers, police, religious figures. A quick court martial and that was that. I don't see any mention of that here, Dan. And I don't see any mention of the cinemas and restaurants they bombed in Saigon. The innocent women and children the VC killed. Fuck them, Dan. Fuck them all!" He shouted the last curse and his words echoed around the room. Judy stopped her commentary and looked over at the two men. Horvitz snorted and stamped out of the room. Lehman saw Tyler slip away from the group and follow him.

Lehman stayed with the group as Judy continued her guided tour of the exhibition, and was surprised at her vehemence as she needlessly described what was going on in the different photographs. She hadn't acted that way at the Military Museum or the Revolution Museum; her commentaries there had been straightforward and unemotional and Lehman wondered if she was putting on a performance for the museum employees who were standing at various points around the exhibition.

She led them to another room which contained a display of American weapons, including M16s, M14s, M18s, mortars, an M72 anti-tank rocket launcher, M20B1 and M9A1 bazookas and shotguns. At the far side of the room sat a bored museum employee, a young girl in a yellow *ao dais* and white pantaloons, who studied her nails and yawned. Tyler and Horvitz were standing by a cluster of mortars. Tyler was whispering to Horvitz, who appeared to be a good deal calmer than when he'd stormed out of the other room. They both looked up when the rest of the group appeared and wandered away outside.

Speed and Henderson took it in turns to pose in front of the anti-tank weapons while the other took pictures, and the salesman from Seattle told his wife war stories. Cummings and his wife walked arm in arm, she asking him quiet questions, he answering and occasionally resting his forehead on her shoulder. Judy continued to harangue the American actions in Vietnam, reading out the notices on the walls and then embellishing them with more details before leading them to yet another room, this one with an exhibition of America's attempt to defoliate the jungles of Vietnam.

She showed them flight plans of the planes which had criss-crossed the countryside dropping eighteen million gallons of herbicides on the forests of South Vietnam, and photographs of victims who, years later, had developed cancers. There were photographs taken through microscopes showing the effects the dioxin in Agent Orange had on human chromosomes, and there was a morbid display of specimen bottles containing deformed human foetuses. "The legacy of American poisons continues to kill our children," said Judy as if accusing each and every one of them for the birth defects. Carmody giggled nervously at the back of the group and Lewis turned round and glared at him.

"Man, this isn't funny," he hissed. "We had no right to do this. No right at all." His eyes were blazing and Lehman thought that he might take a swing at Carmody but then the anger seemed to be replaced by sadness and the black man turned away, waving his hand in the air as if swatting an annoying insect.

Lewis listened carefully to Judy as she catalogued the number of cases and types of cancer that were still being reported, and the number of babies that were born dead because of the poisons in the ground and in the water, especially around what had been the demilitarised zone. As he listened he slowly rubbed his stomach.

Lehman came up behind him. "Are you okay, Bart?"

"Yeah, I'm fine. Just fine."

"Don't let this stuff get to you. It's propaganda, that's all."

Lewis shook his head. "It's more than that, Dan. Yeah, I know that a lot of the rest of that crap about torture and stuff don't mean nothing but this is different. We did this, we dumped millions of gallons of poison on their land. At the time I didn't know what we were doing."

"None of us did, Bart. We were just obeying orders. They didn't give us time to think about what we were doing. Hell, they probably didn't even know themselves. I mean, they knew it was a defoliant but I don't think they knew what the long-term effects would be."

Lewis looked at him with watery eyes. "You think that would've stopped them?" he asked. "Shit, they'd probably have used even more of the stuff. Scorched earth, they called it. Ain't that the truth?"

Judy called the group together and told them that the tour of the museum was over and that it was time to return to the bus. Lewis was the last to go and he walked slowly, his head down and his right hand massaging his stomach.

Neil Coleman sifted through the computer printout which listed all the stolen cars which had been recovered over the past twenty-four hours. He also had a list of cars which had been stolen since the beginning of the year, and he methodically crossed off all those which had been found. Normally he would have given the task to Yip or Hui but both were conveniently absent.

His eyes were starting to ache so he leaned back in his chair and looked out of his window. Offices were emptying and the streets were crowded to capacity. The sound of horns and shouts and the rattle of trams penetrated the double glazing. There was always noise in Hong Kong, Coleman thought. There was always noise and there were always people around you, you couldn't escape either. Down the corridor he could hear the chatter of Cantonese, three women gossiping by the coffee machine. Cantonese was a language that was shouted, never whispered.

There was a black lamp on his desk and he reached forward and switched it on. He leaned back again and ran his fingers through his thick, sandy-coloured hair. With the desk lamp on he could see his reflection in the window, superimposed on the bustling scene outside. His hair was short and parted on the left and continually stood up at the back no matter how much he smoothed it down. It was always easier to keep his hair under control when it was long, but the Royal Hong Kong Police Force required it to be kept to regulation length. He reckoned he was fairly good-looking, in a boyish way, though he thought that his lips were a bit too thick so he tried to smile a lot because that made his mouth look better. His ears stuck out a bit too, but not so much that anyone had commented on them. Not since he'd left school, anyway. His eyes were deep blue and his eyebrows were as sandy and as bushy as his hair. It wasn't the face of a movie star, he admitted to himself, but it didn't send girls screaming for the exit, either.

He wondered how Debbie Fielding felt about his looks. She still hadn't called even though he'd left several messages. The previous evening he'd gone to the disco where he'd first met her, hoping to see her again, but there'd been no sign of her and he'd ended up drinking too much. He'd got back to his apartment at two o'clock in the morning and decided that it would be a good idea if he called her again. He came to his senses when a man's sleepy voice answered and he slammed down the receiver before collapsing back on his bed and falling asleep. It must have been her father, William Fielding.

Coleman drummed his fingers on the desk. He wanted a cigarette, badly, but he settled for a coffee instead. He waited until the chattering in the corridor tailed away before fetching himself a cup. As usual the hot brew burnt his fingers by the time he got it back to his office. He found Phil Donaldson, a senior inspector from Serious Crimes, lounging in Yip's chair.

"Whotchya, Neil," said Donaldson in his east London accent.

"Hi, Phil, what's up? You want a coffee?"

Coleman put the plastic cup on his desk.

"That stuff makes me wanna puke," said Donaldson, rubbing his black moustache with the back of his hand. He was balding and had taken to combing hair from the left side of his head across his crown in a vain attempt to cover his bald patch. Donaldson had been on the force for twelve years, and it was his rough manner and lack of tact which had held him back from rising above the rank of senior inspector. Now it was too late: the government's localisation policy meant that he, like Coleman, would rise no higher.

"I know what you mean," agreed Coleman, taking his seat. "But I get withdrawal symptoms if I don't have coffee every couple of hours."

"Honest?"

"Sure. It's the caffeine, I guess."

"And you can't give up?"

"I suppose I could, but I'm trying to give up smoking and that's more than enough for me to handle. So what's up?" He sipped his coffee.

Donaldson grinned, clasping his hands together and resting his elbows on his knees. Like Coleman he worked in plain clothes and was wearing a dark blue suit which had gone baggy around the knees. His black shoes were scuffed, his shirt had gone several days without a wash and his Foreign Correspondents Club tie was loose and his top button was undone. Donaldson's dress sense was as sloppy as his manners, but he was well liked by his colleagues and reckoned to be a first-class detective. His Cantonese was virtually perfect, and Yip had told Coleman that when he spoke he had a Chinese accent.

"I've just heard from a pal over in Tai Po," he said. "They've just caught a ship trying to smuggle a BMW out of Tolo Harbour."

"So what?" said Coleman, frowning. "Happens all the time. Tolo, Tai Long, Double Haven, all those east-coast ports are used by the triads."

Donaldson shook his head, his grin widening. A long wisp of hair slid along his bald patch and down the left side of his head. "No, mate, you don't understand. They were smuggling it underwater! They were towing it behind a small junk."

"Underwater?"

Donaldson nodded. "You're not going to believe it, but they put the fucking thing in a rubber bag. A huge rubber bag. They sealed it, leaving enough air so that it floated about twenty feet down, and they towed it."

"So how did they get caught?"

"The bag snagged on a rock before they'd gone more than a few hundred yards. The car dragged the back of the junk in the water and it started to sink. Marine Police had to rescue them. Massive loss of face, Neil, massive loss of face all round." He laughed, throwing back his head and wiping his hands on his trousers. Coleman laughed with him. It was funny, no doubt about it. Donaldson sighed and shook his head. "You'll probably get a report on your desk, but you'll see it in tomorrow's *Hong Kong Standard*. One of their photographers lives out there and he took pictures of them dragging the waterlogged BMW on to the shore."

"What the hell can they have been thinking of?" asked Coleman. "Most of the stolen cars we know about are whisked over on speedboats, so fast that even the Marine Police can't catch them. Why use bags?"

Donaldson shrugged. "Amateurs maybe. Maybe they were just taking a gift over for relatives on the mainland. According to the boys in Tai Po, they weren't triads, just fishermen. Whatever, it's a bloody laugh, isn't it?"

"Sure is," agreed Coleman.

Donaldson looked at Coleman and raised an eyebrow. "How's business?" he asked.

"Overworked, underpaid, you know how it is."

"How's the group, staff-wise?"

"We're about thirty per cent understaffed right now. Two constables are working out their notice. I've been promised a transfer from one of the district offices, but I doubt it'll come through. Recruitment is down about eighty per cent from three years ago. Hell, Phil, I'm not telling you anything you don't know already. They just can't get the people."

"What about you? You got anything yet?" Both men had been looking for other jobs for at least a year. It had already been made clear to them that they, like the rest of the expatriates on the force, had no future with the Royal Hong Kong Police. Any promotions were to go only to locals, in preparation for the handover in 1997. And only Beijing knew what would happen then.

Coleman snorted. "Two rejection letters, one from Avon and Somerset, another from Devon and Cornwall."

"You gotta thing about the West Country, or what?"

"It's not that, it's just that I've already been rejected by the big city forces. It's down to the provinces, now. What about you?"

"I've given up on the UK," said Donaldson. "But I was never keen on going back, anyway, not with the taxes they have over there. I'm trying Taiwan."

"Taiwan? What's there?"

"Pat Dugan set up a private detective outfit over there some years back, after his brother-in-law got killed. I've been on the blower to him and he's given me a few leads. There's a couple of American firms hunting down counterfeiters in the region; it sounds like fun. I'll give them a try."

"Good luck," said Coleman. "I'm getting nowhere. It doesn't make any sense, does it? They say that they want to phase out the expats, but they can't get enough locals to sign up. So the strength of the force keeps falling, morale is at an all-time low, and meanwhile the crime rate is going through the roof as the triads try to milk Hong Kong for everything it's got. You know robberies are up forty per cent this year? There are almost twice as many cars being stolen than three years ago. And more and more of the criminals are carrying guns. They're getting to the stage where it's all or nothing. Their only chance is to make a big score now and buy their way off this stinking island. I tell you, Phil, I know just how they feel."

"Life's a bitch," said Donaldson, sympathetically.

"And then you marry one," added Coleman.

"Speaking of which, how's the lovely heiress?" Donaldson had met Debbie Fielding on Coleman's second date with her, and he'd been impressed with her beauty, and with her money.

"Debbie? She's fine. I think. I haven't spoken to her for a few days."

"Path of true love not running smooth, huh?"

The phone on Coleman's desk rang and Donaldson magnanimously waved him to answer it.

"Neil?" said a girl's voice.

It took a moment for Coleman to recognise her, then his heart leapt. "Debbie!" he exclaimed.

"How are you?" she asked.

"Great. Fine. God, you must be psychic. We were just talking about you."

"We?"

"Phil Donaldson's here. You met him at Hot Gossip, remember?"

"The cute guy with the bald patch? Sure I remember." Coleman felt a sudden surge of jealousy at her description. He'd never considered Phil Donaldson as cute and he was annoyed that she did. "So what were you saying?" she continued.

Coleman flushed as he remembered what Donaldson had said. "Oh, just how much I was missing you, that's all." On the other side of the room, Donaldson pretended to make himself vomit by putting two fingers down his throat. Coleman looked away and tried not to laugh.

"That's nice," she said.

She sounded cool and distant. "How are you?" he asked. "I've been trying to get hold of you for days."

"I bet," said Donaldson.

"Have you been away?" asked Coleman. Debbie worked as an advertising sales rep for a glossy travel magazine and spent a lot of time jetting around South-East Asia. The travel was her main reason for taking the job; she sure as hell didn't need the money.

"Just busy," she said. Her offhand reply was like an ice dagger plunging into his heart. He wanted to ask her where she'd been and why she hadn't called him, but he couldn't, not with Donaldson listening and making obscene hand gestures. "Hey, Neil, I've got a favour to ask."

His heart soared. He was sure she was going to ask him out.

"It's my father, he's had his car stolen."

Coleman's spirits slumped. He reached for a pen and his notebook. "What happened?" he asked, the two words loaded with bitterness.

She didn't appear to notice. "His car was stolen from outside our house. Last night. He's furious."

"I'm sure he is," said Coleman. "I thought he had a chauffeur."

"He does but it was his day off and the bank's got a shortage of drivers. Dad prefers to drive himself rather than use one of the pool drivers, most of them haven't been with the bank for long. You know how it is, they're always moving jobs for more money. Anyway, he parked it outside our house and sometime during the night it was stolen."

"Was it locked?"

"Of course it was locked," she said sharply.

"Okay, give me the details."

"Details?"

"Make, model, colour, registration number."

She gave him the details. It was a blue Mercedes 560SEL.

"Was it the bank's car, or his own?" he asked.

"The bank's, of course," she said testily.

"Debbie, are you okay?" he asked. Donaldson pulled a face from across the room. Coleman gave him the finger.

"Sure, why do you ask?"

Coleman sighed. "I don't know. You sound a bit brittle, that's all."

He heard her laugh, a harsh, dry sound. "No, but you can imagine what the atmosphere is like here. Dad's furious."

"Yeah, I bet."

"Do you think you'll be able to get it back, Neil? I promised Dad I'd ask you."

Great, thought Coleman. The recovery rate for Mercedes was about fifty:fifty. And she'd told her dad that he was on the case. "There's a good chance," he lied.

"Oh, Neil, it'd be great if you could find it. He'd be so grateful."

"I'll give it my best shot," he said. "Hey, are you doing anything tomorrow night?"

"Tomorrow? Saturday? Oh yeah, I'm seeing a girlfriend, she's just got back from the States."

His heart fell. He wanted to try to persuade her to go out with him instead but he knew it would sound like begging and he didn't want to do that, not in front of Donaldson. "Okay, what about next week sometime?"

"Oh sure," she said brightly. "I'll give you a call. Bye." She cut the connection and he replaced the receiver.

"Thanks for the privacy, Phil," he said.

Donaldson grinned. "Sounded like business to me, mate. Father of the bride mislaid his motor, huh?"

"Yeah."

"Can't have the chairman of the Kowloon and Canton Bank without any wheels, can we?" said Donaldson. "Still, with ace sleuth Neil Coleman on the case it shouldn't be too long before the car has been recovered and returned to its rightful owner, the bad guys are languishing in Stanley Prison and our hero is in bed with the girl."

"I wish," said Coleman. "Say, are you doing anything Saturday night? Fancy a drink?"

"Darling, I thought you'd never ask," simpered Donaldson.

"Phil," said Coleman, "fuck off, why don't you?"

Lehman showered as soon as he got back to the Floating Hotel. He felt dirty and it wasn't just the heat and the dust, it was as if he'd been tainted by the exhibition of war crimes and Judy's biased commentary. He soaped himself all over, shampooed his hair, and then repeated the whole process but he didn't feel any cleaner.

Tyler had suggested that they go for a drink later on that evening and they'd arranged to meet in the lobby at nine. Lehman looked at his watch and saw that he still had ten minutes to kill. Rather than sit in his room he decided to wait in the lobby bar with a glass of beer. Lewis was already there, sipping a Perrier water and wearing another of his multicoloured shirts.

"You on the wagon, Bart?" Lehman asked, sitting down opposite him.

"My stomach doesn't feel so good," said Lewis, raising the glass of bubbly water in front of him. "Thought I'd give it a chance to settle down, get some heavy drinking done later."

Lehman ordered a beer from a slim waitress with shoulder-length hair and studied Lewis as he sipped disdainfully at his Perrier. "That exhibition sure was something, wasn't it?" said Lehman.

Lewis shuddered, and Lehman wasn't sure if it was the water or the memory. "Brought back some of the pain," he said. "Brought back a lot of memories."

"You were drafted, right?"

"No, I got no one to blame but myself. I couldn't get a job in sunny Baltimore so I signed up to get a trade. I got that all right. Army trained me as a mechanic and then put me on helicopters once they became the rage. Never thought I'd end up fighting another man's war, just went in to learn to fix engines so that I could set up my own place. Then The Man invited me on an all-expenses tour of South-East Asia and told me it was an offer I couldn't refuse. Even when they shipped me over I still thought I'd be sitting in some fortified behind-the-lines camp with the rest of the Rear Echelon Mother Fuckers. Came as a hell of a shock to find myself at the sharp end. I guess it would've worked out the same way, even if I hadn't joined up. I was everything Uncle Sam wanted for battle fodder. I was young, healthy and poor."

"And black?"

"Yeah, you noticed that, right?" He lifted his glass to Lehman and then took a mouthful. He looked as if he was deciding whether to swallow it or spit it out but eventually gulped it down with a pained expression on his face.

"So why did you come back?" asked Lehman.

Lewis shrugged. "Through the Veterans Administration," he said. "I went to see them about a . . ." He paused as if checking himself. "A medical problem," he

155

finished. "A few days later I got the offer of a free trip to Nam."

"Free?" said Lehman, surprised.

"Yeah, some psychiatrist involved with something called the US-Indochina Reconciliation Project fixed me up. Same guy got Horvitz on the trip, too."

Lehman frowned. "A guy called Marks? Dick Marks?"

"Yeah, that was the guy. Don't tell me he picked you, too."

"I was planning on coming anyway, but the day after I spoke to a travel company he rang me up and said he represented an organisation which would pay for the trip, providing I was flexible about the timing and that my service record met their criteria."

"Flexible?"

"Yeah, they had a spare slot and it meant leaving almost right away. That suited me just fine."

The lift doors opened at the far end of the lobby and Tyler and Carmody came out. Tyler was wearing a light blue safari suit and Carmody was in shorts and a grey sweatshirt on which was printed in large black letters, "Vietnam Veteran And Proud Of It". Above the lettering was a leering black skull.

"Oh, man," sighed Lewis. "Don't he ever give it a rest?"

"Doesn't appear so," said Lehman.

Tyler and Carmody sat down and ordered beers.

"Anyone else coming?" asked Lewis.

"Just Eric," said Tyler. "Where do you guys fancy going?"

No one had any ideas so they decided to ride around in cyclos until they made up their minds. They were listening to a four-piece Filipino band tuning up when Horvitz stepped out of the elevator in black Levi jeans and a white shirt. "Let's go," said Tyler. They stood for a few moments outside the hotel while cyclo drivers rushed up like flies attracted to dead meat. Carmody did the haggling and seemed determined to squeeze every last dong out of the deal until Tyler sat in his cyclo and told his driver just to go.

The sky had darkened and the cyclos were constantly swerving to avoid cyclists who were driving without lights. Lehman's driver caught up with Tyler's cyclo and the two drivers synchronised their pedalling so that the two Americans could talk. Despite the gathering gloom Tyler had put his sunglasses on and the lenses shone blackly as he looked at Lehman. "Something distinctly colonial about this, isn't there?" he said.

"Like the last days of the Raj," agreed Lehman. "It must be one of the few places in the world where they still use human power. Legacy of the French, I guess."

"Enjoy it while you can," said Tyler. "This country is about to take off, take my word for it. It's got huge undeveloped oil resources, coal, minerals, and a population that'll work its balls off once communism is killed off. The Japs are already in here, and the Hong Kong Chinese. In a few years it'll be taxis and five-star hotels and high-rise office blocks. It'll be as if the war never happened. Like the Germans and the Japanese these days. Sometimes you wonder just who won the Second World War."

"You think they should be punished for ever?"

"I think that we fought to preserve democracy in this country. And the politicians wouldn't let us fight it to the finish. They wouldn't let us win. So I don't see why we should start co-operating now, I don't see why we should help them out of the mess they dug themselves into. What do you think, Dan?"

Lehman thought for a while as he listened to the breathing of the drivers and the clicking of the cyclo chains. "I think it's been pretty well proven that communism doesn't work. It didn't work in Russia or Eastern Europe and it sure as hell won't work in South-East Asia. If the Vietnamese have come to realise that, then maybe we should help them. Show them that capitalism and democracy are the only way to go."

"And we forget what happened during the war? The boys who died?"

Lehman leant forward in his cyclo. "That's not what I'm saying, Joel. I lost a lot of friends in the Nam, and I'd do anything to get them back. No, I don't want to think that they died for nothing. I can't ever forget that these people were our enemies. That's one of the reasons I came here, to see if they are still the enemy, or if it's time to stop hating. When I flew out on the Freedom Bird I left something behind and I want to straighten that out."

Tyler nodded, and smiled. "Is that the only reason you came back?" he asked quietly.

"What do you mean?" said Lehman, frowning.

"You look like a man who's running away from something, Dan. That's all. Problems back in the States, maybe?"

Before Lehman could answer, a young girl on a Honda moped zipped up, her long hair streaming behind her. She was wearing a tight blue T-shirt and a black miniskirt. "Hey, you American?" she shouted.

"Yeah," said Carmody.

"You want girls?" she called, swerving to avoid a man on a bicycle loaded with baskets of dead chickens. "I know where many girls. You follow me?" She kept twisting the accelerator to keep the moped level with the cyclos. The man who was driving Tyler shouted over at the girl and she called back and then drove off.

"Hey, what did you say to her?" asked Carmody.

"You want girls?" said the driver. "I know much better place. Better girls. Very clean."

"What do you gentlemen think?" asked Tyler. There was a chorus of whoops and whistles and Carmody waggled his legs in the air. Tyler turned round to look at his driver. "I think that means yes," he said.

The driver shouted to his companions and the cyclos turned left at the next junction in almost perfect formation.

"Where are we going?" Lewis asked Tyler.

"No idea, Bart, but I think we're in good hands."

The cyclos made their way through a series of badly lit side-streets, turning left and right until the Americans had no idea of where they were or where they were going. Despite the late hour the streets were still full of mopeds, bicycles and cyclos, and the sidewalks were thronged with people eating, talking or reading under flickering oil lamps. Faces looked up when the Americans went by and small children jumped up and down and waved and called out: "*Lien Xo! Lien Xo!*"

The convoy eventually came to a halt outside a roadside bar which had a sign saying "Hot Bar" outlined in red light bulbs. Two young girls in tank tops and miniskirts came out of the bar and stood giggling as the Americans climbed out of their cyclos. The bar was open to the sidewalk and inside, bathed in red lights, were half a dozen low tables and wooden stools. Country and Western music crackled from a teak-veneer speaker fixed to the wall and a middle-aged woman with short, curly hair polished a glass with a cloth that had seen better days. When she saw the Americans she called into a back room and four more girls came into the bar, one of them wiping her mouth with a tissue. The girls surrounded the Americans like pilot fish around sharks, touching them and giggling and following them to a corner table.

The men sat around the table and the girls pulled in extra stools to sit close to them while another woman put bowls of peanuts and crisps in front of them and asked what they wanted to drink.

"Beers," said Tyler. "Five beers."

Lehman was now used to Tyler taking charge, and it seemed that the rest of the group didn't mind him making their decisions for them. Lehman was certain that Tyler had been more than a pilot during the war. He was clearly a man who was used to giving orders

160

and to seeing them obeyed. A natural leader. Or one who'd been well trained.

The girls spoke next to no English but the woman who brought the beer did so Tyler asked her to sit down and join them. She said her name was Annie and when Tyler complimented her on her English she told them that she had worked in bars when the Americans had been in Vietnam.

"Bad day for Saigon when Americans go," she said. "Communists kill my husband, take my son to work in fields." She shrugged. "I still here, still run bar. Now Americans come back." She said she was forty-three years old but she looked a lot older; her upper lip was lined and she had deep grooves either side of her mouth and folds of skin around her chin that settled over the string of cheap pearls she wore. Her smile was too eager and her eyes kept flicking from man to man to check that they were happy and that they weren't making a move to go. When Carmody got to his feet to go to the toilet she mistook it for a sign that he wanted to go and she reached to grab his hand and pull him back.

"Was this bar here during the war?" Lehman asked her.

"No. The communists closed down all the old bars. Took away the girls. Took away the managers. Took away everybody to re-education camps."

"What about you, Annie?"

She grimaced. "I had a friend, an NVA officer. He took care of me."

"Where are we?" asked Lewis. "What part of town?"

161

"This Dong Khoi Street," she said. "Before NVA come it was Tu Do Street. The French call it Rue Catinat."

"Tu Do?" said Lehman. "Christ, that was where all the bars were. It was the hottest street in Saigon. There were more fights here than in the jungle."

"And probably a higher body count," said Tyler, sipping his beer from the bottle.

"It's changed, all right," said Lehman. He walked to the entrance of the bar and looked up and down the street. So far as he could see the Hot Bar was the only such drinking establishment in the street. Last time he'd been in this road he couldn't move for pimps offering him their sisters and girls offering him their virginity. There wasn't a vice or drug or perversion that wasn't available in Tu Do, at a price. The place had been packed with Jeeps and soldiers, war-weary grunts with wild eyes and hair-trigger tempers on their first R&R and Saigon-based military with crisp fatigues and new boots. Now it looked like every other road in Saigon, run-down and decaying. The garbage had gone, though. There were always piles of it during the war because the government couldn't match the salaries paid by the American bases so they never had enough workers to carry it away. There was no anti-blast tape on any of the windows either. And the beggars had gone. The street used to be packed with widows and disabled ex-ARVN soldiers asking for handouts and gangs of child pickpockets. Maybe the changes weren't so bad after all, he mused. Annie appeared at his shoulder, fearful that he was about to leave.

"You sit," said Annie. "You sit, I get you nice girl."

Lehman turned to her and smiled, saddened by her over-eagerness to please. "Annie, it's okay, I'm not going anywhere. Relax."

She nodded too quickly and held him by the arm until he sat down again. The girls noticed his Mickey Mouse watch and giggled.

Carmody came back from the toilet and sat down again. The girl next to him, a teenager with her hair in two long braids tied with blue ribbons, leant over and whispered to her friend sitting on the other side of Carmody and the two of them burst into a fit of giggles, covering their mouths with their hands.

"What are they laughing at?" Carmody asked Annie.

"She wonder how you go to the toilet," she said.

"Because of my claw?"

Annie nodded. "You not angry?" she asked anxiously.

"No, I'm not angry," said Carmody, putting down his beer. He held his claw in front of the girl with pigtails and her eyes widened, not sure how to react. Annie spoke to her in rapid Vietnamese and the girl smiled and reached out to touch the stainless steel. Carmody twisted it out of her grasp and ran the cold metal softly down her cheek and then along her neck and down to her blouse. The smile froze on her face as the claw traced a line along her collar and then slowly scraped across the material and moved down between her small, firm breasts. All conversation had stopped, and everyone was looking at Carmody. The claw reached the first button on her blouse and he made a small flicking movement that popped it open. He pushed the claw against her skin and drew it down, parting the material and revealing a white lace bra. When the claw encountered the second button he popped it as easily as he had the first and moved down to the third, but before he reached it he looked over at Annie and grinned. "That's how I do it," he said, and cackled.

Annie laughed and the girls joined in, but the girl with the pigtails kept her eyes on the claw and her laugh had a nervous edge to it.

Carmody ran the claw along the line of her jaw and she flinched. He turned to Annie. "Tell her that's not all I can do with it," he said.

Annie spoke to the girl and she nodded but didn't smile.

"How much to go with her?" Carmody asked.

"She very young girl," Annie said. "She not been here very long. Other girls better. Better in bed. I think you be more happy if you choose them." She pointed at a thin girl with long straight hair who sat opposite Carmody. "She very good girl. Very clean."

"I believe you, mamasan, but I want this pretty little thing." He put the claw on the girl's bare leg and moved it up her thigh, dragging the skirt with it. She tried to push it down and whimpered, tears welling up in her soft brown eyes.

Annie looked at Tyler as if appealing for help. "Go easy, Larry," he said quietly.

Carmody held Tyler's gaze for a second or two and then nodded. He withdrew the claw and picked up a red and white pack of Marlboro cigarettes. He opened it with the claw, took out a cigarette, put it in between his thin lips and then, still using the claw, took a gunmetal Zippo lighter from the pocket of his cut-off jeans. He spun it around in the grip of the claw, snapping it open and flicking a flame into life. He lit the cigarette, put the lighter back on the table and then used the claw to hold the cigarette while he blew a plume of smoke up towards a slowly revolving ceiling fan. Annie clapped and the rest of the girls joined in the applause. Carmody went on to show them how he could use the claw as a bottle opener and they all clapped again. Lehman noticed that at the first available opportunity Annie motioned the girl with pigtails to go into the back room where she stayed until the Americans had left.

A moped drove by, its engine buzzing like a dying insect, then its brakes squealed and there was the crunch of a badly timed gear change and it came back and stopped by the kerb. There were two men on the moped. The driver stayed at the kerb while the passenger, a young Vietnamese guy in his late teens or early twenties, dismounted and walked into the bar. He was wearing a black T-shirt, jeans and light brown cowboy boots and had slicked-back hair that glistened redly under the lights. He had a used car salesman's easy smile and the swagger of a pimp with a stable of eager whores. Annie said something to him but he waved her away with a grin and walked over to the Americans.

"Hi, you guys Americans?" he asked.

"Maybe. Who wants to know?" said Carmody.

"Hey, no sweat," said the man. "My name's Ricky. I was just wondering if you guys wanted to do a little business."

"What sort of business?" asked Lewis suspiciously.

"Currency," he said, brushing his oiled hair back behind his ears in a gesture that was almost feminine. "I'll give you a better rate than you'll get in the hotels. What hotel are you staying at?"

"The Floating," said Carmody, lifting his beer with his claw and keeping it raised until he was sure that Ricky had seen it. Then he drank and used the sleeve of his other arm to wipe away the foam from his upper lip, watching Ricky all the time.

Ricky raised his eyes and looked at the ceiling. "Hey, I guarantee that I can do you a better deal than you got there. They're pirates, real pirates. How many dong do they give you to the dollar?"

Carmody was going to answer but a crafty look flashed across his face. It was so transparent that both Lehman and Lewis noticed it and they began laughing. Carmody glared at them. "What are you offering?" he asked Ricky, and took another drink.

Ricky looked at the faces of the men around the table as if hoping they would offer some hint but five pairs of cold eyes looked back. He pulled a face and ran his hands through his hair again. "I'll give you 6,000."

That was considerably better than the rate offered by the hotel, but Carmody wasn't satisfied. "Eight," he said.

166

"Eight thousand dong for one US dollar!" exclaimed Ricky, his hands on his hips like a flamenco dancer. "You are crazy!"

"Yeah, and you're a black marketeer," answered Carmody.

Ricky's lips tightened as if he'd just tasted something very sour. "How much you want to change?" he asked.

Carmody unzipped the money pouch he carried around his waist. Because the Trading with the Enemy Act forbade the use of American credit cards in Vietnam, all the Americans had to carry lots of cash around. They'd found that many places accepted US currency quite happily, but always gave a lousy exchange. They always got a better deal if they paid in the local money, the dong, but as there were several thousand dong for one US dollar and as the biggest Vietnamese banknote was just 5,000 dong, it usually meant carrying a wad of currency around about the size of a house brick. Carmody's pouch was fairly light so nobody was surprised when he looked up and said he wanted to change 250 dollars.

After several minutes of bartering they agreed on two million dong and Ricky went out of the bar to confer with the moped driver. The driver kicked the moped into life and drove off in a cloud of grey smoke while Ricky waited at the roadside. Five minutes later he was back with a small plastic bag which he handed to Ricky. He kept the moped engine turning over with occasional blips on the accelerator as Ricky brought the bag inside and motioned to Carmody to go with him to a table at the back of the bar.

Carmody sat down and placed five fifty dollar bills on the table and laid his claw on top of them. Ricky swung the plastic bag on the table and took out stacks of notes. They were all 5,000 dong notes in piles of nine with the tenth folded around them. Two million dong meant forty piles, and Ricky slowly counted them out. He took one of the piles at random and spread the notes out to show that they were all 5,000 dong bills. He chose another and did the same, and another. Carmody nodded and lifted his claw from the American bills and began scooping the Vietnamese money back into the bag.

"Maybe we'll do business again, Ricky," he said.

Ricky laughed, pocketed the bills and stood up. He froze when Tyler's hand clapped him on the shoulder. "Wait just a minute, Ricky," said Tyler quietly. He pushed down, hard, and Ricky's legs buckled. He crashed back on to the stool, protesting loudly.

"Hey, man, what's your problem?"

"Dan, keep an eye on his chauffeur, will you?"

"Sure thing," said Lehman. He got to his feet and went over to the entrance of the bar where he leaned against the wall as if he had nothing more on his mind than a breath of fresh air. The moped driver looked at him and Dan raised his bottle of beer in friendly salute.

Ricky continued to protest but Tyler's grip was like steel and he remained on the stool. "Larry, why don't you slide those bills back out of the bag and have another look at them?"

Carmody picked the bag up by its bottom and spilled the dong on to the table. He picked up one of the small piles and examined them. "They're okay," he said.

"Try another."

Carmody looked at a second pile. It too was made up of ten 5,000 dong notes.

"Another," said Tyler quietly.

Carmody pushed the piles around with his claw and then took a third wad of notes. "This one's cool . . ." he stopped mid-sentence and glared at Ricky. "You cheating fucking slope!" he hissed. "You stinking fucking cheating bastard!"

"What's up?" asked Lewis, walking over to the table with his beer in his hand.

Carmody held up a handful of bills. The one on the top and the bottom and the one that had been folded around it were 5,000 dong bills, but the rest were five dong notes.

"This fucking gook was trying to con me," he said, and threw the notes in Ricky's face.

"Count them, Larry," said Tyler. "Let's just see how much the little fuck was trying to stick you for."

Carmody went methodically through the untidy stack of banknotes, putting the ones which were all 5,000 dong bills on one side, the ones containing five dong on the other. The genuine bills accounted for less than a third of the total.

"Well, Larry, I reckon that young Ricky here was trying to get your 250 dollars for about one million dong, give or take a few. About half the rate he promised you."

"Bastard!" shouted Carmody. "Give me my fucking money back you slant-eyed little shit."

Ricky made as if to slip his hand into his back pocket but at the last minute he thrust it instead under the table and pulled a black-handled knife out from one of his boots. He pushed Tyler away and held the knife out in front of him, the other outstretched for balance. He shuffled away from the table so that his back was against the wall. Lehman heard the commotion and looked quickly over his shoulder.

"Everything's just fine, Dan," said Tyler calmly. "Just keep your eyes on Tonto there. We'll handle the Lone Ranger."

Ricky waved the knife under Tyler's nose and made short, sharp jabs at his face, but the American didn't flinch.

"Let me have him, Joel," hissed Carmody, stepping around the table. Ricky kept the knife moving between the two men, bending forward at the waist as if preparing to spring.

"I don't know if that's such a good idea, Larry," said Tyler, keeping his eyes on Ricky. "He looks as if he knows how to handle that knife."

"Yeah, well I'm not exactly defenceless," answered Carmody. "I can look after myself."

"No offence meant, Larry," said Tyler, stepping away from the Vietnamese. Tyler motioned to Lewis and Horvitz to move back.

Ricky grinned when he saw that he was being given the opportunity to fight one on one and he focused all his attention on Carmody, who eased himself into a fighting crouch, his claw forward. He made small circling movements with it as he made soft, animal-like grunting noises. Ricky moved away from the wall in shuffling steps, swishing the knife left and right at stomach level. Carmody sniffed and jabbed with his claw and then spat into Ricky's face, a shower of saliva that sent the Vietnamese's hand automatically up to protect himself. Carmody stepped forward and kicked Ricky between the legs, sending him smashing into the wall. Carmody kept moving forward and brought his arm down with enough force to plunge the points of his claw deep into Ricky's hand. Ricky screamed and the knife clattered to the ground. Carmody swung him around and pulled his arm up behind his back, blood streaming from where it was still impaled by the claw. Tears were streaming down Ricky's face and he was shrieking with pain. Carmody wrenched the injured hand up higher and then rammed his knee into the back of Ricky's leg so that the Vietnamese almost collapsed. With his good hand Carmody grabbed Ricky's hair and began to pound his face into the wooden panels of the wall until they all heard cartilage crunch and the man's screams stopped. Only then did Carmody let go of his hair and let him slump to the ground. He had to bend with the fall because his claw had become entangled in the bones and tendons of Ricky's hand and he knelt down to twist it out of the torn flesh. He stood up and took a paper napkin from one of the tables and used it to wipe the blood from his claw, then screwed it up and threw it to one side.

He grinned at Tyler and walked to the entrance of the bar to stand by Lehman. The man on the moped stared at Ricky's limp body, then gunned the engine into life and sped off, his feet dragging on the road as he fought to control the bucking handlebars.

Ricky groaned. Carmody walked back over to him and pulled the US dollars out of the man's back pocket, then kicked him in the ribs.

"That's enough, Larry," said Tyler. "We don't want a dead gook on our hands. Not now."

Carmody nodded and left Ricky alone. "Whatever you say, Colonel." He picked up the carrier bag and scooped the dong back into it.

Lehman turned to look at the two men. He was no longer surprised at the ease with which Tyler controlled the actions of the group.

"I think we'd better all saddle up and move on out," Tyler said and the vets headed for the door where their cyclo riders were already climbing into their saddles.

"Hey, GIs, what do we do with him?" Annie called after them.

They ignored her and swung themselves into the cyclos.

"Where shall we go, Joel?" asked Lewis.

"Gentlemen, how about a race?" suggested Tyler.

"A race?" repeated Carmody.

Tyler turned to speak to the five cyclo drivers. "Do you all speak English?" He was greeted with five smiling, nodding faces. "Right then." He took out his wallet and removed a twenty dollar note. He waved it in the air. "We want to go from here to the Rex Hotel,

172

then along Le Loi Boulevard to the statue of Tran Nguyen Hai, down Pho Duc Chinh Street and along Ben Chuong Duong Street and then to the Floating Hotel."

He looked across at the rest of the vets. "I reckon that's the best part of a mile."

He turned back to the drivers. "We'll only be paying one fare, and that's this twenty dollar bill. The winner gets it all. Okay?"

The men all nodded eagerly. It was more than they normally earned in a month.

"Are you ready? Get set. Go!" Tyler shouted, and fell back in his seat as his driver accelerated. The drivers pounded their legs around and around, bending low as they pushed their rusty cyclos along the roads, steering with one hand and ringing their bells with the other to warn cyclists they were coming through. They varied in age from late twenties to early fifties but all were fit and all appeared to want to win the prize. By the time they reached the Rex Hotel they were all perspiring heavily and the pace had slowed with Lehman slightly in the lead, followed by Tyler, Horvitz and Lewis virtually neck and neck. Carmody was last and he was rocking backwards and forwards trying to get more momentum and to encourage his driver, the youngest of the group. Lehman leant over and waved his fist at Carmody as they rounded the corner into Le Loi Boulevard watched by curious pedestrians who wondered what the crazy Americans were up to. Lewis and Horvitz were yelling at their drivers to increase the pace and they rose up out of their saddles to get greater leverage on the pedals. Lehman's driver kept looking over his shoulder to see if they were gaining.

"No problem. We win," he grunted at Lehman, who could see that he was barely out of breath. His upper body was bathed in sweat and water was dripping off his forehead but that seemed to be more to do with the hot, clammy night than with the physical exertion. A small Yamaha motorcycle cruised up next to Lehman and a teenager with a pudding-basin haircut and thin moustache shouted over to his driver, obviously asking what was happening. The driver shouted something back in Vietnamese and the teenager laughed and whooped and then fell back to taunt Carmody and his driver for lagging behind. Tyler's cyclo began to draw away from Lewis and Horvitz, probably because he was lighter than they were and the slight incline of the road was starting to tell on the drivers.

By the time they reached the statue of Tran Nguyen Hai Lehman's lead had been narrowed by Tyler, who was urging on his driver. Lewis and Horvitz were neck and neck and risking life and limb by reaching over and trying to pull the rear brakes of each other's cyclos, narrowly escaping getting their fingers chewed up in the wheels. Carmody had taken a ten dollar bill from his wallet and was screaming to his driver that if they won he could have that, too. The man was nodding and grinning and doing his level best, but he was clearly not as fit as the other four drivers and Carmody slumped back in his seat, grinding his teeth in frustration. The teenager on the Yamaha revved his engine and laughed until Carmody lashed out with his leg and knocked the machine into a roadside hawker's noodle soup stall which promptly collapsed amid a cloud of steaming broth.

As the cyclos turned into Ben Chuong Duong Street and raced parallel to the Saigon River, Lewis finally managed to jam the brake on Horvitz's cyclo and it skidded to a halt by the side of the road. The driver cursed at Lewis and jumped off to free the back wheel while Lewis's driver put on a spurt and managed to catch up with Tyler who was still waving his twenty dollar bill in the air. With the drivers of both cyclos matching each other pedal for pedal the two cyclos began to gain on Lehman. Carmody's driver had managed to increase his speed in response to his passenger's cursing and shouting. Lehman's driver was gasping for breath and rocking in his saddle as his thighs pumped up and down and Lehman could feel his hot breath blowing against the back of his head. The hotel came into view in the distance and in front of it he could see bicycles circling the statue of Tran Hung Dao in Me Linh Square. Carmody had grabbed a bicycle pump from his cyclo and was trying to jam it in between the spokes of Lewis's nearside wheel.

"Leave it alone, man," yelled Lewis. "You'll turn us over."

Carmody laughed harshly. "Screw you!" he shouted. He jabbed the pump at Lewis's face and then threw it at the cyclo driver. It bounced off the driver's head, but he ignored it, concentrating on trying to catch Lehman.

"What the hell's wrong with you?" shouted Lewis.

Carmody was about to reply when Horvitz's cyclo drew level. Horvitz began to kick at Lewis. "That was a bastard trick back there," shouted Horvitz, each word coinciding with a hefty kick at Lewis's cyclo. While Lewis was distracted, Carmody leaned over and clipped him around the head with his claw, drawing blood. Lewis put his hand on his injured ear, his eyes blazing at Carmody, then he lurched forward as Horvitz kicked the wheel brake. As the cyclo squealed to a halt, Lewis leapt out and chased after Carmody who raised his good hand and gave him the finger. "Up yours, Lewis!" he yelled, then turned and urged his driver to pedal faster.

Realising that he wasn't gaining, Lewis stopped and waited for his own cyclo driver to catch up. His stomach ached and he bent double, trying to ease the pain.

"Can't take it any more, bro?" jeered Horvitz.

"Fuck you," said Lewis. He climbed back into his cyclo and rejoined the race.

Lehman was still in the lead. "Nearly there," gasped his driver.

"Go for it," said Lehman, suddenly embarrassed by the man's enthusiasm for the race. He wasn't doing it out of any competitive instinct, any desire to be first, he was doing it purely and simply so that he could put food on the table for his family, as opposed to the Americans who seemed to want to win for the sake of victory itself. Lehman sensed with a tightening of his stomach that Tyler was manipulating the Vietnamese the way an animal trainer can make sea lions do tricks by tempting them with pieces of fish. He folded his arms across his chest and settled back in his seat, his lips tight together, not caring any more whether or not Tyler and the rest were catching up. He was still sitting like that when his cyclo screeched to a halt in front of the hotel, closely followed by Horvitz and Tyler. Carmody was a full thirty seconds behind them and he glared at his driver while putting his ten dollars back into his wallet. "You weren't fucking trying," he said to the man who was bent double over his saddle and panting. Carmody climbed out of the cyclo and stormed off towards the entrance to the hotel where a young Vietnamese in a sailor suit opened the glass door for him and wished him a good evening. "Fuck off," Carmody muttered and jabbed at the lift button with his claw, hard enough to scratch the plastic.

Outside, Lewis arrived, his ear still bleeding, and Tyler made a big show of handing the twenty dollar bill to Lehman's driver, then the four vets walked after Carmody.

"I thought that would get them going," said Tyler.

"Yeah, that was some ride," agreed Lewis. "I think Carmody was taking it a bit too seriously."

"Just goes to show that capitalism gets results," said Tyler.

Lehman smiled ruefully. "How do you explain that, then?" he asked, pointing back to the parked cyclos. The five Vietnamese men stood together and Lehman's driver was handing out money to the other four. "They're sharing the prize," said Lehman. "It didn't matter who won, they all get a piece of it."

Horvitz frowned. "Now why the hell would they do that?" he mused.

Tyler shook his head and snorted disparagingly. "Who knows?" he said. "Looks like they haven't quite got the hang of the free market after all."

The four Americans walked together to the lifts. Carmody had already disappeared upstairs.

"Drink?" asked Tyler.

Lehman declined, saying that they had a busy schedule for their last full day in Vietnam. Judy had arranged a visit to a local factory, an orphanage, a Saigon hospital and in the evening they were to attend a dinner with a number of local dignitaries.

"I'll see you guys tomorrow," said Lehman as the others went through to the lobby bar.

In the lift on the way up to his room Lehman thought about the Vietnamese and the way they'd shared the prize. It didn't make sense.

Debbie Fielding walked down the stairs and straightened her hair in the hall mirror. She leant forward and pursed her lips, checking that her lipstick hadn't smudged.

"You look fabulous," said her mother. Anne Fielding was standing at the doorway to the lounge, a drink in her hand. She was wearing an Yves Saint Laurent gilded brocade silk dress, gold, black and red, caught at the waist with a delicate gilt chain, but she was standing barefoot. Her toenails were painted the same dark red as her fingernails. She looked tired, thought Debbie, and the drink in her hand clearly wasn't her first of the day. Debbie looked at her watch. It was eight o'clock. "That look was loaded with criticism, young lady," chided Anne, raising the gin and tonic and tilting the glass from side to side.

"That's not what I was doing, Mum, honest," said Debbie. "I was just looking to see if he was late, that's all." She smoothed the pale green velvet dress over her hips. It was split up the sides to the top of her thighs and cut low across her chest.

"He?" queried Anne. "Are you going out with that policeman?"

"Neil? Oh, God, no. He's history, Mum."

"So who's the lucky guy tonight? He must be pretty good to merit the Gaultier."

Debbie playfully stuck her tongue out at her mother. "You haven't met him. His name's Anthony. Anthony Chung." She walked by Anne into the lounge. Her father was sitting on one of the sofas, a pile of bank papers at his side and an open briefcase at his feet like a loyal dog.

"Hi, Dad," she said.

William Fielding looked up and smiled. "Hello, Debs. Party?" He had a gold pen in his hand, a present she'd given him for his fiftieth birthday, eight years earlier. Her mother had given her the money but she'd chosen the pen and ordered the engraving on it. Her father had carried it with him ever since and had already gone through three gold nibs.

"Date," she said.

"Chung, did you say?" said her mother, following her into the lounge. "Did you say Anthony Chung?" She

179

put the emphasis on the surname, and Debbie knew exactly what her mother meant by the inflection.

"Yes, Mum, he's Chinese."

"What does he do, this Anthony Chung?" asked her father, putting the pen down on top of the pile of papers.

Debbie shrugged. "I don't know, Dad. This is our first date."

"Where did you meet him?" asked Anne.

"Mum!" wailed Debbie, plaintively. "It's just a date. I'm twenty-three years old, you know."

"I know you are," said her mother. "I just wondered who he was. You've never been out with someone Chinese before." She took a big swallow of her gin and tonic.

"Mum, I have so. Several times." She resented the veiled accusation of racial prejudice, though she knew that her mother was right. She'd never been out on a date with a Chinese, not one to one, though she'd often been part of mixed-race groups.

Anne frowned. "Well if you have, you kept it a secret," she said.

"I don't tell you about everyone I go out with," said Debbie, beginning to feel defensive.

"I think what your mother means is that we worry about you, especially the way things are going in Hong Kong just now," said William. "The streets aren't as safe as they used to be. The police are undermanned and there's a great deal of anti-British sentiment among the locals."

180

"I wasn't aware that I needed a translator, William," said Anne frostily, crossing the room to the drinks cabinet where she refilled her gin and tonic.

"I hardly think Anthony is going to attack me because I'm British," said Debbie.

"That's not what I meant, Debs, and you know it," said her father. "If you intend to go out late at night, your mother and I would like to know where you're going and who you're with, that's all. I don't want to sound like a Victorian father, but I do expect you to keep your mother and me informed."

He pushed his horn-rimmed spectacles up his nose. With his grey hair and plump face he looked like a kindly schoolmaster, the effect increased by the sleeveless pullovers he wore at home. He looked over the top of his glasses at his daughter, the action giving him a double chin. "Understand?"

Debbie wanted to argue but she knew it wasn't the time, not with her date expected at any moment. "Yeah, Dad, I understand."

He smiled benignly, nodded as if he were concluding a meeting of his board of directors, and then returned to his paperwork.

Anne sat down on the sofa facing the fireplace, at a right angle to where her husband was working. As she crossed her legs, the silk dress slid across her thighs. Anne Fielding had long, shapely legs and she dressed to show them off, but it had been a long time since her husband had appeared to notice. She tapped a fingernail against the glass. "What time is Mr Chung expected?" she said.

Debbie walked over to the white marble fireplace and turned so that her back was to it. "Mum, call him Anthony, please. 'Mr Chung' makes him sound like an old man. He said he'd pick me up at eight. You'll really like him, I'm sure. He's cute, really cute. And he drives a Ferrari."

"A Ferrari?" said her father, lifting his head from his work.

"An F40," said Debbie. "It's the best, and he said I could drive it."

"Only if you're insured," her father said, giving her the schoolteacher look again.

Debbie sighed. "Yes, Dad." A car growled outside, crunching on the gravel as it drove up to the porch. It was the unmistakable throb of a thoroughbred racing car. "That'll be him," said Debbie.

"Invite him in, then," said William Fielding.

Debbie knew that her parents were more interested in inspecting Anthony than they were in being sociable, but she knew it wouldn't be a good idea to refuse. Besides, she was certain Anthony was more than capable of handling their scrutiny.

"Okay," she said, and skipped to the door, beating Maria, their Filipina maid, who had rushed from the kitchen at the sound of the car door slamming.

"That's okay, Maria, I'll get it," she said, and opened the door just as Anthony was reaching for the doorbell.

"Good evening," said Chung with a wide smile. He looked her up and down. "Nice dress."

"You don't think it'll clash with the Ferrari?"

"Green and red? My favourite colours."

182

"Would you like to come in?" she said. "And meet my parents?" she added in a whisper so that they couldn't hear.

"Sure," he said, and winked.

He was wearing a black, faintly pinstriped double-breasted wool suit with a green wool roll-neck sweater which Debbie would have thought too hot for the time of the year, but Chung showed no signs of discomfort. She stepped aside to let him across the threshold, closed the door and showed him through to the lounge. Her father put down his pen and papers and got to his feet. He held out his hand to Chung but waited for the younger man to close the distance between them. William Fielding was a man used to subordinates coming to him. Chung crossed the room in easy strides and shook his hand firmly.

"It's a pleasure to meet you, Mr Fielding," said Chung.

"Good evening," said Fielding. "This is my wife, Anne."

Chung turned to face Debbie's mother. She remained seated but held up her hand for Chung to shake. He stepped forward, took the outstretched hand in his, and bent at the waist to kiss it. "*Enchanté,*" he said. Anne looked surprised at his action. "Forgive me," he said, seeing her confusion. "But in France that is how we always greet a beautiful woman."

Anne smiled and took back her hand. "You spend a lot of time in France?" she asked.

"I am French," he said. "At least, I have a French passport. Whether or not I could ever truly be French is another matter."

"You speak French?" asked Fielding.

"I was educated at the Sorbonne, and I lived there for several years after I graduated," said Chung, "so yes, I'm fluent, and I'm told I have a good accent. It's a marvellous language, so expressive."

"The language of lovers," said Anne.

"That's what the French say," said Chung. "But I think the Italians might dispute it."

They all laughed and Fielding asked Chung if he wanted a drink.

"Not when I'm driving, sir, but thank you for the offer," said Chung.

Debbie was quietly amused by the skilful way Chung was handling her parents. He'd had no qualms about drinking and driving when he'd met her at the California. Kissing her mother's hand was pushing it a bit, though.

"Very sensible," agreed Fielding. He looked over the top of his glasses at Debbie.

"Yes, Dad, I know. Don't drink and drive. Don't worry, I won't."

"Where are you going tonight?" asked Anne.

"I've booked a table at Charlotte's, in Tsim Sha Tsui," said Chung. "It's one of my favourite restaurants."

"In the Ambassador Hotel?" said Fielding. "You're right, it is good. I use it myself whenever I'm over in Kowloon."

Chung looked at his watch. "We'll have to go, I'm afraid," he said to Debbie. "I booked for eight thirty and we've got to go through the cross-harbour tunnel."

"Great," said Debbie.

Chung took Anne's hand and kissed it again. "It's been a pleasure meeting you, Mrs Fielding." He straightened up and went over to shake hands with her husband. "And you, too, sir. I won't keep her out too long."

"That'll be a first," said Anne.

"Thanks, Mum," laughed Debbie, walking through to the front door and opening it. She and Chung walked to the Ferrari. "Can I drive it now?" she asked.

"Later," promised Chung. "I don't think your father would approve."

"I won't tell him," said Debbie.

"They're watching," said Chung, holding the passenger door open for her and helping her to buckle herself in.

Debbie glanced back to the house and saw a curtain twitch at the lounge window. She couldn't see who was there but she'd have bet a month's salary that it was her father.

Chung drove confidently and quickly down the Peak to the towering office blocks of Central where he joined the queue of cars waiting to use the cross-harbour tunnel. It took them a full thirty minutes to cross to Kowloon, twice the time it took the humble Star Ferry.

Chung parked at the New World Hotel car park and walked with Debbie across Salisbury Road and along Nathan Road to the Ambassador Hotel. As they walked, Chung told Debbie about his time in France, his studies, and how he now spent his time running a number of factories in the Shenzhen Special Economic Zone, making computer parts for American companies, as well as looking after his family's extensive Hong Kong property interests. She told him of her job with the travel magazine, how it allowed her lots of foreign travel but that it was just to fill time while she decided what to do with her life.

They went into the hotel and up the stairs to Charlotte's where the maître d' showed them to a booth and handed them leather-bound menus. Charlotte's was one of Chung's favourite Western restaurants and he was pleased to discover that it was the first time Debbie had been there. He recommended she try the salmon, and chose the wine without looking at the wine list.

"I thought you weren't going to drink and drive," she said.

"That was for your father's benefit," said Chung.

"I thought so," said Debbie. "You handled him really well. I think he really likes you, and that's unusual."

"Because I'm Chinese?"

"No, because you're a guy. He's very protective of me. He normally puts prospective boyfriends through the third degree. You got off lightly."

"Is that what I am?" asked Chung. "A prospective boyfriend?"

Debbie blushed. "I mean anyone who asks me out," she explained. "Usually I try to keep them away from my parents."

Their appetisers arrived, cream of zucchini soup with fresh basil for him, smoked chicken for her. Chung tasted the wine and pronounced it excellent.

"I liked your mother," said Chung. "Is she much younger than your father?"

"About twelve years younger," said Debbie. "Dad's fifty-eight, Mum's forty-six next birthday."

Chung raised his eyebrows. "She looks younger," he said.

"Why, Anthony, are you interested in my mother?" asked Debbie in mock horror.

"Of course not," he said, breaking a fresh bread roll apart. "I just felt there was a bit of an atmosphere, that's all. Have they been arguing?"

Debbie's fork stopped on its way to her mouth. "What makes you say that?"

"A feeling, that's all."

She nodded. "They argue, sure, but I don't think that they're worse than any other married couple. They're both under a lot of pressure, but for different reasons. Dad is worried about what's going to happen to the bank, before and after 1997. He's trying to arrange a merger with a foreign bank so that they'll be less vulnerable when the communists take over, but he's finding it difficult because of the loss of confidence in Hong Kong. The stock market keeps falling and the low share price means he can't cut a good deal. His negotiating position just keeps on getting weaker."

"And your mother?"

"All her friends are leaving, and she feels as if she's been left behind. You know what it's like at the moment

— everybody's bailing out. They're either going back to Britain or switching to Thailand or Singapore. Soon there won't be anyone left. That's how she feels, anyway."

"She may be right," said Chung. "How many are leaving now? It's something like 70,000 every year, almost 200 every day of the week. The brightest and the best."

"But you're staying?"

"I'm Chinese," said Chung. "I help earn foreign currency for China, they need me more than I need them."

"Plus you have a French passport."

Chung grinned and raised his glass to her. "That I do," he agreed.

They chatted all the way through the meal, and Debbie found herself genuinely enjoying his company. Chung was articulate, well read, and had a very dry, almost British, sense of humour. It turned out that he was an ardent fan of *Fawlty Towers* and had all the episodes on video tape.

The food was superb and after coffee Chung suggested they go along to Hot Gossip, a bar cum disco on Canton Road. As they walked she slipped her arm through his. He was tall for a Chinese, and well built. She noticed that they attracted quite a bit of attention on the streets. She'd like to have thought that it was because they were a well-dressed, good-looking couple, but in her heart she knew that it was because he was Chinese and she was white. If it had been the other way round, if she'd been the local and he'd been British, then no one would have given them a second look, but there was still resentment when a pretty blonde was seen on the arm of a Chinese male. The resentment came from both sides. The British found it strange that one of their own would be attracted to a Chinese man, the Chinese felt that it was a snub to their own women. It was so two-faced, thought Debbie. Everyone knew that the reason single expats liked Hong Kong so much was because they could go out with so many pretty, Oriental girls. But when a white girl went out with a Chinese, it provoked whispers and nudges. Debbie smiled up at Chung and held his arm tighter. She didn't care what anyone else thought.

Hot Gossip's upstairs bar was packed so they went straight to the downstairs discotheque. Chung found her a seat and then went off to get them drinks. He returned with a bottle of Moët et Chandon in an ice bucket and two glasses.

"A celebration?" asked Debbie.

"I just felt like champagne," he said, pouring it for them. He raised his glass and clinked it against hers. Debbie was drinking when she saw Neil Coleman come into the disco, with his friend Phil Donaldson in tow. They were both sweating and had the look of men who'd been drinking heavily for most of the evening.

"Oh shit," said Debbie, under her breath. She turned away and tried to blend into the wall but Donaldson spotted her. Out of the corner of her eye she saw him grab Neil by the arm and whisper something to him.

"Are you okay?" asked Chung.

"An old boyfriend just walked in," said Debbie. "I hope he doesn't make a scene. He's a bit possessive."

"Don't worry," said Chung calmly.

Debbie saw Neil head over in her direction, a fierce frown on his forehead. Donaldson followed him, grinning maniacally and hoping for trouble.

"He's a policeman," added Debbie. "So's his friend."

"I'll bear that in mind," said Chung. He took a slow drink from his champagne glass and gave her an easy smile.

Coleman bumped into a Chinese couple but didn't apologise. He kept on heading straight towards Debbie like a guided missile. He stood in front of her, swaying unsteadily on his feet. He was wearing baggy brown cotton trousers and a white linen shirt and his sandy hair was unruly, as usual. Neil always blamed Hong Kong's humidity but Debbie reckoned he just didn't spend enough on his haircuts.

"Debbie," said Coleman. Donaldson appeared at his shoulder.

"Hiya, Debbie," he said.

"Hello, Neil. Hello, Phil," she said.

"I thought you were seeing a girlfriend tonight," said Coleman.

"There was a change of plans," said Debbie. Her mouth felt dry and she swallowed some champagne.

"Champagne?" he said.

"We're celebrating," said Chung. He held out his hand to Coleman. "Hi, we haven't met before. My name's Anthony Chung." The gesture took Coleman by surprise, and he shook Chung's hand. "I work with Debbie's father, on the corporate finance side," continued Chung. "We finished a major deal this morning and we were supposed to go out celebrating tonight. He's gone down with a bad stomach, though, so he insisted that Debbie take me out instead. It's not every day that the bank gets a ten million dollar fee. Can we get you a glass?"

Coleman looked confused and turned to Donaldson for support. Debbie wondered why Chung had lied. For whatever reason Chung had decided not to tell the truth, his words seemed to have defused the tension now that Neil regarded him as a bank employee rather than as a rival for her affections. It was a smart move, she saw, because Neil was drunk and in the mood for an argument if not a fight.

Chung introduced himself to Donaldson and after they shook hands offered him a glass of champagne. Both Coleman and Donaldson refused, saying they'd prefer a beer. Chung offered to get them beers, laughing that it was all on the bank, but they refused.

"I'll call you tomorrow, okay?" Coleman said to Debbie.

"Sure," said Debbie.

"What time are you leaving?" asked Coleman.

"I don't know," said Debbie, annoyed at the question. She wanted to tell him it was none of his business but she figured that she'd follow Chung's tactful lead. "Anthony will give me a lift back, he's left some papers at our house."

Coleman nodded as if satisfied with her answer. "Okay," he said. "Nice meeting you, Anthony. I'll call you," he repeated to Debbie.

"Come on, Neil, let's hit the bar," said Donaldson, tugging at his arm. Coleman looked as if he wanted to say something else to Debbie but then decided against it, shrugging off Donaldson's hand and following him back to the bar.

Debbie waited until the two men had gone before turning to Chung. "Thanks for not antagonising him," she said.

"I could see he was looking for trouble," said Chung. "I figured you wouldn't want a scene here, not in front of all these people."

The way he said it left Debbie in no doubt that if Coleman had come across them in an out-of-the-way spot Chung would have had no hesitation in getting physical. His body was well muscled and he'd told her that he'd studied kung fu as a teenager. Coleman, on the other hand, was starting to run to fat and had given up all sports the day he left school.

"You were so smooth," she said. "How did you learn to lie so well?"

Chung laughed. "The knack of doing business with the mainland is to blend truth and half-truth and never to believe what your opposite number tells you. You get used to saying one thing and thinking another. I'm sure your dad knows what I mean, he must spend a lot of time dealing with the Chinese."

"It sounds funny hearing you say that."

"Saying what?"

"Criticising the Chinese."

"You mean, when I'm Chinese myself? Sure, I'm Chinese, but I was educated in the West. There's a difference. Do you think we should go, just in case your boyfriend has a bit more to drink and decides to come back?"

"He's not my boyfriend!" protested Debbie.

Chung patted her bare arm. "I was joking," he said. "Come on, let's go back."

They walked back to the car park, arm in arm. It was getting late but the streets were crowded. The Mass Transit Railway had shut for the night and the few taxis that had their "for hire" lights on were being frantically waved at, and couples were jostling each other to get to the door handles first. There was no queuing system for catching a Hong Kong cab, it was survival of the fittest, the victor being the one who could open the door first. There was no shame in running alongside a moving taxi and elbowing aside others to be next to the rear doors when it finally stopped. All that mattered was getting the cab. It was, thought Debbie, so typical of Hong Kong. Everybody rushing and fighting to get the best for themselves and their families and to hell with the rest.

As they reached the Ferrari, Chung pulled out his keys. He threw them in a gentle arc to Debbie and she caught them in both hands. "You mean it?" she gasped.

"I promised, didn't I?" he said.

"Yes, but I didn't think you meant it," she said, opening the driver's door.

"Hey, just because I lied to your boyfriend doesn't mean I'll lie to you."

"He's not my boyfriend . . ." she began, but Chung cut her off with a wave and a smile.

"Get in," he said, walking round to the passenger side.

Debbie was surprised at how harsh the clutch and brakes were on the Ferrari, and how tight the steering was: the slightest touch on the wheel had the car moving left or right. But it was the accelerator that took her breath away. Just touching it with her right foot had the Ferrari leaping forward like a springing cat. Chung said nothing, letting her learn from her mistakes, and she was grateful to him for that. Even when she felt she had the car under control she could sense that it was straining to get away from her. It wanted to fly along the road, turbines screaming, and she could tell that it hated to be confined in traffic. "God, Anthony, it's beautiful," she gasped.

She hadn't anticipated how noisy the car would be, and she could see why there was no sound system like most cars had. Music wouldn't be heard over the growl of the engine, and besides, it would be totally out of place in such a car. It was built to race, not to cruise.

She edged the car carefully through the night-time traffic and towards the cross-harbour tunnel. Twenty minutes later they were on Hong Kong Island and driving up the Peak.

"It's like riding a wild animal," said Debbie, her voice loaded with admiration. "I've never felt anything like it. You know that if you put your foot down it'll fly."

"You drive well," said Chung.

"For a girl, you mean?"

Chung shook his head. "No, that's not what I meant. I meant you drive well, by any standards."

Debbie grinned, pleased at the compliment. She reached over and ran her hand along his thigh. She slowed the car and turned off the main road. She stopped the car and switched off the engine before unbuckling her harness and turning to face Chung. She stroked the side of his face and then slipped her hand behind his neck and pulled him towards her, kissing him fiercely. His mouth opened and she probed inside with her tongue. His hands reached up to hold either side of her head, brushing her blonde hair clear of her face. Debbie made small, moaning noises and began to climb over the gear stick to Chung's side of the car. Her head banged on the roof and she giggled. She bent her head and kissed him hard as she tried to straddle him, her hands struggling to pull down his zipper.

"Whoa!" he said, pushing her away.

"What's wrong?" she said, surprised. Chung appeared confused. There was a smear of her lipstick across his left cheek. Debbie licked her thumb and rubbed it away.

"Don't be in such a hurry," he said, caressing her cheek. She tried to bite his hand but he moved it to the side. She bent down to kiss him again but he put his hands on her shoulders and held her away. "No," he said firmly.

Debbie put her hands down between his thighs and rubbed him. "You want it as much as I do," she said, her voice husky with passion.

Chung grinned and his eyes sparkled. "I can't deny that. But this isn't the time or the place."

"The time's perfect," said Debbie. "I want you, Anthony. I want you now."

"Debbie, I'm not going to make love to you in a car. When we make love we'll do it properly. There's no rush, we've plenty of time."

"You're turning me down?" said Debbie, stunned.

Chung kissed her, and this time his tongue invaded her mouth before he broke away. "I'm not turning you down, I'm just taking a rain check," he said. "When I make love to you, I want to do it properly, that's all."

Debbie sat back in his lap, her shoulders sagging. Chung was the first man ever to have refused her, and she found it difficult to come to terms with.

"Don't look so offended," said Chung.

"I'm not," said Debbie, "I'm just surprised, that's all." She slid off his lap and back into her seat. She shook her head as she restarted the Ferrari, put it in gear and pulled a tight U-turn. She didn't say anything until the car was parked outside her house. Chung got out first and walked around to the driver's side to open the door for her. Debbie slid her legs out first and Chung helped her up. He kept hold of her hand and pulled her close, kissing her before she had a chance to react. She put her arms around his neck and pressed the full length of her body against his. It was with no small sense of satisfaction that she could feel him hard against her groin. She ground herself into him, pushing her hips from side to side, and then moved away, a sly smile on her face.

"That'll give you something to remember," she said. "Until next time."

"I'll call you," he said.

"You'd better," she answered, and ran to the front door. She unlocked it and disappeared inside without looking back.

Chung stood by the side of the Ferrari and looked up at the house. It was three storeys tall, white-painted stone with large sash windows and a flat roof. There was a light on in one of the upstairs windows, and as he leant back against the car the curtains drew back and a figure appeared, a black silhouette against the light. The figure's hair appeared as a golden halo, and he realised it was Anne Fielding. She was wearing a nightdress and the light streamed through it, clearly showing her figure, the swell of her breasts and her trim waist. She moved slightly and he saw her breasts ripple under the nightdress. He wondered if she knew how she was revealing herself to him, and if she cared. He couldn't see her face but he knew that she was looking down at him as he stood in the light from the porch. Chung smiled, but he couldn't tell if she smiled back. He gave her a small wave, but she didn't react. He shrugged and climbed into the driver's seat of the Ferrari. He looked up again before starting the car; the curtain was back in place and Anne Fielding had gone.

He drove back down the Peak Road, much intrigued by what he had seen.

"You my father?" asked the small boy, his hair light brown and naturally curly, his skin lighter than the Vietnamese the vets were accustomed to seeing.

Lehman ruffled the boy's hair. "No, kid, I'm not your father," he said.

The boy grinned, showing brilliant white teeth, perfectly even. "You know him? My father named Hans. From Holland. You come from Holland?"

Lehman shook his head. "From America," he said. "We're from America."

The boy nodded thoughtfully as if considering a difficult problem. "Okay," he said. "Me go America. You take me?"

"I can't, kid," said Lehman gently. He turned to the nun who was showing the group of Americans around the orphanage. Her white habit was stained at the front as if she'd spilled something down it, something brown or maybe red, and the area around the stain was grey and smudged as if she'd tried to get the stain out but had failed. "They speak such good English, Sister Marie," Lehman said to her.

"We hope that one day they will be adopted by a family in Europe. Or perhaps even America," she explained. "We teach them English, and we teach them as much as we can about other countries. Their future is not here, in Vietnam."

The nun was Irish, and Lehman would have bet money that hidden under the white cowl was a head of the reddest hair that would have perfectly complemented her pale green eyes. The rest of the nuns who ran the orphanage were all Vietnamese and spoke English poorly, she had explained, so she had been sent over from Ireland to help teach the children.

The group was standing in a cobbled courtyard which had been worn smooth by countless generations of feet. Lehman heard a door slam and then the courtyard was filled with the chatter of excited children. On each of the floors was a corridor which ran around all four sides of the courtyard, off which were doors to the various rooms, and in the corners where the corridors met were steps to the floors above and below, also open to the elements. The children, as many as twenty boys and girls, filed down the stone steps and into the canteen where Sister Marie had shown the vets the wooden tables and benches where they took all their meals. On the top floor were the dormitories where the children slept and on the two other floors were the rooms where they took their lessons. The nun had taken them round the poorly equipped kitchens and the canteen and the pantry with its meagre supplies of rice and dried fish, all of them on the ground floor, and as the children continued to pour into the canteen she led the Americans across the courtyard and through another, smaller, archway to a neat kitchen garden where the nuns grew their own fruit and vegetables.

"How many kids do you have here?" asked Speed.

"Just over one hundred," said Sister Marie.

"Are they all Amerasians?" asked Janet Cummings.

"If by Amerasians you mean children of American soldiers, then the answer is no," said Sister Marie. "The last Americans left in 1975, so the children of the war are now at least twenty years old. There were about 25,000, of whom more than half have already gone to the US under the Amerasian Homecoming Act. In effect, America has been bribing the Vietnamese to let them go. It costs the US 137 dollars each time an Amerasian is allowed to leave. They go first to the Philippines for six months to learn English and a trade, and then they go to America, along with their mothers and any other close family. Most of the Amerasians had already left by the time I arrived here five years ago. There were many thousands, most of them dependent on charity or living on the streets of Saigon. They were treated so very badly, those children. They were half white or half black and the Vietnamese do not take kindly to the children of mixed marriages. They called them *bui doi*, the dust of life. They were denied even the most basic education and health care, they were beaten, many were even locked away in the re-education camps. In the early eighties America agreed to resettle the Amerasians in the United States under the Orderly Departure Programme and now most of those who wished to go have gone."

"Which is as it should be," said Judy.

"So who are these children?" asked Janet Cummings.

"They are the children of the original Amerasians," said Sister Marie. "Many of them were abandoned in the same way that their mothers and fathers were abandoned. Those children who could be taken for Vietnamese were accepted into society, but those with non-Asian features were simply left on the streets. Many were left on the doorstep of this orphanage."

"But can't they go to America too?" asked Henderson, lowering his camera.

"If their parents acknowledge them, then of course. But many were abandoned before the programme was announced, and many of the mothers are already in the United States. Matching up the orphans with their mothers is next to impossible. They already have new lives in the States. Many of the Amerasian girls were working as prostitutes and the children would be reminders of the lives they left behind."

A small boy with dark skin and curly black hair came bowling into the vegetable garden, arms flailing and legs skidding on the soil. His eyes searched the group of Americans as if he were looking for someone and when he saw Lewis he grinned and rushed over and grabbed his leg.

Lewis bent down and scooped him up in his arms and held him so that their heads were on one level. The boy put his arms around Lewis's neck and hugged him.

"That's Samuel," said Sister Marie. "He's never seen anyone like his father. Black, I mean."

That explained his rush to the garden, thought Lehman. Some of the other children must have told Samuel that there was a black visitor. The kid's delight at seeing an adult with skin almost like his own was heartbreaking.

"Other children here are the unwanted children of Vietnamese prostitutes and their customers. Some American, some European, and a lot of Russians. The more tourists who come, the more illegitimate children there will be and the more they will be left in our care. We have been trying to educate the prostitutes about using contraceptives, but it is not easy. They are expensive, and not readily available."

A young Eurasian girl called Sister Marie's name and ran over to speak to her in Vietnamese. The nun answered, also in Vietnamese, and then she told the group that the tour of the orphanage had come to an end. Another nun, Sister Agnes, would show them around the hospital part of the building. She pointed to the stairs at the far side of the courtyard and told the Americans that Sister Agnes would meet them on the second floor. The Americans thanked the nun and then followed Judy across the courtyard, leaving the children behind.

Lehman and Lewis lingered until last and Lewis handed the nun a fifty dollar bill. "I know it's not much, Sister Marie, but please take this," he said.

He was rewarded with a wide smile and her green eyes sparkled.

"Why, thank you," she said, surprised by his generosity. "Money is always a problem here. The government has little time for those who are not pure Vietnamese. I did not wish to say more while your guide was listening. You know of course that she is a cadre from North Vietnam? She wields a great deal of power in the South. Many are afraid of her."

"Yeah, we guessed as much," said Lehman.

"So the government doesn't help you at all?" asked Lewis.

202

Sister Marie smiled sadly. "You know, shortly before I came here, the Vietnamese were actually bribing Amerasians to say that they were related to them."

"Say what?" said Lewis.

"Unbelievable, isn't it? For years they treated the Amerasians as if they didn't exist. Treated them worse than animals. Mothers of Amerasian children used to dye their hair black with boot polish, cut off their eyelashes, and rub soot into their white skin. Then the Americans announced that they would allow all Amerasians into the United States and that they could take their Vietnamese families with them. Suddenly the Amerasians found themselves wanted by everyone. Rich Vietnamese would pay thousands of dollars to Amerasians — to adopt them, in effect — so that they could also go to America. That's what happened to many of the orphans who were brought up here. Most were in their late teens or early twenties. Some were strong enough to resist the temptation, but many took the money." She shook her head sadly. "As soon as they got to the States they were abandoned once more by their new-found families. I have letters from some of them. You have no idea how hurt they are. How unloved, even now."

"But don't they go to stay with their fathers in the States?" asked Lehman.

"Rarely," said the nun. "Almost all were disowned by the fathers. There have been some cases where former soldiers have come back to search for their former Vietnamese girlfriends and wives, and taken them and their children back to the States. But for every one who wants to find his past there are a thousand who want to forget. It was a long time ago."

"If I knew I had a child in Vietnam, I'd move heaven and earth to find it."

"When did you leave Vietnam?" Sister Marie asked Lewis.

"Nineteen seventy," answered Lewis.

"And what makes you think you didn't leave a child behind?" she said. "Did you tell all the girls you knew that you were leaving? Did you say goodbye to the girls you met in the bars while you were on R&R?"

"No. No, I didn't," said Lewis thoughtfully.

"Then you don't know," said the nun.

Lewis looked at Lehman and both felt uneasy under the nun's scrutiny. She was absolutely right, of course, Lehman realised. Any of them could have children they didn't know about. And, as Lewis had said earlier, any of the vets could be the grandparents of the children now playing in the orphanage.

"Sobering thought, isn't it?" asked Sister Marie. She looked at them sternly, and then in a swish of material she was gone, floating across the courtyard with three small children in tow, like a mother swan being followed by her cygnets.

"Wow," said Lewis.

"Yeah," agreed Lehman. "She's a tough cookie, all right."

"For a nun."

"Yeah. For a nun."

They rejoined the rest of the group who were being addressed by a small Vietnamese nun in halting English in the corridor on the second floor. She told them that the hospital was for children only, but that they were not necessarily orphans. She led them into the first ward, which was little more than a large room with eight beds up against the walls and a lacklustre fan grating rustily overhead. Paint was peeling off the damp walls.

The beds were occupied by children with broken bones, several were in traction, but all were smiling and curious about their visitors. From several came the same questions that they'd been asked so many times before. "You my father? You take me home?" Again and again the Americans said no.

Sister Agnes gathered the Americans together before speaking to them in a low, measured voice. "The next ward is for children who are dying, and there are men and women there too. They are patients for whom nothing can be done in other hospitals. They come here to die. I tell you this so that you will not be shocked. You are welcome to visit, but please be quiet."

"What's wrong with them?" asked Stebbings.

Sister Agnes frowned and spoke to Judy in rapid Vietnamese. Judy replied, and listened while the nun spoke again. Judy nodded, and then addressed the group.

"Agent Orange," she said. "They are women and children who are dying from Agent Orange. The defoliant. Some have cancer. Some of the children were born sick. All will die."

There was a sharp intake of breath from Lewis, followed by a sigh as he allowed the air to escape.

"Where are they from?" asked Speed.

This time Judy spoke without waiting for the nun to reply. "Mostly from what used to be the Demilitarised Zone. That is where America used most of the defoliants. But some of those affected have not lived there for many, many years. Some moved south in the seventies, but still they get sick."

"Can't anything be done?" asked Stebbings.

Judy shook her head. "Those for whom there is a cure are sent abroad for treatment, but for these people there is no hope. It depends on the cancer. Sometimes it is not cancer. Sometimes babies are born defective. Sometimes the defects are small and can be cured by surgery. Sometimes their brains are outside their skulls, or organs are missing. Many die at birth. The abnormalities we see are similar in many ways to those which were seen in Japan after America dropped the atomic bombs there. It will be a long time before the effects of the American poison disappear."

Most of the vets stood with their heads bowed, not wanting to meet her gaze and equally unwilling to look at the patients. Most of those lying in the beds were conscious and Lehman wondered how many understood English and whether or not they knew what Judy was saying about them. This was clearly part of the tour and he guessed that Judy had brought many groups to this ward before. There was something heartless about using the patients as an exhibit, something macabre and repulsive. Even Sister Agnes appeared to be embarrassed by the guide's moralising. One of the near-skeletons coughed and a nun went over and sat on the edge of the bed and put a hand on a forehead and said soothing words in Vietnamese. Lehman couldn't tell if the figure was a man or a woman.

There were two men in the ward, both in their late forties, one sleeping fitfully, the other half sitting, his back propped up against a pillow. His face was pinched and drawn, his eyes sunk so deep into his face that they were in deep shadow. His bedsheet had slipped down to his waist and the vets could see his ribs clearly etched through the blotchy, paper-thin skin.

He smiled at the Americans, and Sister Agnes took Lewis and Henderson over and introduced them.

"This is Mr Chau," she said. "Mr Chau fought with the Americans. He speaks good English."

Mr Chau's smile grew wider, showing chipped and yellowed teeth, and he nodded a greeting to the two Americans. He coughed quietly, his chest making small, heaving movements. The coughing grew louder and he bent forward, cupping a hand under his bony chin and then red, frothy liquid trickled from between his lips. Sister Agnes darted forward with a cloth and dabbed at his face while the coughing spasm continued.

"Cancer of the lung," she said to Lewis. "Very bad. Mr Chau's wife already die. Cancer of the liver."

"Christ," said Lewis, under his breath.

The coughing fit tailed off and the nun used the now bloody cloth to clean Mr Chau's hands. He smiled again and this time his teeth were red.

"Welcome to Vietnam," he said slowly, enunciating each syllable as if he had not spoken English in a long time.

Lewis and Henderson looked at each other, not knowing what to say to the dying man.

"Thank you," Lewis said eventually.

"Yeah. Thanks," added Henderson.

Lewis took out his wallet and placed a twenty dollar note on the man's bedside cabinet. Mr Chau thanked him, but made no attempt to pick up the money. Lewis knew that there was probably nothing the man could buy. He wanted to ask the nun how long he had to live, but didn't want to ask in front of the man. And part of him didn't want to know the answer to the question because it would remind him all too clearly of his own mortality. He remembered the conversation with the doctor back in Baltimore. Christ, it seemed years ago, almost as if it had happened to someone else, but the gnawing ache in his guts hadn't gone away and he was finding it progressively harder to eat. It wasn't that it hurt to eat, it was simply that he seemed to have lost his appetite. He looked at the living skeleton in the bed in front of him and wondered how long it would be until his own powerful body looked the same, the muscles wasted away to nothing, the skin hanging off the bones like melted wax. He promised himself for the millionth time that he would not allow himself to get to that stage, that he would take his own life long before he became helpless and bedridden.

Lewis wanted to give the man some medicine, anything to ease his pain or prolong his life, but he had nothing like that. He patted down his pockets and came up with a foil packet of disposable wipes which he'd taken from the hotel and a tube of sunblocker. He put them next to the banknote, knowing that the two items were almost as useless as the money but wanting to give the man something none the less.

The children were the worst to look at. Two were little more than babies and Lehman wouldn't have given much for their chances even in an intensive care unit in an American hospital. Lying naked on soiled sheets with nothing more than the prayers of the nuns and whatever drugs were at hand, he doubted that they would survive the week. One of the small ones was being cared for by a young girl who Lehman assumed was its mother, wiping its forehead with a damp towel. Another lay silently on its back, its head turned to the side, making almost no movement, only the occasional twitch of its feet showing that it was alive. Lehman stood by the baby's bed and looked down. Two lines of blue stitches ran along its stomach forming an almost symmetrical cross. Someone had put large cotton mittens on the baby, obviously to stop it plucking at the stitches and injuring itself.

Sister Agnes appeared at Lehman's shoulder. "This girl we call Jessica," said the nun.

"Where is her mother?" Lehman asked.

"Mother must work. She know there is nothing more we can do for baby. She come every day, but now is the time she must work."

"What happened?" Lehman asked.

"Her liver was outside her body when she was born. It grew much bigger than normal because it wasn't inside. Mother used to live in North Vietnam. Much Agent Orange there."

"What are her chances?"

The nun screwed up her face, not understanding what Lehman had said.

"Will she live?"

"The baby?" The nun crossed herself. "Please God, I hope she does. Our doctors did the best they could, and her defect was not as serious as many we see here."

"You see worse?"

"Many are born dead, many die soon after they are born. Many women come from the North to have their babies in Saigon because they know they will get better care here."

Lehman looked around the poorly equipped ward and shuddered at the thought of what it must be like in Hanoi.

"How could they?" said Janet Cummings, under her breath. "How could they do that to a little baby?" The rest of the group came over to the bed. "War shouldn't be about killing babies."

"It isn't," said Horvitz quietly, his eyes on the infant. "Sometimes they just get in the way. Innocent bystanders."

"I can't believe that it's still happening now, all these years later," said Speed.

"Believe it," said Lewis, his voice loaded with bitterness.

"I think we've seen enough," said Tyler at the back of the group. Speed and Henderson nodded in agreement and they moved out into the corridor. Lehman and Lewis were the last to walk down the stone staircase to the courtyard.

"I can't work out what Judy's up to," said Lehman.

"In what way?" replied Lewis.

"It's like she's trying to rub our noses in all the bad stuff that happened, as if she wants to have us continually apologising for what America did. Yet the people we meet all seem so pleased to see us. It's like she has a personal axe to grind. She's obviously been vetted by the government, so they must know what she's like. Maybe she's even been told how to act. Maybe this is how the government wants us to be treated, like criminals returning to the scene of the crime."

They took their places on the coach and sat in silence as they were driven back to the hotel. One image stuck firmly in Lehman's mind, and that was of Eric Horvitz looking down at the baby with the stitches in its stomach. There was sorrow in Horvitz's eyes, and pity. But there was something else, something that worried Lehman. He saw anger, a deep, burning anger, and he had felt that if Tyler hadn't chosen that moment to suggest that they leave, then Horvitz would have lost control. The one thing that Lehman couldn't work out was who or what his anger would be directed at.

Anne Fielding put her head under the shower and rinsed her hair in the hot, stinging stream of water. She lathered up the white bar of soap and bent down to wash her legs, rubbing the lather up and down her thighs and around her backside. She soaped her stomach and then washed her breasts, feeling her nipples harden as her fingers brushed against them. She didn't wash her face with the soap, believing that it was bad for her complexion. Instead she let the water play across her closed eyes and her cheeks, enjoying the sensation. She put the soap back on its shelf and rinsed the suds off, turning slowly under the spray, raising her arms and lifting her legs one at a time.

The muscles in her legs and her right arm were already starting to ache. It was a healthy ache, a reflection of the effort she'd put into the tennis game. It was one of the last chances she'd get to partner Sally Remnick before she left Hong Kong for good and she wanted to make sure she played well. She'd run for every ball, hit her services a lot harder than normal, and damn near run herself into the ground, but they'd won, two sets to one. She turned the shower off and wrapped a fluffy pale green towel around her waist before leaving the cubicle.

Sally was still showering, as were the two women they'd beaten, Phyllis Kelley and Claire Pettier. She left the shower area and padded into the changing room, leaving behind a trail of wet footprints on the tiled floor. To the left were metal lockers and at the far end of the room was a waist-high shelf on which were hairdryers, pretty boxes of tissues, and a selection of brushes and combs. Running along the wall above the shelf was a mirror and she walked over to it. She stood in front of it, her hands on her hips, and studied herself. She raised her chin slightly and turned her head from side to side. She had a good neck, almost no wrinkles, and the skin on her face was smooth and tight. As she turned her breasts swayed and she was pleased with the way they moved and that there were no signs of sagging or ugly veins. Her skin was in good shape too, there were no folds above the towel, no middle-aged spread like she saw on so many women of her age, no indication that she'd ever given birth. She'd worked so hard to keep her figure after Debbie's birth, swimming every day, exercising in the gym, doing all she could to get back to her normal weight and avoid stretch marks. It had paid off.

"God, Anne, you're so narcissistic," said Sally Remnick as she came out of the shower room, a towel around her shoulders, another wrapped like a turban around her long, black hair.

"It's not narcissism, it's practical," said Anne. "It's like examining a car to see if it's got any problems, mechanically or bodywise."

"You've got a fabulous body," said Sally.

"If you add 'for your age' I'll kill you," warned Anne with a smile. Their opponents came out of the shower room and Anne smiled at them. "Drinks upstairs?" she asked.

"Sounds good," said Phyllis. Phyllis Kelley was about the same age as Anne, a tall, buxom redhead who was married to a British stockbroker. Their three children were at boarding school back in England and she had too much spare time on her hands. She played tennis at the Ladies' Recreation Club every day and had a mean first serve. She was also a dedicated shopper and had accounts at most of the city's top boutiques. Even her daily tennis and shopping sprees failed to dent the huge amount of free time she had, and it was no secret that she had had a succession of lovers. Phyllis and her second husband, Jonathan, had been married for almost fifteen years and little love remained. She told Anne time and time again that they only stayed together for the children's sake, but that seemed curious in light of the fact that they were in England for nine months of the year. Anne thought that the Kelleys actually enjoyed their lifestyle: a safe, if dull, marriage, three beautiful children, a very healthy bank balance, and sexual adventures on the side. There were times when she half wished that she and William had come to a similar understanding.

"I can't stay long," said Claire. Claire Pettier was the youngest of the four, a brunette with a homely, round face and a figure which could be best described as chunky. Claire was an American and the only one of the group to have a job. She worked for a public relations company which had some of the biggest firms in Hong Kong on its client list. She was a workaholic, and tennis was about the only social life she had. She was in a perpetual rush, and Anne often envied Claire her sense of purpose and the fact that she hadn't succumbed to what she had labelled the Expat Wives Syndrome. In Hong Kong you either worked, or you were married to someone who worked. And if you fell into the latter category, time was something to be filled, rather than used. Expat wives lived lives of pampered luxury with servants and chauffeurs at their beck and call, but they were often empty lives — trophies on the arms of their rich and successful husbands, or mothers to children they hardly saw. It was hardly surprising that so many followed the example of Phyllis Kelley and looked for fulfilment in other men's beds. Anne was one of the few women she knew for sure who hadn't had an affair. Not because she hadn't wanted to, or because she hadn't had the opportunity. Anne hadn't strayed because she knew that Hong Kong was too small and incestuous a place to have an affair in secret, and that if she were ever discovered it would hurt her husband. Like Caesar's wife, the wife of the chairman of the Kowloon and Canton Bank had to be above reproach.

Anne finished drying her hair and threw the second towel in the basket. She walked naked to her locker, conscious that Phyllis was watching her enviously.

She dressed slowly and carefully and then admired the Armani pale aqua silk suit, the jacket long and the skirt short, in the mirror.

"That's gorgeous," said Sally. "Is it new?"

"So new that William hasn't even got the bill yet," laughed Anne.

"I'm sure he won't mind when he sees how good it looks on you."

"Ha!" exploded Anne. "He hardly notices when I'm around, never mind what I'm wearing." She added despondently, "He's more interested in how his racehorses look."

"Oh, Anne, I'm sure that's not true."

Anne shook her head and smoothed down the jacket. "No, he's only able to concentrate on one thing at a time, and at the moment it's the bank that's occupying his mind. And to be honest, I don't think I even come a poor second. Come on, I need a drink."

The two women headed for the door. "We'll get a table," Anne said to Phyllis and Claire who were still towelling themselves dry. Anne and Sally found an empty table upstairs from where they had a good view of the tennis courts below. A waiter came over and asked if they planned to eat.

"Just drinks," said Anne. "I'll have a gin and tonic, what do you want Sally, a Bloody Mary?"

"Just a tomato juice," said Sally, looking at the slim gold watch on her wrist.

"Jesus," said Anne, under her breath. "Why is it that every time I order a drink someone always looks at their watch?"

Sally reached over and put her hand on Anne's elbow. "Hey, don't be so sensitive. I only wanted to see what time it was because I promised to meet Michael at three." The waiter remained at their table, his pen in his hand. Sally looked up at him. "A gin and tonic and a Bloody Mary," she said.

"I'm sorry," said Anne as the waiter went away.

"What's wrong? I've never seen you like this before. Is it William?"

"That's partly it, but things haven't been right between us for so long that I've almost become used to it." She looked across the table at Sally and Sally could see there were tears welling up in her eyes. "I'm going to miss you, Sally. You're my best friend and I'm going to miss you like hell."

"It's only Singapore," soothed Sally. She took Anne's right hand in hers. "It's a two-hour flight," she said.

"Three," said Anne.

"Whatever. It's not as if I'm going back to the UK."

"I know that," said Anne. She slipped her hand out of Sally's and took a small, white handkerchief from her purse. "It's just that you're my last real friend here," she said, dabbing the handkerchief at her eyes. "Who am I going to talk to? Who am I going to tell my secrets to? I'm starting to feel so alone."

Sally nodded. "Hong Kong isn't the same as it used to be," she admitted. "To be honest, I'm actually looking forward to the move because we've now got more friends living there than we have here. It seems as if everybody's relocating."

"Except me," said Anne bitterly. She saw Phyllis and Claire walking towards their table and waved over to them. "Did you order your drinks?" she asked.

"We caught the waiter as we came in," said Claire, as they sat down.

"You two played really well today," said Phyllis.

"Yes, I'm going to miss Sally when she goes," said Anne.

"When are you going?" asked Claire.

"Three weeks," said Sally.

"So soon?" said Phyllis.

Sally nodded. "The office and computer systems were set up two months ago and the support staff have already been hired. We're going over next weekend to look at houses. It's going to be so nice to live in a real house with a garden and a private pool instead of a high-rise apartment. No more mah jong parties above my head, no more screaming conversations in the lift, no more rude shop assistants or surly waiters. Singapore, here I come."

"Isn't there anything you'll miss?" asked Claire.

Sally looked at Anne and smiled. "My friends," she said quietly. "Only my friends."

"And the shopping," said Phyllis, wagging a warning finger at Sally.

"Well, yes, I suppose the shopping," Sally admitted. "But Singapore is almost as good as Hong Kong."

Their drinks arrived. Anne was pleased to see that Phyllis had ordered her usual vodka martini. Claire, a confirmed teetotaller, had an orange juice.

Phyllis raised her glass. "To 1997," she said. The three other women clinked their glasses to hers and repeated the toast.

"The end of an era," said Sally.

"The end of everything," said Anne.

They drank and laughed. Phyllis leant back in her chair and shaded her eyes with her left hand as she watched the tennis players below.

"Isn't that Richard Marsh?" she asked.

"Where?" said Sally.

Phyllis pointed. "There, on the left."

Sally squinted. "Yes, it's him."

"Who's he?" asked Anne.

"Oh, you must know him," said Phyllis. "He works for the Securities and Futures Commission, he's one of their high-flyers."

"The SFC?" Sally nodded. "That'd be right. It's one of the few organisations where they still promote gweilos instead of locals."

"Only because they don't trust the Chinese to run their own stock exchange," laughed Claire.

"Ah, I remember him now," said Anne. "He came to one of the bank's cocktail parties a few weeks ago. Pretty wife, what's her name?"

"Pauline. He's having an affair, you know."

"No!" said Sally.

"Who with?" asked Claire, sipping her orange juice.

Phyllis looked at all their faces one by one, making sure she had their full attention. "Mary Russell," she said.

"Not Dan Russell's wife?" said Sally, her mouth open.

Phyllis nodded.

"How on earth do you know that?" asked Anne.

Phyllis leant forward and whispered conspiratorially over the table. "Well, I saw the two of them in a booth at Charlotte's last month."

"In the Ambassador Hotel?" said Claire.

Phyllis nodded again. "And his car was seen parked outside the Russells' house about a month before that when Dan was in Taiwan."

"No!" said Sally.

"Yes," said Phyllis. "And last week they were seen together in the Hyatt Hotel in Macau."

"Oh, Phyllis, if anyone was having an affair they'd hardly be likely to go to Macau," protested Anne.

"That's what you think," said Phyllis, raising an eyebrow.

"You have not," said Anne.

Phyllis raised both eyebrows. "I'm not saying I have, and I'm not saying I haven't," she said in a little girl's voice.

"People do get careless," said Claire. "I mean, they know Hong Kong is too small a place to have an affair, but they still do it. It's a sort of death wish, I suppose. They know you can't go into a restaurant without meeting at least three people who recognise you, but they try to have candlelit dinners. They know that everyone goes to Macau at least six times a year but they meet in the hotels there. They're crazy."

"It's all right for you," said Phyllis. "You're single."

"You wish," said Claire. "Have you any idea how hard it is to find a single man in Hong Kong? They're all chasing the pretty little Asian girls, their doe-eyed, submissive dream girls. At least you've got a husband."

"Several, by all accounts," said Sally, grinning. Phyllis laughed with her. She made no secret of her affairs, and had often reduced the three of them to tears with the details.

"What about the Chinese men?" asked Sally. "Surely there's no shortage of them?"

"Oh please, have you ever been out with a Chinese male?" asked Claire. "They're so full of themselves, they've no idea how to treat a woman. Any woman."

"And they're lousy in bed," said Phyllis.

"Oh God!" shrieked Sally. "Phyllis, you have not!"

"Come on Phyllis, spill the beans," said Anne.

220

"Girls, girls, you know that I never kiss and tell."

"Oh right," said Sally.

"Well if you insist," said Phyllis. She took a long pull at her martini. "The first was a banker from New York."

"American Chinese don't count," said Claire.

"His parents still live in Shanghai," said Phyllis.

"Well . . ." said Claire, unconvinced.

"He was very articulate, a good talker, dressed well, but in bed . . . lousy. Two minutes from start to finish, didn't know the meaning of foreplay."

"Details," said Sally. "I want length, width, duration."

"You've had duration, two minutes. Width, well I suppose it was about two inches."

"Two inches in diameter?" said Sally. "That sounds about average."

"Who said anything about diameter?" said Phyllis. "We're talking circumference."

"Oh my God," said Anne.

"And length?" said Claire.

"About the same," said Phyllis. "Two inches."

"No!" said Sally. "You're not serious."

"Maybe it was three inches then," admitted Phyllis. "I hardly felt it. It was like being made love to by a mosquito."

Sally, Anne and Claire laughed loudly, attracting the attention of several neighbouring tables.

"Shhhhhh!" said Anne, dabbing at her eyes with her handkerchief, though this time it was to wipe away tears of laughter, not sadness.

"And the second one?" prompted Claire.

221

Phyllis shook her head sadly. "A Hong Kong Chinese. He works for the Stock Exchange. Married with three children, but God only knows how he managed it. He thought he was one of the world's great lovers, you know? Used his finger for thirty seconds, climbed on top, pumped away for three minutes, collapsed on to his back, lit a cigarette and then asked how it was for me. I ask you. How was it for me? Not great, I told him. He was mortally offended. Asked me if I was frigid. He told me that his wife had an orgasm every time he made love to her."

"Maybe that's why our men like Asian girls so much," said Claire. "Maybe they come on command."

"Wouldn't that be great?" said Sally. "It takes me at least half an hour, and even then it's not guaranteed."

"I don't think I can remember what an orgasm is like," said Anne. She drained her glass and waved over the waiter to order another round of drinks.

"This was quite a few years ago," continued Phyllis. "But I've never been with another Chinese. Two were enough for me. But from what I've heard, they're all the same."

"Phyllis, you're impossible," chided Anne.

"What's sauce for the goose . . ." said Phyllis. "I know what Michael gets up to on his so-called golfing weekends in Thailand and the Philippines. He barely tries to hide it any more. At least he takes precautions."

"How do you know that?"

"The little darling takes condoms in his washing kit, and I'm on the Pill so I know they're not for me."

222

Anne shook her head sadly. Despite the jokes, she was sure that Phyllis would have preferred a loving marriage to the sexual one-upmanship games she was forced to play with her errant husband.

Phyllis looked over Anne's shoulder and licked her lips. "Well now, maybe I was being a little hasty," she said.

"Hasty?" said Anne.

"About Chinese men," said Phyllis. "Take a look at him. Now he is a hunk."

"Where? Where?" said Claire.

Phyllis nodded towards Anne. "Over there," she said. "And he's coming this way." She took a deep breath and smiled.

Anne turned to look at the object of Phyllis's desire. It was Anthony Chung. He was wearing tennis whites and carrying two black Wilson racquets. On his wrist was a slim gold watch and around his neck was a thin gold chain. He looked fit, tanned, and wealthy, three attributes that Anne knew Phyllis found most attractive in men. He raised his racquets in salute to her and walked over to stand by Anne's chair.

"Anne," he said, "so nice to see you again."

Her head was level with his stomach, which she noticed for the first time was flat and firm under the tennis shirt, a far cry from William's pot belly. His thighs were muscular and he looked like he played tennis to win.

She looked up at him and smiled. "Anthony," she said. "I didn't know you played tennis."

"It keeps me fit. And this is a beautiful club. It's just a shame that men aren't allowed to be full members here." He transferred his racquets to his left hand and held out his right to her. She offered her hand instinctively, and before she knew what was happening he had held it and bent at the waist to kiss it, the merest brush of his lips against her flesh. She felt a small tremor of excitement ripple down her spine and she almost gasped in surprise, so unexpected was the feeling. He straightened up, still smiling. Anne felt herself blush, something that hadn't happened since she was a teenager.

"Well it is the Ladies' Recreation Club," said Phyllis, with the emphasis on Ladies. "Anne, you're being terribly remiss in not introducing us."

"I'm sorry," said Anne. "Phyllis Kelley, this is Anthony Chung." Phyllis proffered her own hand to be kissed, and Anthony obliged, then Anne introduced Sally and Claire.

"Do you play here often?" asked Anne. "I don't think I've seen you at the LRC before."

"Several times a month," he said. "I'm playing an American friend today. He's over there by the bar waiting for me."

"Which court are you on?" asked Phyllis.

Chung pointed to the playing area below. "The court on the right," he said. "Will you be watching?"

"Oh yes," sighed Phyllis. "Definitely." Anne kicked her under the table but it had no effect, Phyllis continued to make puppy dog eyes at Anthony.

"Anyway, it's been nice meeting you all," Anthony said, making eye contact with them one at a time. His eyes lingered on Anne and she felt her spine tingle again. "I hope to see you again soon, Anne," he said.

She smiled back. "That would be nice," she said. She recalled that he'd twice called her Anne whereas when he'd been at their house it had been "Mrs Fielding". Had he been so formal for Debbie's benefit or for William's?

Chung waved goodbye to them all and went over to his friend and they left the bar together.

"Wow," sighed Phyllis, fanning herself with a menu. "Hot, hot, hot."

"Oh, pull yourself together, Phyllis," said Anne, crossly.

"Now, now, not jealous are we?" said Phyllis. "I'm not intruding, am I?"

"Of course not."

"Oh come on, you saw the way he looked at you," said Phyllis. "And he kissed your hand."

"Phyllis, he's French. He kisses everybody's hand."

"French you say? That's unusual," said Claire. "How do you know him?"

"He's a friend of Debbie's. He came to the house last week to pick her up. In a Ferrari of all things."

"A Ferrari?" said Phyllis. "It gets better."

"Is he a boyfriend?" asked Sally.

"I'm not sure," said Anne. "I'm not sure Debbie's sure, either. He's the first Chinese she's been out with."

"I bet William's not happy," said Phyllis.

"He hasn't said anything," said Anne. "At least it's a step up from the policeman she was dating. So long as she doesn't get serious about Anthony, I don't think he'll mind."

"And what about you, Anne?" asked Phyllis mischievously.

"What do you mean?"

"I mean, surely you noticed the electricity between the two of you. Come on, admit it, aren't you the least bit tempted?"

"Tempted?"

"To have an affair with him? To find out what it's like?"

"Oh Phyllis, don't be ridiculous," said Anne. She took a mouthful of her drink and found to her surprise that the glass was empty. "I have a wonderful husband. I wouldn't dream of doing anything to hurt William." While Anne would reveal her innermost thoughts to Sally, whom she trusted with her life, there was no way she would ever discuss her personal problems with a woman like Phyllis Kelley. Phyllis could no more keep a secret than she could keep her legs closed when she was with an attractive man. "I've never had an affair, and I don't intend to," said Anne.

"Quite right," said Sally, supportively. "You've got the perfect husband. Why risk it?"

Anne looked at her friend gratefully.

"Well, in that case, you won't mind if I go for it, will you?" said Phyllis.

"There are times when I'm not sure if you're joking or not," said Anne. Chung and his partner appeared on

226

the court below and began hitting balls to each other over the net.

"Oh, I'm quite serious," said Phyllis, watching Chung practise his serves.

Anne felt a flash of jealousy, as if Phyllis was indeed encroaching on her territory. She felt confused, not sure why she felt that way about her daughter's boyfriend. She suppressed the feeling and smiled brightly. "Go for it," she said, holding up her empty glass to attract the waiter's attention. "Who's for another drink?"

Anthony Chung looked at his reflection in his bathroom mirror and smiled. The reflection smiled back. He nodded to himself, amused at the way he looked. He hadn't washed and his hair was lank and greasy and pulled over his forehead like a fringe. He was wearing an oil-stained T-shirt which had once been white but which was now grubby and frayed at the neck. On the front was the insignia of the Caltex oil company. He had on faded black Levi jeans, a brown leather belt and an old pair of Reeboks. He looked like a triad thug.

On his way out he went into the pristine white kitchen and took a hammer out of one of the drawers and an imitation leather briefcase with gilt metal corners from the table.

On the way down in the elevator he swung the hammer from side to side, hoping that he wouldn't bump into any of his neighbours. He took the elevator down to the car park and went over to where the

Ferrari stood. The Porsche was parked behind it and he took the keys from the back pocket of his jeans as he went over to it. He opened the door on the passenger side and threw the briefcase on to the narrow back seat.

The Porsche was a dark blue except for the nearside wing which he'd sprayed black the previous day. He examined the paint job, and once he was satisfied he screwed in the light fittings which he'd removed before spraying. When he'd finished it looked as if the Porsche had been fitted with a replacement wing. He took the hammer and began hitting the hood until there was a large, oval dent in the front, and then he scraped the claw of the hammer along the driver's door several times until the paintwork was scratched and gouged. He walked to the back of the car and hit the rear bumper hard until it was dented and misshapen. He was sweating by the time he'd finished and the brand-new Porsche looked as if it were ten years old and had a particularly careless owner. Chung threw the hammer underneath the Ferrari and climbed into the driver's seat of the Porsche. He put the key in the ignition and turned. It started the first time. Chung had expected nothing less. Despite its tatty appearance, the Porsche was in perfect working order.

He put the car in gear and drove out on to the road. It was late evening and the street lights were on. He drove a hundred yards or so before another driver flashed him to remind him to switch on his own lights. He cursed himself and flicked the switch that operated his headlights.

The car purred along the road as he headed out to the New Territories. The Porsche had cost Chung more than 350,000 US dollars including the punitive import tax that Hong Kong levied on new cars. Unlike the Ferrari, he hadn't been able to lease the Porsche, but he planned to repair it and sell within a few months. He would have no trouble finding a buyer in quality conscious Hong Kong. The Porsche was a twin-turbo Ruf TR, modified by the car wizard Alois Ruf from the common or garden Porsche 911. By the time the Ruf Automobile company had finished tinkering with the masterpiece of Teutonic engineering it had almost doubled in price and had a top speed of just over 196mph. It could do the standing quarter of a mile in twelve seconds dead and could accelerate from nought to 100mph in 8.4 seconds. Following Chung's cosmetic changes the car looked like a second- or third-hand 911 Carrera which most enthusiasts would expect to have a top speed of about 160mph. Chung was driving a car which could do 35mph more than it was supposed to, and the Carrera's acceleration was well below the Ruf's blistering performance, too. The standard Carrera, Chung knew, took more than 14 seconds to reach 100mph and would need the same amount of time to cover a quarter of a mile from a standing start. He was driving the ultimate dark horse.

Michael Wong had told him that the racers would be meeting in a lay-by overlooking Plover Cove Reservoir, about ten miles from the border that separated the New Territories from China. He drove with a watchful eye on the speedometer through the Lion Rock Tunnel to the tower blocks of Shatin, and around Tolo Harbour to the reservoir. Chung had no wish to be pulled up by a traffic cop, though he knew the chances of coming across one were slim. Like most of the Royal Hong Kong Police Force, traffic was woefully understaffed.

Wong had told him that up to a dozen racers would be taking part, each putting up a stake of 100,000 HK dollars, though he wasn't able to name more than three of them.

"No one will ever admit to taking part before they meet," Wong had said. "Unless it's a grudge match. It's part of the psychology."

Chung had asked for details of the course, but Wong had just smiled. It seemed that everything about the race was kept under wraps except for the stake. It was understandable, thought Chung. The police would love to put some of the illegal road-racers behind bars. Eight had been killed in the previous twelve months and they were responsible for several multiple pile-ups on the treacherous roads of the New Territories.

He saw the lay-by ahead and pulled in behind a line of cars. To the right of the lay-by, overlooking the large stretch of unruffled water, was a picnic and barbecue area where families thronged at weekends and on public holidays. There were small stone circles set into the ground where fires could safely be lit and clusters of roughly hewn benches and tables. There were no picnicking families on the benches as Chung climbed out of the Porsche with his plastic briefcase. Instead they were filled with young casually dressed men and their girlfriends. Most were chain-smoking and

230

drinking Coke and Sprite and Chung could feel the tension in the air as he closed the car door. It seemed that every head turned to look at him as the door clunked shut. He looked down the line of cars in front of his Porsche. He could see a red Porsche 928GT up ahead, a car that was capable of 169mph with its five-litre 32-valve V8 engine, and another red model, a Toyota MR2 Turbo which would be hard pushed to reach 150mph and which would take about six seconds to reach 60mph from a standing start. Chung had borrowed one once in Europe, and while it was a pleasure to drive its two-litre engine would be no match for either Porsche. He could see a BMW, which surprised him, because he couldn't imagine anyone bringing a German sedan to a road race, but as he walked up to it he realised it was a BMW Alpina B10 Bi-Turbo, a real wolf in sheep's clothing. Chung knew that the 535i-based car had dual Garrett T25 turbos and could almost break the 180mph barrier. It was built to cruise the German autobahns at a speed which would match many light aircraft and still allow the driver to hear the near-perfect quality of the CD player. Also in the line-up were an Audi V8 Quattro, a Lotus Esprit Turbo, a Nissan 300ZX Turbo, and a Mazda MX-5 Miata which Chung could only imagine belonged to one of the girlfriends. The rest of the vehicles were too far away for him to identify.

He turned away from the cars and looked around the picnic area. At first sight he'd presumed that there were only racers and hangers-on there, but over to the left was a small group of middle-aged men in sharp suits who he guessed were the organisers of the event. Chung walked over to them, swinging his briefcase and very conscious of the fact that all conversation had stopped.

He put the briefcase on the picnic table in front of the four men. The one with his hand in his jacket was the youngest of the group, and Chung had the feeling that he was some sort of bodyguard; he had broad shoulders and a thick neck and his nose had been broken several times. He took a step towards Chung but before he could speak Chung clicked open the locks of the briefcase and opened it.

"I want to race," he said, holding the lid up so that the men could see the bundles of banknotes inside.

"We do not know you," said the man on the right. He was about fifty years old, portly and balding. He was sweating and after he spoke he took a large, red handkerchief from his top pocket and mopped his forehead.

"My name is Anthony Chung and I want to race," said Chung.

"How do we know you are not *chi-lo*?" asked a tall, thin man whose suit was at least one size too small for him. His wrists protruded from the sleeves and there was a good inch of sock showing above his shoes.

"Police?" said Chung, grinning. "If I were police, why would I race? If the police knew there was a race on tonight they'd just set up roadblocks and catch you all."

"We still do not know you," said the thin man. The tendons were clearly visible in his neck and he had a hooked nose, like a bird.

"But you know this," said Chung, pushing the open briefcase towards them. "The stake you require is 100,000 dollars. I appreciate you do not know me, so I am prepared to put in 200,000 dollars."

The men looked at each other. The balding one nodded but the thin man seemed unconvinced. "We have not seen you before," he said. "You say your name is Chung?"

"Anthony Chung," said Chung.

"You have identification?" asked the thin man.

Chung smiled. "Driving licence?" he asked. "This is like Hertz, right? If I were police, wouldn't I have false ID prepared?"

"Show me your ID card," said the thin man.

"That can be faked, too," said Chung. "But I don't have an ID card. I have European citizenship. I am not a Hong Kong resident."

The thin man smiled evilly. "Why would a man with an overseas passport want to race?" he asked. "They race to make enough money to leave Hong Kong. Nobody comes from overseas to race."

"I race for the excitement," said Chung. "For the kick."

"Not for the money?" said the thin man.

"For the kick and for the money," agreed Chung.

The balding man tucked his handkerchief back into the top pocket of his jacket. Sweat was already beading on his brow again. "Surely no *chi-lo* would come with a story as weak as his," he said, nodding at Chung.

"I agree," said the thin man. The bodyguard visibly relaxed and his hand reappeared from within his jacket.

The fourth man, a stocky middle-aged man with bad skin, also nodded.

The balding man reached for the briefcase and pulled it towards him. He picked up one of the bundles of red notes and flicked through it. "Very well," he said. "There are eleven cars taking part, including you. The total stakes amount to 1.2 million dollars, and the organisers retain 200,000 dollars. There will be one prize for the winning driver, and that will be one million dollars. There is no prize for second, none for third. The race will start at midnight at Sha Tau Kok. We leave here at ten minutes before twelve and meet at the outskirts of the town. The course is from Sha Tau Kok to Fanling, down to Tai Po, up through Shuen Wan, past here and up to Sha Tau Kok. The course is about thirty kilometres, and the race is three circuits. Once the race starts it will continue until there is a winner, no matter what happens. If you are involved in an accident you must take care of yourself. If you are stopped by the police you must deal with them yourself. We three are the organisers and our word is final. Do you understand the rules, Mr Chung?"

"I do," said Chung.

The balding man looked at his watch. "In that case, you should prepare your car. We will be leaving here in fifteen minutes."

Several drivers had already gone over to their cars and were revving their engines, eager to get started. Chung walked along the line of parked cars, checking out the opposition. He realised that his first impression — that the race was between high-powered luxury cars

— was mistaken. There were several Toyotas and a Saab, and some of the cars were far from being in top-notch condition. He noticed, too, that the drivers of the more expensive cars were accompanied by older men, and he decided that they were probably sponsors, whereas the drivers of the older cars were on their own. The drivers with sponsors were almost certainly driving the cars for a set fee, or a percentage of the winnings, but the guys with their own cars would be risking everything for a chance of a big win. He wondered where they had got their stakes from. As he passed by, drivers turned to look at him but no one spoke. He could understand why, they were all competitors and there was no prize for second place.

Several of the drivers began sounding their horns and Chung decided he'd better go back to his car. A girl in a tight red dress and bright red lipstick smiled at him and he winked. He slid into the driver's seat of the Porsche and started the engine. The first of the cars pulled out of the lay-by and headed for Sha Tau Kok and he followed them. They stuck religiously to the speed limit, indicated well before all turns, kept their distance from the car in front and in all respects were model drivers. As he drove, Chung reached into the glove compartment and took out a stick of gum. He unwrapped it and popped it into his mouth and chewed slowly. The gear change was slick and the engine ticked over nicely. He would have liked to have driven the Ferrari in the race but he knew that if he won in the F40 they'd give more credit to the car than to the driver.

The start area was an open-air car park on the outskirts of the town. There were five cars there when Chung arrived and within ten minutes all eleven cars were there. Several groups of men and women were standing around, openly staring at the cars, and Chung saw several men with bundles of banknotes in their hands. Wong had explained that while the drivers raced for the prize, friends and relatives would go to watch and there was an active betting scene. There must have been upwards of fifty spectators gathered in the car park, and Chung was sure that if it hadn't been for the secrecy surrounding the event there would have been thousands. Hong Kongers loved to gamble, and they'd have a field day at a road race. There was a sharp knock at his window and he turned to see the balding man standing by the side of his car, mopping his brow. Chung lowered the window.

"You will be number eight," he said. "A very auspicious number. The gods, it would seem, are smiling on you."

"For that I am grateful," said Chung. "How were the numbers chosen?"

The man wheezed. It sounded as if he was having trouble breathing. "We have a lottery," he explained. "The cars will line up at the entrance to the car park in twos. You will be in the fourth pair."

Chung nodded and thanked the man. He put the Porsche in gear and edged it to the starting area, stopping the car behind numbers five and six, the BMW and a Toyota. He blipped the accelerator to keep the turbine warm. On his right the Audi purred up and

236

its driver, a boy barely out of his teens, nodded and smiled thinly. Chung smiled back.

When all eleven cars were lined up Chung took a quick look at the cheap Swatch watch on his wrist. Less than one minute to go.

The girl in red who'd smiled at him in the lay-by tottered to the front of the group of cars on white high heels and raised her arms above her head. From where he was sitting he could see that she didn't shave her armpits. She was laughing and wiggling her hands and then with a shriek she dropped her arms to her sides and the race was on.

The engines roared and the cars leapt forward into the main street. Chung slipped the Porsche into gear and followed close behind the BMW. The BMW could go as fast as 173mph and in Hong Kong cost somewhere in the region of 1.5 million HK dollars. Assuming that it hadn't been stolen, Chung reckoned that it was such an expensive car that it would only have been entered by someone who was confident of doing well and driven by someone who knew the rules and the terrain. He planned to keep in the BMW's slipstream for the first two circuits while he got a feel for the course.

The roads were fairly clear and the few cars that were around soon pulled over to the side when they realised that there was a high-powered race underway. All the residents of the New Territories knew about the illegal road-racing and most had seen what happened to cars that got in their way. The driver of the BMW kept his car above 100mph as they sped towards

Fanling, and as he struggled to keep up with him, Chung knew that he'd made the right choice. Less than two miles out of Sha Tau Kok they had overtaken a Toyota and the Saab. On the straights Chung had no problem in keeping up with the BMW, but he consistently fell behind when they entered turns. The driver seemed to assume that there would be nothing coming in the opposite direction and before the turn he would swing out to the far side of the lane, wheels over the white line, and brake well in advance, slowing but not locking the wheels, as he downshifted. The brake lights would go off as the BMW was about one third of the way through the turn and it would begin accelerating, surging ahead as it left the turn.

They slowed as they reached Tai Po where there was more night-time traffic and the BMW had to brake sharply to avoid a green and grey New Territories taxi which pulled out in front of them. Chung almost ran into the back of him but the Ruf's brakes matched its high performance and he slowed and steered on to the sidewalk. Chung had to drive back on to the road and by the time he'd got into second gear the BMW was 200 yards ahead of him and the Porsche had been overtaken by the Audi.

The road twisted and turned as it ran alongside Tolo Harbour and Chung started to take risks, driving straight through S bends and paying no attention to the lane lines. As the road swung away from the reservoir and towards Sha Tau Kok, Chung's confidence grew. On a long straight stretch he decided to challenge the Audi. He put the pedal to the floor and took the

238

Porsche up to 140mph, pushed it to within ten feet of the Audi's rear bumper and checked that the road ahead was clear. He flicked the Porsche to the side, steadied it and then accelerated, watching the speedometer pass 145mph then 150mph. The Audi tried to keep up with him, but Chung passed him, the white dotted lines blending into a single white streak and then he had to brake as he entered a long right-handed curve. Once he could see the Audi in his rearview mirror he flicked the Porsche back into the correct lane — just in time, because ahead he saw a minibus. It flashed past and he had to slow again for a series of bends, the water of Starling Inlet on his right speckled in the moonlight. The driver of the Audi put his headlights on full, out of spite Chung was sure, and he was momentarily blinded. He concentrated on the road ahead as he raced towards Sha Tau Kok and as he reached the outskirts of the town he could see the rear lights of the BMW. He braked sharply as the car park loomed up. He saw the BMW go through the entrance, turn sharply and screech out of the exit. There must have been 200 spectators, shouting and cheering. Chung turned into the car park, had a brief glimpse of the girl in red shouting and pumping her fist in the air, and then he was back on the road, the BMW just eighty yards ahead of him.

By the time they were racing through Tai Po, Chung and the BMW had overtaken two more of the racers, the Nissan 300ZX and the Lotus Esprit. Chung waited until they were at the straight stretch after Plover Cove Reservoir before making his challenge. He knew that

239

his Porsche's top speed was more than 15mph more than the BMW, so all he had to do was to find a section of road long enough and keep his foot to the floor. The manufacturer's specifications would do the rest.

The road was clear and he swung the Porsche out on to the wrong side of the road. He pressed the accelerator down and felt the twin turbos kick behind his shoulder. He drew level with the black BMW and out of the corner of his eye he saw the driver, jaws clenched and eyes fixed straight ahead, trying to squeeze more speed out of the car. The speedometer ticked off 130mph, 135mph, 140mph, and Chung knew that the BMW was getting close to the limit of its 360 brake horsepower. It weighed some 700 pounds more than the Porsche and top speed had been sacrificed for luxury. Chung began to pull away from the BMW just as he was forced to slow because the road started to curve. The BMW had to slow, too, and he continued to pull away, then, just as he thought he was clear, he heard a metallic crunch and felt the rear of the Porsche skid to the right. The steering wheel jerked in his hand and Chung's first thought was that he'd blown a tyre. He fought to control the car as the tyres screamed like a tortured animal. Before he could straighten the Porsche he felt it lurch again and his neck whipped back and forth. Chung realised that he was being rammed, that the BMW driver was trying to push the Porsche off the road at more than 120mph. He tried to accelerate away but the road conditions wouldn't allow him to go much above 120mph, which was well within the BMW's capabilities. Chung braked slowly and guided the Porsche to the right of the lane, giving the BMW ample room to pass, at the same time bracing himself for another ramming attempt. The BMW driver decided to try to get by and Chung watched him disappear from the rearview mirror as it accelerated. He risked a quick look to the side and saw the nose of the black BMW was level with his rear wheel arch. Chung chose his moment carefully, and when he was satisfied that he was in the right position he moved the steering wheel firmly through ninety degrees, swinging the Porsche smoothly at an angle and cutting across the front of the BMW. The full weight of the Porsche pushed the bulkier BMW to the side, towards the pavement. Chung could feel the BMW try to force its way back on to the road and he kept the pressure on the steering wheel so that it was forced up on the pavement with a crash and the sound of tearing metal. He swung the Porsche back into the middle of the lane and accelerated hard. In the rearview mirror he saw the BMW brake furiously and try to swerve to avoid a concrete-stemmed street light. The driver failed and the BMW slammed into the post, its hood exploding upwards in a cloud of steam. The road turned sharply to the left and Chung could no longer see the BMW.

The road curved to the right and he saw Starling Inlet for the second time in the race. Despite the hammering the Porsche had taken, it still handled well. Chung experimented with the steering and with the accelerator until he was sure that there was nothing amiss. As he played with the controls, the Lotus Esprit and then the Audi spurted past him. The Audi beat him to the Sha Tau Kok car park by at least fifty yards, but as Chung turned in there was no sign of the Lotus. The crowd of watchers was even bigger this time as news of the race had spread through the town.

He caught up with the Audi a mile outside Fanling. Its young driver swerved from side to side in an attempt to block the Porsche but Chung faked to pass on the right, swerved to the left and jammed down hard on the accelerator. As he roared past the driver put his quartz lights on full again, but this time Chung was prepared and the blinding lights had no effect. He kept the Porsche up to 100mph as he sped through Tai Po, cutting through a red traffic light and scaring the hell out of two taxi drivers. On the road to Shuen Wan he saw the rear lights of the Lotus and he sped after it, pushing the Porsche to the limits of its road-holding. Yard by yard he gained and he made his challenge before the reservoir, zipping past it in fourth gear. His hands were sweating on the wheel and his chewing gum had lost its flavour. The muscles in the back of his neck were aching and he knew it was more from the tension than from the whiplash of the BMW ramming.

He saw the Porsche 928GT in the distance and as he left the reservoir behind him he gradually caught up like a fisherman hauling in on a line. He kept an eye on the speedometer and when he was within fifty feet it was showing 160mph, the theoretical limit of a standard 911 Carrera and about 10mph less than the 928 could manage. He moved over to overtake, pushed the accelerator pedal down and surged forward. He could easily take the 928GT, there was more than a mile of clear road ahead and the Ruf had power to spare but he eased off. He saw the lights of Sha Tau Kok in the distance and he slowed to let his rival take the lead. Chung pulled in behind the red Porsche and kept close to its rear bumper. He kept one eye on the car in front and the other on the speedometer, taking care not to pass the 160mph mark. If the driver of the car was a typical Porsche owner he probably knew the performance characteristics of most of the different models and if he was overtaken by a 911 when he was on full throttle he'd know that Chung wasn't driving a standard model. Besides, Chung had known from the start that it would be better not to win his first race. He was there to win the confidence of the road-racers, not antagonise them.

The red Porsche pulled into the car park and was immediately engulfed by a crowd of well-wishers. The driver climbed out and was hoisted on to the shoulders of two well-built youths in leather bomber jackets and tight jeans and they proceeded to carry him on a lap of victory around the tarmac car park. Chung parked his own Porsche some distance away and got out. He leaned against the side of the car and watched the celebrations. The thin man in the suit who'd spoken to Chung earlier went over to the winner and presented him with a blue nylon holdall which Chung guessed contained the prize money.

"You raced well," said a voice by his side. He turned to see the balding man with his ever-present handkerchief in his hand.

"As you said, there is no prize for coming second," said Chung, watching the winner being lowered to the ground. The girl in the red dress put her arms around him and kissed him full on the lips. "Winner takes all," said Chung.

"Ah, Winnie Lo. Yes, she is attracted only to winners. Perhaps one day you will win her favours."

Chung laughed sourly. "It isn't a girl I want to win. It's a race."

"And the money," said the bald man.

"And the money," agreed Chung. "Next time I hope you won't expect a double stake from me."

"Indeed not," said the bald man. "If you wish to race again, I will contact you before the next one. You will give me your telephone number?"

Chung gave the man his number. "Tell me," he said, nodding over in the direction of the winner, who was still being embraced by Winnie Lo, "who is he?"

"Ah, he is Simon Li. He has won the last two races. An independent."

"Independent?"

"He has no one backing him. Some of the racers belong to triads, others have wealthy sponsors. A few fund their own cars. Which category do you fall into, Mr Chung?"

"The latter. I can pay my own way." He smiled. "Though not if I continue to lose."

"For a first performance you did admirably."

"Thank you," said Chung. "I had a run-in with a black BMW. He tried to force me off the road."

The bald man laughed dryly. "That is the cut and thrust of racing, I'm afraid," he said.

"I'll know next time," said Chung. "Who was the driver?"

"Ricky Leung, a veteran of many races. He was one of tonight's favourites."

"A sore loser," said Chung. "He had a terrific car, though. Who was his sponsor?"

The bald man wiped his forehead. "I was," he said. "But no longer." He smiled at Chung's obvious embarrassment. "Do not worry, Mr Chung. I am not a sore loser. I will find another driver. Once I have repaired my car."

The intercom on William Fielding's large oak desk buzzed, catching him by surprise. He had been so engrossed with the computer print out in front of him that the rest of the building might as well not have existed.

"Yes, Faith," he said.

"It's Charles Devlin," said his senior secretary.

"Send him in, please, Faith," said Fielding, concertinaing the print-out and pushing it to the left side of the desk next to a rosewood-framed photograph of Anne and Debbie, taken a year earlier. He stood up and walked around his desk as Devlin came in. The two men shook hands warmly. They had worked together for almost twenty years, though Fielding had joined the bank ten years before Devlin. Devlin was in his mid-forties and was the bank's head of corporate finance. He had been appointed by Fielding and it was an open secret that he was to be his successor when he retired in two years.

Both men were Scots and had a love for single malt whiskies and as it was early afternoon Fielding asked Devlin if he wanted a drink.

"I could be tempted to a small one," said Devlin, a knowing smile on his lips. Devlin had the rugged looks of an amateur rugby player, which he had been in his younger days. He had played for the bank in his early years in Hong Kong but had switched to golf when he'd discovered that most members of the bank's board were scratch golfers. He'd worked his handicap down to five and regularly played with Fielding.

Fielding poured two measures of an Islay malt that he was especially fond of. He held out a glass to Devlin and motioned to the two grey leather sofas in the corner of the office. He put his own glass on the black wooden coffee table in front of the sofa and sat down.

He waited until Devlin was also seated before asking him how his trip to Bonn had gone.

"Not as well as we'd hoped, William," said Devlin, and Fielding's heart sank.

Devlin had spent three days in Germany meeting with leading bankers in an attempt to initiate merger talks. It was the latest in a series of exploratory talks which had taken Devlin to London, New York and Tokyo, so far with little or no success. "They made encouraging noises, but the general drift was that they're too tied up with the opening up of Eastern Europe to get involved in the Far East right now. In five years, maybe ten . . ."

246

"Blast them!" said Fielding. "They know that it'll be too late then. They know as well as we do that we need a merger to protect ourselves. If we thought we could survive on our own for the next five years we wouldn't need a partner."

"All four of the banks showed me figures to back up what they were saying, William. It's going to take billions of Deutschmarks to stabilise East Germany, never mind the rest of the countries that Russia has let go. The Germans are scared stiff that if they don't help them modernise they'll be faced with immigration on an unimaginable scale, a flood of economic migrants that will swamp the developed countries. All the EC countries are pouring money into Eastern Europe, partly because it'll create a huge market for their own goods, but also to safeguard their own standards of living. They just don't have money to spare to invest in Asia. Not right now."

"You didn't get the feeling that they were just trying to talk the price down?" asked Fielding as he swirled the glass of whisky between the palms of his hands. "Or that they are just waiting for our share price to fall?"

Devlin shook his head. "Frankly, William, we never got round to talking about money. They don't appear to be interested at any price. I'll prepare a full report for the board, but that's the gist of it. One of the Munich think-tanks has come out with a report which suggests that one in four Soviet citizens would rather live in Germany. Another survey says that more than two million Turks want to emigrate to the West. The Germans are having to deal with hundreds of thousands of would-be immigrants each year. They've got their own version of our Snakeheads, gangsters who smuggle people from Bulgaria and Romania into West Germany, just as ours sneak mainland Chinese over the border. It's amusing in a way. They're having to face what we in Hong Kong have had to deal with for years. We were condemned by everybody for sending Vietnamese boat people back to Vietnam because they were economic and not political refugees. Now the Germans are sending back more than ninety per cent of their refugees. It's ironic, really."

"It's ironic, but it doesn't help us with our problem," said Fielding.

The two men sat in silence and drank their whisky. Devlin looked at the large screen television in the corner of Fielding's office. On top of it was a video recorder and several video cassettes labelled with various advertising campaigns. The bank had been trying to restore confidence with a series of optimistic television commercials, but market research showed that they just weren't working.

Fielding looked out of the huge window which ran the full length of his office. It offered one of the best views in Hong Kong, the Star Ferry terminal with its green and cream-coloured ferries plying their trade across the ship-packed harbour, the glitzy hotels and shops of Tsim Sha Tsui across the water, and the hills of Kowloon beyond. And behind the hills, less than twenty-five kilometres away, was communist China, patiently watching and waiting to take back the colony and its six million inhabitants. Fielding saw a Cathay

Pacific 747 begin its final approach over the Kowloon tower blocks, dipping its right wing and swooping so low that it seemed sure to crash, then levelling out and heading for the single finger of runway which poked out into the harbour.

"Are those the projections?" asked Devlin, pointing to the print out on Fielding's desk.

"Yes, and damn depressing reading it is, too."

"Still bad?"

Fielding snorted at the understatement. "We've lost about ten per cent of our customer base over the past three years, and the rate of lost accounts is accelerating. Our industrial loan book is in a steady decline because no one wants to buy new plant or buildings. Home ownership is in a tailspin, and prices are down. The only people buying property in Hong Kong are the mainland Chinese, and they're funding their purchases through the Seven Sisters. None of their business is coming our way. The only section that's on the up is our gold bullion business and our foreign exchange accounts. The Kowloon depository is pretty much full to capacity. I tell you, Charlie, it's as clear as the nose on your face what's happening. Our customers are either putting their money overseas or they're switching into gold or foreign currency, and they're sticking that in our vaults in preparation for the day when they leave. And when they go, they'll take their gold with them. It's the old refugee mentality, I'm afraid. They have no faith in the banking system. You know what section of the retail sector is showing the best return at the moment?"

Devlin shook his head.

"Luxury boats," said Fielding. "Big ones. Fifty-footers and longer. And you know why? Because a boat offers escape. I tell you, Charlie, the world is going to have to deal with another type of boat person in a few years. And they're not going to be so easy to turn away."

"That's the impression they have in Europe," agreed Devlin. "All they read in the press there is the fact that Hong Kong is the Jittery City: the city that's living on borrowed time. And they don't want to take the risk of investing here. They want to know what it's like under Chinese rule. If the Chinese make a success of it, they'll invest here. But with everything they have on their plates at the moment, they're not prepared to risk their capital."

"And who can blame them?" said Fielding. He drank his whisky and placed his empty glass on the table. "If we had any confidence in the Chinese we wouldn't be going around Europe, cap in hand."

"It's a safety net, William, that's all. If we show the world that we have a safety net they'll be more confident of our prospects."

"Aye, Charlie. And I still believe in Father Christmas."

A young Thai boy in a white uniform walked up to the poolside loungers and asked the Americans what they wanted to drink.

"Four beers," said Carmody. The poolboy giggled and went back to the bar, returning a while later with four glasses and four opened bottles which were beaded with condensation. He poured each one, giving each glass a thick, frothy head, and after placing them on the tables adjacent to the loungers held the bill out for Carmody to sign, which he did with a flourish. The boy looked at his claw with open curiosity as Carmody used it to hold the pad.

"Pretty, isn't he?" he said as the boy walked away.

"Yeah, they're very feminine, the boys," agreed Lehman.

"Real pretty," said Horvitz.

"Hey, I didn't mean that I was attracted to him, or anything like that!" said Carmody, holding his glass away from his lips.

"Didn't mean to imply you were, Larry," said Lehman. "Just stating a fact."

"Yeah. Well they're not as pretty as the girls here, that's for sure," said Carmody. He took a deep drink of his beer and smacked his lips greedily. "Mind you, I reckon they're better looking than those German women over there. Hell, Lewis there has got more going for him than the German bitches."

They both looked at the near-comatose Lewis, his broad, black back rising and falling in time with his laboured breathing.

"You think he's having a wet dream?" said Carmody, and he cackled like an old witch.

Lehman didn't think so. Lewis's face was turned towards him and away from Carmody, and if Carmody had been able to see the expression he wore, Lehman knew he wouldn't have made a joke about it. His eyes were screwed up tight as if he were in pain and his lips were moving, though it was impossible to hear anything intelligible. His head was resting on his folded arms and Lehman could only see one of his big, square hands but it was clenched tight as if he was preparing to strike someone. His left leg twitched and Lehman could see that his toes were drawn back, the tendons in his heel stretched taut.

Lewis began to grind his teeth and a vein pulsed in his forehead. Lehman wanted to wake him, but knew it was better not to, that if he were to awake mid-dream it could be traumatic. Lehman still suffered from his own nightmares and flashbacks, and they were almost a thousand times more vivid and painful if they weren't allowed to work through to their own conclusion. By far the worst was when somebody woke him up. His two ex-wives had both learned the hard way and had accepted that no matter how much he ranted and raved in his sleep it was better to leave him be, but casual girlfriends had often left his apartment in tears after trying to wake him up. It wasn't that he wanted to hurt them, it was just that he often came out of the dreams fighting. And it wasn't as if he could explain in advance, because he couldn't imagine anything less romantic than a warning that there was a good chance that he'd lash out in his sleep. Lewis's hand remained locked into a fist and Lehman didn't relish the idea of fending off the big man.

It was their second day back in Bangkok after being seen off in Saigon by a stony-faced Judy. She had clearly been glad to be rid of them. There had been no conversation from her in the coach and no goodbye speech at the airport, though several of the Americans had tipped her and Hung with American dollars. Lehman himself had given them both ten dollar bills, though all they'd got from Carmody and Horvitz was a scowl. What had surprised Lehman was seeing Tyler slip Judy an envelope, which he guessed contained money. It had been as they were about to go through immigration. Tyler had held back so that he was last and it was only because Lehman was idly looking around while a pretty Customs girl went through his passport page by page that he saw the envelope and Tyler's smile and nod of thanks.

Their flight back to the States wasn't for another week, giving them time to wind down after Vietnam. They spent most of their time sitting by the pool and drinking beer. The salesman, Cummings, Stebbings, Henderson and Speed had stuck to themselves on the plane to Bangkok, and from the conversations Lehman overheard he gathered that they had enjoyed their visit and had all felt they had benefited from the experience. Certainly Henderson and Speed seemed a good deal more relaxed and didn't appear to have to stay as close to each other as they did before their visit. Cummings, too, seemed more at ease and not so dependent on his wife. For them, maybe, it had been a worthwhile endeavour. For the rest of the group, however, the trip to Vietnam seemed to have done more harm than good. Carmody's anti-Vietnamese rhetoric was worse than it had been, and Horvitz kept falling into long, sullen silences as if trying to deal with uncomfortable memories. Lewis had confessed that he'd been having more nightmares since he'd returned to Vietnam, and Lehman had to admit that memories which he thought had long since lost their sting were now troubling him once more and he was getting flashbacks — bad ones, images which he'd hoped had faded. Apparently they hadn't, they'd been lying somewhere in his subconscious waiting for the trigger to bring them to the surface: the night attack when two Hueys had collided just yards in front of him; the morning when his co-pilot, a nineteen-year-old farm boy called Ted, took a sniper's bullet in the face; the marine sergeant who walked into the rear rotor of Lehman's Huey and died in his arms, the top of his skull crushed into mush.

"You okay, Dan?" said a voice and Lehman looked up to see Lewis sitting and stretching. The tension had faded from his face.

"Bad memories," said Lehman, rubbing his cheeks with the palms of his hands as if he were putting on aftershave.

"Yeah, tell me about it. They worse for you, after Vietnam and all?"

Lehman nodded. "Yeah. It's to be expected, I guess. It was twenty-five years ago, I was just about coming to terms with it."

"Man, you don't ever come to terms with it. Never. Hey, you wanna go look round the city?"

"Yeah, I reckon I've been in the sun long enough. Do you want to eat?"

Lewis patted his stomach. "No. I'm okay. Just fancy a look-see. Check out the markets maybe. See if I can find a souvenir for my boy."

254

"Didn't know you had a son," said Lehman.

"Eight years old," said Lewis proudly. He fished his wallet out of his shorts and took out a small colour photograph. He showed it to Lehman. A crinkly-haired boy with a mischievous grin beamed out of the tiny picture. He had his father's wide forehead and square chin. A good-looking boy.

"He's definitely your son all right," said Lehman. "Looks just like you."

"Yeah. I don't see much of him these days. One weekend in four."

"Divorced?"

"Yeah. Wife couldn't take it any more, she said. The nightmares. The flashbacks."

Lehman stood up and draped a towel over his shoulders. "Come on," he said, "we need a change of atmosphere. This is starting to get too depressing."

"Ain't that the truth," laughed Lewis. He got to his feet and asked if Horvitz or Carmody wanted to go along. They both declined but Carmody reminded them that they'd promised to meet Tyler later that night for a tour around Pat Pong, Bangkok's red light area. Rest and Recreation, Tyler had said. Rape and Run, Carmody had called it.

Lehman and Lewis left the poolside to go back to their rooms to change. On their way through the hotel lobby they met Tyler. He wore a light blue safari suit and a pair of gold-rimmed sunglasses.

"Where are the boys?" he asked them.

"By the pool," said Lewis.

"You guys still okay for tonight?"

"Sure thing," said Lewis. "Nine o'clock, right?"

"On the dot," said Tyler, grinning. "You going somewhere special?"

"Check out the shops and stuff," said Lewis. "Present for my boy, maybe."

"You should look at the computer stuff they've got here," said Tyler. "Pirate copies. Dirt cheap. Anyway, see you both later."

He nodded a farewell and headed for the pool.

"What do you make of him?" asked Lehman as Tyler disappeared through the door.

"Tyler?" said Lewis, frowning. "What do you mean?"

"He's nothing like any pilot I ever met," explained Lehman. "I feel like I should salute every time I see him. And have you noticed that Carmody has started calling him 'sir'? There's more to him than meets the eye, I'm sure of it."

"Yeah, well I think he talks a lot of sense. I thought he handled himself really well with Judy. He stood up for himself. Hell, he stood up for us all. I think if he hadn't been there we'd have all laid down like Henderson and Speed. Yeah, I like Tyler. We could have done with more officers like him in Nam. You know who he reminds me of? Oliver North. Marine Corps through and through. A professional soldier, someone you can rely on, somebody who'd die to protect his men and who'd expect them to do the same."

"But not a pilot?" pressed Lehman.

Lewis shrugged. "Pilot. Marine. Who gives a fuck? He's just an A-One guy. Come on, let's go get changed and get a tuk-tuk."

"Hell, can't we get a cab? You die of fumes in the back of those things. And they're dangerous, too."

"Come on, man," laughed Lewis. "Who wants to live for ever?" He slammed Lehman on the back hard enough to rattle his teeth and pushed him towards the elevator.

They got back to the hotel just after dark, their shirts soaked in sweat after a thirty-minute ride in the back of a two-stroke tuk-tuk, the hybrid of a scooter and a rickshaw which buzzed like a wasp in a bottle as their driver recklessly weaved through the dense Bangkok traffic.

They arranged to meet at the bar at just before nine o'clock and went upstairs to shower and change.

When Lehman arrived in the bar in a clean red polo shirt and white slacks, Tyler was already there talking to Horvitz and Carmody at a table in the far corner. All three looked up when Lehman walked in and for a moment it seemed to Lehman that they were sharing a secret and that he was an intruder. Horvitz and Carmody quickly turned their faces to Tyler as if seeking his advice but his expression didn't change and he asked Lehman what he wanted to drink.

Lehman asked for a beer and Tyler waved over a slim waitress in a tight-fitting purple and gold dress which covered her from the neck to the floor and asked for four Singha beers.

"Make that five," he said as Lewis arrived. He was wearing a short-sleeved green and white striped shirt and blue jeans.

"Like it?" he said, holding out his arms and modelling the shirt. "It's a fake Yves Saint Laurent, cost just thirty baht."

"A bargain," said Lehman. Two waiters in jacket and trousers made from the same purple and gold material as the waitress's dress scurried over with two more chairs which they arranged around the table and before the beers arrived they had placed a wooden bowl of crisps and another of salted peanuts in front of the Americans.

"Isn't the service here just out of this world?" asked Carmody. He was the only one of the group wearing a long-sleeved sweatshirt, and it covered up all of his artificial arm except for the claw at the end. He scratched his bare leg with the claw. He was also the only one of the Americans to be wearing shorts. His sweatshirt had a large orange sun on the front with "Bangkok" written in oriental script.

"Unbelievable," said Lewis as the waitress returned with the tray of drinks. She knelt skilfully by the side of the table and poured the beers into cold glasses with small, economical movements, all the time smiling and averting her eyes demurely.

"Can you imagine them doing this in Baltimore, Bart?" laughed Carmody.

Lewis rolled his eyes. "Just wouldn't happen, not in a million years," he agreed.

"So," said Tyler, helping himself to a handful of crisps. "First we eat, then we hit Pat Pong. How does that sound?"

"Sounds perfect," said Horvitz. Despite the darkness of the bar he was still wearing his sunglasses.

They finished their beers and made their way to the front entrance of the hotel where they discovered that Tyler had hired a white Mercedes for the journey. "I thought you might like to go in style," he explained.

"All right!" cheered Carmody, climbing into the back seat.

Tyler opened the front passenger door and got in while Horvitz, Lewis and Lehman joined Carmody in the back. The Mercedes was the large 560SEL model so there was plenty of room for them.

"Where we going?" Lewis asked.

"A place I know," said Tyler and he spoke a few words of Thai to the driver. The driver, a middle-aged Thai in a white uniform with gold buttons, nodded and started the car.

"You speak Thai?" Lehman asked.

"Not so you'd notice," replied Tyler. "I asked the concierge to tell me how to pronounce the name of the road."

"Your tones sounded good," said Lehman.

"Let's wait and see where we end up before you start complimenting me on my Thai," said Tyler, good-humouredly.

The Mercedes was air-conditioned so they were insulated from the choking fumes and dust of the crowded city streets, but even through the closed windows they could not escape the night-time sounds: the sing-song Thai voices of the street hawkers, distant police sirens, car engines racing as impatient drivers kept their feet hard on the accelerator even when the roads were blocked, the ever-present buzzing of the tuk-tuks, nipping in and out of the stationary cars.

The Mercedes turned off the main road and into a narrow alley devoid of street lights, bumping and bucking over potholes. Lehman looked out of the side window but all he could see were pockmarked walls and sacks of rubbish. He saw a dark shape scuttling along the side of a building but he couldn't tell if it was a small cat or a large rat. The car turned right and into another alley and then drove out of the darkness and on to another well-lit area, a street full of restaurants and shops with bright neon signs and the ever-present tuk-tuks outside.

"Here we are," said Tyler as the Mercedes pulled to a halt. As the Americans piled out of the car, Lehman heard Tyler speaking to the driver in Thai. Lehman couldn't understand what was being said, but he doubted that it was anything Tyler had learned from the concierge and the tones sounded as good as they'd heard on Thai radio. Tyler's fluency with South-East Asian languages was something that Lehman would love to have had explained.

Lehman stood with Horvitz, Carmody and Lewis at the door to the restaurant where they waited for Tyler to join them.

"The car was a great touch, wasn't it?" said Lewis.

"Yeah, Tyler has style all right," agreed Carmody, his voice loaded with admiration.

"You guys don't think there's something strange about the fact that he speaks Vietnamese and Thai?" asked Lehman.

"So he's good at languages, so what?" said Carmody, defensively.

"So how did a pilot get to be so good at Vietnamese and Thai?" said Lehman.

"What the fuck does it matter?" said Carmody. "Maybe he studied languages at college. Maybe he was in intelligence and doesn't want to let us know. Maybe he was in the CI fucking A. All I know is that he's a great guy. And that's enough for me."

Horvitz and Lewis were nodding agreement so Lehman raised his hands in surrender. "Hey, I'm not arguing with that," he said. "I was just wondering, that's all." As they went in, he wondered what Tyler had been saying to Carmody to inspire such loyalty, and why Lewis and Horvitz had been so quick to align themselves with him. He felt as if the three of them had been allowed into some secret that he was still not privy to. He remembered the guilty looks on the faces of Horvitz and Carmody when he'd walked into the hotel bar, and of the whispered conversations he'd caught glimpses of in Vietnam. Tyler walked up to the door, wiping his forehead with the back of his arm, perspiring from the evening heat, the climate hot and clammy compared with the ice-cold air-conditioning of the Mercedes.

"I asked him to wait," Tyler explained. "We might not get a cab here and we'll be sweating like pigs if we take tuk-tuks from here to Pat Pong."

The restaurant was busy but it appeared that Tyler had had the foresight to book a table. They appeared to be the only tourists there. As they walked to their table three Thai girls in long white dresses bowed, their hands pressed together under their chins like children saying their prayers. Lewis copied their movement and they smiled at his antics, though their smiles faded when they saw Carmody doing the same, his claw up against his good hand. He grinned at their discomfort.

Tyler ordered five beers as they took their seats and a young maître d' in a dinner jacket which was one size too large for him handed out red leather-bound menus.

"Would you guys mind if I ordered?" Tyler asked. "I'm a big fan of Thai food."

The rest agreed and drank their beers while Tyler went through the menu with the maître d', pointing at dishes on other tables and asking his opinion.

The food, when it arrived, was first class and more than justified the long trip from the hotel. There were small fried fish-cakes with a sweet, orangey sauce, crisp spring rolls with lettuce and mint leaves to wrap them in, and a spicy clear sauce with sliced chillies to add flavour, a hot, spicy prawn soup with a strong lemony tang which Tyler explained was a Thai speciality, prawns fried in garlic, and a huge fish which lay on a long metal tray under which charcoal glowed redly. The fish was in a clear liquid which tasted of liquorice. The rice was mixed with small pieces of seafood and came in half a hollowed-out pineapple.

There were no chopsticks to be seen and the Thais eating at the other tables were using just a spoon and fork. The fork was used to load up the spoon which was then transferred to the mouth. The Americans followed their example.

262

"God, this is good food, all right," said Carmody, his mouth full. He gestured at Lewis with his fork. "Come on, Bart. Eat up."

Lewis was disconsolately pushing a prawn around his plate with his fork. "I'm not really hungry," he said.

"More for the rest of us," said Carmody.

"Are you okay?" Lehman asked.

Lewis raised his eyebrows. "Yeah, I'm fine. Honest. I just haven't much of an appetite, that's all. I think maybe I picked up a bug in Nam."

"Yeah, standards of hygiene there aren't what they should be, that's for sure," agreed Carmody, grains of cooked rice spilling from between his lips as he spoke.

When the bill came, Tyler picked it up before any of them could reach for it and he dumped a wad of notes on to the tray. "My treat," he said, waving away their protests. The Mercedes had the engine running and the aircon was on full blast. When they'd all climbed in Tyler twisted around in his seat and grinned. "Well, gentlemen, are we ready for Pat Pong?"

Carmody whooped and Lewis slapped the back of the driver's seat. Even Horvitz was smiling.

The Mercedes threaded its way through the parked tuk-tuks and motorcycles which were waiting outside the restaurant. Even though it was well past the rush hour the roads were still packed with cars and it took almost an hour to reach the red light area.

Pat Pong was actually two roads — Pat Pong One and Pat Pong Two — both lined with garish bars and massage parlours. Tyler asked the driver to stop at the head of Pat Pong One and not to bother waiting for them.

"I reckon we'll be here for a fair while," he said to Lehman. "And there are always taxis waiting. Besides, we might not all be going home at the same time." He winked at Carmody. "Or to the same place."

The five Americans stood on the sidewalk looking around as the Mercedes pulled away. The air was filled with raunchy music and high-pitched shouts and yells, blended together with the omnipresent rumble of traffic and buzz of motorcycles and scooters. Young Thai boys were calling out to tourists as they wandered down the strip. "You want girl? You want see show? Real sex show. No charge. You want massage?" Down the centre of the road was a line of stalls selling cheap clothes, cassette and video tapes and souvenirs. Lehman breathed in the night air, a heady mix of exotic spices, sweat and exhaust fumes. A teenage Thai boy tugged at the back of his shirt and grinned when Lehman turned to look at him.

"Sex show?" the boy said, nodding encouragingly.

Lehman shook his head.

"You want boy?"

"Christ, no. Definitely not."

"Go on, Dan," leered Carmody. "Go for it."

Lehman said nothing, but he scowled and gave Carmody the finger.

The Americans were soon surrounded by a group of young Thai men entreating them to try the various delights of Pat Pong, which seemed to consist of sex shows, young girls, young boys, and one very seedy-looking individual who promised the participation of a very large dog. They became increasingly vocal and aggressive until Tyler spoke to them sharply in their own language and they backed away.

"Come on, a friend of mine used to run a bar down here," Tyler said to the Americans. "Let's see if he's still there." Without waiting for them to agree he made off down the crowded sidewalk, ignoring the hustlers and pimps who stood at every doorway alongside girls in bikinis and miniskirts. The vets followed close behind, weaving their way through the crowds.

"Here it is," said Tyler and he veered left, through a doorway and up a flight of steep wooden steps. Lehman had no time to catch the name of the bar, but it seemed to be no different from the scores of others they had walked by. From somewhere above their heads they could hear a pulsing beat, and as they climbed higher it grew louder and clearer. It was the Rolling Stones' "Paint It Black".

At the top of the stairs were a pair of wooden doors with small glass windows set into them. The glass was criss-crossed with embedded wires but through it the Americans could see flashing lights, red, blue and green. On either side of the doors sat pretty young Thai girls wearing bright orange bikinis, smoking cigarettes and giggling. Judging their ages was next to impossible: their skins were golden brown and unlined, their hair jet black and glossy, with the muscle tone of teenagers but the world-weary eyes of girls who'd slept with too many men at too young an age. Lehman would have put them at between sixteen and twenty-eight years old, but wouldn't have been surprised if he'd been told that some of them were in their thirties. They jumped to their feet as they saw the Americans coming up the stairs, flashing white smiles and stubbing out their cigarettes.

"Welcome, welcome," they sang, like startled songbirds, and pushed open the double doors. Music billowed out like fog, and they blinked as they walked into the main bar. It was almost too much to take in at once, a sensory overload that made their minds whirl. To the left was a raised oblong dance floor, about one metre wide and ten metres long, on which stood four girls, naked except for identical pairs of black high-heeled shoes, gyrating in time to the music and smiling at no one in particular. Lehman felt something warm and dry slide into his hand and squeeze, and when he looked down it was to see a small girl looking up at him. She was wearing the same orange bikini as the girls outside and it did little to conceal her breasts which she jiggled against his arm as she grinned up at him.

"Hello," she said.

"Hi," replied Lehman. She had shoulder-length hair, as black as tar, parted in the middle with a small, black and white bow at the back. Her eyes were a melting brown and wide, her nose was slightly flattened as if she were pressing her face against a glass window and she pouted her lips as if someone had told her that it was the way to a man's heart. She was pretty, but in a girlish way, and Lehman felt slightly uneasy at his hand being held by such a young girl wearing little more than her underwear. He had the feeling that if it had happened in a bar in Los Angeles he'd be jumped on by the Vice Squad, but as he looked around he could see that the bar was full of middle-aged men being similarly attended to by teenage girls.

"You like me?" she said, and giggled when Lehman said that he did. Horvitz and Lewis had also been grabbed by equally attractive girls and Tyler had been seized by two. From where Lehman was standing they looked like twins, tall for Thais with close-cropped hair and large breasts which they rubbed against his chest as they whispered to him.

Tyler was ignoring the twins and looking over at the main dance floor which was circular and in the middle of the bar. Girls in white blouses and jeans were serving drinks to predominantly middle-aged male customers who sat on stools and watched the dozen or so naked girls dancing. Several of the girls were holding on to gold poles which ran from the ceiling to the floor and smiling whenever a customer caught their eye. Some of the girls were clearly very young, their bodies as sleek as baby seals with next to no hair between their legs, their smiles open and guileless. More girls were standing next to the drinking tourists, their hands rubbing and probing as they alternated between talking and pouting.

"My name Lorn," said the girl at Lehman's side. She pressed her hand against her flat stomach and moved it from side to side.

"Hello, Lorn. My name's Dan."

"Shall we sit down?" Tyler said, his voice carrying over the music without shouting.

The vets nodded and Tyler spoke in the ear of one of his twins. She nodded eagerly and led him over to the bar where she began moving girls aside and asking customers if they'd mind moving until she managed to arrange five empty stools. Tyler took the middle seat, with Carmody and Horvitz on his left, and Lewis and Lehman to his right.

Lorn snuggled up next to Lehman, her hand slipping deftly between his thighs as she rested her cheek against his arm. The twins stood behind Tyler, both with their arms around his waist and before their drinks had been placed in front of them, Horvitz, Lewis and Carmody also had company. Two spotlights above the bar were flashing different coloured beams of light which were reflected off a mirrored wall behind the bar and the reflections of the girls were swathed in red, blue and green light as they danced.

"You like me?" asked Lorn again.

"Of course," said Lehman. "How old are you?"

He felt her shrug against his arm. "Seventeen," she said. "What hotel you stay at?"

Lehman told her and she nodded wisely. "Good hotel," she said. "We go now?"

"Go where?"

"Your hotel. We make love." The hand squeezed him and pushed deeper between his legs.

"Looks like you've scored," grinned Lewis. He had been taken over by a plump girl with waist-length hair who was stroking his arm and nuzzling his neck. "Brings back memories this, doesn't it?"

"Yeah, sure does," agreed Lehman, though the thought flashed through his mind that most of the memories weren't all that pleasant, and he regretted the times he'd bedded hookers — not because he'd ever caught anything but because he always felt so goddamn empty after the act. He looked down at Lorn's pleading eyes and he was tempted, no doubt about it, but he knew that if he took her back to his room and made love to her, no matter how physically satisfying it was, he would feel disgusted with himself afterwards as she showered and dressed and left him in the empty bed.

She misread the look in his eyes and her smile widened. "We go now?" she said, bouncing up and down like a puppy wanting to go for a walk.

He smiled at her enthusiasm. "Maybe later," he said. "Let me buy you a drink."

She nodded and spoke to one of the waitresses in rapid Thai. "You buy for my friends?" she asked and Lehman agreed. Small glasses of clear liquid appeared in front of the girls, six in all. Lehman lifted up Lorn's and tasted it. It was sweet and obviously non-alcoholic.

"Seven Up," she said and smiled like a child.

"So you won't get drunk," said Lehman.

"Me not like drunk," she said seriously and sipped at her drink.

The bill arrived in a blue plastic beaker which a waitress placed in front of Lehman. He lifted it out and looked at it. It was about a third of the price a round would have cost him in Los Angeles, and the company there wouldn't have been anywhere near as pretty.

The music stopped with the sound of a needle being scraped across a record and the girls on the podium scrambled off and were replaced by a thin girl with pock-marked cheeks which she'd tried to conceal with make-up. She was wearing a black bikini which she peeled off as she moved lethargically around the stage to Frank Sinatra singing "New York, New York". Her hands moved around her groin and then one finger slipped inside her vagina and emerged with a thin length of string as if she were about to pull out a sanitary towel. It grew longer and longer until she had almost eighteen inches pulled out and then something metallic slipped out from between her legs.

"Christ!" gasped Carmody. "That's a fucking razor blade!"

The blade glinted wetly under the lights as it swung on the string. The girl pulled again and another six inches of string emerged followed by a second blade. The girl gyrated her hips and opened her legs wider and carried on pulling. A third blade slipped out, and a fourth, and a fifth. By the time she'd finished there were eight blades hanging on a piece of string which was a good five feet long. She held it above her head like washing on a line as her audience clapped enthusiastically.

"They can't be real," said Carmody. "They'd cut her to fucking bits."

The girl smiled sweetly at Carmody and spoke to one of the waitresses who then handed Carmody a sheet of paper and asked him to hold it out in front of him. He

270

did as she asked and then the girl on the stage knelt down and took one of the blades in her hand. She drew it slowly down the paper and it cut it cleanly into two pieces.

"Looks real enough to me," laughed Lewis, raising his glass.

"Well I'll be fucked," said Carmody, looking at the two pieces of paper.

"Larry, considering where we are I'd say that was a distinct possibility," said Tyler.

"I'll drink to that," said Carmody, raising his glass.

The five Americans clashed their glasses together, raised them in salute, and drank.

"Dan, how you spell your name?" asked Lorn.

"Pardon?"

"Your name. How you spell?"

Lehman spelled his name and Lorn repeated it and then she leaned across the bar and spoke to the girl on the stage who was laying a large sheet of paper on the dance floor as Frank Sinatra was replaced by the Beach Boys. Lorn slid back off the bar and grinned at Dan. "What's happening?" he asked.

"Watch," she said and waggled her eyebrows suggestively.

The girl squatted over the paper and held out her hand to one of the waitresses and took hold of a thick felt-tipped pen, holding it up for everyone to see.

"What's going on?" Carmody asked.

"Watch," said Lehman, raising and lowering his eyebrows. By his side Lorn giggled and pinched his arm.

The girl took the cap off the pen and slowly inserted it, backwards, into her vagina. Carmody began making whooping noises and banged his claw on the bar, rattling his glass. The men watched the pen gradually disappear until just two inches remained visible, then the girl positioned herself over the sheet of paper and began using small movements of her hips to write.

"Oh my God," said Carmody. "A cunt that can write."

The men watched, transfixed, as the girl, her tongue between her teeth, carefully bobbed up and down over the paper. When she'd finished she sat back on her hips and held the paper over her head. "WELCOME TO BANGKOK, DAN" it said.

"How about that!" yelled Carmody as another group of ten or so naked girls ran on to the stage and began dancing to a Rod Stewart song. The girl dropped down off the podium and presented the sheet of paper to Lehman.

He took it, shaking his head in amazement and totally lost for words.

"Give her money," whispered Lorn.

"What?"

"Give her money. Fifty baht okay."

"Sure," said Lehman, pulling out his wallet and handing over five green notes. Nothing in Bangkok came free. Even the welcome had to be paid for.

"Something to hang on your wall back home, Dan?" asked Lewis.

"I must dance now," said Lorn. "I come back, okay?"

"I'll count the minutes," said Lehman.

272

Lorn screwed up her face, not sure what he meant. "You not take another girl, Dan," she said earnestly. "You wait for me, okay?"

"Yes, okay, Lorn. You go and dance."

"You watch, okay?" she said, nodding.

"Of course."

She pinched his arm gently and ran around the bar and up on to the stage, slipped out of her bikini and dropped the two tiny bits of orange material on to a chair. She looked even younger without the swimsuit, her thighs plump with puppy fat, her breasts firm and with no trace of sagging. Lorn gave him a beaming smile and shook her shoulders at him and blew him a kiss. Lehman smiled back and raised his glass to her.

The Americans sat in silence, watching the dancers on the stage and drinking their beer. Occasionally a man would leave with one of the bargirls dressed in a simple dress or blouse and jeans, presumably back to the guy's hotel or to one of the many short-time hotels which were in the buildings above the bars and restaurants of Pat Pong. After twenty minutes all the girls on the stage skipped off and were replaced with a new shift.

Lorn popped up at Lehman's side and slipped her arm around his waist. She was wearing her bikini once more. Her hand crept inside the back of his trousers where she stroked his skin.

"You see me?" she whispered into his ear.

"Oh, yes, I did that," said Lehman.

"You pay my bar fine? You take me out?"

"Maybe," answered Lehman.

A thick-set Thai man with a chunky gold chain around his neck and wearing a gold Rolex came out of a side door. He went behind the bar and checked the till. He saw Tyler and threw up his hands, a wide grin on his face. He practically ran around the bar and shook Tyler fiercely by the hand. "Joel Tyler," he said. "Good to see you back."

"You couldn't keep me away from the best bar in Pat Pong," said Tyler.

"In Bangkok, please," said the man.

Tyler introduced the burly man to Lehman as the owner of the bar and when they shook hands Lehman could feel a chunky ring bite into his flesh. The grip was firm and slightly damp and the smile seemed artificial. The man's name had about six syllables and when Lehman asked him to repeat it Lehman was still unable to pronounce it.

"My *farang* friends call me Josh," he said.

"*Farang?*" said Lehman.

"It's what they call foreigners," explained Tyler.

"It's quite friendly," said Josh. "It carries no racist overtones, I can assure you. Some of my best friends are *farangs*." His belly rolled as he laughed, big booming guffaws that cut through the rock music. Several of his back teeth had been replaced with gold ones.

"Little Lorn is looking after you, Dan?" Josh asked.

Lehman could feel Lorn tense as if she were frightened. Lehman sensed that a less than enthusiastic response would end up with her being hurt. He put his arm around her shoulder and pressed her to him.

"She's terrific," said Lehman, detesting the Thai man for the effect he was having on the girl. She was trembling.

"Good, good," said Josh. He spoke to Lorn in Thai and she replied in a faltering voice, shaking her head. Josh asked her something else and she nodded and he laughed again and then took Tyler off to one side for a private conversation. "Your drinks are all on the house," he called over his shoulder.

"What did he say to you?" Lehman asked Lorn once Tyler and Josh were gone.

"He ask me if I sick," she said.

"Sick?"

"If I have AIDS, or VD. I tell him I okay."

"But doesn't he stop the girls working if they get sick?"

She shook her head. "No, he not care. Many girls here have AIDS. They must work, must send money to their families. They very poor. Even if sick, still must work."

"You mean, if a girl gets infected with AIDS she still works?"

"Of course. What she do?"

"And Josh doesn't stop them?"

"Why he care? All girls use condoms. And most customers are tourists. Most not come back. That is why he ask me. He not want you get sick. You friend of friend. He must take care of you."

"What else did he say to you?"

She blushed. "He say I must treat you like king, and not ask you for money." Lehman disliked the man even more, for scaring Lorn and for pimping for him. "I come to your hotel?"

"I don't think so," said Lehman.

"You not like me?"

Lehman sighed. "Yes, of course I like you. I like you a lot. You're very pretty, very sexy, I'm sure I'd have a great time with you. But I can't."

"Why not?" she pressed. "If I not make love with you, he very angry. Maybe he hit me."

"Lorn, I'm married," Lehman lied. "I love my wife very much and I cannot sleep with any other girl. You understand?"

She nodded earnestly. "I understand. You very good man, Dan. Your wife very lucky."

"Lorn, if Josh tries to hurt you, you must tell me." He tore off a corner of the "Welcome To Bangkok" poster and wrote down his hotel and room number on it. "If he gives you any trouble, I want you to call me."

She took the piece of paper and slipped it inside the briefs of her bikini. Lehman got off his stool and she hugged him around the waist. On the stage a girl was lying on her back and using her vaginal muscles to blow steel-tipped darts through a silver pipe at balloons held at arm's length by two seedy-looking tourists. Her stomach tensed and the dart flew through the air and one of the balloons popped with a loud bang. "Don't go," pleaded Lorn.

"I have to," he said. He took out his wallet and tried to give her another 500 baht note but she put her hands behind her back and refused to take it.

"I not want your money," she pouted.

276

He folded the note and slid it down her orange briefs, next to the piece of paper. "A present," he said.

Lehman patted Lewis on his shoulder and told him he was going back to the hotel. Lewis was having his thighs massaged by a plump girl with her hair tied in two braids. He said he'd stay for a while. Horvitz was similarly occupied with a bargirl while Carmody was trying to pay a girl's bar fine. Lehman removed Lorn's hand from his arm and headed towards the entrance. Tyler caught up with him just as he reached the door.

"You going, Dan?" he asked.

"Yeah, thought I'd have an early night."

Tyler looked at his watch. "It's not that early," he said, "it'll be midnight in a few minutes. I think I'll call it a night myself. Let's get a tuk-tuk together." He waved a goodbye to Josh and Josh's gold bracelet glistened under the spotlights as he waved back. Girls in bikinis made a half-hearted attempt to stop them leaving as they descended the stairs and one was bold enough to stand in front of them, hands on hips, demanding that they go back and buy her a drink. They moved either side of her, pressing their backs to the wall, and her small hands wandered over Lehman's thighs. They fluttered around his groin and then he felt his wallet being slid out of his pocket. He clapped his hand to his pocket but the girl was so cute he found it impossible to be mad at her. She held her hands up in the air as if surrendering, then stood up on tiptoe to kiss his chin. Her breath smelt of fish and garlic and he heard her sniff as she kissed him. He slipped by her and followed Tyler out into the street where he was being harangued by three youths who were offering to show him the charms of night-time Bangkok. He spoke to them in Thai and they stepped back, surprise on their faces, then they burst out laughing and walked away.

"What did you say to them?" asked Lehman.

"Something along the lines that the only women I wanted were their mothers and what I'd like to do to them. It loses a lot in translation."

"Yeah, I bet it does," said Lehman. "Your Thai is pretty good, isn't it?"

"I can get by." Tyler beckoned to a tuk-tuk driver who kicked his machine into life and pulled up next to the two men.

"You said you couldn't speak Thai," said Lehman as he climbed into the back of the tuk-tuk.

Tyler got in and held on to a guard rail as the tuk-tuk moved away. He turned and looked at Lehman, fixing him with his cold blue eyes. "You've got to have some secrets, haven't you, Dan?" he said.

"I can't argue with that," said Lehman.

"I mean, life would be boring if we all knew everything there was to know about each other, wouldn't it? A little mystery makes life that much more exciting." He smiled and his eyes crinkled. Tyler's smile was quite warm, it was the confident, "I can be trusted" expression which Lehman had seen on the faces of boiler room salesmen all over California.

The tuk-tuk accelerated through the traffic, the driver skilfully switching back and forth between the road lanes whenever he spotted a gap. "Are you planning to stay out in Asia for a while, Dan?" asked Tyler.

"What makes you ask that?" replied Lehman. The tuk-tuk lurched to the left and ducked in front of a rattling old bus which slammed on its brakes.

"Problems back home, maybe," said Tyler quietly.

The tuk-tuk driver accelerated so quickly that Tyler and Lehman were pushed back into their seat, then he braked and they were thrown forward. Behind them another driver angrily sounded his horn.

Lehman looked at Tyler, frowning. Before he could speak, Tyler held up his hand. "Hear me out first, Dan," he said. "I gather you're in a spot back in LA, and that it probably isn't a good idea for you to show your face there, not just now . . ."

"How the hell do you know about that?" Lehman said angrily.

"I have contacts all around the world, Dan. And when I meet someone who interests me, I make enquiries."

"What the fuck is going on, Tyler? What are you up to?"

The tuk-tuk turned off the main road and into a darkened sidestreet where it bumped over potholes and weaved from side to side to avoid piles of garbage.

"I'm pretty sure we can both help each other. You have skills which I need, and I think I can help you out of your present predicament."

"Predicament?"

Tyler smiled, and this time his smile lacked warmth, it was a brief showing of teeth that reminded Lehman of a shark preparing to attack. "There's a contract out on you, Dan. I'm sorry to have to break it to you like this, but that's the way it is. If you go back to California, you won't last ten minutes."

"That's ridiculous!" said Lehman, but his stomach churned with the realisation that Tyler might be right.

"Mario Cilento doesn't piss around," said Tyler. "He's put a 10,000 dollar contract on your head. It's not much, I know, but there's plenty of folks around who'd kill for Mr Cilento free of charge just to get on his good side."

Lehman felt devastated. He knew that Mario Cilento would be furious at him for hitting his brother, but he'd never expected him to order his death, not over 125,000 dollars and a knee in the groin. Max would certainly bear a grudge, but he didn't have the authority to order a hit and his elder brother had always had a cooler head. A beating, maybe, a broken limb, that was the most he'd expected. But a contract? Lehman shuddered despite the hot Bangkok night. He leant forward in the tuk-tuk and put his arms protectively around his chest, his mind a whirl. "You must be mistaken," he said eventually.

Tyler shook his head. "There's no mistake, Dan."

"But it was only money," said Lehman. "Barely six figures. I thought that if I laid low for a while, then went back and promised to make up for it —"

"It's more serious than that," interrupted Tyler. "You hit Max harder than you thought."

"Oh Christ, he's dead?"

"No, he's not dead. But when you kneed him between the legs, you damaged one of his testicles. You damaged it so badly that they had to operate and Max Cilento is now walking around with just one ball. Well, from what I hear, walking isn't actually the right word. Limping would be more appropriate."

Despite the seriousness of his situation, Lehman couldn't stop grinning. "One ball?" he said. "Max Cilento is one ball short of a full pair?" He laughed out loud and Tyler laughed with him.

"Yeah, they've started calling him the Eunuch and he's having a real hard time. Mario is being called the Sultan and Max's crew is tagged as the Harem. It isn't so much the damage you did, it's the embarrassment factor. If Mario Cilento was Chinese you'd call it loss of face. You've made the family a laughing stock and they'll never forgive you for that."

Lehman leant back in the seat. "Yeah, I see what you mean." The tuk-tuk lurched to a halt outside the hotel and Lehman climbed out while Tyler paid the driver. They walked together through the hotel lobby.

"Can I have a word with you before you turn in?" asked Tyler. Lehman agreed and the two men took the elevator to his room. Lehman opened the door and Tyler sat on a beige sofa while Lehman knelt down by the side of the mini-bar.

"Singha okay?" asked Lehman.

"I'd prefer a bourbon," said Tyler.

"Ice?"

"Straight."

Lehman gave him a miniature Jack Daniels and a glass and helped himself to a beer. He sat down on the corner of the queen-size bed as he poured the Singha. A large mirror hanging on the wall opposite the bottom of the bed reflected his actions. The whole hotel seemed to be geared up for guys picking up girls. The reception desk asked to see the IDs of any girls brought into the hotel so that guests could be protected from theft, every room had a huge bed, two robes in the bathroom and a mirror close to the bed. Business cards with the names and addresses of local massage parlours appeared under his door as if by magic and even the chambermaids smiled invitingly as if they'd be prepared to share the bed rather than simply make it up.

"Dan, I don't want you to think that I've been prying into your personal life," said Tyler. "I'm not playing some sort of game with you, I want you to know that." He took a long pull at his Jack Daniels. "You seem like the sort of guy I could use, and I wanted to have that confirmed before I approached you with what I have in mind. I just made a few phone calls, that's all."

"Who did you call?" asked Lehman.

"I have friends," said Tyler. "That's all I can tell you."

"Everyone must have their secrets?" said Lehman sarcastically.

"Something like that. But you've no need to worry, the people I use are discreet. There's no way that Mario Cilento will know that you're out here. At least, he won't find out from me. Does anyone else know you're here?"

Lehman shook his head.

"I asked you before how long you planned to stay here. Can you answer me now?"

"I'm not sure," answered Lehman. "Not now you've told me about the contract. I'd assumed that it was just a matter of lying low for a while then going back and taking my medicine. A beating, maybe. Possibly a broken arm and a promise that I'd make good the money. I'm a good operator, you know, and I'd just put in the extra time until I cleared it."

"The way I hear it, that's not on the cards," said Tyler.

"Yeah. So I guess I will stay put for a while, while I figure out what to do." He drank his beer but it had no taste. He grimaced and so did his reflection.

"Dan, I can help you," said Tyler.

"Help me make up my mind, or help me get straight with Cilento?"

"I can help you get enough money maybe to persuade Cilento to take back the contract. Or to start a new life somewhere else. Plastic surgery if necessary, new ID, the works."

Lehman snorted. "Plastic surgery? You think I need a nose job, Joel, is that it?"

Tyler smiled grimly. "You know what I mean. You could get enough money to stay hidden for ever. And you never know, if you were to offer Mario Cilento half a million bucks and a fulsome apology, he might figure it was worth the loss of face."

"Half a million bucks?" said Lehman. "Where am I going to get money like that?"

Tyler sipped at his bourbon. "That's what I want to talk to you about." He paused long enough to make sure that he had Lehman's undivided attention. He did. "Dan, what would you be prepared to do for two million dollars?"

Lehman rolled his glass between the palms of his hands as he considered the question. "A lot," he replied eventually.

"Would you kill?"

"No," said Lehman emphatically. "Not cold, I'd never kill for money."

"You killed in Nam, though?"

"Twice. I was a chopper pilot, remember? I killed when I had to, when my Huey went down and we had to fight off an NVA patrol, but I was never in the jungle with an M16 in my hand. But that's not what we're talking about, is it? You're talking about killing for money, and the answer is that I wouldn't. Not for two million dollars, not for twenty million dollars."

"A point of principle?"

"Yes."

"Would you break the law for two million dollars?"

Lehman laughed. "Come on, Joel. Everyone breaks the law. We've all driven above the speed limit, we've been at the wheel with a few too many beers under our belts, we've smoked grass and done a hell of a lot more besides. I've no problems with breaking the law, it just depends on what law it is you want broken. Why don't you tell me what's on your mind?"

"What I'm trying to do, Dan, is to ascertain just what you'd do for money. You've told me that you won't kill, and that's fine, the job I have in mind doesn't involve murder. But you can't expect me to come right out with what I've got in mind, not until I know where you stand. For all I know, you might go running straight to the police, and then where would I be? No, you'll have to bear with me, for a while."

"If you've been asking questions about me back in California you'll know that I'm not exactly on the best of terms with the police. And you'll know what it is I do for a living."

"You sell non-existent investments. Fraud."

"It's a grey area, but I wouldn't quibble too much with your description."

"Would you fly a helicopter for money?"

"Depends."

"On what?"

"On what it is you want to fly. I wouldn't want to get involved in drugs." He grinned. "Other than for occasional recreational use," he added. "But I wouldn't fly drugs in from South America. Too risky."

"But if I could guarantee you wouldn't get caught? Would you do it then?"

"For two million dollars? And no chance of getting caught?" He took a mouthful of beer as he thought about it. "Yeah, I would. I've nothing against the idea in principle. Is that what you have in mind, Joel?"

Tyler shook his head. "I'm still feeling my way, Dan. Bear with me. Would you steal?"

"Steal what?"

Tyler shrugged. "I don't know. From a shop, maybe. Would you throw a brick through a jeweller's window and take a two million dollar necklace?"

"Too risky."

"Okay, if I could put together a team which was breaking into a jeweller's shop at night, and if I could guarantee that there was a ninety per cent chance of us getting away clean and that your share of the take would be two million, would you do it?"

Lehman waggled his head from side to side and chewed his lip like a schoolboy trying to solve an algebra problem. "It's too hypothetical," he said.

"Gut feeling," pressed Tyler. "Give me your gut feeling."

"Yeah, I'd do it."

"And what if it meant going in during the day, with guns but not planning to use them. If I could guarantee the same odds of success. Would you do it then?"

"Depends on the team," said Lehman.

"Good guys. Guys like you."

"Vets?"

Lehman felt Tyler's eyes bore into his own like blue ice daggers. "Yes. Vets like you."

"Who?"

Tyler smiled tightly. "First we have to decide whether or not you want to be part of it, Dan. It wouldn't be fair to the rest. If you'd already agreed you wouldn't want me to be telling someone who might run off and spill his guts, would you?"

"It sounds like you don't trust me, Joel."

"I don't trust anybody. Not completely. Not until I know them."

"Tell me one thing. Is Bart Lewis part of this?"

"Would it make a difference?"

"No, I guess not." Lehman studied his own reflection in the mirror. Middle-aged, grim expression as usual, slightly hunched over his glass of beer, sweat stains under the arms of his shirt, seven o'clock shadow around his cheeks. A man on the run, not knowing how long it would take until Mario Cilento's contract was fulfilled. That wasn't how Dan Lehman wanted to end his days, on the receiving end of an assassin's bullet. "It's a robbery?" Lehman asked.

"It's a robbery," confirmed Tyler.

"Where?"

"I can't tell you."

"When?"

"Weeks rather than months. You'd have to stay in South-East Asia. But that's not a problem for you, is it?"

Lehman ignored the question, figuring it was probably rhetorical anyway. "And the chance of success is ninety per cent?"

"Who can tell, Dan? I was using that as an example. I don't plan to get caught, that's for sure. And I'll explain everything to you nearer the time. But I can say that as far as I'm concerned it'll be a completely successful operation. And if it all goes to plan, nobody will get caught. If it goes wrong, I would hope we'd be able to abort safely. And I should stress that all I want you for is your helicopter experience, nothing more.

You won't be carrying a weapon, not unless you want to."

"Was the two million dollars hypothetical, too?"

Tyler shook his head. "No, that'll be your cut. Two million dollars. Cash. Are you in?"

Lehman looked at his reflection again. He straightened his back and smiled. "Yeah, I'm in. Who else is in on it?"

"Bart Lewis. Eric Horvitz. And Larry Carmody."

Lehman frowned.

"Something wrong?" asked Tyler.

"I guess I'm just surprised that you'd want Horvitz and Carmody. I mean, Bart's a regular guy, and if you're planning to use a chopper then he's obviously useful, but Horvitz and Carmody?"

"They've both seen combat, they can handle the pressure. Sure, they've got problems, but that's more because they've had trouble adapting to life back in the States rather than anything intrinsically wrong with them. They'll be fine, believe me. I've seen their files, their war records. And Lewis is more than just a regular guy — he's a decorated crew chief and was one of the army's best mechanics. I'm an excellent judge of character, Dan. That's why I chose you."

"Did you arrange for them to come on this trip?" Lehman asked.

Tyler smiled. "Secrets, Dan," he said quietly.

"What about me? Did you know about me before I left the States?"

"What do you mean?"

"I mean that Lewis, Horvitz and I were all approached by a guy called Dick Marks, saying he was some sort of psychiatrist with an organisation that helped vets return to Vietnam. What was it called? The US-Indochina Reconciliation Project?"

Tyler nodded. "The organisation exists, but Dick Marks works for me, not for it. And his name isn't Marks, either."

"I don't understand what's going on here," said Lehman.

"I needed a pilot, a good one," explained Tyler. "I needed a mechanic, and I needed two men who know how to handle themselves in combat. I had you all checked out in the States, but I wanted to see for myself before I approached you. I wanted to feel you out. See what sort of condition you were in, physical and mental."

Lehman shook his head. "That doesn't make sense," he said. "You didn't know until the last minute that I was coming. Hell, I didn't know myself."

"To be honest, Dan, you weren't my first choice. I'd already contacted a chopper pilot in Phoenix but he broke his leg three weeks ago. I already had Lewis, Horvitz and Carmody lined up. Marks and I were trawling all over the place looking for a suitable pilot. You were a godsend."

"I had the skills you need, and I have a good reason for needing cash."

"That's about it," agreed Tyler.

Lehman wondered what Tyler had said to convince Lewis, Horvitz and Carmody that they should take part in whatever it was that he had planned. Tyler was a control freak, that was for sure; he seemed to enjoy manipulating people, and while he claimed to be able to spot people's strengths he had an uncanny knack of finding people's weak points. The carrot and the stick. In Lehman's case the carrot was the two million dollars. And the stick? The fear of the contract hanging over him, and the unspoken threat that Tyler could quite easily inform a certain Mr Cilento of Lehman's present whereabouts. "So what happens now?" asked Lehman.

Tyler smiled, stood up, and placed his empty glass on top of the mini-bar. "I have to keep some secrets, Dan. You'll get the details soon enough." He stepped towards Lehman and Lehman got to his feet. Tyler stuck out his hand like a car salesman wanting to seal a deal with a handshake. They shook hands and Tyler patted Lehman on the back. "I'm glad you're on board, Dan. Really glad."

Lehman saw Tyler out and then poured himself another beer. He went over to the window and pulled back the blinds. The water in the swimming pool glinted far below. Someone was swimming a slow breast stroke, pale white skin in the blue water.

Lehman hadn't been too surprised by Tyler's choice of men. He'd spent a great deal of the trip in Vietnam talking to Lewis, Carmody and Horvitz, and now it was clear why. He'd been sounding them out, getting the measure of them and working out which buttons to press to get them to agree to join him. Lehman nursed his beer and wondered what buttons Tyler had pressed.

Carmody would probably have been the easiest to persuade; from what Lehman had seen the man was bordering on psychotic and had a lot of anger inside. Tyler would have offered him a way of expressing that anger, of getting it out of his system and of making money at the same time. Horvitz? Eric Horvitz was a real mystery. Something was burning inside him, it wasn't anger, it was something else, something colder. Lehman didn't know much about Horvitz but he supposed that Tyler had managed to go deeper into his psyche. Maybe he'd offered him a chance to relive his glory days. A last hurrah. Even Lehman could appreciate the fact that most of the vets had never been so alive as they had been during their time in Vietnam and maybe that was what Horvitz missed. The robbery might give him the adrenaline rush that life after Vietnam denied him. That left Bart Lewis. He seemed a straight enough guy, but Lehman couldn't imagine him wanting to take part in a robbery, even though there was little doubt that he needed the money. He'd said several times that his garage business in Baltimore wasn't doing too well and he had a young son who he wanted to put through college when he was old enough. Lewis would have been easy to hit with an investment programme. All Lehman would have had to do would be to tell him it was a sure thing, that it would provide a nest egg for when his kid needed to go to college, tell him that his son would be proud of him and Lewis would already be reaching for a pen to sign the cheque. Lehman felt a sudden wave of emotion for Lewis, a desire to protect him from life's sharks.

There was a knock at the door and Lehman stood up to answer it. Lorn stood outside in a black shirt and yellow wrap-around skirt. She looked up at him and gave him a beaming smile. "Hello," she said brightly.

"Hello," he said.

Her smile widened, showing perfect, white teeth. "I come see you," she said.

"I can see that," he answered. He frowned. "Are you okay? The manager didn't give you a hard time, did he?"

"No, I okay," she said. "I want see you." Her eyes seemed to sparkle as she smiled. She looked shorter than when Lehman had seen her in the bar and he realised it was because she'd swapped her high heel shoes for a simple pair of sandals.

She pouted, her lower lip pushed forward as she waited for him to ask her in. He could feel her eyes pleading and he melted. He stepped to the side and opened the door wider. "Come in," he said.

She stepped inside the room and looked around. "Bathroom there?" she asked, nodding towards a door.

"Yeah," said Lehman. Part of him wanted to ask her to leave, but he could feel himself growing hard at the thought of being in bed with her.

She dropped her brown leather handbag on the dressing table by the television and headed for the bathroom. "I shower," she said gaily over her shoulder. "You want come with me?"

Lehman wrestled with his conscience for about ten seconds before following her.

Neil Coleman sat at his desk with a grin from ear to ear, luxuriating in the warm feeling of a job well done. He swung his feet up on to his desk and sipped his fifth cup of coffee of the day. The one thing that would make his morning perfect would be a cigarette, but he was determined to quit once and for all. On his desk was an internal memo from the Commissioner's office, congratulating him on the previous night's work. The glowing praise would look good on his record, even though he knew that it wouldn't lead to promotion, but it was the speed with which it had reached his desk that had impressed him. Normally it was only bad news which travelled quickly through the police bureaucracy.

Coleman yawned and closed his eyes. He had been up all night, and spent most of it in the front seat of a police van overlooking Chek Mun Hoi Hap, the narrow channel which linked Tolo Harbour with the sea. Hui had been with him, and there had been six uniformed constables sweating in the back. Hui had offered Coleman a cigarette on at least three different occasions, and each time had expressed apologetic surprise when he had refused. Coleman was sure he was doing it on purpose.

They'd spotted the men loading the cars on to three high-powered speedboats at two o'clock in the morning. Coleman had parked the vehicle at Wu Kai Sha from where they could see most of the harbour and the landing area where they'd been told the stolen cars would be loaded. The tip had come from one of Coleman's contacts, a triad member who'd been feeding him information in exchange for cash for the past couple of years. He'd phoned Coleman and said that a rival triad was planning to send six stolen cars to China and had given him detailed instructions on where and when. Coleman had the feeling that his informer was more interested in the police damaging a rival triad than he was in the money, but he'd take information any way he could get it.

He'd requisitioned a pair of night-vision glasses — the sort the army used to spot illegal immigrants trying to sneak across the border from China — and had watched a group of young men drive three Mercedes, a Nissan saloon and two Toyotas off the Tolo Highway and head towards a gently sloping beach. They were accompanied by two green trucks which drove right up to the water's edge. As a dozen men climbed out of the back of the trucks, Hui had called up the Marine Police on his radio. They had six launches in position, three just beyond the channel at Bluff Head, one off Chek Chau and two more on the apex of Ocean Point. The launches could effectively seal off the channel when required.

The triads had been incredibly well organised. In the space of ten minutes they unloaded several dozen planks of wood and steel barrels from the trucks and had constructed a rough pier stretching thirty feet out to sea. Coleman scanned the harbour and eventually spotted the three speedboats bobbing close to Ma Shi Chau, a small island about three kilometres offshore. Coleman pointed them out to Hui and he radioed the details over to the Marine Police.

One of the triads aimed a torch out to sea and flashed the beam. On-off. On-off. On-off. There was an answering flash from one of the speedboats and then all three began coursing through the waves.

"It's going down," said Coleman, under his breath. It was rare for there to be any sort of excitement in the Stolen Vehicles Unit and he relished every moment.

The first speedboat cut its power and made a long, arcing turn to take it parallel to the home-made pier. Ropes were thrown to moor the boat and a Mercedes was driven gingerly along the wooden planks. The driver timed his final approach to the swell of the waves, surging forward at just the right moment and driving up to the front of the boat. Coleman tried to make out the registration number, hoping that it was William Fielding's car, but it was too far away.

The driver got out of the car, climbed out of the boat and ran back along the pier as the second car, a Toyota, made the trip. When it was safely in the boat and the driver back on the pier, the boat surged away and out towards the channel.

Coleman nodded and Hui called in the Marine Police. Their instructions were to apprehend the boats one at a time as they reached the mouth of the channel.

The second boat was loaded with two Mercedes and it also headed for the open sea. Coleman waited until the fifth car was driving along the pier before telling Hui to bring in the rest of the team, four vanloads of uniformed constables who had been waiting in nearby Ma Liu Shui.

A voice crackled in Cantonese over the radio and Hui translated for Coleman, the sole gweilo occupant of the van. "They have the first two boats in custody," he said, a wide grin on his face. He flicked a Marlboro out of its pack and lit it with a blue disposable lighter. He offered one to Coleman who shook his head and pointedly wound down his window.

From their viewpoint on the Wu Kai Sha peninsula they were able to see the four police vans roar up to the beach and the constables dash out to round up the men. They were armed but no shots were fired and within five minutes the triads were being marched to the vans with their hands handcuffed behind their backs.

"Let's go," said Coleman. Hui started the van's engine and they drove quickly to the Tolo Highway to help collect the evidence they needed: the cars, the pier and the triad vans. It had been a major success and those who took part in the operation had been on a high ever since.

One of the drivers was already offering to talk to them about other vehicles if they didn't press charges and he promised to blow the smuggling chain wide open. The threat of a criminal record was a potent weapon against potential informers because countries like Canada and Australia always insisted on proof that new immigrants were not law-breakers. The triads were as keen as the middle classes to leave Hong Kong, and within the next day or so Coleman hoped to persuade more of the triad soldiers to open up. It had been a great day. The only disappointment had been that

296

William Fielding's Mercedes hadn't been among the cars they'd recovered.

Thoughts of the chairman of the Kowloon and Canton Bank brought Debbie to mind. Coleman swung his feet off his desk and reached for his phone. He dialled the Fielding house and he tapped his fingers against his in-tray. Debbie answered, to his surprise.

"Debbie? It's Neil."

"Oh. Hello, Neil. How are you?" She sounded distant, as if she were thinking about something else. Coleman felt tongue-tied. He'd expected one of the maids to pick up the phone.

He told her about the bust and how they'd recovered the stolen cars.

"That's great," she said. "Was one of them my dad's?"

He had to admit that he hadn't recovered her father's Mercedes yet and he could tell that she was disappointed.

"Anyway, I was wondering if we could go out one day this week and celebrate," Coleman said.

"I'd love to, Neil, but I've a really hectic work schedule. We're up against a deadline so it's nose to the grindstone all week."

"Okay," he said, trying to hide his frustration. "What about Saturday?"

She sighed. "Can't, I'm afraid. Mum and Dad are giving a dinner party for a couple of their friends who are leaving Hong Kong. I have to be there."

"Can't I come?" asked Coleman, trying not to sound like he was pleading.

"You wouldn't enjoy it, Neil. I'll call you next week, okay?"

Coleman bit his lip, hard enough to make himself wince. "Debbie, is something wrong?"

"Wrong?" she said. "What do you mean?"

"We haven't been out for weeks now. I miss you."

"That's nice," she said.

"Don't you miss me?" he said, squeezing his thighs together. He knew he sounded like a teenager and he hated himself for it.

"Neil, I had a great time with you, and I'm happy to go out with you again . . ."

"But?" he said.

"What do you mean?" She was beginning to sound tense.

"It sounded like there was going to be a 'but' there."

She sighed deeply. "What I was going to say was that you shouldn't take what we did so seriously."

"Debbie, you made love to me. That means something."

"Yes, it means something to me, too. It means we had a good time. And I like that, I like having a good time. But you scared me when you asked me to get engaged, Neil. I mean, we'd only been out four times."

"Six," corrected Coleman.

"Okay, six. But I'm too young to settle down. I just want to enjoy myself."

"That's what I want, Debbie. But I want to enjoy myself with you. I don't want to go out with anyone else."

"But I don't want that, Neil. Not right now. When I'm your age, maybe I will, but right now I'm only twenty-three and I don't want to be committed to one person."

"Not even to me?" asked Coleman. She didn't answer. "Debbie, I want to talk to you."

"We're talking now," she said sharply.

"I mean face to face. I want to see you. I want to touch you."

"I told you, I'm busy. I'll call you next week."

"Jesus, Debbie, I can't believe you're like this," complained Coleman. "No one has ever made love to me like you did. You can't turn me away now. I love you . . ." Hui walked into the office, sat down at his own desk and opened a file. Coleman flushed, wondering if Hui had been listening outside the door.

"Neil, don't be so immature," said Debbie. "We had fun, that's all."

There was so much that Coleman wanted to say to her, but he couldn't do it while Hui was in the room. "You'll call me next week?" Coleman asked.

"Yeah," she said. "Look, I've got to go. Bye."

The phone went dead. "Yeah, that'll be great," Coleman said to the buzzing line. "I'm sure we'll have a terrific time. Bye for now."

Hui looked at him as if he'd seen right through the charade. "You seen this?" Coleman asked, walking over to Hui's desk and handing across the congratulatory memo.

Hui nodded and grinned. "Got one myself," he said without reading it. "Good to be appreciated, isn't it?" He passed it back to Coleman.

Coleman went back to his desk, crestfallen. He'd assumed that he'd been singled out for special treatment. He hadn't thought that everyone involved had got a memo.

"Great bust, Neil," said an east London accent behind him.

"Whotchya, Phil," said Coleman, without looking round. He sat down and picked up his cup of coffee. "News travels fast."

"Twenty triads under arrest, six stolen cars recovered and three smuggling boats impounded! You should be bloody pleased, mate. You going to be at the press conference?"

Coleman frowned, a sick feeling in the pit of his stomach. "What press conference?"

Donaldson looked at Hui and back to Coleman. "Three o'clock this afternoon. The Commissioner's meeting the press. They're putting the cars on display; it should get a great show in tomorrow's papers."

"Yeah," said Coleman, confused. He looked at Hui. "Did you know about this, Kenneth?"

Hui looked embarrassed. "The press office called earlier. I have been asked to attend."

"They didn't say anything about me?" Hui shrugged and said nothing. "Fucking terrific," said Coleman. He scowled at Donaldson. "You know what's going on, don't you?" he said.

"Yeah, I know," said Donaldson sympathetically. The force was continually playing down the importance of the expats and it was clear that Coleman's role was being sidelined. Neither wanted to voice their opinions in front of Hui, however.

"Shit," said Coleman.

"Maybe the Commissioner will give you an honourable mention," said Donaldson.

"I've already got a memo," said Coleman bitterly.

"Yeah, well that and a dollar will get you a ride on the Shau Kei Wan tram," said Donaldson.

"Hey, can you do me a favour?" asked Coleman.

"Maybe," said Donaldson cautiously. "What is it you want?"

"Can I borrow your car for a few days? I'll be careful." Donaldson owned a six-year-old Suzuki Jeep which he mainly used to go windsurfing at weekends.

"Till when?"

"Saturday morning? Is that okay?"

Donaldson considered his request for a while and then nodded. "Just take care of it, okay? And put petrol in it, will you? And please, please, please, don't fuck up my police radio."

"Thanks, Phil," said Coleman.

"The lovely heiress not picking you up in the Jag?"

"Don't ask," said Coleman.

"You know me, mate. The epitome of tact. So what's wrong, not getting your leg over, then?"

"Just give me the keys, Phil. Just give me the keys."

★ ★ ★

The small plane banked steeply and dropped like a stone towards the airfield far below. Lehman's stomach lurched and he grimaced at Lewis. Lewis scowled back. "I hope this guy fucking knows what he's doing," he said.

The wings waggled up and down giving Lehman a good view out of both sides of the plane as it made its approach. There were rice paddies with men and women in wide conical hats tending green shoots, and bullocks pulling wooden ploughs through brackish water. In the far distance were hills which were too rugged to cultivate and which had been left to the jungle. Overhead the sun beamed down from a cloudless sky.

"Yeah, I hate small planes," agreed Lehman. "Give me a helicopter or a Club seat in a 747. Anything in between makes me want to heave."

"You're always complaining, Dan," laughed Tyler from the front, where he sat next to the pilot — a middle-aged Thai who gave the impression of having trained on air force dive-bombers and who hated having to ferry three *farangs* around in a thirty-year-old single-engine Helio-Courier. "Beautiful little planes these," continued Tyler as the pilot lined up the nose with a thin dirt runway. "CIA used hundreds of them during the war. You can land one of these babies in just 120 feet."

"I'll just be grateful if we get down in one piece," said Lehman.

302

"No problem, my friend," said the pilot, dropping another hundred feet and slowing the airspeed so that the tiny plane was going no faster than a family car. He dropped the right wing and put his foot down hard on the left rudder pedal which put the small plane into a forward slip, allowing him to lose altitude at a faster rate. The altimeter spun around and the ground rushed at them. At the last minute the pilot straightened the plane so that it was aligned with the runway. The wheels kicked up puffs of dust on the bone-dry dirt and the plane came to a dead stop in next to no time, just as Tyler had predicted. "See," said the pilot, beaming. "No problem."

The only buildings on the airfield were a corrugated iron shack, a big circular fuel storage tank and an empty hangar large enough for three planes the size of the Helio. In front of the hangar was an old blue Mercedes covered with a thin layer of reddish dust. It crept forward towards the plane and stopped about twenty feet from it, its doors closed and its engine purring.

"That for us?" asked Lewis.

"Yeah, we've still some way to go," said Tyler.

"I hope it's got air conditioning," said Lewis, breathing in the hot, humid air. He mopped his wide brow with the sleeve of his khaki shirt.

Tyler had been secretive about their ultimate destination, telling Lehman and Lewis only that they would be going north for a couple of days and that they were to bring with them just a flight bag with a change of clothes. They'd left Horvitz and Carmody in Bangkok and picked up the Helio at Bangkok Airport.

"You want to tell us where we are now?" Lehman asked.

"Nearest town is called Udon Thani," said Tyler. "The border with Laos is about fifty klicks to the north. We're heading east." He spoke to the pilot in Thai and the man nodded.

"The plane's going to wait for us?" asked Lewis.

"Hell, Bart, we can walk if you want to," said Tyler, grinning.

"Plane's fine by me," said Lewis. New beads of sweat were already forming on his forehead and he wiped it again with his sleeve.

"Let's get in the car," said Tyler, "you're gonna melt."

The driver of the Mercedes had switched on the air conditioner for them and Lewis and Lehman climbed gratefully into the back of the car and stretched out, enjoying the cold air. Tyler got into the front and spoke to the driver in Thai. They set off down the road which led away from the airstrip and towards the wooded hills. Tyler took a piece of paper from his back pocket and unfolded it. Lehman peered over his shoulder and saw that it was a hand-drawn map.

"When are you going to tell us why we're here?" Lehman asked Tyler.

"We're here to get a helicopter."

"Out here?"

"If my sources are right, and they usually are, we should find just what we need about twenty klicks away."

"I don't understand," said Lehman, frowning. "Why do we have to come all the way out here to get a chopper? We could hire one for a few hundred bucks."

"Because we can't hire one without a hell of a lot of paperwork, and while we could fake it there's too big a chance of us leaving a trail that can be followed. There's another reason, too. We're going to be using it in Hong Kong and it's a very small place. If we fly a chopper in it'll be noticed and recorded."

"You're saying we're not going to fly it to Hong Kong?" said Lehman, totally confused.

"That's right. Assuming the chopper we're gonna see is okay for the job, I'm going to arrange to have it shipped to Hong Kong. That way, when we come to use it it'll come as a complete surprise. You see what I mean? If we take off from Kai Tak, we'll be followed all the way by air traffic control. But if we keep it under wraps in the New Territories and only fly it on the day of the mission they won't know what it is or where we've come from. Confusion, Dan, that's what we're aiming for. We want the enemy confused so that we have time to get in and out before they can get their act together."

"And what sort of chopper is it?"

Tyler winked. "You've got to let me have some secrets, Dan. Besides, I want to see the look on your face when you see it." He settled back in his seat and concentrated on the road ahead while Lehman looked out of the side window at the farmers in their rice fields. The road they were driving on was practically deserted. Once they overtook a rusting yellow bus loaded with villagers and livestock but other than that they saw only farmers with bullock carts and once an elephant being ridden by a small boy. The car climbed away from the rice farms and up into the mountains where whole areas had been stripped by slash-and-burn hill-tribe farmers, leaving the red soil exposed. In some places attempts had been made to repair the damage done by the farmers by replanting acres of fast-growing pine trees, giving the area the look of a poorly patched quilt.

As they drove through the hills they kept catching glimpses of small villages tucked away in the valleys, pretty wooden houses with steep roofs, and everywhere there were small farms with men, women and children working in the fields.

The Mercedes began to descend, the double-track road winding down through the hills until it plateaued. There were farmland and rice fields on either side of the road, but in the distance they could see semi-evergreen forests which had yet to fall victim to the slash-and-burn farmers, rich green mixtures of chestnuts and oaks, ferns and bamboos.

After half an hour's driving, Tyler spoke to the young driver in Thai and the Mercedes turned off the road and on to a narrow dirt track clearly designed for foot traffic rather than cars. The Mercedes rocked like a boat as it bucked from pothole to pothole. Lehman wondered how Tyler knew that a helicopter could be found in the middle of nowhere. His thoughts were interrupted when the Mercedes braked suddenly, throwing him and Lewis forward so violently that Lewis banged his face on the headrest in front of him.

"Fuck's sake, man, what's happening?" he said.

"Elephants," said Tyler. "They get right of way in these parts."

Lewis rubbed his nose, tears welling uncontrollably in his eyes, as two big, grey elephants strode slowly across the track, waggling their ears and swinging their trunks to and fro. A bare-chested teenage boy, sitting with his legs either side of the first elephant's neck, grinned and waved at the driver of the Mercedes with a small stick. Thick chains around the necks of the two giant beasts were attached to logs which they dragged behind them. When they had crossed, the Mercedes started up again, following the track as it twisted and turned through the countryside. Tyler kept looking at the milometer and peering out of the window to the left, and after they crossed a small stone bridge over a clear blue stream he spoke to the driver in Thai. The driver nodded and pulled the Mercedes off the track. He switched off the engine while Tyler twisted around in his seat.

"Okay, this is it," he said to the two men in the back.

"This is it?" said Lehman, looking around. He couldn't see anything that looked remotely like an airport or a landing strip.

"Assuming I'm reading the map correctly," said Tyler. "Come on."

The three men got out of the car and stood on the dirt track. Lewis wiped his brow with his shirt sleeve again. "Just like Baltimore in the summer," he said. "Hot and wet. Weather like this, one murder a day, guaranteed."

"This way, guys," said Tyler, striding down a narrow path which led away from the track. An old woman carrying a wicker basket looked at them with wide eyes, astonished to find three *farangs* walking through the remote countryside. Tyler put his hands together under his chin and bowed and said something to her in Thai and the woman almost dropped her basket in surprise. Tyler spoke to her and she pointed along the path, nodding her head vigorously. "Yeah, this is the way," Tyler said to Lehman and Lewis.

The path took them through a rice field and alongside a small farm where all the buildings had low, thatched roofs. A group of naked children were playing in a stream, jumping in and splashing each other, their laughter carrying across the fields.

The path took them away from the farm to a large lake, fringed by tall palm trees and ferns. In the centre of the lake was an island, and on the island was a collection of buildings built haphazardly around a stone pagoda-like structure. It was capped with a gold spire which gleamed and sparkled in the light. Between the shore and the island was a long, narrow wooden bridge, wide enough to allow two men to pass shoulder to shoulder. Where the bridge met the island were two large dragons, their bodies covered with glazed tiles of the deepest blue and turquoise.

308

"Wow," said Lehman. "What's that?"

"It's a *wat*," said Tyler. "It's a sort of a monastery and a place of worship for the local villagers. The tower in the middle, with the gold spire, is what they call a *chedi*. It goes back to the twelfth century and is supposed to contain a real relic of the Lord Buddha. It's a holy place, but so isolated that it doesn't get many visitors. The other buildings are a school, a library and an *ubosoth*, where they ordain novices."

Five thin monks in saffron robes were walking slowly around the *chedi*, heads bowed, and they could hear the banging of a drum.

"And these monks are going to lend us a helicopter?" said Lehman in disbelief.

"Are you saying you don't believe in miracles, Dan?" said Tyler. He winked at them. "You guys wait here. There's someone I have to speak to."

He slipped off his shoes and socks and walked barefoot along the wooden planks. Lehman and Lewis sat down on the lush green grass at the side of the lake to wait.

"You believe this?" said Lewis. "He brings us all the way out here to speak with a group of monks. Are we crazy or is he?"

"I dunno, Bart. He's come through so far, but this is weird. Really weird."

They watched Tyler walk slowly along the bridge and on to the island. Lehman shaded his eyes with his hand. He could see a bespectacled old monk, bow-legged with sagging shoulders, hobble from one of the buildings to where Tyler stood. Tyler put his hands under his chain again and bowed low; the monk returned the bow, but it was the merest inclination of the head, an acknowledgment of Tyler's respectfulness and nothing more. They spoke for a while and then the monk led Tyler away into the shade of a wooden building with a red-tiled roof.

They waited. The hot afternoon sun became unbearable so they moved underneath a large palm tree and sat in its shade. They watched colourful birds fly from the jungle and across the lake, flashes of blue, red and yellow, and they saw huge dragonflies and butterflies, the insects almost equal in size to the birds. Lewis lay back in the grass, closed his eyes, and soon was snoring gently. Lehman sat with his back to the palm and put his hands behind his neck. Like Lewis, he couldn't understand why Tyler had brought them to north-east Thailand. What use would monks have with a helicopter? And what would tempt them to part with it so that the Americans could use it in a robbery?

His thoughts were interrupted by the sight of Tyler walking out of the building with another monk. Like the first, he wore a saffron-coloured robe which went over his left shoulder, ending just above his knees, but this monk was only an inch shorter than Tyler. They walked together to the wooden bridge, Tyler speaking and the monk nodding. They stopped when they were halfway along the bridge and stood facing each other. The monk's bald head had a dark halo around it as if it had been several days since he'd shaved. He had pale skin for a Thai, suggesting that he spent most of his days indoors, and he had a slight stoop as if he resented his height. His hands were clasped in front of him as he spoke and he seemed to be asking Tyler for something because Tyler was shaking his head and holding his hands out as if trying to ward him off. The monk shrugged and made as if to go back to the *wat*. The American reached out to touch the monk but then jerked his hand back as if realising that it would be sacrilege to lay a hand on the holy man. Tyler said something to the monk, and the monk nodded and smiled. Tyler spoke for some considerable time, his face serious. All his body language was negative, he folded his arms across his chest, he kept turning away from the monk and twice he clasped a hand to the back of his neck which Lehman knew was a subconscious signal that Tyler was suppressing violent thoughts.

The two men moved along the bridge towards the shore. Lehman patted the sleeping Lewis on his shoulder.

"What's up?" asked Lewis, sleepily.

"He's coming back," said Lehman. "With a monk."

"A monk?"

"Yeah. A monk." Lehman got to his feet and helped Lewis up. As Tyler and the monk approached, Lehman saw that Tyler's face was red and covered in a sheen of sweat.

"Gentlemen, I'd like you to meet Chuck Doherty," said Tyler.

Lehman thought Chuck seemed a hell of a strange name for a Thai monk until he saw with astonishment that the features of the bald-headed man were Caucasian. Lehman instinctively extended his arm to shake hands but the monk ignored it; instead he bowed with the palms of his hands placed together under his chin. Lehman and Lewis copied the action, feeling slightly ridiculous.

"Chuck has something to show us," said Tyler.

"This is starting to feel like an episode of *The Twilight Zone*," Lewis whispered to Lehman as Tyler and the monk headed along a track which ran around the lake. They were soon sweating profusely and Lewis picked two large leaves from a bush to use as makeshift fans. The monk took them to the opposite side of the lake and then cut through the undergrowth where at least they could walk in the shade. The monk spoke to Tyler in Thai and Tyler shouted back to Lewis and Lehman that they should keep an eye out for snakes.

"Most of them are deadly," called Tyler.

"Terrific," growled Lewis.

They followed the track through the undergrowth until it veered to the right, at which point the monk pushed his way through broad-leaved bushes which came up to his shoulders.

"We're going in there?" said Lewis. "Ah, shit, man. What about the snakes?"

"Chuck's legs are bare, so if there was anything to worry about he wouldn't do it," said Lehman.

"Fat lot you know," said Lewis. "Man's a Buddhist, and Buddhists don't care what happens to them in this life because they know they've got a better one coming round."

"Maybe you're right," said Lehman, stamping through the vegetation, banging his feet down to scare

312

off any snakes that might be lurking there. "But how many Buddhist monks do you know who are called Chuck?"

Lewis hummed a few bars of the theme from *The Twilight Zone*. He stopped abruptly when they emerged from the bushes into a wide clearing in the centre of which was a hut made of reeds, about twenty paces by ten and about fifteen feet high. There were no windows in the structure, and as far as the men could see, no way in or out.

Lewis and Lehman walked around it while Tyler and the monk stood at the edge of the clearing, talking in quiet voices.

"No door," said Lehman.

"None that I can see," agreed Lewis. "It's like a giant box."

"I suppose you just pull out part of the wall to get inside, and rebuild it when you leave," said Lehman. "Question is, what's inside?"

"I think I know," said Lewis. "I think I know but I don't believe it."

"I think I know, too, and I don't believe it either."

Doherty began pulling away bunches of the reeds. They were attached to a framework of bamboo poles which had been bound together with straw braids and came away easily. He cleared a space about six feet square before Tyler asked Lehman and Lewis to give him a hand. They ripped handfuls of the dried reeds away from the framework and threw them on an untidy pile behind them.

"Jesus Christ," said Lewis under his breath. "Would ya look at this."

"I'm looking, Bart," said Lehman. "How the fuck did it get here?"

Standing in the framework, covered in a layer of thick dust, was a helicopter. A Huey. They were looking at it side on, the Plexiglas cockpit to their left, the tail to the right. The rear of the main rotor had been tied to the tail to stop it swinging around and bits of reed were hanging from the wire. Lehman stopped stripping away the reeds and stepped forward to peer through the Plexiglas. A family of mice had made its home in the co-pilot's seat and they scampered away in a flurry of dust. Spiders had constructed elaborate webs between the Huey's controls and the seats, and a centipede was walking nonchalantly across the top of the pilot's station. Despite the dirt and the animals, nothing appeared to be missing from the Huey, it hadn't been stripped or vandalised, and Lehman couldn't see any signs of damage that would have caused it to crash. He knelt down and looked at the skids. They had sunk a couple of inches into the ground but there was no buckling so it looked as if it had landed under control. He took a couple of steps back and examined the side of the helicopter. There were no markings, which was strange. There was no number stencilled on the tail assembly and nothing on the fuselage; it didn't even have "Navy" or "Marines" or "Army" to denote which of the services it had belonged to, and there was no insignia anywhere to be seen. He frowned and ran a hand through his hair.

314

"How the hell did it get here?" said Lehman, breathing heavily from the exertion.

"I flew it here," said Doherty, throwing an armful of reeds on to the pile.

"You?" said Lehman incredulously.

"I was a pilot. During the war." His words came slowly, as if it had been some time since he had spoken English.

"But that must have been twenty years ago!" exclaimed Lewis.

Doherty nodded. "Twenty-two," he said.

"You've been in the monastery for twenty-two years?" said Lehman.

Doherty nodded again. "That has been my privilege," he said.

"Jesus Christ," said Lewis.

"Hardly," said Doherty. "The Lord Buddha would be more appropriate." There was no trace of irony in his voice.

They cleared virtually all of the reeds away from one side to reveal the entire length of the helicopter. Lehman could see a row of bullet holes on the underside of the rear of the fuselage, but on closer examination he could see that they'd passed through the skin without doing any serious damage, certainly not enough to bring it down.

"Why are there no markings?" Lehman asked Doherty.

"It was an Air America slick," he explained. "The serial numbers have been removed, too."

"Untraceable," said Lehman.

"That was the idea," said Doherty.

Lewis pulled open the cargo door and peered inside. A small, startled bird flew out chirping loudly, tried to fly up, banged into the reed roof, and then flapped out through the side and off into the trees. Lewis climbed in.

"So what's it doing here?" asked Lehman.

Doherty didn't answer. Tyler stepped forward and put a hand on Lehman's shoulder. "The point is, Dan, do you think you can fly her?"

Lehman looked at him in amazement. "You're not serious?"

Tyler's blue eyes stared back at him. "I'm quite serious. Can you fly her?"

"If she was working, sure. But, Joel, she's been standing unused for close to a quarter of a century. She'll have rusted away to nothing. There's no way on earth she's airworthy."

Tyler smiled. "Bart, what variant of the Huey would you say this baby is?"

Lewis whistled through his teeth. He stuck his head between the two pilot seats and looked at the controls, then up at the radio. He climbed out of the cargo area and studied the turbine and the rotors. He looked at Tyler and grinned. "Yeah, I see what you mean." He looked at Lehman and smiled. "It's a UH-lE. The Marines used them for assault support, flying them off ships."

"So?" said Lehman, confused.

"The original Huey had lots of structural magnesium components," said Lewis. "It doesn't react well to

316

sea water. In fact it disintegrates quite quickly on exposure to salt and water. So when the Marines wanted their own Hueys they came up with the UH-lE. They used aluminium instead of magnesium. It's heavier, but Bell got around that problem by using a more powerful engine."

"I must be obtuse, but I don't see what that's got to do with getting it airborne."

"It won't rust, Dan," said Lewis. "It's practically corrosion-proof." He frowned and then turned back to Tyler. "But I doubt that the turbine'll still work," he said. "That's almost certain to have seized up."

"I can get us a new turbine unit," said Tyler. "That's the least of our problems."

"Transmission, too. And the tail rotor gearbox and the tail rotor intermediate gearbox. We might be lucky, but I'd feel safer knowing we had replacements."

"I can get them, too," said Tyler. "Parts aren't going to be a problem. Nor are the hydraulic fluids and the fuel. Leaving that aside, and assuming I can get us a place to work, can you make her airworthy?"

"Sure thing," said Lewis. "We used practically to take these babies apart and put them back together in the field."

"And what about you, Dan? If Bart gets her airworthy, can you fly her?"

Lehman shook his head as if he were awakening from a dream, trying to clear the growing sense of disbelief that was clouding his mind. "I guess so," he said.

"Guessing isn't good enough," said Tyler, sharply. "I need to know for certain."

Lehman nodded. "If Bart can fix her up, I can fly her," he said slowly.

"Good man," said Tyler. "That's what I wanted to hear."

"But fly it where, Joel? What is it you're planning?"

Tyler smiled. "Soon, Dan. I'll fill you in when we get to Hong Kong."

Doherty pulled the door to the pilot's station open and climbed in. He had to hitch up his robe, revealing thin, brown legs, and he wiped the seat with his hand, scraping off bits of grass and cobwebs. He looked over the instruments as if seeing them for the first time, and gently placed his hands on the controls.

"How did you know it was here?" Lehman asked Tyler.

"Josh told me about it," said Tyler. "He comes up here a couple of times a year for girls. Buying trips, you might say. He takes young girls from the farms and gives them jobs in his bar. They can earn more there in six months than in twenty years on a farm. He told me that he'd heard about a *farang* who'd arrived with a helicopter and become a monk. It sounded crazy, but I asked him to make a few discreet enquiries."

"Had you seen the helicopter before?"

Tyler shook his head. "No. But Josh had a look at it. He's not an expert but he told me enough to make me think that we could use it. Think about it, Dan! It's practically untraceable. Like Doherty said, it was an Air America slick, they'd have used it for all sorts of covert missions into Cambodia, Laos, Thailand. The spooks will have removed any identifying marks that could link it with the American forces. If we use it, nobody'll have a clue where it came from."

"You said you could get parts for it. How come?" Doherty was playing with the controls, a faraway look in his eyes. Lewis had gone to the rear of the helicopter and was checking the tail assembly.

"There are many South-East Asian armies using the Huey these days," said Tyler. "They were one of the few American successes during the war. The Philippine army, for instance, has almost a hundred. Money talks, the parts walk. It's as easy as that. I've got contacts in the Philippines, and so has Josh."

"You seem to have contacts everywhere," said Lehman.

"Everywhere that counts," said Tyler.

"And how do you plan to get this baby to Hong Kong?"

"Josh will take care of it for us. He'll drive it down in a container, one of the big things they load on to ships. We'll have to take off the rotor and the skids, but most of it should go in in one piece. They're easy to strip down, anyway. It won't be a problem. The container will be labelled as containing machine parts and Josh'll bribe the Customs people both ends, in Thailand and in Hong Kong. It'll take two weeks, max."

"How big will this container be?" asked Lewis.

"I think they're a standard size, Bart, something like forty feet long, eight feet wide, eight feet six inches high. But don't hold me to that, we'll check with Josh. Why, is there a problem?"

"The Hueys were all about forty feet long. The UH-lD was forty-one feet six inches, the early UH-lEs were based on the UH-lB and the later ones on the UH-lC. The Bs were just over thirty-eight feet long; I'm not sure about the Cs."

"So if it's longer than forty feet it won't fit?" said Lehman.

"It'll fit, but we'll have to take the tail off," said Lewis.

"You can do that?" asked Tyler.

"Anyone can," said Lewis. He went to the portion of the tail behind the cabin and unlatched a panel. He waved Tyler over and pointed inside. "There are four bolts, here, here, here and here," he said. "Unscrew them and the whole assembly comes off. If you can get new replacements it'd be better."

He took a few steps back. "It's too tall to fit in as it is, so the rotor mast will have to come out. You'll have to take the rotors off anyway, and then it's just four bolts to slip the rotor itself out. And you'll probably have to remove the skids. Then the Huey can be lifted right off. You can use the rescue hoist mounted in the roof. One thing: you mustn't put it flat on the ground without the skids or you'll damage the gear on the bottom. You'll have to design some sort of trolley which supports the cab at the same point as the skids. You could put it on small wheels so that the fuselage will slide in and out of the container." He looked at Tyler, his eyes bright with enthusiasm. "But it'll fit, all right."

Tyler clapped him on the back.

"And Josh can have the container shipped straight through to Hong Kong," said Lehman. "It's that easy?"

"It's not easy, but it happens all the time," said Tyler. "Hong Kong is a major clearing centre for a good percentage of the heroin from the Golden Triangle, and most of it goes by sea. Arms, too. You'd be amazed at how many weapons go through Hong Kong's ports, and most of them are described as heavy machinery or spare parts. It's just a matter of knowing who to bribe and how much. This is Asia, remember, and bribery and corruption are a way of life here. When somebody gets caught smuggling it's usually because they haven't greased the right palms, not because of smart detective work on the part of the authorities."

Lehman nodded thoughtfully. "You've obviously got it all thought out," he said.

"That's the key to a successful operation, Dan. Planning. Taking care of all contingencies. Thinking ahead. I promise you, I've pre-planned every step of this mission. Nothing can go wrong."

Doherty had put on the flight helmet and was looking up at the radio switches. Lewis finished his inspection of the Huey and walked over to join Tyler and Lehman, wiping his big hands on his trousers. "It's going to work," he said. "I'm sure it's going to work." His enthusiasm for the project was obvious.

"Good," said Tyler. "When we get back to Bangkok you can write out a full set of instructions for Josh and his men. They'll do all the work."

"But what about the mad monk?" asked Lehman, nodding towards Doherty.

Tyler's eyes narrowed. "He wants to come back with us," he said quietly.

"Say what?" said Lehman.

"He says he wants to come with us. To Hong Kong. He wants to be part of it."

Lehman turned to face Tyler. "Let me get this straight," he said. "This guy is a spook pilot with Air America. He flies his slick to Thailand, builds a hut around it and joins a monastery. He shaves his head, goes native for twenty years, and yet within minutes of meeting you he wants to sign up for the robbery of the century. Are we supposed to buy that?"

Tyler shrugged. "I'm as surprised as you are, Dan. It wasn't my intention to have him along. I knew about the helicopter, that was all. Josh told me Doherty had become a Buddhist and I figured that I could persuade him to part with the Huey. He's in the country illegally so I was sure he wouldn't take too much convincing. He agreed to let us take it, but he insists that he comes along."

"Why? Why would he give up what he's spent more than twenty years achieving?"

"Part of it is that he feels he's gone as far as he can within the community here. Despite their willingness to accept him as a novice, they never let him forget that he is a *farang*. He has always been an outsider, and I think that seeing me brought that home to him. I was the first non-Thai he had spoken to since he arrived here. But there's more to it than that. I think he's frightened that others will trace him here. If we found him, others could, so this place is no longer a sanctuary for him.

And I think he realised that if we could get his Huey out of the country, we could do the same for him. He doesn't have any papers, you see. No passport. No visa. Nothing. He's been pretty much a prisoner in Thailand."

"Can you do that?" asked Lehman. "Can you get him out?"

"Oh sure. Josh can fix him up with all the papers he needs, good enough to pass muster anywhere in the world. He can probably get him a Social Security number as well. He can have a whole new identity, and with that he can go back to the States."

"That's what he wants? To go back?"

"I think he's confused," said Tyler. "I don't think he knows what he wants. But the one thing he's sure of is that he wants to be part of what we're doing."

Lehman shook his head in bewilderment. "It doesn't make sense," he said. "He's a monk. Monks don't steal."

"He's confused," said Tyler. "Besides, he's so unstable it'd probably be a good idea to have him in Hong Kong where we can keep an eye on him. God knows who he'll tell if we leave him here."

"That's a good point," said Lewis.

"I guess so," agreed Lehman. The three men watched Doherty play with the controls like a kid in an amusement arcade.

"And if it doesn't work out, we can always kill him," said Tyler. Lehman jerked his head round, his mouth open. Tyler held up his hands. "Just joking," he said. "Honest."

The Thai Airways Airbus seemed reluctant to descend into the thick white clouds which obscured Hong Kong and the South China Sea some 10,000 feet below. It was as if the pilot didn't quite believe his instruments, but eventually the nose dipped down and, like a timid swimmer who has decided to jump in and get it over with at once, the plane swooped down towards the ground. Lehman leaned his forehead against the window and peered into the white nothingness, unconsciously counting off the seconds. It was impossible to tell if he were looking a hundred yards or just a few inches, there was no depth or substance to the cloud.

The plane vibrated and shuddered and they felt it bank to the right and then suddenly they were out of the cloud and Horvitz breathed deeply and grinned across at Lehman. The grin vanished when he saw a tower block swing past the left-hand wing, not more than a hundred feet below.

"Jesus H. Christ," he said. "Did you see that?"

"The television programme they were watching, you mean?" laughed Lehman. "Yeah, I saw it. And the dinner on the table."

A metal hook banged down in the gap between their seats and Carmody's face followed it.

"Is it always as hairy as this?" he asked.

"It only looks hairy," said Lehman. "It's one of the most difficult approaches in the world, but because it's tough the pilots take more care. They hardly ever have an accident."

"You've been to Hong Kong before?" asked Horvitz.

"Sure," he answered. "I came for R&R in the mid-seventies and I've been here as a tourist twice, in 1982 and again in '86, I think. Before they opened Vietnam up."

The plane levelled out and then they saw a flash of water and then they were down, rumbling along the single finger of runway which pointed out into the bustling harbour. Horvitz could see fishermen throwing out what looked like lobster pots from a trio of tiny dinghies and a motorised junk with its deck piled high with wooden crates bobbing in the waves and making next to no progress. Hong Kong Island was virtually obscured in a thick, cloying mist which had rolled down from the Peak, though he could make out indistinct shapes of exotic skyscrapers like some hastily done watercolour. The plane turned around through 180 degrees and headed back to the terminal building while a stewardess welcomed them all to Hong Kong in English, Thai and Cantonese over the intercom and said she hoped that they'd fly with her again.

The four vets were through immigration and Customs within twenty minutes and they queued together at the taxi rank. Tyler, who had remained in Bangkok with Doherty, had booked them into the Eastin Valley Hotel on Hong Kong Island but had warned them that most taxi drivers probably wouldn't know its English name so he'd given them all a card with its name and address in Chinese. On the back of the card was a map which showed where it was and they'd all commented on its proximity to the Happy

Valley Race Course and its distance from the harbour. It was clear they wouldn't be able to get all four of their suitcases into one of the red and grey Toyota cabs so they took two, Horvitz and Carmody travelling in one, and Lewis and Lehman in another. Both taxis were soon in thick traffic and driving through the built-up areas of Kowloon. Neither cab had the air conditioner switched on and all four were sweating profusely. To Lehman it seemed that every breath was an effort, almost as if he were breathing underwater. He tapped the driver on the shoulder and asked him to switch on the air conditioning. The driver laughed at his discomfort and did as asked while Lehman and Lewis wound up the windows. The interior of the cab was soon almost chilly and both men could feel the sweat drying on their skin.

"You tourists?" the driver asked, looking at them in the mirror.

"Yeah," said Lewis.

"You Americans?"

Lewis nodded.

The driver laughed. "I have two cousins in America," he said. "In San Francisco. Good country. Maybe I go one day." He slammed on the brakes and narrowly missed crashing into the rear of a truck loaded with baskets of green vegetables. In the back of the lorry sat two young men whose bare chests were covered in brightly coloured tattoos of roaring tigers and fire-breathing dragons. They grinned good-naturedly at the taxi driver and made obscene gestures.

"Triads!" said the driver contemptuously.

"How do you know?" asked Lewis.

"Can tell," he answered. "The tattoos. Only triads have tattoos like that."

The traffic moved slowly through ugly high-rise industrial buildings and after thirty minutes they reached the toll gates for the Cross Harbour Tunnel. The driver thrust a green note into the hands of a young girl in a black and white uniform and a white filter mask hiding the bottom of her face and then drove down the double-track road that led to Hong Kong Island. In the distance Lehman and Lewis could see the taxi containing the two other vets.

They emerged into the open air on the island among high-rise blocks that were several times higher than those in Kowloon and whose shapes seemed more imaginative than the boring cubes that were stacked around the airport district. There were tall, thin spires, towering oblongs with circular windows, mirrored blocks in blue, silver and bronze, buildings with hard edges, others with curves, each different from its neighbour as if the architects had been in some sort of competition. They had plenty of time to look at their surroundings as the taxi had to slow to a crawl to negotiate a series of roadworks. Young men without ear-protectors were drilling away at the tarmac while others attacked it with pickaxes. Like the men in the back of the vegetable truck, many were bare-chested to reveal their tattoos. The taxi was suddenly filled with a foul odour and both men looked at each other.

Lewis raised a hand. "Hey man, it's not me!" he protested.

"Well it's not me either!" said Lehman.

Both men looked at the driver. He grinned at them in the mirror, showing the glint of a gold front tooth. "Smell from typhoon shelter," he said. "Many people live there on boats. Much shit!" He cackled and swerved to avoid an old man on a bicycle.

Lehman and Lewis grimaced and tried to breathe through their mouths until they were away from the junk-filled shelter and its offensive odours. Eventually both taxis turned away from the harbour and the roads grew narrower and more crowded, with housewives and delivery men spilling off the sidewalks and wandering in between the traffic without looking where they were going. Their driver pounded on his horn and on his brake pedal with increasing regularity, cursing good-humouredly. They went around a bend and then, on the left, they saw a huge multi-tiered grandstand facing away from them. Around what appeared to be a group of soccer and rugby fields were powerful floodlights atop spindly metal poles.

"Soccer?" asked Lewis.

"No, it's the racetrack," said Lehman, craning his neck to get a better look. There was a line of black letters set in the wall above the entrance announcing "The Royal Hong Kong Jockey Club" and he saw that there were two tracks running around the playing fields, the inner one of sand and the outer of grass. Around the racecourse was a haphazard forest of residential tower blocks, each appearing to be trying to peer over the shoulder of its neighbour to get a better view of the track below.

Ahead of them they watched the first taxi turn right and followed it. It turned right again, then stopped outside the hotel. Horvitz and Carmody got out of the first cab and waved at Lewis and Lehman before paying their driver and manhandling their suitcases into the lobby. Lewis and Lehman followed them. They checked in and two young bellboys in smart white uniforms helped them take their bags upstairs. Tyler had booked them all on to one floor, the eighteenth.

Lehman tipped the bellboy and closed the door behind him. It was a large, comfortable room with a king-size bed, a marble-topped desk by one window, a small sofa and two small side tables by a second window. A neat dressing table with a padded seat faced a large wall-mounted mirror. A large wooden cabinet housed a television and a mini-bar, and behind sliding louvred doors he found a closet and small safe. He opened the door to the bathroom and smiled at the telephone on the wall next to the toilet. It would be a pleasant enough place to stay for a while; Tyler hadn't scrimped, that was for sure. As Lehman suspected, there wasn't much of a view. His room overlooked a steep wooded hill at the bottom of which was an untidy line of old buildings, each between three or five storeys high and peppered with air-conditioning units. The roofs of the buildings had all been put to use: several had been packed with pots of tall green plants, one was used as a child's play area with a swing and a red and blue plastic slide, others had been turned into pleasant sitting areas with seats and large, spreading umbrellas.

He leaned closer to the window and far over to the right he could see half of the racetrack.

The phone rang and he picked it up. "Yes?" he said.

"Dan? That you?" It was Lewis.

"Yeah, it's me. What's up?"

"Man, can you believe this place? My room is fantastic. You see the size of that bed? Have you ever seen a bed as big as that? I've never been in a place like this before. It's just mind-blowing."

Lehman smiled at the man's open enthusiasm. "Yeah, it's great," he said, not wanting to burst his optimistic bubble.

"And what about the phones? Two phones. And one of them in the john."

"Yeah, ain't that something," said Lehman. "Look, why don't you ring around the rest of the guys and tell them to meet downstairs in an hour. We'll go out and get some food, maybe hit a few bars later on. That sound good?"

"Sounds great to me, man."

When the vets met in the lobby, nobody had any idea where they should go. Lehman was the only one who'd been to Hong Kong before so they all looked to him for guidance.

"Come on, guys, it's been almost ten years since I was here."

"Yeah, yeah, yeah. Come on, Dan," chided Lewis.

"Yeah, you must know where the action is," said Carmody.

"Okay, okay. Let me think," laughed Lehman. "The red light area was Wan Chai, and I guess it still is. And

330

there were some pretty good places over the harbour in Kowloon. It all depends on what you guys wanna do. I mean, do you want to eat, drink, have a massage, see a movie?"

"Or E, all of the above," said Carmody.

"A drink would be a good start," said Lewis.

"What about you, Eric?" Lehman asked Horvitz who had barely said a word since they'd arrived in Hong Kong.

"A drink's fine by me," said Horvitz. He'd tied his long hair back in a ponytail but it didn't make him look at all feminine.

"McDonald's," said Carmody. "I feel a Big Mac attack coming on."

"McDonald's?" repeated Lehman. "You're in the food capital of the world and you want a burger?"

"Not just a burger," said Carmody. "A Big Mac."

"Sounds good to me," said Horvitz. Lewis shrugged his shoulders as if to say he didn't care.

"I don't believe it," said Lehman, shaking his head.

"Come on, Dan. Don't tell me you're not fed up with all this noodle and rice crap. Think about a nice, thick, juicy burger with all the trimmings," said Carmody.

"And French fries," said Horvitz.

"And a thick strawberry milkshake," said Carmody.

"I give in," said Lehman. They went outside the hotel and flagged down a cab.

"Where you want to go?" the driver asked, chewing a toothpick.

"McDonald's," said Lehman who had taken the seat next to the driver while the other three crammed in the back.

"Americans?" said the driver as he slammed the cab into gear and roared off.

"How did you guess?" asked Lehman. Behind him he heard three sniggers.

The driver dropped them off outside the familiar Golden Arches. The only difference between it and any of the thousands back in the States were the Chinese characters up on the sign next to McDonald's. There was even a life-size Ronald McDonald standing to the left of the entrance. They walked up together to the counter and waited until it was their turn to be served.

Lehman had a cheeseburger and white coffee, Carmody ordered two Big Macs, a large fries, a chocolate sundae and a strawberry milk shake, Lewis had a regular burger, fries and Coke and Horvitz asked for a double cheese-burger and black coffee.

They paid for their order and carried it over to a table. "Ketchup," said Carmody. "We forgot the ketchup." He went back to the counter and came back with three packets of red sauce. He ripped one open and dribbled it over his fries, picked up one of his Big Macs and took a big bite. He chewed and rolled his eyes. "Home," he sighed.

"Oh God," moaned Lehman, not sure whether or not Carmody was being serious. But after he'd taken a few bites of his cheeseburger he had to admit, albeit reluctantly, that he had missed junk food all the time they'd been in Vietnam and Thailand. Rice and noodles were all well and good, but there came a time when a man needed to get his teeth around a good old all-American burger. Lewis didn't seem to feel the same way. He left most of his.

When they'd finished eating they walked to the Star Ferry Terminal and caught a green and white ferry across the harbour to Kowloon. They sat at the back of the ferry and watched the sky darken over the towering office blocks of the island, turning the hills behind them from green to purple. Lights were coming on in most of the blocks, the sign of office workers staying late. The city that never sleeps, thought Lehman.

Before the ferry docked at the Tsim Sha Tsui terminal housewives and businessmen got up from their seats and stood impatiently by the gangway while the ferry's ropemen helped manoeuvre the ferry against the dock.

"They're always in such a hurry," said Carmody. "Why is that?"

"Borrowed place, borrowed time," said Lehman. "This whole place gets given back to China in 1997. Everyone's just trying to pack in as much as they can before the communists take over. Remember what the communists did to Saigon? Think what they'll do to Hong Kong."

"You think it'll go that way?" asked Lewis.

"Hell, Bart. I know nothing about it, just what I read in the papers back home. But I do know that tens of thousands are leaving every year, just like it was before the Americans pulled out of Vietnam. You don't get panic like that unless there's something in the wind."

They stood up and walked across the gangplank and up a concrete slope to the outside. The first thing they saw as they walked out of the terminal was another McDonald's outlet. The shops of Tsim Sha Tsui were all still open, despite it being after 8.30p.m., and the Americans had to weave their way through the crowds. It wasn't just tourists who were wandering around, there were Chinese families out for a promenade, grandparents, parents and young children walking and talking, stopping to stand and stare as if window-shopping was a hobby the whole family could enjoy.

"Where are we going, Dan?" asked Lewis, dodging a girl pretty enough to be a fashion model who was talking into a portable telephone and checking out the display of a jewellery shop as she walked, seemingly on autopilot.

"A surprise," said Lehman.

He led them past the Peninsular Hotel and its display of green Rolls-Royces, and then turned left into Nathan Road and threaded his way through side-streets, looking for landmarks that would let him know he was heading in the right direction. He took a couple of wrong turns, fooled by the fact that the streets were all so similar, lined with shops selling high fashion, others touting cheap T-shirts, some selling gold jewellery and precious gems, others offering cheap watches, windows full of jade and coral, others full of colourful plastic earrings and brassy hairclips, and everywhere the eagle-eyed salesmen in sharp suits standing in their doorways trying to tempt them inside.

There were restaurants, too, of every nationality: Chinese, Thai, Indian, Vietnamese, Western, Singaporean, Korean — a bigger variety than Lehman had ever seen together in one place before. Even the gaps between the buildings had been put to use, with shoeshine boys squatting beside the tools of their trade and hawkers behind trolleys covered in red cloth on which were spread out gold-plated jewellery, digital watches and key-rings that buzzed when you whistled at them. Above the shops were the metal-framed windows of apartments, scattered with air conditioners supported by rusting metal stands. Between the apartment windows and the ranks of shiny shops were jungles of colourful signs that reached halfway across the roads below, signs that seemed almost to defy gravity in their attempts to draw attention to themselves. The Star Gem Company. Khyber Indian Cuisine (Members Only). KO's Jewellery. Bob Tailor. Tuxedos For Hire And Sale. And then he saw the one he was looking for: a sign in the shape of a pair of pouting red lips with white lettering which announced "Red Lips Bar". He pointed at the sign and urged the group across the road along which crawled taxis full of businessmen, cream and green minibuses loaded with schoolchildren and housewives, and tour coaches packed with holidaymakers heading back to their hotels. In among the traffic, bare-chested youths manhandled cardboard boxes from wooden-sided trucks into the shops, their tattoos writhing on their backs as if alive. The traffic had been slowed by construction which had been surrounded by yellow-painted metal barriers and red and white plastic cones. There were piles of earth, broken tarmac and exposed cables, but there was nobody working in the hole.

"Red Lips Bar?" said Lewis. "What den of iniquity is this you're taking us to, Dan?"

"I think you'll like it," said Lehman, ducking into a dark alley. The entrance to the bar was a hole in the wall guarded by a frumpy Chinese woman of indeterminate age wearing a jet black wig which seemed to have slipped on her head. She had on thick black mascara and too-red lipstick which overlapped the edge of her lips and gave her a clown-like smile.

"Welcome to Red Lips," she said in accented English.

"You have got to be joking," grinned Lewis. "You have really got to be joking." He stood with his hands on his hips and looked around the bar, with its scratched and stained tables, dimly lit cubicles and smoke-stained ceiling, and at the women in ill-fitting evening dresses, none of whom could have been under fifty years old. The Rolling Stones were on the jukebox. "Paint it Black." It was the same record that had been playing in the bar Tyler had taken them to in Bangkok, and Lehman took it as a good omen. The record was scratched and the sound was down low enough so that they could hear the conversation from the only booth that was occupied in the bar, where two Australians with bottles of Fosters lager were arguing over who got the best deal on their cameras. They looked up almost guiltily as they became aware of the new arrivals, as if they were ashamed of being caught in such a dive. They were accompanied at the table by two women who must have been in their sixties, one with grey frizzy hair and a face that was criss-crossed with wrinkles and the other with hair so black that it could only have been dyed. They were listening attentively to the Australians and sipping from small glasses. From where he was standing Lehman could see that one of the women, the one with grey hair, had her hand on her tourist's thigh where a gnarled nail slowly scratched the material of his jeans. Lehman felt he could hear the coarse scratching sound all the way across the bar.

"Sit here, sit here," said an emaciated woman in a purple dress speckled with silver threads which draped around her thin frame as if it were still on a hanger. She fastened her bony fingers around Lehman's forearm and it felt like the touch of a skeleton. Her eyes were deep-set and there were thick lines around either side of her mouth as if it were set amid two fleshy parentheses. When her lips drew back in a parody of a smile, they revealed that the two front teeth at the top of her mouth were gold. "Sit, sit," she repeated and Lehman felt the talons tighten on his arm. A chubby woman with shoulder-length hair wearing a scarlet dress with a high neck and puffed-up sleeves attached herself to Carmody's arm and began edging him towards a booth like a collie rounding up a stray sheep.

"What the hell is this place?" asked Lewis.

"Like the lady said, it's the Red Lips Bar," replied Lehman. "It was one of the R&R hangouts during the war, but this one never changed. They never decorated

337

and they claim that it's the original bargirls still working here."

The skeleton on his arm nodded enthusiastically. "Yes, yes. Same bar. Red Lips never change. You American, yes? I think I remember you, GI. What your name?"

Lewis and Carmody laughed and even Horvitz managed a rueful smile. "She says that to all the guys," said Lehman. "I never came here during my time in Nam, but a friend brought me here ten years ago or so. It certainly hasn't changed since then. But I don't recognise this woman, I swear to God." He put his hand over his heart and raised his demonic eyebrows but Lewis and Carmody continued to taunt him as the aged bargirls nudged them into the booth. There was enough room to fit two of the Americans either side with a woman between them, and two more pulled up stools and sat at the end of the table, blocking their escape route. The Stones finished "Paint It Black" and Leonard Cohen took their place with a mournful dirge which Lehman didn't recognise.

A woman who was even older than the bargirls came over and took their order. Lewis asked what the local beer was and she said San Miguel and they decided they'd all try it. The old woman shuffled off to the bar and came back with four cans and four glasses which looked as if they'd been in service for at least twenty-five years. The four women sitting with the Americans dutifully poured the beers and watched as the men drank.

338

"It's good," said Carmody, putting his half-empty glass back on the table where a round-faced woman with more than a hint of a moustache and spectacles with thick lenses refilled it for him.

"You buy girls a drink?" the old woman asked, flashing them a gummy smile. She could have been anywhere between seventy and a hundred years old, with a high forehead and lifeless hair that had been combed straight back as if she'd been riding a motorcycle without a helmet. Her wrinkled skin was peppered with brown patches and her hands were so clawed with arthritis that she'd had difficulty putting the cans of beer on the table.

"Girls?" shouted Carmody. "Where?" The old woman glared at him and muttered something in Cantonese.

"Yeah, why not," said Lewis. "Bring the little ladies some refreshment."

The old woman beamed and nodded and whizzed off to the bar as if on wheels. When she came back she was carrying four glasses on the tray, each containing an inch of brown liquid. She began to put them on the table with trembling hands. Carmody reached over and picked one up with his claw and held it under his nose. He sniffed. "It's tea," he said.

"Of course it's tea," said Lewis. "You know the way it works. That's how they make their money."

"Just once I'd like to see one of these bitches have a real drink," said Carmody.

"Come on, Larry, it's just a way of buying their time, you know that. They've got to live. And it's not as if their drinks are expensive," said Lehman.

Carmody laughed. "Yeah, and it's not as if we can't afford it, is it? Not with the money we're going to get, huh?"

"I'll drink to that, all right," said Lewis, raising his glass. Lehman, Horvitz and Carmody did the same and they clinked glasses above the centre of the table. It was the first time any of them had mentioned the reason why they were in Hong Kong. There had been an unspoken agreement that the subject wouldn't be raised until Tyler had rejoined the group. Before they'd left Thailand, Tyler had told Lehman and Lewis not to mention Doherty or the Huey. Lehman had assumed that Tyler had revealed to the other three as little about the forthcoming operation as he himself had been told: that it was a robbery, that it was a big one, and that it was to be in Hong Kong. He didn't even know what sort of money they'd been promised. Lehman had given a great deal of thought to what the mission might be, but he couldn't think of any way in which their four individual skills could be used. One helicopter pilot, a helicopter mechanic, a doorgunner, and a Special Forces killer. It was a potentially dangerous team, but Tyler had promised that nobody would get hurt.

His thoughts were interrupted by a bony finger running down his spine. He turned to look at the cadaverous woman sitting on his right. She smiled at him. "You want massage?" she asked in a voice as dry as a death rattle. His mouth fell open as a horrific image of being given a rub down by the old crone flashed through his mind.

340

"Oh no," he said. "Oh no. I couldn't. I mean, it's a very tempting offer, but no. No thanks." Carmody giggled and urged him to take advantage of the woman's offer. "Carmody, you can be a real pain sometimes," said Lehman.

"Yeah?" replied Carmody, the smile vanishing from his face. "You wanna do something about it, Danny Boy?"

Lehman could tell from Carmody's tone that he wasn't joking.

"Don't be so fucking touchy, Larry," said Lewis, moving quickly to defuse the situation. Lehman was sure he could handle the man if they came to blows, but he had no wish to get into a fight. He was grateful for Lewis's intervention because he had no intention of backing down. He'd met enough characters like Carmody to know that if he didn't stand up to him then he'd keep pushing him into a corner and that sooner or later they'd be trading punches anyway.

Carmody looked at Lewis, and then at Lehman. Lewis poured more beer for Carmody and gestured at the glass. Carmody's smile returned and he shrugged. "No offence," he said to Lehman.

"None taken," said Lehman, and he clinked his glass against Carmody's. Lewis looked at both men as if to confirm that they'd both cooled down and then announced he was going to the toilet. He winced as if in pain when he stood up. One of the women sitting on the stools swung her legs to the side to make way for him.

Carmody did his cigarette lighting trick with his claw and the women watched, entranced. They took it in turns to stroke the shiny metal and discussed it in Cantonese with much nodding and face-pulling.

Horvitz was as quiet as usual and as Carmody amused the women, he sat with a faraway look in his eyes. His hand gripped his glass tightly and Lehman could see the muscles in his arm tightening up. His left eyelid began twitching, a barely noticeable flicker as if he were subconsciously fighting to control it. Lehman wondered what was going through his mind.

"You okay, Eric?" asked Lehman.

Horvitz didn't react so Lehman spoke to him again. This time Horvitz's eyes seemed to refocus as if he were awakening from a dream, and he relaxed the grip on his glass. The muscle in his eyelid continued to twitch, however.

"Sorry," he said to Lehman. "What did you say? I was miles away."

"I asked if you were okay, that's all."

"Oh sure. This is one hell of a bar."

"Brings back memories?"

"Not really, no. I was never much one for Rape and Run. I only took R&R when the medics insisted."

"Insisted?"

"Stress, they said. Combat fatigue, that sort of crap. They didn't know what the fuck they were talking about. The nearest they ever got to a bullet was holding one with a pair of forceps. Stress is what keeps you on your toes. Keeps you alive. Take away the stress and you're nothing. You've just got to wait until your body adapts to it, until it accepts that the stress is normal. Necessary even." The twitching intensified and then suddenly stopped as if Horvitz had become aware of it and had, by an effort of will, put a stop to it.

Lehman nodded, but he didn't agree with what Horvitz had said. Continual stress was totally destructive, and he had no doubt that that was why Horvitz was as tense as he was now. It was the first time he'd seen Horvitz like that; before he'd always appeared calm and relaxed. Lehman could only imagine the inner tension that had gripped the man. Carmody wore his heart on his sleeve and his flashes of temper were just that, quick outbursts that disappeared as quickly as they flared, but Horvitz was always so tightly controlled that when he exploded it would be devastating.

"When they eventually forced me to take a break, I stayed in Nam. Hung around the beaches, went swimming, stuff like that. Never much cared for the bars or what went on there. Never seemed real, not after the jungle. Nothing has seemed real since. You know, sometimes I think that I died back in Nam and that everything since has been some sort of dream. Or a nightmare."

"That's why you went back?"

Horvitz shrugged and took a drink from his glass. "It wasn't my idea. A guy from the US-Indochina Reconciliation Project in Philadelphia got me on the trip. Paid for the whole thing. Some sort of project they've got going to help vets with PTSD."

"PTSD?"

343

"Post Traumatic Stress Disorder, which I guess is just a fancy shrink's term for combat fatigue. They reckoned that by going back I'd maybe come to terms with it. With what happened."

"Do you think it worked?"

Horvitz looked at Lehman, his stare even and empty. "Too much happened to me back there, Dan. I think about Vietnam every day of my life. Every hour. Too much happened for me ever to forget."

"No one's saying forget. Just accept."

Horvitz smiled grimly. "The things I did aren't the sort of things a man can ever accept. Not if he wants to stay sane. It's safer just to pretend that they happened to someone else. A twenty-year-old kid who didn't know any better."

"Maybe you should try sharing it with someone."

"You, Dan? You wanna share some of my memories? You wanna go rooting around in the black bits of my mind and see what I've got hidden there?" Horvitz dismissed Lehman's offer with a snort and took another pull on his beer.

They drank for a while, listening to the songs that crackled out of the antiquated stereo system, all of them from the late sixties and early seventies. The Rolling Stones. The Doors. Leonard Cohen. Each and every one brought back memories for Lehman as if the music offered a direct line into his subconscious. He kept recalling faces of men who were long dead, places he'd been, missions he'd flown, until the bar faded away and he was back in his Huey flying low and fast over the jungles of South Vietnam, the roar of the turbine filling his ears, the fear and excitement turning his bowels to liquid, feeling more alive than he'd ever felt before. Music often had that effect on him, wiping away the years the way a sponge removes dirt, leaving only streaks behind. Smells worked the same way, too. The sweet smell of pot always took him back to the Nam, as did hot oil fumes and shit. And burnt meat. Burnt meat was the worst.

Often an odour seemed to be even more effective than music in stimulating his memory, catching him unawares with its force. There was a logic to the memories that flooded back with the songs of the sixties and the seventies but the smells often took him by surprise. He'd drive into a filling station and open his hood and the oil fumes would billow out and he'd be standing next to his Huey with George Lambert, his crew chief for six months until his face had been blown apart by a sniper's bullet. Lambert had been holding a monkey wrench, his hands caked in grease which he'd also managed to smear across his left cheek, and he'd been laughing with Lehman about God knows what when his face had exploded in a shower of crimson blood and white bone fragments. Lehman didn't remember hearing the crack of the bullet but he'd never forgotten the feel of the wet blood on his own face and how it had felt gritty and sticky as he instinctively reached up to wipe it off. Lambert hadn't died immediately because the bullet hadn't gone through the skull. It had just taken away most of his left cheek and he hadn't been able to talk or even scream, he'd just thrashed around a lot and thrown what was left of his head from side to side as Lehman had held him in his arms, screaming for a medic but knowing that there was nothing that could be done. All it took was the smell of oil, and it all came back.

Lehman blinked and looked up, realising that Carmody had spoken to him.

"Say what?" said Lehman.

"I said, do you wanna drink?" Carmody repeated.

"Sure," said Lehman. The glass in his hand was empty, but he didn't recall finishing his beer.

"Should I get Bart one, too?"

Lewis's glass was half full where he'd left it before going to the toilet. It had been almost fifteen minutes since he'd left the table.

"Yeah, I would," said Lehman, getting up. "I'll go see if he's okay."

"Maybe old Bart can't hold his booze," laughed Carmody. "He's certainly not keeping up with us."

Lehman went through the bamboo curtain that led to the toilets, and pushed open the swing door that had a small figure of a man on it. There was nobody at the urinals and for a moment Lehman thought that Lewis had gone back to the hotel, but then he saw that the door to one of the stalls was shut, but not locked. He went over to it and stood by the side. He bent down and could see the soles of Lewis's shoes. The man was obviously kneeling in front of the bowl, and as Lehman listened he could hear retching sounds.

"Bart, you okay?" he called.

346

He heard Lewis clear his throat and spit, and then the toilet flushed. Lewis began to get to his feet but he groaned and threw up again.

"Bart?" repeated Lehman.

"I'm okay, I'm okay," Lewis said, spitting again.

There was a scuffling noise and then the door to the stall opened and Lewis came out, wiping his mouth with the back of his hand. "That burger didn't agree with me," said Lewis, grinning sheepishly at Lehman. "Or maybe I drank too much beer. I was just throwing up, that's all."

"Yeah?" said Lehman. "Maybe you should take a look in the mirror."

"What do you mean?" asked Lewis. He turned to look at his reflection in the ageing mirror which was screwed above the wash-basins. His lips were red with blood. Lehman pushed open the door of the stall where Lewis had been sick and he lifted the black plastic lid of the toilet. The water there had turned red.

"What the hell's going on, Bart?" asked Lehman. "Are you sick, or something?"

"I've just thrown up, that's all," said Lewis, turning on the cold tap and splashing water on his face. It streaked redly down his chin.

"Bullshit," said Lehman. "You don't throw up blood just because you've had a bad burger. Have you seen a doctor?"

Lewis looked up and studied Lehman in the mirror. "Just forget it, Dan, all right?"

"Does Tyler know about this?"

Lewis shook the water off his hands and turned round to face Lehman.

"This is none of your business," he warned.

"Bart, you're sick. You need help."

Lewis threw back his head and laughed. "You're telling me," he said, his voice bitter.

Lehman walked up to Lewis and put his hands on the black man's wide shoulders. "How sick are you?" Lehman asked. He felt the big man's shoulders shrug.

"The big C," said Lewis.

"Oh Christ," said Lehman.

"Yeah. Oh Christ," agreed Lewis.

"What sort of cancer?" asked Lehman.

"You know that sort that they can treat with chemotherapy?" said Lewis. Lehman nodded. "Well it's not that one," said Lewis. He laughed and then his laugh turned to a wince and he put his hands on his stomach. "Get outta my way," he groaned and rushed back to the toilet. He leant over and retched again, his hands against the wall as if preparing to be frisked.

Lehman stood by the mirror feeling quite helpless and intensely sorry for Lewis. He really liked the man. When Lewis returned to the wash-basins and cleaned himself up again, Lehman asked if there was anything he could do to help.

Lewis shook his head. "It's in my stomach and my pancreas, and God only knows where else," he said. "They can't operate and it's too far gone for chemotherapy or radiation treatment. It's my own fault, I guess. For months I thought I just had a bad stomach, you know? I used to take stuff to settle my stomach

348

every morning, and I was swallowing painkillers like M&Ms. If I'd gone to the docs five years ago, then maybe they could have done something. Maybe. But not now."

"Do they have any idea how you got it, Bart? Smoking?"

Lewis grimaced as if the thought was painful. "Agent Orange. That's what I reckon."

"Agent Orange? You mean you got it in Nam?" Lehman sounded horrified.

"I used to use the stuff to keep the perimeter of our firebase clear of vegetation. We used to spray the stuff everywhere, no masks or gloves or nothing. It had no smell, there was no irritation or nothing. No one ever told us it was dangerous."

"And it gave you cancer?"

"That's what I think. But it's damn near impossible to prove. I went to the VA back in Baltimore but they don't think I stand much chance of getting compensation out of the government. I wasn't part of any deforestation programme, we just used it now and again as a weedkiller. It's not as if it says I used Agent Orange on my service record, or anything like that. The only way I'll get compensation is if I take them to court."

"Couldn't you get a lawyer to take on your case on a percentage basis?"

"Oh sure. But it takes time. And time is something I don't have much of right now."

Lehman nodded and then suddenly realised the implications of what Lewis was saying. "Oh shit, Bart. How long have you got?"

Lewis shrugged and rubbed the back of his neck. "Months rather than years. That's all the doc could say. He gave me painkillers but I try not to take them."

"Does it hurt?" asked Lehman, instantly regretting the banality of the question.

Lewis grinned. "Yeah, Dan. It hurts. It hurts like fuck. And to answer the other question that's on your mind: yeah, Tyler knows."

"And he doesn't care?"

"What, you think maybe I'll hold the team back? Worried that you won't get your money?"

Lehman held up his hands. "Hey, ease up, Bart. That's not what I meant at all. I just meant that if you're hurting, maybe you should just be at home. With your family."

"All the family I've got is my ex-wife and kid, and I don't think she'd be too keen to have me around. We didn't get on too well when I was healthy and I was damned if I was going to tell her that I was sick. The best way I can help my kid is to go through with Tyler's plan. It means I'll be able to put Victor through college, give him something to remember me by than just the rows and the fights I had with his mother. She's remarried, to a computer programmer in Boston. He's got money, more than I ever had, but I want to be the one who gives him his start in life, you know? In years to come I want Victor to know that I helped him, that I was his father and that I came through for him. I need this chance, Dan. I need it bad. It's the only way that I'll be able to get any money together in the time I've got left. I cashed in all my life insurance policies when I got divorced, and there's no way I can get cover now."

Lehman nodded. "Okay, I understand," he said. It was uncanny, he thought, the way in which Tyler seemed to know exactly how to press the right buttons to get people to do exactly what he wanted. Lehman was used to getting a fix on a person's weakness and then using that weakness as a way of manipulating them; that was why he had been so successful at talking investors into parting with their money. But Tyler was something else. It was one thing to convince an elderly couple in Florida to put their money in platinum futures, quite another to persuade four completely different Vietnam veterans to take part in a robbery in Hong Kong.

"Something else, too. You remember that hospital we went to in Saigon, the one where we saw all those people dying of cancer?"

"Yeah, I remember," said Lehman.

"Well, I figured I could do something to help them, you know? Do something to right the wrongs we did out there."

"You're a hell of an idealist, Bart."

Lewis grinned. "Yeah, well, dying does that to a man, I guess. Time to stock up a few brownie points before I meet my maker."

"You believe that?"

Lewis shook his head, suddenly serious. "No, I don't. Any belief I might have had in God went out of the window in Nam. But I want to do something for them, and this is the only way I can get money. I'm not sure which is the most important reason, helping Victor or giving money to the Vietnamese. I just know that I'll feel a hell of a lot better. Come on, let's go back. And don't tell the guys, okay? I'll do the job. I'll give it my best, I promise."

"Okay, Bart. I won't say anything."

The two men went back to the bar. Lewis began to tell a joke as soon as he'd slipped back on to his seat and there was no outward sign of the cancer that was eating him up. He winked at Lehman and Lehman tried to smile back but his heart wasn't in it.

Neil Coleman drummed his fingers on the steering wheel of the Suzuki Jeep and looked at his watch. It was almost midnight. Where was she? Coleman had telephoned Debbie at her office at six o'clock and been told that she'd left for the day. He'd called the Fielding house at six-thirty and again at seven-thirty and both times the maid had told him she wasn't at home. At first he'd felt anger that she'd lied to him. She'd quite distinctly told him she'd be busy all week, and yet here she was out on the town. He'd only wanted to call her and tell her how much he was missing her and how sorry he was for nagging her on the phone. He wanted to say he understood that she had to work and that maybe they could go swimming on Sunday afternoon. And what did he find? That she was out enjoying herself. He'd wanted to go looking for her; there were only so many places she could be and most of those would be in Lan Kwai Fong, but then he decided he'd wait for her to drive home. He'd parked at the side of

Old Peak Road, turned off his lights and waited. Over the hours the burning anger had subsided, replaced first by bitter resentment and then by indignant curiosity. He'd switched the police radio on and listened to the crackling conversations between the men on the beat and their stations. Most of them were in Cantonese and he could barely understand what they were saying, but every now and again he'd hear another *gweilo* on the air. It was better than listening to the Canto-pop crap the commercial radio stations put out.

A red and grey taxi, its "For Hire" light off and two girls in the back, growled up the hill. They were both brunettes. Where the hell was she? It wasn't fair, he thought. All he wanted to do was to take care of Debbie, to settle down with her and build a life together. She had no right to treat him like this. His nails bit into the palms of his hands and he realised he'd been squeezing the steering wheel so hard that his knuckles had gone white. His jaw ached too, as if he'd been biting down too hard and too long. He massaged his chin with his hands and sighed.

In his rearview mirror he saw a red car drive round the bend of the road below and he stiffened. As it drew closer he felt as much as heard the engine, a deep-throated rumble that vibrated the Suzuki. He turned and peered through the driver's window. He recognised the car as a Ferrari — a sharply sloping hood, the sides pockmarked with air scoops and a wing mounted on the rear deck. It was the sort of car that turned heads, even in Hong Kong which had more

Rolls-Royces per mile of road than any other place on earth.

The driver was blonde, the passenger a Chinese. As the car flashed by he saw with a jolt that it was Debbie who was driving. He fumbled with the ignition key, and by the time he'd started the engine and put the Suzuki into gear the Ferrari was already out of sight. Coleman pushed the accelerator pedal to the floor but the four-wheel drive wasn't built for speed and he couldn't get it above 50mph. He bobbed backwards and forwards as he drove, trying in vain to urge the Jeep to go faster.

The road swerved sharply to the right and he felt the Suzuki sway as he took the corner. He had a sick feeling in his stomach and in his mind was a picture of Debbie, her eyes wide, a smile on her lips, her hair tucked behind her ears, her hands light on the wheel. There was passion in her eyes, and his hands tensed as he thought of what happened when she'd driven him up the Peak. How she'd driven down the side road and climbed into the passenger seat. He felt himself grow hard at the thought of it, and was immediately disgusted with himself. As he approached the side road he slowed but when he drew level with it he could see that it was deserted. Relief washed over him like a tidal wave and he accelerated up the hill.

He cut the engine about a hundred yards before he reached the Fielding house and switched off the lights before coasting to a stop. Through the gates he could see the Ferrari parked in front of the house. The lights of the house were on and the drapes drawn, and in the soft glow that seeped through the material he could see the two figures standing by the car. Debbie was wearing a black miniskirt and a gold halter top and her hair was loose around her shoulders. As Coleman watched she kissed the man on the lips, waved goodbye, and let herself in through the front door.

All Coleman could see of the man was his back: black hair and a well-fitting dark blue suit. If he hadn't seen him coming up the Peak he wouldn't have known he was Chinese. He wasn't as thin as Chinese usually were; he had the shoulders of an Olympic swimmer, broad and muscled. The front door closed and there was a flicker from an upstairs window as if a drape had been disturbed. There was something shadowy at the window, a figure maybe, and the man at the Ferrari had seen it, too, and gave a small wave. The drape fell back into position as whoever was at the window went back into the room. Coleman figured it was probably old man Fielding, checking that his daughter was safely home.

As the Chinese turned to get back into his car, Coleman saw his face clearly for the first time. It was the man that he'd seen with Debbie in Hot Gossip. What was his name? Chung, that was it. Andrew Chung or something. He was a smoothie, that much Coleman remembered. They'd been drinking champagne. What was it they'd said? Yes, he remembered, he was a friend of William Fielding and Debbie had been helping him celebrate, that's what he'd told Coleman. Another lie, he thought, triumphantly. They'd both lied to him, but he'd been too clever for them. He'd caught them out. A friend of the family? Then why the kiss on the lips? And the sexy outfit? She shouldn't have lied to him, Coleman thought bitterly. He hated that more than anything else in the world.

The Ferrari rolled forward through the gates and Coleman sat back in his seat so that his head was in the shadows. He took a cheap ballpoint pen from the pocket of his jacket and jotted the registration number of the Ferrari on the palm of his left hand. "I'll have you, you fucking Chink," he muttered to himself as the Ferrari roared down the hill like an angry lion.

Tyler arrived at the Eastin Valley Hotel just after three o'clock on Wednesday afternoon and checked into the penthouse suite after arranging a room for Chuck Doherty on the ninth floor. He tipped the bellboy and waited for him to leave before he opened the French windows which led to a small sun-drenched patio. He stood and stretched in the warmth, looking down at the racetrack far below. In the centre of the track he could see a huge colour screen and two black tote indicator boards either side. There were big patches of brown in the middle of the soccer pitches as if the grass there was thirsting for water, while the turf on the racetrack was lush and green. He went back into the bedroom and took a pair of powerful binoculars and scrutinised the course, the deserted multi-tiered grandstand, the nearly empty car parks and the various buildings around. Silent for the moment, he knew that once the horses began running the stands would be full of screaming Chinese, urging on their horses and waving their betting chits in the air while the tote boards flashed the latest betting results and the colour screen showed a live close-up of the action.

He walked into the bedroom, put the binoculars on the desk, and called the four vets one after the other. All were in their rooms except for Lehman and he told them to be ready in reception at half past six, with their passports. He left a message for Lehman and was a little annoyed because he'd made it clear to all of them that they should be ready and waiting all Wednesday afternoon. He made a mental note to speak to Lehman later and then called down to room service and ordered a club sandwich and coffee before running a hot bath.

When he stepped out of the elevator with Doherty, the four men were waiting for him, sitting on the overstuffed sofas in the reception area. All had dressed casually in slacks and short-sleeved shirts, except for Carmody who had on a Mickey Mouse sweatshirt which covered most of his artificial hand. All had slightly bemused looks on their faces because Tyler hadn't told them where they were going and the fact that they had to bring their passports suggested that they were going on a trip.

The men got to their feet and Tyler nodded his approval. He introduced Doherty to Horvitz and Carmody, without explaining where he'd come from. Both men looked curiously at his shaven head. "Right," said Tyler. "Fall out." He led them out the door and along the sidewalk towards the racetrack.

Lehman fell in step beside him as they walked. "Sorry I wasn't in the room when you called," he said.

357

Tyler looked across at him. "No sweat," he said. He was impressed that Lehman had apologised. It showed professionalism, so Tyler decided not to press it.

"It's the racetrack, isn't it?" asked Lehman. "We're gonna hit the track, right?"

"Maybe," said Tyler. "For the moment we're just a group of good old boys out on the town. We'll get down to specifics later."

Lehman smiled, satisfied that he was right.

Wong Nai Chung Road, which circled the racecourse, was packed with cars and taxis and the sidewalks were thronged with pedestrians, many of them carrying Chinese newspapers. The sky was beginning to darken and the harsh white floodlights gave the racetrack a cold, clinical look. They joined the crowds but were soon split up as they were jostled and pushed by impatient racegoers rushing towards the turnstiles which led to the public stands. Tyler stood head and shoulders over most of the crowd so the rest could easily follow him as he made his way along the side of the grandstand towards the members' entrance. Three security guards were slumped by the turnstiles languidly checking that those who went through had the correct badge dangling on their chests. Pouring through were well-dressed Chinese in dark suits, elegant Chinese women in their best dresses and jewellery, and well-to-do expats. But there were scruffier racegoers too, indistinguishable from those in the mob who had been pushing through into the public stands. There were two ticket offices, one on the left away from which stretched a long queue, and one on the right, which was clear. Tyler waited until the vets had gathered around him.

"Right, gentlemen. This is Happy Valley racetrack. Consider this rest and recreation, nothing more. We're here to enjoy ourselves, place some bets, hopefully win a few dollars. I plan a full briefing back at the hotel at 2300 hours, so at this stage I just want you to have a look around and get a feel for the place. If you show your passport to the gentleman at the counter there and give him fifty dollars he'll issue you with a members' enclosure badge which will give you access to most of the grandstand. If you'll follow me up to the second floor I'll show you how the betting works."

One by one the men handed over their passports and cash, attached their badges, and pushed through the turnstiles. Fast-moving escalators were whisking racegoers up to the higher levels and the men followed Tyler up to the second floor. The escalator took them to a large hallway. To the left were full-length windows beyond which they could see the brightly illuminated racetrack and to the right were cashiers' desks behind security glass screens which stretched the full length of the hall. Behind the screens sat young men and women in wine-coloured pullovers and cream shirts taking bets from the racegoers. The system seemed fast and efficient. Gamblers were taking small cards from dispensers, marking their bets by what appeared to be a series of small pen strokes and handing them to the cashiers. The cards were stamped and returned.

The men stood together while Tyler walked over to one of the ticket dispensers and came back with a

359

handful of cards. All were the same size but had different coloured stripes along one side. "Okay," said Tyler, "these are the betting cards. You fill them out and give them and your stakes to one of the guys at the counter. They run the card through a computer terminal which records the bet and prints the details on the back of the card."

The men nodded. "Seems simple enough," said Carmody.

"It is," said Tyler. "But most people go for exotic combinations, and they're a bit more complicated. I'll give you a quick rundown, but don't worry if you don't remember it all. The guys behind the counter will help you and there's an information desk too." Tyler looked at his watch. "The first race starts at seven forty-five," he said. "Let's buy some programmes and get down to it."

They each took a handful of tickets and a programme and walked out of the air-conditioned betting hall and into the seating areas, rows and rows of plastic bucket seats facing the floodlit track. They filed along to a section of empty seats and sat down.

"Bart, why don't you get us all some beers?" Tyler said. It was more of a command than a question, and Lewis didn't hesitate. He disappeared back up the steps while the rest of them studied the programme. It contained everything but the name of the winning mount — there was a full rundown on the form and the stakes won by each horse, a description including its breeding history, its placing so far during the season, and the weight of the rider. It took a while to figure out what all the information was, but the Jockey Club had even included a guide on how to read the programme. It was almost an idiot's guide to betting, which made Tyler all the more certain that there was no way of coming out ahead. The Jockey Club effectively had the system rigged through its tote system so that it couldn't lose, deducting its own commission and government betting duty before dividing the rest of the betting turnover among the winning tickets. The more that was bet, the more they paid out, and the more their commission grew. The club's percentages added up to about three billion HK dollars a year. The only winner in Hong Kong racing was the Jockey Club; everything else was just redistribution of wealth.

Lehman looked around at their fellow racegoers. Some were obviously tourists, skin reddened by unaccustomed exposure to the sun and wearing clothes they wouldn't be seen dead in back home, weighed down with new camera equipment fresh from the rip-off shops in Tsim Sha Tsui. Others were cocky young expats in sharp made-to-measure suits drinking gin and tonics and laughing with their heads thrown back, rich Chinese with Rolex watches studying Chinese newspapers and marking favourites with gold pens and poor Chinese slurping noodles from plastic bowls as they waited for racing to start.

"Strange mix, isn't it?" said Lewis as he came back with a tray of beers.

"Yeah," agreed Tyler. "Hardly seems like the sport of kings, does it?"

"I thought racing was just for the top people, for the British," said Carmody, who was sitting on Tyler's left. "It seems like every man and his dog is here. The place is almost full. There must be 100,000 people here."

"No," said Tyler. "Normal raceday attendance is about 36,000. More for the big meetings. And there'll be another 10,000 or so at the other racetrack in Shatin, watching it on a live screen there."

"They must be racing mad," said Lewis as he handed out the beers.

"It's not the horses they like, it's the gambling," said Tyler. "Gambling is illegal in Hong Kong, with two exceptions — horse racing and the Mark Six Lottery. And the Jockey Club controls them both. The Chinese love to gamble, that's why they're here."

"Speaking of which, I'm going to place a bet," said Carmody, sliding by. "Fifty dollars to win on Galloping Dragon."

"A hot tip?" asked Tyler.

"A hunch," said Carmody.

Over at the end of the row Lehman was in deep conversation with a middle-aged Chinese man with horn-rimmed spectacles. The man had several newspapers and a notebook full of small handwritten figures and he was wagging his finger at Lehman as he talked. As Tyler watched, the man helped Lehman fill out a card with a series of ticks, nodding and grinning, obviously pleased at being asked advice by an American tourist. Lehman thanked him, and then followed Carmody up the steps.

Lehman stood behind Carmody in a short queue in front of one of the cashiers. He looked at his watch.

362

There were ten minutes to go before the first race was due to start and Lehman could feel the tension growing in the betting hall.

Carmody reached the front of the queue and handed his ticket and money over with his claw, enjoying as he always did the look of surprise on the young girl's face. She couldn't take her eyes off the stainless-steel claw and her fingers trembled as she fed his card into the computer terminal. Carmody smiled at her discomfort and slowly raised the claw to scratch his cheek. Her eyes widened and she gave him back the card, pulling away her hand as if frightened of getting burnt. Carmody held her gaze for several seconds before moving away.

Lehman smiled at the girl, trying to ease her fear, but she was still shocked at what she'd seen and kept her eyes down at the counter as she processed his betting ticket. Lehman's bet was a complicated one done on the advice of the man he'd been sitting next to. It was an All Up Win bet, where any winnings on the first race were automatically put on the next, and so on. Under the man's guidance, Lehman had chosen a horse from each of the six races and was placing a 500 dollar bet. If all his six selections came home first he wouldn't need to go any further with Tyler and his plan. It was the sort of gamble that Lehman relished. All or nothing. As far as he was concerned, there was no point in wagering fifty dollars to win back a hundred. There was no satisfaction in a small win.

He took his stamped card from the girl and turned to see Tyler behind him.

Tyler looked down at the card with its distinctive brown strip. "I didn't even tell you about that one," he said.

"I guess you can't tell us everything," said Lehman.

"Not all at once, that's true," agreed Tyler, looking steadily at Lehman. "Though the key to making big money isn't gambling. It's planning. Careful planning followed by faultless execution."

"That's what you're doing?"

Tyler nodded. "The planning has already been done, Dan."

"And the execution?"

"Later. I'll tell you all later."

"It's here, isn't it?"

"Later, Dan." Tyler stepped to one side to allow Lehman by and then placed his own wager, a hundred dollar eachway bet on the favourite. When he retook his seat the horses were on the track warming up, the jockeys wearing brightly coloured shirts, the horses well groomed and eager for the off. The crowd was buzzing, there was an announcement over the loudspeakers in Chinese which sparked a chorus of good-natured cheers and whistles, and the crowd began rushing down the stairs to take their seats.

The large screen in the middle of the track was showing close-ups of the various runners and the two tote boards carried all the betting details, including the winning odds of the different horses and the odds of the various combination bets.

With a minimum of fuss the horses were encouraged into the starting gates and then they were off, hooves kicking up small plumes of sand from the artificial track. The start was at the far side of the track and as the horses came pounding around the second curve and in front of the grandstand everyone got to their feet and began screaming and shouting, then in a thunder of hooves they were gone, curving around to the right. All eyes then were on the screen where the order of the first four runners was indicated by large numbers. The favourite was running second. Of Galloping Dragon there was no sign. Carmody was shrieking, his eyes fixed on the screen, his one hand clenched tight, the hook making small pumping movements. The drumming of the hooves got louder as the horses rounded the bend for the last time and galloped towards the finishing line, nostrils flaring and tendons straining. The spectators were at fever pitch as the favourite slipped into third place and a chestnut challenged the leader, its jockey bobbing backwards and forwards like a man possessed, but his challenge failed by just half a length as they flashed across the finishing line.

"Shit!" said Carmody, slumping down into his seat. "Shit, shit, shit!" Lewis ripped up his ticket and dropped it on the floor. Lehman was smiling so Tyler guessed he'd backed the winner, and his suspicion was confirmed when the Chinese bettor who'd given him the tip turned to him and shook his hand.

"You not gambling, Eric?" Tyler asked Horvitz.

Horvitz shook his head. "Never been one to get a kick from betting, Colonel," he said. "Watching the racing is fine, but that's as far as it goes with me."

"Having money on the outcome gives it an edge," said Tyler. "Means you've got an interest in the outcome."

"I've lived on the edge, Colonel. I've walked the line and I came back." He spoke in a dull monotone voice like a spirit talking from beyond the grave, a presence that had no interest in the petty occupations of the living. The two men looked at each other for a second, and then Horvitz smiled thinly. "Besides," he said, "I want to keep hold of my cash."

Everyone but Horvitz placed bets on the second race, Tyler backing the favourite with an each-way bet again, Carmody going for another hunch, Lewis and Doherty putting 500 dollars on the favourite to win and Lehman going for a combination bet on the advice of his newfound friend. The favourite romped home at two to one which saw Doherty and Lewis jumping up and down and slapping a disgruntled Carmody on the back. Tyler was showing a decent profit and he went into the betting hall to collect his winnings from the first two races. Lehman followed him and stood at an adjacent window.

"How are you doing?" asked Tyler.

"Okay," said Lehman, accepting a handful of yellow notes from the cashier.

"Is your All Up bet still on?"

Lehman grinned and nodded. "Fingers crossed," he said. He winked at Tyler and then slowly walked along the betting hall towards the escalators. He went up another floor and found an identical betting hall filled with people watching the results on a bank of television sets and queuing to place their bets. Handfuls of red and yellow notes were being shoved across the counters and betting tickets eagerly grabbed. A lot of money was changing hands. A hell of a lot of money. There were dozens of cashiers watched over by supervisors behind them. The money was placed in drawers in front of the cashiers but he didn't see any of it being collected and taken to a central point. There didn't seem to be much in the way of security, either. The same cashiers who accepted bets also paid out winnings after checking the tickets, and from a cursory glance Lehman had no idea how much cash there was behind the windows at any one point. He went back to his seat and chatted for a while with his neighbour, picking up several more tips in the process. The man was an amateur tipster and was pleased to have found an attentive listener in Lehman. Lehman reckoned that the man didn't often get a chance to show off his knowledge, and he was happy to lend him an ear because over the next few races he won several thousand dollars. The All Up bet fell at the fourth race, by which time there had been 8,000 dollars riding on his horse. His companion had gone for the more conservative All Up Place bet and by the time the last winner crossed the finishing line he'd turned a 400 dollar stake into a quarter of a million dollars. Hong Kong dollars, that is, equivalent to about 32,000 US dollars. The man was pleased at winning, but not as overjoyed as Lehman would have expected considering the size of the windfall. Lehman got the impression that the man was used to winning big sums. He himself ended the night a couple of thousand dollars richer, though at one point he'd been up about 10,000 HK dollars. Tyler walked away with a similar amount, though he had steadily won small sums throughout the meeting. Doherty admitted to being down a few hundred dollars while Lewis was cagey about his performance. Lehman reckoned he'd lost overall, while there was no doubt about what had happened to Carmody. He was sitting slumped in his bucket seat surrounded by a pile of torn-up tickets.

The men walked back through the crowds streaming out of the racecourse. There was a row of Mercedes and Rolls-Royces awaiting their wealthy owners and taxis with their roof lights on were having no trouble touting for business. When they reached the hotel they were sweating from the exertion of walking uphill in the hot, moist air and Tyler invited them all up to his suite for a drink.

There was a small, circular table on the patio and the vets gathered chairs around it and sat down, laughing and joking about the night's racing while Tyler fetched them cans of Carlsberg, Tsing Tao and San Miguel from the mini-bar fridge.

When they all had a beer in front of them the conversation gradually died and they waited expectantly for Tyler to speak. Far below the floodlights still illuminated the racetrack and the air was buzzing with the sound of thousands of people making their way home. Tyler stood behind his chair, leaving his beer on the table. He stood for a while and looked down on the throngs in the streets below and then switched his glance to the five men, looking at them one by one and nodding at each as if acknowledging them for the first time.

"I suppose you've all realised by now that the visit to the track wasn't just a chance to win money." He smiled at Carmody. "Or to lose it." The vets laughed, and Lewis slapped Carmody's leg. "When I approached you all in Bangkok, I made it clear that what I have planned is a robbery. A big one. One of the biggest. And tonight you've all seen that there's a stack of money at the Happy Valley track, there for the taking. You don't have to have an IQ above room temperature to put two and two together. What you gentlemen have to decide is whether or not you want to take part. There's obviously a limit to how much I can tell you before you decide whether or not to commit yourself, but I can give you a few basic facts."

He took a mouthful of beer from his can of San Miguel. "More money is wagered at the racetrack in Hong Kong than anywhere else in the world. The average amount wagered at a race meeting is 725 million HK dollars — that's about ninety million US dollars."

"Excuse me, Colonel, that's ninety million US dollars during the season, right?" interrupted Carmody.

Tyler shook his head. "That's a negative, Larry. Betting turnover for the season is more than seventy billion HK dollars. In US dollar terms that's almost ten billion. The record take for one raceday is more than 900 million HK dollars; 115 million US dollars. Think about that, gentlemen. Savour those numbers."

Lewis whistled softly and Lehman nodded slowly.

"Now, not all that money sits at the racetrack. The average attendance at the track is about 36,000, as I told you before. Another 10,000 or so place bets at the Shatin track while racing goes on down there. But one million bets are placed at the Jockey Club's off-course betting centres which are spread all over the colony. And another half a million bets are phoned in. But even so, more cash is bet at that track than anywhere else in the world. Gentlemen, I have a foolproof plan to acquire a sizable portion of that money. I already have a number of associates but I need your particular expertise to ensure that the operation proceeds successfully. I can't tell you any more until you decide whether or not you wish to enlist."

He put down his beer and surveyed the five men. "Gentlemen, it's time to shit, or get off the pot." He folded his arms across his chest and waited.

Carmody was the first to speak. "I'm in, Colonel," he said. Carmody looked around the faces of the four other men. Lewis was nodding. So was Doherty.

Lewis and Carmody looked at Lehman. He shrugged. "I wouldn't have come to Hong Kong if I hadn't already decided that I was in," he said.

"Way to go!" said Carmody, and Lewis reached over to shake his hand.

Tyler looked at Horvitz, who seemed to be the only one of the five who was actually thinking about the proposition. He seemed to be mentally wrestling with himself, his forehead deeply lined. In the distance dogs were barking from the hillside that loomed above the hotel. Horvitz's eyes seemed to blank out as he thought, then he lifted his chin and grinned. "Yeah, I'm in," he said. "You can count me in."

Tyler smiled. He walked through into his bedroom, lifted his suitcase and hefted it on to the bed. He flicked its catches and took something from inside. The vets watched him curiously. Whatever he had taken from the case he held behind his back as he went back to the patio.

"I knew before we arrived in Hong Kong that we'd make a good team, and I expected you'd all say that you wanted to take it further. But you have to understand that we have now reached the point of no return. You can't say that you want to go ahead with this and then decide later that you want to drop out. If you have any doubts, any doubts at all, then now is the time to express them and to walk away. At the moment all you know is where. You don't know when, or what the plan is, or who else will be taking part. We can part now as friends and I won't feel threatened. You don't know enough to be a danger to me or to my plans. You can take the money I've given you and go back to your lives in the States."

From behind his back he took a large handgun. He held the butt with his right hand and caressed the barrel with his left. The gun dwarfed his hand. It was a powerful gun, a Smith & Wesson Model 19 Combat Magnum weighing thirty-five ounces. He'd picked it up earlier in the day, before he'd checked in at the hotel.

"If you go now, there'll be no hard feelings. But if you try to leave once the operation is under way, there will be only one way out." He nodded his head at the gun. "Gentlemen, if you have any doubts, any doubts at all, then go now."

The five vets sat in silence, all of them looking at the menacing weapon. Tyler looked at them, searching for any sign of reluctance. He saw none, and smiled.

"Very well. From this moment on consider yourself on the payroll. I'll now take any questions you may have."

Horvitz took his eyes off the Smith & Wesson and ran his hand along his chin. "Yeah, I've got a question," he said. "When do we do it?"

Tyler smiled. "Happy Valley's busiest day," he said. "The last race of the season."

Lehman nodded. "I've a question. How do we get away? How do we get away with the money once we've got it?"

Tyler walked across the patio and rested his hands on the wall. He felt rather than saw the rest of the vets get up and follow him, standing behind him in a semicircle and looking down at the track. Tyler pointed at the grandstand, and then raised his hand up skywards, between the towering apartment blocks. "We get away the same way we used to in Nam," he said quietly. "We fly."

Anthony Chung had long held the view that the best Cantonese food in Hong Kong was to be had at the Dynasty Restaurant in the New World Hotel in Kowloon. Pretty much everything about the restaurant was perfect: the service was impeccable, the decor was smart with none of the tacky glitz that spoiled so many of the local restaurants, and the food was always superb. Chung had never tasted river fish as fresh and succulent as was served at the Dynasty, and even their steamed rice was a step above anything else that could be obtained in the city.

The captain greeted him warmly by name and escorted him to a corner table set for three. He waited until Chung was seated before snapping out a white napkin and placing it over his lap and handing him two menus, a regular à la carte menu and an additional one with the chef's specials.

"Your usual?" the captain asked. He was young, in his late twenties with slicked-back hair and a ready smile, and he never forgot the name or the preferences of his regular clients.

"Please," said Chung. As the captain left, Chung glanced around the restaurant. As usual it was virtually full; he wasn't alone in appreciating the high standards of the Dynasty's chefs. He recognised faces at several of the tables: a sprinkling of high-powered businessmen with their wives or mistresses, the editor of one of the city's leading Chinese newspapers, and two successful horse trainers. There were tourists, too, probably eating there because they were staying at the hotel and not aware they were dining in one of Hong Kong's premier restaurants. He'd seen tourists asking why chow mein wasn't on the menu, or ordering four portions of the same dish and each eating their own with a fork while the waitresses giggled in the kitchen.

A smiling waitress came over with his brandy and ice. She was pretty, with long wavy hair and large eyes and a good figure which was accentuated by the tight-fitting green and gold *cheung sam* she wore. Chung watched her hips move under the dress as she walked away. As she went through the double swing doors that opened into the kitchen, Chung saw his guests arrive at the entrance to the restaurant. The man was short and portly, his face pockmarked with old acne scars; straggling hairs grew from a mole on his round chin. His face was virtually circular, his nose a small bump in its centre, the fleshy lips forming a straight line until he smiled. His distinctive features had led to Paul Chau being saddled with the nick-name "Pizza Face" at school, but he had had the last laugh on his schoolmates. He'd gone on to become one of Hong Kong's most successful — and richest — showbiz agents, and he had some of the city's most glamorous actresses and singers as his clients and companions, a five million dollar house on the Peak and a Canadian passport. The suit he was wearing had clearly cost several thousand dollars and even across the restaurant Chung could see the glint of a gold Rolex on his left wrist.

The four businessmen sitting at the table next to Chung all turned to get a better look at the new arrivals, but it wasn't Chau who had attracted their attention. It was his companion they were straining to look at, a truly stunning girl, tall and willowy in a figure-hugging black dress which ended a couple of inches above shapely knees and which was cut to reveal tanned shoulders and an expensive gold necklace. Her hair was up, showing a long neck and small ears and a

374

pair of dangling, gold earrings which swung gently as she moved her head. She was used to being admired. Though Chung hadn't actually seen any of the four movies she'd appeared in, Chau had told him that Yo-yo Yip was one of Hong Kong's rising starlets. Ten months ago she'd won a Miss Photogenic award in a beauty competition run by one of the local television stations and Chau had arranged for her to be signed up by a major Hong Kong film studio. Hong Kong film-makers rarely took more than a month to put together a movie and the stars on the payroll of the big studios worked seven days a week, often shooting several films at the same time. The films were shown in local cinemas and then sold on to Taiwan and Singapore, but returns on the movies were nowhere near that of Hollywood blockbusters and the Hong Kong stars were poorly paid by comparison. It often took budding starlets like Yo-yo several years of hard work before they earned serious money, but they usually had expensive tastes and were short on patience. Many were amenable to taking a few short cuts to increase their bank balances.

Yo-yo walked down the restaurant, following the captain. Behind her Chau kept a hand on her waist like a trainer leading his favourite racehorse out of the paddock. She didn't look to the right or left as she walked but Chung knew that she was all too well aware of the effect she was having on the men at the tables. Some of them obviously recognised her — Chau had said that her last appearance in a kung-fu comedy had earned good reviews and she'd been featured on several magazine covers as a result — but others were just looking because she was such a stunning beauty: high cheekbones, rosebud mouth and wide eyes which seemed to be half closed.

Chung got to his feet before she reached the table. He shook hands with Chau who then introduced him to Yo-yo.

"You look even prettier than you do on screen," Chung said to her in Cantonese.

She smiled prettily, showing white, even teeth that could have graced a toothpaste advertisement. "You saw my last movie?" she asked.

"Of course," lied Chung. Chau had briefed him on her last two films and the roles she'd played.

"What did you think?" she asked as the captain helped her into her chair.

"You were marvellous," said Chung. "I thought you handled the comedy really well, too. Did you do the action scenes yourself?"

She nodded enthusiastically. "Yes. And I've still got the bruises." She giggled and raised a hand to cover her mouth.

Chau took his seat and ordered a Heineken for himself and a Perrier for Yo-yo. "Nice suit, Anthony," he said approvingly.

"Armani," Chung said. He'd worn it because he knew Chau would notice and comment on it, and because it would be a name that Yo-yo would be sure to recognise. Chau had said that he would arrange the introduction, but it would be up to the girl how the evening developed. It was important to make the right impression.

Their drinks arrived and the waitress smiled at Chung again. "Do you have any preferences?" he asked Yo-yo.

"I love shark's fin soup," she said. "And seafood. All seafood."

"Seafood is a great aphrodisiac," said Chau. "Especially oysters."

Yo-yo smiled coyly. "I love oysters," she said. She saw Chung smiling and averted her eyes. Chung had the distinct impression that she was playing out a scene from one of her movies.

The captain returned to take their order: a large steamed grouper, prawns in hot and spicy sauce, shark's fin soup with chicken, roast duck and plum sauce, baked aubergine in garlic, and their special white rice. Yo-yo asked if they had *bat choi tsari*, a vegetable she was especially fond of, but the captain apologised, saying that they had only *bat choi*, a larger variety. She pouted, her eyes magically became moist, and the captain stammered that he'd go and have a word with the chef and see what could be arranged; she wasn't to worry, if they didn't have any in the restaurant he would personally go out and get some. She smiled bravely and thanked him. She was, Chung had to admit, drop dead gorgeous.

They talked of passports while they waited for the food to arrive. She expressed envy at Chung's possession of a French passport and said that she hoped to obtain Australian citizenship within the next year. Chau asked why she hadn't considered getting Canadian citizenship and she shuddered prettily and said it was too cold. "Besides," she said, "most of my friends are going to Australia. I want to be somewhere where I have friends."

"But you don't have to stay for ever," said Chung. "Three years is all you need to get your residency, then you can come back and live in Hong Kong."

"Ha!" she snorted. "No one wants to live here after the Chinese take over. After 1997 there will be no one left. No one that matters, anyway. Almost all the big stars have Australian or Canadian passports already. Isn't that true, Paul?"

"All my clients who can afford it have bought their way in, yes," agreed Chau.

"And those who can't are doing everything they can to earn enough before 1997," said Yo-yo. "That's my plan, anyway. To work as hard as I can and to earn enough money to emigrate."

"Did you apply for a British passport?" asked Chung. The British government had offered passports to up to 50,000 heads of households and their families based on a points system.

"I asked for an application form, but you should have seen it," laughed Yo-yo. "You needed a university degree to understand the explanatory book that came with it. They made it as difficult as they could. Besides, who wants to live in Britain? The climate's lousy and the people hate us, you know that. They took what they could from Hong Kong and now they want to throw us back to the Chinese. They don't want us in their country."

"I didn't know you were so political," said Chung as waitresses arrived bearing their food.

"It's not politics, it's common sense," said Yo-yo. "It's every man for himself." She breathed in the fragrance of the fish and nodded approvingly. The captain himself came over to lift the silver lid off the plate of *bat choi tsai* and was rewarded with a stunning smile and a murmur of thanks.

"Hong Kong is finished," she continued. "Some of the big studios have already moved to Singapore and I think the rest will follow soon. The record industry here has pretty much gone. Everybody I know has either got a passport or is planning to get one, either by earning enough to buy one or by marrying someone."

"You'd do that?" asked Chung, surprised. "You'd marry someone for their passport?"

"But of course, if I had to," she said, spooning hot prawns into her bowl. She reached over and took Chung's bowl and filled it with prawns, too. He nodded his thanks. "I have offers, many, many offers," she said.

"I can believe it," said Chung, popping a prawn into his mouth with a deft movement of his chopsticks.

"But I don't want to be owned by anyone," she said. "I want to depend only on myself. It would be a last resort, that is all." She looked at Chung earnestly. "But I would do it, if I had to. There's no way I'll be sitting here waiting for the communists to take over. There's no way I'd trust them. Anyone who puts their faith in the communists deserves whatever they get."

Chung was surprised by her vehemence and changed the subject, not wanting to upset her. They talked of the heads of the various studios, their forthcoming films and their mistresses. There were no secrets in Hong Kong. She was soon laughing and giggling, and occasionally she reached over and tweaked Chung's arm. Once her foot touched his beneath the table and she smiled when she caught his eye. When the plates and bowls lay empty before them and waitresses began to clear the table and serve small cups of fragrant tea, Yo-yo asked to be excused and picked up her small black handbag. Both men watched her walk to the Ladies room. A dozen other men in the restaurant turned to watch her go and at least one got his hand smacked by a jealous girlfriend.

"She's lovely, isn't she?" asked Chau.

"No doubt about that," agreed Chung. "I was surprised how anti-communist she is. She really seems to hate them."

"One of her cousins was killed in Tiananmen Square," explained Chau. "At least the family assumes he was. He was with the demonstrators when the troops opened fire. They never found his body, but that's hardly surprising because as soon as they'd cleared the square they used bulldozers to pile them up and then they poured petrol over them and burned them." His mouth suddenly dropped. "What am I saying?" he said, embarrassed. "You were there, of course. Anthony, I'm sorry, I don't know why I forgot. Your father, how is your father?"

Chung shrugged. "He's as well as can be expected, under the circumstances," said Chung, looking down at the tablecloth.

"Is there anything I can do?"

Chung shook his head. "Everything that can be done, is being done. You know how these things work."

"I understand, but if there is anything I can do, let me know. I mean it."

"I know you do, Paul, and I appreciate it." The subject of his father still pained him so he changed the subject. "Will Yo-yo get a passport, do you think?"

"She earns good money." He laughed. "I should know, I get to keep twenty per cent of it." He wiped his fleshy lips with his napkin. It came away smeared with thick, orange-coloured sauce. "Seriously, though, she's cutting it close. She earns about 100,000 Hong Kong a film, which means she's not in the big league yet, and time's running out. She spends like there's no tomorrow, as well. You should see her closets, they're full of clothes, most of them with designer labels. She has friends, though, and I think if she really has a problem they'll help her. She's the occasional girlfriend of the chairman of one of the big hongs here. He'll take care of her if she needs it, I'm sure."

"Who is it?" asked Chung.

"Anthony, Anthony, surely you don't expect me to betray a confidence, do you? Let's just say my friend is one of the ten richest men in Hong Kong and that he reckons that Yo-yo is one of the best lays he's ever had."

"You bastard, tell me," grinned Chung.

"Okay, you've twisted my arm," laughed Chau. He gave Chung the name and Chung raised his eyebrows in surprise. The man was a pillar of the Chinese community and had been tipped as the man who would run Hong Kong once the Chinese took over. Chau had been modest when he said the man was one of the ten richest in Hong Kong. Chung knew of only one or two who could possibly be richer.

"You're joking!" exclaimed Chung.

"No, it's the truth," said Chau. "Cross my heart and hope to die."

"You have no heart," said Chung. "And he said that Yo-yo was the best lay he'd ever had?"

"The absolute best."

"This isn't just a sales pitch, is it?" asked Chung. "You're not trying to raise the price?"

"The price is as we discussed," said Chau. "Ten thousand Hong Kong."

"For the night?"

"For as much of the night as you want her for," said Chau. "But remember she has to be on the set at eight o'clock tomorrow morning."

"That's fine by me," said Chung.

"And Anthony?"

"What?"

"Don't mark her, okay?"

Chung looked suitably offended. "Paul, what are you suggesting?"

"Just remember what I said, that's all."

The door to the Ladies opened and Yo-yo came out, pausing for dramatic effect before beginning the walk back to the table. Both men got to their feet. Chau placed his napkin on the table as Yo-yo and Chung sat down.

"I have to be going," he said, holding out his hand to Chung. Chung shook it firmly. Yo-yo looked up and Chau gave her a small, almost imperceptible, nod, letting her know that the fee had been agreed. Pimping was an ugly word, but, whichever way you cut it, that was what Chau did for Yo-yo, and for a handful of other top starlets. She relaxed and Chung felt her small foot press against the back of his calf.

Chau left and Chung and Yo-yo made small talk while they waited for the bill to arrive. He paid with his gold American Express card and she linked her arm through his as they walked together to his car. Chung was conscious of the number of heads she turned and the way her hip touched his as she held his arm.

She squealed when she saw his car and squeezed his arm so tightly that she practically cut off his circulation. "It's a Ferrari!" she said. She unlinked her arm and ran a hand along the side of the car. The red paintwork gleamed under the fluorescent lights, giving it a cold, hard look.

"Oh, it's lovely," she cooed. "It's fabulous. How much did it cost?"

Chung wasn't surprised at her directness. Like most Hong Kongers, Yo-yo had no qualms about asking the price of anything she saw. "Sticker price is about 400,000 US dollars, but dealers can get more than 700,000 US dollars for them. But you want to buy one in Hong Kong, you've got to pay one hundred per cent car tax."

She looked at him with wide eyes which were full of admiration. "One and a half million US dollars?" she said.

"Give or take a few," said Chung laconically. In fact the car was leased and he didn't expect to have it for more than a few months.

She put her arms around his neck and kissed him full on the lips. He felt her small breasts against his chest and her warm tongue forced its way gently between his teeth. Yo-yo Yip was clearly turned on by money in a big way, he decided, but then so was almost everybody in Hong Kong. He broke away and opened the passenger door for her. She slid into the spartan interior and smoothed the grey flannel which covered the dashboard.

"It's just like a racing car," she said as he buckled himself into his bucket seat.

"It is a racing car," he corrected, helping her fasten the six-point racing harness.

"How fast does it go?" she asked.

"It'll do 197mph, but there's nowhere in Hong Kong where you can get it up to that speed," he said. "But it'll do nought to sixty in 4.2 seconds."

"Wah!" she said. She rubbed her thighs together and Chung heard the whisper of silk.

He edged the car out of the car park, gunning the accelerator to keep the revs above 4,500 so that the plugs wouldn't foul. He drove away from the harbour towards his apartment in Kowloon Tong. Out of the corner of his eye he saw her face fall when she saw where they were going. Kowloon Tong was a high-class residential district, home to some of the richest families in Hong Kong, but it also had hundreds of love motels, short-time hotels which were perfect for afternoon assignations and where many businessmen took their mistresses if they were too tight-fisted to buy them their own apartments.

She had obviously assumed that Chung was taking her to a love-motel, judging by the way she pouted and looked moodily out of the passenger window. Her face brightened when Chung guided the Ferrari through the wrought-iron gates which led to the residential block where he lived. He parked the car in the underground car park between a Rolls-Royce and a convertible BMW. The pout evaporated and she ran her fingernails down the back of his jacket as they walked to the lift. The doorman in the lobby looked up from the racing paper he was reading and nodded at Chung. The walls and floor of the lobby were finished in green-veined marble and the elevator doors were made of a dark, highly polished wood. There was a tall palm in a gilt urn towering in a corner and two large leather sofas where guests could wait. Yo-yo nodded approvingly.

The doors hissed open and Chung stepped to the side to let her in first, her high heels clicking on the hard marble floor. Chung pressed the button for the penthouse, the doors closed respectfully, and the elevator whisked them twelve floors. Kowloon Tong was under the flight path to Kai Tak Airport and there were rigid height restrictions on all buildings, another reason for the apartments being so expensive. The elevator doors opened to reveal a small marble-lined lobby and a single mahogany door. Chung took his keys and opened the two high-security locks and showed Yo-yo inside.

She sighed appreciatively as she walked along the hallway and into the lounge. The far wall was virtually all glass and it looked down on a courtyard full of lush green trees and bushes around a small pool which was lit by discreet spotlights. The walls and ceiling of the room were painted white, the floors were wooden and stained a pale beige, and there were vertical white blinds which had been pulled back to either side of the window. It was a stunning room during the day, when the sun streamed in through the double-glazed glass wall, and even at night Chung knew Yo-yo would be impressed and that it wouldn't be long before she asked him how much it had cost. Like the Ferrari, the apartment was leased. So was the furniture, which, like the car, was Italian and very expensive. There were three sofas covered in a cream fabric, a coffee table made of an oblong sheet of toughened glass balanced on three black marble spheres, and a long, low black table on which were lined up the components of a Bang and Olufsen stereo system, a Hitachi video recorder and a large, flat screen television. At either end of the table stood tall, thin speakers which were as tall as Yo-yo. Two paintings, modernist splashes of red, black and green on pure white canvas were highlighted by track-mounted spotlights on the ceiling and to the right of the door was a black, oblong dining table, around which were eight high-backed chairs.

"It's lovely," she said. "It's fabulous." Chung wondered if she realised that they were exactly the same words she'd used about the car.

"I like it," he said. He'd left a couple of glossy car magazines on the coffee table next to a copy of the *Hong Kong Standard*, and there was a squash racquet leaning next to one of the speakers, small touches which made the rented apartment look more like a home.

Yo-yo put her handbag next to the CD player. "Mind if I put something on?" she asked.

"Help yourself," said Chung. "The CDs are in a drawer under the amplifier."

She slid open the drawer and ran a finger over the CD collection. "You like Bryan Ferry?" she asked.

"Sure," said Chung. The CDs came with the apartment and he hadn't even looked at them. Yo-yo took the shiny disc out of its holder and pressed the button which opened the player.

"Can I get you a drink?" Chung asked. She shook her head and pressed the "play" button. Ferry's deep, rich voice oozed out of the speakers.

She slipped her shoes off and padded over the wooden floor, walking on the balls of her feet so that her legs still seemed long. She took him by the hand and he felt her sharp nails bite into the skin. "Which way's the bedroom?" she whispered. Chung nodded towards a door and she pulled him in that direction.

Unlike the lounge, the bedroom was carpeted, a thick, pale purple pile which matched the drapes that had been drawn across the window. Yo-yo flicked the light switch and the room was bathed in soft light. The whole of the left wall had been given over to walk-in closets with white louvred doors and along the right was a long, low dressing table of white wood and two matching stools.

The bed was against the wall facing the door, a queen-size on a brass frame with a thick quilt in a dark purple cover and two big pillows in purple cases. The quilt was unruffled and the pillows were perfectly smooth as if the bed had never been slept in. Yo-yo took off her gold earrings and went over to the dressing table, running her stockinged feet through the carpet. She put the jewellery on the table next to a circular mirror and then took off her necklace. She was humming softly to the music playing on the stereo outside.

There was a lamp by the side of the bed, a thin, black stem, about six feet tall, which opened out to a bowl shape. At its base was a plastic brightness control which Chung had already set to the level he wanted. He switched on the lamp and turned off the main overhead light. The lamp illuminated most of the bed but left the corners of the room in near darkness.

"You want the light on?" said Yo-yo, turning to face him across the room.

"I want to be able to see you," said Chung, slipping off his jacket. He opened one of the closet doors and put his jacket on a wooden hanger.

388

Yo-yo reached up to unclip her hair and shook it so that it flowed around her shoulders. She walked slowly towards Chung, taking her time because she knew that men liked to watch her move. When she stood in front of him she removed his tie, watching his face as she slipped it out of his collar and dropped it on the floor. She ran the fingernail of her right index finger slowly down his chest and then used both hands to undo his belt, her eyes never leaving his face. Chung moved his chin forward to kiss her but she had already begun to move down on to her knees as her small hands pulled down his zipper. Her hair glistened as she looked up at him; he felt her cool hands on his skin, stroking and holding, and he gasped. She smiled at his obvious enjoyment, then opened her mouth, lightly licking her full lips with her small, pointed tongue. Chung groaned and placed both hands gently on the sides of her head. He could feel her ears through her hair. Her hands moved again, pushing his trousers down, and he felt cold air as she slipped open his silk boxer shorts and took him in her warm, wet mouth. She made soft groaning sounds and closed her eyes. Chung moved his hips backwards and forwards, turning his head away from the closet doors so that the video camera hidden there wouldn't film his features, its gentle whirring sound masked by Bryan Ferry's vocals.

"Got you, you bastard," said Neil Coleman under his breath. He'd just got off the phone from the luxury car rental company which had leased the Ferrari to Anthony Chung. He'd run the registration number through the Department of Vehicle Registration computer and discovered that the car was owned by the leasing company. All it had taken was one phone call and he had Chung's name, date of birth, address and bank details, along with his French passport number. He apparently had no Hong Kong identity card, which was interesting in itself. Where the leasing company had asked Chung to fill in details of his employment he had written "self-employed". So much for his claim that he was a colleague of William Fielding.

The address was an apartment in Kowloon Tong, a high-class residential area which was a far cry from his own tower block in Wan Chai. He put through a call to the Hong Kong government's Rating and Valuation Department which informed him that the flat was owned by a mainland Chinese company and was leased out on a monthly basis.

It took several calls to the Inland Revenue before he was satisfied that Chung paid no tax, either personal or through a company, and one call to the Births and Deaths General Register Office to confirm that he had not been born in Hong Kong. He telephoned through to Criminal Records and asked them to run a check on Anthony Chung. He waited on the line while they typed in his details and after a moment or two he was told that there was nothing on him, not even a parking ticket. His next step was to phone through to the Immigration Department. According to them, Chung had arrived in Hong Kong a month earlier on an Air France 747 from Paris and had been given a six-month visa. He had not applied for employment in the colony and had given the Sheraton Hotel in Tsim Sha Tsui as his address.

Coleman sat back in his chair and studied what he'd written down. Anthony Chung was the same age as Coleman, thirty-four, a French citizen, had no visible means of support but was driving one of the most expensive cars in the world and living in an apartment which probably cost at least three times Coleman's salary. What Coleman wanted to know was whether Chung had been born in France or if he was from mainland China. And he wanted to know what he was up to; once he found out, he'd stop him. And that was a promise.

Anthony Chung swung his bare feet up on to the coffee table and rested the clipboard on his thighs. He was wearing a black polo shirt and black jeans and he hadn't shaved that morning. He pointed his remote control unit at the video recorder and froze the picture on the large flat-screen television. He tapped his gold fountain pen against his chin as he studied the figures on the screen. Yo-yo could clearly be seen, sitting astride him, her back arched and her eyes closed. Chung's arms were up and he was caressing her breasts, but his face was in shadow at the end of the bed. There was no way of telling the identity of the man she was so energetically making love to. Chung made a note on the clipboard and pressed the remote control. Yo-yo jerked into motion again, grinding herself against the figure on the bed, gasping and panting and throwing her head backwards and forwards. Chung picked up a mug of black coffee and took a mouthful as he watched.

The Chung on the screen moved to sit upright, pushing Yo-yo on to her back and positioning her legs up on his shoulders, either side of his neck. He froze the picture and noted on the clipboard that at no time had his face been revealed to the camera lens. All that could be seen as he moved was the top of his head, and once her legs were around his neck his face was totally hidden. He started the video again and watched as his video image pumped in and out as Yo-yo grunted in time with her movements, her toes clenching and unclenching. Chung pressed the fast forward button and smiled as the lovemaking lurched into overdrive. He slowed it down again when the figures changed position. The screen Chung reached up to move her legs back around his waist where she interlocked her ankles and squeezed him. Yo-yo scratched her nails down his spine and kissed his neck like a vampire taking blood. The Chung on the video kissed her on the mouth but as he did the left side of his face was revealed to the camera. Chung stopped the video and noted the fact on the clipboard. When he kissed her left ear his face was hidden but as soon as he kissed her mouth he could be identified. He'd have to be careful in that position, but it was a good one because all of her face was in the light. If he put her across the bed he'd be able to kiss her on the mouth without his face being seen.

He started it again. The screen Chung lifted himself off Yo-yo and gently eased her on to her front, lifting her hips and taking her from behind. It was the position which gave him the most pleasure but it achieved the exact opposite of the effect he wanted: his face was in full view of the camera while Yo-yo had her head down. Earlier on, after he'd unzipped her dress and unfastened her stockings, he'd made her kneel on the end of the bed and he'd made love to her while he stood behind her and that had worked really well because his whole body had been in the dark. Yo-yo pushed herself up and held on to the brass frame of the bed, forcing herself back on to Chung. The whole frame of the bed rocked, so aggressive were his movements. It was a good picture, he could clearly see the sweat dripping down her neck and hear her panting, but he could equally plainly see his own face. He wrote on his clipboard and took another drink from his coffee mug.

The figures on the screen changed positions again, Chung sitting on the bed with his back to the closets, her sitting on him, her legs around his waist, lifting herself up, and then dropping down, making them both gasp. All that could be seen of him was his back. Perfect.

She threw back her head and moved faster and faster, her hair swinging from side to side and then she cried out and shuddered. She stopped moving and held her arms tight around his neck but the screen Chung hadn't finished with her. He took her arms and pushed her down on to the bed again where she lay with her eyes closed, her body glistening under the light from the lamp, her nipples hard and erect, her hair in disarray. Chung lay on top of her, kissing and licking at her small breasts, then moving slowly down her body, running his lips across her stomach and down to her thighs. As he watched he remembered how salty she'd tasted and how smooth her skin had been. The man on the screen eased himself off the side of the bed so that he was kneeling on the floor with his back to the closets, and pulled her with him so that she lay half on and half off the bed, her thighs either side of his face. He slipped his hands under her backside and kissed her thighs, licking the flesh from her knees to her groin, teasing her until she grabbed his head and pushed his mouth where she wanted it. Chung stopped the picture and studied it and made a note on his clipboard. When he started it again Yo-yo was going wild, bucking her hips and throwing her head from side to side so hard that he had to hold her tightly as he flicked his tongue in and out. It had been the first time that he felt that Yo-yo had actually taken pleasure from their lovemaking. Up until then he'd felt that she was simply being an actress, going through the motions and making the appropriate noises, but he'd known when he kissed her between the legs that she really had come, so much so that she'd almost strangled him with her thighs. Her passion had pushed him over the edge too, and he knew that the next section of the film, the last, showed him rolling Yo-yo on to her front and taking her roughly from behind, his hand over her mouth and her biting his index finger and thrusting herself against him as he grunted and pounded into her. Chung was embarrassed by the sudden recollection of his loss of control and he stopped the video and hit the rewind button, reluctant to see the evidence of his own passion. The screen went blank as the video recorder whirred.

He studied the notes he'd made on the clipboard. Yo-yo might have been just going through the motions most of the time but she'd been exactly what he'd wanted. She'd willingly made love in all the positions he'd asked of her and as he read through his notes he knew that when he had to do it for real he'd be able to keep his face hidden from the camera.

Lehman and Lewis sat on a hard wooden bench and watched as Doherty knelt in front of a gold Buddha with a benevolent smile, its hands cupped at its waist. They were sipping warm Coke as they watched the shaven-headed man light sticks of incense and pray. Tyler had said that he didn't want Doherty out on his own and had asked that one or other of them always be close by.

"I still don't understand why we need him or his Huey," said Lewis. "How much would it cost to buy one?"

An old Chinese woman wailed and waved a wooden tube of fortune-telling sticks as she knelt on a rush mat. Lehman sipped the metallic-tasting Coke. "A few hundred thousand dollars," he said. "But it's not as easy as just putting your money down and flying away. You have to show that you have insurance, and supply details of the pilot. There are all sorts of rules and regulations tied up with owning any sort of aircraft."

"So we're stuck with the Huey?"

"Yeah. And we couldn't have had the Huey without taking Doherty with us. He was the key to our robbery, and we were his ticket out of Thailand and back to the real world."

"I can't figure out why he wants to go back," said Lewis. "He was telling me that he got to read Western newspapers left by tourists who visited Udon Thani, so he knows what's going on. When Tyler first introduced us I thought he was going to be sort of trapped in the past, you know, like he'd stepped out of a time warp, and that we were going to have to fill him in on everything that happened over the past twenty years. But he seems to know more about world affairs than I do."

"Yeah, can you imagine explaining how Ronald Reagan got to be president?"

The two men laughed and clinked their red and white cans together. Doherty came over, stopping to slip his sandals back on his dusty feet. He looked like a bird that had been stripped of all its feathers. He was scrawny, slightly stooped and had a large nose and deep-set eyes. If it wasn't for his easy smile he'd look quite sinister, Lehman thought.

"Thanks for waiting, guys," said Doherty.

"No sweat," said Lewis.

"You guys want a beer?" He tossed them bottles.

"I still can't get over you being a monk and drinking," said Lewis.

Doherty shrugged his slight shoulders. "Being a Buddhist monk isn't the same as being a priest," he said. "The Thais are more flexible about their religion.

Being a Buddhist has more to do with finding your own path than it has with following prescribed rituals. You don't get thrown out just because you down a couple of Singha beers or go with a woman. It's more important that you reach a peace with yourself than screw yourself up by resisting temptation."

"Sounds like the perfect religion," said Lewis.

Doherty turned and fixed him with his deep-set eyes, his eyelids half closed like a basking lizard. "In many ways it is, Bart. It was the meditation side that I was drawn to. I'd been interested in it ever since I was a kid, but the monks taught me to do it properly, really to get inside myself. You reach the stage where your meditation is so pure, so uncluttered, that you stop succumbing to the temptations of the real world. That's why the older monks are celibate. It's from choice."

"But you never reached that stage?" said Lehman, throwing his empty can in the bin.

"No, Dan. I never reached that stage." He grinned and Lehman noticed that two back teeth were missing on the right side of his mouth, clearly the result of primitive dental facilities in northern Thailand.

Lehman looked at his Mickey Mouse watch. Tyler had said that he wanted to see them back at the hotel at four o'clock so they'd have to leave the temple soon and cross the harbour to Hong Kong Island.

"I've got to visit the men's room, guys," said Lewis, lifting himself up off the bench with a groan. Lehman and Doherty watched him walk away.

"He seems troubled," said Doherty.

"He's got personal problems," said Lehman. "His wife left him and he misses his kid."

"I think the worry is giving him an ulcer," said Doherty. "He's always rubbing his stomach and he doesn't eat so good."

Thoughts of Lewis's cancer filled Lehman's mind and he quickly moved to change the subject. "You're not in this for the money, are you, Chuck?"

"Are you?" Doherty replied calmly.

Lehman thought about it for a few moments. "Yes," he said. "Mainly for the money." And to make sure that Bart Lewis doesn't get out of his depth, a voice whispered inside his head.

"So why are you so surprised that money should be a motivating factor in my case? Because you found me in a temple?"

"Not just in a temple. You were a monk."

"I was a Buddhist. I still am. Becoming a monk was just a way of achieving what I wanted."

"Which was?"

"To stay in Thailand. And to come to terms with myself."

"And you've done that?"

Doherty nodded. "I think so. I think I learned as much from them as I could. I know I don't want to spend the rest of my life among the monks. I want to go home. I wanted to leave for some time, but it wasn't possible without the right papers. The colonel's contact in Bangkok has given me a new passport, the genuine article, too. He's given me a whole new identity. What the colonel is doing is a chance that only comes along once in a lifetime and I intend to grab it with both hands."

"You've got family back in the States?"

Doherty shook his shaven head. "None that I care about. That's one of the reasons I joined the army. To get away from them. I sure as hell won't be going back."

"You enlisted?"

"Yeah. Even though I knew it meant going to Nam. In a way I think I wanted to go right from the start. To test myself."

"So how did you end up in Thailand?"

"I'd had enough," said Doherty wistfully. "I'd seen too many things I didn't want to see. Too much hate. Too much needless killing."

"That's what wars are about," said Lehman.

"Maybe. But you were what, an army pilot, right?"

Lehman nodded.

"I flew for Air America, Dan. And they were a different bunch, believe me."

Lehman said nothing, he sat with the beer bottle held between both hands and listened. Doherty's eyes seemed to blank out as he spoke in a soft, even voice. A Chinese family walked past carrying a roast pig on a platter which they placed on the ground and began surrounding with burning sticks of incense.

"I was a good helicopter pilot, one of the best. I signed up because I wanted to fly. I wanted to fly more than anything else in the world, but while I was in Vietnam I became totally disillusioned with the army, with all its inefficiencies and its egos. I got into a fight with one of my commanding officers. He was faking his log book to make it look as if he was flying missions when he was safely in his tent, making himself look good so that he picked up medals while I was seeing my friends shot to pieces. I beat the shit out of him and after that I ended up with only the most dangerous missions. I knew that it was just a matter of time before I didn't come back. My tour of duty came to an end in '73 and I was approached with an offer to join Air America." He smiled. "Nobody actually mentioned the CIA but it was an open secret that it was funded by the CIA and handled most of the covert operations into the countries around Vietnam. It meant more money and I could continue flying slicks. I thought I was made. That was what I thought, anyway. Turned out that Air America was no better organised and flying for them was every bit as dangerous as flying for the army. I kept being told to ferry Special Forces units into Cambodia and Laos, always as a volunteer but if you didn't volunteer you didn't stay hired. There was as much incompetence among the men of the CIA and Special Forces as there was in the army, only they were a hell of a lot more vicious. I was flying a slick once when two CIA men threw out a North Vietnamese prisoner they were interrogating. I'd already decided that when my twelve-month contract with Air America was up, I was going home. I'd had enough. Then I saw kids killed. Women and children blown away in a country where we shouldn't even have been.

"I picked up a group of Special Forces men in the Huey you saw. I was supposed to ferry them into Laos, wait while they delivered a consignment, and then bring them back. Ship to ship. Turned out the mission was a drugs deal, the men I carried were delivering gold and picking up drugs, heroin I suppose. There was a double-cross, I don't know who or why, but they started firing and didn't stop until everyone was dead. Women and children, shot in the back. I saw the whole thing, and then they tried to kill me. I managed to get back to the Huey, but it was a close call."

Doherty fell silent, watching the Chinese family pin small pieces of coloured paper to the roast pig. "I could have gone back to Vietnam," said Doherty eventually. "But I figured that I'd either be court-martialled for leaving them behind, or they'd get out of Laos and come looking for me. Either way, I decided to call it a day. I went to Thailand."

"You flew all the way from Laos to Thailand?"

"It's not that far," said Doherty. "And the Huey had been fitted with extra fuel tanks. I kept flying until I was sure I was well inside Thailand and landed where you found it. A few days later I built the hut around it and shortly afterwards I joined the monastery. I'd been interested in Buddhism for some time. I started by doing odd jobs for the monks and after five years they allowed me to join as a novice." He grinned. "The rest is history."

"That's a hell of a story, Chuck," said Lehman.

"And it's true," said Doherty. "Monks don't lie." He ran his hands over his scalp. "It still feels strange talking to an American again."

"What about the tourists? The ones who visited your monastery, the ones who left the newspapers you read?"

Doherty shook his head. "I kept out of the way. News of an American monk would soon have got around, especially when the man involved was a deserter from the Vietnam War."

"You weren't a deserter," said Lehman. "You flew for Air America, not the army."

"You're splitting hairs," said Doherty. "And I couldn't let the monks get in trouble for looking after me. We always knew well in advance when visitors were coming. I just remained in my room. It was no hardship."

Lehman stood up and stretched, screwing up his nose at the sickly sweet smell that saturated the air around the temple. "You know what Tyler has planned?" he said, his back to Doherty.

"A robbery. A big one. We're going to hit the racetrack and we're going to use my old Huey. So far that's all I know. Except that no one will get hurt."

"He told you that?"

"I insisted. As I said, I am a Buddhist. I won't be a party to killing. Not any more."

Lehman turned to face Doherty. He shook his head, a confused smile on his face. "Robbery is okay, but killing isn't. I don't understand."

"You don't have to, Dan. They're the rules I live by, I'm not forcing them on you or anyone else."

"Did Tyler say what part you'd be playing in the heist?"

"I don't think he's going to let me fly the slick, if that's what you mean. I haven't been at the controls of a helicopter since 1974. You'll be flying her, I'll just be a passenger."

"You really think she'll fly again?" Lehman asked.

"You've got doubts?"

Lehman shrugged. "It depends on Lewis, and the parts. And a good dose of luck."

Doherty shook his head. "You've got to have faith in the colonel, Dan. You've got to have faith."

Lehman saw Lewis walking back, rubbing his stomach, and he looked at his watch. Mickey Mouse grinned up at him. "We're going to have to go. Let's catch a cab," he said.

Within an hour the three men had showered and changed and were standing outside the door to Tyler's suite. "Dan. Bart. Chuck. Come in," he said, holding the door open for them. He was wearing a khaki military-looking shirt with epaulets and sleeves neatly folded above his elbows. As they entered, Lehman saw a man he didn't recognise sitting on the patio with a glass of beer on the table in front of him. The man smiled and gave him a half wave. He was in his late thirties with a round, boyish face and hair that was neatly cut and combed. He looked like a Mormon missionary. Lehman was about to ask Tyler who the new man was when he suddenly saw he was holding the glass with a metal claw. It was Carmody, without his unkempt beard and trademark wraparound sunglasses.

"Larry?" said Lehman in amazement.

"No!" exclaimed Lewis in disbelief. "What happened to the beard? The hair?"

"Big difference, huh?" said Carmody. "It was getting on my nerves, what with the humidity and all."

"It's good," said Lehman, sitting down at the table. Carmody looked a lot less threatening without the facial hair and the shades, Lehman decided. His eyes were a pale grey and there were smile lines radiating from the edges. His cheeks were plump and the skin looked surprisingly soft. Carmody self-consciously rubbed a hand against his cheek.

There was a knock at the door while Tyler was fetching beers for Lehman and Lewis.

"Get that will you, Bart?" Tyler asked.

Lewis reacted immediately and opened the door to admit Eric Horvitz. Like Carmody, Horvitz had changed. He was still wearing his sunglasses but his hair had been trimmed so that it was shorter and a good deal tidier, and his beard had been cut and shaped.

"What's up with you guys?" asked Lewis, stepping aside to allow Horvitz into the room. "You visit the same hairdresser or something?"

"Something like that," said Horvitz and went out on the balcony to sit between Lehman and Carmody. "We had time to kill and thought we'd try out the barber shop in the Mandarin Hotel. Pretty good cut, huh?"

Lewis ran a hand through his own greying, curly hair. "Think I should give it a try?" he asked.

"Couldn't hurt, Bart," said Horvitz. "Couldn't hurt."

"Beer, Eric?" asked Tyler.

404

"Please, Colonel," said Horvitz. Tyler uncapped a bottle of San Miguel and handed it to him. When everyone had a drink he stood with his back to the window and told Horvitz and Carmody about the Huey in Thailand.

"A real Huey?" said Carmody. "We're going to use a Huey from Nam? Amazing."

"It'll arrive next week," said Tyler. "I've already arranged a factory out in the New Territories where we can carry out the repairs with no risk of being seen. We'll check out of the hotel tomorrow morning. Larry, have you got your driving licence?"

"Yes, Colonel."

"Good. You'll come with me first thing tomorrow to hire a couple of vehicles. I'll meet you in the lobby at nine."

"Yes, Colonel."

Lehman could see that Carmody's appearance wasn't the only thing that had changed. He was sharper, there was more confidence in his voice and bearing and he seemed to have lost some of his bitterness. He did everything but salute Tyler.

Tyler stood with his legs shoulder-width apart, his back ramrod straight and his hands clasped behind him. "As of tomorrow, you gentlemen should consider yourself on active duty. I don't expect you to stand to attention or to salute, but I want you to act as if this were a military operation. When I give orders I expect you to carry them out speedily and without question. This operation has been planned down to the minutest detail, yet it will be revealed to you only on a need-to-know basis. If there is anything you are unhappy about, talk to me, but there will be occasions when I cannot give you the whole picture. I'm sure you understand why. I'm equally certain you know that you must not talk to anyone about what we are doing here in Hong Kong.

"Let me summarise the position so far. Next week the helicopter will be delivered to our factory. At about the same time the replacement turbine and gearboxes will be shipped over from the Philippines along with the other spare parts you wanted, Bart. We will have a little over three weeks to get the Huey into shape, at which point I will give you further technical details of the operation. I can tell you that it will involve us flying from the New Territories to the track here in Happy Valley, and then out to sea where there will be a ship waiting for us. Dan, you have no problem in landing at sea?"

"It's pretty straightforward," said Lehman. "But I'd like to get some practice in."

Tyler shook his head. "Not possible, I'm afraid. In fact we'll only be able to test the Huey on the ground. The first time it flies is on the day of the operation. Is that a problem?"

Lehman sniffed. "It's not a problem, but you're not making it easy."

"I'd like us to be able to run through the whole thing from start to finish, but it's just not possible. If we fly the helicopter we lose the element of surprise."

"Understood," said Lehman.

406

"Bart, I'm arranging for you to have a little extra help," Tyler said to Lewis. "We'll have a Chinese mechanic with us; he'll be able to operate the lathes I've had installed in the factory." He looked around all the men sitting at the table. "Bart will be in charge of the refurbishment of the helicopter and I'd like you all to assist him. There will be a great deal of work to do and you'll all have to pitch in. Does anyone have a problem with that?" He was faced with a row of shaking heads.

Neil Coleman ordered a beer and leaned against the bar. He felt something cold and damp soak into the sleeve of his jacket and he straightened up, cursing.

"Fucking hell, CK, why don't you ever clean the bar?"

The wizened old barman grinned at Coleman and half-heartedly wiped a cloth over the Formica surface before plonking down a bottle of Heineken so hard that the lager inside foamed and bubbled over.

"Thanks, CK," said Coleman through tight lips. He looked around the police social club at the twenty or so expatriate officers, nodding to a few, studiously avoiding others. He saw Phil Donaldson drinking a Heineken from the bottle as he listened to one of the anti-triad officers. After a few minutes, Donaldson joined Coleman by the bar.

"Hiya, Neil, how are they hanging?" he asked.

"Straight and level," said Coleman. "What's new?"

"Not much. Loved the show the *Hong Kong Standard* gave the car bust. Did I miss it or weren't you mentioned?"

Coleman scowled. "I didn't even get a fucking invite."

"I saw they interviewed your little spy, though."

"Hui? Yeah. I'm starting to wonder if it's the Commissioner he's spying for and not the commies."

"Could be. You said so long and farewell to Ian?" Ian Cormack was an inspector with Serious Crimes who was leaving after twelve years of service to join a private security firm in Bangkok. Coleman, Donaldson and the rest of the expat police contingent had been invited to his leaving party. There were, Donaldson noticed, no Chinese there except for CK, the surly and ageless barman.

"Not yet," said Coleman. "I tell you, Phil, these get-togethers are getting more and more depressing."

"They're getting smaller and smaller, that's for sure. It won't be long before there's just you and me."

"Will you come to my leaving do?"

"Will you come to my mine?" asked Donaldson.

"Sure."

"That's good, because I'll be out of here long before you."

"Bastard!"

"There's Ian now. Ian!" Donaldson waved his beer bottle in the air to attract Cormack's attention. He came over, a portly man who, like Donaldson, was beginning to lose his hair. Unlike Donaldson, he made no attempt to cover his bald spot and, if anything, had his hair cut shorter to emphasise it. He shook hands with both men.

"Thanks for coming, guys," he said. Whisky slopped over the edge of his glass and trickled on to the worn green carpet.

"Another rat deserts the sinking ship," said Donaldson.

"It was an offer I couldn't refuse," said Cormack.

"I bet," said Coleman. Everyone knew that Cormack had been looking for another job for at least twelve months, just like every other expat on the force. "I'm glad for you, Ian." He raised the bottle and clunked it against Cormack's glass. More whisky slopped to the floor. "If you hear of any other openings . . ."

"The only openings he's going to find are in Pat Pong," jeered Donaldson. "Between the legs of the hookers there."

"Yeah, I'll miss you, too," said Cormack. "Anyway, thanks for coming, guys. I've got to work the room."

"Not much of a room to work," said Coleman.

"It's to be expected, I suppose," agreed Cormack, "the rate the guys are leaving. And they're only hiring Chinese."

"Huh!" snorted Donaldson. "They can't get Chinese to work for the police. I heard from a girl in Personnel that they wanted to hire 2,900 constables last year and only signed up 657. They wanted 160 to make up its inspectorate intake and you know how many they found? Twenty-six! Twenty-fucking-six! They're crazy. They block our promotion, they say they want to localise the force so that everything'll go smoothly after 1997, and what happens? I'll tell you what happens, every police station in the fucking colony is undermanned, they're down to about two-thirds of their establishment level and morale is lower than it's ever been."

Heads began to turn as Donaldson raised his voice, and Cormack backed away. "Hey, calm down, Phil," said Coleman.

"Yeah, there's nothing we can do about it," said Cormack. "Nobody cares any more. Shit, I used to be so proud of the force, I really did."

"The best police force money can buy," said Coleman, with a grin.

"And look at it now," continued Donaldson, ignoring Coleman's interruption. "At a time when Hong Kong needs a strong police force, it's weaker than it's ever been. Hell, do you remember when the Commissioner's house was burgled in broad daylight?"

"Yeah, and he assigned four uniformed constables to stand guard, round the clock," said Cormack. "That's more than they have patrolling most of the housing estates in Hong Kong. The man has no shame."

"Who has, these days?" said Donaldson. "It's every man for himself. And the last one out's a sissy. I tell you, there's going to be blood on the streets before long. Full-scale riots, the works. You know, Hong Kong used to be one of the safest places in the world, for expats anyway. There was trouble between the triads, sure, but they kept the violence among themselves. Europeans never got mugged, tourists could walk through the streets at midnight and be one hundred per cent safe, guaranteed, and it was almost unheard of for an expat's house to be broken into. Now look at it. That

410

woman on Disco Bay, the New Zealander, gang raped and cut up with a machete. Her house smashed to bits. That was just mindless. The Cathay Pacific pilot who was robbed at gunpoint. They roughed him up and trashed his house as well as robbing him. Tourists are being mugged every day, cars owned by Brits are being vandalised in front of their homes, their kids are getting beaten up at school. There's an anti-British feeling the like of which we've never seen before and it's going to explode. And who's going to contain it when it does? The army's pulling out, the police are leaving in droves. I tell you, it'll be the little yellow men in green uniforms, they'll be the ones restoring law and order and they'll do it like they did in Tiananmen Square."

"Oh, come off it, Phil," said Coleman. "The Chinese would never send the army in. They wouldn't dare."

"They wouldn't dare?" said Donaldson. "They wouldn't care. They own this place, remember. That's what Thatcher confirmed when she said they could have it in 1997. They're the landlords and we're the tenants, and if we can't keep the place in order they'll do it themselves. Trust me on this. You know that new highway that cuts right through Shenzhen. Tailor-made for tanks." Donaldson was practically shouting, and Coleman put his hand on his shoulder. Cormack moved away, embarrassed, as Coleman tried to calm him down.

The two men turned to face the bar, their folded arms resting on the Formica. Donaldson sighed. "I've got to get out, Neil. This place is killing me."

"It's killing us all," agreed Coleman.

"Huh! At least you've got your heiress," said Donaldson. "Play your cards right and she'll bail you out, you lucky bastard."

"I don't think so," said Coleman. He explained how he'd seen Debbie and Chung in the Ferrari.

"The same guy we saw in Hot Gossip?" asked Donaldson.

"Yeah."

"The one who said he was a colleague of her dad's?"

"Yeah."

"Shit. He lied, huh?"

"Wow, you ought to be a policeman, Phil," said Coleman.

"Don't get bitter and twisted," said Donaldson. "What have you found out about this guy Chung?"

"What makes you think I've found out anything?"

"Come on, Neil, I know you too well. I bet you've already run him through all the computers. You probably even know his shoe size."

"Nine," said Coleman, grinning. "Yeah, I found out some stuff." He told Donaldson what his enquiries had revealed. "But I want more. I want to know what he's up to."

"Have you tried Special Branch?"

"Special Branch?"

"They've got files on most of the people who deal with China. And anyone from the mainland who comes through Hong Kong goes on their computer."

"He's French," said Coleman.

"Fuck that, they're Chinese for ever, no matter what their passports say. If he wasn't born in China his parents were, or their parents. Or they'll have relatives in China. Try Special Branch."

"You know anyone who'll let me have a look at their files? They're a pretty secretive bunch."

"With good reason, mate. All their informers and agents are on those files. They're all due to be destroyed long before the Chinese move in. Some of the names in those files wouldn't last a minute if the Chinese knew about them."

"That's why I was asking if you knew anyone."

Donaldson looked over his shoulder. "Terry McNeil over there is your best bet. He's a solid enough guy, and he owes me a favour."

"You want to introduce me?"

"Now? Shit, mate, I'm pissed."

"Yeah, I guess you're right. Tomorrow maybe?"

"Tomorrow," agreed Donaldson. "You want another drink?" He held up his empty bottle and waggled it from side to side to attract CK's attention.

When Lehman stepped out of the elevator the following morning, Lewis and Doherty were already in the lobby sitting on an overstuffed sofa reading the *South China Morning Post*.

"Hi, guys," he said. "You eaten breakfast?"

"I'm not hungry," said Lewis, putting down his paper.

"I ordered on room service," said Doherty. "First time I ever had room service. In fact, this is the first time I've ever stayed in a hotel."

Lehman looked around the lobby. "Is Eric up?"

"He went out for a walk," said Lewis.

"In this heat? He must be crazy."

"Said he felt caged in. Needed his space."

They heard a car drive up to the front of the hotel and they all looked round to see Tyler at the wheel of a large white Toyota sedan. As he opened the door and climbed out Carmody arrived in a black Wrangler Jeep with the top down.

"Are we all ready, gentlemen?"

They nodded and Tyler told them to take their luggage and put it in the vehicles while he settled the bill. Horvitz returned while Lehman was putting his suitcase in the boot of the Toyota.

"We're checking out?" he asked.

"Yeah," said Lehman. "You got your case?"

"The bell captain's looking after it for me." He went to retrieve his suitcase and put it on top of Lehman's.

"We all ready?" asked Tyler, putting a sheaf of hotel computer print out into his jacket pocket. Everyone nodded and took their places in the vehicles: Horvitz, Lewis and Lehman joining Tyler in the Toyota, Doherty and Carmody in the Jeep.

The sky was cloudless and blue and the temperature was in the high eighties. Tyler had the air conditioning on full. He drove the car down the hill, past the racetrack and towards the tower blocks of Causeway Bay. They reached the entrance to the tunnel, the road dipped down and they drove under the fluorescent lights, the waters of the harbour above their heads. The road climbed up and they were soon outside with clear blue skies overhead. They queued at one of the toll booths and Tyler handed over the toll fee to a young man in a sweat-stained uniform with his ears plugged into a Sony Walkman. Lehman looked behind him and saw the Jeep with Carmody and Doherty. Carmody saluted and Lehman gave him a thumbs-up. Tyler drove the car through Tsim Sha Tsui, the roads between the luxury hotels and tourist shops packed with slow-moving traffic. A Singapore Airlines 747 roared overhead, its flaps down as it prepared to land.

The Toyota and the Jeep left Tsim Sha Tsui behind and headed through the countryside of the New Territories. The change in scenery was dramatic: in just a few miles they had gone from one of the most crowded cities on earth to a place of green hills and secluded valleys, small farms and villages where mangy dogs scavenged for scraps. The roads they drove on were wide and well built, as good as any they'd seen in the States. In the distance they saw more tower blocks and as they came closer it became clear that they were apartments and not offices or hotels, homes to thousands upon thousands of workers. The buildings were covered in poles on which the occupants hung their washing and they looked for all the world like thousands of ragged, multicoloured flags. Lehman wondered what sort of people would want to spend their lives living on top of each other like battery chickens, but realised they probably didn't have a choice. He wondered too whether life would be all that different for them under a communist regime.

The road wound its way through a range of hills and then alongside the sea. The water was overlooked by three-storey pretty white houses with orange-tiled roofs and large balconies, around which were clustered expensive cars. The setting was idyllic and Lehman figured that it was probably an area where expatriates lived. Seen in isolation there was no way of knowing that the area was so close to China; it looked more like Europe, Greece perhaps.

The scenery became more rural, but they saw no evidence of large-scale agriculture — just small family farms with little in the way of livestock. Lehman asked Tyler if he knew why and Tyler explained that the colony depended on China for most of its food and water, that labour and land was so cheap across the border there was little profit in growing crops in Hong Kong, even in the rural New Territories.

Tyler indicated to turn right and left the main highway down a two-lane road, slowing to make sure that Carmody followed. The two cars were alone on the road and they didn't see another soul until they turned off, this time along another two-lane road which ran alongside a shale cliff face which had been strengthened with concrete. They followed the road as it curved around the bottom of the cliff and then Tyler signalled a right turn down a single-track road which ran through uncultivated fields peppered with palm trees and bushes. Half a mile down the road they saw a two-storey prefabricated metal warehouse with a gently sloping roof, set back in a field and surrounded by a metal link fence about twelve feet high. There was a large sign by the entrance with the name of a construction company and across it was a banner which said "For Sale or Rent" and the telephone number of a real-estate agency. Tyler brought the Toyota to a stop in front of the metal gate and he switched off the engine. Carmody pulled up in the Jeep.

"No need to get out, I'm just going to get the gate," Tyler said. He got out of the car and took a set of keys from his pocket. The gate was locked with a thick chain and a large padlock which he unlocked. He slipped the chain out and pushed the gate open. It rasped angrily as if it hadn't been used for some time. He opened it as far as it would go and then got back into the car. He handed the keys to Lewis. "I'll drive us through, Bart, and then you can get out and lock it behind us. You can walk up to the building."

"Sure, Colonel," said Lewis, weighing the bunch of keys in his hand.

Tyler started the car again and drove it thirty feet inside the compound, and stopped to let Lewis out. Carmody drove through and followed the Toyota and parked at the front of the building. All the men climbed out as Lewis dragged the gate shut and re-padlocked it.

"This is going to be home for the next few weeks," said Tyler. He had two portable telephones. "I haven't had a phone put in," he explained. "I'll carry one of these and I'll leave one inside."

The men looked the building over. There were no windows and the metal panels were ribbed for extra strength. It stood on a concrete base which extended to a few feet from the link fence which surrounded it. There was a huge sliding door which took up half the front of the building and which reached more than twenty feet high, almost to the roof. Set into the sliding door was a normalsized door which had three locks and a letter box and the name of the construction company stencilled in white paint.

"They used to repair equipment here," explained Tyler. "The company pulled out of Hong Kong a few months ago."

He waited for Lewis to walk over with the keys and used them to open the three locks. He pushed open the door and went in. It was stifling hot inside and pitch dark. As the men followed him in, Tyler fumbled for a panel of light switches and one by one a series of fluorescent lights flickered into life. The building appeared to be even larger from the inside, almost the size of an aeroplane hangar. The roof was a network of steel girders from which were hanging a number of chains, hooks and pulleys. The strip lights were above the girders, hanging from the roof. The walls were featureless, the same ribbed steel panels as on the outside, and the floor was dusty concrete. There were bits of scrap metal and machine parts scattered around and oil stains that made irregular dark shapes in the grey concrete. By the side of one wall was a row of workbenches and above them was a wide selection of tools fixed to wooden boards. Most of the tools appeared to be new. Over in the far corner was a pile of cardboard boxes and to the left were what looked like a row of offices, single storey and made of wood.

"God, this is like an oven," said Carmody, wiping the sleeve of his sweatshirt across his brow.

"It's too big a space to air-condition, unfortunately, but I've had some fans brought in. They're over there." He nodded at the cardboard boxes. "Once we get set up we can use them to keep cool. As you can see from the lights, I've arranged for the electricity to be connected. Over there" — he pointed at the offices — "is where the firm had its supervisors. Those rooms are air-conditioned and there is a toilet with a shower room." He walked with the men across the floor to the offices, and pushed open the door which led to a carpeted corridor. There was another light switch by the door and Tyler turned on the lights. Half a dozen doors led off the corridor and there was another door facing them at the end. "That's the bathroom," said Tyler, nodding at the end door. He waved at the row of doors to the left. "I've had camp beds put in these offices and some basic furniture — chairs and somewhere to hang your clothes. There's an air conditioner in each room. Bart, why don't you take this one, I'll be in here, then Dan, Eric, Chuck and Larry. If anyone's unhappy with the arrangements, let me know, but don't expect four-star luxury."

"Cooking facilities, Colonel?" asked Carmody.

"There's a microwave in one of those cardboard boxes, and a coffee machine. There's some food there but once we're organised here you can drive to the nearest town and bring back some provisions. First we open the main door and get the cars inside. I want us to keep a very low profile while we're here. The nearest village is two miles away, our only neighbour is an old people's home about half a mile away at the end of the

419

road outside. We stay indoors while we're here. In this part of the New Territories non-Chinese are quite rare, so you'll stick out like sore thumbs. No sunbathing outside or fooling around. Understood?"

He was answered with a chorus of "Yes, Colonel" and he nodded as if pleased with their response.

"Marie, I'm sure you can do the flowers better than that," said Debbie Fielding, her hands on her hips and an exasperated expression on her face. Marie was a good, hardworking maid but she had not an ounce of creativity. Her big, brown eyes began to well up with tears. God, thought Debbie, Filipinas can be so sensitive. She smiled at the maid and leaned across the table. "Look, watch me," she said, and rearranged the floral display. "Put the larger orchids in the middle, like this. See?"

Marie nodded enthusiastically. "Yes, Miss Fielding. I am sorry."

"Everything's got to be perfect tonight, Marie. You know this dinner party is very important for my mother. Nothing must go wrong. How is Somsong getting on in the kitchen?" The Fieldings' Thai cook was famed for her cuisine and more than one visitor to the house had tried to lure her away with promises of more money.

"She is fine, Miss Fielding," said Marie.

Marie, Somsong and the Fieldings' other maid, Theresa, lived in small rooms at the back of the house. Debbie had missed having maids while she was studying in the UK. It had come as quite a shock when

420

she found she had to do her own washing and ironing and that ovens and bathrooms needed cleaning. She found that maids could be a pain and were naturally lazy unless kept on their toes, but they made life so much more civilised. She scrutinised the long rosewood dining table and its fourteen place settings, the solid silver candelabra and the silver cutlery glinting in the overhead lights. Once the meal was ready and the guests had all arrived the candles would be lit and the lights extinguished. The dining room was impressive — tall ceilings, her father's favourite gilded Thai wood carvings on the walls and the French window with its breathtaking view of the harbour and Kowloon beyond.

Debbie looked at her watch. Seven-thirty. The invitations had said eight though Sally and Michael Remnick would be at the house earlier to greet the guests. The dinner party was in their honour, a last chance for their closest friends to say goodbye. They were flying out to Singapore on Monday.

Debbie went up the wide, curving staircase and along the hallway to her bedroom. She stripped off her sweatshirt and jeans and walked into her large closet in her bra and pants. She ran a hand along the lines of shirts and dresses wondering what to wear. She pulled out a Chanel her mother had bought for her but dismissed it as too serious. A Kenzo was too frivolous, a Ralph Lauren too formal. She wanted something that would be sexy because she'd invited Anthony Chung to be her partner at the party, but nothing too flashy because the evening was for the Remnicks. Her hand touched leather and she pulled out the hanger. It was a black leather dress by Isaac Mizrahi, backless and ending mid-thigh with a chrome zipper running diagonally across the front. She held it up against herself and looked at her reflection in the mirror. A mixture of demure evening wear and cycle slut from hell. It was perfect. She picked out a pair of fishnet stockings and black high-heeled shoes and changed into them. She went into her bathroom where the light was brighter and inspected herself. Satisfied, she sat in front of her dressing table and brushed her hair. Downstairs she heard the doorbell ring and Theresa hurry to answer it. She put the hairbrush on the dressing table, checked her make-up in the mirror, and went down to the lounge where Sally and Michael Remnick were standing by the mantelpiece.

"Sally, Michael," said Debbie, holding out her arms. "We're going to miss you so much." She rushed to hug Sally and kissed her on both cheeks, then did the same to Michael. Sally Remnick had on a long black dress, high at the neck and cut low at the back and her skin looked deathly pale in contrast. Other than during her games of tennis, she rarely exposed her skin to the burning Hong Kong sun. Michael, on the other hand, loved to sunbathe and his skin was bronzed and tending to become leathery, even though he was barely into his forties. He looked like a 1930s matinee idol in his tuxedo and with his slick-backed hair, greying at the temples. Michael Remnick was a favourite on the cocktail party circuit, charming and always ready with a funny anecdote when the conversation flagged.

Hostesses loved to have him and his wife on their guest list.

Theresa was handing them drinks when Anne Fielding came into the room, closely followed by William, who was brushing lint off the shoulder of his dinner jacket. Anne was wearing her favourite Calvin Klein strapless evening dress, a long slip of gold lace which hugged her figure and showed off her neck and shoulders and a good deal of cleavage. She wore her hair up at the back, held in place with a gold clip and there was a gold link chain around her neck, a present from William on their twentieth wedding anniversary.

The Fieldings greeted Sally and Michael, both of whom complimented Anne on how beautiful she looked.

Anne looked Debbie up and down. "That looks good on you," said Anne. "It's a bit 'Mistress of the Dungeon', but I'm sure Anthony will be impressed."

"Anthony?" said Sally, one eyebrow raised. "Not Anthony Warmington at Schroeders?"

William Fielding shook his head and accepted a tumbler of whisky and water from Theresa without thanking her. "I wish it was," he said.

"Dad!" exclaimed Debbie.

"I meant he's a sharp young man, that's all," said Fielding. He took a drink from his glass and savoured the Scottish malt. "Anthony Chung is Debbie's new boyfriend," he explained to the Remnicks.

"Well, he's hardly a boyfriend," said Debbie, sighing in exasperation.

"Well you have been out with him several times," said Anne. She took a gin and tonic from the tray held by Theresa.

"Three times, Mum," said Debbie.

"What would you like to drink, Miss Fielding?" asked Theresa.

"White wine, please," said Debbie, not looking at the maid. "Three times hardly constitutes a boyfriend," she said to her father.

"At least he's a big improvement on that policeman," said Fielding. "He still hasn't done anything about my car."

"Your Mercedes?" said Remnick.

"It's been stolen," said Fielding.

"God, another car theft," said Remnick. "Vandalism is way up, too. Our neighbours had the tyres of their Jaguar slashed last week. The attacks seem to be centred on British-made cars, have you noticed?"

"British shops, too," said Anne. "There was an article in the *South China Morning Post* about a campaign of harassment against British retailers, supergluing their door locks, spray-painting slogans on the windows."

"One of the few articles in the *Post* you can believe," laughed Remnick. "It's not the most accurate of organs, is it?"

"They can't get the staff, I suppose," said Fielding. "They're being hit by the exodus like the rest of us."

The doorbell rang and Theresa went to answer it. She opened the door to admit two couples, mutual friends of both the Fieldings and the Remnicks, and soon the lounge was full of laughter and gossip.

424

Anthony Chung arrived promptly at eight. Theresa let him in and Debbie saw him from across the room. It was the first time she'd seen him in a dinner jacket, and he looked stunning. He looked around the room confidently, like a lion looking for the weakest member of the herd, and when he saw her he smiled and headed over in her direction.

She kissed him on the cheek and smelt his aftershave, spicy and seductive. "You look fantastic," she said, linking her arm through his.

"You too," he replied.

"Why thank you, kind sir. Come and say hello to my mother."

She took Chung around the room, introducing him to everybody and impressed by the way he handled himself. It was only when they were going through to the dining room that she noticed that he was the only Chinese there.

William Fielding sat at the head of the table with Sally Remnick on his right and Debbie on his left. Anne Fielding sat at the far end of the table, opposite her husband, with Michael Remnick on her right and an American lawyer on her left. The food was superb and the conversation was typical of any Hong Kong gathering: the future of the colony after 1997; falling property values; the disintegration of law and order; and who was leaving.

Sally Remnick asked Chung for his view of what was happening to Hong Kong and he studied her face before answering. "I think that the laissez-faire attitude which has allowed Hong Kong to flourish will be stifled under Chinese rule," he said. "I think it will be a slow death. A gradual increase in bureaucracy, higher tax rates, more interference, until eventually Hong Kong loses all the advantages which made it so successful."

Ronald Sager, a senior editor on one of the colony's more successful business magazines, nodded in agreement as he helped himself to more salad. "And the people here know it," he said. "That's why so many are leaving. I had to get an American visa in my new passport, and you know how long I had to queue at the consulate? Nine hours! The queue starts at four o'clock in the morning. I got there at six o'clock and I didn't get to the front until the afternoon. The line winds all the way up Garden Road, and they're all Hong Kong Chinese wanting to emigrate. America, Canada, Australia, they don't care where so long as they get out. Tell me, Anthony, what sort of passport do you have?"

"French," said Chung.

"See," said Sager, looking around the table. "That proves my point. Any smart Chinese already has his safety net, just in case. Isn't that right, Anthony?"

Debbie rubbed Chung's leg with her own under the table, letting him know that she sympathised with him and was sorry that he'd been adopted as the token Chinese viewpoint. He smiled at her and didn't seem over-worried.

"You have to understand that we are all refugees here in Hong Kong. Either refugees or the children of refugees. The people here fled from China, either for economic reasons or because they felt they couldn't live under communist rule after the communists took over in 1949. They know all too well what life is like under communism and have no wish to go back to it."

"It's unusual for a Hong Kong Chinese to have a French passport?" asked Sally Remnick.

Chung nodded. "Most Chinese don't like Europe, it's true. They feel happier where there are established Chinatowns in cities like Vancouver, Sydney, San Francisco. But I love Paris, I am very comfortable there."

"It's a beautiful city," agreed Sally.

"And the food is good," said William Fielding.

"But not as good as this," smiled Chung, indicating his empty plate. "I have never eaten such excellent Thai food."

"We have a superb Thai cook," said Fielding. "A real treasure."

"Speaking of treasure, Mr Fielding, I wonder if you, or rather your bank, might be able to offer me some assistance."

"In what way?" asked Fielding. He showed no signs of irritation at business being raised at the dinner table. In Hong Kong, there were no restrictions on when or where business could be discussed.

"I am expecting a delivery of Chinese antiques from the mainland, and I will have to have them placed in a high-security area until I am ready to ship them to France. Does the bank have such a facility?"

"We do have a depository in Kowloon, Anthony, but it is expensive. You might not find it worth paying the charges. What would the value of the shipment be?"

Chung shrugged. "In the region of two million dollars," he said.

"Hong Kong dollars?" asked Fielding.

"Oh no, US dollars," said Chung. Fielding raised his eyebrows, impressed. "They are very valuable pieces," continued Chung. "Small but extremely valuable."

"How small?" asked Fielding. "The charges would depend on their size."

"I suppose in total they would take about as much room as two cabin trunks. They're mostly jade, so they don't take up too much room."

Fielding nodded. "I don't think they'd be a problem," he said.

"But how secure is the depository? I can't afford to lose them."

Fielding smiled. "It's the safest place in Hong Kong, I can assure you of that," he said confidently. "It's even more secure than the vaults of the Hongkong and Shanghai Bank. Look, if you've any doubts I can arrange a tour for you."

"That would be great," said Chung.

"I'll speak to our head of security, George Ballantine. I'll tell him to expect your call on Monday."

Marie and Theresa began to clear away the dishes and Anne Fielding led the guests back into the lounge for coffee and liqueurs.

After tending to the Remnicks, Anne went over to Chung with a silver coffee pot and a cup and saucer.

"Coffee?" she asked.

"Please," he said, holding the cup and saucer while she poured.

428

"I thought it was illegal to take antiques out of China," she said.

"It is, without an export licence, and they're hard to get hold of."

"So you managed to get a licence?" she asked.

"No," he smiled, "unfortunately I didn't. That dress is lovely. It's a Calvin Klein, isn't it?"

"My, you have a good eye for clothes," said Anne, genuinely surprised. "I doubt if any of the women in this room would be able to identify the designer just by looking at the dress."

"He's almost never wrong," said Debbie, walking up to them.

"It looks stunning on you," said Anthony. "You have excellent taste."

"He's right, Mum. It's a gorgeous dress."

Anne held the coffee pot out to her daughter. "Here, Debbie, can you give this to Theresa? I'm fed up with playing at waitress. And send Marie over with a brandy, please."

"Another brandy?" said Debbie.

"Watch it, young lady," warned Anne.

Debbie took the empty coffee pot and moved away, giving Chung a big smile as she went. Anne took her own coffee cup off the mantelpiece.

"Your husband is a very lucky man, having such a beautiful wife," Chung said once Debbie was out of earshot.

Anne smiled and felt her cheeks redden at the unexpected compliment.

"And such a pretty daughter," he added.

Anne studied Chung over the top of her coffee cup. "Are you trying to flatter me, Anthony?" she said.

He smiled disarmingly. "Me, Anne?" he said. "What on earth makes you think that?"

"And why, Anthony, am I 'Mrs Fielding' when either Debbie or my husband is around, and 'Anne' when they're not?"

Chung thought about her question as he sipped his coffee. "I suppose because a woman is often defined by the people she surrounds herself with. When you're with your husband you are his wife, when you're with Debbie you're a mother."

"And when I'm with you?"

"Then, Anne, you can be yourself." He looked at her and she felt his eyes bore deep inside her as if he were rummaging through her closets looking for secrets. "Tell me, Anne, how long has it been since you've been able to be yourself?"

He waited for her to answer, but they were interrupted by Debbie's return.

"So what are you two so engrossed in?" Debbie asked.

"I was asking your mother where she got her clothes," said Chung. He looked at Anne as he spoke and she felt the lie bind them together like an invisible chain.

"The Landmark," said Debbie. "She's there almost every afternoon visiting one boutique or another."

"Oh, Debbie, you make it sound as if I do nothing but spend money," scolded Anne. Marie came over with a balloon glass of brandy which she handed to

430

Anne. She held it up to her nose and breathed in its heady bouquet, her eyes on Anthony Chung.

Anthony Chung telephoned George Ballantine on Monday morning, just before noon. His secretary put Chung through straight away so he figured that William Fielding had been as good as his word and paved the way for the tour of the depository. Ballantine spoke with a Scots accent, but with a guttural tone as if he was a heavy smoker.

"Aye, Mr Chung, I was told to expect your call," said Ballantine. "Would you be able to come over some time this afternoon? Say three o'clock?"

"Three o'clock will be fine," said Chung. "But there's one problem — I've no idea where the depository is."

"I'm glad to hear that," chuckled Ballantine. "We do try to keep a low profile." He gave Chung the address and told him to telephone if he had any trouble finding the building. "I warn you, there's no sign on the outside," said Ballantine. "Not even the bank's logo."

Chung thanked him and hung up. He spent the morning working on the Porsche. He had taken part in three races including his first meeting, and he'd won the most recent, taking the one million dollar prize and a kiss from Winnie Lo. She'd made it quite clear that she was willing to give him more than a kiss but he'd politely declined. The money would go some way to deferring his expenses and he'd put the briefcase of cash under his bed. The racers were used to seeing his Porsche and he'd begun to open up the throttle and show them what it was capable of. He'd also compiled a list of the best drivers and had already approached five to see if they'd be willing to help him. None had so far refused.

At three o'clock he drove down the road in Kowloon where Ballantine had said the depository was located but couldn't find it. He parked the Ferrari in a multi-storey car park and retraced the road on foot. The area was mainly residential blocks with some low-rise offices, featureless buildings which were a far cry from the glass and marble towers of the Central business district.

There was no block which matched the number Ballantine had given him, but he found the building eventually, more by elimination than anything. It was on the corner, and when he walked a few yards down the side street he saw an entrance where vans could drive through a metal gate. Each wall of the building bordered the sidewalk and it had none of the barbed-wire-topped security walls which he'd expected. There were no windows on the ground floor but from the second floor up it looked like every other office block in the area. He stood back and shaded his eyes so that he could scrutinise the upper floors. Only then did he see the concealed cameras set into the walls, covering all the approaches.

He walked back to the main road and along the front side of the building. Ballantine had been right — the bank kept the lowest of low profiles. The main entrance was a metal and glass door through which he could see a simple lobby with a grey carpet and a teak reception

432

desk. There was a print of an old sailing ship on the wall and a potted palm which was beginning to go yellow from over watering. There was a grey metal elevator door but Chung noticed that there was no strip of lights above it to indicate which floor the elevator had stopped at.

Chung pushed open the door and walked into the lobby, feeling the sweat on his face dry under the fierce air conditioning. Behind the reception desk sat a middle-aged Chinese woman in a light blue blouse and a floppy red scarf. There were no guards but Chung saw a closed-circuit camera fixed to the wall behind her. Other than an appointments book and a telephone the woman's desk was empty. She smiled but said nothing, waiting for him to speak.

He introduced himself and she checked his name in the appointments book before asking to see his identity card. Ballantine had explained that he'd need some form of identification so he'd brought his passport with him and he handed it over to her. She compared his face to the picture, smiled again, and gave it back. She asked him to take a seat and pointed to the sofa under the sailing print. As he sat down she picked up the telephone and two minutes later the elevator doors hissed open and a grey-haired man in his early fifties stepped out. His face was fleshy and his cheeks and nose were criss-crossed with broken red veins as if he were over-fond of alcohol. He had a pot belly which was accentuated by the tightness of his grey suit. He'd fastened all three buttons and the material was stretched taut. Clipped to his breast pocket was a laminated security badge which contained his picture.

He introduced himself as George Ballantine in the rough Scottish brogue which Chung had heard over the phone. Ballantine's handshake was moist and limp and Chung had to resist the urge to wipe his hand afterwards. Chung followed Ballantine into the lift, the doors hissed closed, and Ballantine pressed the upper of the two buttons on the control panel. There was no indication of which floor the elevator stopped at, though Chung could tell from the way his stomach lurched that they had travelled up. The doors opened on to a white corridor and Ballantine led him along to a large corner office with windows which looked down to the streets below.

"You managed to find us all right," said Ballantine, handing Chung a business card.

"As you said, it wasn't easy," said Chung.

Ballantine walked around his large black desk and sat down in a high-backed leather swivel chair. Chung sat in one of two smaller chairs on the opposite side of the desk. On the wall behind Ballantine were a number of framed photographs of him standing in front of different vault doors, most of which were bigger than he was.

Ballantine saw Chung looking at the pictures. "They're the vaults we have in our various branches," said Ballantine. He leaned back and pointed to one of the photographs. "That's the one we have here. I'll take you down and show it to you later."

"They look impressive," said Chung.

"To be honest, Mr Chung, looks can be deceptive. The size or thickness of a vault door is, more often than not, nothing more than a public relations exercise. Very few professionals would even try to go in through the door, they'd go in through the top or bottom or the sides. But people expect to see a big door, so we give it to them. Now, William tells me that you have Chinese artefacts you wish to store. Is that right?"

Chung nodded. "They're fairly small, but there's quite a few of them."

"I think you'd be better off keeping them in our safe-deposit box vault. You might need several boxes, but I'm sure we'll be able to accommodate you."

"How is business at the moment?"

"It's hectic," said Ballantine. "Do you want a coffee?"

"Please," said Chung. Ballantine pressed the intercom switch on the telephone and asked his secretary to bring in coffee for two.

"We've never been so busy," continued Ballantine. "Everyone seems to be switching their savings into gold or valuables and it's not safe keeping them at home, what with the rising crime rate and everything. They're coming in every day with gold, diamonds, paintings, even cash."

"They?"

"People who don't trust bank accounts, people who remember what happened in 1949 when the communists took over China. It happened in Vietnam, too, when the South fell. Any money in bank accounts was as good as lost."

"You're not saying that you believe that's going to happen in 1997?" said Chung.

Ballantine held up his hand and shook his head. "No, no, of course not," he soothed. "But that is the perception that many Chinese have. And you know as well as I do how rumours can get spread here. Like wildfire. You must have heard the story about the tram that broke down during a typhoon. Everyone on the tram had to get off and the only place they could find to shelter was in front of a bank. People walking by assumed they were queuing to take their money out and within hours there was a run on the bank."

Chung smiled thinly. "An apocryphal story, Mr Ballantine," he said.

"That may well be, but the run on the Standard Chartered Bank in 1991 wasn't apocryphal. There were rumours, just rumours mind, that Standard Chartered was connected to BCCI. There were queues of depositors withdrawing all their savings. And Citibank faced a similar run. They happened, Mr Chung. I saw the lines. The Chinese have a tendency to believe any rumour that affects their savings. You can tell them until you're blue in the face that money can be sent around the world at the press of a button, but if they can't hold it in their hands they don't believe in it. It's the old refugee mentality."

"Once bitten," said Chung.

"Exactly," said Ballantine. "They'd rather have 100,000 American dollars in a safe-deposit box where they can touch it when they want to rather than the same amount in a foreign currency account earning interest. We can offer them paper gold, a sort of bank passbook which is equivalent to gold and we link the value of their investment with the price of gold on a daily basis, but they'd still rather have physical gold, either bars or gold coins. They sell more gold coins in Hong Kong than anywhere else in the world. Safety-deposit boxes have always been popular in the colony, but I've never seen it at this level before."

"What do you think will happen after 1997?" asked Chung.

"To the stuff in our vaults? My personal opinion is that most of it will be moved overseas before then. Sure, it might come back, but I doubt it. These are nervous times, as you're probably all too well aware. Mr Fielding tells me that you'll be taking your antiques abroad before too long." He looked at Chung expectantly, as if he'd just proved a complicated mathematical theorem and was expecting a pat on the back.

"I think they'll be more appreciated overseas, that is true," said Chung, not wanting to deflate the man's pompous self-regard. The more self-important he felt, the more he'd let slip information which would be of use. "But from what I've seen they should be perfectly safe here."

Ballantine smiled. "You haven't seen the half of it, Mr Chung," he said. "For instance, we saw you walk down the side-street and survey the building and the delivery entrance."

"You saw me?" said Chung, expressing the desired amount of surprise.

"Upstairs in our control room, we have a team of men monitoring the screens linked to the various surveillance cameras. I'll take you up and show you. But basically it's impossible to get within a hundred yards of this building without being seen. The entrance you came in is one of only two ways into the building, the other being the vehicle entrance at the side. The lift we came up in stops only at this floor. To go down to the vaults or up to the control room you have to use the other elevator at the far end of the building which means going by a second reception desk, and again that involves being observed by at least three more cameras. The elevators also have hidden cameras, concealed in the ceiling lights. There is an elevator override system operated from within the control room, and the garage door can only be opened by our controllers. Basically, it is impossible to get into, or out of, the building without bank staff supervision."

There was a knock on the door and a small, plump secretary appeared with two mugs of black coffee. Chung stirred his coffee as the secretary left the office.

"Does the bank store its own money here?" asked Chung.

"Not our normal day-to-day cash deliveries, no," said Ballantine. "The facility isn't big enough for the sort of through traffic we'd need. We can get armoured cars in downstairs, but no more than three at a time and the roads don't really give us enough room outside. So far as getting cash to our various branches is concerned, we have a vault under our head office in Central and a larger vault out in the New Territories at a secret location."

"More secret than this one?" said Chung with a smile. He drank his coffee, suppressing a shudder when he discovered it was instant and not freshly ground.

"Oh yes, it has an even lower profile than this one," said Ballantine. "How's your coffee?"

"It's delicious," said Chung, taking another mouthful and sliding the mug on to Ballantine's desk. "So this is wholly a safe-deposit centre?" he said. "That the bank doesn't use this to store its own resources? I find that a little troubling."

"Oh no, that's not what I meant to suggest at all," said Ballantine, putting his own steaming mug on the desk. "I was referring to storage and delivery of cash, the notes which are printed by the Hongkong and Shanghai Bank and by Standard Chartered. Our gold stocks, which are considerable, are held here, as are our stocks of foreign currency. Why don't I give you the tour? We can finish our coffee later."

"That would be marvellous," said Chung. He stood up and followed Ballantine out of the office and along the corridor. Ballantine walked to a second elevator and hitched up his trousers while he waited for it to arrive. Like the elevator that had ferried them up from the reception area, there were no floor indicators. When it arrived and the two men had stepped inside, Chung saw that the buttons inside weren't labelled either.

"I'll take you to the main vault first," said Ballantine. "I think you'll find it quite impressive." He pressed the lowest button and Chung felt the elevator descend smoothly. When the doors opened they stepped out into a large lobby. To the right was a long, low desk behind which sat a man in a light grey suit and wearing a bank tie. He stood up when he saw Ballantine.

"Good afternoon, Mr Law," said Ballantine. "This is Mr Chung. He is considering becoming a client of ours. Could you give him a badge, please?"

"Certainly, Mr Ballantine," said Law. He took a laminated badge marked "Visitor" from a drawer and affixed it to the breast pocket of Chung's suit.

Ballantine took Chung past the desk and stood in front of a door composed of thick, vertical, metal bars, each the diameter of a man's wrist. Ballantine looked over his shoulder and nodded at Law who pressed a button on a control panel mounted in the top of the desk. The door slid smoothly sideways, revealing a corridor lined with steel which led to a huge circular vault door which Chung recognised from the photograph in Ballantine's office. The door itself was about eight feet thick and it was wide open, revealing the metal-lined vault beyond. Chung could see the thick metal rods set into the door which would slot into the sides of the vault when the door was closed and the locks turned. The door itself was tiered, like a steel wedding cake put on its side, and there were corresponding grooves in the wall of the vault so that there was no way anything could slip through the sides of the door when it was shut.

"Wow," said Chung. "It's massive. Is it solid steel?"

Ballantine nodded. "Yes, and it has the latest in time locks. Once the door is locked and the clocks set, it can't be opened. By anybody."

"Surely there must be some way? What if someone is locked in by mistake?"

Ballantine laughed. "Mr Chung, you've been watching too many movies. It would be impossible for anyone to be locked in. But — and it is a huge but — if anyone were foolish enough to get themselves trapped, the vault has its own air supply. He would just have to wait inside until the time locks open the vault door. There is no way to open the doors any sooner. If he were to be locked in on Friday evening, it would be Monday morning before the door opens. He would be very thirsty and hungry, and the vault would probably stink to high heaven, but he'd be alive."

"So it's locked right through the weekend?"

"That's right. That's one of our best safety features. Even if anyone were to get into the building, they wouldn't be able to open the vault door."

Ballantine stepped into the vault and motioned for Chung to follow him. The vault itself was about the size of a basketball court, with the floor and ceiling composed of seamless metal. Around the walls were racks containing polythene-wrapped parcels which Ballantine said were foreign currency stocks. "Sterling, Deutschmarks, yen, dollars, francs," he said as he walked around the vault. In the centre of the vault was a line of four blocks, each as high as a man's stomach and each covered with a light green cotton sheet. "And here," he said, indicating one of the piles, "here is where we keep the gold." He pulled back the cloth to reveal a steel rack filled with gold bars which gleamed dully under the subdued lighting. The stack was ten bars wide and ten bars deep and the rack was ten bars high. There were 1,000 bars in the single stack, and each bar weighed one kilo. "This is where we keep the bullion; the various coins we sell are in the racks over there."

He picked up one of the bars with both hands. "This is a one kilo bar, 99.99 per cent pure," he said. Chung took it from him and lifted it to his chest.

"There's something so powerful about gold," said Chung. "It has an aura about it that you just don't get with money."

"I know what you mean," said Ballantine. "I can understand why you Chinese are so attracted to it."

Chung looked at Ballantine coldly and wondered if the man knew how offensive he found his racist comments. Almost certainly he didn't. And Chung had no doubt that if he were to tell Ballantine, the man would put his hand on his heart and say that of course he wasn't racist and that some of his best friends were Chinese. Chung smiled. "This is all the bank's gold?"

"Some of it is kept on behalf of our customers, private investors and companies who wish to keep some of their assets in gold. But most of it is the bank's. Of course, we have no idea how much gold is stored in the safety-deposit boxes upstairs. It'll be tens of millions of dollars, I'm sure. I would think that the gold exceeds the cash."

"How much gold do you have here?" asked Chung, waving his hand at the cloth-covered stacks.

"You'd have to ask Mr Law for an exact figure," said Ballantine. "But I would think it would be of the order

442

of thirty-five million pounds." He said the figure slowly, as if wanting Chung to be impressed.

Chung whistled softly. "Wah!" he said, hating himself for playing the dumb Chinese but knowing that he had to play along with Ballantine. There was still information he needed.

"So you can see, the bank is more than happy with the security arrangements here. And I'm sure you will be, too. Let me show you our safety-deposit area. I think it should be suitable for your antiques, but if not we can arrange to have them stored here."

They went out of the vault and Chung handed his badge back to Mr Law, smiled and thanked him, and followed Ballantine to the elevator. Their next stop was the floor above the vault. The elevator door opened on to another lobby which was identical to the first, though this time there was a young girl with shoulder-length wavy hair wearing a white blouse and dark blue skirt behind the low desk. Like Mr Law she stood up when she saw Ballantine, and she pinned a security badge to Chung's breast pocket. She patted the lapel of Chung's suit after she'd attached the badge and she gave him a warm smile. Ballantine didn't introduce her, he walked past her without a word and stood in front of the barred door. She pressed the button to open the door and it slid open. The two men walked into the waiting area. Along the wall were a number of booths, each with two metal chairs with padded leather seats in front of a wooden shelf. Several of the booths were occupied with customers, all Chinese, Chung noted, bent over their safety-deposit boxes. Opposite the booths was another vault door, almost as big as the first one.

"This one has time locks as well?" asked Chung as they walked through it into the vault.

"Just like the one below," said Ballantine. "This one is monitored, too, and there are alarms connected to the control room."

The walls of the vault were lined with thousands of safe-deposit boxes, varying in size from small ones a few inches square, which could contain nothing bigger than a few papers, to ones on the lower levels which were the size of large cabin trunks. Each box had two locks. Ballantine walked over to one wall and showed the locks to Chung. "When you rent a box, we give you one key, and we keep the other," he explained. "When you come to open your box we match your signature against our records and we use our key and yours to open the box. That way no one else can open your box."

"What if I lose the key?" said Chung.

"We do have a way of opening the boxes if absolutely necessary, Mr Chung, but people rarely lose their keys. And if they do, the signature is an extra safety check."

Chung turned around and looked at the open vault door. "Upstairs, you mentioned that the door was mainly for show," he said.

"Perhaps I was being over-simplistic," said Ballantine. "What I meant was that any robber worth his salt wouldn't try to get into a vault through the door. He'd come in through the floor or ceiling, or the walls. They tend to be the points of least resistance. Though in the

444

case of our vaults, we have incorporated extra features which will make entry there next to impossible."

"Really?" said Chung.

Ballantine nodded. "There are sensors inside both vaults which pick up any movement. The smallest movement will set them off. There are also temperature sensors which monitor any change in temperature."

"Impressive," said Chung.

"But before they can even get inside the vault to set off the sensors, they'd have to get through the outer walls which are a combination of reinforced steel and concrete. On the outside we have the entire vault covered with a network of thin wires through which we pass electricity. Any breakage of the wires sets off an alarm in the control room."

"And you said the control room is manned twenty-four hours a day?"

"Even on Chinese holidays," said Ballantine. "I'll take you up and show you round."

They went back to the elevator, Chung giving up his badge and receiving another warm smile in return, and Ballantine pressed the top button. On the way up he explained how the bank ran most of its security operations, including fraud investigations, from the building, and that most of the upper floors were used by administrative staff.

To get to the control room they had to pass through two security doors, both of which were monitored by security cameras and which Ballantine opened by swiping a magnetic card through a reader. "This is the nerve centre of the depository," he explained as he led

Chung down a carpeted corridor to a third door which was composed entirely of glass on which was stencilled "CONTROL ROOM".

"Bullet-proof glass," said Ballantine. "Totally unbreakable." He waved at the uniformed man sitting at a console behind the door and the door opened. There were five men, all in light blue uniforms with the bank's insignia over their breast pockets. Chung took the trouble to introduce himself to all five of the men as he toured the control room, and he looked at the identity card each man had clipped to his chest, memorising their names as he shook their hands. The men studied ranks of television screens, some black and white and some colour. Some of the screens showed a constant picture, such as the ones covering the corridors, but others were continually moving and changing their viewpoint. Others clicked from view to view every few seconds. Ballantine had one of the men demonstrate how a picture on one of the small black and white screens could be called up on one of the big colour screens if there was something they wanted to see in more detail. Some of the cameras could be moved by operating tiny joysticks on the console.

"Very impressive," said Chung. On the wall behind the men were half a dozen shotguns in a cabinet. "Very impressive indeed."

"We don't expect the men here ever to use the shotguns, of course," said Ballantine, seeing Chung's interest in the weapons. "The telephones over there are direct lines to the police station, and to a private security firm."

"A private firm?" said Chung. "Why is that necessary?"

Ballantine smiled. "The police are stretched to breaking-point these days," he said. "We can't depend on them always responding as quickly as they used to, so to be on the safe side we have a private firm on hand. Just as a precaution."

"Are the alarms linked directly to the police?" asked Chung.

"Yes. And to the security firm. If the alarms go off here they also go off there. Our staff here call them either to confirm there is an emergency or to tell them it's just a test. The function of the men in this room is to bring in outside help, not to protect the vaults themselves. They do not leave their posts during their shift. They even set the electric time locks on the vault doors from here."

"It seems a faultless system," said Chung.

"It is, Mr Chung. It is. Now, let me take you back to my office and I'll give you an application form and some leaflets."

Chung spent ten minutes in Ballantine's office listening to his views on bank security and drinking his awful coffee before thanking him and leaving. On the way to his car, Chung removed a gold pen from his inside jacket pocket and on the back of Ballantine's business card he wrote down the names of the men he'd seen in the bank's control room.

Neil Coleman took the lift to the floor which housed Terry McNeil's office in Special Branch. McNeil was sitting hunched over a computer terminal. By his side was a red and gold-patterned mug with a lid on it. When McNeil saw Coleman he switched off his screen and sat back in his chair. He lifted the lid off his mug and the fragrance of jasmine filled the small office. Unlike Coleman, McNeil was not required to share office space. He had personalised it with several tall green plants and a variegated spider plant which tumbled either side of his computer screen and there was a large parchment scroll behind his desk on which was a vertical line of Chinese characters. On a table behind the chair on which Coleman sat was a Pioneer portable television and underneath it, on the floor, a video recorder of the same make.

"Pull up a pew, Neil," said McNeil. "And close the door, would you?"

Coleman pushed the door to and sat down. He envied McNeil his privacy and his plush office with its view of the bustling harbour, and the fact that he worked for the one area of the police where expats were still top dogs; with the family connections which all local Chinese had on the mainland, there was no way they could be trusted to handle the sensitive intelligence information which passed across the desks of Special Branch every day.

"Anthony Chung took some tracing, I can tell you," said McNeil. He took a sip of hot tea and Coleman got the feeling that he was being strung along, that McNeil was taking a perverse pleasure in making him wait. "Do you want tea? Or a Coke or something?"

"I'm fine, Terry. I had a coffee just before you called."

McNeil put the lid back on his mug.

"It's unusual for a Chinese not to have a Hong King identity card," said McNeil. "Even the ones who emigrate must have had a card, and the ones who come back usually get one once they arrive. It makes travel in and out much easier, both here and in China. That and the French passport gave me the clue."

"Clue?" said Coleman.

"Yeah. You said you thought Chung was part of a car ring?"

Coleman had decided not to tell McNeil the truth, not the whole truth anyway. "I saw him driving a Ferrari, an F40. I thought it was worth checking him out."

"But the F40 was leased, right?"

"Yeah. But then I found he had a French passport and thought maybe there was a European link."

"You thought he was smuggling cars from Hong Kong to France? Give me a break, Neil."

"I'm not sure what I thought. I just wanted to check him out, that's all."

McNeil looked thoughtfully at Coleman and chewed the inside of his lip. Coleman cursed Donaldson for suggesting he try Special Branch for information on Anthony Chung, and for recommending Terry McNeil. McNeil was the same age as Donaldson and Coleman but looked five years younger. He had curly brown hair and light green eyes and spoke with an Irish accent that was beginning to irritate the hell out of Coleman.

"You see, Neil, Anthony Chung shouldn't be in Hong Kong," said McNeil. "If he had any sense at all he'd be in France, keeping his head down, the lowest of low profiles. He's risking his life being this close to China."

Coleman leaned forward in his seat, his hands on his knees. He rubbed the sweat from his palms on to the grey material of his suit.

"It was the French passport that provided the clue," continued McNeil. "It's not the normal place where Hong Kong Chinese try to emigrate. France doesn't really have any attraction for them. The Vietnamese go there because Vietnam used to be under French control, but not Hong Kong Chinese."

"Too close to Britain," said Coleman, smiling.

"Maybe," said McNeil. "But there is one group of Chinese who are very keen to move to France. Chinese dissidents."

"Dissidents?" said Coleman, bewildered.

"France has always been prepared to offer sanctuary to people persecuted for their beliefs, more so than Britain or Germany. Remember Tiananmen Square?"

"Sure." Images flashed through Coleman's mind. The earnest student demonstrations in the Chinese capital. The peaceful marches, the speeches delivered by young men and women who wanted to taste democracy for the first time, the warnings from the old men in power, and then the tanks. Hundreds of unarmed protesters were machine-gunned or crushed to death as the uprising was put down by the army, and for months afterwards news of executions and long prison sentences continued to reach Hong Kong. Yes, Neil Coleman remembered Tiananmen Square. Nobody who had been in Hong Kong on the night of June 4, 1989, would ever forget.

"Afterwards it was the French who did most to get the ringleaders out. Their embassy in Beijing helped smuggle them out and gave them sanctuary. Many still live in Paris."

"And you're saying that Anthony Chung was one of the dissidents?"

"No, that's not what I'm saying."

Coleman wanted to reach across the desk, grab McNeil by the throat and squeeze the information out of him. Instead he smiled and raised his eyebrows.

"But he was smuggled out of China by the French and given French citizenship. Not because of what he'd done, but because of his father."

"His father?"

"Zhong Ziming. Zhong was one of the top men, an aide to Deng Xiaoping for many years and a close associate of Zhao Ziyang, the former Communist Party General Secretary. Switch the TV and the video on and hit the 'play' button, will you?"

Coleman turned in his chair and did as McNeil asked. The recording was from a television news broadcast, clearly taken a few days before the army was sent into Tiananmen Square. It showed a balding, bespectacled old man moving through the crowds of smiling students, shaking hands and patting them on the back. The voice-over was a woman with an American accent saying that the presence of the Communist Party General Secretary in the square was being taken as a sign that the party leadership was giving tacit support to the calls for more democracy.

"Hit the pause button, will you?" asked McNeil.

Coleman did as he'd been asked and the picture froze. Zhao was standing with his hand outstretched, about to greet a tall young man with fiery eyes and a white scarf tied around his head. The scarf had Chinese characters written on them in bold, black strokes. There were two old men behind Zhao, men in dark blue Mao-style suits, who were watching Zhao and smiling.

"See the old guy on the left?" said McNeil.

Coleman pointed to a bald man, fairly stout with a thick, bull neck and wide shoulders, a man who could have been anywhere between fifty and seventy years old so featureless was his face. "Him?"

McNeil nodded. "That's Zhong Ziming. He made several appearances in the square before June 4, both with Zhao and on his own. He made several speeches in support of the democracy movement."

"What happened to him? Executed?"

McNeil shook his head. "Zhao Ziyang was removed from power, but he had too many friends to be punished. Zhong Ziming wasn't as well connected, and Zhao wasn't able to protect him. The last we heard was that he is being held in solitary confinement, but that was twelve months ago. There were a number of unidentified executions of dissidents just before Christmas and there is a chance he was killed then."

"Okay, but I'm not getting this, Terry. That guy's name is Zhong Ziming. I asked you to check out an

Anthony Chung. What makes you think they're related?"

"That's easy. Zhong is the Mandarin Chinese version of Chung. Zhong's son is Zhong Juntao, but he took the name Anthony when he went to Paris to study. It's not unusual for Chinese to use Anglicised names, nor for them to use the Cantonese version of their family names. Zhong Juntao. Anthony Chung. They're one and the same, Neil."

"And you're saying that Chung was given French citizenship after Tiananmen?"

"Chung, that's Chung the son, was in Beijing for several months before the demonstrations, though we have no evidence that he was one of the ringleaders. He went into hiding on the day the troops opened fire and it appears that the French got him out two months later. His father was arrested on June 6."

Coleman put his head in his hands and tried to come to grips with what McNeil had told him. As McNeil had said, Hong Kong was the last place Chung should be. The Chinese secret police would have no qualms about grabbing Chung and taking him back over the border if they located him.

"Thing is, Neil, he's not exactly your run-of-the-mill car thief, is he, this Anthony Chung? He's political rather than a law-breaker. Is there any other reason you're suspicious about him? Anything I should know about?"

Coleman cursed himself for having raised the subject of Chung with Special Branch. There was no way he could tell McNeil or anyone else that he'd been using police time to investigate a rival for his girlfriend's affections.

"No, I just saw him in the Ferrari, that's all," said Coleman. "It was the car rather than the man. Maybe he's just here on holiday or something."

"Possible," said McNeil, not convinced.

"Maybe he's got friends in Hong Kong."

"That's likely," said McNeil.

Coleman got to his feet. "Anyway, I'm going to drop it right here," he said, hoping that McNeil would do the same. "As you say, he's not a car thief. I'll leave it."

"I guess so," said McNeil, looking at the frozen television picture. His head jerked up as if he'd just thought of something. "Hey, good bust by the way. That car smuggling gang was a good one."

"Thanks. I was pleased with the way it went," said Coleman as he opened the door.

"Didn't see you at the press conference, though," added McNeil, but Coleman had already left.

Tyler's portable telephone bleeped and he answered, speaking quietly with his back to the rest of the vets. When he finished the call he turned round, a wide smile on his face.

"The Huey will be here in less than an hour," he said. "The container has just been cleared from the Kwai Chung container terminal, unopened."

"Great!" said Lewis. He gave Lehman a high five.

"I'm gonna make coffee while we wait," said Carmody. He threw away the old grounds and replenished the filter machine. When the coffee had

454

brewed he filled mugs and handed them out and they drank as they waited. Forty-five minutes after Tyler had taken the phone call they heard a horn sound outside.

"Okay, that'll be it," said Tyler. "Bart, Dan, open the sliding door, we're going to back the container right inside. I don't want the delivery men to know what they're delivering. Eric, Larry, can you drive the cars out? We'll park them outside until we've got ourselves organised."

Tyler went through the small door and walked over to unlock the gate while Lewis and Lehman pushed the sliding door back. A large truck with three men in the cab was waiting by the gate, a long, red container on its back. The driver waved at Tyler and he waved back before unlocking the padlock and slipping the chain. He pulled the gate open and held it back as the truck slowly turned in and drove towards the warehouse.

Once the rear of the truck had passed through the gate, Tyler closed it and jogged after it. He flagged it down and explained to the driver that he wanted him to reverse the truck so that the rear half was inside the building. The man wasn't wearing a shirt and he had a huge tattoo of a tiger across his chest, its claws out, ready to strike. He grinned and told Tyler he understood. He carefully steered the truck and backed the container through the open door. The driver and his two companions made to get out of the cab but Tyler told them to stay where they were.

"We could use their help, Colonel," said Lewis. "It's going to be heavy."

Tyler shook his head. "No, it's enough that they know we're here. I don't want them to know about the Huey. I'm told they can be trusted, they're triads and have sworn an oath of secrecy, but I don't want to take any risks."

"Okay, Colonel, it's your call."

"Besides, Josh had the skids removed and the Huey mounted on trolleys, as you suggested. He slid it in and all we have to do is to slide it out. Bring over some ropes while I open up the container."

Tyler took a pair of pliers and cut the metal seals around the padlocks. He fished his set of keys from the pocket of his trousers and unlocked the padlocks one by one. "Josh gave me a duplicate set of keys before I left Bangkok," he explained. Once he'd removed the locks he pulled open the rear of the container to reveal the cockpit of the Huey, staring out at them like an insect emerging from a chrysalis.

"That's one hell of a tight fit," said Lewis, scratching his head.

"Flashlights, Larry," said Tyler.

Carmody went over to one of the workbenches and returned with two flashlights. He turned them on and handed one to Tyler. The other he gave to Lewis who had already climbed into the back of the container and was carefully squeezing alongside the helicopter.

"They had to take the tail assembly off, like I thought, Colonel," said Lewis, his voice echoing inside the metal box. "Skids are off too and it's on flat trolleys. The wheels on the trolleys have been locked so that they wouldn't move while the container was in transit.

456

The rotors are off, we should unpack them first." They heard the crash of metal and after a few seconds Lewis emerged from the container. "The main rotor mast has been taken out, and there's a bag in the pilot's station which I guess contains all the bolts and things. They've done a good job taking her apart. There are reinforced metal sheets on the side which must be what they used to slide the Huey in. We can use them as a ramp to get it out," he said.

"Josh thinks of everything," said Tyler. "Let's do it."

"Dan, can you pull the slide out of the other side? I'll get this one."

"Sure," said Lehman. He scrambled up into the container and, while Tyler directed the beam of his torch down the length of the container, pulled on a long, thin metal sheet, about three feet wide and twenty feet long. "No way, Bart. It's going to take two of us to handle one of these."

Lewis clambered down to the rear of the Huey, ducked under the tail, and helped Lehman manhandle the heavy metal sheet out. Once the end of the sheet projected out of the container Horvitz and Doherty helped slide it. They leaned it so that it sloped from the edge of the container down to the concrete floor.

When he was satisfied, Lewis had Lehman help him manoeuvre the sheet on the other side of the container. They were all sweating by the time the two lengths of steel were in position.

"I think we should clear the rest of the stuff out first, the rotors and the skids," said Lewis.

The vets pulled out the main rotors, the rotor mast and the tail rotors and the metal skids and put them carefully on the ground by the workbenches. The tail assembly was locked behind the main fuselage and would have to be taken out last. When they'd cleared the floor of the container Lewis instructed the vets to tie the ropes to the Huey, looping them around the cockpit and through the cabin.

"Now what?" said Carmody.

"I'll unlock the brakes on the trolleys, then Chuck and Larry can go to the rear of the fuselage and push. The colonel and Eric can push the middle and hold on the rope through the cabin, Dan and I will take the front and hold the ropes around the cockpit. As soon as it gets to the top of the ramps we stop pushing and put all our weight on the ropes. It'll have more than enough momentum to keep it moving; all we'll be able to do is to slow it. Watch out for rope burns, don't let it slide through your hands."

The men took their positions. Lewis released the brakes and at his command they began straining against the helicopter. The wheels grated and gradually the Huey began to move, the trolleys rattling against the metal floor of the container.

"Careful, we're almost there," said Lewis. The trolleys banged against the steel ramps and for a moment it looked as if they'd stick there but the small wheels rolled over the join and the front of the Huey began to dip down. "The ropes!" shouted Lewis. "Hold the ropes. She's going."

458

All of them stopped pushing and pulled back on the ropes as if they were in a tug-of-war contest. Horvitz grunted and wound his end of the ropes around his waist. Lehman could feel the rope slide through his hands and he gripped it tighter. The Huey picked up speed and Lewis shouted for them all to pull harder. The wheels began to skid on the ramp and Lehman strained against the load.

Tyler's feet began to slide along the metal floor and Lehman could feel his own begin to lose traction. He bent at the knees and tried to push back with all his might. The rear of the Huey bobbed up as the nose dipped down and it banged against the roof of the container before it slid out. Lehman was pulled to the edge of the container and he released his hold on the rope as the Huey reached the bottom of the ramp; he watched as the two trolleys supporting the helicopter rolled on to the concrete floor. The stub of tail section scraped along the ramp in a shower of sparks as the Huey levelled off and then it was clear and the helicopter came to a halt under the overhead fluorescent lights.

The six men stood at the open end of the container and looked down at the helicopter.

"Looks really bizarre without its tail," said Carmody. "It really just fixes on with four bolts?"

"That's all," said Lewis. "Come on, let's get the tail section out."

The tail assembly was surprisingly light and the men carried it easily out of the container and down the ramp. Lehman had both hands on the stinger at the rear, the long metal spike which prevented the tail rotor from chopping into the ground. They placed the tail section carefully on the floor next to the rotors.

"Now the hard work starts," said Tyler. He walked down the ramp and the others followed him. They all pulled the ramps clear of the container and Tyler relocked the door. He went round to the front of the truck where the three Chinese men sat talking and smoking. He told them they could go. The driver scratched the mouth of his tiger tattoo and put the truck into gear. It lurched out of the warehouse and out of the main gate as Lewis and Lehman rolled the huge sliding door shut.

"Now, push the Huey to the back so that we can drive the cars in as well," said Tyler.

All six of the men pushed the helicopter on its two trolleys until it was just ten feet away from the offices, leaving more than enough room for the Toyota and the Jeep. Carmody and Horvitz drove the two vehicles inside and parked them just inside the warehouse.

"What's the first step, Bart?" asked Tyler.

Lewis gestured at the overhead pulleys. "We rig up a system for pulling the turbine and the gearboxes out. Then I plan to strip her completely. Everything comes out and we'll lay it down on the floor over there. I want to go over all the electrics and strip the hydraulics down. We can get to work on that while we're waiting for the new turbine to arrive."

"Let's get to it," said Tyler.

Neil Coleman popped a couple of painkillers into his mouth and washed them down with his coffee. A uniformed constable opened the office door without knocking and dumped a stack of files into his in-tray before leaving without saying a word. Coleman groaned and picked the files out one by one. A blue Mercedes. A green Mercedes. A white Toyota. Another blue Mercedes. Another green Mercedes. A red Nissan. A black Mercedes. Coleman scratched his nose. What the hell was it with Mercedes Benzes, he thought to himself. They were usually a popular choice with the car smugglers, but the rate of Mercedes car thefts was getting ridiculous. In the past month at least fifteen had gone missing, which was well above average for the time of the year. Almost double, in fact. In the past the increase in car thefts had coincided with booms in the Chinese economy: when the cadres and mainland businessmen had money to burn they usually put in orders for cars with the Hong Kong triads, but he'd seen nothing to suggest that the country's economic woes were anywhere near being solved. And something else was worrying Coleman — the thefts of other car makes were pretty static, it was just Mercedes thefts which were on the increase.

He decided to go over to the Central police station for a chat with CID there and ask them if they had any thoughts about the spate of car thefts. Most of the Mercs had been taken from their patch. He caught the Mass Transit Railway to Central. During peak periods the MTR could be hell on earth. He hated being packed shoulder to shoulder with office workers: nobody smiled, nobody apologised for physical contact, nobody stepped aside to allow passengers on or off. It was every man for himself and all he could see were unsmiling, inscrutable faces. He hated it and always planned his journeys so that he avoided rush hour. During early afternoon the MTR was a totally different experience, fast, efficient and clean with no more than a couple of minutes between trains and a ticketing system that put the London Underground to shame. The only thing that spoiled the Hong Kong system was the people, thought Coleman, not for the first time, as he left Central MTR station and stepped into the burning hot sunshine.

He took off his lightweight jacket and slung it over his shoulder but he was still sweating after a few steps and he decided to cool off in the Landmark Centre. He sat down by the fountain and looked around the multi-level shopping mall, home to some of the most prestigious names in the world: Chanel, Rolex, Louis Vuitton, Gucci, Bally, Nina Ricci — a roll-call of the shopping favourites of the rich and famous. The Landmark was busy, as always. As far as Coleman could tell, the average Hong Konger had only two interests: making money and spending it. If they weren't at work they were walking around the city's shopping areas, even if they weren't actually planning to make a purchase. In Hong Kong, window-shopping had been elevated to an art form. Coleman sat by a bubbling fountain while he got his breath back. He looked up at the second and third levels of shops and boutiques. The shoppers were a mixture of sunburnt tourists in shorts and cheap dresses and rich Hong Kong wives, expatriate and Chinese. Long escalators ferried people up to the different levels. A young Chinese girl with waist-length hair caught his attention. She was on the down escalator and as Coleman looked she swished her hair like a horse shaking its mane. She was wearing a leather miniskirt and a white silk jacket and her legs seemed to go on for ever. Coleman smiled as he saw the number of men who turned to watch her go by on the escalator. Several were rapped on the shoulder by their wives.

Suddenly Coleman jerked out of his reverie. On the up escalator was Anne Fielding, Debbie's mother, in a red jacket and dress, her blonde hair loose around her shoulders. As always she looked perfectly groomed. She looked exactly what she was, thought Coleman a little enviously, a rich man's wife. She was attracting almost as many turned heads as the young Chinese girl. He stood up and craned his neck to see if she stopped at the second floor or if she was going higher. If he could "accidentally" bump into her then he could start a conversation — not about her husband's still-missing car he reminded himself — and find out how Debbie was. Maybe even ask her to pass on a message to her.

He ran his fingers through his hair and headed towards the escalator, but stopped abruptly when he saw someone else he recognised. A Chinese man in a flash suit. Anthony Chung. Coleman held back and watched Chung go up the escalator, after Anne Fielding.

"Anne, this is a surprise," said a voice.

Anne Fielding turned to see Anthony Chung standing by the shop window, an easy smile on his face.

He reached up and brushed an unruly lock of hair from his forehead. "Why, Anthony, yes, this is a surprise," she said. "And I notice that it's 'Anne' today and not 'Mrs Fielding'. I suppose that's because Debbie's not here."

"Isn't she?" said Chung.

Anne felt that she was being toyed with, and she was more than a little suspicious about their supposedly chance meeting. Debbie had already told him at the dinner party that she could be found most afternoons shopping in the Landmark Centre. Debbie had meant it as a joke but there was an element of truth to it. Anne enjoyed the act of spending money, especially her husband's money. If she couldn't have his affection, at least she could have his credit cards, and the Landmark was without doubt the best place to shop. If she was one hundred per cent honest with herself, Anne would have had to admit that she'd half expected to bump into Anthony Chung on one of her shopping expeditions. It was nothing he'd said, but a look had passed between them when Debbie had made the joke about the Landmark, a look that suggested that the information had been stored away for future use.

"You look lovely today," said Chung, looking her up and down. From a less chivalrous male Anne would have taken offence at the way she was being appraised, but she knew that Chung was observing the dress as much as he was her figure.

"Thank you," she said. "I feel as if I should ask you if you come here often."

Chung laughed and nodded. "I must confess to having charge accounts at several of these boutiques."

"Me too," she said. "Are you looking for anything in particular?" In her head she seemed to hear him say "Just you" but his lips didn't move and she knew that he was considering her question.

He shrugged. "To be honest, I buy most of my clothes in Paris. I find the service better there."

"Oh God, yes, save me from Hong Kong shop assistants," said Anne. "They stand next to you, say nothing, and follow you around the store like they suspect you of shoplifting. And they're usually so beautiful and so slender. They make me feel positively defensive about my figure."

"Anne, I think you're fishing for compliments," said Chung. "You know perfectly well you have a superb figure."

"For a mother," said Anne, ruefully.

"For any woman," said Chung. "But I'm not going to let you draw me into this. How about we go for a drink and I'll tell you about Paris."

Anne blinked. It was the first time in a long while that somebody had suggested to her that she have a drink. Normally she was the one to suggest it, and it produced either a not-so-subtle look at the watch or a raised eyebrow. It was so refreshing to have someone else take the initiative.

"That would be lovely," said Anne.

"Gin and tonic?" said Chung. "With ice and lemon?"

"My favourite," said Anne.

"I knew that," said Chung. "Shall we go?"

Coleman followed Chung and Anne Fielding down the escalator and out into the busy street. They were talking

465

and laughing as they walked and Coleman knew that there was little chance of them noticing him; they were too engrossed in each other. He wondered what they were talking about and envied Chung for the easy way in which he seemed to be dealing with Debbie's mother. He'd only been introduced to her once and he'd been tongue-tied. She made him feel that he wasn't worthy of her daughter, even though she was charming and polite. It was just a feeling. Coleman felt anger flare inside him as he wondered how close Chung was to the Fielding family. The way he was deep in conversation with Debbie's mother suggested that this wasn't the first time they'd met. It wasn't fair, thought Coleman; he'd be just as confident with her if she had time to get used to him.

They walked along Des Voeux Road and into the Mandarin Hotel. Coleman dashed along the road and got to the lobby just in time to see them walking into the Captain's Bar. Coleman bought a copy of the *South China Morning Post* and found himself a seat in the far corner of the lobby where he could see the entrance to the bar. He opened the paper and looked over the top of it.

Anne put her empty glass on the table and it was replaced by a full one almost immediately, the bubbles of the tonic sticking to the cocktail stick. She stirred her drink, poked at the slice of fresh lime, and licked the stick. She was aware that Chung was watching her and she slipped the stick out of her mouth and on to the table.

466

"Sorry," she said, feeling like a little girl being caught doing something wrong by her father.

"No need to be sorry," said Chung. "A gin and tonic is a very sensual drink. It deserves to be enjoyed."

"Oh, I love it," sighed Anne. "I love the taste of the gin, the coldness of the ice cubes, the bite of the lime. I love the way the tonic bubbles against the inside of my mouth as I swallow. You're right, it's a sensual pleasure. Not many people know that."

Chung was sipping at a whisky and ice. She thought of what William would say if he saw ice in Scotland's finest export, and smiled.

"What are you thinking?" asked Chung quickly.

She gestured at his drink. "Ice and whisky. William would hate that."

"William's not here," said Chung. She looked up at him sharply and his eyes looked deep into hers.

"No," said Anne thoughtfully. "No, he isn't." She wondered what the time was but didn't want to look at her watch in case Chung thought she was dropping a hint. She was enjoying his company, and relished the fact that she was with someone who was totally uncritical of her drinking. William always sighed when she ordered a second or third drink, and even Debbie had started to pull a face. Chung was a real gentleman; as soon as she finished one drink he would order her another without her even asking. How many had she had? She tried to remember. Three or four. There were three cocktail sticks on the table next to her glass but she knew the waiter had removed some earlier.

The waiter put a bowl of roasted peanuts on the table and Chung pushed it towards her, but she shook her head. "No, no thank you," she said, "they spoil the taste of the gin."

"Are you hungry?" he asked.

"I am, but not for peanuts," she said.

"Can I offer you lunch?" he said.

She put her head on one side and looked at him. "You're offering to buy me lunch?" she said.

"No," he said. "I'm offering to cook for you. It'll be the best Chinese meal you've ever had."

"Oh, I couldn't," said Anne. She sipped at her drink but found that there was only ice left in the glass. A waiter unobtrusively took it away and replaced it with a fresh one. Was that five or six? She couldn't remember. She felt totally relaxed, all the more so for the pleasant time she was having with Chung. Debbie's boyfriend, she reminded herself harshly.

"It'd be my pleasure," said Chung. "And I would like very much to show you my home. Think about it. We'll have a couple more drinks and then you can let me know what you've decided."

Coleman checked his watch. It was three o'clock and if Chung and Debbie's mother didn't appear soon he'd have to give up. He couldn't stay out of the office all day, not with Hui around. Coleman was becoming more and more convinced that Hui was an informer for the Commissioner rather than the mainland.

As he looked over the top of the sports section of the paper he saw Anne Fielding appear, closely followed by

Chung. Anne appeared to lose her balance and Chung reached over to steady her arm. She smiled at him and Coleman had the feeling she'd drunk a little too much. Her cheeks were slightly red, though that could have been light reflecting off her red jacket and dress. Chung said something to her and Coleman could hear her laugh clear across the lobby.

They left through the main entrance of the hotel at the opposite side of the building from where they'd entered. Coleman thought that they might join the taxi queue so he looked cautiously through the glass doors before he left. Three men in dark suits and an old woman in a too-tight green dress were the only people waiting for a cab. A doorman in a red coat resplendent with gold braid was standing at the roadside trying in vain to hail taxis for them. Coleman looked right and left and saw Anne and Chung on the pavement, walking slowly. He followed and saw them walk into a multi-storey car park.

He looked at his watch again. More than anything he wanted to know where they were going. He had a feeling of dark dread in the pit of his stomach. He wasn't sure what they were up to, but he had a bad feeling about it. Policeman's intuition, he thought. A prickling of the hairs on the back of his neck. He loitered outside the car park until he saw the Ferrari growling slowly down the spiral driveway towards the exit. He started frantically to look for a cab and sighed audibly as he saw one cruising up with its "For Hire" light on. He flagged it down and slid gratefully into its air conditioning. His cheeks and forehead were beaded with sweat and he could feel damp patches under his arms.

"See that car, the red one?" Coleman asked the driver, who nodded. "I want you to follow it, but not too close, okay?"

"Where they go?" asked the driver.

"I don't know," said Coleman. "If I knew, I wouldn't have to follow them, would I?"

"Me not know," said the driver, shaking his head. "Not care. Maybe they go Kowloon. Me Hong Kong taxi. Me not go Kowloon."

Hong Kong taxi drivers were supposed to go anywhere in the colony if asked, but most preferred to stick either to the island or to Kowloon, not because they'd get lost but because they didn't like driving through the cross-harbour tunnels. Traffic always moved slowly and a slow taxi meant a smaller fare. Coleman thought about showing the man his warrant card but instead he promised him an extra twenty dollars and that he'd use the cab to come back to the island later on in the afternoon. The driver seemed satisfied by that and they lurched into the traffic, about a dozen cars behind the Ferrari.

"How long have you lived here?" Anne asked as Chung drove through the wrought-iron gates to the building's car park. He climbed out of the driver's seat and walked quickly around the back of the car to open the door for her. He reached down and took her hand. She squeezed it as she pulled herself up.

470

"It's hard to get out and still look like a lady," said Anne. Her head felt woozy and she steadied herself by resting her left hand on the roof of the car. She shook her head but that made her feel worse and she almost dropped her handbag. She felt Chung's arm around her waist and they walked together to the lobby. On the drive over from Hong Kong island he'd asked her about her taste in food and told her what he intended to prepare for her, though Anne had said she'd be quite happy with another gin and tonic and a look around his apartment. She'd stopped feeling hungry and besides, she knew she'd only end up paying in the gym for the extra calories.

The doorman was talking to a mailman and he nodded a greeting to Chung as he went by. The lobby looked expensive, thought Anne, but there was too much marble for her taste. It was a little ostentatious, and the wooden elevator doors seemed out of place. The elevator arrived and she stepped inside with Chung. She saw Chung press the penthouse button.

"The penthouse?" she said.

"I hope you like it," said Chung. She could smell his aftershave, a sweet, masculine fragrance that she vaguely recognised. Anne smiled when the elevator doors opened to reveal another, albeit smaller, marbled lobby. Definitely too much marble, she decided.

She looked at her watch and for a moment had trouble focusing. "I think I've had a little too much to drink," she said.

"Nonsense," soothed Chung, opening the two high-security locks. "Welcome to my humble abode," he said, pushing the door open.

"Welcome to my parlour," Anne said, under her breath. She knew that she was asking for trouble by going to Chung's flat, and knew that it was wrong to lead him on, but she wanted to know more about the man. She wanted to see him on his home turf so that she could find out what made him tick.

"I beg your pardon?" said Chung.

"Nothing," she said brightly, and walked past him, conscious that he was looking at her legs as she went by. She swung her hips just a little, excited by the fact that he was watching her. Did he ever compare her with Debbie? she wondered. Who did he prefer? Debbie was younger, and slimmer, and her skin was better, but she knew that she was the more voluptuous. And she had the legs.

She looked over her shoulder as she got to the middle of the room and felt a sudden rush of disappointment when she saw that Chung had his back to her and was closing the door.

"Anthony, this is lovely," she said. She went over to the floor-to-ceiling window and looked down on green trees and bushes around a small pool. "This room really catches the sun, doesn't it?" She turned to look at him.

"It has a good feeling," he agreed. "I'm not so sure about the decor."

"You don't own it?" she asked.

"No, it's leased. I reckon now is not a good time to own property in Hong Kong." He shrugged. "You know the way it's going, Anne. Nobody trusts the Chinese, and the property market is always the first to suffer."

"Well, whoever did the interior design did a marvellous job. I love the coffee table. And the paintings are interesting."

"Music?" asked Chung.

"Sure," said Anne.

She watched Chung walk over to the CD player. He looked so good in Armani, she thought. He moved like a model. No, not a model, there was always something self-conscious about a male model on the catwalk. Chung seemed totally self-controlled, not caring if he was being watched or not. He was like an actor on a stage. She wondered why he hadn't tried to kiss her. She thought he might have tried in the car, and then again when he opened the car door for her to get out. And when they were in the elevator she'd watched him out of the corner of her eye, expecting him to put his hands on her shoulders and draw her to him. He hadn't, and that had surprised her. When he'd opened the door to the apartment and she'd walked by him, she had half expected a kiss on the cheek, but he hadn't made a move. He was the perfect gentleman, she thought, a little resentfully. She wouldn't allow him to kiss her, of course, but she was a little put out that he didn't even try.

Bryan Ferry's voice filled the air, singing to a tune she couldn't put a name to.

"Okay?" asked Chung.

"Fine," said Anne.

She turned to look out of the window. She heard Chung's footsteps and when she looked over her shoulder again, he'd gone. She swayed slowly in time with the music. She wanted to dance, and just then she wanted very much to dance with Anthony Chung. She knew instinctively that he would be a superb dancer. He had the body for it, the timing, and the confidence. He'd be superb in bed, too, she decided. The qualities that made a good dancer also made a good lover. She snorted and silently scolded herself for such stupid thoughts. William Fielding was the only man she'd made love to in almost a quarter of a century, and before him there were only two others. And one of them didn't really count.

William had never been much of a dancer, she thought ruefully.

"Penny for them?" said Chung. She turned and smiled at him, shaking her head. He was holding out a glass of gin and tonic and she took it from him.

"Nothing," she said. She sipped the drink, savouring the tang of the lime and the bursting freshness of the tonic bubbles against her nose. "You make a terrific gin and tonic," she said.

"And you're a connoisseur," said Chung, raising his glass to her.

If William had said that, she would have taken it as a criticism and been wounded, but coming from Chung with his confident smile and raised eyebrow, it was funny. She clinked glasses with him. "To connoisseurs,"

474

she said, and drank again. "Anthony, can I ask you something?" she said.

"Of course. Anything."

"Have you slept with Debbie?" The question had come out in a rush and until she'd taken the second mouthful of gin and tonic Anne didn't even know she was going to ask it. She must have had too much to drink. She kept her eyes fixed on Chung, waiting for him to answer.

He looked her straight in the eyes. "No," he said, and shook his head.

She believed him, though she wasn't sure why it mattered whether she believed him or not. He took the glass from her hand and placed it on the coffee table, and then before she knew what was happening he'd taken her in his arms. She raised her chin and opened her mouth slightly, but he didn't kiss her, he began to dance with her, slowly guiding her around the floor. He danced well, exactly as she'd thought he would, guiding her with his strong arms. There was none of the faltering and fumbling there was with William when he insisted they lead the dancing at the bank's annual Christmas party. The combination of the gin, the soft music, and the warmth of Chung's body was hypnotic, and she closed her eyes. He held her close and without realising she was doing it she rested her head on his shoulder and sighed gently. She felt a light touch on the top of her head and she knew that he'd kissed her.

The hand around her waist pushed her ever so slightly and she pressed her thighs against his. She could feel him, hard, wanting her, and she pulled away but the hand was insistent and she allowed it to push her back. As they danced she moved her hips from side to side, rubbing against him and feeling him grow harder and bigger. Her mind was in turmoil. She didn't want to betray her husband, she really didn't. He'd been so good to her, so loyal, so trusting, she couldn't be unfaithful to him. And Chung was her daughter's boyfriend. Her daughter's, for God's sake. How would she ever be able to look Debbie in the eye again? Every fibre of her mind screamed that what she was doing was wrong, and that she was playing with fire, but she continued to press against him as Bryan Ferry sang. It had been so long since she'd felt a man against her, wanting her, wanting to possess her. It took William so long to get aroused, and it was never a success, hadn't been for many years. Hadn't been from the very start, she admitted to herself. William had never reacted in the way that Chung had. She rubbed her thigh harder against him and she felt him twitch. She felt a surge of power, knowing that it was up to her; she could break away, tell him that she had to go, and it would stop right there. She had proved to herself that she was still attractive and that she could arouse a young man like Chung. It would be a boost to her confidence, there was no need for her to take it any further. She moved her right hand up and down his broad back, feeling the muscles under the smooth material of his fitted jacket. She wondered how his flesh would feel, and how it would smell. She thought of how pale and unhealthy William's skin appeared, how wrinkled it was around his waist, and how thin his arms were. He had long

476

since stopped bothering about the state of his body, took no exercise and shunned the sun. She used to nag him, but in recent years she had given up. It was his own fault, she thought. He could have looked after himself better. He could have tried harder in bed. She'd asked him often enough, made suggestions, tried to take the lead. If he didn't respond, well, that was his fault, not hers.

She pressed harder with the flat of her hand and his chest pushed against her breasts. She felt her nipples harden under the pressure but there was no embarrassment, she wanted Chung to know that he'd aroused her. She wanted him to know that she wanted him, that she was wet between her legs, that she was ready for him. She wasn't going to do anything, she wasn't going to take it any further, she just wanted him to know, that's all.

She used her whole body against him: she nestled her head against his shoulder, rubbed his back with her hands, pressed her breasts against his chest and her thighs against his groin. She kept her eyes closed, her mouth slightly open. Just one more minute, she promised herself, one more minute of dancing and then she'd go home. Back to William. And to Debbie. She wanted so much to drop her hand, to slip it between his legs and feel him. She wanted to rub him and feel him grow, to know for certain the effect she had on him. Why hadn't he kissed her properly? Why hadn't he pushed back her head and pressed his lips to hers? She wanted to raise her head and look at him but she was frightened that he'd take that as a sign that she wanted him to kiss her. She didn't want to lead him on. One more minute, she promised herself. One more minute and she'd go home.

She felt his hand slide up her back and gently stroke her hair. She put her hands on his shoulders and raised her head, pushing him away slightly. He smiled boyishly.

"Anthony," she began, meaning to tell him that she wanted to go.

He raised one eyebrow. "Yes?" He made no move to kiss her or to pull her back to him. She knew that if she said she wanted to go, he'd let her. It was her choice.

"Anthony . . ." Her mind was spinning. She felt as if she was going to faint. She couldn't betray her husband, but he didn't deserve her loyalty. She was almost fifty years old and she'd never enjoyed sex, never had the sort of adventures Phyllis Kelley had. She could practically count the number of orgasms she'd had on the fingers of one hand. It wasn't fair. She'd soon be too old, it wouldn't be long before no one would find her sexy and she and William would settle down to a quiet old age. "Anthony . . . why don't you show me the rest of your apartment?"

She hadn't meant to say it, she really had planned to tell him that she was going, but once she'd spoken she felt flushed with excitement. Her stomach went liquid, knowing that she'd just offered herself to Chung, knowing that she was going to touch him, kiss him, explore his body and enjoy him. For one moment of panic she thought that he was going to refuse her, but then he smiled and led her by the hand to a door at the far end of the room. She could hardly walk, her legs were trembling so much. William Fielding had been the only man to see her naked for almost twenty-five years, never mind make love to her. She felt strange, as if her body no longer belonged to her. Her heartbeat was pounding in her ears and she could hardly breathe. The door seemed to loom larger and larger ahead of her, and she knew that if she went through it her life would never be the same again. It wasn't too late, she could still back out and go back to her husband an honest woman. William would never know.

She pulled at Anthony's hand and he stopped. He looked at her without speaking. Her eyes involuntarily dropped to his groin. She could see how aroused he was. His chest was rising and falling and he licked his lips.

"Anthony . . ." she said, her voice sounding husky with passion.

He stepped forward and held her and she rubbed herself against him again, harder this time. She wanted him to make the decision for her, to grab her and take her so that she could tell herself that he'd forced her, but she could tell that he wouldn't do that. He was leaving it to her. "Anthony . . ." she said. His deep brown eyes looked right into her and her heart melted. "Anthony, nobody must ever know," she said, quietly.

He shook his head. "Nobody ever will, Anne," he said. "I promise."

"Nobody must ever know," she repeated, quieter this time.

He didn't reply a second time, he just bent down slightly and swept her up off her feet. She put her arms around his neck as he carried her into the bedroom and kicked the door closed behind him with his heel. The drapes were drawn to block out the afternoon sun and it was dark inside.

Chung carried her over to the bed and laid her down, then bent to switch on a lamp. It was a soft light which illuminated the bed but not the corners of the room. It was a light to make love by. William never made love with the light on, he said it made him feel uncomfortable. Anne had no qualms about showing her body to Chung, she knew she looked good, and she wanted to see him. She looked up at Chung as he took off his jacket and hung it on the handle of one of the louvred doors of the closets behind him. She didn't know what to do, whether she should help him undress or take off her own clothes. At home she and William had their own bathrooms, and she couldn't remember the last time he had tried to undress her. She sat up, slipped off her jacket and let it slide off the bed as she reached out her hand to stroke his shirt. It was silk and felt slippery under her fingers. She felt a hard button and she undid it and then slipped her hand inside. His skin felt dry and warm. As he took off his tie she undid several more of his buttons and then she stood up and put her arms around his waist, under his shirt. She slipped off her high heels and stood on tiptoe, offering her mouth to him. He bent his neck and kissed her, softly at first, and then with passion, his tongue forcing its way into her mouth. She gasped. William had never kissed her like that. Ever. She tasted him and sucked on his tongue as it invaded her, and she made small grunting noises. Eventually she couldn't breathe and she broke away, panting, but Chung grabbed her and kissed her hard. She allowed her right hand to slide down his chest until it came to the belt of his trousers. She couldn't believe what she was doing. She had never in her wildest dreams imagined that she would be unfaithful to her husband. She undid the belt and opened the top of his trousers. She had only ever touched two men there. She wanted Chung to know that, she wanted him to know that she wasn't like Phyllis Kelley. She moved her hand slowly, almost frightened to touch his flesh. He was wearing silk boxers that slid against his hardness. She held him first through the silk, rubbing the material up and down, grasping him so hard that he gasped.

She felt one of his hands pull down the zip of her dress and then his hands eased the material down over her shoulders. It slid down and caught on her hips but she wiggled her legs and it fell to the floor. She released him and helped him off with his shirt, kissing his nipples and scratching his chest with her nails. He put his hands behind her back and unclipped her bra, and she shook her shoulders as it came away. His hands reached for her breasts and he held her nipples, caressing them so that they hardened. She sighed as he bent and kissed both breasts, light touches of the lips, nothing more. Anne groaned. The last person to kiss her breasts had been Debbie when she was ten months old. The thought made her sad but it lasted for less than a second because Chung's right hand moved down her stomach and slid under her panties. His index finger stroked her hair and then slipped between her legs. God, she hadn't realised how wet she was. The sensation of him inside her sent chills down her back and with both hands she pushed down his boxer shorts and reached for him. He felt huge, and he continued to grow as she stroked him. He felt much bigger than William, bigger than she'd imagined a man could ever be. She looked down but he was standing so close she couldn't see him. In one smooth movement Chung pushed her tights and panties down then he gently eased her back on to the bed and slipped them off her feet. He watched her as he kicked off his trousers and shorts and removed his socks. He stood naked before her, the light casting shadows across his face. For the first time she could see how big he was. He stepped forward and she opened her legs, assuming that he was going to lie on top of her. She reached up with her arms, wanting to enfold him and take him inside her, but he smiled and gently turned her over so that she was lying on her stomach. She tried to turn, wanting to see him, but his hands held her firmly. She could see across the room to a low dressing table of white wood and two matching stools. The bed was very feminine, with a brass frame with a thick dark purple quilt and big, fluffy pillows in purple cases. She wanted to imprint everything on to her memory, she never wanted to forget this afternoon. It would be her one and only fling, she'd already decided.

She felt Chung's hands pull her back so that she was on her knees, facing away from him, her feet over the edge of the bed. She turned to look over her shoulder and flicked the hair from her eyes. He was standing at the side of the bed, his hands on her hips, smiling. She tried to roll over on to her back again but he wouldn't let her. For a frantic moment she thought that he had something else in mind, something unsavoury, but then he slipped a finger inside her and she knew it was going to be all right. He moved up against her and she faced forward again, pushing herself back. No one had ever made love to her this way, from behind. She felt so vulnerable, so open to him. She felt him nudge her legs further apart and she moaned, wanting him inside her but wanting to prolong it too. His finger slid out and she could feel her flesh try to hold him in. Then his finger was out and before she knew it he was inside her, buried in as deep as he could go. It happened so quickly that she gasped out loud and there were tears in her eyes. He withdrew slowly, both of his hands back on her hips, until he was almost out. He lingered there, moving gently from side to side. She quivered in anticipation but he made no move to enter her again. She opened her legs wider and rocked back, but he moved back, too.

"Please," she said. Still nothing. "Please," she repeated, her voice thick with desire. She felt the hands tighten and pull her back and at the same time he thrust into her, pounding away at her, harder than anyone had ever made love to her. "Oh God," she moaned. "Yes, yes, yes." No one had ever been so deep inside her. She'd never really known what it was like to be made love to. Everything she'd ever experienced before had been a sham.

She wanted so badly to turn and to kiss and hold him, but she didn't want the sensations she was feeling to end.

It was Chung who decided to move. He slowed his strokes and then withdrew. She felt empty and pushed herself back, trying to recapture him, but he rolled her on to her back and helped her move into the centre of the bed, lying across it so that his back was to the closets. He stood at the side of the bed looking down at her. She looked at him, glistening wet and erect under the light, and she held out her arms to him, begging him to take her. She opened her legs as he came to her and she lifted her head to kiss him. He entered her as his tongue slid between her lips, his mouth stifling her gasps. His hands moved under her and he squeezed her as he moved in and out, tightening her so that she could feel every inch of him inside her. He covered her face with kisses and whispered in her ear.

"Put your legs higher," he said, nibbling at her ear lobe.

She did as he asked and felt him go in even deeper.

"Link your ankles together and squeeze me," he said.

She followed his instructions and she felt herself tighten inside so that she felt all the ridges along him.

"God," she gasped. "This is incredible." William had never told her what to do to give him pleasure, he'd hardly talked at all when they were having sex, just grunted when he'd come. This was something totally different. She wanted to do exactly what Chung asked of her, and she wanted to experiment too. She raked her nails along his spine, not hard enough to break the skin but hard enough to hurt him, and she was rewarded by him groaning and moving faster. She slid her hands down his back and held his buttocks, squeezing them as he ground against her.

She was sure that he was about to come, and she revelled in the power she had over him. As he continued to move inside her he took her legs and positioned them on his shoulders, moving slowly so that it didn't hurt. She didn't think she'd be flexible enough but to her surprise her legs came up higher and higher until her knees were almost level with her face. He continued to make love to her, filling her like she'd never been filled before.

"It's too deep," she gasped. "It's too deep."

"It's how it should be," whispered Chung, his face next to her cheek. With her legs up around his shoulders she couldn't move, she was totally at his mercy. He moved back and forth, alternating between slow, controlled strokes that made her whimper with pleasure, and fast, almost brutal, stabbing motions that drove her to a frenzy. Sweat was pouring off her and she could feel damp fronds of hair across her forehead.

"No one has ever made me feel like this," she moaned.

"Not your husband?" he whispered into her ear.

"No, my husband never made me feel like this," she said, her voice shaking with each pumping movement he made.

Chung levered himself up on to his elbows and slipped out of her. He moved her again, sitting on the bed facing the dressing table, and positioning her over his lap, her legs either side of his. His mouth was open and he was breathing heavily. She could smell his sex, a perfume more intoxicating than any aftershave. He reached between his legs and guided her on to him. Just as the tip entered her she reached down and removed his hand. Her eyes sparkled. "Let me," she said. She rotated her hips in small circles, allowing him in an inch at a time, then withdrawing, teasing him in a way she'd never done to a man before. She couldn't believe how sexy she felt, how much she was enjoying having Chung inside her. She could feel that she was soaking wet between her legs, and hotter than she'd ever been. She arched her back and closed her eyes, concentrating on the way she moved. It was all so new to her. Chung reached up and caressed her breasts, his face shadowed by the lamp.

She kissed him, pushing her tongue deep into his mouth, biting his lips and licking his skin. "Can you feel me?" she asked, her hair swinging back and forth as she ground herself against him. He nodded. He was panting too much to speak. She raised herself up and held herself above him so that just the tip of him was inside. She had never in her life felt so powerful. She could feel Chung strain to get back inside her but she rode him, holding him at bay. She looked deep into his brown eyes and saw herself reflected there. She put her hands on his wide shoulders and felt his muscles bulge as he, tried to take her. She made him wait, until she could see a longing in his eyes which was so intense that it burned. Only then did she allow herself to drop on to him, driving herself down so hard that the breath was forced out of her. She pounded up and down, scratching his shoulders, her eyes wide and her nostrils flaring, wanting nothing more than to have Anthony Chung come inside her. Faster and faster she rode him, and then when she sensed that he couldn't hold it back any longer she put her hands on either side of his face, sucking and kissing his lips until she felt him explode inside her. Even when he'd come she continued to move, but slowly and more gently than before, wanting to squeeze every last drop out of him. She rested her forehead on his shoulder as she had when they'd danced in the lounge. It seemed an age ago. A drop of sweat ran down her left breast and hung on her nipple as if reluctant to let go. Her body suddenly felt cool and she was aware of the film of sweat which covered her skin. She hadn't come, but that didn't matter to her. It had been many years since she'd had an orgasm, and the pleasure Chung had given her was more than enough. She licked his shoulder, the tang of salt on her lips. She smiled to herself, wishing she could tell Phyllis Kelley that her view of Chinese men was hopelessly inadequate. Admittedly her own experience was limited to just three men, but she couldn't imagine Phyllis ever having anyone better than Anthony Chung. God, how she'd love to give the details to Phyllis and see her mouth drop. Length. Width. Duration. It had all been so perfect. "Perfect," she said out loud. Chung stroked the back of her neck. Anne knew that she'd never be

487

able to tell anyone what she'd done, it was a secret she'd have to lock away inside herself for ever. She had no regrets, not after the joy she'd experienced. To think that she could have gone to her grave not knowing what real lovemaking was. She was glad that she'd done it, but it had been a one-off, she'd never do it again. Not with Anthony Chung. Not with anybody. Except for her husband of course. She sighed. Chung's hand came up and caressed her breast at the same time as he massaged her neck. She felt him shift beneath her and she made to slip off him, thinking that he wanted to get up. Instead he pushed her on to her back and crawled backwards off the bed, licking her breasts and planting soft kisses on her nipples. They stiffened and she stroked his thick, black hair. He slowly moved down the bed until he was kneeling on the carpet, his head on her left thigh. She could feel his warm breath on her skin and then his hands held her knees and pulled her towards him so that her legs were hanging over the edge of the bed. He ran his tongue through her pubic hair and she put her hands up to her mouth.

"No," she said quietly.

She felt his tongue run the length of her right thigh, from her hair down to her knee, and then his mouth moved back the way it had come, only slower.

"No, you mustn't," she said, but she reached down and stroked his hair and opened her legs wide for him. Chung kissed her other thigh and licked the inside of her knee, driving her wild with anticipation. She knew what he was going to do, and she trembled at the thought of it. William had kissed her between the legs

488

once, a year after they'd married, but it was a half-hearted attempt and neither of them had particularly enjoyed the experience. Anne remembered how embarrassed they'd both been afterwards, and how red-faced William had been. He'd never tried it again.

Chung nibbled at the flesh where her leg joined her groin, then he ran his tongue along the groove there, his breath hot and warm. Anne closed her eyes and tightened her fingers in his hair, surrendering herself to the sensations that he was creating within her.

Chung's hands slipped under her backside and his face pressed against her thighs as his tongue worked its way inside her. He licked her and then pushed his tongue in and out, rubbing it against her wet flesh. She groaned and bucked her hips, pushing herself against his face. She was amazed by Chung's creativeness. He nibbled at her, he sucked, he kissed, he licked, he alternated between using his tongue and pushing his finger in; she felt herself go impossibly wet and it seemed to go on for ever, building and building until a white light seemed to explode inside her head and she shuddered and screamed.

"We go now?" asked Coleman's driver.

Coleman checked his wristwatch for the thousandth time. He was going to have to go back to the office, he couldn't afford to hang around Chung's apartment block all afternoon. He cursed himself for following Anne and Chung in the first place. He'd seen them at the Landmark, they'd had a drink in the Mandarin Hotel, and they'd gone back to his apartment. What he'd seen raised more questions than it had answered. For all he knew Debbie could also be in the apartment, or even William Fielding. There was a multitude of possibilities but Coleman still had a sick feeling in the pit of his stomach.

"Yeah, let's go," said Coleman.

The driver wound down his window, spat noisily on to the pavement, and started the taxi.

Lewis was microwaving a cup of beef soup when Tyler came up to him and tapped him on the shoulder.

"Beef soup?" said Tyler. "Is that all you're having for breakfast, Bart?" he asked.

"I haven't got much of an appetite," said Lewis.

"You look like you're losing weight," said Tyler. "Are you in pain?"

"It's bad, Colonel, but not too bad. Honest."

"Painkillers?"

"I'm taking them. I'm okay, really."

"Let me know if it gets too much," said Tyler, clearly concerned. "How's the work going?"

"It's going well, better than I thought," said Lewis. The microwave pinged and he took the steaming mug out. He blew on the surface and sipped it before walking over to the dismembered Huey with Tyler.

"The damage to the tailboom was superficial," said Lewis. "The bullets passed straight through it. I tell you, Colonel, Chuck was lucky. Any one of those slugs could have snapped the tailplane control linkage or the drive shaft and the Huey would have spun itself into the ground. They weren't even nicked. Didn't touch the

490

main rotor, either. God must have been smiling on him that day."

"Buddha, you mean," said Tyler.

"Yeah," said Lewis, grinning. "Buddha. The final drive right-angle gearbox, that's the one right by the tail rotor, is totally seized, though the bevel drive gearbox in the tailboom seems to be serviceable. Assuming we get a complete set of parts, I'd feel safer if we replace both, but we could get away with using the original bevel drive."

The two men moved from the rear of the helicopter to the middle. Where the turbine had been on the top of the Huey was now a gaping hole. "There was a surprising lack of rust in the powerplant," said Lewis. "Not that I'd want to fire her up after twenty years, but it looked to be in good condition. When will the new one get here?"

"That's what I was coming to tell you," said Tyler. "They'll be here within the next couple of hours."

"We're getting everything?" asked Lewis.

Tyler nodded. "The works. And a bonus, too. Remember you said you were having trouble operating the lathes?"

"Sure. Still am."

"The mechanic will be arriving with the parts delivery."

"Great," said Lewis.

"He's Chinese, but he can be trusted," said Tyler. "But he doesn't know what we're planning, so I don't want any idle talk in front of him. Tell the others, will you?"

"Will do, Colonel," replied Lewis. "Sure will be useful to have an extra pair of hands around."

"How's the main gearbox?" asked Tyler, standing on the cabin floor and peering at the top of the Huey.

"It's seized, but if we were to take it apart and put it back together again I think it'd work. Again, I'll be happier with it replaced. The swashplate mechanism is okay, and so is the main rotor mast. Rotor blades, too. I'll tell you, Colonel, they really knew what they were doing when they built the Huey. You could just about get this bird in the air as it is. I'm not saying that you'd get me up in it, but . . ."

"That's great, Bart, just great." He clapped Lewis on his back. "What's the main job at the moment?"

"The electrics," said Lewis. He took Tyler over to a large, green tarpaulin which had been spread out on the ground. Yards of wiring were laid out on the tarpaulin like the blood system of some strange prehistoric monster. "It's basically sound but we're checking it inch by inch and renewing the contacts. We're looking good though, Colonel, we're looking damn good."

"Glad to hear it, Bart," said Tyler. He looked at Lewis and frowned. "Are you sure you're feeling okay?"

Lewis gave him a beaming smile. "Never felt better," he said. He went over and supervised Horvitz and Carmody as they painstakingly checked the wiring. Doherty was sitting in the cockpit of the Huey, his hands and feet on the controls and a faraway look in his eyes. Lehman was standing at the side of the helicopter watching him. Lewis took another sip at the beef soup, but he had no appetite. Tyler was right, he had been

492

losing weight, though he hadn't thought it was noticeable. He simply wasn't hungry, and any food he forced down seemed to increase the pain a hundredfold. At first he'd put off taking the painkillers the doctor had prescribed for him back in Baltimore, but now he was taking the maximum dose, six tablets a day. He had said that once Lewis had reached the maximum dose he should go back for another check-up and he'd prescribe stronger medication. Yeah, right, thought Lewis. All I have to do is pop on a plane back to the States and get a new prescription. Colonel Tyler would just love that. A searing pain ripped through his stomach and he winced. His arm began to shake with the effort of not screaming and the beef soup slopped over the side of the mug. He took deep breaths and willed the pain to subside so that he could take another pill, fighting to stop himself from bending double. The tablets were back in the section of the office he used as a bedroom and he walked slowly over to it.

He sat down on the end of the camp bed and used the beef soup to wash down one of the tablets. He looked at the label on the plastic bottle then spilled them out into his palm. He counted them one by one. There were twenty-one. Enough for three and a half days. What then? Just the pain, the gnawing, biting, searing pain. The thought made him shudder. He'd lied to Tyler about how bad the pain was; he didn't want him to think that he wouldn't be able to go through with the mission. He slid the tablets back into the bottle and screwed the cap on, then sat with his head in his hands while he waited for the pain to subside.

He was disturbed by a knock on his door. "Bart! The parts have arrived." It was Dan Lehman.

"Yeah, okay, I'm coming," said Lewis, slipping the bottle under his pillow. He stood up and went out into the corridor where Lehman was waiting.

"You okay?" asked Lehman.

"God, I wish everyone would stop asking me if I'm okay," snapped Lewis.

"Hey, cool it," said Lehman, holding his hands up as if blocking a blow. "It's me, remember?"

Lewis glared at Lehman but the tension visibly drained from his body and he apologised. "I'm not feeling good, Dan. It hurts."

"I know," said Lehman, not knowing what else to say. He had no idea of the pain Lewis was going through.

"Come on, let's go," said Lewis. They went along the corridor and out into the warehouse. The small door was open and they headed for the oblong of bright sunlight. Outside was a small truck which had been reversed up to the sliding door. The truck was painted green with white Chinese characters on its wooden sides. There was a metal framework over the back of the truck which could be covered with a tarpaulin when the weather was bad but it had arrived uncovered and the two men saw two large wooden crates. As they got closer they saw that they both had "Machine Parts" stencilled on the side in black capital letters and an address in Manila.

"Close the door, Dan," said Tyler. He was standing at the end of the truck and watching three bare-chested

494

men with dark skins trying to push one of the crates with little success.

"How did they get them on?" asked Carmody.

"Fork-lift truck," said one of the men in heavily accented English. "You no have?"

"No, we no have," said Carmody, clicking his claw.

"Easy, Larry," said Tyler. An old Chinese man, small and plump, was standing next to Tyler with his arms folded across his broad chest. The skin on his head was sprinkled with small purple birthmarks, each separate and distinct from the others, like a map of the world where the continents had been separated. There were folds of skin along the back of his neck and around his waist as if he were a couple of inches shorter than he used to be and his skin hadn't taken up the slack. He was wearing faded blue denim overalls with a bib which seemed to be straining to hold in his pot belly.

The old man turned to Tyler. "You have a winch inside? A pulley perhaps?"

"Good idea, Mr Tsao," said Tyler. "Could you tell them that we'll back the truck inside and unload it, and then drive it out. I'd like them to wait at the fence."

Tsao nodded and spoke to the men in quiet Cantonese. They grinned and seemed happy to leave the work up to the Americans. They jumped off the truck and swaggered over to the fence. As they walked their tattoos rippled on their backs as if they were alive: a screaming eagle, a scorpion preparing to strike, and a dragon breathing fire. The tattoos looked old, the colours were fading and the edges blurring as the inks seeped through the cells of their skin, but the men themselves couldn't have been more than twenty-five. One of them took a pack of Marlboro from the pocket of his jeans and handed cigarettes around and they squatted together by the fence, smoking and laughing.

"Larry, can you drive the truck in?" asked Tyler. "Dan, Eric, will you two get the door?"

Horvitz and Lehman closed the small door and then pushed back the sliding door until the space was wide enough to drive the truck through. Tyler motioned to Carmody and he started the truck and began reversing. Tyler guided it under the largest pulley system and told Carmody to stop. Lewis clambered on to the truck, fixed a thick chain under and around the larger of the two crates, and fastened it to the metal hook below the pulley. He began winching it up, grunting as he pulled on the chain which ran through the pulley, and Lehman climbed up to assist him. Together they heaved on the chain and soon the crate creaked and groaned and lifted off the truckbed. Once they had it six inches above the truck Lewis and Lehman clambered down and shouted to Carmody to move the truck forward. He jerked the truck forward ten feet and stopped it with a squeal of brakes. Lehman and Lewis lowered the crate to the floor then slid the pulley over so that it was poised above the truck again. They repeated the process with the second crate and when it was also on the concrete they banged on the tailgate of the truck and Carmody drove it out of the warehouse and up to the fence where he climbed out of the cab and handed over the keys to one of the Chinese labourers. They drove

496

off, still smoking and laughing, black fumes belching from the exhaust.

Tsao picked up a large black holdall and walked with Tyler into the warehouse as Lehman and Lewis pushed the sliding door shut. When they'd finished Tyler asked them all to gather around. "This is Mr Tsao," said Tyler, by way of introduction. The old man nodded and put his bag on the floor. "Mr Tsao will be helping us get the helicopter ready."

Tsao shook hands with each of the men in turn. He had a round face and his plumpness smoothed out any wrinkles he might have had. He reminded Lewis of the Pillsbury Dough Boy. When Tsao smiled at him Lewis saw that his back teeth had been replaced with gold caps and one of his canines was also gold. After he'd shaken hands with all of them he went over to examine the Huey.

Tyler took a crowbar and pried the lid off the smaller of the two crates. The Americans watched as Tyler began scooping aside handfuls of polystyrene shells as if he were looking for something. "Here we are," he said triumphantly. He pulled out four thick books wrapped in clear plastic. There were also four dark green plastic binders which he held out to Lewis. "A little bonus courtesy of the Philippine military machine," said Tyler.

Lewis took the books and flicked through the pages. "Workshop manuals," he said. "They're all here: Operators Manual, Airframe Manual, Parts Manual, and Engine Manual. The full set. Terrific."

"I thought they'd make your day," said Tyler. "Look, will you show Mr Tsao around. There's a cot for him in the office next to mine."

"He's sleeping here?" said Lewis.

"It's the best way to maintain security," said Tyler. "He lives in Shatin but he's told his family he's working on a contract over the border. He's being well paid and he comes highly recommended by one of my contacts here in Hong Kong."

"That's good enough for me," said Lewis.

"Just don't forget what I said about talking in front of him," warned Tyler. "The less he knows about what we're doing, the better."

"Understood, Colonel."

Tsao stood at the side of the Huey, gently stroking the war machine, wonder in his watery eyes.

Michael Wong put his knife and fork together on the empty plate and patted his stomach. "An excellent meal, Anthony. Truly excellent."

"I'm glad you enjoyed it," said Chung, dabbing at his lips with a starched white napkin.

A waiter appeared as if by magic and whisked away both plates. "Have you noticed how much better food tastes when you don't have to pick up the check?" Wong asked.

Chung grinned. "Not recently, no."

Wong laughed good-naturedly. He was about five years older than Chung, and looked more like a successful businessman than a triad leader, or Dragon Head. His hair, like Chung's, was expensively cut, and he wore spectacles with Yves Saint Laurent frames. His face was squarish and he had a prominent dimple in the centre of his chin. The one clue to his violent background was a small raised scar which ran for about two inches down the side of his chin but he always held his head so that it couldn't be seen. Chung knew that under the light blue suit there were worse scars, laying testament to an attack on his life ten years earlier when Michael Wong was a simple triad foot-soldier, a Red Pole. Wong had taken Chung to a high-class Chinese-only sauna in Wan Chai and as they'd sat together in the steam he'd seen Wong's scars stay white as the rest of his skin went pink. They were wicked wounds, hatchet cuts that ran from his neck to his waist, criss-crossing like the tramlines at Kennedy Town tram terminal. Michael Wong was lucky to be alive, and he lived life to the full, as if every day was his last.

"Dessert?" offered Chung as the waiter pushed over the sweet trolley.

Wong patted his trim waistline. "Got to keep my figure, Anthony," he said. "Amy won't let me into the bed if my waist is an inch over thirty-three."

Wong had been happily married for almost fifteen years and had three children, all girls. He doted on them all.

"Coffee then?" asked Chung, waving away the trolley.

"Coffee would be good," said Wong.

Chung nodded at a waiter who was hovering with a silver coffee pot and he stepped smoothly forward and began pouring. They waited until he'd finished before continuing their conversation, which up to that point had been about the forthcoming races at Shatin, the relative merits of Taiwanese girls compared with Japanese, and whether Wong's daughters should go to school in the UK or the States.

"So, Anthony, how is everything going?"

Chung nodded and smiled. "Very smoothly," he said. "This man Tyler is a true professional. I must confess to having some misgivings when you suggested that we use a gweilo, but he is every bit as good as you said. His idea of using the helicopter was genius, sheer genius. And the team he has put together, it's perfect, absolutely perfect. I tell you, Michael, if you really wanted to mount a raid on the Happy Valley racetrack, Tyler would pull it off. He really would. Your man Tsao has started working with them, and the helicopter will be ready in plenty of time."

"Good," said Wong, stirring his coffee. "You have the names for me?"

Chung slipped a folded piece of paper across the table and Wong pocketed it, unread. "There are five," said Chung.

"I shall make enquiries," said Wong. "You had a good look at the security arrangements?"

"You should have been there," said Chung, leaning back in his chair and toying with his saucer. "Their head of security is a racist gweilo. He was an arrogant pig who was more than happy to lord it over an ignorant Chink. He told me more than he should."

"They do love to underestimate us, don't they?" mused Wong. "I'll arrange for my man Lee to come

500

round and talk to you. He is an alarms specialist, and he can brief my men. But you envisage no problems?"

"None at all," said Chung. He waved at a waiter to attract his attention and made a quick scribbling motion with his hand. The waiter rushed off to get the bill. "I already have eight drivers lined up. I am going to meet another right now. What about the vehicles?"

"I have nine so far," said Wong as the waiter arrived with the bill. Chung took it off the silver plate, scanned it, and put it back with his gold American Express card. "I should have the last one within a day or two. Five are already modified, the rest will be completed well in time."

"All Mercs?"

"We thought it best. They are the most reliable, and the easiest to modify."

"Excellent," said Chung, dropping his napkin on the table and getting to his feet. "No," he protested as Wong made to leave. "You stay and finish your coffee."

Wong reached up and shook hands with Chung and wished him luck.

"You make your own luck, Michael," said Chung, patting him on the back. "You know that."

On Chung's way out the captain approached him and handed him a small leather holdall. Chung took the bag and smoothly slipped a banknote into the captain's waiting hand.

Uncle Fung took his cloth and carefully polished the chrome tap, taking extra care where the metal joined the sparkling white marble. That was where a dirty crust sometimes built up. He'd seen it in other, less well-tended, men's rooms, but it would never be allowed to develop in his. When he was satisfied that the tap was as clean as it could be, he lined up the hairbrushes on the marble shelf in front of the mirror so that they were all exactly one inch away from the glass and perpendicular to it, before straightening the bottles of aftershave so that their labels faced ahead. There were small drops of water on the floor below one of the wash-basins and he knelt down to mop them up. When he straightened up he saw the door open and a well-dressed Chinese man in his thirties came in, carrying a black leather holdall. Uncle Fung's eyes remained downcast but he quickly scrutinised the man. A pale green suit, well tailored, either French or Italian, and good quality tan shoes which were definitely Italian. As the man walked by him to one of the cubicles, the one he'd most recently cleaned, Uncle Fung thought happily, he noticed the man's expensive haircut and caught the fragrance of an expensive aftershave, all suggesting that a good tip would be forthcoming.

As the cubicle door closed, Uncle Fung checked that the urinals were sparkling clean and that there were plenty of clean white hand towels by the door. Uncle Fung took pride in his work, a pride which his wife always said bordered on obsession. She now lived in Canada, in a luxury apartment in Vancouver overlooking the Strait of Georgia, with their four children. The apartment was full of expensive antiques which he and his wife had collected over their forty years together and was twice the size of the one they used to share in Causeway Bay. It was stunning, but Uncle Fung had never actually seen it, only Polaroid photographs sent along with letters from his family. He would join his wife and children before 1997, that had already been decided. Until then, there was still much money to be made.

Uncle Fung had worked as a toilet attendant in the hotel for the past twenty years, and it had been profitable work. Very profitable. At a conservative estimate he was worth almost two million dollars. Two million American dollars, most of which was in Canadian bank deposit accounts, and all of which he'd earned as a result of his diligence in the hotel's washroom. The hotel was close to the Hong Kong Stock Exchange, and its restaurants and coffee shops were well frequented by the colony's stockbrokers and share analysts. Barely a day went by without Uncle Fung picking up some useful titbit of gossip or other as brokers relieved themselves at the urinals or washed their hands at the basins. In the men's room, Uncle Fung was invisible. Occasionally he would overhear inside information, news of a forthcoming takeover or deal which wasn't common knowledge, and he would use the information to good effect, buying and selling shares and always making a good profit. Life had been good to Uncle Fung, and in many ways he regretted not being able to pass the post on to one of his sons, but the forthcoming communist takeover made that impossible. Uncle Fung had escaped over the border in 1956, his wife a year later, and he could not take the risk of living under Chinese rule again. They had long memories, the communists.

He heard the rustle of toilet paper in the cubicle and put a hand on one of the taps. As he heard the toilet flush he turned the tap on so that the water would be hot when its occupant emerged. Uncle Fung averted his eyes as the door opened. He'd discovered long ago that the more subservient he appeared, the bigger the tip that was proffered. His eyes widened when he saw the cheap, grubby training shoes that were on the feet that emerged from the cubicle. Above them were blue jeans, torn in several places, the sort worn by street vendors. Uncle Fung could not keep his eyes averted any longer. The figure was carrying the same black bag but now it was being held by a young man with unruly hair, a stained T-shirt and a denim jacket that was as scruffy as the jeans. There was a streak of oil on the man's left cheek. He nodded at Uncle Fung and leant towards the mirror to check his appearance. He reached up to smudge the oil on his face and Uncle Fung noticed for the first time that there was dirt under the man's fingernails. He hadn't seen it when the man had entered the washroom, if indeed it was the same man. The man ruffled his hair so that it looked even more untidy, smiled at Uncle Fung, and headed for the door, swinging the holdall. Uncle Fung was so staggered by the transformation that he completely forgot to open the door. He stood in the centre of the washroom, shaking his head. After a minute or so he walked slowly over to the cubicle and looked apprehensively around the door, half expecting to see the man in the pale green suit dead on the floor. It was empty, of course, and Uncle Fung scratched his head. Maybe now was the time to go to Canada, he thought. Life in Hong Kong was becoming far too complex.

Lehman stretched his back and groaned. It had been a long time since he had done any physical work, and refurbishing the Huey was proving to be laborious. He went over to the workbenches, where Lewis was tinkering with the radio which he had removed from the Huey. Bits of it were spread all over a wooden bench.

"No joy?" asked Lehman, looking over his shoulder.

"The colonel says we don't need the radio but I'd feel safer if we had it working," said Lewis. "We could listen for other aircraft, maybe pick up air traffic control when we're airborne. It'd let you know if we had to face anything unexpected."

Lehman nodded. "It'd be useful, all right. We could call ATIS and get a weather report from Kai Tak, too."

"ATIS?"

"Automatic Terminal Information Service. It's a recording of weather and runway information, it goes out on VHF. But are you saying you can't fix it?"

"Not a hope. Mr Tsao's had a look at it as well, but he's not really an electronics expert. I think the crystals have given out, but I'm not really an electronics expert either, not at that level anyway. In Nam if it stopped working, we just slotted in a new one. And besides, these things were tuned to individual pre-set frequencies before each mission. It's unlikely that they'd correspond to any frequencies that are used here."

"So?"

Lewis looked up, a red-handled screwdriver poised above the electrical parts. "Well, I reckon we could buy a scanner here and patch it into the Huey's aerial and the intercom system. I could mount it in the roof, no problem."

"Let's do it then," replied Lehman. "Do you want to go into Tsim Sha Tsui and pick one up? I'll drive."

"Sure. You think we should tell the colonel? He went out an hour or so ago."

"I don't see why," said Lehman. "The guys have got plenty of work to do, they won't miss us. We can be there and back in an hour."

Lehman drove the Wrangler Jeep to the main shopping area of Tsim Sha Tsui and parked in a multi-storey car park. The shops selling electrical equipment all followed the same format: big colourful signs bearing the names of the big Japanese manufacturers, window displays of the latest products, mostly from Japan, and inside were counters set up in a U-shape behind which sat earnest young men wearing short-sleeved shirts and gold-rimmed spectacles who kept their eyes trained on the entrance to their domains like hawks searching for pigeons.

The two men stood for a while looking into the window of one of the larger shops. Black shelves were lined with every conceivable sort of consumer electrical equipment: hand-held computer games; cameras; camcorders; digital tape recorders; walkie-talkies;

506

computer notebooks; miniature television sets; short-wave radios. Not one had a price tag or any indication of how much they would be expected to pay. The sales assistants inside perked up, scenting prey.

They walked out of the bright sunshine and into the air-conditioned shop. Other than two middle-aged men examining a Hitachi camcorder while their stomachs hung over their too-tight shorts, they were the only customers.

"Yes, can I help you?" asked a sales assistant who looked about fifteen years old. He motioned for them to sit on high stools on their side of the counter.

"We're looking for a radio receiver. A scanner," said Lewis. "Something that can pick up aircraft transmissions, police, emergency services, stuff like that."

"No problem. For America or for Australia?"

Lehman and Lewis looked at each other. Lehman thought of lying but quickly realised that then they might end up with unsuitable equipment. He turned back to the salesman who was looking at the digital watch on his wrist as if he had better things to do than waste his time serving customers.

"For use here," said Lehman. "In Hong Kong."

The salesman sucked air in through his teeth. "Cannot," he said.

"Why not?" asked Lehman.

"For export only," the salesman said. "Cannot use in Hong Kong."

Lewis frowned. "But these new scanners can pick up almost everything. They should work here same as anywhere."

"Need licence to use in Hong Kong. For export only."

Comprehension dawned. "Ah, you mean we mustn't use them in Hong Kong. They do work here but we're not allowed to use them. Right?"

The salesman nodded and smiled as if a particularly stupid child had just told him that two times two was four. "Right," he said. "Need a licence from the post office."

"Okay," said Lehman. "What we want is a scanner that will work in Hong Kong. But we won't use it here. We'll be taking it to the States with us."

The salesman grinned. "I have several that will do," he said. He slid back a glass panel and brought three different models from out of the window display. He demonstrated all three to the Americans with casual familiarity. All seemed to be able to monitor the same frequencies, the only difference being size and range.

Lehman haggled for a while over the cost of the biggest and managed to get the price down by almost thirty per cent. Before he handed the money over to the young salesman he asked him if he could supply a list of frequencies of local radio users, the police and such like.

"You must not listen to police broadcasts," the man said. "I already told you."

"Yeah, yeah, I know. But if I promise not to listen, could you give me a list?"

"How do I know you're not police yourself?"

"How many Americans are there in the Hong Kong police?" replied Lehman.

The salesman thought for a minute and then nodded. "Okay, okay, I'll see what I can do." He took the money from Lehman and shouted over to one of his colleagues in Cantonese who disappeared into a back room. He came back a few minutes later with a sheet of paper which he gave to Lehman without saying a word. "That has most of the frequencies," explained the salesman as he detached the flexible antenna from the scanner and put them both into a box. "But don't say where you got them from. Or this. Don't tell anybody you buy here, okay? This for export only."

"I understand," said Lehman. He gave the list a quick look. It appeared to be a computer print-out composed of two long columns. The left was a list of police stations, divided into Kowloon, Hong Kong, New Territories and Marine Police and consisting mainly of names that Lehman couldn't even begin to pronounce. Some were obvious though, like Emergency Unit East Kowloon, Airport, and Traffic. The numbers all appeared to be six-digit VHF frequencies.

"Okay," said the salesman impatiently. "You want batteries?"

"Doesn't it come with batteries?" asked Lehman.

"No. Or a case. You want a case?"

"No, no case. But I'll take a set of batteries."

"What about a mains adaptor?"

Lehman looked at Lewis. "What do you think, Bart?"

Lewis shook his head. "Batteries will be fine. I might patch it into the electrical system, but it's not vital. It won't use that much power, the length of time we have it on."

Lehman paid for the batteries, slipped the list of frequencies into his back pocket and walked with Lewis back to the car park. On the way they walked past a McDonald's. Lehman looked over at Lewis, his eyebrows arched.

"Big Mac attack?" asked Lewis.

"No doubt about it," said Lehman. "You?"

Lewis grimaced. "I'm not hungry, but you should get burgers for yourself and for the guys in the factory. I've got to buy some stuff from the drugstore."

Lehman's face filled with concern. "What's up?"

"I'm almost out of painkillers. I had some with me that I brought from Baltimore, but they're practically gone. I thought I'd try a drugstore, see if they had anything."

Lehman frowned. "Do you think they'll sell you stuff that's strong enough over the counter?"

Lewis shrugged. "I'll give it a try. If they won't I guess I'll visit one of the local doctors. Whatever you do, don't tell the colonel, okay? He doesn't know how much pain I'm in, and I don't want him to know, either."

"Hey, my lips are sealed. I just don't like thinking of you in pain, that's all."

They arranged to meet outside the restaurant. Lehman had to wait five minutes for Lewis to return, and he had a small paper bag in his hand.

"He sold me a selection of painkillers, and gave me the addresses of a couple of doctors," said Lewis. They went back to the Jeep. On the way Lewis uncapped one of the bottles and chewed on a couple of white tablets. Lehman said nothing.

Tyler still hadn't put in an appearance by the time they got back with their bags of burgers and fries. "All right!" cheered Carmody when he saw what they'd brought. Lehman and Lewis shared out the food and while they ate Lehman unpacked his scanner, screwed in the antenna and slotted in the batteries. Lehman offered Lewis a pack of French fries but he shook his head and said no. Lehman shrugged and put the scanner down on the bench next to the radio from the Huey that Lewis had been working on. Carmody watched, munching a Big Mac as Lehman switched it on. He spent a few minutes programming in some of the frequencies, the Emergency Units for the four areas of Hong Kong, the Traffic and Fire Service frequencies, and the Marine Police's harbour frequency. The scanner raced up and down the airwaves looking for a transmission and then a torrent of Chinese crackled through the speaker. Lehman pulled a face and pressed a button to send the scanner searching again. It locked on to another Cantonese channel. Then another. And another. Lehman tried for ten full minutes but he couldn't get anything other than Cantonese.

"Useful, man. Really useful," said Lewis. "You think maybe I should have tried it out in the shop first, right?"

Tyler drove to Sai Kung and to the beach where he'd arranged to meet Michael Wong. He was five minutes early, but he could see that Wong and his bodyguards had already arrived. On the beach he could see a middle-aged man in tartan trousers, golfing shoes and an expensive dark blue short-sleeved shirt swinging a golf club. He was wearing a black golfing glove on one hand, a large gold watch, and gold-rimmed sunglasses. Crouched down in front of him was a man in a brown suit holding a plastic carrier bag. The man dipped his hand into the bag and came out with a golf ball which he placed on a plastic tee.

The golfer eyed up the ball, shifted his feet from side to side, swung back the club and sent the ball curving out to sea. The man in the suit took another ball and placed it on the tee and shuffled back as it, too, was walloped out over the waves, some ten feet or so to the left of the first.

Tyler got out of his car and when he closed the door two well-built Chinese bodyguards looked over at him. The golfer didn't appear to notice his arrival and continued to hit balls seaward. Tyler started to walk towards him and wasn't in the least surprised when the bodyguards moved to intercept him.

"I'm here to see Michael Wong," he said. One of the guards spoke to his companion in rapid Cantonese and he nodded back. "My name is Joel Tyler." He wasn't sure if the men spoke English but the one who had spoken turned away and walked over to the golfer. He waited until another ball had been whacked into the waves then whispered into his ear. The golfer turned, saw Tyler, and waved his golf club in greeting.

"Mr Tyler!" he called. "Good to see you again."

Tyler wondered whether the man really had been unaware of his arrival, or if he was just playing some sort of power game. He hoped it wasn't the latter because he and Michael Wong were going to be working closely together and it was important that they trusted each other. Game-playing would just get in the way. Wong walked over, smiling and swinging his golf club under his arm and holding it there like a sergeant-major's swagger stick. He held out his other arm and shook Tyler's hand fiercely.

"Everything is well?" he asked the American.

"Everything is fine," said Tyler.

"The Smith & Wesson is good, yes?"

"It's an excellent weapon," agreed Tyler.

"And Mr Tsao. How is Mr Tsao doing?"

"He is a real asset," said Tyler.

"A trustworthy man," said Wong. "You play golf?"

"I'm afraid not."

"My handicap is fourteen now," said Wong.

"You have a good swing," said Tyler.

"You think so? I am trying to improve it. That's why I come here each day, to improve."

"It's working," said Tyler.

The two men walked together along the seashore, Tyler shading his eyes from the bright sunshine.

"Everything is going according to plan?" asked Wong.

"The helicopter? Sure, we're on schedule. No problems. What about your end?"

"My men are in place. I have a good feeling about this, Mr Tyler. A very good feeling."

"Me too," smiled Tyler. "How are you getting on with the weapons I asked for?"

"The M16s will be here shortly. They are being delivered from Singapore. I should be able to deliver them within two days. Is that satisfactory?"

"That'll be fine," said Tyler. "Will you deliver them? I'd like the men to meet you."

Wong looked across at the American. "To what end?" he asked.

"It'll make them feel more relaxed to meet the man who's helping them to commit the robbery of the century," said Tyler.

Wong began to laugh. He stopped walking and threw back his head and gave full vent to his deep-throated laughter.

Neil Coleman took a file from his in-tray and opened it with a sigh. He rubbed the bridge of his nose and closed his eyes. "What is it with Mercs?" he muttered to himself.

"Something wrong?" asked Hui.

Coleman looked up. "Another sodding Mercedes has been stolen. That's ten over the past week. I can't understand it."

"It is a popular car," said Hui.

"I know that," snapped Coleman. "I meant that they're making up a higher percentage of stolen cars than this time last year."

"Ah," said Hui, nodding thoughtfully. Coleman waited for him to comment further but Hui simply turned back to his desk.

"Great," muttered Coleman. "Thanks for your input, pal." He leant back in his chair and looked at the teeming crowds down below. He was sick to the back teeth of Hong Kong: the people, the heat, the noise. When he'd got up that morning he'd discovered three cockroaches inside his fridge. He'd been infested with the things for the past three months. He hated the insects and had put roach traps under his bed and behind the fridge, but they seemed to have got wise to them. The only way to get rid of them was to spray but he didn't have the money to bring in exterminators and that meant speaking to his landlady, an elusive Chinese woman who lived on one of the outlying islands. He'd left message after message on her answering machine but she hadn't called back yet. He made a mental note to tell the bank not to pay next month's rent if she didn't get in touch.

His telephone rang and he picked it up, hoping that it was his landlady finally returning his call. It wasn't, it was a call from the manager of one of the colony's Mercedes suppliers, a Mr Leung. He was very apologetic for bothering the police, but thought they ought to know that they had been selling a surprisingly larger number of parts for Mercedes cars.

"What would those parts be?" Coleman asked as he doodled on the notepad on his desk. He couldn't understand why Leung had called. The squad was interested only in stolen vehicles, not retailing.

"Tinted windows," said Leung.

"Tinted windows?" repeated Coleman, frowning.

"Yes, tinted windows. You know, with dark glass," said Leung patiently.

"Yes, I know what tinted glass is," said Coleman, sitting up straight in his chair. "How many windscreens have you sold?"

"Not just windscreens," said Leung. "Complete sets. Windscreen, side windows, rear windows. Everything. For three cars."

Coleman's interest waned. "Three isn't a very large number, Mr Leung," he said.

"No, no, you not understand," protested Leung. "Three sets from my shop only. I call round other dealers. All have sold tinted windows in the past two months. Twelve sets in all."

"Twelve?" said Coleman. "Is that unusual? How many would you normally sell?"

"In one year, perhaps one set. Tinted windows not very popular in Hong Kong. People think only gangsters drive cars with black windows."

"You mean really black, not just tinted to block some of the sun?"

"Completely black, so no one can see through," said Leung. "They make the car appear very sinister."

"I see," said Coleman. "Look, Mr Leung, were all the sets of glass supplied to the same customer?"

"No, I had thought of that. They were all to individual customers, different addresses. Also, the orders were placed at different times. We had to order from Germany each time."

"Strange," mused Coleman.

516

"As you say, strange. I do not know what to make of it."

"Me neither, Mr Leung. But I promise I will look into it. Would you do me a favour, would you please fax me a list of the customers who have requested the parts?"

"So you can check if they own Mercedes cars?" asked Mr Leung.

"Exactly," said Coleman. He gave the man the office fax number and took down Mr Leung's phone number before thanking him for the information and hanging up. He sat back in his chair and tapped the eraser at the end of his pencil against his front teeth. Why in God's name would twelve different people suddenly decide to install black glass in their Mercedes cars? And was it connected to the rash of missing Mercs?

Lewis and Mr Tsao were kneeling either side of the turbine and peering at its innards. "Is there anything I can do to help you guys?" asked Lehman.

Lewis looked up and shook his head. "Once we've got this sorted out we're going to need another pair of hands to help get it in place, till then we can handle it," he said.

"I thought I'd go to the races at Shatin, get the feeling of the track there."

"No problem with me," said Lewis. "Better check with the colonel, though."

"Yeah, I guess so," said Lehman. Lehman knocked gently on the door to Tyler's room.

Tyler opened it with the portable phone in his hand. "Hiya, Dan, how's things?" he said.

"Fine, well on schedule," said Lehman. "I was thinking of going to the races. Is that okay with you?"

Tyler nodded. "I don't see why not. Take any of the guys who want to go with you, they deserve a break."

"Thanks, Colonel," said Lehman. As he walked down the corridor to his own room Lehman realised that it was the first time he'd called Tyler by his rank. It had slipped out naturally, and Tyler had accepted it without comment.

Lehman changed into jeans and a blue polo shirt. There was a knock at his door and Carmody stuck his head in the room.

"Hey, Dan, you going to the races?"

"Yeah, you wanna come?"

"Sure. I'll see you at the Jeep."

"Okay, see if Eric wants to go."

Five minutes later Lehman was driving the Jeep out of the compound, with Carmody next to him and Horvitz on the back seat. As soon as they reached the main road into Shatin they hit traffic, all of it heading for the races. They parked a quarter of a mile away from the track and walked among the throngs of racegoers, almost all of them Chinese and most of them reading Chinese newspapers. They filed into the public stand, which was every bit as efficient and modern as the Happy Valley complex. They bought racecards and sat alongside a husband and wife who were eating cold chicken wings from a plastic tub, talking as they chewed.

"Hey, guys, Galloping Dragon is running today," said Carmody.

"Yeah, I'm surprised it wasn't shipped off to the glue factory after its last performance," said Horvitz.

A group of four teenagers on the seats in front of them were shouting at each other and jabbing their fingers at each other's newspapers. The stand was buzzing with good-natured arguments and laughter as the crowds anticipated the forthcoming races.

"Are you going to bet today?" Lehman asked Horvitz.

"I might give it a try," said Horvitz, running a hand through his beard.

"I'll go and get us some cards," said Lehman, standing up. He threaded his way along the line of seats and walked up to the betting hall. There were queues of bettors at each of the many tellers, handing over bundles of notes and shuffling betting cards. Lehman walked along the line of betting tellers and watched them taking in the money, faces impassive.

He went over to a betting card dispenser and helped himself to a handful of cards. A figure approached him from behind and coughed quietly. "Ah, Mr Lehman. You remember me? I am Dr Chan."

Lehman turned round to see a middle-aged Chinese man with horn-rimmed spectacles carrying a pile of newspapers, Chinese and English, and a notebook. It was the racing fan who'd helped him out on his visit to Happy Valley.

"Of course I remember, Dr Chan," he said. He stuck out his hand to greet the man and Dr Chan transferred his stack of papers to his left arm. He fumbled and they spilled to the floor. Lehman knelt down and helped him pick them up. When they'd both straightened up they shook hands.

"You are becoming a regular," said Dr Chan.

"Do you have any tips?" asked Lehman.

"Oh yes," said Dr Chan, flipping through his notebook, "let me see. Yes, I calculate that Red Pearl has a ninety per cent probability of winning the second race." He looked at Lehman over the top of his spectacles. "And Shining Wind is worth a bet in the fourth. Other than that, there is nothing I would recommend today."

"I'll certainly back them, Dr Chan. Thank you."

"How long will you be in Hong Kong for, Mr Lehman?"

Lehman shrugged. "A few weeks, I think."

"Ah, then you will be here for the last race of the season. That is always a big day."

"I'd love to see it. You'll be at Happy Valley?"

Dr Chan frowned. "Oh no, last race is here, at Shatin, not at Happy Valley."

"Are you sure?"

Dr Chan looked pained, as if Lehman had suggested that he'd written a wrong prescription. "I would not be mistaken about such a thing, Mr Lehman. The last race is always at Shatin. Tradition."

Lehman's mind whirled, wondering why Tyler had said that the robbery would be at the Happy Valley track. Dr Chan could not possibly be mistaken, and

Tyler had been right on everything else. Why the conflict? It was bizarre in the extreme.

"You seem puzzled," said Dr Chan.

Lehman forced a smile. "No, I just made a mistake, that's all. Well, I hope you have a good day's racing, Dr Chan. I must get back to my friends."

They shook hands and Lehman took the betting cards to Horvitz and Carmody.

"Red Pearl in the second and Shining Wind in the fourth," said Lehman as he passed out the cards.

"Hot tip?" asked Horvitz.

"Yeah, I met a guy who gave me some advice last time. He seems to know what he's doing."

"Okay, I'll put a hundred dollars each way on both of them, and fifty bucks on Galloping Dragon," said Carmody, scribbling on his card.

An announcement in Chinese over the loudspeakers resulted in a rush towards the betting hall and Carmody dashed off, a wad of red banknotes in his hand. From their seats Lehman and Horvitz looked out over the track and across to the sea. Like Happy Valley there was a massive video board on the far side of the home straight and there was a grass track and an inner dirt course.

"It's a beautiful track," said Horvitz. He pointed out to sea. "Be a hell of a lot easier to get away from the place, wouldn't it?"

Lehman nodded. He had been thinking along the same lines. If the last race of the season truly was being held at Shatin, the heist would be a good deal less complicated than the cross-harbour flight that going to

Happy Valley would entail. Lehman was confused, but he didn't want to discuss his fears with Horvitz. Or with Carmody for that matter. Over the past few weeks both men had grown much closer to Tyler and Lehman suspected that the colonel trusted them more than he did Lehman.

Tyler came out of the offices with his portable phone in his hand. "The guys gone to Shatin?" he asked Lewis, who was lying on his side by the turbine. Mr Tsao was kneeling by his toolbox and handing tools to Lewis as he asked for them.

"They left about an hour ago," said Lewis.

"Good. Chuck go with them?"

"No, he's in his room. Meditating, I think."

"Okay. I'm going to take the Toyota into town. I'll be back in a couple of hours. When do you think you'll be ready to install the turbine?"

Lewis rolled away from the turbine and sat up, grunting. "Tomorrow, I guess. And we're going to have to test it."

Tyler nodded thoughtfully and tapped the antenna of the phone against his leg. "It'll be noisy," he said.

"But it's got to be done. If we don't get the settings right there's no guarantee she'll fly."

"If we must, we must," said Tyler. "But let's wait until the Huey is fully assembled. I don't want to test the turbine more than once. Get the gearboxes and the electrics in and the rotors attached. We'll test them all together."

"And there's the fuel," added Lewis.

"The fuel will be here within the week," Tyler promised. He headed towards the door. "See you guys later," he said over his shoulder.

Lewis groaned and rubbed his stomach, his eyes closed and his mouth half open. He put his spanner on the concrete floor and took out a bottle of codeine tablets he'd bought at the drugstore. They barely took the edge off the pain and they made him feel nauseous, but they were better than nothing.

Mr Tsao squatted back on his heels and watched Lewis with watery eyes. "You are sick?" he asked.

Lewis winced as he chewed and swallowed two of the white tablets. "Headache," he muttered.

"I think not," said Mr Tsao. He wiped the back of his hand under his nose and sniffed. "I think problem your stomach. You are in much pain. And you not eat much."

"What are you, my mother?" said Lewis, putting the bottle of tablets back into the pocket of his overalls.

"Not mother," said Tsao, his hands on his knees. "Friend. I not like see you hurt."

Lewis got to his feet and pulled a face. "I'll be okay. We'll be finished soon."

Tsao raised his thin eyebrows. "Maybe I can help," he said.

Lewis looked at him and massaged his stomach. "I don't think so, Mr Tsao. If the tablets don't help, I don't think there's much you can do."

Tsao pressed his hands against his knees and stood up, his joints cracking like dry twigs. He took a step closer to Lewis and he could smell garlic on his breath.

"So, pain is bad?" said Tsao.

"Yes, all right, it hurts," said Lewis. He knew that Tsao had seen him wincing as they'd worked on the turbine and the gearboxes, so there was little point in continuing the charade. He had grown to like and respect the Chinese mechanic; he was hardworking, a skilled metalworker and he had a dry wit that Lewis appreciated.

"You have cancer, I think," said Tsao.

Lewis was stunned by the man's perception and his jaw dropped. "How . . ." His voice faltered before he could finish the question.

"How I know?" Tsao said. "My wife died two years ago from cancer of the stomach. She not eat, she lose much weight. Before she die she in much pain. Always rubbing stomach."

"I'm sorry," said Lewis.

"We married long time," said Tsao, a faraway look in his eyes. "She give me many sons. She cry all the time, at night she screamed. Begged me to take away the pain."

"I'm sorry," Lewis repeated. He shuddered involuntarily at the thought that, in all probability, that was how he himself would end up, lying on a bed somewhere screaming for the pain to be taken away. The way Dr Jordan had described it back in Baltimore, the pain he was feeling now was just a shadow of what was to come.

Tsao's eyes seemed to refocus and he smiled thinly at Lewis. "Towards the end I give her something to dull pain. If you wish, I get same for you."

"What is it?" asked Lewis.

"Opium," said Tsao softly.

Lewis threw his hands up in horror. "Opium?" he said. "You mean heroin. No way, Mr Tsao. No way. I've seen that shit destroy too many lives to get involved with it. My home town is riddled with heroin and coke and crack and all the rest of that crap. I'll have nothing to do with it."

Mr Tsao shook his head patiently. "We are not talking about heroin. No need inject. I show you. Chinese use opium for long time."

"I don't think so," said Lewis. "I've seen too many addicts panhandling on the streets."

"I think you need not worry about long-term effects," said Tsao, his voice little more than a whisper. "I think you not have to become addict."

Tsao's words made Lewis feel cold deep down inside and he licked his lips nervously. He couldn't say anything so he just nodded.

Tsao took that as acceptance. "I will call number two son. He will bring opium here."

Tsao used the second portable telephone, which Tyler had left on one of the workbenches, and the two men worked on the turbine while they waited for Tsao's son to arrive.

After an hour they heard a car horn sound and Tsao went outside. He returned with a small polythene packet, about two inches square, which contained a small amount of white powder.

"I'm not sure this is a good idea," said Lewis.

"Try," said Tsao. "No need inject. You can chase the dragon."

"Chase the dragon?" said Lewis.

"I show you," said Tsao. He went over to the area of the warehouse the men used as a kitchen. He put the packet on top of the microwave and picked up a roll of kitchen foil. He tore off a strip about four inches wide and eight inches long and then folded it in half lengthways. He bent the oblong strip into a V-shape and sprinkled a small amount of the powder into the groove. There was a disposable cigarette lighter on the bench next to a butane gas burner and Tsao took it in his right hand. "Watch," said Tsao. He held the foil strip up to his face so that one end was about three inches below his nose. He ran the lighter along the underside of the foil. "You do this with flame, flame burns powder, you sniff smoke," said Tsao. "You must move face over strip to keep up with smoke. That is why we call it chasing the dragon. You understand?"

Lewis nodded and Tsao handed the foil and the lighter to Lewis. He lifted the foil and flicked the lighter on. Tsao nodded encouragingly, and Lewis played the flame under the end of the foil closest to his face. It bubbled and smoked and he breathed in deeply.

"Not so fast," cautioned Tsao. "One slow breath is best."

Lewis moved the lighter up the foil and more of the powder turned into sweet grey smoke. It began to drift up into his eyes, making them water, and he moved his head forward, chasing the fumes. He continued to inhale the smoke. He was so busy concentrating on catching the fumes that he inadvertently played the flame over his fingers and he yelped and dropped the foil.

"Shit!" he screamed and put his scorched hand under a running tap.

"Chasing the dragon needs practice," said Tsao sympathetically. "How you feel?"

Lewis dried his hand on a paper towel. He could feel a warm glow concentrate around his chest and spread through his veins, taking with it a feeling of well-being, of peace. It seemed to fold around the searing pain in his stomach and envelop it like a cotton wool shroud and gradually it began to diminish until the pain became an ache and then the ache became just a memory. "It feels good, Mr Tsao," he said gratefully.

"I thought so," said Mr Tsao. He picked up the small bag of powder and handed it to Lewis. "Use only when pain very bad," he cautioned. "When this finished, I get you more."

The roads in Kowloon were clear of traffic as William Fielding drove the Saab out of the Lion Rock Tunnel and into the early morning sunshine. Even crowded Hong Kong had to sleep, and at five o'clock on a Monday morning the colony's roads were no busier than an English country town's.

The Saab handled well, but the car felt claustrophobic in comparison with the Mercedes, and the air conditioning was nowhere near as efficient. He could have requisitioned a Mercedes from one of the bank's senior employees but decided instead to use his wife's car. The visit to the Shatin stables was, after all, a private one.

The white grandstand loomed ahead of him and he waved his pass at the security guard at the entrance to the stables. The old man in the dark blue uniform barely glanced at the pass and he saluted as he recognised Fielding at the wheel. It was just one of the perks of being a steward of the Royal Hong Kong Jockey Club. He parked between a white Rolls-Royce and a dark green Bentley and walked over to the stable block where his horses were based. Fielding's two horses cost him more than 25,000 HK dollars a month in stable fees and brought in only a fraction of that in winnings, but he relished being an owner, both for the excitement of watching them race and the social cachet it brought.

He showed his pass to another security guard outside the block but he too saluted without looking at it. One of his horses, Bank On It, was in its stall being brushed by his *ma-foo*, or stable boy. The stable boy, actually a fifty-year-old man, greeted Fielding. Under the system operated by the stables, a *ma-foo* was allocated two horses and he cared for them for as long as they raced in Hong Kong. The stable was air conditioned to a constant twenty-two degrees and gentle piped music seeped out of concealed speakers and the floors were covered with an expensive Japanese floor-covering so that they wouldn't have to walk on bare concrete. The racehorses lived in better accommodation than most Hong Kong workers.

"Galloping Dragon in pool," said the *ma-foo* as he brushed Bank On It's glossy coat with long, firm strokes.

"Is Mr Kwan with him?" asked Fielding.

The *ma-foo* nodded without looking up. Unlike the security guards, the *ma-foo* was not impressed by Fielding's presence. He lived for his horses and cared little for the owners.

Fielding went over to the swimming pool. His trainer, Archie Kwan, was walking along the poolside watching Galloping Dragon swimming. The horse was midway along the pool as his *ma-foo* matched its pace, holding a tether in his hand to keep it centred in its lane. Kwan said something to the *ma-foo*, another middle-aged man, and both men looked at the animal's rear legs. The *ma-foo* nodded and said something in Cantonese.

Archie Kwan was one of the most successful trainers in the colony with thirty-six horses under his control and more than his fair share of winners. He was forty-three years old, had a wife and two teenage mistresses, a Rolls-Royce and Canadian citizenship. He was the Hong Kong dream personified, thought Fielding as he walked up behind the man.

"William!" said Kwan, extending a hand. He referred to all his owners by their first name, no matter who they were. He trained horses for some of the richest and most powerful Chinese businessmen in the colony and Fielding was one of just a few gweilos he had agreed to take on. "What brings you out so early?"

"I thought I'd watch trackwork for a while," said Fielding.

"Sure," said Kwan. He nodded at the horse in the pool. "He didn't do us any favours at Shatin," he said. "That tendon is still worrying him."

"He'll be okay, though?"

Kwan sucked air through his teeth. "He'll be fine by next season, but before . . . I don't know, William. Maybe, maybe not."

"I'd really like him to do well in the last race of the season," said Fielding.

"Me too, but there's only so much we can do. If you like, I can rest him until the final meeting."

"That might be best," agreed Fielding. A win would be nice. It was about time something went his way, he thought to himself. Nothing had gone well for him for some time. He'd drawn a blank with every merger opportunity he'd pursued, his car was still missing, and Anne had been decidedly frosty over the past few days. He knew that he hadn't been spending enough time with his wife but she didn't seem to appreciate just what a difficult time the bank was going through. That was one of the reasons he'd made the early morning drive to Shatin — he was finding it harder to sleep and he knew that his tossing and turning annoyed Anne.

"So, I'll hold back Galloping Dragon until the last meeting," said Kwan. "Maybe I'll see you in the winner's enclosure."

"That would be a treat," said Fielding. He looked at his watch. "I'll go and watch the trackwork," he said. "Keep up the good work, Archie."

Kwan gave him a thumbs-up and a grin. Fielding walked outside, his head downcast and his hands in his pocket. He went and stood by the edge of the track and leaned on the barrier. Three chestnut geldings cantered around, their Chinese jockeys talking to each other and grinning. Fielding watched the horses as they worked up a sweat, but his thoughts were confined to the problems facing the Kowloon and Canton Bank.

Lehman could see that the Huey was going to be finished well on time. Under Lewis's supervision the vets had stripped out the helicopter's wiring, checked every inch, and refitted it. Lewis had installed the scanner they bought from the Tsim Sha Tsui tourist shop after discovering that several of the channels did use English on occasions. It seemed that when British officers were talking on air they would use their own language, but Chinese speaking to Chinese would always use Cantonese. They had also used the scanner to pick up conversations between airline pilots and Kai Tak control tower — all air traffic communication was in English.

The turbine and gearboxes had been given a clean bill of health and installed after Lewis had fitted the skids. The rotors, main and rear, were still lying on the floor, and Lehman wasn't fully happy with the response of the hydraulics, but he doubted that they faced any major hurdles. The bird would fly.

Mr Tsao and Lewis had turned in, tired from their labours, and Carmody was in the shower. Tyler had taken the Toyota and said that he wouldn't be back until after midnight. Lehman walked slowly round the Huey, touching the warm metal with his hand. He was eager to be at the controls, to feel the surge of power as the rotors bit into the air and the Huey surged forward. He had flown helicopters in California to keep his licence up to date but he had not flown a Huey since he returned from Vietnam and he was looking forward to it. Tyler had promised them that they would test the turbine within the week, though he would not allow them to take the slick outside the warehouse.

Lehman went to the kitchen area and opened the fridge. There were several cans of beer inside, American and local. He took out a Budweiser, closed the door, and stood for a while in front of a free-standing fan, allowing the cool air to blow across his face as he popped the can and drank.

He felt edgy as if sleep would be a long time coming and he decided to take a walk outside. When he reached the door he saw Horvitz sitting with his back to the wire fence around the compound, staring up at the night sky. He was wearing his dark glasses as usual, Lehman noticed. He went back to the refrigerator and took out another can of Budweiser for Horvitz who nodded his thanks and put the can by his side, unopened.

"It was a hot one today," said Lehman, sipping his beer and looking up at the stars.

"It was that," said Horvitz.

"What do you reckon it is now? Seventy degrees?"

Horvitz shook his head. "Seventy-three," he said confidently.

532

"How can you be so sure?" Lehman asked.

"Hear the crickets?" said Horvitz. Lehman had the feeling that Horvitz had his eyes closed behind the sunglasses.

The insects were chirping furiously. "Yeah?" said Lehman.

"Count the number of chirps in fifteen seconds. Add forty to that figure. That gives you the temperature."

"You're kidding!" said Lehman.

"Try it."

Lehman looked at his watch and counted the cricket chirps as his second hand moved from twelve to three. Thirty-three. "Okay, so there are thirty-three chirps. Thirty-three plus forty is seventy-three. But how can I check what the temperature is?"

"Trust me, Dan. It works. It's an old country trick."

Lehman shook his head in bewilderment, not sure if Horvitz was pulling his leg or not. Lehman drank in silence. An airliner boomed overhead, heading towards China. After a while Horvitz opened his Budweiser and drank deeply, his Adam's apple bobbing like a fishing float as he swallowed.

"What are you doing here, Dan?" asked Horvitz.

"Just wanted a drink," said Lehman.

"No, I mean what are you doing in Hong Kong?"

"The heist, you mean? I need the money. I need a lot of money, quickly, or bad things are going to happen to me. It's complicated."

Horvitz nodded and drank again. "We're a mixed bunch, aren't we? You, me, Carmody and Lewis."

"And Doherty. Let's not forget the mad monk."

"Yeah. And Doherty. Do you ever wonder why the colonel chose us?"

Lehman shrugged. He rolled the Budweiser can between the palms of his hands. "He wanted me because I flew Hueys and because I still fly helicopters. Bart Lewis is a first-class mechanic and crew chief. Carmody I'm not sure about. He's the sort of guy who's prepared to take a risk."

"You mean he's got nothing to lose?"

"Yeah, maybe that's what I mean. Maybe none of us have anything to lose."

"You know that the colonel fixed it for Carmody to go on the trip to Vietnam?"

"No, I didn't know that."

"Yeah, he told me when he'd had too much to drink one night. Met the colonel in a bar in Cleveland. Larry and his Purple Heart. Shot in the line of duty." His voice was bitter.

Lehman turned to look at him. "Are you saying he wasn't wounded? What about his arm?"

"You might ask yourself how many doorgunners got to be shot in the hand," he said quietly. "Not many. Not unless they were self-inflicted."

"You think so?" said Lehman.

"Yeah, I think so."

"Is that what you were thinking — you were wondering why Tyler would choose Carmody?"

Horvitz drained his can and squeezed it with his right hand. The thin metal tube crumpled like paper. "I wonder why he chose Carmody, sure. But I'm even more curious to know why he wanted me."

534

"Why did you go back to Vietnam?"

"A guy from the VA came to see me, said I could go back for free. All expenses paid. He pretty much talked me into it. I was happy enough in the woods."

"The woods?"

"Yeah, I was living rough just over the Canadian border. There are quite a few vets there. People leave us alone, we hunt, fish, take care of ourselves."

"And they found you there?"

"The guy said they were looking for war heroes. Said that with my medals the Vets Association would pay for the whole shooting match."

"You've got medals?"

"Have I got medals?" said Horvitz, throwing the crushed can backwards over the fence. "Yeah, Dan, I've got medals. I've got a Silver Star, a Purple Heart with Oak Leaf Clusters, three Bronze Stars for valour, two of them with Oak Leaf Clusters, the Army Commendation Medal for valour with Oak Leaf Clusters. I've got enough oak leaves for a whole fucking tree, but I still got spat on when I got home. I still got called Baby Killer."

He pushed himself up off the ground and wiped his hands on his overalls. "I guess that's why I agreed to work with the colonel. It gives me a chance to get even."

He smiled thinly and turned his back on Lehman. Lehman watched him walk back to the warehouse. He sipped his Budweiser and counted the cricket-chirping. There were consistently thirty-three chirps every fifteen seconds.

Lehman sat for half an hour on his own, then went back inside. He walked around the Huey again and sat for a while in the pilot's station, fingering the glass fronts of the various instruments on the panel in front of him: the altimeter, the vertical speed indicator, the altitude indicator, the airspeed indicator, the heading indicator, the torque indicator, and the dials which showed the levels of fuel and the oils in the various transmissions. Lehman would have liked the opportunity to test fully all the instruments but Tyler had insisted that the first flight would be on the day of the robbery.

He pushed down on the rudder pedals and held the collective and cyclic gently. He badly wanted to fly; being in the air was almost an addiction for him and it had been several months since he'd been at the controls of a helicopter. He yawned and closed his eyes. When he opened them he saw Tyler standing in front of him, a wry smile on his face.

"Sleepwalking, Dan?" asked Tyler.

"Couldn't sleep," said Lehman. He was surprised that he hadn't heard Tyler walk across the concrete floor.

Tyler climbed into the co-pilot's station on Lehman's left.

"It always amazes me the way you guys keep these things in the air," said Tyler. "All those opposing forces working against each other: the rotors trying to pull themselves off, the fuselage trying to spin the opposite way to the rotors, the tail rotor pushing it back, the whole thing trying to shake itself to pieces. And in the middle of it all, one man, using both hands and both

536

feet and one pair of eyes." He shook his head. "You guys have my admiration, Dan."

Lehman looked across at Tyler. The words sounded right, but Lehman knew he was being spoken to in the same manipulative manner in which he'd addressed hundreds of others, playing to their vanities, their weaknesses.

"It's just a matter of technique," said Lehman. "You could train a monkey to do it eventually." He looked sideways at Tyler. He was wearing a short-sleeved khaki safari suit that was military in appearance, epaulets on the shoulders and button-down pockets on the chest. His hair seemed shorter than when they'd first met, but he couldn't recall exactly when Tyler had had it cut.

"Something on your mind, Dan?" asked Tyler quietly. He was scanning the instrument panel and playing with the controls, not looking directly at Lehman. He pulled the cyclic back and the duplicate moved in between Lehman's legs.

"We're gonna fly this to Happy Valley, right?" said Lehman. "On the last raceday of the season?"

"That's right," said Tyler, his voice soft and level.

Lehman turned to look at him. "So how come the last race of the season is always held at Shatin?"

Tyler looked up sharply, his eyes narrowed. His lips were two thin horizontal lines and he studied Lehman like a surgeon weighing up where to make his first incision. Lehman felt his insides tighten. Tyler's face gradually softened, the lips opened and turned up at the edges and the eyes crinkled. "So who've you been talking to, Dan?"

Lehman shrugged. "Does it matter?" he said.

"It matters if it means you don't trust me," said Tyler. "This whole operation, from start to finish, depends on you trusting me."

"What about you trusting us?" asked Lehman.

"Need to know," said Tyler. "It's on a need-to-know basis, I said that right from the start. Everything has been planned down to the last detail, but I can't reveal it all."

"Because you don't trust us?"

"Because if one of you — Lewis, Horvitz, Carmody, Doherty, or you — is compromised, then the whole operation is blown. That's too big a risk to take." He moved the cyclic in small, tight circles. Lehman looked down at his own cyclic moving in identical circles. "You're right, of course," continued Tyler. "The last race is at Shatin. Normally. But I'm arranging for it to be switched to Happy Valley."

Lehman laughed coldly. "So you carry weight with the Royal Hong Kong Jockey Club now?" he said.

"No, that's not it," replied Tyler. "Some friends of mine will be setting fire to the Shatin grandstand two days before the race is due to be held. They'll have no choice but to switch venues."

"That doesn't make sense, Joel. Shatin is a hell of a lot easier to get to than Happy Valley. We wouldn't have to go near Kai Tak, and we could fly straight out to sea. The crowds are bigger at Shatin, too."

Tyler nodded. "That's true, but there are three reasons why Happy Valley is better. First, there are components to the operation I haven't told you about.

538

We're going to be relying on help from inside, and we only have that inside help at the Happy Valley track. We're going to need someone to get us inside the back offices, and we can't do that at Shatin. Second, they'll all be geared for the meeting to be at Shatin, so it'll throw all their security arrangements into disarray. And third, we're going to be leaving to the south which means Happy Valley is closer. All we have to do is fly over the Peak and we're away. Does that make sense to you?"

Lehman thought about it for a moment or two. He sighed. "Yeah, I guess so. I just thought . . ." He faltered, not sure what to say.

"You thought what?" said Tyler.

Lehman put his hands up. "Okay, okay, I didn't know what to think, Joel. It's just that you were gearing us up for Happy Valley, and then I heard that the last meeting was at Shatin. I was confused, that's all."

"You wouldn't have been confused if you'd trusted me, Dan."

"That's difficult to do when I don't have the full picture," said Lehman.

Tyler nodded. "You know the rules on that," he said. "There are other people involved, not just the guys here. As soon as I can tell you everything, I will. But, Dan, I promise you that I won't lie to you. Okay?"

Lehman looked at Tyler and slowly nodded. "Okay," he said.

Tyler smiled and patted Lehman on the shoulder. "Good," he said. "I'm hitting the sack." He swung easily out of the helicopter seat and walked away.

Lehman watched him open the door to the offices and close it behind him.

He sat in the cockpit for another half an hour, idly playing with the controls as he thought over what Tyler had said. It was hard to trust a man he barely knew who was planning to lead a group of virtual strangers into the robbery of the century. He looked at his watch. It was almost one o'clock. He decided to follow Tyler's example and go to bed.

He showered and went to his room with a large pink towel wrapped around his waist. He sat on the end of his camp bed as he dried his hair on a second towel. He heard groaning sounds from the room to his right, the room where Horvitz was sleeping. The partitions between the rooms were cardboard thin and Lehman had often lain at night listening to Lewis's resonant snoring, but the noises from Horvitz were completely different. He was muttering something, incoherent words Lehman first thought, but then he realised that Horvitz was talking in Vietnamese. He stopped drying his hair and stood up, bending his ear to the wall and straining to listen. Lehman could hear sobbing, as if Horvitz were crying as he talked, then he heard a scream, a shout of pure terror that shocked him away from the wall as if he'd been slapped in the face.

He threw open his door, crossed to Horvitz's room in three strides and burst through his door. Horvitz was still asleep, one arm clawing at the air in front of his face, the other thrown across his forehead. The scream had died as suddenly as it had begun and he was crying and talking again, partly in Vietnamese and partly in

540

English. Lehman heard the words "sorry" and "killed" and something that sounded like "maybe" as Horvitz tossed and turned on his camp bed. Sweat was pouring off him and Lehman could see that almost every tendon and muscle in his body was stretched tight. His breathing was fast and erratic and his chest was heaving. He began making stabbing movements with his right hand, each jab in time with a Vietnamese word as if he was poking someone in the chest. Suddenly Horvitz's eyelids sprang open, his eyes wide and staring but he was still asleep and still talking Vietnamese. He began mumbling and tears welled up in his eyes. It was the first time Lehman had ever seen Horvitz display any real signs of emotion, and the first time he'd even seen the colour of his eyes. They were pale grey.

Horvitz began grinding his teeth as if he were in great pain, and then he opened his mouth and Lehman knew he was about to scream again. He knelt down quickly and reached out to touch his shoulder, hoping to wake him before he cried out. He shook the sleeping man and said his name quietly but barely had he got the name out when Horvitz's hand was clamped around his neck, as tight as a vice. Lehman fought to loosen Horvitz's grip, but his two hands could make no impression on the fingers which clawed into his throat, the nails biting into the skin, the fingertips cutting off the blood supply to his brain. He tried to speak but he couldn't get the air out of his lungs. He tried to twist Horvitz's wrist but the deadly grip was unbreakable. His throat burned and he felt himself slide into unconsciousness. As his vision began to blur he

541

released his hold on Horvitz's wrist and dropped his hands on to his shoulders. He started to shake him, so hard that his head was lifted off his pillow, and to his relief he saw Horvitz's eyes refocus and his hand drop away from Lehman's throat.

Lehman fell back, gasping for breath as he massaged his aching throat. Horvitz lay back on his bed, his hands against his face, his hair in disarray and his cheeks wet with sweat and tears.

"Jesus, Dan, you shouldn't wake me when I'm having a nightmare," Horvitz said.

"Yeah, well I know that now," said Lehman, his voice a dry croak.

"You don't want to do that again." Horvitz wiped his forehead with the back of his arm.

"I know, I know. Now I know, okay."

Horvitz sat up and looked at Lehman as if seeing him for the first time. "I'm sorry, Dan. I didn't know what I was doing."

"I thought you were going to scream," said Lehman. "I need some water." He padded down the corridor to the bathroom and reappeared with a glass of water. He sipped it as he sat down. "Do you have nightmares a lot?" he asked.

"Most of the time," said Horvitz, rubbing his eyes. He picked up his sunglasses and put them on and looked at Lehman through the dark lenses. "It's been a long time since I was woken up while I was having one, though. When I came back from Nam I nearly killed a couple of girls in my sleep. Ever since I've made sure I sleep alone."

Lehman nodded, knowing exactly what the man meant. "Probably best," he said and smiled. "You wanna talk about it?"

"The nightmare?"

"Yeah. It might help."

"It might," said Horvitz. He put his hands behind his head and lay back on the pillow, staring at the ceiling. He looked like he was lying under a sunbed, working on a tan.

It was some time before Horvitz spoke again. Lehman waited, sipping at the tepid water. "Remember I told you about Billy Wills?"

"The guy who was killed when you were in the Lurps?" Lehman remembered Horvitz telling him the story about the young soldier who'd been disembowelled while they were out on patrol in the Iron Triangle. It hadn't been a pleasant story.

"Yeah, that was it. We never found the VC who did it, they just disappeared. Vanished. Turns out they'd gone underground, into the tunnels. A while after that I pulled a few strings and got myself assigned to the Tunnel Rats of the 1st Infantry Division. It took some doing because I was a bit heftier than the average volunteer but I had acquired some skills that they knew would be useful. They let me join one of the teams, six men in all. Two stayed at the tunnel entrance to pass in supplies or pull out the wounded, and four of us went in. I always went point. Always. The man on point was always at least twenty feet ahead of the second man so that if he hit a booby trap there'd only be one fatality. We each had a flashlight with a red light so it wouldn't destroy night vision, a knife, wire, and a pistol. That was it. No grenades because an explosion would burn up all the oxygen, no equipment because there was no room for it. I was too big as it was. The gun I used was a beauty, a Hush Puppy, ever heard of it?"

Lehman shook his head.

"Great weapon, for close-up fighting, anyway, and that was the only sort I ever got involved in. Smith & Wesson made it especially for the Navy Seals, to kill guard dogs, would you believe? It was based on the Model 39 automatic pistol, 9 mm calibre, weighed just under a kilogram. You screwed in a specially made silencer which was good for about thirty shots before you had to replace the insert. What made it really special was the ammunition they designed for it, a subsonic round which was much heavier, and slower, than the normal 9mm bullet. You could lock the slide mechanism so that it only fired one shot and the mechanism stayed closed and didn't make a clicking noise. You could carry it underwater, which was an added bonus. But it was perfect for the tunnels; the sound hardly carried at all, whereas a normal round fired underground would deafen you for ages. And down there, your ears were your most valuable equipment because you could hardly see a thing, even with a torch. Anyway, a torch gave your position away more than anything so we tended to move in the dark."

Lehman shuddered. He couldn't even begin to comprehend the horror of moving through a small tunnel in complete darkness, not knowing if there was a

544

VC in front or behind ready to blow your brains out or stick a bayonet into your guts.

"Most of the tunnel system was based on three levels: the top levels were the main communication tunnels leading to the outside entrances and to kitchens and conference chambers; the second levels were sleeping chambers and air-raid shelters; and the third was where they stored their weapons and food and treated their wounded. When the VC knew there were rats in the tunnel they'd clear out of the upper layer and go deeper. The tunnels there were narrower, so narrow that the slimmest of the rats couldn't turn round. You could imagine what it was like for me."

Lehman shuddered. He could visualise all too clearly what it would have been like.

"The most dangerous areas of the tunnels were bends, because you never knew what was around them, and trapdoors, because they were usually booby-trapped. It was the point man's job to make the trapdoors safe. It was the sort of thing I was used to doing with the Lurps, but it was a hell of a lot harder underground, in the dark. Sort of clarified the mind, you know. You get to know what's important, and what isn't."

He fell silent for a minute or two and Lehman had no way of knowing if his eyes were open or closed behind the sunglasses.

"Whenever we got to a fork, or to a trapdoor, one of the team would stay there in case the VC were leading us into an ambush. I never stayed, I always went point. I was there to kill VC, nothing else. For Billy Wills, you understand. It was something I had to do. The first trapdoor was clean, but the second had a Russian grenade attached to it, its pin halfway out. I almost missed it. I went down, alone. I knew there was a VC close by, I just knew it. It was completely dark, darker than any darkness you can imagine. The walls were damp, the air was so thick that you could almost chew on it, and I could smell sweat. Their sweat is different, because their diet is different. We used to eat rice and dried fish so that we'd smell the same as them. No C rations, no chocolate. No toothpaste. Nothing that would leave a chemical signature. I squeezed through a tunnel into a large room, lined with what felt like parachute silk. The room was big. I followed the left side, knife in one hand, pistol in the other, flashlight tucked into the back of my trousers. I heard a noise, a rustling sound, and I heard breathing. The sound was about ten feet away, maybe more, too far away to use the knife. I fired the gun, three times so that I could get a spread of shots, then I lay low and waited. I heard a crying noise, and thought I'd just wounded him, so I crawled closer and put another bullet into him. The crying didn't stop, but I couldn't have missed. I held the torch out to the left, well away from my body, and switched it on. There was a body in the far left corner of a chamber which was about twenty feet square. There were three tunnels leading to the chamber, the one I came through and two others. I went over the body, certain that he was still alive because of the crying sounds. He was wearing black pyjamas and sandals and I was sure he was VC even though there was no weapon. There was blood; I couldn't see the colour because of the red light but I could see it glisten, but even so he could have been faking, so I used the knife, going for the kidneys and twisting the blade, and then I rolled him over. It wasn't a man, it was a woman, an old woman, skin all wrinkled, cheeks sunken, rotting teeth. She must have been in her seventies. She was curled up around a bundle, rags I thought. That's where the crying was coming from. It was a baby. The old woman had rolled up around the baby to protect it. I pushed away the rags from around its face and the little face smiled up at me. I'm sure it was a girl, just a few months old. She stopped crying. She smiled up me, Dan. I'd killed her grandmother, and she smiled at me. She started to gurgle, like babies do."

Lehman rubbed his chin, wanting to comfort Horvitz but not sure what to say. "It was a war," he said eventually. "She must have been involved with the VC or she wouldn't have been down the tunnels. And at least the baby wasn't hurt."

"I haven't finished, Dan," said Horvitz, and Lehman's blood chilled. Horvitz swallowed. "I heard someone moving down one of the tunnels and I killed the light. There were three, maybe four, moving slowly. They'd probably come to see what the noise was. The baby wouldn't stop gurgling, it was as if she was trying to tell them that I was there. Then she stopped gurgling and began to cry. I had to stop her crying, Dan. I had to stop her. So I did. I stopped her crying and then I killed all three of the VC, one with the knife and two with the Hush Puppy."

Horvitz sat up in a smooth movement as if he were doing sit-ups in a gym. His arms dropped to his side and the cotton sheet that had been covering him fell around his waist revealing his tanned chest. "They called me Baby Killer when I got back to the States," he said, his voice softer and quieter than before. "They called me Baby Killer and they were right. That's what I am. That's what I have nightmares about, Dan."

Lehman stared at Horvitz, trying to find the words to say that would ease his pain, but knowing that there were no words. A single tear trickled from under the sunglasses and ran down Horvitz's left cheek. Lehman said nothing. He leant forward and put his arms around Horvitz and hugged him.

Marie answered the phone on the third ring and called up the stairs to Debbie Fielding that it was for her. Debbie asked who it was but Marie had already gone back to the kitchen. She picked up the extension in her bedroom. Her heart fell when she heard Neil Coleman's voice.

"Oh, hello, Neil," she said, knowing that he was going to ask her out and wondering how she could get out of it without provoking him. The last couple of times he'd called they'd ended up rowing, usually over her relationship with Anthony Chung. What made Coleman's accusations all the more annoying was that she'd hardly been out with Chung, and on the four occasions they had dated he'd done nothing more than kiss her, despite her making it clear that he could go as far as he wanted. Anthony Chung had been the perfect gentleman, though Debbie still hoped to corrupt him.

"Hiya, Debbie. How are you?"

"Busy, as usual," she said, sitting down on her bed. She reached for her toy lion, a graduation present from her mother, and stroked it on her lap.

"I'm sorry about last time," he said. "I didn't mean to snap at you. I just lost my temper."

"You should be careful about that," said Debbie. In fact he'd screamed an obscenity into the telephone and then hung up on her. Debbie had actually been relieved because she thought that meant he finally understood that she didn't want to see him any more. Men were so crazy sometimes, she thought. You slept with them once or twice and they thought they owned you. She'd liked Neil Coleman at first, and she'd needed little encouragement to have sex with him, but he'd taken that as a sign that she wanted to settle down with him and have his children.

"I didn't mean to," whined Coleman. "I was just upset because I missed you so much."

Debbie saw her reflection in the mirror of her dressing table. She stuck her tongue out and crossed her eyes.

"I am sorry, Debbie, really."

"Apology accepted," said Debbie.

"So, can I take you out again? This weekend maybe?"

Debbie closed her eyes. "I can't, Neil."

"Where are you going?" His voice had hardened and she could sense they were heading for another row.

"I've just got a lot of work on, that's all."

"Okay, what about next week?"

"Can I get back to you?" she said.

"Aw, come on, Debbie. You said that last time. You said you'd call me and you never did."

"Neil, the way I remember it, you slammed the phone down on me."

"The time before that, I meant," he said.

"Whenever. You can't expect me to call you when you're behaving so badly."

"I said I was sorry," Coleman said. "Look, Debbie, I love you. I really do."

"That's nice," said Debbie. She rolled her eyes at her mirror.

"So why can't I see you?"

Debbie sighed. "Maybe next week," she said.

"Debbie, don't you love me?" He said it in a plaintive whine that made her want to throw up.

"Neil, I hardly know you," she said.

"You know me, Debbie. Jesus, have you forgotten what we did in your car?"

"No, I haven't forgotten, Neil."

"Well surely that must have meant something to you?"

"Apparently it means more to you than it does to me, Neil."

"You sound like you're mad at me," he said.

"Not mad, just disappointed. I thought you'd be more mature, you being so much older than me."

"I'm not that much older, it's only ten years. Plenty of girls marry guys ten years older. It's not much of a gap."

550

"Neil, I don't want to get married."

"So why did you make love to me? Why did you do that if you didn't love me?"

"Christ, I just wanted to have fun," she hissed. "I'm twenty-three years old, sometimes I like to fuck, okay? I wanted to lay you, that's all. Why can't you accept that?"

"Have you made love to that Chink? Is that why you don't want me?"

"Chink? You mean Anthony Chung?"

"You know who I mean. Tell me, I have a right to know. Have you made love to him? Have you?"

Debbie held her breath, wondering what to say. She knew there was only one way to get rid of Neil Coleman once and for all. "Yes I have," she lied.

"You bitch!" Coleman yelled. "You fucking bitch!"

The line went dead. Debbie looked at herself in the mirror and brushed her long blonde hair behind her ears. She wondered why men behaved the way they did. She'd have been perfectly happy to have gone out with Coleman now and again, and she quite enjoyed having sex with him, but like most men he wanted more and more of her. She put the lion back on her pillow and stood up to check her reflection in the mirror. She was wearing black leather jeans and a white shirt, and she turned so that she could see her backside. She knew men liked her legs and her rear, features that she'd inherited from her mother. She looked at the mirror face-on and stuck out her chest. Pity she hadn't inherited her mother's breasts, she thought ruefully. She really envied her mother's figure. When they went shopping together Debbie saw the reaction her mother's low-cut dresses had on men and she wished she could do the same. She went downstairs into the lounge where her parents were.

Anne Fielding was sitting by the fireplace, wearing a blue silk dress and holding a large gin and tonic in her hands. Debbie resisted the impulse to look at her watch, but she knew it was early. Her mother seemed to be hitting the gin bottle earlier and earlier these days. She wondered why her dad didn't say anything to her. He was sitting on another sofa, a stack of bank papers by his side, polishing his spectacles. He signed a memo with a flourish and put it on one side.

"Are you going out?" Anne asked Debbie.

"Not tonight," she replied. "I'd rather just read. And I've a couple of videos I want to watch."

"Not going out with Anthony?" said Anne.

"He hasn't called in a while," said Debbie. "Do you think I should call him?"

"He seemed like a nice guy," said Anne. "But it's never a good idea to chase a man. Let him do the chasing."

"That's what your mother did with me," said William Fielding, looking at Debbie over the top of his spectacles.

"Works every time," said Anne. She tapped the side of her crystal tumbler with a red-painted fingernail.

"I was thinking, Dad. Would it be all right to invite Anthony to come to the races with us, on the last meeting of the season? He told me he was a big racing fan."

552

"That's this weekend," said Anne. "It's a bit short notice."

"I know. I thought if it was okay with you I'd ask him. You said I could go and there's plenty of room in the box." The Kowloon and Canton Bank's boxes at Happy Valley and Shatin were lavish affairs, ranking in prestige alongside those of the Hongkong and Shanghai Bank and Jardine Matheson, and invitations to the major meetings were eagerly sought after.

"I don't see why not," said William Fielding, "he seems a perfectly presentable young man. A big improvement on that policeman, anyway. Has he found my car yet?"

"I'm afraid not, Dad. So I can ask Anthony?"

"Yes. I thought I just said yes."

Debbie went over and kissed him on the cheek. "Thanks, Dad."

"You're not getting serious about this man, are you?" asked Anne.

Debbie shook her head. "You know me, Mum."

"Yes, young lady, I do," said Anne. She drained her glass and walked over to the drinks cabinet to fix herself another gin and tonic, her heels tapping on the floor.

Woo Bik-kuen held his bowl up to his lips and used his chopsticks to shovel roast pork and rice into his mouth, his eyes never leaving the television screen. He guffawed as the fat lady on the screen tried to squeeze into a lift full of Filipina maids, and rice grains sprayed out over the Formica table. His wife didn't mind, she was laughing as heartily as him at the on-screen antics.

They were both fans of the Cantonese comedy programme and never missed it. He reached for his bottle of San Miguel and took a mouthful, swilling it round to wash down the rice. He belched appreciatively and his wife pointedly leant over and switched up the volume.

The doorbell rang, but neither of them moved. Woo put the bowl back under his chin and shovelled in more food. His wife could cook only a limited number of dishes, but what she cooked, she cooked well, and Woo only liked simple fare anyway. Give him dim sum, or roast pork, or roast goose, or won ton soup, and he was happy; that and a little rice was all he needed after a hard day's work. His job wasn't demanding, but it was boring, and he looked forward to his evenings in front of the television set, especially when his three sons were out of the apartment. Their home was small, two bedrooms and a cramped lounge, and when everyone was home there was barely enough room to sit around the television. It was hot; too, even with their tiny electric fan on full power; it couldn't cope with the humid night air and five sweating bodies.

The doorbell rang again, three impatient buzzes this time, and Woo glared across the table at his wife. He worked all day, she should be the one to answer the door while he was eating, he thought. She ignored his angry look and stared at the television, chuckling as she swallowed. The elevator doors had closed on the fat woman and the maids were complaining in sing-song pidgin English. The doorbell rang, one long continual buzz as if someone was leaning against it. It was clear that they wouldn't stop until the door was opened.

Woo pushed back his chair and wiped his mouth with the back of his hand. Thirty-five years he'd been married, and the woman was as stubborn as the day he'd put his ring on her finger. She pretended not to see him walk to the front door and open it, but risked a sly look over her shoulder. She was curious to see who was calling so late in the evening, but not curious enough to spoil her viewing pleasure.

Two young men stood in the doorway, one a good-looking man in his forties in a dark blue suit and a red and white striped tie, a man who looked like a television presenter or a successful insurance salesman. The other was younger and more muscular, his leather bomber jacket straining across his broad shoulders. His hands swung easily at his side and he had an arrogant tilt to his chin. Woo had seen the pose many times among the rough young men who stood outside the off-course betting shops. It was the stance of a Red Pole, a triad fighting soldier. The man in the suit nodded at Woo and introduced himself as Mr Chan. He said he was a Grass Sandal for a triad gang, the name of which Woo was all too familiar with. He didn't introduce his leather-jacketed companion.

"What business does the triad have with me?" asked Woo. "What have I done that they send along an illustrious messenger to my humble home?"

Mr Chan smiled. "We wish only to speak with you, Mr Woo. We seek a favour only you can grant."

Woo felt suddenly sick. His wife was openly listening, her chopsticks poised halfway to her mouth. Triads did not request favours, they demanded them, no matter how flowery the language.

"I am just a working man," said Woo. "I am a poor man; if it is money you want I can raise some, I am sure, but times are hard and . . ."

Mr Chan held up a hand to silence Woo. He was wearing a thick gold bracelet around his wrist and his nails were neatly clipped. "Mr Woo, we do not wish to take money from you. Indeed, fortune has smiled on you this day because the favour we will ask will result in riches for you and for your family. Riches the like of which you have never imagined in your wildest dreams." His eyes hardened. "But they are not the sort of riches that should be discussed outside, in a corridor."

The man in the leather jacket slowly clenched and unclenched his fists, his nostrils flaring like an angry bull.

"Of course, of course," said Woo, stepping to the side. "Please excuse my impoliteness. Please come into my humble home."

Woo's wife was already clearing away their supper dishes and wiping the table top down with a greasy cloth. She pulled out three chairs and busied herself making a pot of *bo lay* tea for the visitors. She served the fragrant brew in small bowls and then scurried away into the sanctuary of the main bedroom, wanting to stay and listen but knowing that it was no place for a woman.

"Such fragrant tea," said Mr Chan, sipping at his bowl.

"I wish I had something better to offer my illustrious guests," said Woo, his head bowed.

"This is perfect, refreshing on such a hot night."

"My humble home has no air conditioning, and for that I apologise," said Woo, getting to his feet and moving the fan so that the cool breeze blew across the visitors. The man in the leather jacket swallowed his tea in two mouthfuls, and tapped the table three times as Woo refilled his bowl, the traditional way of showing thanks without the effort of speaking.

Mr Chan took another sip of tea, smiled, and put his bowl on the table top. "So, to business, Mr Woo." Woo nodded and suppressed a shudder. "You enjoy your job with the Kowloon and Canton Bank?"

"I hold a very lowly position, but it is undemanding work," said Woo.

"It is a key position. You are responsible for a great deal of money, Mr Woo."

"I am but a small cog in a great machine," said Woo.

"You are close to retirement, are you not?" said Mr Chan.

"I am an old man, it is true, and I will not be working for many more years," said Woo. "Perhaps you seek a younger man —"

"No," interrupted Mr Chan. "You are the man we seek, Mr Woo. You will be working next weekend. And on Friday. Is that not so?"

"Yes," said Woo.

"That is what we thought," said Mr Chan, straightening the cuffs of his shirt. He had large gold cufflinks, Woo noticed. "We wish you to ensure that the time locks to the depository vault doors are set to open twenty-four hours earlier than usual," said Mr Chan.

"It is not possible!" said Woo.

Mr Chan slapped his hand down on the table, hard enough to rattle the three tea bowls. "Mr Woo, do me the courtesy of assuming that I know what I am talking about. You are responsible for the time locks, you set them to open on Monday morning. We wish the time locks to open on Sunday morning."

"But why would you want me to do such a thing?"

"You are not a stupid man, Mr Woo," said Mr Chan. "And it does not require a genius to work out what we are planning to do. I do not wish to burden you with the details. All I require of you is that you do as we ask regarding the locks. And one other thing. There will be visitors to the depository on Sunday. You will recognise one of the visitors, but you will not allow them access until you have checked with your head of security, the gweilo called George Ballantine. He will give permission to admit the visitors. In all respects you will act as normal, do nothing unexpected. The only out of the ordinary act we ask of you is the setting of the locks. Do you understand me?"

Woo nodded, knowing that resistance would be futile. The Grass Sandal was a messenger, the Red Pole was an enforcer, and he would have to deal with one or the other. He was an old man and had no wish to fight. "Yes, I understand."

"And you agree?"

"Yes, I agree," said Woo, his hands under the table, his head bowed.

"In that case, Mr Woo, we can do business. Once this is all over, you will receive one million Hong Kong dollars, enough for you and your family to start a new life, wherever you want. It will be a golden opportunity for you, Mr Woo. A golden opportunity for your wife and your three sons. How are your sons, Mr Woo?"

Woo looked up. "My sons are fine, strong boys," he said.

"I hope they stay that way, Mr Woo. I hope they stay that way."

Mr Chan stood up and pushed back his chair. His companion stood up awkwardly and his chair fell back, cracking into the wooden floor like a pistol shot. The bedroom door was flung open and Mrs Woo rushed out, fearing the worst. When she saw that her husband wasn't hurt her face reddened and she stood in the doorway, wringing her hands.

Woo showed his visitors out, closed the door, and then leaned against the wall with his head in his hands. His wife came over and stood in front of him, asking what was wrong but receiving no reply.

Tyler had given Mr Tsao the night off, not out of any concern for his well-being but because Michael Wong was coming round to help with the briefing and he didn't want the old man to know what was going on. Wong arrived at just after ten o'clock in a large white delivery van with the name of a Kowloon electronics retailer stencilled on the side. He sounded his horn at the entrance to the compound and Tyler went out to let him in. Tyler opened the gate, pulled it back so that Wong could drive in, and then relocked it behind him. Wong gunned the engine while he waited for Tyler to slip the chain through the gate and click the padlock shut and he waved for the American to climb in so that they could drive the fifty yards or so to the warehouse. They sat talking for a while before Tyler got out and called the four vets over. He introduced them one at a time, and then Wong slid open a side door on the passenger side of the vehicle. He showed two long wooden crates to Tyler, each the size of a small coffin with rope handles at either end.

"Right gentlemen, let's get them inside," said Tyler. Horvitz and Carmody carried one, Doherty and Lehman the second. Once inside they put them down on the floor next to the worktables.

"Can you open them, Eric?" asked Tyler, handing a crowbar to Horvitz. Horvitz nodded and forced the end of the crowbar in the edge of one of the crates and forced the wood up with a splintering sound. He used his hands to tear away a piece of wood, revealing straw packing underneath. He pushed it aside, reached in and pulled out an assault rifle.

"Jesus, an M16," said Carmody.

"Four M16s, actually," said Michael Wong. He had brought a large black briefcase with him from the van. "Ammunition, too. And you'll find tear-gas canisters and smoke and stun grenades in there."

"Everything we need for a party," said Horvitz.

"Let's do it over here," Tyler said to Wong. The two men went over to the wall near the workbenches, where Wong put down his briefcase and popped its combination locks.

"Gather round, gentlemen," said Tyler, as Wong began taking out two cardboard tubes from the case. He unscrewed the caps and slid out a series of charts and photographs. He pinned them up on the wall with small thumbtacks as the vets stood around him in a tight semicircle. One was an aeronautical chart centred around Kai Tak Airport, another was a large-scale street map of Kowloon and Hong Kong Island. Lehman studied the chart carefully as Wong took several large glossy colour photographs out of one of the tubes. He pinned up a series of photographs which had obviously been taken from a plane showing the airport, Kowloon, the island, and several of the Happy Valley racetrack. Below them he lined up another series of pictures, all ground-level views of the racetrack, some of them close-ups of the grandstand.

"Gentlemen, we have now reached the point where I can reveal the full details of the operation," said Tyler, as Wong stood to the side of the pictures and maps, his arms folded across his chest. "I am sorry you have been in the dark for so long, but I'm sure you can understand the reason for secrecy. You will hear tomorrow that the Shatin racecourse was damaged in an arson attack. You'll probably see it on your television sets if you're not out celebrating in the seamy bars of Wan Chai." The vets nodded. Tyler had brought in two portable colour televisions in an attempt to alleviate their boredom during the periods when they weren't required to work on the Huey. "Mr Wong here, you might have guessed, will be responsible for the closure of the racetrack, and the subsequent switching of the last race of the season to the Happy Valley track on the island." Tyler looked pointedly at Lehman. "Because the Shatin video screen will also be damaged in the attack tonight, there will be no video link between the two tracks, which means that all the high rollers will be going to Happy Valley on Sunday. It's going to be a record take, and we're going to be the beneficiaries. I haven't discussed with you the details of the operation before, partly because we were still in the process of finalising the arrangements. An important component of the operation involves assistance from within the Jockey Club, and for that we have to thank Mr Wong here. He has in place a number of his people who will be working as tellers and supervisors on Sunday. They will give us the access we need. You gentlemen will enable us to get the money out. It will be a very profitable combination, I can assure you."

Both he and Wong smiled.

"The timing of this operation will be the most important thing," said Tyler. "The passage of money to and from the tellers is like the ebb and flow of the tides. Before each race money flows into the tills of the tellers, after the race it flows back to the winners, with the Jockey Club retaining its cut. It flows in, it flows out, with the Jockey Club retaining progressively more money as the meeting goes on. The amount of money in the tills reaches a peak just before the last race. If we move too soon, all the bets won't be in. If we move too late, the tellers will have paid out to the winners. There are eight races scheduled for Sunday. Mr Wong's men on the inside will admit members of his triad into the offices five minutes before race eight starts, but they will not move until the race has actually started and the horses are running. All eyes will be on the track, the betting halls should be practically deserted and anyone in there will be watching the race on the television screens. The men will hit each betting hall, take the money to the elevator, where they will transfer it to the roof of the grandstand. You gentlemen will leave the warehouse so that the Huey arrives at the track just after the race starts. Dan, the timing on this is going to be critical, so I want to go over the flight plan with you. We'll get a full weather report on the day so that we know what sort of winds to expect. You'll fly the Huey on one circuit around the field, dropping the smoke and stun grenades where they will cause maximum confusion. You'll then fly to the top of the grandstand and pick up the money. Again, Dan, we'll need to do the weight calculations beforehand so that we know how much we can take on board."

Lehman nodded in agreement.

"Question, Colonel," said Horvitz.

"Yes, Eric?"

"Do I gather that you won't be flying with us?"

"That's affirmative. I'll be at the track, helping Mr Wong here. I'll RV with you on the roof of the grandstand. You'll pick me up along with the cash."

Horvitz nodded.

"Another question, Colonel," said Lehman.

Tyler raised an eyebrow and looked at him.

"The guns," said Lehman. "What are the guns for?"

"For effect, Dan. I don't expect them to be used. But we have to show that we mean business."

"So they won't be fired?"

"Not unless the Huey is fired upon," said Tyler.

"Is that likely?"

"It's unlikely in the extreme," said Tyler. "The only weapons the guards have are shotguns, and beyond fifty feet they're practically useless. They're certainly not going to be able to bring down a Huey. Dan, we're not trying to cause a bloodbath here. We want to get in and out with the minimum of trouble. You fly in, drop the smoke and stun grenades, you pick me up on the roof. Then we fly."

"To where?" asked Lehman.

"I was coming to that," said Tyler. "I want to go over the grandstand first. I don't want the Huey actually to touch down; keep it in a hover about six inches to a foot above the surface. Here." He pointed to one of the photographs of the grandstand. "This is where we'll come out with the money. We'll have packed it in canvas bags in the elevator. Larry, Eric and Bart, you'll exit the helicopter and provide cover here, here and here." He jabbed at the photograph three times. "I'll have loaded the bags, with the help of two triad soldiers. I'll then board the Huey, and the three of you join me, providing covering fire if necessary. Is that clear?"

564

The vets nodded. Lehman heard Carmody's claw click.

"Our route after that will be due south, over the Peak, and down below Lamma Island." He traced the route on one of the maps with his forefinger. "From here we'll fly south-west for fifty klicks where we'll RV with a ship, a freighter which will have a specially constructed landing ramp. Dan, you'll land the Huey on the ship, we unload the cash, and then we push the Huey overboard. The ship will take us to Thailand, the captain is a friend of Josh's. Josh will arrange for the Hong Kong dollars to be converted into any currency we wish. Gold even, if that's what you prefer. Questions?"

Carmody shook his head. Horvitz ran a hand through his beard. "What happens to the triad soldiers we leave behind?" asked Horvitz.

Wong stepped forward. "The men we have on the inside will not be compromised," he said quietly. "They will admit the armed Red Poles without being noticed."

"Red Poles?" said Horvitz, his brow furrowed.

"Red Pole is the name we give to our triad fighters," explained Wong. "They will be masked and they will wear overalls, no one will be able to identify them. Once they reach the elevator they will dispose of their overalls and in their place they will wear police uniforms."

"I should have made that clear. I will also be wearing a uniform, that of an inspector in the Royal Hong Kong Police," said Tyler. He smiled. "Please don't shoot me by mistake." He turned to Wong. "You have the uniform?"

Wong nodded. "In the van," he said. "I'll give it to you before we leave."

"Any other questions?" asked Tyler.

"I have some, but they apply mainly to our flight plan and to our loading," said Lehman. "We'll go over those tonight?"

"That's affirmative," said Tyler. "And tonight we'll also test the turbine. That okay with you, Bart?"

"Fine, Colonel," said Lewis. "Been looking forward to it."

"I think that brings this meeting to an end, gentlemen," said Tyler. "I'll leave these charts and photographs on the wall tonight for you to familiarise yourself with them."

Wong put his cardboard tubes back in his briefcase and relocked it. He said goodbye to the vets and wished them well, and then went out with Tyler. A few minutes later they heard the van start up. The vets studied the M16s as they waited for Tyler to return.

"The good old poodle-shooter," said Horvitz. He picked one up. "Never trusted them myself. They were always fouling unless you kept them spotless, and how could you keep them spotless in the jungle?"

"What did you use, Eric?" asked Lewis.

"An AK-47 usually," said Horvitz, running a hand down the metal barrel. "That way, if the VC heard you firing, they figured it was one of their own. The AK-47 never jammed, even if you treated it like shit." He turned to look at the men. "You know Mattel used to help make this weapon?" He raised his eyebrows. "You know, the company that made Hot Wheels and the Ken and Barbie dolls?"

"Come on, Eric," laughed Carmody. "That was just a rumour."

Horvitz shook his head. "Saw one myself, Larry, in 1972. Most M16s had the Colt logo, but I saw a couple of grunts who had M16s with the word Mattel in the centre of a serrated circle on the handgrip. Wasn't a rumour, I saw it with my own eyes."

"Mattel, huh?" said Lewis. "Makes you wonder, doesn't it?"

Tyler returned, swinging the bunch of keys and holding a blue nylon suit-carrier which Lehman assumed contained the inspector's uniform. "Everything okay?" said Tyler. "Anything you gentlemen didn't want to ask in front of Mr Wong?"

"It seems straightforward enough," said Lehman.

"We're sure no one is going to get hurt?" said Doherty.

"Chuck, you'll be sitting up front with Dan. The only person you'll hurt is yourself if you screw up on the controls."

Nobody else had any comments so Tyler said he wanted to test the Huey. "Dan, can you get ready? You'll need a fire guard, right?"

"Yeah, someone with a fire extinguisher. They'll have to stand here, by the fuel filler, until we're sure there's no chance of a hot start."

"Bart, can you get that? There's an extinguisher on the wall over there." Lewis went over to get the red fire extinguisher. "Okay, I want us all to get into the back," Tyler said to Horvitz and Carmody. "And you too, Bart, once the turbine is up and running. All four of us will be in the back to give Dan the feel of the weight. That okay with you, Dan?"

"Sure, it's a good idea," said Lehman.

He began to walk round on his pre-flight inspection, even though the Huey wasn't going anywhere. He checked the left side of the helicopter, and knelt down to push the fuel-drain valve on the underside to check that there was no water in the fuel. He checked the tail rotor was free and then climbed up on to the top so that he could inspect the main rotor, the mast, the rotor hub, the swash plate, the transmission mounts and the control rods. He took extra care over the nut at the top of the mast. The Jesus nut, they called it, because if it failed it was all over. Only when he was completely satisfied did he climb down using the concealed foot holes next to the pilot's door. Tyler took the crew chief's seat just behind where the pilot and co-pilot would sit. Carmody and Horvitz sat at the back, facing forward. Lehman climbed into the pilot's station and watched as Doherty swung awkwardly into the seat on his left. They both put on their helmets and nodded that they were ready. Doherty opened the operator's manual and placed it on his lap.

Lehman clicked the radio trigger switch on his cyclic with the index finger of his right hand. "You okay?" he asked through the headphones in Doherty's helmet.

Doherty clicked his radio mike on. "I'm fine," he answered.

"Okay," said Lehman, "let's rock and roll."

Doherty grinned and placed his finger on the manual. "Ext LTS switches," he read.

"Set," said Lehman, flicking them into position.

"Battery switch," said Doherty.

"On," said Lehman, clicking the switch.

"GPU."

"Connect for GPU start."

"Fuel switches," said Doherty.

"Set," said Lehman.

"Fire guard."

Lehman twisted around to check that Lewis was standing by the helicopter with the fire extinguisher in his hands. "Posted," said Lehman.

"Rotor blades," said Doherty.

"Clear and untied."

"Throttle."

Lehman twisted the throttle to the starting position. "Set for start."

"Engine," said Doherty.

"Start engine," said Lehman. His left hand tightened on the collective and he pressed the starter trigger switch there. The electric starter motor whined and the turbine began to hiss like a boiling kettle. Lehman's eyes flicked automatically to the exhaust-gas temperature gauge as the rotors began to turn above his head. Flick, flick, flick, the rotors speeded up into a blur and the gauge went briefly into the red danger zone and then slid back into the green.

"INVTR switch," said Doherty, his voice clear in Lehman's ear above the noise of the turbine.

"Main on," said Lehman.

"Engine and transmission oil pressures," said Doherty.

Lehman scanned the gauges. "Check," he said. The oil pressure was in the green for the main transmission and the gear boxes in the tail.

"GPU disconnect," said Doherty.

"Disconnected," said Lehman. He scanned all the gauges on his side of the instrument panel. All were green. He looked over to Doherty's side and checked there were no problems there. Doherty gave him the thumbs-up, then turned and signalled to Lewis that there was no more need for the fire extinguisher. He stepped back, the downdraught from the spinning rotors kicking up clouds of dust around him. He put the extinguisher by the wall of the warehouse and then joined Horvitz, Carmody and Tyler in the back of the Huey.

Lehman studied the gauges, checking that the torque, exhaust and oil levels were all within limits and the electrical system was performing as it should. From somewhere in the back he heard a tapping sound and he focused on it. It wasn't mechanical, it sounded like something knocking on the side of the Huey.

Tyler had said that he could lift the Huey a few inches off the ground to check if the rotor shaft was stable and that the Huey could generate sufficient lift. He pulled slowly on the collective and gave the cyclic the merest hint of a push.

570

He could still hear the tapping. Dit-dit-dit daa. Dit-dit-dit daa. He realised it was someone in the back tapping nervously. He looked over at Doherty. He was sitting with his hands almost touching the controls, but obeying Lehman's instructions not actually to take hold of them. They only had a few metres of clearance above the whirling blades and there was no margin for error, the sort of error that two decades in a monastery could induce. Doherty was looking out of the front of the cockpit, his mouth open as if in shock. The tapping stopped. Lehman gave all the gauges a final check and increased the pressure on the collective. The nose rose first and he quickly compensated, bringing the tail up. The Huey tried to swing clockwise and he pressed down on the left pedal, keeping her straight. Lehman looked over to Doherty again, hoping that he'd confirm that there were no problems, but the man was still sitting motionless, his eyes wide. Great, thought Lehman, that's all I need. A frozen co-pilot.

He lowered the collective and slowly brought the Huey down on to the floor. He miscalculated at the last second and the tail dropped. The stinger scraped the floor before the Huey settled on to the heel of the right skid, then the heel of the left. Lehman breathed deeply, thanking the Lord that it was the stinger that had touched the ground and not the rear rotor. Contact with the stinger was untidy, with the rotor it could be fatal. He shut the helicopter down on his own because Doherty still hadn't moved.

The vets scrambled out of the side doors, bending their heads low because the rotors were still turning.

Lehman applied the rotor brake and brought them to a halt. Lehman took off his helmet and climbed down to see Tyler shaking hands with Lewis and congratulating him. He pumped Lehman's hand when he walked over. "Great job, Dan," said Tyler, his eyes sparkling. "I'm really proud of you. I want to take all you guys out for a beer."

"All right!" cheered Carmody.

"I'll pass, Colonel," said Lehman. He jerked a thumb at Doherty, still in the co-pilot's station. "Chuck and I want to go over the controls again, and we'll get to work on the route planning. We can go over it with you when you get back with the men."

Tyler slapped him on the back. "Sure, Dan, sure."

"I'll stay, too, Colonel," said Lewis. "My stomach's not feeling too good tonight. I don't think I'd be good company on a beer run. Besides, I'd like to give the slick another going over."

"Okay, Bart. Eric? Larry? You guys on?"

"Sure, Colonel," Horvitz and Carmody chorused.

"Then fall out, gentlemen. Fall out." He dumped the suit-carrier on the workbench under the maps and photographs and went out with the two men. Lewis and Lehman watched them go.

"Something wrong, Dan?" asked Lewis.

"It's Chuck. He's frozen."

They waited until they heard the Toyota drive out of the compound before they went over to Doherty. He was sitting rigid in the co-pilot's seat, his hands loose on the controls.

"Chuck, are you okay?" whispered Lehman, not sure how the man would react to sudden noises.

Doherty closed his eyes. "There's something wrong," he croaked, his voice little more than a dry rattle. "There's something very wrong."

"What? What's wrong?" asked Lewis.

Doherty used both hands to take off his flight helmet and put it on the pilot's seat. He kept looking out of the front of the Huey all the time. "I didn't catch on at first," said Doherty. "It was just a knocking, somewhere in the back."

"The tapping?" said Lehman. "Yeah, I heard it."

"What? Something wrong with the turbine?" asked Lewis.

"No, someone was tapping," said Lehman. "Didn't you hear it?"

Lewis shrugged. "I was too busy checking everything was okay," he said. "So what's with the tapping?"

"Three short taps, one longer tap," said Doherty.

"Morse code?" said Lehman. "The letter V?"

Doherty slumped forward and put his head in his hands. "That's what it sounds like, but it's not Morse. It's just nerves. Somebody who doesn't like flying in Hueys."

"So?" said Lewis. "So what's the beef?"

For the first time Doherty looked at the two men. "I heard it before," he said quietly. "I heard it before, a long time ago."

Lewis looked at Lehman as if to ask what the hell was going on. Lehman shrugged. He was just as confused. "What do you mean, Chuck?" he asked.

"Remember I told you about the Special Forces team I dropped into Laos? The guys who killed the women and kids?"

"I remember," said Lehman. "That was when you took the Huey to Thailand."

"What I didn't tell you was that one of the guys was tapping when I took off, exactly the same tapping I heard today. Three short taps, one long one. One of the guys was nervous."

"What, you're saying that one of the men you left in Laos was in the back of the Huey tonight?"

"Dan, what the fuck is going on?" asked Lewis, totally mystified.

"I'll fill you in later, Bart," hissed Lehman. "Chuck, you think one of the men was on that CIA operation?"

"That's what I think," said Doherty.

"So who is it?"

Doherty slapped the cyclic. "I don't know!" he said. "That's what's burning me up."

"You didn't see the guy in Nam?" asked Lehman.

"I saw him, but, Dan, that was more than twenty years ago. It was night, remember. And they had camouflage paint on their faces and they were wearing bush hats. Dan, they could be anyone. All I can remember is that he had blondish hair. He took his bush hat off to put on the flight helmet. Or maybe it only looked blond because it was cut so short."

"Well, we can narrow it down to three," said Lehman. "I take it the guy wasn't black, right?"

Doherty smiled, the tension beginning to drain from his face. "Yeah, that much I do know."

574

"So it's either Tyler, Horvitz or Carmody," said Lehman. "Or a coincidence."

"It doesn't feel like a coincidence to me," said Doherty.

"You guys want to tell me what's going on here?" asked Lewis.

Lehman briefly explained about Doherty's abortive mission in Laos. When he'd finished Lewis ran one of his big, square hands through his curly, greying hair. "Shit," he said. "Horvitz was in the Special Forces, we know that."

"But Carmody might just be mad enough to shoot women and kids," said Lehman. "We know what he's like now. Imagine what he would've been like twenty years ago."

"Yeah, but don't forget one thing," said Doherty. "It was Tyler who knew where the Huey was. Where I was."

Lewis and Lehman nodded.

"And there's another thing," added Doherty. "Whoever it was, he knows that I left him behind, left him and his friends to the VC. I can't imagine he's going to forgive me for that, can you?"

Lehman clucked his tongue and frowned. "Chuck, it might be nothing more than a coincidence. Let's just be calm, just take it easy. In forty-eight hours we're going to be very rich, and nobody's going to do anything to spoil that. You stick with me all the time, and we'll keep our eyes open. Bart'll be in the back when we take off and he can keep an eye on Horvitz and Carmody, see if they start tapping. If it isn't one of them, it might be Tyler. But, Chuck, they won't do anything until after this is all over. Okay?"

Doherty nodded, but said nothing. His eyes were afraid.

"Are you okay?" asked Lehman.

"I'm okay," Doherty said eventually, but he didn't sound convinced.

"Look, Chuck, if you want you can go now. Just go. I can fly this without you; we'll tell Tyler you took off."

Doherty frowned as if considering Lehman's offer, but after a few moments he shook his head. "No, I'll stay," he said. "Maybe you're right, maybe it's nothing."

"Good man," said Lehman. "Come on, climb down and we'll check her out." As he turned away from the cockpit he looked at Lewis and grimaced. Lewis rubbed his stomach and looked equally unhappy.

The men in the rubber dinghy paddled slowly towards the sea wall, taking care to disturb the surface of the water as little as possible. There were four of them in the boat, all dressed in black. In between them were four nylon bags. Engines throbbed some distance behind them as a junk made its way towards the mainland. They had paddled the boat from Tide Cove in Tolo Harbour, along the Shing Mun river channel which ran alongside the reclaimed land on which the racetrack had been built. One of the men at the bow made a waving motion with his hand and pointed, and they paddled in the direction he'd indicated. When he was close enough to the wall he jumped from the boat and scrambled silently on to the stones, his rubber soles making no sound. He lay down flat, one hand holding a nylon rope which was tied to the bow. He looped the rope around a metal post and motioned for the three others to join him. There was a line of bushes between the sea wall and the track and they regrouped in the vegetation. The throbbing of the junk's engines faded into the distance and the only sounds were the sea slapping against the wall and night insects chirping and clicking. With only two days to go before raceday, security was tight at the Shatin stables. The horses were under constant video surveillance to ensure that no drugs were given to them, and there were guards at all the entrances and exits. The men weren't going near the stables, but they'd been warned to take every precaution. Their target was the grandstand, directly opposite where they lay.

The leader nodded and the four men crawled slowly away from the bushes and across the grass track, taking care not to snag their bags. They waited at the barriers around the dirt track until they were satisfied that they hadn't been observed, then dashed across. In the centre of the track were more bushes and they crawled through them to the opposite side. They were all sweating and breathing heavily. One of the men spotted a guard smoking a cigarette and he tapped the leader on the shoulder and pointed. They waited until the man had ground the butt under his heel and gone back into the building before moving across the two tracks and up to the barriers separating the grass track from the public stands.

They spread out, each moving to his prearranged position, and then they dashed up the steps to the top of the stand, bent low. When they were all in position they opened their nylon bags and took out the explosive devices inside, each wrapped in protective plastic. The timers had already been set for thirty minutes, all that was needed was to press a small black button on the clock to activate the devices. Each had been especially built by one of the triad's explosive experts and had been designed to damage the stand structurally but not to start a major fire. Several hundred horses were stabled at the Shatin complex and the idea was to have the venue switched, not to destroy the livestock.

Each man put a device at the top of the stand, and another in the middle, then they crawled back to the bushes in the centre of the tracks. The leader had three additional devices, smaller than the ones in the stand, and he put one each at the base of the giant video screen and the tote screens before signalling to his men to return to the sea wall. They took their empty nylon bags with them, ducked through the line of bushes and slid down the sea wall to the rubber boat. They paddled quickly to put as much distance between themselves and the racetrack as they could. By the time the explosions ripped through the night air the dinghy was back in Tolo Harbour and the men were climbing into a high-powered speedboat.

William Fielding swirled his malt whisky around the crystal tumbler and savoured its peaty bouquet. Charles Devlin was sitting on one of the grey leather sofas while

Fielding stayed seated at his desk. Next to Devlin was an overweight, balding man in his late thirties, Alex Perman, the bank's top public relations executive, who was nursing a gin and tonic. Fielding sipped his whisky, a frown on his forehead. The three men were in the middle of a brain-storming session, trying to come up with ways of strengthening the bank's share price in a falling market. As the share price continued to decline it was becoming increasingly harder for Devlin even to find overseas bankers willing to talk with him, never mind begin negotiations. If the downward spiral continued, the market value would be so low that they would become a full takeover target. There were already rumours in the stock market that one of the Chinese trading hongs was planning to put together a consortium to mount a raid on the bank's shares. The *Hong Kong Economic Journal*, one of the colony's most prestigious Chinese newspapers, had run the rumour three times now, and Fielding knew that where that paper was concerned, there was no smoke without fire.

They'd been talking for the best part of an hour but had little in the way of a concrete strategy. Fielding was privately thinking that Perman wasn't up to the job. When the bank had been doing well, Perman's shortcomings hadn't been obvious, but now that they were in a slump it was all too clear that they needed someone with more experience in handling the media. If they could turn around the financial analysts and journalists they might be able to generate an air of confidence that would see them through the next few months. So far the only suggestion that Perman had made was that they bring in an outside firm of public relations consultants. Devlin had squashed it immediately, quite rightly pointing out that it would be perceived as a panic measure and do more harm than good. This dirty linen was going to have to be washed in private.

Devlin had suggested that they use the Hong Kong rumour mill themselves and plant a story in one or more of the Chinese newspapers that a definite suitor had emerged. The English press often followed up stories in their Chinese counterparts and so did the wire services based in Hong Kong. Assuming the story appeared to be true, it would spread around the world. That, Devlin said, might give them a breathing space, and attract other would-be investors. Fielding had considered the idea seriously, but decided that it could also backfire if a real suitor didn't appear.

"If these stories of a Chinese takeover are true, we might have to consider looking for a white knight," said Devlin.

"I want a full partnership," said Fielding sharply, "I don't want us to become a subsidiary of another bank, even if it's on a friendly basis. I haven't been with this bank for thirty years only to see it taken over. And I don't think you want that either, Charlie."

"I want to stay independent as much as you do, William. But if it ever comes to a choice between being taken over by an English clearer and being allowed to run our affairs, or being taken over by the Chinese, I know which I'd choose."

Fielding nodded. "You're right of course, but God willing it won't come to that. I don't want to end this meeting on a sour note, but we seem to be going around in circles. Alex, I'd like you to prepare me a full report on the PR ramifications of the problems we've got at the moment. And any suggestions you have." Perman looked decidedly uncomfortable. "Charlie, you're going to have to put your thinking cap on again. I know we've turned down overtures from the Australian banks in the past, but maybe we should be reconsidering." Devlin pulled a face, but nodded none the less. "I'd like to see both reports by next Wednesday, and I'll call a full board meeting on the following Friday. I'll speak to our brokers beforehand and see if they can come up with some ideas. We pay them enough, for God's sake."

Fielding stood up and walked round his desk, his hands in his pockets. Devlin had never seen him looking so dejected, and wondered if perhaps the chairman was having trouble at home. He opened the office door and held it wide for them as they left.

Fielding's secretary, Faith, slipped inside as Devlin and Perman left. "Don Bedford's been outside for fifteen minutes," she said.

"I know, I know," said Fielding, going back behind his desk. Faith picked up the empty glasses from the black wooden coffee table and took them over to the drinks cabinet where she put them on a lacquered circular tray. "The meeting with Charlie and Alex ran on, I'm afraid," said Fielding. He wasn't looking forward to seeing Bedford. He was head of Personnel and for the past three years he'd had to cope with a flood of resignations, half from Hong Kong Chinese emigrating, the rest from workers being poached by other banks. They'd tried increasing salaries, by twenty-five per cent last year, but, as all the other banks did the same, the defections had continued. Almost all the bank's computer operators had resigned over the last twelve months, and most of them had gone to Australia. As quickly as the bank trained them they were off. It was a never-ending cycle, and the closer they got to 1997, the faster the pace. Bedford never had any good news for Fielding. They'd already lowered the entrance qualifications to the point where the youngsters taking deposits from customers could barely speak English. Standards were falling all round, as they were in almost all the colony's service industries. Most of the hotels were running at staffing levels almost twenty per cent below the early nineties and everyone knew that the police were massively understaffed.

"I'll tell him to come in," said Faith, carrying the tray to the door. "Oh, one more thing, you heard about the fire at Shatin?"

"The racetrack? Yes, it was all over the papers. It was lucky no one was hurt. My trainer was on the phone at six to let me know that my horses were okay. There was some panic in the stables, a few horses hurt themselves kicking against their stalls, but none was badly injured. Hellish lucky. Has anyone claimed responsibility?"

"No," said Faith. "There was talk on the radio that it was just the latest in a long run of anti-British protests and there could be more. They've just announced that

Sunday's meeting is being switched to Happy Valley. Do you want me to tell all your guests? And shall I have the catering arrangements changed?"

"Of course," said Fielding. "You're quite right. I tell you what, if the race is going to be on the island, I might as well have some of them around for drinks first. Invite Charlie and Diane, and Phyllis and Jonathan Kelley. Maybe another two couples who live on the Peak, you know who's best. Say drinks about two hours before the first race. And can you arrange for a car and driver to take Anne and me to the track? Unless Hong Kong's finest have finally managed to find my car."

"No news yet, I'm sorry, William."

"The best police force money can buy," said Fielding. "Where are they when you need them?"

"Oh, William," said Faith briskly, heading for the door. "It'll turn up eventually." She held the tray with one hand and opened the door with the other. Don Bedford was sitting in her outer office, a thick file on his knees and a look of despair on his face.

Chung drove his Porsche to Kwai Chung, the huge container terminals that handled the bulk of Hong Kong's imports and exports on his left. Huge mobile cranes straddled the containers and moved them around like robots playing some surreal game of checkers. He had arranged to meet Michael Wong in an underground parking garage which his triad controlled. Like most of Hong Kong's criminal organisations, Wong's triad had moved into many legitimate business operations including parking, delivery services, video rentals and property, though the bulk of its income still came from drugs, prostitution and extortion. Wong had shut down the parking garage and was using it to modify and store the stolen cars.

The sign above the garage said "Closed Until Further Notice" in Chinese and English and there was a surly young man sitting in the attendant's booth cleaning his nails with a penknife. The man glared at Chung when he pulled up and pointed to the sign with his knife. Chung wound the window down and in Cantonese told him he was there to see Wong, the Dragon Head. The man nodded and pressed a button on the console in his booth. The metal grille at the entrance rattled up and Chung drove down a sloping ramp into the car park. Two big Chinese heavies with leather jackets were lounging next to a concrete pillar and they straightened up when they saw Chung in the Porsche. One of them put his hand inside his jacket and held it there, and both looked at Chung with hard eyes. The grille slowly closed behind him.

The ramp turned to the right and Chung braked because he couldn't see what was ahead of him. As the ramp straightened up it opened out into a parking area about the size of a football field, with square concrete pillars every few yards and the parking spaces marked by white lines. There were ten large Mercedes cars at the far end of the parking area, gleaming under the overhead fluorescent lights. Eight were lined up against a wall, one was on a ramp, its wheels off while men in overalls worked on it underneath. Another was on the ground and all of its windows were out. Two men were fitting a black windshield into the gaping hole at the front. To the left were two security vans bearing the logos of the Kowloon and Canton Bank.

Chung parked the Porsche twenty feet from where the mechanics were working under the ramp. As he climbed out he saw that one corner of the parking area, well away from where the cars were being worked on, had been converted into a makeshift lecture theatre, with a dozen folding chairs facing a big bulletin board. A large-scale map of Kowloon and the New Territories had been pinned to the board. Almost all the chairs were occupied, but Chung couldn't see any faces because all the men had their backs to him. He closed the car door and a few heads turned to get a look at him.

Chung was wearing a black polo shirt and jeans, and a gold Rolex glittered on his left wrist. He saw Michael Wong standing at one end of the line of Mercs and walked over to him.

"Anthony!" called Wong. He went over to Chung and shook hands with him. "Good to see you."

"Everything on schedule?" asked Chung.

Wong waved his arm towards the eight shining cars. "These eight are already done," he said. "The remaining two will be finished tonight."

"Good," said Chung, nodding. Wong took him over to the line of cars. There was something decidedly sinister about the top-of-the-range Mercs with black glass, Chung thought. It was because you had no idea who or what was within, he decided. But you knew that anyone inside could see you perfectly.

Wong opened the passenger door of one of the cars and told Chung to take a look inside. Chung put his hand on the roof for support and stuck his head inside. The plush interior had been completely stripped out, including all the seats. A simple bucket seat and seat belt had been installed for the driver, but other than that the car was empty. The carpets had been stripped out and Chung could see metal reinforcing struts had been welded to the floor and thick wire mesh overlaid on top.

He stood upright. "Excellent job," he said.

"The suspension has been strengthened, and special heavy-duty shock absorbers fitted," said Wong. "You can see how high the cars are riding now, they'll settle down once they're loaded up."

"And each car will carry how much?" asked Chung.

"Up to 1,100 pounds," said Wong. "At today's price, that would be equivalent to about seven million US dollars."

"Ten cars, seventy million dollars. That's a lot of gold, Michael. An awful lot of gold. And the vans?"

Wong pulled a face. "It depends what we find in the boxes. Could be cash, jade, lots of currency I would think. We'll take as much as we can."

"The cars go first, of course."

"Of course," said Wong. "They've much further to go."

"Where are you going to hide the vans?"

586

"We'll drive one out to Yuen Long, to a safe house we have there, the other we'll bring back here. We'll split it into several loads and distribute it to other safe houses within the day. We should have the cash out of Hong Kong within six hours, the diamonds we'll keep here. I can't believe it's going so well, Anthony. The gods are truly smiling on us."

Chung grinned. "It's not good joss, and you know it. It's planning, and investing in the right people. Speaking of which, how are the gweilos and the helicopter?"

"I was there yesterday for their briefing. The chopper is ready to go, and so are the men. That man Tyler is a wizard. To find a group of men willing to rob the racetrack was achievement enough, but he's actually got them to the stage where I believe they could really pull it off. I tell you, Anthony, if you change your mind and decide you want to . . ."

Chung held up his hand. "Don't even joke about that, Michael. If we succeed we get everything we've ever wanted, but if we fail . . ."

"I know, I know."

"And for us to succeed, it is imperative that the Americans do not. All attention must be focused on them, the way a conjurer diverts the attention of the audience. Only then can we pull the rabbit out of the hat."

"Don't worry, Anthony. Your plan is perfection itself, and we are following it every step of the way."

"The guard in the depository?"

"Mr Woo. He has been spoken to, and he understands our position, and his own. He has three sons, he will do as we say. And you, have you been invited to the races?"

"Better than that. The Fieldings are having pre-race cocktails at their home. I have been asked to go by their daughter. I suggest we meet at my apartment at eleven o'clock tomorrow morning for a final briefing. Do you think seven men will be enough?"

"Seven and myself. Eight in all. I think that will suffice. The men I have in mind are quite intimidating. They scare the shit out of me, so I think they'll have no trouble persuading the Fieldings and their guests to do as they're told."

The two men laughed as Wong slammed the door of the Mercedes. "The drivers, are they all here?"

Wong nodded and put his arm around Chung's shoulder. "All ten. You did a good job recruiting them." The two men walked over to the group of men sitting on the chairs. Most had turned around to get a better look at Chung and Wong. As Chung got closer he began to recognise faces, and he winked at Simon Li. He was the driver who'd won the first race Chung had entered, and Chung had beaten him once since. Li was the first driver Chung had approached, and he'd readily agreed. Chung had guaranteed him the equivalent of two winner's purses for less than an hour's driving, an offer he had subsequently made to another nine drivers. All had accepted.

Several of the drivers shouted greetings to Chung. Most believed that the operation was being run by

Michael Wong and assumed that Chung was just another hired hand. Chung preferred to keep it that way and he took his seat among the drivers. He looked at the map as Wong walked to the wall and turned to address the group. There were ten routes drawn on the map, all originating from one spot in Kowloon, and all terminating at one of five points on the coast. Wong's briefing was short and economical. He explained that the men were to report to the garage at midday and that they would be leaving at ten-minute intervals to drive to the depository. After being loaded with gold, they would follow one of the assigned routes.

"Drive as quickly as possible, but do not speed or go through red lights," warned Wong. "We expect the police presence in Kowloon to be at a minimum, but there is no point in taking risks. The drivers assigned to the longest route will be leaving first, so we expect all the cars to be at their destination point within two hours from the moment the first car arrives at the depository."

"How do we know which route?" asked one of the drivers.

"They will be assigned on Sunday," said Wong. "You won't be told until you arrive at the depository which your route will be, so memorise all of them. And please don't have any ideas about getting lost on the way."

The drivers laughed. They all knew Wong, or knew of him and his triad, and they knew how foolish it would be even to think about double-crossing him. He had smiled and joked during the briefing, but they knew that under the banter the well-dressed Dragon Head was a cold-hearted killer who would not tolerate insubordination, never mind betrayal.

Chung arrived back at his apartment just after one o'clock. He parked the Porsche next to his Ferrari, and nodded to the doorman on his way to the elevator. The doorman was well used to seeing Chung in his scruffy attire, though he was clearly somewhat confused by it. Chung unlocked his door and went into his apartment. He stripped off his black shirt and went into the kitchen to brew himself a pot of coffee. He looked at the ostentatious Rolex on his wrist. It wasn't the sort of watch he would normally wear, but he'd wanted to show the drivers that he knew how to spend money as well as win it. He took the watch off and placed it on the kitchen top next to his microwave oven.

As he waited for his coffee-maker to run through its cycle he paced slowly around the kitchen, going over the plan in his head, checking for anything he might have missed. It was only last-minute nerves, he knew, because he'd planned it to perfection long before he'd approached Tyler and Wong.

The coffee burbled and he poured himself a mug, spooning in sugar and adding a splash of milk. As he sipped it the doorbell rang. He frowned because he wasn't expecting anyone. He went over to the front door and opened it, the mug of coffee in his hand.

Anne Fielding was just about the last person he expected to find on his doorstep. She was wearing a blue Chanel suit with gold buttons, blue high heels and a delicate gold necklace. Her hair was held back in a ponytail with a dark blue clasp which made her look ten years younger than she really was and which was a contrast to the relatively businesslike cut of the suit. To Chung it seemed that she wasn't sure how to dress for him — as the sophisticated woman she was or the girl he made her feel like.

"Anne?" he said.

"Aren't you going to ask me in?" she said.

"Of course," he said, stepping aside.

She looked him up and down, an amused smile on her face. "I don't think I've seen you so casually dressed before," she said. Chung was wearing his hair in his driver's style, and still had on his jeans and tatty Reeboks.

He grinned and ran a hand through his hair, slicking it back. "Just slumming today," he said.

"You look completely different," she said.

"And you, as always, look gorgeous."

Anne raised her eyes to the ceiling and sighed. "You don't have to say that," she said.

Chung sipped his coffee, an amused smile on his face. Anne walked over to one of the sofas and put down her handbag and turned to face him. "I had to come," she said.

"I'm glad you did," he replied. "Can I get you anything?"

"Like a drink, you mean?" she said. She shook her head. "No, no drinks this time."

"Coffee then?"

"No. No coffee either. I can't get over how different you look."

"Jeans and training shoes, that's all. I suppose I've always been wearing a suit when you've seen me before."

"Or nothing at all," she said, with a smile.

"That's true," he said. He wasn't sure why she was in his apartment, or what she wanted from him.

"Anthony, why didn't you call me?"

"I wasn't sure if you'd want me to," he said slowly.

"Because of what happened? Because I went to bed with you?"

He shrugged, not knowing what to say.

"Was it that bad?" she asked.

He shook his head quickly. "No, it wasn't that," he said. He smiled. "You know it wasn't that." He paused and studied her. "Did you want me to call you, Anne? Is that it?"

Anne went over to the window and looked out, her back to Chung. "When I left here I was so . . . so . . . I don't know how to describe it . . . so . . ." She turned to look at him. "Fulfilled. That's how I felt. Oh, take that amused look off your face. You know what you did to me, how you made me feel."

Chung put his coffee mug down on a side table and stood by his stereo system. "I didn't mean to smile, Anne."

"I left here on a cloud, I hardly remember getting home. I went home and sat down with a gin and tonic and I could still feel you inside me. I didn't shower, because I wanted to keep the smell of you on me. William came home and thought I was ill. I told him I had a headache, but I could tell that he thought I'd been drinking too much. He went to bed early and I sat up most of the night, thinking about what we'd done. The fulfilment gradually evaporated and then I started to feel guilty."

"Because you'd betrayed your husband?"

Her blue eyes flashed. "Because I'd betrayed him, and because I'd enjoyed it." She frowned. "In a way, it would have been better if it had been a disaster, if I'd hated what we did. That would have been easier to deal with. I would have felt guilty and bad about myself, and I could have written it off as a not-too-pleasant experience. At first I didn't want to see you again, but after a few days I started to get angry at you because you didn't call."

"How could I have called you, Anne? Suppose someone else had answered the phone?"

"You could have found a way," she said. "You had no problem finding me in the Landmark. You could have gone there any afternoon and found me. I used to go and look for you, do you know that? I was like a schoolgirl, walking round and round and hoping that you'd come up behind me and surprise me. I went from fulfilment to guilt, to anger, in just a few days. I tell you, Anthony, you put me through more emotions in one week than my husband has inspired in ten years."

"I don't know if I should take that as a compliment," he said.

"You should," she said.

"I still don't understand what it is you want from me," said Chung.

"I'm not sure if I know myself," she said. "I just know that you showed me something I never thought I'd experience."

He raised an eyebrow, but said nothing.

"Passion," she said in answer to his unspoken question. "I felt passion for the first time. Real passion."

"Come on, you make it sound as if you'd never made love before."

"Not like that," she said, shaking her head. "Never like that."

"But you have a child!"

She laughed harshly, her voice as brittle as spun glass. "Anthony, don't ever confuse having children with making love."

"You still haven't told me what you want, Anne."

Anne sighed and folded her arms across her chest. She put her head on one side and gazed at Chung. She looked as if she were going to say something and then shook her head.

"You have a husband, Anne. You're married. And you have a child."

"There you go again, Anthony. I'm a wife, and I'm a mother. And if I'm not careful that's all I'll be for the rest of my life. I want more than that. I want to feel alive. I want to feel . . . passion."

"You want to leave your husband?"

Anne tossed her head and laughed. "Leave William? Good God, no. Of course not. Don't worry, Anthony, I'm not suggesting that I run away with you. I just want to feel the way you made me feel again. I want to be touched, held, made love to."

She took a step towards him. Then another. She kept moving until she was standing in front of him, her arms at her side, her face turned up to his. "I don't want any sort of commitment from you," she whispered. "I don't even want your love. I just want to be touched."

He put his hands on her shoulders and kissed her softly on the lips. "You're the wife of an important man, you shouldn't put yourself in this position," he said.

She reached up with her right hand and put it behind his neck. "Will you promise me you'll never tell anyone?" she whispered.

"Of course," he said.

She pressed herself against him. "Then there's nothing wrong," she said. She stood up on tiptoe and kissed him, forcing her soft tongue between his lips. He returned the kiss but then pressed down on her shoulders, pushing her away from him.

"One thing," he said, his voice thick with emotion.

"What?" she said.

"Your rings," he said. "Your wedding ring and your engagement ring. Take them off."

She looked up at him, frowning. "Why?" she asked.

"Because I want to make love to Anne, not to the wife of William Fielding."

She kept her eyes on his, and nodded. She slowly slipped the two rings off her wedding finger and held them in the palm of her hand.

"Drop them," he said quietly. "Drop them on the floor."

She did as he asked, still watching his face. The rings rattled on the wooden floor, but she didn't look to see where they fell. Instead she pressed a forefinger against his lips. He opened them and gently bit her finger, then licked it sensuously. He reached for her hips and pulled her towards him. She removed her finger and kissed him, her eyes open so she could watch him as she pressed her lips against his. She moaned like an animal in pain and slid her hand down the front of his trousers.

Neil Coleman put his head in his hands and rested his elbows on the table. In front of him were the half-eaten remains of a hamburger and French fries, the plate smeared with ketchup.

"You want another beer, mate?" asked Phil Donaldson.

"Yeah, go on," said Coleman. He ran his hands through his sandy hair while Donaldson waved over a waitress and ordered two more San Miguels.

"You look as miserable as sin, Neil," said Donaldson. "What's wrong?"

"It's that fucking Chink," said Coleman.

"Chung?"

"Yeah. He's still after Debbie. I just can't get to her any more. She's always seeing him."

"Wasn't Terry McNeil any help?"

"No, and it was a fucking terrible idea going to him in the first place. Seems that Chung is related to some Chinese politician. I think McNeil was getting a hard-on, you know? He was starting to wonder if maybe Special Branch should be taking an interest. I had to back-pedal like fuck." He reached into the pocket of his grey suit and took out a packet of Kent cigarettes and lit one with a neon green disposable lighter.

"I thought you'd given up smoking," said Donaldson. The waitress returned with their two beers and Donaldson tried to look down the front of her dress as she poured them. Both men watched her walk away. "Big tits for a Chinese, that one," said Donaldson.

"Good arse, too," said Coleman.

"So what's with the smoking?"

Coleman looked at the cigarette in his hand. "I only gave up to encourage Debbie," he said. "There doesn't seem any point now."

"I can't believe you're going to let that heiress get away from you. All that money. The car."

The mention of the car brought back memories of their lovemaking in the passenger seat of the XJS, the top of her dress around her waist, his hands on her breasts, her eyes closed as she pounded away on top of him. He shook his head. "It's that bastard Chung," he said. "If he wasn't around, I'm sure I could get to her. She loves me, I know she does, it's just that he's getting in the way, you know?"

"We could always plant drugs in his car," said Donaldson.

Coleman looked at him with narrowed eyes. "You serious?"

Donaldson wiggled his eyebrows. "I could get it done," he said.

"I bet you could," said Coleman. "No, it wouldn't work. McNeil would hear about it and he'd remember that I was asking questions about Chung."

Donaldson leaned over the table. "I was joking, you soft bastard," he said.

Coleman took a mouthful of beer and wiped his mouth with the back of his hand. "I knew that," he said. "Thing is, I can't get close to her any more, you know? Last month she said I could go to the races with her, to the last race of the season. The bank's got its own private box and she said I could go. Now she says she's changed her mind. Chung's going with her, I know he is. Bastard. I hate the fucking Chinese bastard."

"Maybe he'll get shot in the robbery," said Donaldson, grinning.

"What are you talking about?" said Coleman, intrigued.

Donaldson bent over the table again, his sleeve scraping against the curry sauce on his plate. "It's all hush-hush," he whispered.

Coleman also leaned over the table so that his head was close to Donaldson's. "Phil, you can trust me. I'm a policeman."

Donaldson guffawed and punched Coleman on the shoulder. "Yeah, right," he said. He kept his head over the table. "We've had a tip from one of our triad contacts that the racetrack is going to be hit tomorrow. An armed gang is going to bust into the betting halls."

"Is that connected with the fire?" Coleman asked.

"Could be," said Donaldson. "We don't have any details. Just the tip that there's going to be a heist. This sort of vague tip is par for the course. It's probably from another triad that's got wind of what's going on and wants to spoil it. It happens."

Coleman frowned and took a long drag on his cigarette. He tried to blow a smoke ring up to the ceiling but it came out of his thick lips as a cloud. He coughed and looked at Donaldson. "They're going to hit the track while the race is on?" he asked.

"That's the tip. We'll be swamping the racecourse with plain-clothes cops and we'll have marksmen in several of the boxes. We've also arranged to have our own people in the betting halls, working as tellers."

"It doesn't make sense," said Coleman. "The way I remember, all the money goes straight from the tellers to an underground vault below the grandstand, right?" Donaldson nodded. "It stays there overnight and then it's taken by armoured car to their underground vault in Kowloon Bay. Why would they hit the track? The money is all over the place during the meeting; it would make much more sense to attack the armoured car. Best place would be while it's in the cross-harbour tunnel."

Donaldson smiled. "You've got a criminal mind, Neil my boy," he said. "But we've got to follow the tip we've been given. And our source tells us that it's the track they're going to hit."

"And where are they going to go with the money? The roads'll be jammed solid for miles around."

"Hell, I don't know. Maybe they'll catch a tram to Shau Kei Wan. Don't tell anyone, all right, or my balls'll be in a vice."

"Of course I won't," said Coleman. "As you said, maybe Chung'll get caught in the crossfire."

"I'll drink to that," said Donaldson. "You want another?"

"Yeah," said Coleman. "And some. By the way, can I borrow your car again tomorrow?"

"Oh shit, Neil, why don't you get your own?"

"Can't afford it, you know that. So is that a yes?"

"It's a yes, but only if you fill the tank this time."

"You drive a hard bargain, Phil." He stabbed his cigarette out in an ashtray, twisting it savagely as if grinding it into the eye of Anthony Chung.

Archie Kwan arrived at the Shatin stables shortly before six o'clock. His *ma-foos* were already there, feeding and watering their charges. He had eighteen horses racing at the afternoon meeting and he had high hopes for ten of them. All the horses had been under constant scrutiny for the past forty-eight hours to check that they weren't slipped any drugs and all the feed and water was checked by Jockey Club officials. He went over to the stall where Galloping Dragon was being prepared. The horse was not one which Kwan thought would win, but William Fielding had been adamant that he race. Face, thought Kwan. Sometimes it seemed that it was the gweilos who were more concerned about face than the Chinese.

The *ma-foo* was checking Galloping Dragon's legs, running his hands expertly over the muscles and tendons. "Too soon to race again," he muttered.

"He'll do okay," said Kwan.

The old *ma-foo* shrugged, a gesture that said everything. He knew as well as Kwan that the horse was being raced for the wrong reasons. Kwan had already decided that next season he would tell William Fielding that he wouldn't be able to train his horses at his stable. He'd come up with some excuse but the bottom line was that Kwan no longer wanted to train horses for British owners. He'd noticed that when British owners entered the winner's enclosures with their horses more often than not they'd attract booing and catcalls from the crowd. There'd be cheers and applause, too, but there was bad feeling, a sense that if the British were pulling out they should leave now, the sooner the better. The fire at the grandstand had been the last straw so far as Kwan was concerned. The Chinese press was saying that the arson attack was a reflection of anti-British sentiment and that more such attacks were expected. Kwan had no wish for his own stables to become a target, so he would train only for Chinese owners in future. Besides, the Chinese generally owned better quality horses.

He went outside to check that the horseboxes were ready. All the horses would be exercised and then driven across the harbour to the Happy Valley stables where they would be prepared for the races. Kwan would also meet his jockeys there. He was concerned about one of them, an Englishman called Reg Dykes who'd been in the colony for just two years and who was having problems maintaining his racing weight. He'd developed a taste for Asian women and Scotch whisky, and the combination had proved disastrous. Kwan hadn't told him yet, but this would be Dykes's last race. He didn't want British owners and he didn't want British jockeys. He wanted to have as little to do with the British as possible. He looked at his Cartier wristwatch. It would soon be time to go.

Woo Bik-kuen lay on his back, his face covered in sweat. He'd barely slept all night. His wife slept curled up in a tight ball next to him, her knees up against her chest, snoring loudly. It wasn't the sound of her snoring which kept Woo awake, nor the stifling heat of their cramped bedroom. Woo was worried, more worried than he'd ever been in his life. He'd obeyed the instructions of the softly spoken Grass Sandal, setting the time locks so that they'd open in two short hours instead of at eight thirty Monday morning. Woo had wanted to call in sick so that he didn't have to be at his post, but he knew that to do so would be sure to attract attention to himself. His only hope of getting through this was to act as if it was just another Sunday. He rubbed his nose and turned on to his side, but there was no relief from the nagging doubts that plagued his mind. In the next room he heard one of his sons cough. If it wasn't for his sons, and his wife, then maybe Woo would have risked going to the police, but he knew that the triads would have no compunction about killing them all, slowly and painfully, just to teach him a lesson. He looked over at the cheap plastic alarm clock on the side table. Only thirty minutes and he would have to get up. He rolled on to his back and rubbed his hands over his face. Maybe they wouldn't come. Maybe they'd decide not to go through with the robbery. Maybe it had all been a bad dream. His wife grunted in her sleep and a thin dribble of saliva ran down her chin. No, it was no dream. Tears of frustration welled up in his eyes and he clenched his fists.

Neil Coleman drove Donaldson's car up the Peak, his right foot to the floor and its engine screaming in protest. He had the mother and father of all hangovers, having stayed drinking with Donaldson until four o'clock in the morning. He hadn't managed to crawl out of bed until just before eleven o'clock and he hadn't bothered shaving or showering, he'd just thrown on a T-shirt and blue jeans and dashed to the car. He was determined to sit outside the Fieldings' house until he saw whether or not Anthony Chung had indeed been invited to the races in his place. He parked close enough to the main gate so that he could see anyone driving in or out, and then settled back to wait. He switched on the police radio and tuned it to 449.625 MHz, the frequency used by the Happy Valley police station, so that he could keep track of what was happening over at the racecourse.

Lehman padded out of the bathroom, a towel wrapped around his waist. He knocked on the door to Lewis's bedroom to tell him that he'd finished with the shower.

603

Hearing no answer, he opened the door and went in. Lewis was kneeling naked on the floor, his back to the door, his head hunched forward. Lehman stepped to the side to see what Lewis was so engrossed in. He seemed to be holding a strip of silver foil under his chin, and heating some white powder in it with a cigarette lighter. He had his eyes fixed on the line of white powder in the foil and as the heat from the flame vaporised it he moved his nose along, inhaling deeply. Lewis suddenly became aware that Lehman was standing in the room and his eyes widened, but he continued to breathe in the white smoke.

"Bart, what the hell's going on?" asked Lehman.

Lewis finished and squatted back on his heels, holding his breath for a full ten seconds before exhaling deeply. He stood up and put the lighter and used foil on his camp bed.

"Bart? What's all this about?" pressed Lehman. He closed the door.

Lewis muttered something incoherent, and rubbed the back of his hand across his forehead.

"What?"

"Chasing the dragon," repeated Lewis.

"What the hell is chasing the dragon?" asked Lehman.

"It eases the pain," said Lewis.

Lehman went over to the bed and picked up the blackened foil. He held it to his nose and sniffed it. "Heroin?" he said.

"Opium," said Lewis.

"What's the difference?" Lehman asked, and Lewis shrugged. He began to pull on his overalls. "Where did you get this crap from?"

"Mr Tsao gave it to me," said Lewis, "and it's not crap, Dan. It's a terrific painkiller. It's the only thing that kills the pain, Dan, the only thing."

"It's bad, huh?"

Lewis held his arms out to the side. "Look at me, Dan. I've lost about twenty pounds over the past two weeks. I can't keep any food down, but that doesn't matter because I've no appetite anyway." He put a hand over his stomach. "I can feel the cancer now. There's a lump about the size of an orange in here, hard and smooth. It wasn't there when I was in Vietnam, I'm certain."

"Shit, Bart, I'm sorry," said Lehman, his voice unsteady.

"So you can see that the dope isn't going to do me any harm," said Lewis, his eyes intense. "Don't tell anyone, Dan."

"If Tyler finds out, he'll hit the roof," said Lehman.

"If he finds out, he won't let me go," said Lewis. "And if he doesn't let me go, I could lose the money."

"Don't be ridiculous, Bart. You've done everything he asked of you. You'll get your money."

Lewis screwed up his face as if he had a bad taste in his mouth. "Maybe, but I'm not so sure I trust him, not after what Chuck told us. I want to be in at the kill, and I want to follow it through. Dan, in ten hours all this will be over. I can last ten hours. I've been controlling the dose like Mr Tsao told me, just so it's on the threshold of hurting. I'm not drowsy or anything."

"I know," said Lehman. He would have noticed over the past few days if Lewis had appeared drugged, and while he had spotted the weight loss he hadn't seen any signs that Lewis wasn't fully competent.

Lewis sat down on his bed and took a pen and small notebook from underneath it. He scribbled, the pen dwarfed by his big, square hands. "I'm giving you the name and phone number of my ex-wife; if anything goes wrong and I don't make it, I want you to make sure my son gets my share." He pulled the sheet out of the notebook and held it out to Lehman.

"Come on, Bart, you'll make it," said Lehman. He reluctantly took the sheet of paper, careful not to get it wet. He was still dripping from the shower.

"Yeah, but if I don't I want you to get the money to my son and let him know it's from his father. And the orphanage in Saigon, remember?"

"I remember."

"Give them some too. You decide how much, half maybe, see what they need. I just want to know that I didn't die without doing something to make amends. Okay?"

"I understand, Bart," said Lehman, feeling uncomfortable about discussing his friend's death.

Lewis smiled. "Okay, thanks. Now get the hell out of my bedroom."

Lehman headed to the door.

"Say, what did you want?" said Lewis. "Why did you come into my room in the first place?"

"The shower," said Lehman. "I was just telling you that I'd finished in the shower."

"Thanks," grinned Lewis. "I did all that a couple of hours ago. I couldn't sleep. The excitement, I guess. It's been a long time since I've been this fired up."

"Yeah, I know what you mean."

"It's ironic, isn't it? I've never been so close to death, and yet I've never felt so alive. I guess that's one reason I want so badly to be in the Huey this afternoon. I miss the excitement, Dan. I really miss it. I didn't know until I met Tyler how much I missed it."

Lehman nodded and fingered the piece of paper Lewis had given him. Lewis's words echoed something he'd been feeling for some time. Tyler had welded the group of disparate personalities into a team which now functioned as a well-coordinated unit. But there was more, Lehman knew. They cared about each other, in the same way that bonds had been forged in the heat of war, bonds that at the time Lehman had thought would never be broken. Lehman wondered what it would be like when the job was over, when the vets had the money and all had to go their separate ways.

"What's wrong?" asked Lewis.

Lehman shook his head. "Just thinking," he said.

"You looked furious."

Lehman grinned. "Yeah, everyone says that," he said. "It's my eyebrows. I was just thinking about what we'll do when all this is over."

"You'll go back to the States?"

Lehman nodded. "Hopefully, if I can persuade some not very nice guys not to blow my head off. Anyway, I'm going to get dressed. I'll see you out at the Huey."

"It's going to work, Dan," said Lewis. "It's really going to work." His eyes blazed with enthusiasm.

Anne Fielding studied her reflection in the full-length mirror. The blue Ralph Lauren was perfect, but she couldn't decide whether to wear simple pearls or the sapphire necklace that William had given her for Christmas five years earlier. She held up the pearls, then the necklace, then the pearls again. She settled for the pearls and put them on.

They nestled comfortably around her neck and she stroked them as she looked at the dress in the mirror. The dress had a simple collar and was cut respectably low at the front, high enough as befitted the wife of a bank chairman, low enough to attract admiring glances. It was a delicate balance, but one she enjoyed experimenting with. She slipped her high heels on and checked her legs in the mirror. The dress ended slightly below her knees, and it swung as she moved. She ran her hands down her slim hips and smiled at herself in the mirror as she remembered her last meeting with Anthony Chung. He'd done things to her she'd only dreamed about before, taken her to a level of passion she hadn't believed possible. And what struck her most was that the second time she'd gone to bed with him there had been no guilt afterwards, none at all. When he'd asked her to take off her wedding ring she'd resisted at first, but he'd been right. With the rings off her finger she had been truly naked with him, and she'd no longer been a wife or a mother, she'd been a lover, his lover, and there wasn't anything she wouldn't do for him. She had become more confident with him on the second occasion, and more willing to experiment. She didn't know why Chung had such an effect on her, but she felt a desire to do things with him that she'd never dream of doing with William. It was partly because she felt safe with him, and partly because there was no feeling of embarrassment. With William she always had the feeling that he wasn't quite sure what to do with her body, that he didn't know how to give her pleasure and was too embarrassed to ask. Anthony inspired her. That was the word, inspired. With him there was nothing she wouldn't try. He'd seemed more relaxed the second time, less rigid in the way he made love to her. He'd taken his time, too, stripping her slowly and kissing her all over until she'd been screaming for him to go inside her.

She didn't want to hurt William, but neither did she want to deprive herself of the pleasure Anthony offered. She'd earned it, she'd raised a child, she'd been a dutiful wife and mother, she'd given William the best years of her life, and she deserved this one transgression. Anthony had sworn that he'd never tell anyone, and she believed him. She wasn't like Phyllis Kelley, she wasn't about to embark on a string of affairs, she just wanted to experiment with the sexuality Anthony had shown her, to find out exactly what she was capable of as a woman. It wouldn't last, she knew that, eventually he would move on, but it would leave her with memories that she could look back on in years to come, when Debbie had left and William was old and she was sitting in a rocking chair. It would give her something to remember, and she would always be grateful to Anthony. Always.

"You look like the cat that got the cream," said a voice. She turned to see William coming out of the bathroom. Her cheeks reddened and suddenly she felt guilt wash over her.

"I'm looking forward to this afternoon," she said. "Do you like the dress?"

"It's fine," he said.

He was already combing his hair in the mirror and didn't even turn to look at her. The guilt evaporated and she felt angry at his indifference. That was one of the things she loved about Anthony. He always appreciated what she was wearing and commented on it. William didn't give a damn; his only comments came when the credit-card statements dropped through the letterbox.

"And the necklace, does that look okay?" she asked.

"It's beautiful," he said.

"Well I'm not wearing it, I'm wearing the pearls," she said frostily, and left the bedroom before he could turn round.

Debbie was down in the lounge, supervising the maids as they prepared the drinks table and the buffet, which was a combination of Thai appetisers and Western finger food. Debbie was wearing a Kenzo dress, buttoned all the way up the front and made from a print of the heads of wild cats: tigers, lions, and pumas. It was striking, but didn't do much for her daughter's figure.

"Love the dress," said Anne, kissing Debbie on the cheek. "Did Anthony say he'd come?" Anne already knew he'd accepted Debbie's invitation: they'd discussed it afterwards as they'd lain naked together on his bed.

"Yes, Mum. He's bringing the Ferrari. Is it okay if we drive it to the track?"

"Your father will be disappointed, I think he wanted you with us."

"Oh, Mum, please," said Debbie, both hands on her mother's arm. "Please."

"Okay, go on then," sighed Anne. "But don't tell your father I said it was okay."

Anne looked at her watch. "The first guests will be here soon," she said. "Tell Marie to start bringing the champagne in. I could do with a glass myself."

Coleman saw a dark green Daimler turn into the driveway of the Fielding house, and a few minutes later a Mercedes roadster arrived. Well-dressed middle-aged couples got out and were admitted to the house. Coleman tapped the steering wheel and craned his neck around to look out of the rear window of the Jeep. There was still no sign of Chung, but Coleman had a gut instinct that he was coming. He could feel it with the same sort of certainty he had when interrogating a suspect he knew to be guilty. It was his policeman's sixth sense, and he trusted it completely. Chung was out to steal his girlfriend and he was going to the races with her. Chung was taking his place, and he was damn sure he was going to stop him. He rubbed his hand along his chin, feeling the stubble growing there. He lifted his arm and smelt his armpit, wincing at the pungent aroma of stale sweat. He figured that it would be smarter not to confront Debbie until he'd showered and changed.

He heard a deep, growling sound and knew without turning that it was the Ferrari. He settled back in the driver's seat and waited. The Ferrari drove through the gate and stopped in front of the house. The door opened and Chung climbed out. He was wearing a dark blue suit and he stretched as if he'd just woken up. He bent down and checked his hair in the car mirror.

"I'm going to have you, Chung," hissed Coleman. "I'm going to fucking have you."

Chung pressed the doorbell and after a second or two he was admitted. Coleman sat bolt upright, his spine rigid with tension. His hands gripped the steering wheel and a small vein was pulsing in his forehead. He wanted to rip Chung's head from his body, he wanted to beat him to a bloody pulp, he wanted to drive his precious Ferrari backwards and forwards over him until every bone in his body was broken.

His vindictive thoughts were interrupted by the arrival of two Toyota Corollas, one white, one red. There were four men in each of the cars, all Chinese and not one dressed as if he were going to the races as a guest of the Kowloon and Canton Bank. They looked to Coleman like triad Red Poles, burly men with bad haircuts and hard eyes, the sort of men who carried hatchets and sharp knives inside their jackets. They both cruised up the driveway and stopped either side of Chung's Ferrari. Coleman frowned. They didn't look like tradesmen, or guests, and he couldn't work out what they were doing there. The car doors opened as one, and the men got out, looking around like tourists. The occupants of the second car walked down the side of the house as if they were going to the garden, while the four men in the first car, the white one, went up to the front door. One of them pressed the doorbell. The door opened and Coleman caught a glimpse of a Filipina maid in a white uniform before the men went inside, out of sight. Coleman's frown deepened and he scratched his chin.

Phil Donaldson stuck his hands deep into his pockets and surveyed the towering grandstand in front of him. He was standing by the barriers at the edge of the grass track with a uniformed superintendent, Paul Penycate, who was talking into a radio mike mounted on his shoulder. The temperature was in the upper eighties and there were damp patches under Donaldson's armpits. A sudden gust of wind made the hair covering his bald patch flap up like a banner and he pressed it down with his left hand.

Penycate was organising one hundred constables who were usually in uniform but who were now scattered around the grandstand in plain clothes. They had been split into groups of six, each group controlled by an officer with a concealed radio who would issue his men verbal instructions. The police had no idea where the robbers would come from, so they had to keep the security as low key as possible.

Twenty men and women from Donaldson's anti-triad squad had been given Jockey Club uniforms and a quick briefing on how to operate as tellers and were already in place in the betting halls with concealed radios. Another fifty members of the Tactical Support Group were sitting in a Jockey Club lecture room listening in to the radio traffic ready to rush to wherever they were needed. Penycate had plain-clothes policemen sitting in cars on all the main roads around the track and another twenty expat officers were scattered around the members' enclosure in their best suits and Jockey Club ties.

"Think we've covered everything, Phil?" asked Penycate. They'd known each other for a long time, and used first names when other ranks weren't close by.

"I can't see any gaps," said Donaldson.

"I still think they'd be mad to try and hit the track today," said Penycate. He nodded at the crowds pouring into the grandstand. "Look at all the witnesses. Thirty thousand of them. And where are they going to go? The roads are jammed solid. If you ask me someone's pulling our leg."

"Our source is normally reliable, Paul," said Donaldson. The radio on Penycate's shoulder crackled in Cantonese and he replied. Like Donaldson he was fluent in the language. A sergeant from the Tactical Support Group was asking about the timing of the first race and Penycate said it was thirty minutes away.

A figure at the far end of the track shouted Donaldson's name and waved. Donaldson shielded his eyes from the sun and squinted. It was Tommy Lai, one of his anti-triad detectives and the man who had picked up the tip about the robbery. Tommy was a thickset Chinese with a pudding-basin haircut and a broken nose, and looked more like a triad Red Pole than a detective. He also had a huge tattoo of a hooded snake on his back and was rumoured to be an honorary member of the 14K triad, though Donaldson knew he was one of the straightest men on the force. His brother, a uniformed policeman, had been killed in a shoot-out with triad thieves who were fleeing from a jewellery store in Tsim Sha Tsui.

"Yo, Tommy, what's up?" Donaldson called as soon as he was within range.

"You're not going to believe this, Phil," said Lai, who was also in plain clothes: a black leather bomber jacket, tight blue jeans, brown cowboy boots and a thick gold chain around his neck. "I've just had a call from my snitch, and he says they're going to use a helicopter."

"A what?" said Penycate.

"A helicopter," repeated Lai, his eyes darting from Donaldson to the uniformed officer. "He said they're going to fly in, just before the last race. And they're going to be armed. With automatic rifles."

"Fucking hell, Tommy, somebody's winding you up."

Lai shook his head fiercely. "This is kosher, boss. Straight up." Tommy Lai had learned most of his English from detective shows on late night television, mainly reruns of *Kojak, Magnum PI* and *The Sweeney*.

"Where are they going to get this helicopter from?" asked Penycate.

Lai gave a Kojak-type shrug and raised his eyebrows like Magnum. "Fucked if I know," he said. "Sir," he added. Penycate glared at him. "Sorry, sir," said Lai. The anti-triad squad was a lot less disciplined than the uniformed branch, and Lai had grown used to the informality.

"The airport?" said Donaldson.

"Could be," said Penycate. "I'll call the airport police and get them to check out any helicopters they have at Kai Tak."

"There's the helicopter service to Macau from the Sheung Wan ferry terminal, sir," said Lai, trying to win back Penycate's goodwill.

"And the army have some, don't they?" added Donaldson.

Penycate nodded. He waved a uniformed inspector over and quickly briefed him to contact all helicopter users, and to get an officer over to air traffic control at Kai Tak Airport so that they'd be guaranteed immediate warning of any unidentified helicopters.

When he'd finished, Penycate looked at Lai. "This had better be right," he warned. "If it turns out that someone's having you on . . ." He left the threat unfinished.

"Tommy's sources are impeccable," said Donaldson. "He's never let us down before."

"He'd better not start now," said Penycate. "I'm going to call in more men from Kowloon and the New Territories. It's going to leave us stretched really thin, but if they do have automatic rifles, we'll have to swamp the area with police."

"You don't think we should cancel the meeting?" asked Donaldson.

"You want to explain to thirty thousand Chinese that the last race of the season is off?" said Penycate. "You'd have the mother and father of all riots on your hands."

Donaldson nodded. He knew how volatile the Chinese could be. There had been street riots when the Star Ferry company had announced it was raising the cost of a trip across the harbour by just a few cents. And the Chinese felt a hell of a lot more strongly about racing than the ferry. "Okay, but you might want to think about getting some marksmen up there." Donaldson pointed up at the residential skyscrapers looking down at the racetrack.

Michael Wong nodded at the Filipina maid who opened the door, and stepped inside before she could react. She was flustered, not sure if he was a rude guest or a gatecrasher, but before she could ask him for his name two more Chinese men appeared behind him, then a third. Wong put his hand across her mouth, whirled her round and pushed her against the wall, hard enough to bang her forehead. He slipped his hand inside his jacket and pulled out a handgun which he jammed up under the side of her chin.

"Keep quiet!" he hissed. He felt her jaw shake under his hand and he tightened his grip around her mouth. The last man through the door closed it behind him. As he turned round he pulled a gun from under his jacket and a woollen ski-mask from the pocket of his trousers. The two others did the same and the three men moved together to the door that led to the lounge.

"If you move, you're dead!" Wong hissed at the frightened woman. "Do you understand?"

The maid nodded and Wong slowly took his hand away from her mouth. He kept the barrel of the gun against her neck while he fumbled for his own black ski-mask and put it on. He seized the back of her blouse and pulled her away from the wall and then pushed her ahead of him, after the three men.

Bart Lewis polished the nose of the Huey with his cloth — small, circular movements that a housewife might use to remove a stain from a coffee table. Carmody and Horvitz knelt by the tarpaulin as if at prayer, bending over the M16s and pushing shells into magazines. Lehman and Doherty walked around the Huey, carrying out the pre-flight check.

The door to the office area opened and Tyler walked out. Lehman looked over and did a quick double-take. Tyler had on his khaki police inspector's uniform, complete with peaked cap and gleaming leather belt. He was carrying a bundle of camouflage material in his arms.

"Nice outfit, Colonel," said Lewis.

"Thanks, Bart," said Tyler. "Gather round, gentlemen. I have something for you."

Horvitz and Carmody stood up, wiped their hands on their overalls and walked over to Tyler with Doherty and Lehman. Lewis flicked his cloth into the back of the Huey and ambled over, his hands in his pockets.

"Fatigues!" said Carmody. "Just like we used to wear in Nam."

Tyler handed them out, making sure that each man got the correct size. Lehman unfolded his and held the shirt against his chest. It seemed like a perfect fit. It appeared to be US Army issue, the brown and light green stripes reminiscent of the fatigues worn by the Rangers in Nam. All that was missing was his name tag.

"I thought you might enjoy wearing the uniform," said Tyler.

"Great idea, Colonel," said Carmody, as he stripped off his overalls and pulled on the fatigues. The rest of the vets followed his example, throwing their overalls on to a workbench and replacing them with the crisp new uniforms. When they'd finished they stood in a group, admiring each other. Lehman had to admit that even with the thickening waistlines and encroaching wrinkles, the fatigues made them appear like a team of professional soldiers.

"Does the Huey check out, Dan?" Tyler asked.

"Like a dream, Colonel," said Lehman. Dressed in the fatigues and facing Tyler in his starched inspector's uniform, it seemed only right to call him "Colonel".

"Any problems?" Tyler asked. All the vets shook their heads. Tyler looked at his watch. "Okay, gentlemen, I'll be leaving. The next time we meet will be on the roof of the Happy Valley grandstand with upwards of twenty million dollars." He threw them a smart salute, his back straight, his left arm stiff at his side. The vets straightened up, pulled their shoulders back, and saluted as one.

Anne Fielding was standing at the buffet table when Anthony Chung walked into the room. He was immaculately dressed as always, a dark blue suit which showed off his wide shoulders, a white shirt with thin blue vertical stripes that was clearly made to measure and a blue silk tie. He saw her and smiled, then Debbie was at his arm and kissing him on the cheek.

"Gorgeous, isn't he?" said Phyllis Kelley, who was standing next to Anne and dipping a large shrimp into a bowl of hot sauce.

"Phyllis, you're insatiable," scolded Anne.

Phyllis popped the shrimp into her mouth and chewed. A spot of red sauce dribbled down her chin and she dabbed at it with a napkin. "Do you think Debbie and he are . . ."

"Sleeping together?" said Anne frostily. "I don't know, and frankly, Phyllis, I don't care. And, incidentally, do you think you might have a word with your husband and ask him to stop feeling up my maids? It's hard enough getting them to work as it is." She walked away, her heels clicking on the wooden floor, leaving Phyllis standing with her mouth open.

"Anthony, so nice to see you," said Anne.

620

"Mrs Fielding," said Chung, extending his hand. "Thank you for inviting me."

Anne gave him her hand and he kissed it, giving her a barely perceptible squeeze as he did so.

"We should have a good day's racing, the weather is perfect," said Anne.

Chung kept hold of her hand until Anne withdrew it, their fingertips touching at the last moment as if reluctant to part. "I understand your husband has a horse running," Chung said, smiling easily. "Do you think it's worth a bet?"

The mention of her husband on her lover's lips made her stomach lurch, but she continued to smile at him. She felt light-headed being so close to him and she had a sudden urge to step forward and embrace him, to press her lips against his and to invade his mouth with her tongue.

"Galloping Dragon's only good for one thing, and that's to feed family pets," giggled Debbie. "The sooner he's pet-food, the better."

"Debbie!" chided Anne. "You're talking about the love of your father's life."

Over Chung's shoulder Anne saw a man in a blue ski-mask push open the door. He had a gun in his hand, which he held above his head. "Nobody move!" the man barked in accented English. "If move, you die!"

The cocktail party chatter died away. A plate crashed to the floor and Anne turned to see Phyllis Kelley with both hands up to her mouth. The man in the mask moved into the room, closely followed by two others.

Behind them Anne could see a fourth man wearing a black ski-mask, his arm around Marie's neck. All had guns held in the air.

"Everyone down on floor! Down!" shouted the man in front. No one moved, and one or two of the men began to protest. The man stepped forward and brought the gun crashing down on the side of Jonathan Kelley's head. He cried out and slumped to his knees, blood streaming down the side of his head. Phyllis Kelley gasped and dashed forward to put her arms around her husband, but the man kicked her in the chest and she fell to the floor, choking and crying. Anne went down on her knees and lay face down, turning her head to the side so she could see what was going on.

"Down!" the man shouted, waving his gun menacingly. One of the men turned and was about to run for the French window which led out on to a balcony overlooking the garden, but before he could even move four more figures appeared wearing ski-masks and carrying guns. They moved methodically through the room, pushing the guests to the floor and making sure they lay face down.

"If you do as we say, no one get hurt," said the man in the black mask. He threw the maid down on the floor. Her skirt rode up her thighs and she tried to pull it down but the man prodded her with his foot and she stopped.

One of the other men pointed to the maid's shapely legs and said something in Cantonese and they laughed. Two of the men went out of the room and

Anne heard them go upstairs and move from room to room.

"Which one of you William Fielding?" the man in the black mask asked. Anne felt cold dread grip her heart. She heard her husband speak and then she heard him being dragged to his feet.

The man in the black mask shouted at Fielding but Fielding shook his head, saying he didn't understand. A slap rang out and Anne lifted her head to see what had happened. She caught a glimpse of her husband spitting out blood and then she felt a foot in the middle of her back and she pressed her face back to the hard wooden floor.

There was an exchange of Cantonese and she heard someone else being dragged to his feet. She recognised the next voice she heard. It was Anthony Chung. The men were obviously using him as an interpreter because the man in the black mask spoke to him, and he in turn spoke to her husband in English.

"They say you must go with them, Mr Fielding," Chung said. "They say you must do everything they tell you, or the people here will be punished. He doesn't say what the punishment will be, but I can tell that he is serious."

"Tell him I'll do as he says," said Fielding. There was a coughing sound, and a spitting noise. "Tell him not to hurt the people here."

Chung spoke in Cantonese and the man in the black mask replied.

"He says I am to go with you to translate. Their English isn't particularly good. They want there to be

623

no misunderstandings. They've asked me to point out your wife and daughter. I'm going to have to do it, Mr Fielding, or they'll start shooting."

"I understand, Anthony," Fielding said, wiping his bloody mouth with a handkerchief. "Don't worry. Just do as they say."

Anne could see the men in masks moving from guest to guest, tying their hands and feet with rope. She felt hands grab her shoulders and she was pulled to her feet. Across the room she saw two men in leather jackets and green woollen masks holding Debbie. Debbie looked across at her mother, fear in her eyes.

Someone forced Anne's hands behind her back and she felt her hands being tied. She saw that Debbie was also being bound.

"What do they want with me?" Fielding asked Chung.

"They didn't say. They want you to go with them, but they didn't say where."

"Can they understand what we're saying?"

The man in the black mask stepped forward and jabbed the barrel of his gun in Fielding's solar plexus. "I understand enough!" he barked. Chung moved to help Fielding stay on his feet. Anne tried to go to him but she felt rough hands pull her back. One of the hands slid over her breast and squeezed her. She turned to face the man and spat in his face. Saliva dripped down his yellow woollen mask and she glared at him. The man drew back his hand to slap her but the man in the black mask shouted something in Cantonese and the hand was lowered. She could see brown eyes glowering at her from behind the yellow mask. As she watched, the eyes stared at her cleavage, which was rising and falling as she panted. She could tell that the man was turned on by her mistreatment. She looked away, fearful of antagonising him any further.

The man in the black mask spoke to Chung again. When he'd finished, Chung raised his voice and addressed the room. "They are taking Mr Fielding and me outside, and they'll be holding Mrs Fielding and Debbie in a bedroom upstairs. At no time will you be left alone, so please don't try anything. They assure me that no one will be harmed if they get what they want."

Anne lurched forward as someone slapped her in the back and she almost stumbled. The man she'd spat at pushed her towards the door. She caught Chung's eye and gave him an anxious smile. He smiled back, but the man in the black mask raised his gun menacingly and he looked away. She and Debbie were herded up the stairs like cattle being rounded up for the kill.

Neil Coleman saw the door to the Fieldings' house open and four men walk out. Two of them had arrived in one of the Toyotas, one was William Fielding, and the other was Anthony Chung. He pushed himself back in his seat as the men walked towards a Mercedes parked in the double garage at the side of the house. It wasn't the one that Fielding had reported stolen, so Coleman guessed he'd arranged a replacement. Coleman scratched his chin thoughtfully. The two Chinese strangers didn't look like racegoers, and he wondered what had happened to the other six who'd gone inside.

Fielding climbed into the driving seat of the Merc, with Chung in the back. One of the strangers took the front passenger seat, the other sat next to Chung. They were talking, and Coleman couldn't see any signs that Fielding and Chung were being coerced. The Mercedes started up and drove down the driveway, indicated a left turn and headed down the Peak towards the Central business district. After a moment's hesitation, Coleman started the Suzuki Jeep and followed it.

Archie Kwan leant his elbows on the barrier and focused his binoculars on the starting gates. Four of the horses were already in but three others, including one of his, Fortune Cookie, was playing up. Reg Dykes was having trouble controlling the horse, and Kwan thought the fault lay more with the jockey than the mount. Dykes was using the crop on Fortune Cookie's flanks and urging him on with his knees, but the horse was rearing and flaring its nostrils. The horse belonged to a mainland Chinese trader and Kwan knew he was watching from a private box and that he would not be happy with what he saw. Dykes really was more trouble than he was worth, Kwan decided. He'd looked half dead at the weigh-in and had only just scraped in. Through the binoculars Kwan saw Dykes whip the horse hard, and he winced. He raised his binoculars and scanned the grandstand, trying to locate the box where Fortune Cookie's owner was. He saw the Jardine Matheson box, packed with racegoers drinking champagne, and he saw several directors of the Hongkong and Shanghai Bank smoking cigars and studying racecards and close by the directors of Hutchison Whampoa, the colony's leading Chinese hong. He saw the box which belonged to the Kowloon and Canton Bank, though he couldn't see William Fielding. An expectant hush fell over the crowd and Kwan saw that all the horses were now in the starting gates. The first race was about to begin.

The drive from the Peak to Kowloon took twice as long as usual because of the cars streaming into Happy Valley for the race meeting. William Fielding drove slowly, his mind working to find some way out of his predicament. Twice he drove by police cars and he thought of jumping out of the Mercedes and turning the two men in his car over to them. But he had little faith in the Hong Kong police being able to rescue Anne and Debbie without it turning into a bloodbath. They had the reputation of shooting first and asking questions later.

The man sitting next to him, the one who'd stripped off the black ski-mask in the hall, had told him to drive to Kowloon, and Fielding was almost sure they were heading for the bank's underground depository. They were wasting their time, he knew, because both vaults in the depository had time locks, and no matter what they threatened or what they did, there was no way they could be opened before Monday morning.

The cut on the inside of his mouth had stopped bleeding but it still hurt, and his chest ached where he'd been prodded by the gun. He hoped that they hadn't hurt Anne or Debbie.

The man in the passenger seat told him to drive down Nathan Road and Fielding knew for certain that they were going to the depository. He wanted to tell them that they wouldn't be able to get into the vaults, but didn't want to antagonise them so he kept quiet. Chung sat in the back, his arms folded across his chest.

Anne Fielding sat on the edge of the bed and flicked the hair out of her eyes. The rope they'd used to bind her arms behind her was biting into her flesh and the pain brought tears to her eyes. Debbie was lying face down on the bed while one of their two guards tied her legs.

The other guard stood at the door to the bedroom, holding a gun in either hand. He was the man Anne had spat at earlier and he was openly staring at her.

"Which one do you like best?" the man at the door asked his companion in Cantonese. Anne couldn't speak the language but she guessed from the way he was looking at her that she was the subject of the conversation. "The mother or the daughter?"

"The younger the better," said the man crouched over Debbie. He stroked her legs. "You think we should do to these two what the British have been doing to Hong Kong for years?"

The man with the guns laughed. "I'd really enjoy giving it to the mother. Look at her breasts. And her legs. Have you ever had a *gweipor*?"

"Never. I hear they don't like sex. Frigid most of them." He finished binding Debbie's legs and stood up, wiping his hands.

"This one doesn't look frigid. She looks like she's built for sex."

"Give her one, then. I'll hold the guns. No one will know. You have the mother, I'll have the girl."

The man by the door tapped one of the guns against his leg. Anne avoided his eyes, keeping her legs pressed together, knowing they were talking about her and hoping upon hope that they wouldn't touch her. She knew she'd be unable to fight them off. She strained at her bonds behind her back but the knots wouldn't budge. The effort of straining made her breasts push up against her dress and she felt the man's stare mentally undress her. She let her shoulders sag and sat slumped on the bed.

"The Dragon Head said he'd kill us if we touched them," said the man with the guns. "Don't even think about it."

"I can dream, can't I?" He went over and stood in front of Anne so that his groin was in front of her face. Anne kept her head down but he grabbed her hair, forcing her to look at him. "She has a wet mouth," said the man in Cantonese and he pushed her face towards his trousers. Anne tried to pull back but he twisted the handful of hair so hard that she gasped. She was off balance and fell forward, her cheek pressing against his thigh. She tried to push herself back, away from him. "See, she's pushing herself against me. She wants it."

The man with the guns shook his head. "If the Dragon Head finds out he'll cut off your balls," he warned.

The man looked down at Anne. He nodded slowly. "You're right," he said, "she's not worth it. No *gweipor* is worth it."

"You have the paper?"

"In my back pocket." He took a sheet of paper and unfolded it before kneeling down in front of Anne. He showed the paper to her. "I want you call box at racetrack. You read from this. You understand?"

Anne nodded. She read the typewritten lines on the paper. "Who do you want me to say this to?" she asked.

"Man in charge of box," he said. "You understand?"

"I understand," she said.

"If you say anything not on paper, your daughter dies," he said. "And you die. But first we have fun with you. Understand?"

"I understand," said Anne. The man's English was slow and hesitant and heavily accented but she could follow what he was saying.

He took the phone from the bedside table and dialled a number. When he was sure it was ringing he held it against her face. Anne could hear Debbie crying softly and she wanted to reassure her but knew that would only provoke the men further.

A man answered and she recognised Alex Perman's voice.

"Alex, this is Anne Fielding," she said.

"Anne? Where are you? The race has already started."

"We've had a small problem at the house, Alex. One of the guests is feeling ill and we're waiting for the doctor to get here. It looks like a diabetic coma so we're going to stay here until we're sure everything is okay."

"Is there anything I can do to help?"

There was nothing on the typewritten sheet to say how she was supposed to answer questions, so Anne continued to read.

"We'll try to get there as soon as possible, but it might not be until the end. William says you're to look after the guests there, make sure everyone's taken care of. He'll call you later. Goodbye, Alex."

The man hung up for her. "Good," he said. "Very good."

The Mercedes stopped in front of the depository's delivery door, though Michael Wong told Fielding to leave the engine running. Wong spoke to Chung in Cantonese, even though his English was perfect. He didn't want Fielding to know how good a grasp of the language he had, and it was important to reinforce the impression that Chung was along as an interpreter.

"He says you are to accompany him to the reception area," Chung explained to Fielding. "I'll be coming, too. You are to tell the person at reception that you wish to show us around. Will they know you?"

"Yes," said Fielding. He was a regular visitor to the depository. "But they won't admit the three of us without authorisation. They have a list of who is scheduled to visit."

Chung spoke to Wong in Cantonese, and Wong replied. "So what will they do?" asked Chung.

"They will check with my head of security," said Fielding.

Chung and Wong conversed again, and Chung leant forward to put a reassuring hand on Fielding's shoulder. "He says you are to speak with the head of security and tell him that you have two guests you wish to show around the depository. You must make sure that he doesn't suspect anything. He says your wife and daughter will be killed if anything goes wrong, Mr Fielding. And I am afraid they mean it."

Wong prodded Fielding in the stomach with his gun. "I know English to hear what you say," he said in pidgin English. "You tell, they die."

"I will do as you say," said Fielding.

Fielding, Chung and Wong got out of the Mercedes and the fourth man climbed into the driving seat. They walked around the side of the building and Wong pushed open the glass door for Fielding. There was always someone manning the reception desk, even when the vault doors were locked, because the control room was always occupied.

Fielding recognised the man at the desk, an elderly Chinese man in a grey suit with a bank tie. "Mr Lee, how are you this afternoon?"

"I am well, Mr Fielding." The man looked down at an appointments book on his desk. "We were not expecting you, were we?"

"No, but I wish to show my friends here around the depository."

632

"I shall have to check with Mr Ballantine," said Lee. "It is the rules, you understand?"

"Of course, Mr Lee. You would not be doing your job if you did anything less. We shall sit over here."

Fielding took the two men over to one of the sofas and sat down, straightening the creases on his trousers. Chung sat on his right, Wong on his left.

Lee consulted a bank phone directory and dialled a number. After a minute or two he called over to Mr Fielding. "Please come to the phone, Mr Fielding," he said.

Wong spoke hurriedly to Chung. "He says to have the call put through to the phone on the table," said Chung.

Fielding told Lee to transfer the call and he picked up the receiver when it buzzed. "William, is that you?"

"Good afternoon, George. Sorry about this, but I had a sudden urge to visit the depository."

"I thought you'd be at the races," said Ballantine.

"I'll be going later," said Fielding. "I have Anthony Chung with me, the man you were good enough to show around for me, but he has a partner with him and they'd both like a quick look around. Does that cause you any problems?"

"Of course not," said Ballantine. "But you know the vaults are sealed until Monday?"

"I've explained that, but they'd still like a look. They have a shipment of antiques arriving tomorrow."

"That's fine by me, William. Enjoy yourself. I'll see you in the office tomorrow." There was a pause. "Are you sure everything is okay?"

Fielding held his breath. It would be so easy to drop a hint that he was in trouble; George Ballantine was no fool, but his first reaction would be to call in the police, and Fielding could not risk the lives of his wife and daughter. Could not and would not. "A head cold, George," he said. "I feel terrible, but business is business."

"I know what you mean," laughed Ballantine. "Go to bed with a hot toddy, that always works for me. Transfer me back to Lee and I'll put him in the picture."

Fielding asked Lee what his extension was and put the call back to him. Lee spoke to Ballantine and then he summoned the elevator for the men. He watched as the doors hissed shut on them.

"There is something he should know," Fielding said to Chung. "Tell him the vaults have time locks, and there's no way they can be opened until Monday morning."

"I'll tell him," said Chung. He spoke to Wong, and Wong replied in a few curt syllables. "He says he knows," Chung whispered.

The lift doors opened and the three men walked along the corridor to the control room. They were admitted through the two security doors, the locks clicking open as they approached, showing that they were being monitored every step of the way by the closed circuit cameras. When they reached the glass door of the control room, Fielding saw three uniformed men waiting for them. The oldest of the three, a man called Woo who Fielding knew had been with the bank for several decades, opened the door for the group. He was sweating, Fielding noticed, even though the control room was air conditioned.

"Mr Lee said you were on your way up, Mr Fielding," Woo stammered. He looked over Fielding's shoulder at Chung and Wong. He stepped to the side and let the three men in. "Is something wrong?"

"No, Mr Woo. We're just here to look around," said Fielding.

Woo closed the door and turned to face the three men. His mouth fell open as Wong pulled the gun from inside his jacket.

"All of you, put your hands on your heads!" Wong barked in Cantonese. The three men did as they were told. "Stand up against the wall, and face it," commanded Wong. The men shuffled round. Fielding stood with his arms at his side, not sure what to do. He looked at Chung and as he did Wong slammed the pistol into his temple, knocking him cold. Fielding slumped to the floor, his head banging against a console as he fell backwards.

"Fuck your mother, you could have killed him!" cursed Chung, kneeling down and feeling for a pulse in Fielding's neck. Chung sighed with relief when he felt a strong, steady heartbeat. Despite Fielding's laboured breathing and the blood dripping down his temple, he was in no danger.

"Up against the wall!" Wong ordered, covering Chung with the gun. Chung backed away and stood next to the three uniformed guards. He put his hands on his head. "You three, turn round," said Wong. The three guards shuffled round. All were sweating and wide-eyed.

"I want to show you that I am to be taken seriously," Wong said in quiet Cantonese. "I want to show you what will happen if you do not do exactly as I say." He smiled tightly, pointed the gun at Mr Woo's chest, and fired twice. The explosions echoed around the soundproof control room, deafening them all. Two red blossoms appeared on Woo's pale blue shirt, dark at the centre, pale at the edges. His hands clawed slowly down his chest, his mouth working soundlessly; his eyelids fluttered and he slid backwards down the wall leaving a bloody smudge on the white paintwork. The two surviving guards stared at their dead colleague, then looked fearfully at Wong. He smiled and pointed the gun at the space between them. "Do exactly as I say, or you will suffer the same fate." The men nodded frantically.

Wong waved his gun at the television monitors. "Which of these covers the delivery entrance?" he asked.

One of the men pointed to a black and white screen and Wong went over to it, keeping a wary eye on his captives. He could see the Mercedes outside.

"Open the door and let the car in," he said. The man who'd pointed at the screen stepped to a console and pressed a red button. Seconds later Wong saw the Mercedes drive in. "And now lower the gate," Wong ordered. "Then get back to the wall and put your hands back on your head." The men did as they were told. "Now, where are the keys to the vaults? Both vaults."

One of the guards shook his head. "The vaults have time locks. They won't open until tomorrow."

"I'll worry about that," said Wong. "Give me the keys."

The guard who had opened the gate, who Wong decided was clearly the more co-operative of the two, went over to a steel box mounted on the wall and took out two key-rings. He placed them on the console near Wong and went back to the wall and put his hands on his head without being asked. Wong kept the gun trained on the men while he waited for the next car to arrive. In less than five minutes a second Mercedes appeared on the screen, this one with black windows. "Open the gate again," he ordered. The second car was admitted.

Wong scanned the monitors and saw the one which covered the delivery area. He saw five Red Poles climb out of the car and head for the exit. The camera in the elevator showed them entering and pressing the button for the control room floor, and he watched as they moved along the corridor. "Open the security doors," Wong ordered, and his instructions were obeyed. Through the glass door he saw the five men come around the corner, guns in hand. He opened the door and let them in.

One of them immediately began tying Fielding up, roughly binding his arms and legs and stuffing a gag in his mouth. Another forced one of the guards to strip off his uniform, while a third tied the other guard's hands behind him.

"Tie him, too," Wong ordered, pointing his gun at Chung.

When the guard was down to his socks and underpants, he was tied up too, while one of the Red Poles took off his own leather jacket and jeans and changed into the uniform. When he was ready he stood in front of Wong who nodded his approval. "Go down and replace the man on reception," said Wong. "Try not to kill him. Bind him and gag him and bring him up to the control room." Another Red Pole had been designated to go down with him, and they left the control room together. Wong explained to one of the Red Poles which monitor covered the delivery gate outside and which was the interior view, and how to operate the gate. Wong kept his gun on Chung, another Red Pole covered the two guards and together they left the control room and went down the corridor to the elevator.

Lehman looked at his watch. "Time to go," he said. Doherty nodded and climbed up into the co-pilot's station. Mr Tsao stood by the workbench, looking at the photographs of the racetrack and the maps. Lewis and Horvitz put their M16s in the back of the Huey and went over to the main sliding door. Together they pushed it back, allowing the bright sunshine to stream in. Lehman put on a pair of sunglasses and slid his flight helmet on. Doherty did the same.

"You got the frequencies?" Lehman asked.

"Sure," said Doherty. He reached behind his seat and showed Lehman a black clipboard. On it were written a list of frequencies for Kai Tak Airport and various police stations they could expect to fly over en route. Doherty programmed them into the scanner. Carmody put his M16 on one of the seats and hauled himself into the back. He sat in the side seat, the one normally used by the door-gunner, and he rested the rifle on his thighs. He gave a thumbs up to Lehman, showing that he was ready.

Horvitz and Lewis jogged back to the Huey, the door fully open. The door was almost as tall as the warehouse and Lehman had already calculated that there was enough room to get the Huey in a hover and move it forward and out under its own power. Horvitz leapt into the back of the helicopter and scooped up his rifle. He pushed his sunglasses up his nose, rubbed his short beard and grinned at Carmody.

Lewis picked up the fire extinguisher and stood by the side of the Huey as Doherty opened the operator's manual and put it on his lap.

Lehman clicked the radio trigger switch. "Let's do it," he said.

Doherty nodded and began reading his checklist out loud. They ran through all the checks and Lehman pressed the starter trigger. The electric starter motor whined and the turbine whistled like a banshee. Lehman kept his eye on the exhaust-gas temperature gauge as the rotors whirled above his head. Tsao turned his back on the maps and watched the helicopter.

Lehman checked that all the gauges were in the green and motioned to Lewis to climb into the back of the Huey. He waited until Lewis was seated and had his rifle in his hands before clicking his radio mike on. "Everything okay?" he asked Doherty.

"Let's do it," Doherty replied.

Lehman pulled on the collective and eased the cyclic forward. The skids grated along the concrete floor and Lehman increased the pressure on the collective. The turbine roared and the rotors speeded up. Lehman allowed the Huey's nose to rise almost a foot before compensating. He pressed his left foot down to stop the helicopter's natural tendency to spin clockwise and pushed the cyclic so that the Huey crept forward. It inched out of the warehouse like a family car leaving a suburban garage.

Once the whirling rotor was clear of the door Lehman increased power and felt the Huey soar upwards. The ground flashed beneath them, then they were over the perimeter fence and banking away from the wooded hill that overlooked the compound. Lehman clicked his radio mike on. "I didn't hear any tapping," he said to Doherty. "You?"

"No, me neither," answered his co-pilot. "Makes you think, doesn't it?"

Lehman kept the Huey less than a hundred feet from the ground and pointed its nose south, towards Hong Kong Island and the racetrack.

Neil Coleman picked at his teeth with his thumbnail and watched the metal gate shudder upwards to admit a Mercedes 560SEL with black windows. It was the fourth he'd seen in the last half hour, and he still had no idea what was going on. He'd arrived at the

640

depository just in time to see Fielding and Chung walk into the front of the building, and a few minutes later their car had driven into the side entrance. It had remained inside, but four more Mercedes cars had arrived, and three had left. Coleman had resisted radioing for reinforcements because he wasn't sure yet what he'd tell headquarters, or how he'd explain his own presence outside the depository. None of the registration numbers matched numbers of stolen cars he was searching for, yet the fact that they all had black windows suggested they belonged to the same people. He wondered if perhaps the bank was secretly moving its assets out of the depository and had chosen to use cars rather than armoured vans. It seemed unlikely in the extreme, but he couldn't think of any other explanation for Fielding's presence. There was another reason for not calling in his observations, and that was that he remembered what Donaldson had said about the police preparing for a robbery at the racetrack. They wouldn't appreciate being called out on a wild-goose chase. He'd have to be one hundred per cent certain that something was amiss before calling it in. He tapped on his steering wheel and waited.

When the dust clouds had settled and the throbbing of the Huey had receded into the distance, Mr Tsao closed the main door to the warehouse. It took all his strength and he was sweating by the time he'd finished. He poured himself a glass of water at the sink and then went into his bedroom to pack his holdall. He checked that he had left nothing in the room, and folded his

641

blankets neatly on the camp bed before leaving. On the way through the warehouse he stopped in front of the maps and photographs. He placed his holdall on the workbench and stared at the wall. He heard a scuffling sound behind him and he turned around, but slowly as if he knew what he'd find. Tyler stood in the centre of the warehouse in his police inspector's uniform, the peak of his cap down low over his nose, his back locked straight as if he were on parade. In his left hand he had a white plastic carrier bag.

"I did not hear you drive up," said Tsao quietly.

"I walked," said Tyler.

"I see," said Tsao, as if he was talking to himself.

Tyler began to walk towards Tsao, his rubber-soled shoes making no sound on the concrete floor.

Tsao nodded, almost imperceptibly, at the pictures pinned up on the wall. "It will not work, of course," he said.

"Of course," agreed Tyler, still walking.

"Ah," said Tsao. "I see."

"You did an excellent job of work, Mr Tsao," said Tyler. "You are a true craftsman."

"Thank you," said Tsao. He turned his back on Tyler and studied the wall. If he heard the sound of Tyler's gun being cocked he showed no sign of it. The bullet exploded through the back of his skull, throwing blood, bone and brain matter across the maps and pictures of Hong Kong.

Tyler went over to the barrels of fuel and oil and took an incendiary device out of the carrier bag. The device consisted of a cheap alarm clock, a detonator and a

642

small amount of explosive, and it was similar to those which had been used at the Shatin racetrack. It had been designed and built by the man who had made the Shatin bombs. Tyler checked that the time was set for ten minutes, placed it by the side of the barrels, and walked away, out into the searing sunshine.

Michael Wong stood in the depository's receiving area and watched his men load up the fifth Mercedes. As each car arrived it brought with it a driver and two Red Poles, and there were now ten men helping to transfer the gold from the main vault.

The guards had been amazed to find that the keys opened the vault doors and that the timing mechanisms had operated twenty-four hours earlier than expected. The two men had looked at each other, surprise written all over their faces, and Wong knew it wouldn't be long before they reached the conclusion that Woo must have set them incorrectly. It didn't matter, Woo was no longer a problem. Wong had opened the main vault first and his Red Poles had begun loading the gold bullion on to metal trolleys and then into the lift up to the ground floor and along to the loading area. He'd then taken the two guards, their hands bound behind their backs, to the safety-deposit box vault. It had opened and Wong had asked them where the keys were.

One of the guards, the one in just his shorts and socks, had protested that the bank's clients had the only keys and that without them they couldn't get into the boxes. Wong had shot him in the foot and asked the other guard. He had shown Wong where the replacement keys were kept. Wong knew that the bank kept duplicate keys in case of loss, though it tended not to broadcast the information. They had brought electric drills with them as a precautionary measure, but there had been no need. Two of the Red Poles were methodically working their way through the boxes, starting with the large ones. Two more triad soldiers were emptying the boxes and dividing the contents into four piles: gold; cash; valuables; and rubbish — legal papers and the like. The two guards had been bound and gagged and left in the safety-deposit box reception area. Chung had been put on the sofa, his arms still tied.

The men finished loading the Mercedes and one of them operated the gate, allowing the driver to ease the car out into the street. As it left, another Mercedes arrived and drove straight in. Two Red Poles climbed out and helped unload the next trolley.

Wong looked at his watch. It was all going to plan, five cars loaded up and on their way: a total of thirty-five million American dollars. Two were being loaded up, another three would arrive within the next half hour. Tyler was due within the next fifteen minutes so Wong went to check the men in the safety-deposit-box vault. As part of his pay-off, Tyler was picking up five million dollars in gold and currency. Wong caught the elevator and went up one floor. He walked by the two bound guards and nodded at Chung.

More than half the boxes were open and the pile of cash was now almost waist-high. There was a large canvas bag at the entrance, the sort used by sailors to stash their gear, and Wong took it over to the banknotes. He knelt down and began putting bundles of hundred and thousand American dollar notes into the bag. It didn't take him long before he had four million dollars and he hefted it on to his shoulder and took it back to the elevator.

When he arrived back at the receiving area another Mercedes was arriving. He dropped the canvas bag on the floor and told one of his Red Poles to put aside one million dollars in gold bullion.

The air traffic controller looked at his radar screen and blinked his eyes, twice. A small blip had appeared from nowhere on the screen, showing that something was in the air about five miles north of the airport. Whatever it was it was not using a transponder. It moved like a small plane or a helicopter but no one had filed a flight plan from that direction and there were no airfields nearby. He flicked his microphone on. "Unidentified aircraft flying five miles north of Hong Kong International, this is Hong Kong Approach, please respond on 119.1." There was no reply. He flicked over to the tower frequency, 118.7 MHz, and tried again. Still no response. He flicked back to 119.1 MHz.

"Unidentified aircraft flying four miles north of Hong Kong International, this is Hong Kong Approach. If you can hear me turn left and enter a holding pattern. If you can receive but not transmit, squawk 7600."

He studied the blip on his screen. It was moving inexorably south. He repeated the message on the tower frequency. No effect.

The controller called his supervisor over and explained what was happening.

"Are you sure it isn't a student pilot from one of the flight schools?" asked the supervisor.

The controller shook his head. "It appeared from nowhere. And there are no Cessnas out at the moment."

"No radio contact?"

"No, and no transponder signal. I've asked him to squawk 7600 if his radio is out but his transponder is still inactive. If he has one."

"Where did it come from?"

The controller shrugged. "Heading south, but it appeared from nowhere. Near Shatin, I guess."

The supervisor nodded. "Try him on the Guangzhou Control frequencies, 132.4 and 123.9, just in case he's reading his charts wrong."

He called across the room to a controller who was about to take a break and asked him to phone through to Guangzhou to see if they had any information on the rogue aircraft. He turned back to the controller tracking the blip and put his hand on his shoulder. "You concentrate on the unidentified aircraft," he said calmly once the man had tried the Guangzhou frequencies unsuccessfully. "Hand over your aircraft to Danny and Eric." He shouted over to a controller sitting at the far left of the tower. "Danny, we've got an unidentified aircraft three miles north. Have you anyone there who can give us a visual?"

"I've a 747 inbound for landing at 1,500 feet, due west."

"Try them," said the supervisor. "Put it on the speaker."

A uniformed police sergeant sitting at the side of the radar room stood up and walked over to the supervisor. "This could be it," the supervisor said in anticipation of the man's unspoken question. The wall speaker crackled into life and the whole room listened as Danny Tse hailed the 747. "Five-Eight-Two, this is Hong Kong Tower. Report if you see traffic at ten o'clock at three hundred feet."

"Hong Kong Tower, please confirm three hundred feet, Five-Eight-Two."

"Five-Eight-Two, that's affirmative, traffic at three hundred feet, ten o'clock your position."

There was a pause then the pilot of the 747 came back on the air. "Hong Kong Tower, traffic in sight, Five-Eight-Two."

"Five-Eight-Two, please identify traffic."

"Hong Kong Tower, it's a helicopter, flying low. It looks like a green Huey. And you're not going to believe this, but I can see men in uniforms carrying rifles. Five-Eight-Two."

Tse looked over at the supervisor and raised his eyebrows.

"Warn all traffic that we have an unidentified helicopter in the area," said the supervisor. "Give it lots of room. God knows what the lunatics are up to."

The sergeant switched on his own radio and began speaking to the airport police station while the controller continued trying to contact the helicopter.

Coleman had counted nine Mercedes in, and eight had left. With the tinted windows it was impossible to tell who was driving, or how many passengers there were. For all he knew Fielding or Chung could have left in one of them. After he'd waited for ten minutes, he'd taken a walk by the front of the building, but everything had seemed in order. A uniformed guard was sitting behind the desk in the small reception area and he'd looked up as Coleman went past.

He'd gone back to the Jeep and tuned his radio to the Happy Valley frequency, 449.625 MHz. He heard nothing about the supposed robbery so he flicked to the emergency unit frequencies, 449.525 MHz for the east of the island, and 449.250 MHz for the west. Still nothing, not that he could understand, anyway. His Cantonese was really abysmal, he knew, but, as he had no long-term plans to stay in the force, it didn't worry him overmuch.

He was toying with the idea of calling up one of the Kowloon stations and getting them to run a check with the Kowloon and Canton Bank when a uniformed police officer drove up in an unmarked car, a white Toyota. Coleman got a side view of the guy as he drove past, but didn't recognise him: he had a prominent hooked nose and cold, blue eyes. He had short grey hair, cut in a military fashion and he looked to be in his fifties. Coleman thought he knew most of the expatriate officers so he racked his brains for who it might be.

The man beeped his horn and the metal gate rattled up. A Mercedes drove out and the man slowly guided the Toyota inside. Coleman frowned. The fact that a Royal Hong Kong Police officer was involved made him feel a little easier, but he was still in a state of total confusion.

Lewis moved his head in the airstream, enjoying the feel of the cold air rippling across his face and through his hair. He closed his eyes and his mind spun back to Vietnam, to the countless missions he'd flown as crew chief, back in the days before he'd had a son to worry about and a cancer eating away at his insides. A burst of gunfire jolted him out of his reverie. He opened his eyes to see Carmody firing into the sea below, a satisfied grin on his face. He turned and gave a thumbs-up to Lewis. "Just checking," he mouthed.

They'd avoided the tower blocks of Kowloon by flying to the west, over the container terminals of Kwai Chung and the countless freighters moored around Stonecutters Island. They were so low they could see the looks of surprise on the faces of the Asian sailors below. Several even waved, and Carmody had waved back, then pointed his M16 at them and laughed when they'd ducked.

Once they'd reached the sea Lehman had taken the Huey even lower as they flew east over Victoria Harbour, the bustling shops of Tsim Sha Tsui on the left, the office blocks of Central on their right. They flashed over a wooden Chinese junk bobbing in the water, where three fishermen in coolie hats looked up open-mouthed and then were gone, and they banked steeply to avoid a Star Ferry which was ploughing towards Hong Kong Island, packed to the gills with housewives, schoolchildren and tourists. Lewis saw a man in a T-shirt and shorts aim his camcorder at the Huey but doubted that he managed to get a shot. In Nam there were two safe ways to fly over the jungle: so high that the VC fire couldn't reach them, or low and fast so that they didn't have time to react.

Lewis looked over the island, at the glittering glass towers, shiny bright against the green peaks behind them. The sun sparkled off the tallest tower in the island, a twisted knife of glass and steel which stood head and shoulders above the rest, made even taller by a twin-pronged structure on top that looked like a massive television antenna. To its right was the futuristic grey steel headquarters of the Hongkong and Shanghai Bank, and behind it a building shaped like an elongated wedding cake which was topped by the logo of the Kowloon and Canton Bank. Lehman put the Huey into a steep bank to the right so that Lewis felt as if he were suspended over the water and they flew between the towers, their reflection speckling off a dozen different surfaces, metal, glass and marble, as if they were flying in formation, while the throbbing thud of the rotors echoed back from the buildings. Lewis reached for the cardboard box which contained the smoke and gas canisters and he began removing the small wire clips which stopped them going off accidentally. When he had prepared twenty of the canisters he repeated the process with the box of stun grenades.

He looked up to see Carmody grinning at him. "Yeah!" yelled Carmody above the beat of the rotors. "Rock and roll! Rock and fucking roll!"

Phil Donaldson watched the horses being coaxed into the starting gate for the last race. He was starting to wonder if perhaps somebody really had been pulling Tommy Lai's chain. None of the anti-triad men posing as tellers had reported anything unusual and in another half an hour the grandstand would be empty and the Jockey Club's millions would be safely locked away in the underground vault. Donaldson looked across at Paul Penycate and realised that exactly the same thought was going through the superintendent's mind.

The damp patches under Donaldson's armpits had grown steadily larger throughout the afternoon and he could feel sweat trickling down his back and soaking into his boxer shorts.

Tommy Lai had disappeared during the fifth race, saying that he wanted to try to contact his informer. Donaldson reckoned he was just keeping out of the way in case the whole thing fell apart. Penycate now had more than 300 men at various points around the track and was growing more nervous by the minute. Donaldson was considering making his own excuses and leaving.

Penycate's radio crackled and he answered in fluent Cantonese. It was Kowloon headquarters, relaying a message from the sergeant they'd sent to sit in on Air Traffic Control at Kai Tak.

"It's happening," said Penycate. "They've spotted a helicopter, heading this way. I'm going to call in more men."

Donaldson nodded, he'd heard and understood the transmission. And he'd heard that the men in the helicopter were carrying rifles. Penycate was already talking into his radio mike, warning the marksmen to be ready.

Michael Wong and Joel Tyler surveyed the gold bullion which had been placed into three metal cases, the sort used by professional photographers.

"Takes up a surprisingly small amount of space, a million dollars," said Tyler.

Wong nodded. "It's heavy, though. I'm surprised you want any of it in gold."

"Where I'm going, gold is a better currency than cash." Tyler was planning to use a triad speedboat to take him out to sea where he would rendezvous with a larger boat which would take him to Thailand. Josh had stipulated that he would expect payment in gold, and Tyler had readily agreed. The two men watched as the gold and a canvas bag of dollars were loaded into Tyler's car.

"Are you going to keep the uniform on?" asked Wong with a smile. Tyler's appearance in the depository had caused something of a stir, and one of the Red Poles had actually levelled his gun before Wong had shouted a warning.

"It has its uses," said Tyler. "I'll change when I reach the boat."

Wong smiled. "It suits you, Colonel Tyler."

The gate rattled up and a van in the livery of the Kowloon and Canton Bank drove in. Wong shouted over to two of his Red Poles to begin loading the valuables from the deposit boxes. "This is going well," Wong said to Tyler. "We already have nine cars on their way, the tenth is being loaded now. We'll have the two vans loaded within five minutes." He looked at his watch. "I would think that the first of the cars are already in Chinese waters."

"You've cleared the vaults?" asked Tyler.

"As good as," said Wong. "We'll have stripped them of all their gold, and most of the cash. I'm not an expert but I think we've found diamonds and precious stones worth in the region of thirty million dollars. Some bearer bonds, too. We don't have the space for the small bills, or for the antiques, and we've had time to open only eighty per cent of the boxes. But even so, I would say the operation has been a complete success."

"It should be, it was planned to perfection," said Tyler. "Where is Chung?"

"He is in reception on the floor below us. He thought it best we maintain the illusion that he is our prisoner."

"That makes sense," said Tyler. "Well, I shall leave you now." He shook hands with Wong. "Give him my regards and tell him I'll be in touch when it's all blown over."

Wong grinned. "Somehow, Colonel Tyler, I don't think this will ever blow over."

The Huey flashed between two residential tower blocks, so close that Lehman could see the items of clothing hanging out to dry on poles below the kitchen windows. Through the Plexiglas he looked down across the track to the grandstand. He pushed the cyclic forward and eased off on the collective, swooping down like a hawk. He could see racehorses in the starting gate and knew that the last race was just about to start. His timing had been perfect, and he felt a professional pride in the fact that he'd got his wind drift and weight calculations dead on. He took the Huey down to fifty feet above the ground and put her in a gentle bank so that the underside of the helicopter swung towards the thousands of spectators. He turned so that he was flying parallel to the grandstand and slowed the speed down so that the men in the back could throw out the smoke and gas canisters every ten feet or so. He took a quick look over his shoulder and saw Lewis, Carmody and Horvitz activating the canisters and lobbing them into the crowds. Within seconds thick, choking smoke had obscured the spectators on the lower levels and by the time the Huey had reached the far end of the grandstand people were pushing and fighting to get to the exits. Horvitz lifted up the box that had contained the smoke bombs to show that it was empty and Lewis pushed over the box of stun grenades.

Carmody screamed obscenities at the panicking crowds as he grabbed for a stun grenade with his good arm. He pulled out its pin and threw it into the stand like a baseball pitcher with something to prove, and as Lehman put the Huey in a steep bank it exploded with a deafening roar. Lehman flew back along the grandstand, higher this time because the smoke was obscuring the ground, while the men in the back tossed the stun grenades down. The Huey was followed by a line of explosions which intensified the panic below. Men and women were screaming and shouting and for a wild moment Lehman flashed back to Nam, landing in a hot LZ to pick up wounded grunts, shells from VC mortars thumping into the ground like a giant's footsteps. He shook his head and pulled and twisted the collective to gain height as he reached the end of the grandstand. The Huey soared up as Horvitz threw out the last of the stun grenades.

The crowd had spilled over on to the track in an attempt to get away from the choking smoke and the thunder-flashes. They left behind others motionless on the ground, trampled in the stampede. Lehman saw startled faces in the private boxes, men in dark suits and women in long dresses, backing away from the helicopter with fear in their eyes, holding their hands up as if trying to ward the Huey away. Horvitz and Carmody waved their M16s and pretended to fire as the helicopter climbed higher.

Donnie Choi grated the gears of the truck as he fumbled with the gear stick. His hands were sweating and he wiped them one at a time on his cut-off denim jeans. There was a small fan mounted on the dashboard and plugged into the cigarette lighter socket and Choi turned his face to it. He was bare-chested and there was a sheen of sweat over the tattoo of a hawk which swooped between his nipples. Four lines of traffic were merging into two which then moved slowly into the tunnel like burrowing snakes. A Nissan driven by a middle-aged *gweipor* drew up alongside Choi's truck with her indicator flashing but he pretended not to see her and moved forward a foot or so, refusing to allow her in. The truck he was driving was old and the sides were scraped with a dozen different paints. The woman decided that she didn't want to risk her Nissan's paintwork and let Choi go first. He smiled to himself. He hoped the *gweipor* would be behind him in the tunnel.

On the back of the truck were twenty barrels of concentrated acid, tied with ropes. A warning notice on each barrel, in English and Chinese, warned that the fumes were not to be inhaled. Choi looked at the cheap digital watch on his wrist. He was making good time. He wondered how Rocky Kan was getting on in the eastern harbour crossing.

The traffic ahead of him began to speed up and he drove out of the bright sunlight into the fluorescent lights of the tunnel. Choi leant down and picked up a piece of rope under the dashboard. He held it on his knee and steered the truck with his right hand. He slowed to allow the car in front to get further ahead, then as he reached the low point of the tunnel he pulled hard on the rope and accelerated. The barrels spilled out of the back of the truck and crashed on to the ground, breaking open. Acid gushed out and white fumes began to stream into the air. One barrel spun to the left and hurtled into the front of a taxi in the opposite lane and the car crashed into the wall as it tried to avoid it. A delivery van hit the taxi and a minibus slammed into the car. Within seconds the tunnel was in total disarray. The acid had begun eating into the tyres of the cars just behind Choi's truck and the drivers were panicking, sounding their horns and attempting to reverse. Choi slammed on his brakes, pulled the rope completely into his cab, stashed it under his seat, then climbed out and stood watching the chaos he'd caused.

Neil Coleman fingered the mike on the police radio and studied the metal gate leading to the inside of the depository. He had counted ten Mercedes in, all of them with darkened windows, and nine had left. Coleman had noticed that the cars which came out were lower to the ground than when they went in, as if they were loaded with something heavy. Two vans with Kowloon and Canton Bank livery had also gone inside, and both had yet to reappear. And then there was the uniformed inspector in his Toyota. Something was clearly wrong, but Coleman couldn't for the life of him figure out what it was. If he called it in, he'd have to explain how he came to be sitting outside the depository and that would mean telling them about Chung. And then it would all come out — the way he'd mixed his personal and professional life and used Special Branch to check out the rival for his girlfriend's affections. But if he didn't call it in and something illegal was going on then he'd have just as much explaining to do.

He keyed in the frequency for Kowloon East and spoke to their control room. He identified himself and his location and asked them to contact the Kowloon and Canton Bank to see if they were moving assets out of their depository. He was told curtly that he'd have to wait, there had been accidents in both cross-harbour tunnels and all available men were already on Hong Kong Island.

"Haven't you got anybody you can spare?" Coleman asked.

"As soon as we have, we'll get on to it," a female Chinese voice answered. "The robbery at Happy Valley takes precedence."

"The robbery's happening?" he said. When Donaldson had told him about the triad tip, he'd only half believed him.

"The grandstand has been bombed and dozens of people have been injured. Emergency services are having trouble getting to the track, and we have to deal with dead and injured in the tunnels. And we have a major fire at a warehouse in the New Territories. That's why your request for information on the bank has such a low priority, Inspector Coleman. I'm sorry. I'll get back to you when we have time."

The gate began to open and Coleman placed the mike back on the radio unit. The last Mercedes rolled out, closely followed by the Toyota. Coleman had a brief look at the driver, the grey-haired inspector, and then both vehicles turned into the main road. That only left the two vans inside, and the vehicle that had taken Chung and Fielding. The clue to what was happening, Coleman decided, lay in what was inside the Mercs, and he decided to follow the two cars. He started the Jeep and reached for the mike again, this time to run the licence plates of the Mercedes and the Toyota through vehicle registration.

Lehman could hear the screams of the crowds above the thud of the rotor blades, and as he banked the Huey to the left he saw hundreds of men and women pour into the streets like a river that had burst its banks. He heard the rattle of gunfire and jerked his head round. Carmody was firing into the sky, the brass shell cases of his M16 bouncing off the roof of the helicopter. He had a manic gleam in his eye and Lehman knew it wouldn't take much for him to begin spraying the crowds with bullets. He turned the Huey so that Carmody was facing away from the grandstand and up into the sky where he couldn't do any damage. He pulled harder on the collective and twisted it, taking the Huey above the grandstand so that he was looking down on it from about twenty feet. He put the helicopter into a hover and edged the cyclic forward, skimming along the surface until he was close to the point where Tyler was due to appear with the money. There was a small square-shaped structure on the top, with a door in it marked "Maintenance". He eased off on the power and flared the rotors, dropping the Huey so that its skids were just inches above the concrete.

Lewis, Carmody and Horvitz jumped out and crouched below the spinning rotor blades, their M16s at the ready. They fanned out, keeping their heads down, and moved away from the helicopter. Carmody reached for the maintenance door with his claw, and pulled its handle. It wouldn't move and he pulled harder. He turned to look at Horvitz, and he moved over to help. Smoke began to curl up over the edges of the grandstand, like an encroaching fog.

Lehman turned to Doherty, but Doherty was busy flicking through the channels of the scanner, a worried frown on his face. Lehman clicked his mike on. "What's wrong?" he asked.

Doherty shook his head and his frown deepened.

A small hole appeared in the Plexiglas in front of Lehman's face, and small cracks radiated out from it. He looked at it, wondering what had caused it. A second hole appeared, slightly higher and to the left. Realisation hit him like a cold shower.

He clicked his mike on. "We're under fire!" he yelled. He kicked the pedals, left and right, swinging the tail of the Huey from side to side the way he had in Nam when flying into hot LZs, and he increased the power so that the Huey rose up.

The three men on the roof heard the increase in rotor speed and turned to see the Huey rise above them, its tail swinging erratically.

"What the fuck's going on?" screamed Carmody, stepping back from the door.

660

Horvitz pounded against it with his shoulder. "Something's wrong," he said. He looked at the rugged diving watch on his wrist. "The colonel's late."

"Dan's throwing the Huey around like he's gone crazy," shouted Lewis. "I say we go back."

"No!" yelled Horvitz. "We don't leave the colonel. We wait until he gets here."

Lewis backed away, the downwash from the rotors rippling his fatigues. "Let's wait in the Huey," he shouted.

"Our orders were to wait for the colonel here!" Horvitz yelled. "That's what we do."

"Tyler isn't here."

"He will be," shouted Horvitz. He turned back to the door and fired a burst of bullets at its lock. The wood splintered and sparks showered off the metal fittings. Horvitz kicked the door and it caved inwards, sagging on its hinges. Beyond was a small storage room and concrete steps leading down. Horvitz stuck his head inside but there was clearly no sign of Tyler. He looked at Carmody and shrugged.

"What do we do?" asked Carmody.

Above them the Huey was careering from side to side and backing up like a frightened cat.

"We wait," shouted Horvitz.

Lewis began to protest when he suddenly fell backwards, blood streaming from his throat. Horvitz and Carmody stood transfixed as Lewis slumped to his knees, the rifle clattering on the roof. Lewis put his hands to his neck and blood seeped through his fingers, running in rivulets down his tiger-striped fatigues. Two more red patches appeared on his chest, ragged, black holes in the material, wet with blood.

"We're being fired at!" screamed Carmody. He looked around but they were the only men on the roof and they'd heard no shots above the roaring thud of the rotor blades. Horvitz was calmly surveying the apartment blocks which looked down on the racetrack. The nearest was 400 yards away, a thin white tower with small, semicircular balconies. A small puff of dust kicked up near Carmody's left foot and he jerked it away as if he'd been burnt. "That's why Lehman's jerking the Huey round!" he yelled. "They're firing at us."

"Back to the slick," said Horvitz, still running his eyes over the tower blocks. He hefted the M16 in his hands and licked his lips. "Take Bart with you. I'll cover you."

"Cover me! You can't even see where the shots are coming from, how the fuck are you gonna cover me?"

Horvitz didn't look at Carmody. "Do it," he said. "Do it or I'll be the one to shoot you." He raised the stock of the M16 to his shoulder. He'd seen one of the marksmen, dressed in dark blue overalls, kneeling on a balcony close to the top of the building which gave him a clear shot at the whole grandstand. Horvitz was amazed he'd missed Carmody. Maybe he'd never killed before and the shot at Lewis had shaken him. It was one thing to be a crack shot on the range, quite another to take lives calmly when under pressure. Horvitz still hadn't heard any of the shots and he knew that the marksman he'd spotted wouldn't be alone and that even as he stood and focused his mind there was a good chance that his heart was in the crosshairs of another telescopic sight. He concentrated all his thoughts on the man on the balcony, steadied his breathing, and relaxed everything but the finger on the trigger. Four hundred yards was a hell of a long shot with an M16, and he had the gusting wind to allow for. He fired a short burst and saw a line of bullet marks appear in the concrete above the balcony. He saw the police marksman get hurriedly to his feet and Horvitz held his breath and fired again. Three red dots spotted the man's chest and he fell back. Horvitz brought the gun down and went to help Carmody, who was doing his best to support Lewis. Horvitz gave Carmody his rifle to carry and swung Lewis across his shoulders in a smooth movement, grunting as he took the strain. He staggered towards the Huey which was slowly descending, taking care to keep well away from the tail rotor and the stinger which was swinging to and fro like a deadly scythe.

As Horvitz reached the cargo door, Lehman stabilised the Huey so that Lewis could be rolled inside. A third hole appeared in the Plexiglas, closer to Doherty, and Lehman felt the helicopter shudder as bullets hit the tail section.

"We've got to go," he screamed, but his voice was lost in the sound of the rotors. He turned to see if Carmody was on board and he saw Lewis lying on his back, just behind the co-pilot's seat, his hand clamped to his neck in a vain attempt to stem the flow of blood. His mouth moved soundlessly and his eyes had a glassy, faraway look about them that Lehman had seen time and time again on the faces of dying grunts. Carmody threw his M16 on to one of the canvas seats and hauled himself in as Horvitz leapt into one of the side seats, firing a burst from his rifle at the tower blocks. More bullets thudded into the side of the Huey and Lehman saw small holes appear in the roof of the helicopter.

He pulled and twisted the collective, pushed the cyclic forward and pressed his right pedal so that the Huey rolled to the right, away from the racetrack.

Doherty clicked his mike on. "It was a trap," he said to Lehman.

"It couldn't have been," said Lehman, increasing power to the rotors so that he could get as much distance between them and the marksmen in the towers. "They couldn't possibly have known we'd be coming in by helicopter." He concentrated on flying the Huey, keeping the tail twitching as he climbed over the hills that divided the island. He was so involved in the controls that he couldn't hear what Doherty said next, but he did hear the radio conversation that Doherty put through his headphones.

He heard an English voice giving a description of a uniformed inspector, close-cropped grey hair and a hooked nose, in his early fifties, driving a white Toyota. The man was answered by a Chinese woman speaking English with a thick accent who told him that the car had false registration plates, as did a Mercedes the man was following.

"What the hell's that?" interrupted Lehman.

"I'm feeding in what I've been listening to on the scanner," said Doherty. "Does that description remind you of anyone?"

"It's Tyler," said Lehman.

"That's right, it's Tyler," said Doherty. "Some police guy over in Kowloon has been calling in his description and asking for information about a bank depository. It's where one of the big banks keeps all its money."

"And Tyler's there?"

"He's just left it. In the Toyota."

"And who is the English guy?"

"A police inspector. Coleman his name is, I think. He's trying to call in police reinforcements but they're telling him that they're too stretched because of the robbery. And because there have been two pile-ups in the cross-harbour tunnels. All the cops are stuck on the island."

"Where we were," said Lehman, realisation dawning.

Doherty nodded. "Exactly. Where we were. There's more."

"More?"

"There's a major fire out in the New Territories. A warehouse."

Lehman looked across at Doherty. He clicked his mike on again. "We're going to have to tell the others," he said. "They have to know."

Doherty nodded in agreement.

"I'm going to set this bird down."

"Not here," said Doherty. "Take us back to Stonecutters Island. It's closer to Kowloon and I've got a feeling that's where we'll want to go next."

"What about Bart?"

Doherty shook his head. "You saw the wounds, Dan."

Lehman wanted to protest but knew that Doherty was right. He hauled the Huey into a tight left turn and sped over the western end of the island, back to Victoria Harbour.

Tears were streaming from Phil Donaldson's eyes, and his ears were ringing from the deafening explosions of the stun grenades. One had gone off just yards from where he had been standing as he was trying to calm people down and get them to file out of the exits in something approaching an orderly manner. Trying to get the excitable Chinese to calm down was an impossible task and he'd been pushed, jostled and ignored by the frantic racegoers. One old woman had elbowed him in the stomach and told him to go fuck his mother, a common Cantonese curse which would have sounded amusing coming from the toothless maw of the wizened face under any other circumstances. The Chinese were reluctant to queue for anything, least of all when they thought they were in danger, and it was every man, and woman, for themselves. He'd seen the Huey fly the full length of the grandstand dropping smoke canisters and by the time he heard the dull crumping thudding sounds it was obscured by the thick smoke. At first he thought the explosions were the sound of cars crashing in the road but they were heading in his direction and getting louder. He'd thrown himself to the ground, thinking that they were fragmentation grenades, and a dozen spectators had trampled over him. He'd put his hands over the back of his head and curled up and when the grenade had exploded close by he thought he'd been killed for sure. He lay where he was for a full thirty seconds after the explosions stopped, then he slowly uncurled and checked himself for broken bones or bleeding. The damp patches on his suit were only sweat, and he got to his knees, staring up through the smoke and trying to see what had happened to the Huey.

Through the irritating white fog he saw Paul Penycate, his superintendent's cap on the ground, waving at his uniformed men to try to stem the panic and shouting in his radio mike in Cantonese. He was telling the marksmen in the apartment blocks to fire at will. Donaldson heard the crack of high-velocity bullets and seconds later returning machine-gun fire from the roof of the grandstand.

Penycate was speaking to someone else on his radio and Donaldson went over to him. "Nothing's been taken?" the superintendent was saying in Cantonese. "All the money is secure? You're sure?"

There was a small cut on Penycate's temple, dripping blood. "There's been no robbery, no inside job," Penycate explained. "The helicopter's on the roof; God knows what they think they can do up there. There's a maintenance staircase, that's all. They use it to check the elevator switch gear and the air conditioning."

They heard more firing and a Cantonese voice crackled over Penycate's radio that one of the men on the roof had been shot. The engine note changed and a few seconds later another Cantonese voice reported that the helicopter was leaving, empty-handed.

Penycate spoke to Central headquarters and told them to alert Air Traffic Control that the helicopter was on the move. "We've got the bastards now," he hissed at Donaldson. "What goes up has to come down somewhere, and we'll be waiting for it."

The Red Pole named Willie Lee waited until the four men had climbed in the back and settled down among the canvas bags before slamming the door of the van. He jumped into the front passenger seat and nodded to the driver that everything was ready. The gate rattled up and the van drove slowly out into the afternoon sunshine.

Michael Wong watched it go and looked at his watch. There were now only two vehicles in the loading area: the last remaining van and the Mercedes in which he'd arrived. The remaining Red Poles were now loading the last van with canvas bags of cash and jewellery. Wong had pulled his men out of the control room and he'd had them seal the trussed-up guards in the main vault along with Fielding, who was now conscious but blindfolded, gagged and bound.

They were just minutes from leaving. He took the elevator down to the floor containing the safety-deposit boxes and walked to the reception area. Anthony Chung was sitting with his arms tied behind him, a bored look on his face. He grinned when he saw Wong step out of the elevator.

"Finished?" asked Chung.

"Two minutes and we'll be gone," said Wong. "Tyler has just left with his money."

Chung nodded. "Fielding?"

"He's in the vault below this, trussed up like a chicken."

Chung stood up and waited while Wong undid his bonds. He rubbed his arms to restore the circulation. "I wonder if it was worth you being tied up like this," said Wong.

"It made the guards think I was an unwilling hostage, an innocent bystander," said Chung, shrugging. "And Fielding saw me tied up. He was quite sympathetic."

Wong grinned. "Such an awfully nice chap," he said in a mock upper class English accent.

The two men laughed. Wong slid his gun out of its underarm holster. "Are you sure you want to do this?"

Chung took off his tie and pulled a large white handkerchief from the top pocket of his jacket. "It's the only way," he said. "It's the only way of convincing everybody that I'm not part of this. Just be careful you don't hit the bone."

Wong nodded. "Are you ready?"

Chung smiled and stuck out his hand. Wong shook it firmly. "It's been good, working together," said Chung. "I couldn't have done this without you."

Wong grinned. "Anthony, you've made it more than worth my while."

Chung transferred his tie and handkerchief to his right hand and held his left arm out to the side. Wong lifted his gun and shot Chung in the forearm. Chung stifled a scream by biting down hard on his lip as the bullet tore through his flesh and embedded itself in the wall by the elevator. Wong helped him take off his jacket and Chung pressed the handkerchief against the wound. Wong made a makeshift tourniquet from the tie and then eased Chung down on to the sofa. The blood flow stopped quickly and Chung nodded that he was okay.

"I'll call the police in five minutes," said Wong. "There'll be an ambulance here in fifteen."

"I'll be fine," said Chung, his face ashen. He breathed deeply, knowing that the pain would get a lot worse when the shock had worn off. "Good luck, Michael."

The supervisor looked over the controller's shoulder and studied the small flashing blip on the radar screen. The uniformed sergeant had told him of the attack on the race-track so they had given up trying to contact the helicopter, their task now to keep tabs on it and make sure that all other aircraft were kept out of its way. The blip was moving to the north-east, heading for the final approach used by aircraft landing at Kai Tak. The controller had already put two Cathay Pacific 747s into a holding pattern and he was preparing to do the same with a KLM jet. The supervisor stood and beckoned the sergeant over. "Tell your boss it looks like they're heading for Stonecutters Island."

"Stonecutters Island?" said the sergeant. "That doesn't make sense. There's nothing on Stonecutters Island."

670

Lehman flew over the road which ran around the island and climbed up into the green hills at its centre. He saw a large field with no buildings or livestock and he flew in a large circle around the area to check that there was no traffic in the air or on the tracks around the field. When he was satisfied that there was nothing nearby he eased off on the collective and circled down to the field, flaring at the last minute so that the skids brushed the grass and the Huey settled down. He left the rotors turning and unbuckled his harness. Doherty climbed out of his seat as Lehman dashed around to see how Lewis was. Horvitz shook his head. Lehman climbed up and knelt on the metal floor and looked down on his dying friend. The wound in his neck was still spurting blood despite a pad of cloth Horvitz had pushed against it. It was soaked, and so was the front of Lewis's shirt, and blood was trickling from either side of his mouth. The man's eyes refocused and he pulled back his lips as he saw Lehman above him. His teeth were red as if he'd been drinking cranberry juice. "Dan . . ." he said, his voice little more than a moan.

"I'm here, Bart," said Lehman, taking one of the man's big hands in his own. The flesh felt cold and waxy and had little strength left in it.

"Don't forget my boy," wheezed Lewis, his eyelids fluttering. Lehman felt the chilled hand squeeze once and then go still. The eyelids stopped moving and the chest shuddered once and then went as still as the hand.

"I won't, Bart. I promise," whispered Lehman.

"What's going on, Dan?" asked Horvitz, who was leaning against the back of the co-pilot's seat with his M16 on the floor next to him.

"We've been betrayed, right from the start," said Lehman.

"What are you talking about?" said Carmody.

"This whole operation has been a fake from day one. Tyler set us up so that he could betray us."

"What?" said Horvitz, stunned.

"It's true," said Doherty. "We've been monitoring the police frequencies on our radio. A man answering Tyler's description is tied up with what looks like a robbery in Kowloon. A bank job."

"That's crazy," said Horvitz. "If there was a job he wanted to do in Kowloon, he'd use us."

"Not if he expected us to get caught," said Lehman. "Not if he wanted to use us as bait."

"Bait?" said Carmody. "What do you mean, bait?"

"How many police do you think were waiting for us at the track?" said Lehman. "There were marksmen all around the place, and I bet the track was swamped with plain-clothes cops. I bet they've got the roads sealed off, too."

"Why would they seal off the roads if they knew we were using a helicopter?" asked Carmody, frowning.

"Maybe they didn't know about the Huey, just that there was going to be a robbery," said Doherty. "There's something else. Both cross-harbour tunnels have been wrecked. That effectively seals off the island. All the police there are stuck. Hell of a coincidence, wouldn't you say?"

672

"Unless someone wanted to keep all the cops on the island while they robbed a bank in Kowloon," added Lehman.

"One more thing," said Doherty. "Our warehouse has gone up in flames."

"And you think the colonel did that?" asked Carmody.

"Jesus, Larry, will you try and get the big picture on this," said Lehman. "We've just flown into a hail of lead, there was no sign of Tyler at the RV, a man answering his description is driving his car in Kowloon, our warehouse is on fire and half of Hong Kong's finest are marooned on the island."

Horvitz nodded and ran a hand through his beard. Lehman looked at his reflection in Horvitz's glasses. "What about you, Eric? You convinced?"

Horvitz nodded slowly. "Yeah. I'm convinced." He looked over Lehman's shoulder at Lewis. "We gonna get the bastard?"

"That's what we've got to decide. Larry, what about you?"

Carmody hefted his M16 on his hip. "Let's go see if we can find him. If he really is in Kowloon, I say we waste the fucker."

"Chuck?"

"You know what I think, Dan. It explains the tapping, that's for sure."

"Tapping?" said Horvitz, frowning.

"It's personal," said Lehman. "Okay, that's unanimous. Chuck, do you have an idea where we'll find him?"

"Last I heard, the cop was still following him. He'll be calling in his position, and we've got maps. We'll find him."

"Okay," said Lehman. "We go."

"Rock and roll," said Carmody, slotting in a new clip of cartridges, "let's do it."

"What about Bart?" said Doherty. "Do we leave him here?"

Horvitz looked at the body. "Not here," he said. "Over the water, that's all we can do. We don't have time for a burial." He saw Lehman looking at him. "I'm sorry, we just don't have time."

"I understand," said Lehman. He nodded. "We have to go." Doherty climbed back into his seat and began buckling his harness. Lehman walked quickly around the Huey, checking the extent of the damage. There were fresh bullet holes, more than a dozen in all, but the damage was mainly superficial. Horvitz and Carmody clambered back into the Huey and Lehman buckled himself in and ran his eyes over the instruments and gauges. When he was satisfied he pulled on the collective and took the Huey up, circling around before heading east, over the crowded streets of Kowloon.

Neil Coleman was having trouble keeping up with the Mercedes. The driver seemed to have the knack of knowing just which lane to be in, and without appearing to break the speed limit it was soon twenty cars ahead of Coleman's Jeep.

674

The Toyota was driving along the same road, heading east, and the inspector was just half a dozen vehicles ahead, stuck behind a cream and red minibus. Coleman reached for his radio mike and called Kowloon East Emergency Unit, asking them if they had any men to check out the depository. The officer on duty told him that they had just received an anonymous telephone call that a man had been shot during a robbery there and that they were already sending a team over. Coleman sighed with relief after hearing confirmation that he really was on to something. He radioed a description of the Mercedes and the Toyota and said that he was in pursuit.

"Which direction are they headed?" he was asked.

"East," he said, "towards Tolo Highway."

Coleman was told that all the cars were tied up at the cross-harbour tunnel disasters but that they'd send the first available one as back-up. Ahead of him he saw the Toyota and the Mercedes continuing along the road, towards the coast. Coleman suddenly recalled the last time he'd been in the area, when he'd masterminded the capture of the car smuggling gang. He now knew he'd been looking at the fleeing car from the wrong perspective: he'd been wondering what it was doing leaving the bank building rather than concentrating on where it was going. It was going towards the sea, and that meant a boat. And presumably that was where the other nine Mercs had gone.

He retuned his radio to 52.650 MHz, the frequency used by the Marine Police in the east of the New

Territories, and identified himself. To his surprise there was an expatriate inspector on duty, a Liverpudlian named Guy Williamson he remembered meeting once at a leaving party in the police social club. Coleman explained where he was and that he was in pursuit of a car which could have been involved in a robbery at the Kowloon and Canton Bank and which was now heading for Tolo Harbour. "Can you get a boat to Ma Liu Shui, on the coast, in about ten minutes? I'll meet it there and we should be able to cut them off once they've loaded the car."

"You're sure they're going to put it on a boat?" asked Henderson.

"There's nowhere else they can go," said Coleman. "There's a Toyota, too. He's probably arranged to meet a boat as well. Guy, how many launches have you got near the Tolo Channel at the moment?"

"The one I'm sending to pick you up, Neil. That's it at the moment. Cutbacks, you know. Smuggling is pretty low on the Commissioner's priority list."

"Yeah, tell me about it. Well, his cutbacks have probably lost us the first nine Mercs. I bet they're already in Chinese waters. How much gold do you think a top-of-the-range Merc could carry, Guy?"

"A hell of a lot, I suppose. Okay, Neil, let me talk to the boat. Ten minutes, right?"

"Ten minutes it is."

The Merc was about a quarter of a mile ahead of him, but Coleman turned off the road and headed towards Ma Liu Shui. He radioed Kowloon East Emergency Unit again and told them he was leaving the Merc and heading straight to the coast. He was told there was still no car available, but that as soon as one was free they'd head out to Tolo Highway.

Doherty pressed the trigger to activate his radio mike. "You hear that?"

"I heard it," replied Lehman. "Can you find Tolo Highway on the map?"

Doherty had a sectional chart of the airport and its surroundings, and a large-scale road map of the area. They were fluttering in the wind and he folded them as best he could and kept them pressed to his knees as he scanned them, looking for the roads they'd heard the police inspector name on the radio. Lehman flew at less than a hundred feet over the container terminals of Kwai Chung, then kept as low as he could over the apartment blocks and high-rise factories of Tsuen Wan. He increased the power so that he'd have enough height to clear the hills that separated the Kowloon peninsula from the rest of the mainland.

"Fly a heading of zero eight five," said Doherty. "We're about ten miles from them. I think. Maybe nine."

Lehman banked the Huey to the right. "Whatever you say, Chuck," he said.

He levelled the helicopter and took a quick look over his left shoulder. Horvitz was sitting at the back of the Huey, cradling his M16 in his arms like a baby. Carmody was sitting at the side, in the position the door-gunners used to favour, scanning the buildings below. They were alone in the back. The only reminder of Lewis was a red smear on the floor and a pool of glistening blood which rippled with the vibrations of the engine. When they'd left Stonecutters Island Lehman had put the Huey into a hover above the waves and Carmody and Horvitz had weighed the body down with ammunition and rolled it out of the cargo door. There had been no other way. He'd seen many shorter goodbyes in Nam.

Lehman was keeping the Huey as low as possible, hoping to minimise its radar profile, but the rugged hills were causing turbulence that had them rocking and shaking like a roller-coaster. To their right, a thousand feet or so above them, Lehman saw a 747 swooping down, its flaps extended.

"I've got it," he heard Doherty crackle in his ear. "That peak to our left is Needle Hill, and that's Beacon Hill on our right. At the end of this valley is Shatin. Before you get to the town head up to zero one five, we should see Tolo Harbour ahead of us."

"Good work, Chuck," replied Lehman. He was getting the feel of the Huey now and had begun relying less on the instruments and more on how the controls responded. He took the Huey down to within fifty feet of the ground, following the contours of the landscape and increasing his speed. Ahead he saw the high-rise blocks of Shatin, much taller than those of Kowloon because they were well away from the airport. Lehman turned until the heading indicator showed zero one five. Over his headphones he heard the English policeman talking to a Marine Police launch, confirming an RV at Ma Liu Shui.

"Have I got this right?" asked Doherty. "Tyler and this other guy are heading for the sea, and they're going to be picked up by boats?"

"That's what it sounds like to me, Chuck. And this policeman is trying to head them off in a police launch."

"Why don't they just run him off the road?" asked Doherty.

"All the cops are tied up at the track, I guess," said Lehman. He was scanning the roads below, looking for a Mercedes followed by a white Toyota. There was little traffic now that they'd left the built-up areas, and there were none of the luxury cars that they'd seen so many of in Kowloon and Hong Kong Island. Instead there were battered old trucks loaded with farm produce, minibuses and green and grey taxicabs. Below them the Huey's shadow followed them, its black silhouette flying silently along the ground.

"I think I see them," said Doherty. "Ten o'clock, about one mile away."

Lehman pushed his left pedal and eased the cyclic to the left and the nose of the Huey turned anti-clockwise. In the distance he saw a large dark blue Mercedes with darkened windows, and about three hundred yards behind it, a white Toyota. "I see it," said Lehman. "I'm going to take us closer, to get a better look. Tell the others to look out of the right side. We don't want to make any mistakes here."

As Lehman flew the Huey towards the cars, Doherty turned round and by shouting and pointing indicated that the two men in the back should see if they could identify the driver as Tyler. Horvitz gave him a thumbs-up and he and Carmody knelt by the open door, the wind streaming through their hair, their guns at the ready.

Lehman took the Huey to about fifteen feet above the ground and kept to the right of the Toyota and behind it while he matched its speed. The road was a double-lane highway which was heading almost due east, to the sea. North of the road was a hill topped by a rocky outcrop, a fringe of spindly trees around its summit. To the south were uncultivated fields with a sprinkling of small stone buildings which looked like they might once have been homes but which now stood abandoned. The road curved gently to the left and Lehman put the helicopter into a slight bank, scanning the route ahead to make sure there were no obstructions. All it would take would be one stray electricity pylon or telephone cable and it would all be over.

The Toyota was being driven at about seventy mph and the Mercedes must have been going faster because it was pulling away. The road straightened out and Lehman levelled the Huey, then he increased his airspeed so that the helicopter began to gain on the car. He took the Huey in at a forty-five-degree angle from behind, and had Doherty count off the distance in feet so that he could concentrate on the road ahead.

"Fifty, forty-five, forty," Doherty said over the radio. "It's a guy driving, Dan. It's definitely a guy. And he's got grey hair."

Lehman increased his pressure on the left foot pedal and eased the helicopter to the left, dropping down so that the skids were whizzing along just six feet above the grass. "He must have seen us," said Lehman. "He must have heard us by now."

"He hasn't turned round," said Doherty. "Thirty-five feet. Thirty." The road ahead curved to the right and the Mercedes was already around the bend, out of sight. There was a cluster of buildings on the bend, a filling station and some wooden shacks with old, rusting cars in front of them. He had only a few hundred yards before he'd have to climb to get above them, so he increased his speed and in a smooth movement drew level with the Toyota. Lehman's vision was completely obscured by Doherty and the left side of the slick but he heard Doherty's excited voice in his helmet. "It's him! It's him all right!"

The filling station loomed up and Lehman hauled on the collective and twisted it. At the same time he pulled the cyclic to the right, taking the Huey up and away from Tyler's car, soaring over the obstructions so they were once again looking down on the white Toyota. He heard the rattle of gunfire and took a quick look over his shoulder. Horvitz had his M16 to his shoulder and was firing short, controlled bursts at the car below. Empty shells scattered over the floor of the Huey.

"He's still wearing his police uniform," said Doherty over the radio. "It's definitely him."

The filling station disappeared behind them and Lehman put the Huey into a dive, swooping down on the Toyota like a hawk diving on a rabbit.

"He's got a gun!" Doherty shouted. "Pull away!"

Lehman swung the helicopter to the right and as he did a bullet smashed through the Plexiglas in front of Doherty and thudded into the electrical equipment in the roof of the cockpit. He took the Huey higher and flew over the Toyota so that they were on the opposite side to Tyler, who had accelerated and had just one hand on the steering wheel. In his right hand he had his Smith & Wesson, the gun he'd shown them all in the Eastin Hotel, and he poked it through the open window and fired a second shot as the Huey flew overhead. Lehman saw him twist in his seat and scowl, then press the button that electronically opened the windows on the passenger side of his vehicle.

Horvitz slid across the Huey and took up position at the doorway, bracing his M16 against the bulkhead and firing short sprays. Bullets thudded into the doors of the Toyota and the tail light exploded into a shower of red and orange plastic. Tyler bent low across the front seats and fired up at the helicopter, but his shot went wide and he almost lost control of the speeding car.

There was a bullet-proof metal sheet that could be raised to protect the pilot from side-on shots, but Lehman couldn't take his hands off the controls. He pressed himself back against the seat to make himself a smaller target and tried to hold the Huey steady so that Horvitz could take aim. He kept his eyes on the road ahead and tried not to look at Tyler and his powerful handgun.

He heard the rattle of Horvitz's rifle and then heard the squeal of tortured metal and when Lehman looked to his right he saw Tyler fighting to keep the Toyota on the road. Steam was pouring from under the hood and the windscreen had shattered. Both tyres on the left side of the car were tattered ribbons of rubber and the front wheel hub was grating along the road in a shower of sparks. The rear end of the car began to slide as the Toyota lost speed and for a moment it looked as if it were going to roll, but Tyler managed to straighten it up and it stopped.

Carmody was pumping his claw in the air and screaming obscenities at the Toyota, wisps of smoke feathering from the barrel of his M16. Horvitz had his M16 still at his shoulder, covering the wrecked car. Lehman pulled the helicopter around in front of the Toyota, keeping it at an angle so that both Horvitz and Carmody could cover the car with their rifles. He took the Huey lower so that its skids were only inches above the road's surface.

The hood had buckled and steam still hissed around it as water pooled under the engine. The windscreen had completely shattered and the downdraught from the thudding rotors blew glass cubes along the road like hailstones. There was no sign of Tyler. Lehman moved the cyclic a fraction of an inch to the left and edged the Huey to the side, compensating with his pedals to keep Horvitz and Carmody facing the car as he moved to check out the driver's side. The door was still closed.

Doherty pressed his radio mike switch. "You think he's hurt?"

"I don't know, Chuck," replied Lehman. "Just keep your hands clear of the controls in case I have to move fast."

He kept the Huey moving, aware of the sweat on his hands and the dryness of his mouth, trying not to blink because he knew that when Tyler moved he'd move fast. A minibus packed with gawking housewives drove up behind the Toyota and slowed, the driver watching open-mouthed. He put the vehicle in reverse and screeched away, eventually turning round and driving back towards Shatin. A chunk of shattered windscreen fell down and broke into tiny cubes on the hood and then Tyler was up, both hands on the gun which he stuck through the hole where the windscreen had been. Lehman saw him as if frozen in time: the policeman's khaki tunic, the whiteness of the knuckles as the hands tensed, the crow's feet around Tyler's eyes as he took aim, the smear of blood across his grey hair. Lehman heard the M16s crackle and he saw a flash from the barrel of Tyler's gun at the exact moment that a hole appeared in the Plexiglas in front of him. He jerked the controls to the left, at the same time as Tyler ducked out of sight. Lehman felt a cutting pain in his right arm as if someone had plunged a hot knife into his flesh and was twisting it deeper.

Both Horvitz and Carmody had missed Tyler though several shots had hit the headlights of the Toyota. "They missed him!" shouted Doherty.

Lehman felt his arm burn and the strength began to ebb out of his right hand. He clenched his fingers tighter around the cyclic and when he pulled the trigger of his radio mike switch he almost screamed, so intense was the pain in his forearm.

"I've been hit," he said.

"Where?" said Doherty, turning to look.

"Right arm," hissed Lehman, biting down his lip.

The driver's door flew open and Tyler used it as cover to scramble to the back of the Toyota. He stood up and fired a shot at the Huey. It went wide and Lehman fought to keep control of the helicopter, every movement of the cyclic making him wince. Tyler moved away from the car, keeping himself facing the nose of the Huey so that Horvitz and Carmody couldn't get a clear shot. Neither Doherty nor Lehman had guns, and Tyler knew it. He faced them with the gun held in both hands, waiting to see what they'd do next.

Lehman could feel wetness crawl down his sleeve and he knew that his right arm would soon be useless. He felt it begin to tremble and the nose of the Huey wobbled left and right. Tyler could obviously see the wound and he smiled thinly, raising the gun. Lehman wanted to turn the Huey to the side so that Carmody and Horvitz could open fire but he knew that he wouldn't be fast enough with the injured arm, that Tyler would see it coming and would have all the time in the world to put several bullets from the high-powered handgun into the cockpit. Tyler began to walk forward, towards the Huey, as Lehman fought to keep the Huey steady.

"I've got it," he heard Doherty say, and in the periphery of his vision he saw him reach for the controls.

"No!" he said, but his fingers had gone numb and he couldn't pull the mike switch. He took his right foot off the pedal and used it to press down on the second radio mike switch on the floor, but it was too late, he could feel Doherty's hands and feet take over. The Huey immediately began to rise as Doherty twisted the collective too much, then Lehman's stomach fluttered as he brought it down too hard so that it slammed into the ground and then bounced up again.

"I've got it," repeated Doherty.

Tyler stood where he was, about twenty feet in front of the hovering helicopter, and smiled as he stood, legs shoulder width apart, the gun in both hands. He took aim at Doherty, but as he fired the Huey dropped again and the shot went high. Lehman looked across at Doherty. The man seemed totally calm, totally at peace, as if unaware of the horrendous position they were in. He looked almost as if he were meditating. The nose of the Huey dipped and for one wild moment Lehman thought that Doherty was trying to attack Tyler with the whirling rotor blades. That would be fatal because the Huey would immediately lose lift and crash into the ground. He reached for the cyclic but before he could extend his injured arm Doherty had increased the power to the rotors and levelled the Huey, its skids a couple of feet off the ground.

Lehman looked at Tyler and saw that he was taking aim with the gun again. Doherty was breathing deeply, his hands and feet moving on the controls as if they had lives of their own. The tail twitched to the left and Doherty pushed his foot down on the left pedal to

686

correct it. Lehman heard the turbine roar as Doherty increased the power to the rotors and the needle flickered in the torque gauge. As the power increased, the Huey's tail twitched to the left until Doherty remembered to compensate by pushing down on the left pedal. The Huey had a natural tendency to turn in the opposite direction to the rotors. Following Newton's law that for every reaction there is an equal and opposite reaction, the Huey wanted to spin clockwise. The tail rotor pushed the tail against the torque, and it was operated by the pedals. The faster the main rotor span, the more pressure was needed on the left pedal to keep the Huey pointing straight ahead. Doherty's flying skills had gone rusty, to say the least, thought Lehman. Then, in a sudden moment of clarity that was almost telepathic, Lehman knew what Doherty was going to do. It was as if Doherty had spoken to him out loud, though he knew that no words had passed the man's lips since he'd said that he had taken the controls. Lehman slid his own feet off the pedals so that he wouldn't interfere. He looked straight ahead, willing Tyler not to fire for just another second. He saw Tyler's arms come up, and he saw him turn his head slightly to one side as he aimed, and then Doherty took his foot off the left pedal and pressed the right pedal right to the floor, increasing power because the sharp turn would cause a loss of lift.

With no pressure on the left pedal, the Huey whirled around like a top, the nose spinning to the right, the tail acting like a whip. As the Huey began to spin Tyler saw what was happening and took a step back, his gun still aimed at the cockpit. Lehman heard a crack as the bullet hit something metallic but the Huey continued to spin and all he could see were the fields and the hills beyond. The Huey dropped as it spun but Doherty pulled on the collective and the skids only scraped the surface of the road before rising into the air again. He tried to stop the spin but overcompensated with the pedals. Lehman put his feet on his own controls and helped bring the Huey into a level hover. Directly in front of them was Tyler's body lying awkwardly on the road, his head almost severed by the Huey's stinger which had slashed through the skin and tendons like a scythe. Doherty's lethal manoeuvre was one which Lehman had seen happen time and time again by accident in Nam, with over-hasty pilots turning their slicks too fast and spinning their tails into unwary grunts, with often fatal results. He'd never seen it done deliberately, though. This was a first.

Doherty regained control and gently put the Huey on the ground. He looked over at Lehman and smiled thinly.

"I've waited a long time for that," he said, forgetting to use the radio mike. Lehman understood, even though the words were lost in the beat of the rotors.

Horvitz and Carmody leapt out of the stationary Huey, their M16s at the ready, and raced over to the bloodstained body. Horvitz crouched down but it was clear that Tyler was stone dead.

Carmody went over to the crippled Toyota and peered in through the open driver's door. He called Horvitz over and pulled the rear door open.

688

Lehman clicked his foot mike switch on with his left foot. "You think you can fly her?"

"How bad are you hit?" Doherty asked.

Lehman tried to move his right arm but a bolt of pain lanced through his entire right side. "I can use the pedals, and probably help with the collective, but my right arm is useless."

Doherty took off his helmet, unbuckled himself and climbed out of the Huey, then rushed around to Lehman's side. He examined Lehman's wound, tearing the shirt open. The flesh was wet with blood but the bullet seemed to have missed the bone. Doherty lifted the arm, slowly because Lehman cried out in pain, and saw that there was an exit wound, slightly larger than where the bullet had gone in.

"It might hurt, Dan, but there's no major damage," he said. "It didn't touch the bone and it doesn't look like it tore any major blood vessels." He ripped a strip of material from Lehman's shirt and used it as a makeshift tourniquet. "Keep it tight for ten minutes or so, then loosen it for a while before tightening it," said Doherty. "Keep doing that, it should stop bleeding eventually. We'll clean and sterilise the wound later."

"Later? Where the hell are we going to go?"

"We'll head out to one of the outlying islands, west would be the best bet. It'll mean flying over Kowloon again, but if we keep low it won't be a problem."

"Think you can manage it?"

"I'll need your help, Dan. But I think between us we can do it." He tore off a piece of his own shirt and wrapped it around the still-bleeding wound. "You okay?"

"I'll be fine. Come on, let's get this bird in the air."

Horvitz had dragged a canvas bag out of the rear of the Toyota and was dragging it along the road. It was too heavy for him to lift with the M16. He heaved it to the cockpit and stood next to Doherty. "You're not going to believe this, but Tyler's car is full of gold and cash. There must be millions of dollars there. Millions. And it's American money, not Hong Kong."

Horvitz had pulled an aluminium box from the car and hefted it over his shoulder, bending double as he hefted it towards the Huey. He dropped it into the helicopter and went back for another. Doherty ran over to help him while Carmody leant his M16 against the skids and used both hands to push his box into the Huey. There were three boxes and the canvas bag, and when they were all loaded into the cargo area Doherty climbed back into his station and fastened his harness. He pulled on his helmet and clicked his mike switch. "You ready, Dan?"

Lehman nodded. He kept his feet on the pedals and slid his left hand around the collective, his right hand he let lie in his lap. As Doherty pulled the collective up and twisted it, Lehman mimicked his action. He pushed down on the left foot pedal, feeling Doherty do the same but too slowly, and he watched his own cyclic move forward. The Huey jumped forward as Doherty was too heavy-handed on the cyclic, but there was nothing Lehman could do, his right arm was effectively dead.

690

Anne Fielding's hands had grown numb, so tight were the ropes which bound her hands behind her back, but she refused to ask the men in ski-masks to loosen her bonds. She didn't want them touching her; it was bad enough the way they kept looking at her with undisguised lust in their eyes. The man in the yellow ski-mask had sat down on the edge of the double bed and he kept reaching over to stroke Debbie's legs.

Their guards were clearly waiting for something, looking at their watches and growing increasingly nervous. There was a brass alarm clock on the small table at William's side of the bed and Anne could see that four hours had passed since the men had burst into the room downstairs. She wondered what had happened to William, and to Anthony.

The telephone had rung only once, and one of the guards had held the receiver to her face. It was a worried Alex Perman, calling to see why they hadn't arrived at the racetrack. Anne had told him that they hoped to be there for the last race and not to worry.

She had racked her brains for any reason why the men in masks should want her husband. If it had been a straightforward kidnapping, there would have been no need to leave the guards behind. And surely it would have made more sense for the kidnappers to have taken her or Debbie so that William could have organised the ransom. And what could have been the reason for them to have taken Anthony? It didn't make sense. She clenched and unclenched her fingers, trying to restore the circulation.

"Something wrong?" asked the man sitting on the bed. He looked at her as he ran a gloved hand down Debbie's calf. She could see his eyes narrow behind the holes in the ski-mask, then she saw his gaze travel down over her breasts to her thighs.

She shook her head. The man was about to say something else when the phone rang, making him start. The other man walked around the bed, nodded at Anne to make sure she understood she was to speak, and picked up the receiver. He tapped her shoulder with the barrel of his gun and put the receiver to her ear.

"Hello?" she said, her heart racing.

"I want to speak to one of the men in the room with you, Mrs Fielding," said a Chinese voice. A man.

Anne pulled her head away and shook her head. "It's for you," she said.

The guard put the phone to his own ear, listened for a while, grunted, and said something in Chinese. He hung up and spoke rapidly to the other man. They both turned to look at Anne and her blood ran cold.

"Lie down," said the one by the phone. "Face down."

Anne swallowed. She felt light-headed, almost dizzy, fearful of what they intended to do. "Please," she begged, "please don't hurt me." Tears welled up in her eyes.

Gloved hands seized her and pushed her face down into the pillow. She tensed, certain that they were about to rip her clothes off. Hands grabbed her legs, lifted them, and she felt rough rope bite into her calves. Her fear subsided a little, knowing that they were unlikely to

692

try raping her with her legs tied together. A scarf, a silk Hermès she'd bought at a boutique in the Landmark, was pushed between her lips and tied behind her neck. She heard the two men muttering to each other, then her bedroom door opened and closed. She listened intently as she breathed through her nose and heard the two men clatter downstairs. A few minutes later the front door banged and the house was silent.

Coleman groaned when he saw the police launch heading towards the pier at Ma Liu Shui. It was one of the Marine Police's older vessels, a Vosper Class launch which was capable of about fourteen knots, on a good day. The smugglers, Coleman knew, usually had thirty-foot needlepoint boats with four 350 horsepower engines capable of up to eighty-five knots, and even loaded with a Mercedes and God knows how much gold and cash it would still be more than capable of outrunning the old police launch. Coleman slapped his steering wheel in frustration and cursed Guy Williamson for not sending him a Shark Cat, which could cut through the waves at more than forty-five knots. He parked the Jeep and rushed towards the pier, arriving just before the boat drew up. The Chinese constables on board were preparing to tie the launch up but he shouted that they were to go straight along the coast. He grabbed a pair of rubber-coated binoculars from one of the men and scanned the coastline as the engines kicked into life.

The men on board were armed with service handguns which would be of little use in the choppy sea, but there were two high-powered rifles on board and Coleman had the crew get them out. He asked one of the men to radio for assistance, and if possible to seal off Tolo Harbour at the channel near Sham Chung. He knew it was a futile request; the smugglers regularly used the channel to get everything from cars to video recorders out into Chinese waters, and they were masters at getting past the police patrols.

Coleman looked at his watch. They were cutting it close, he knew, because the Mercedes and the mysterious Toyota were certain to have reached Tolo Highway already. He motioned for the captain to speed up the launch and to get closer in to the land. He was beginning to feel queasy from the unaccustomed motion of the boat and he put down the glasses and took deep breaths of the cool, salty air. The sky overhead was a clear blue with only the faintest feathers of cloud. Seagulls called and circled overhead, lazily flapping their wings in the breeze.

When Coleman put the glasses to his eyes he saw a boat moored next to a short, stubby pier in the distance. The boat was rising and falling in the waves, and it seemed to be low in the water. There was a mobile crane, mounted on the back of a truck, and its lifting arm was extended over the launch. At first Coleman couldn't see what was being loaded but as the police launch crested a wave he was suddenly able to see the large Mercedes, chains wrapped around it to provide a cradle as it was lowered into place. The police launch dropped down into a trough and the boat and car disappeared from sight.

He pointed in the general direction of the pier and shouted at the captain to take the launch in. As the launch rose again he scanned the coastal road but he could see no sign of the Toyota.

"They're moving," said one of the Marine police.

Coleman craned his neck and saw the boat moving slowly away from the pier.

"Try to cut them off!" Coleman yelled. The launch turned to the right and moved to intercept the vessel. As they got closer Coleman could see that the high-powered boat had steel cladding on the sides and a cockpit of thick glass which he'd have been willing to bet a year's salary was bullet-proof.

"Hail them," he told one of the constables. The man picked up a mike and his amplified voice cut over the rumble of the launch's engines. The boat ignored the Cantonese commands and plumes of white water gushed from its stern.

"Fire a warning shot," Coleman ordered.

One of the policemen shouldered a rifle and fired a single shot, but it had as little effect as the verbal warning.

"Where the hell is the back-up?" Coleman shouted. The man on the radio shrugged and said that they were trying their best. Coleman heard sirens and he scanned the shoreline with his binoculars. He saw three police cars, lights flashing, arrive at the pier. The driver of the mobile crane and three other men tried to escape on foot and he heard the crack of pistol shots.

The smugglers' boat pulled away at an angle to the police launch, and it clearly had no intention of stopping. He told the constables to try to disable the boat's engines and they began to fire their rifles, but Coleman could see the bullets spark harmlessly off the steel plates either side of the boat. It pulled away from the slow-moving police launch and headed through the Tolo Channel.

"Keep after them!" Coleman shouted. "At least we can radio their position to base. Any joy with the back-up?"

"We have a Sea Raider at Crescent Island," replied the radio man.

"That's better than nothing," said Coleman. "Call them up, tell them the boat is heading their way."

Crescent Island was around the corner from Bluff Head at the tip of the channel where it opened out into Mirs Bay. The thirty-knot inflatable Sea Raider stood a better chance of cutting off the smugglers' boat, which was making good speed but nowhere near the eighty-five knots he'd expected. They were still in with a chance.

The flight over the tower blocks of Kowloon was bumpy in the extreme. Without being able to hold the cyclic, Lehman wasn't able to tell if it was the up- and down-draughts caused by the wind around the buildings or Doherty's unfamiliar hands on the controls which were the cause of the rough ride. Doherty had trouble keeping the Huey on a straight heading. Each time he changed the power setting by twisting the collective he forgot to compensate on the pedals, so Lehman was constantly trying to anticipate his movements, and failing miserably. The Huey veered left, then right, like an ailing fish, and Lehman was relieved that Doherty kept the Huey well above the shops, hotels and offices below. It meant that the Huey would be clearly visible on the radar screens at Kai Tak, but at least there was no danger of them hitting a stray television aerial. Doherty had folded the chart of Hong Kong and the surrounding sea over his left leg and he kept looking down at it and cross-checking with his heading indicator. There was a sprinkling of small islands, most with Chinese names, and then further west was a much larger landmass, bigger even than Hong Kong Island, which was shown as Lantau Island on the chart. Beyond Lantau were more islands and Doherty said he thought it best to try one of them; hopefully they'd be beyond the range of Kai Tak's radar and so far from Hong Kong that they'd be unoccupied.

Lehman was finding it progressively harder to control the swinging motions of the Huey and he decided to speak to Doherty about it. He took his left foot off the pedal and went to press the foot mike button. Immediately the nose of the Huey swung sharply to the right.

"Chuck, you're forgetting to compensate for the torque," warned Lehman.

Doherty shook his head and pressed his mike trigger. "It's not me, Dan, honest. My pedals aren't responding as they should."

Lehman scanned the instruments with a growing sense of alarm. His eyes fixed on the gauge which indicated the transmission fluid level in the tail rotor intermediate gearbox, at the end of the tail assembly. It was in the red.

Lehman clicked his foot mike on again. "No oil in the forty-five-degree gearbox," he said. "We must have taken a bullet there. It's going to seize at any time."

Without oil the gears would soon overheat and lock solid or even fly apart, a catastrophic failure that would have only one result. Without the tail rotor working the Huey would spin hopelessly out of control, unable even to autorotate to the ground.

"Chuck, we've got to descend, now!"

"There's nowhere to land," shouted Doherty. Lantau Island was a mile behind them and they were less than 200 feet above the choppy waves.

"Reduce power to cut down the torque," said Lehman.

Doherty hesitated so Lehman twisted his own throttle with his uninjured left arm. The turbine whistle quietened, and almost immediately they heard a metallic grating noise like nuts and bolts in a blender and the Huey began to spin, not as fast as when Doherty had killed Tyler but fast enough to make Lehman nauseated.

"I can't hold it!" shouted Doherty. "I'm losing it! I'm losing it."

Lehman pressed down on his left pedal with all his might but it had no effect. The Huey banked sharply to the right and began to slide. Below him Lehman saw the grey, churning sea and out of the corner of his eye a small freighter, its deck loaded with wooden crates. The cyclic was jerking backwards and forwards between Lehman's legs and he gritted his teeth and grabbed for it with his right arm. He felt the muscles in his upper arm scream and when the cyclic tugged at his fingers he felt as if he was going to pass out. The wound had just about stopped bleeding but the movement of the cyclic ripped it open again and he felt dampness ooze down his arm. He cut the power completely, hoping that would slow down the spinning and he pumped the left pedal until his leg ached. He forced himself to ignore the jagged bolts of agony in his arm as he pushed the cyclic to the left, screaming in pain and frustration as the sea rushed up towards him.

The small green blip on the radar screen winked out. "They're down," said the air traffic controller.

The supervisor stood behind him, his arms folded across his chest. "Any land near their last position?"

The controller shook his head. "They were at least a mile north-west of Lantau. There's nothing there but sea."

"I wonder what the hell they were playing at?" mused the supervisor. They'd watched the helicopter on the screen as it flew across the harbour to Happy Valley, where it had disappeared from the screens for several minutes. It had reappeared and flown to Stonecutters Island where it had landed for almost five minutes. The police sergeant had radioed Marine Police to send a launch to the island, but before they could respond the controller had called out that the helicopter was on the move again. It flew across Kowloon causing the controllers to put several inbound jets into holding patterns and then disappeared off the screens in the New Territories. The police sergeant had radioed its last position to police at Shatin, but shortly afterwards it had taken to the air again, flying an erratic course to the north of the airport. They'd asked for a visual from a Cathay Pacific 737 and had been told that the helicopter seemed to be in trouble.

The supervisor turned to the police sergeant. "They've gone down, into the sea," he said. "They hit the water pretty hard. I doubt there'll be any survivors. Helicopters aren't designed to float."

The smugglers reached Bluff Head and turned north, heading for Chinese waters. The police launch was about a mile behind and Coleman was having a hard time keeping it in sight, even with the high-powered binoculars.

The radio man shouted to Coleman over the roar of the engines. "We have two Shark Cats on the way," he called. "They're off Robinson Island."

Coleman pumped his fist in the air. The Shark Cats were the Marine Police's fastest launches. He offered a silent prayer of thanks to Guy Williamson and whichever God it was who looked after policemen. Robinson Island was about five miles north-west of Bluff Head and the launches there would be in a perfect position to intercept the smugglers.

The police launch rounded the peninsula and the waves grew higher, spray slapped over the cockpit and Coleman had to wipe the lenses of his binoculars. His shirt was soaked in salt water but the day was hot and the sensation wasn't unpleasant. The launch was thrown around by the waves and Coleman had to keep one hand on the guard rail for balance. He turned to the policeman next to him. "Can you see them?"

The young Chinese constable screwed up his eyes. Like Coleman, he was drenched. He shook his head. "Sea's too rough," he said.

"Keep the same heading," said Coleman, "with any luck they'll turn back, then head east when they see the Shark Cats."

The radio operator shouted over to attract Coleman's attention. "They have it in sight, the boat is turning back."

"Yes!" yelled Coleman. He put the binoculars back to his eyes and panned across the waves. In the far distance he saw the needle-point boat crest a wave, the Mercedes clearly visible on the deck, then it nosedived down and was gone. A second later it reappeared, plumes of spray crashing over its glass cockpit. Coleman could make out three men crouched behind the glass plates, one of them at the wheel, one with a walkie-talkie pressed to his ear, the third looking over his shoulder at the pursuing Shark Cats.

The smugglers' boat began to turn in the water, trying to double back to Chinese waters, but the Shark Cats were anticipating the manoeuvre and moved to block it. In the distance he heard the crack of rifle shots.

All thoughts of his heaving stomach were gone as Coleman urged the captain on, banging his fist on the guard rail.

"We're getting close to Chinese waters," warned the constable. "We don't have the authority to cross over."

"Let's just get the bastards," said Coleman, his eyes fixed on the fleeing boat.

"We must not cross the boundary," pressed the constable, but Coleman ignored him.

The Shark Cats were playing cat and mouse with the smugglers, keeping between their boat and the mainland, darting to and fro and firing sporadic bursts at the steel-lined hull. The smugglers made an attempt to get by to the west but one of the Shark Cats got ahead and it turned back, a white wake of foaming water behind it.

Suddenly Coleman heard a loud bang and something exploded a hundred yards ahead of the police launch, kicking up a spout of water twice the height of a man. "What the hell was that?" he shouted.

One of the constables pointed to a large grey launch to the north, about half a mile away. It was flying a red Chinese flag and had two deck-mounted guns, both pointed in their direction. Coleman focused his binoculars on the bridge. He could see four men wearing the uniforms and peaked caps of the People's Armed Police. On the deck below were a dozen men, several of them carrying AK-47 assault rifles. The launch was steaming in their direction, carving cleanly through the waves. The Shark Cats had given up their chase and were following the Chinese launch like ducklings paddling after their mother.

Coleman heard the hiss and crackle of a loudspeaker, then a strident Chinese voice barked across the waves.

702

It was Mandarin Chinese and he didn't understand a word. He turned to the constable at his shoulder. "What do they want?" he asked.

"They say we are in Chinese waters and we must go back."

"Tell them we're in pursuit of smugglers," said Coleman.

"It will do no good," said the constable.

"Tell them!" Coleman insisted.

The constable raised a loudhailer to his lips and spoke to the Chinese launch, which was now less than 200 yards away. When they replied the man lowered the loudhailer. "They say they will deal with the smugglers. They say we must turn back."

In the far distance behind the Chinese gunboat, Coleman could see the smugglers speeding away, totally unchallenged.

"They're getting away," Coleman protested, pointing at the fleeing boat. "Tell them to go after the smugglers. Tell them we'll wait here. They're wasting time!"

The constable shrugged and translated Coleman's outburst. Coleman could tell from the tone of the reply that his request was being denied. "They say we must go," said the constable. "They say that if we do not turn back, the next shot will be across our bows. The one after that will sink us. I think they mean what they say, Inspector Coleman. We are in their waters, after all."

"Damn!" cursed Coleman, slamming his fist into the guard rail hard enough to graze his knuckles. The two Shark Cats drew alongside his launch, waiting for his instructions. He looked over at the stone-faced men cradling their AK-47s, and at the officers on the bridge. They returned his stare and Coleman knew without a shadow of a doubt that they meant what they said.

"Turn back," he said to the men. "There's nothing else we can do." He raised his fist to his mouth and licked the bruised flesh over his knuckles. The launch turned in the water and headed for Hong Kong, the Shark Cats either side. Coleman didn't look back.

The lines began forming outside branches of the Kowloon and Canton Bank before the sun had set. News of the robbery was broken by RTHK on its six o'clock news programme and by nine o'clock both of the colony's television stations had camera crews outside the depository in Kowloon and were showing footage of streams of uniformed police and technicians in overalls passing in and out of the building. William Fielding had been taken to hospital suffering from concussion but a harassed Alex Perman gave an impromptu press conference in which he said that the bank wouldn't be able to say how much had been stolen until they had carried out a full inventory of the vaults. A pushy Chinese interviewer had asked if sixty million US dollars would be a fair estimate and Perman had stuttered and shrugged and said he had no way of knowing.

By nine-thirty every one of the bank's 410 automatic teller machines had been drained of cash. An armoured car was sent out to branches in Shatin to replenish the empty machines but it was attacked by a mob wielding sticks and hatchets and it fled. The bank's head of security, George Ballantine, ordered that no more attempts were to be made to stock up the ATMs. In every one of its branches faxes poured in with instructions to close accounts or to transfer funds overseas.

A small group of the bank's directors began telephoning managers and ordered them to gain access to their branches and to calm investors if possible. Several managers were severely beaten by angry customers. A mob stole the keys from one of them as he tried to get inside his branch in Mong Kok. They looted the branch, smashed its counters and office equipment, and broke into the branch's vault.

Some 50,000 dollars were taken and several people were trampled in the crush. Police with electrified batons, stun guns and riot shields broke up the mob and arrested twenty-three men and women.

Petrol bombs were thrown at a branch in Sham Shui Po and police had to use a water-cannon to break up a howling mob demanding their money. By midnight there were armed police standing outside all of the bank's branches and more than two hundred rioters had been arrested. Following the police clampdown and assurances from the bank that all the branches would be open for business on Monday morning, the crowds began to quieten down and orderly lines formed on the sidewalks with people squatting down and preparing to wait throughout the night. By midnight there was a healthy trade in places in the queue, with those at the front offering to give up their spots for 5,000 dollars. Hawkers began to set up their stalls offering fried food and won ton soup at treble the daytime prices.

The Governor pulled the quilt over his head but the ringing was insistent. He rubbed his eyes and reached for the gold-rimmed spectacles on his bedside table. His wife snored quietly by his side. Ringing telephones never woke her at night: she used to joke that after coping with night feeds for their three children she deserved all the sleep she could get now that motherhood was behind her.

He sat up, slipped the spectacles on, and picked up the receiver. He looked at the alarm clock next to the phone. It was six o'clock in the morning and he'd only been in bed for two hours following an all-night meeting with his Financial Secretary, Banking Commissioner and Police Commissioner.

The voice that spoke to him was Chinese, using slow English, a perceptible pause between each word as if a computer were speaking. The man politely introduced himself but the Governor already knew who it was. There was no mistaking the calculated enunciation of the director of Xinhua, the New China News Agency. The Chinese government had no official diplomatic representative in Hong Kong, but the news agency acted as a de facto embassy, and all communications routed through its spokesman came straight from Beijing. The director was the agency's highest-ranking official and he was, to all intents and purposes, China's ambassador in the colony. He apologised profusely for wakening the Governor but said that he had an urgent matter to discuss. The Governor was in no doubt as to the matter in question.

"It concerns the looting of the Kowloon and Canton Bank," said the director in his measured, emotionless voice.

"We are all very concerned, of course," said the Governor, briskly. "We are doing everything we can to control the situation."

"We are especially concerned about an interview your Commissioner of Banking gave to a Chinese journalist this evening," the director continued, as if the Governor hadn't spoken. "He intimated that the administration was considering the use of the exchange fund to support the Kowloon and Canton Bank. Is that the case?"

The Governor sighed. It sometimes seemed that half the Chinese journalists in Hong Kong were working for Beijing and not their own newspapers. "That is certainly one option under consideration," he said slowly. In fact, it was just about the only concrete suggestion that had emerged after five hours of talks.

"You see, Governor, we feel that the use of the exchange fund should be confined to original intention, and that is to support the link between the US dollar and the Hong Kong currency. We feel it unwise to use the fund for any other purpose."

The Hong Kong dollar was linked to the American currency at the rate of 7.8 HK dollars for every one US dollar, and the government used a huge cash reserve, built up over many years, to maintain that link by intervening on the foreign exchange markets whenever the link came under pressure. "I think the administration would take the view that maintaining the stability of Hong Kong's banking system is in effect maintaining the strength of our currency," said the Governor.

"We would differ," said the director. "We regard the exchange fund as a substantial part of the assets of Hong Kong, assets which will become the property of the People's Republic of China after 1997. We do not wish those assets to be used to support a capitalist bank which has allowed itself to get into trouble. Hong Kong has made much of its independence and its capitalist ways. We do not now want to see a capitalist bank rescued by Chinese money. Let the bank seek the help of its fellow financial organisations, or go to its shareholders for assistance. You do not see the Seven Sisters, the banks that form the Bank of China Group, asking our government for assistance when times are hard. You do not see the Cathay Bank holding out a begging bowl. The Chinese banks stand by themselves."

"Director, I think you do not fully appreciate what the use of the exchange fund entails," said the Governor. His wife snored, rolled over, and tugged the quilt. He allowed it to slide over his legs. "It would be a loan, paid back in full. With interest. It would be a temporary device until we can find some way of stabilising the bank, possibly by arranging a takeover or a merger."

"I understand perfectly," said the director. "We fully endorse the idea of a takeover, but I repeat that we do not wish the exchange fund to be used in such a manner. We do not want to see a repeat of the bad feeling that was caused by the lack of consultation over the airport project."

The Governor ran his hand through his greying hair. His administration was still smarting over the Chinese reaction to the colony's plan to build a new airport on one of the outlying islands as a replacement for Kai Tak, which had just about reached its operating limits. Beijing had at first threatened to veto the project, and had only allowed it to go ahead once it was given authority to award major contracts and franchises over the head of the Hong Kong administration. The agreement was negotiated directly with London and was a massive slap in the face for the colony's bureaucrats, as well as setting a precedent for the Chinese. The British government wanted the handover to proceed as smoothly as possible, and was scared to death of civil revolt and bloodshed. In order to achieve that it had allowed China gradually to backtrack on many of its promises made in the 1984 joint declaration under which Hong Kong was guaranteed an elected legislature and full autonomy, except in defence and foreign affairs, after the handover. Under Chinese pressure the government had already refused full democratic elections of the legislature and was now giving the Beijing cadres a growing say in the affairs of the colony prior to 1997.

"Would such a loan from the exchange fund be possible if the administration were to consult with the Chinese government?" asked the Governor. "It would then, of course, be made clear that the rescue had the backing of China, that China was keen to see the stability of the Hong Kong banking system maintained." In other words, the Governor thought wryly, so that China could claim the credit.

"No, it would not," said the director, dashing the Governor's hopes.

He decided to try a different tack. "The director is of course aware of the localised outbreaks of discontent we have experienced," he said. "The violence is a result of customers of the bank being concerned about their savings. There is a risk that if we do not act quickly to support the Kowloon and Canton Bank, there will be further outbreaks of disorder. There is an added complication in that many of the assets in the looted safety-deposit boxes had been used as security against borrowings which had in turn been invested in the stock market."

There was no response and for a moment the Governor thought that the connection had been cut. Eventually he heard a grunt, so he continued. "Investors lodged certificates of deposit, gold and other valuables, with the bank and the bank in turn loaned them money to buy shares. Now that the contents of the boxes have been stolen, the investors will be forced to sell their shares. If that happens, the Hang Seng Index will fall sharply, perhaps as sharply as it fell during the 1987 worldwide stock market crash. It could be the final blow for Hong Kong, Director. If the stock market does indeed crash, Hong Kong's reputation as a financial centre may be irrevocably damaged. And such a collapse would hit every investor in Hong Kong, not just the bank's customers. I am told that sell orders are already piling up in stockbrokers' offices. There will be a rout when the market opens later this morning. Unless we act."

"I understand, but I repeat that we do not wish the exchange fund to be used to support the bank."

"Director, I must not be making myself clear. If the bank fails, and if the market crashes, there will be civil disorder of the like never seen before in Hong Kong, coming at a time when our police force is in a weakened state. We will be stretched to the limit to contain the discontent."

"We have already considered that eventuality," said the director, calmly. "We are moving a division of the People's Liberation Army to the outskirts of Guangdong. If necessary they will be used to maintain law and order in the colony."

"You can't do that!" exclaimed the Governor without thinking.

"We can, and if necessary we will," said the director, unaffected by the Governor's undiplomatic outburst. "Do not forget that you are only tenants of Hong Kong, we are the landlords. If a tenant does not take care of the property, a landlord has the right to move to make sure that there is no damage. You are also aware how close we came to sending in troops during the stock market crash of 1987. We will do everything we have to do in order to maintain law and order in Hong Kong. Am I making myself clear?"

"Yes, perfectly," said the Governor.

"The Kowloon and Canton Bank must put its own affairs in order," said the director. "That is an end to it.

Good night, Governor, and my sincere apologies for awakening you."

"Good morning," said the Governor pointedly. The line went dead. His wife lay curled up in the foetal position, snoring quietly, the quilt pulled around her like a shroud. The Governor dialled the number of the Financial Secretary, shaking his head in bewilderment.

An angry crowd gathered outside the headquarters of the Kowloon and Canton Bank at six o'clock in the morning, shouting slogans and waving banners. An effigy of William Fielding was soaked in petrol and set on fire. When police moved in with fire extinguishers, the demonstrators started breaking up paving stones and throwing them. One officer was taken to hospital with a cut eye and three demonstrators were injured when the police moved in with stun guns and batons. More than a dozen demonstrators sat in a circle outside the bank building and announced they were going on a hunger strike until they received their money. The Police Commissioner ordered all his men to report for duty, no matter what their status. All leave was cancelled, all men were to work around the clock until further notice. Two hundred constables in riot gear were posted outside the bank's headquarters. Rumours that the government was refusing to bail out the bank spread like wildfire, and several branches in the New Territories reported that their windows had been broken. The Police Commissioner doubled the guard on his home, just to be on the safe side.

William Fielding arrived in his office at seven o'clock, three hours before his branches were due to open. He had needed three stitches on his forehead and they'd been covered with a large sticking plaster. His head throbbed and he had trouble focusing but he'd discharged himself from hospital and called an emergency meeting of his directors, his head of security and the bank's public relations advisers. Following Alex Perman's dismal performance on television after the robbery, Fielding had insisted on outside consultants being called in. They were now into crisis public relations and Alex Perman was clearly out of his depth.

Fielding had needed a police escort to get into the building, and his car had been kicked and spat on. Two policemen had gone with him into the building and ridden up in the elevator with him. Both had been armed. The boardroom had been prepared — notepads and pens distributed around the long, oval mahogany table, and crystal decanters of water set in the centre, with upturned crystal tumblers at each place setting. Most of the directors were there. George Ballantine nodded a greeting and Alex Perman was flanked by two representatives of the public relations firm. Charles Devlin got up from his chair and went over to Fielding as he sat down at the head of the table.

"William, are you sure you should be out of the hospital? You look terrible."

Devlin had been one of the first to visit Fielding in the hospital. He'd also helped Anne and Debbie deal with the police investigating the break-in at their house.

"I'll be okay, Charlie, but thanks for your concern. And thanks for taking care of Anne."

"Is she okay?"

"She's in shock, the doctor's given her a tranquilliser."

"What about the man they took with you?"

"Anthony Chung? He's still in hospital. It seems the bullet did more damage than they thought at first. He might lose his arm."

"Poor devil," sympathised Devlin. "You're lucky they didn't shoot you, I guess."

Fielding put his hand to his injured head and winced. "Lucky isn't exactly how I feel, Charlie, but I know what you mean."

Devlin went back to his seat and the remaining directors arrived and took their places. Fielding opened the meeting, and quickly went over the events of the previous eighteen hours. The story of the depository raid had been all over the front pages of the morning papers, along with the abortive robbery at the racetrack. None of the newspapers, English or Chinese, reported the clash between Hong Kong and Chinese police at sea. The *South China Morning Post* and the *Hong Kong Standard* had both carried editorials calling on the government to use the exchange fund to support the bank, and there were unattributed quotes in their news stories suggesting that the Banking Commissioner would announce such a rescue before the stock exchange started trading. The *Hong Kong Economic Journal* had managed to get quotes from the Banking Commissioner saying he planned to use the fund, but the Chinese paper also suggested that Beijing was unhappy with his proposal. Several of the Chinese papers had investigated the effect the robbery would have on the stock exchange. They had discovered that two of Hong Kong's most aggressive corporate raiders had substantial loans from the bank, backed by gold deposits, which they had used to fund several major acquisitions. The shares were certain to be sold in early trading, the papers warned, and there were quotes from analysts suggesting that share prices could plunge by as much as forty per cent. Estimates of how much had been taken in the robbery varied from 700 million to 1,000 million HK dollars.

"George, do we have a figure on how much was taken?" Fielding asked Ballantine.

George Ballantine looked at him with bleary, reddened eyes. He had had very little sleep, like most of the men around the table. "Virtually all our gold stocks were taken, equivalent to 426 million HK dollars at Friday's closing price. The foreign exchange stocks they took amount to about 125 million HK dollars, depending on the exchange rates. As to the contents of the safety-deposit boxes, well, it's anybody's guess. We've a queue half a mile long outside the depository. We've had clerks taking statements from as many people as we can, but most are reluctant to say what was in their boxes until they know whether they've been broken into or not. It's hundreds of millions of dollars, that's for sure. Tens of millions of pounds."

Fielding nodded. "What about our cash flow? Assuming there is a run on the bank, what shape are we in to pay out?"

The director in charge of operations tapped his pen on his notepad. "We have up to 100,000 HK dollars cash in each branch, minimum. Our larger branches have up to 500,000 HK dollars. That sounds a lot but it could go very quickly once people start closing their accounts. The ATMs alone can pay out 120,000 HK dollars every hour, and we have 410 of them. Assuming they're all in operation, that's almost fifty million HK dollars an hour."

There were whistles of disbelief from around the table.

Fielding nodded. "I suggest that we don't replenish the ATMs," he said, and there were several nods of agreement. "What about getting cash to the branches?"

The director tapped his pen again. "We have sixty-three armoured cars and vans, of which eighteen are out of service. That leaves forty-five, but Personnel tells me we have only thirty-eight drivers."

"We can commandeer more drivers if necessary," said Fielding.

"In that case we have forty-five vans and cars. If it takes each car thirty minutes to make a delivery, it will take just two hours to resupply each branch. I would add, however, that following last night's events, we will need extra security when deliveries are taking place."

George Ballantine coughed. "If I may interrupt, Mr Chairman, security won't be a problem. I have arranged with the police for armed guards as and when

716

we deliver, and I have brought in two private security firms. We will cope."

"Good, good," said Fielding. "The only problem is, do we have enough cash. Charlie?"

Devlin exhaled deeply. "That depends on what the Banking Commissioner decides," he said. "If he comes through and supports us with the exchange fund, we can borrow all we need from the Hongkong and Shanghai Bank and from Standard Chartered. Once the crowds see we're paying out, confidence will soon return."

Fielding nodded. "I hope to hear from the Banking Commissioner within the hour," he said. "I think one of our main priorities must be to inform our customers what is happening. Alex, I want you to arrange radio and television interviews for nine o'clock, and I want posters printed so that we can stick them up on the windows. In Chinese, of course. They should explain what is happening and that their money is safe."

One of the public relations consultants raised a hand. Fielding smiled at his schoolroom approach and asked him to speak.

"I think you should consider the international ramifications of this," said a suave man in his forties, with slicked-back hair and horn-rimmed spectacles. "I suggest you call in the major foreign correspondents — *The Times*, the *Financial Times*, the *Independent*, *Wall Street Journal*, *New York Times*. Get them here and speak to them personally. You're going to need all the overseas support you can get."

"Good idea," said Fielding. "Get on to it, will you, Alex?"

Perman nodded and scribbled on his notepad.

"I'd recommend seeing the analysts, too. They're going to want to know what effect this is likely to have on the share price, short and long term."

"Good thinking," said Fielding. "Charlie, can you organise that? Get one of your boys in corporate finance to talk to them as soon as possible. If the small investors sell, maybe we can persuade the institutions to buy."

"Will do," said Devlin.

A telephone rang just behind Fielding and he turned round in his chair and picked up the receiver. It was his secretary, telling him that the Banking Commissioner was on the line.

"Put him on, Faith," Fielding said, slumping back in his chair. His head was throbbing worse than ever, and it felt as if the stitches were cutting into his skin. As he listened to the voice at the other end of the line, his face went grey and he closed his eyes. The men around the table could tell it was bad news even before Fielding replaced the receiver and addressed them.

"Gentlemen, I'm afraid I have to tell you that there will be no support from the Banking Commissioner. The Governor has ruled out using the exchange fund to support the bank."

There was a chorus of dismay from around the table, and the sound of hands being slapped against the wood. "That can't be right," said one director. Another sat with his head in his hands.

"There's no need for me to tell you that this puts a totally different complexion on the situation," said Fielding. "Without government support we will be unlikely to find anyone willing to lend us cash to see us over the next few days."

"Did they say why?" asked Devlin.

Fielding shook his aching head. "No, but reading between the lines, I think the Chinese government has vetoed it. Ever since they won the airport fiasco they've been dying to flex their political muscles again. I think they want us to go to the wall to prove a point. It's up to us to prove them wrong. Ideas, gentlemen?"

Fielding looked at a wall of blank faces. He raised his eyebrows but the action caused him to flinch with pain. "Gentlemen?" he repeated.

It was Devlin who spoke first. "I can go to the Hongkong and Shanghai and Standard Chartered and see if they'll help us without a government guarantee. I don't hold out much hope, though."

"A rights issue?" said one of the directors.

"With the share price in free fall?" said Devlin scornfully.

"What about asking one of the Seven Sisters for help? Or the Cathay Bank?" said another director.

"You think the Chinese would bail out a gweilo bank?" asked Fielding. "I'd have thought they would take great pleasure in seeing us go under. Especially as most of the depositors who take their funds from our accounts will be putting them straight back into the Bank of China."

The telephone rang and Fielding turned to answer it. It was his secretary again. Fielding nodded as he spoke to her and replaced the receiver.

"Gentlemen, it appears I have visitors. Charles, please chair the meeting in my absence." Fielding eased himself out of his chair and walked slowly to the door of the boardroom, his shoulders sagging as if he carried the weight of the world on them.

Neil Coleman could think of a million things he'd rather be doing than standing in front of the headquarters of the Kowloon and Canton Bank in full riot gear, but he hadn't been given the choice. Every constable and officer had been called in for duty and assigned to one or other of the bank's branches. It didn't matter in the least to his superiors that the previous day Coleman had been chasing a Mercedes loaded with the bank's gold and had almost been blown up by a Chinese gunboat. The priority now was to make sure that a lid was kept on the volatile Chinese population until the banking system had been stabilised by whatever means necessary. Coleman knew that the Chinese had every reason not to trust the colony's British administrators. The last time the Banking Commissioner had said there was no need to panic was at the time of the BCCI scandal in 1991, and thousands of Hong Kong investors had lost their savings by taking the administration at its word. And they remembered, too, the way the Stock Exchange had shut its doors for four days during the worldwide stock market crash in 1987, leaving local investors locked into a falling market while the rest of the world sold shares as if there were no tomorrow. It was eight o'clock in the morning and the queue of anxious investors wound twice around the base of the building and for several hundred yards down Queen's Road. There were 200 men in riot gear, with four expatriate inspectors and a superintendent. Two water-cannons were standing by and there were five dark blue minibuses containing men with the force's latest acquisitions — electronic riot shields which could deliver more than 50,000 volts of electricity. All the men had been issued with 120,000 volt stun guns and there were more than a dozen constables standing close to the superintendent with CS gas grenades.

Like the rest of the men, Coleman was wearing black overalls and a crash helmet with a protective visor and thick rubber boots. His gun was holstered on his side, a thin link chain connecting its butt to the belt. He was soaked with sweat and unable to wipe his brow.

Coleman had been told to write a full report on Sunday's off-duty activities, and he'd had to do more than a little creative writing. There had been no way he could explain why he had been hanging around outside William Fielding's house on raceday, or why he had followed Chung and Fielding to the depository. He'd been economical with the truth and said that he'd been driving by the depository when he'd seen a Mercedes leave, and that it was the car and its darkened windows which had sparked his interest. His report said that he'd waited outside the depository for just half an hour before he called it in and went off in pursuit of the

Mercedes and the Toyota. Nobody had so far queried his description of Sunday's events and if everything worked out he'd end up a hero with a Commissioner's commendation.

He'd assumed that CID would want him to help with their investigation into the robbery, but two Chinese detectives had brusquely told him that he'd be interviewed in due course and that his statement was all they needed at present. He'd only been in bed for five hours when he was ordered to report to Wan Chai police station where he'd been issued with riot gear. When Coleman had been pursuing the Mercedes through the New Territories he'd had no idea that he was involved in something that could lead to major riots and violence in the city. The Chinese seemed to be reacting to the robbery with far more emotion than they had responded to the killings in Tiananmen Square. Then there had been marches, slogans politely shouted and token hunger strikes, but there had been no riots, no petrol bombs, no attacks on police and buildings. When it came down to it, the Chinese cared more about hard cash than democracy, Coleman thought, hefting his long riot baton in his hands.

A young Chinese man standing in line was talking earnestly to an old woman with an empty shopping bag. He was shaking his head but eventually he nodded and she handed over a bunch of yellow notes and he allowed her to take his place in the queue. The price for a spot near the front had now grown to 8,000 HK dollars.

The superintendent came over and stood by Coleman's shoulder. "I've just heard that the government has ruled out a rescue," he said out of the corner of his mouth. "We're bringing more men in. These people are going to erupt when they find out."

Faith was standing by her desk, a worried expression on her face. "William, there are three representatives from the Cathay Bank." She nodded over to the reception area and Fielding looked over to see three men sitting with straight backs and placid faces. She gave him three simple business cards. Each had the logo of the Cathay Bank, one of the most powerful Chinese financial institutions. All three men held the position of director. Fielding went over and introduced himself. They stood up as they saw him coming and each politely shook hands with him. The man in the middle of the trio was the oldest, a short man in a Mao-style black suit, the style simple but the workmanship first class, as if a Savile Row tailor had been commissioned to stitch the material. On the left was a good-looking Chinese man in his mid-thirties who wore a made-to-measure pinstripe suit and carried a slim black briefcase. He spoke perfect English with a mid-American accent and he introduced his two companions to Fielding. The man on the right of the group was mainland Chinese, wearing an ill-fitting grey suit and a white shirt with a worn collar. One of his front teeth was gold and it glinted as he smiled and bowed his head.

The man with the American accent did most of the talking, but it was clear he was deferring to the two older men. He explained that they had come to offer their support during the Kowloon and Canton Bank's period of uncertainty. Fielding asked if they wished to address the whole board but he was told that this was a personal offer and they wished to speak only with him.

Fielding showed them into his office while Faith arranged three high-backed chairs in front of Fielding's desk. Faith offered the men refreshments but they all shook their heads. She closed the door quietly behind her as Fielding took his seat. He linked the fingers of his well-manicured hands across his blotter and looked at his three visitors expectantly. The man with the American accent looked to his left and to his right and received almost imperceptible nods from both his companions.

"Mr Fielding, we are here to make you an offer which will maintain the integrity of the Kowloon and Canton Bank, and which will ensure there is no slump in confidence in the territory's ability to function as a world financial centre. The Cathay Bank is prepared to make a substantial injection of cash into the bank, within the hour, and we will announce that we are prepared to honour all the bank's commitments. Your customers will be able, if they wish, to use their cards at our ATMs and withdraw cash from our branches with their cheques and passbooks. Once such an arrangement becomes public, the panic will be over. The people will know that you have the resources of one of the biggest banking groups in the world behind you."

724

Fielding said nothing, but his interlinked fingers tightened on the blotter. He knew that so far he had heard only half of the deal the visitors had in mind.

The spokesman looked to the men on either side of him to check that he had their approval to continue. Again, the slight inclinations of the heads were barely noticeable. "In return the Kowloon and Canton Bank will become a member of the Cathay Bank Group."

Fielding smiled and shook his head. He fingered his wedding ring as he phrased his thoughts. "I am of course most grateful for your interest in our short-term problems," he said, choosing his words carefully. "But I can assure you the problems are short term. We hope to have lines of credit in place before our branches open for business. I can assure you, this will all blow over."

"I think you are mistaken," said the spokesman. "The Banking Commissioner has decided it would be unwise to use the exchange fund for such a purpose."

"How do you know that?" snapped Fielding.

"It is known," said the man with an easy smile. "We also know that help will not be forthcoming from the British banks. Nor will any of the American banks intervene."

"There are other options," said Fielding.

"I think you will find that any Hong Kong parties who were thinking about making a takeover bid for the bank's stock have now reconsidered their position," the man said, his dark brown eyes fixed on Fielding's. "When the stock market commences trading, your share price will collapse, causing you further liquidity problems. We offer you a way to save the situation. It is your only solution, I am afraid."

Fielding put up his hands, palms outwards, and shook his head vigorously. "No, it is out of the question," he said. "Even if I were to agree, even if the board were to accept your proposal, then it would have to go before the shareholders. And I am certain they would refuse to allow the bank to be taken over by the Cathay Bank."

The man in the Mao suit whispered into the younger man's ear and he nodded. "What we propose, Mr Fielding, is that the Cathay Bank will make a reasonable offer for the shares, or at least for a controlling percentage, based on its net assets rather than the share price. That would guarantee that the shareholders receive a fair price, certainly a much better price than they will be able to obtain in the market if you open for business the way things are. We would intend to keep the bank's listing on the Stock Exchange here, and to go for parallel listings in Tokyo and London. The shares will become more marketable as a result, and shareholders will have the option of selling to us or in the market if they are unhappy with them as an investment. No one will put a gun to their heads."

"The bank has always been independent," protested Fielding.

"By independent, you mean out of China's control," said the spokesman, coldly. "You have been perfectly willing, some might say eager, to sell your independence to a European group."

726

"That may be," said Fielding, "but there can be no question of the board recommending a takeover by the Cathay Bank."

"If you personally were to recommend it, I think you would have no problem persuading the rest of the directors," said the spokesman. "And the shareholders, like your customers, are so panic-stricken that they will clutch at any straw. I might add, Mr Fielding, that we do not anticipate any objections from the Banking Commissioner. In fact, we expect our initiative, and your acceptance of it, to be warmly welcomed by the Hong Kong administration."

Fielding felt as if the three men were inexorably forcing him into a corner.

"I have no desire to recommend your proposal be accepted by the board," he said patiently.

"We are confident that we can change your mind," said the spokesman.

Fielding snorted and leaned back in his chair. He looked pointedly at his watch, not caring if his visitors were offended by the gesture. He wanted to get back to the board meeting.

"Let us explain what we have in mind," said the spokesman. "We would be content with sixty per cent of the bank's share capital, either through a rights issue or by us buying in the market, or through a limited offer. In the meantime we would offer our unconditional support to the bank. We would expect you to stay on as chairman at an increased salary, though the day-to-day running of the bank will come under Beijing's control. The Cathay Bank will have enough directors to maintain control of the board, but you will be free to nominate several existing directors to keep their positions. We will waive the bank's traditional rules on retirement, and you will be guaranteed the chair for so long as you want it. We in China do not believe as you Westerners seem to that a man's qualities become useless after a certain age. We take the view that wisdom comes with maturity, Mr Fielding, and you may hold the post until you are ninety if you wish."

For the first time Fielding was tempted, knowing that even if the bank were to be saved by any other means, his retirement date had been set and whatever happened he would be leaving under a cloud. But he despised the way the Cathay Bank representatives were so keen to take advantage of his bank's misfortunes, and he had no wish to become a lackey of Beijing, no matter how high the salary.

"I am afraid I cannot recommend your proposal to the board," he said finally.

The spokesman whispered to the man in the Mao suit, and then to the man with the gold tooth. All three whispered in Mandarin, and then as one they stood up, extending their hands. Fielding shook hands with them all and wished them goodbye. The spokesman placed his briefcase on the desk and clicked open the locks. He opened the case and took out a video cassette, which he handed to Fielding. His two companions had already reached the door and were leaving the office.

"I will go back to my office; you can reach me at the number on my card," said the spokesman. "All I need is a phone call from you and we will make the announcement. You have heard everything we have to offer you. After viewing this, you will understand what you have to lose if you refuse us. In Hong Kong, a man's reputation, his face, is his most important asset, Mr Fielding. I need say no more. I am sorry it has come to this." He closed his case and lifted it off the desk, nodded curtly, and followed his companions out of the office.

Faith stood at the door, wearing a look of concern.

"William, are you all right?" she asked, wringing her hands like an old Chinese *amah*.

"Everything is fine, Faith," he said. "I just need a few minutes alone. Don't put any calls through."

She nodded, unconvinced, looked as if she wanted to say something, but closed the door.

Fielding walked slowly to the video recorder and slotted the cassette in. He switched on the recorder and the television set and stood in front of the screen, his arms folded across his chest, a sick feeling in the pit of his stomach. The screen was filled with black and white static and then a picture flickered up, two figures on a bed, a man and a woman. The man was in the shadows, his back to the camera, but Fielding could see he was well muscled and had jet black hair. The woman was Anne, naked on the bed, her nails scratching the man's back as she gasped and cried out. Fielding watched as his eyes filled with tears. He kept repeating his wife's name in a soft whisper, over and over.

The announcement of the takeover bid for the Kowloon and Canton Bank came thirty minutes before the bank's branches were due to open, along with details of the cash injection from the Cathay Bank. Police vans toured Hong Kong, broadcasting the details through loudspeaker vans, and Cathay Bank press releases were faxed to the local radio stations. Bank managers began hurriedly pinning notices up in the windows of their branches. Those at the front of the lines were unwilling to leave their places, sensing a trick, but others rushed to Cathay Bank branches and came back to confirm that the rival bank was indeed honouring all transactions. By the time the doors opened for business the queues had all but vanished and the riot police were standing around in small groups, their helmets off, their stun guns and batons holstered.

The stock market opened quietly. There was a flurry of selling in the first half hour, but it was mainly from orders faxed to stockbrokers overnight and the shares were snapped up by institutions. Shares in Kowloon and Canton Bank did especially well, rising ten cents by lunchtime. The announcement that the Cathay Bank was supporting the Kowloon and Canton Bank was taken as a show of Beijing's support for the whole of Hong Kong and not just the beleaguered financial institution. The Financial Secretary and the Banking Commissioner had both issued statements of support for the merger, saying that it heralded a new era of Anglo-Sino co-operation that boded well for post-1997 relations. By early afternoon Neil Coleman was back at his desk, feet up, picking his teeth with a plastic paperclip and deliberating whether or not to call Debbie Fielding and ask her how she was.

There was no need for Anthony Chung to delay the meeting. He could just as easily have gone out to the Roissy-Charles de Gaulle Airport, which was only sixteen miles or so to the north of Paris, to greet the old man. But he knew the airport was a soulless place, clinical and cold and not worthy of such a momentous occasion. The moment had to be savoured, to be tasted and enjoyed to the full. It had been a long time coming, and Chung did not want it to be spoiled by screaming children, bad-tempered departing tourists and business-men rushing for taxis or the RER trains. No, there had to be a touch of theatre about the meeting, and once Chung had given it some serious thought it was obvious where it should be: the place where it all began just six months earlier, when Chung had first set the wheels in motion and handed over the envelope to the now deceased Colonel Tyler.

He stepped out of the Métro station in the Champs-Elysées and sniffed the summer air like a mole emerging from its underground lair, blinking in the bright sunlight. His left arm was still in plaster and supported by a sling. Wong's bullet had taken a piece out of Chung's elbow and the doctors had told him that even when it had healed he'd never be able to extend it fully and it would probably give him pain for the rest of his life, especially during damp and cold weather. Chung was not bitter; it was a small price to pay for his father's freedom. And it went a long way to persuading the Hong Kong police that he had been an innocent bystander caught up in the bank robbery.

The thoroughfare was thronged with tourists: Germans, British, Japanese, and the hawkers were doing a brisk trade in cheap sunglasses and badges. There were few signs that only days earlier the avenue had witnessed the finish of the Tour de France after three gruelling weeks. The French street-cleaning system was nothing if not efficient.

The forecast for the day had been sunny with temperatures in the low seventies, and the view from his apartment in the Rue de Sèvres had borne out the meteorological forecast, so Chung had chosen a lightweight blue linen suit, a white shirt and a flowery-patterned Kenzo tie that he knew would raise his father's eyebrows if not a smile.

There was a spring in his step as he walked down the Champs-Elysées towards Fouquet's because up until he'd received the telephone call from Hong Kong he'd never quite believed that they'd let him go, that even at this late stage the old men in Beijing would go back on their word even though Chung had delivered everything as promised. It wouldn't have been the first time that they'd lied. The 4a.m. phone call had dragged him from a deep dreamless sleep and there had been a moment's confusion before he realised he was being addressed in Cantonese and not in French. It was Michael Wong calling to say that the old man had arrived on a CAAC jet from Beijing, that he was as fit and well as could be expected and that he was now somewhere high above Vietnam in an Air France 747 heading towards Paris.

"First class?" Chung had asked and Wong had snorted and laughed. Of course.

Chung looked at his watch, which he'd transferred to his right wrist, for the thousandth time since the early morning phone call. He'd arranged for a Mercedes with a Chinese driver to be at the airport to collect his father and to bring him to Fouquet's, and before he'd left the apartment he'd called the airline to check that the flight would be in on time. The plane had landed twenty minutes earlier, the old man would have had only the luggage he had carried on with him, and there would be no problems with the immigration officials; the French diplomats in Beijing had had all the paperwork ready for some time. Assuming the traffic wasn't any worse than usual, he should arrive at Fouquet's within half an hour, probably a good deal sooner.

He looked down the avenue towards Place de la Concorde. Place de la Révolution it had been called a little over 200 years ago, when the French people overthrew their cruel aristocracy and they'd killed more than 1,300 over thirteen months of terror during which the smell of blood hung like a cloud over the centre of Paris. Thirteen hundred victims in thirteen months. That had been just about the rate of killings in China in the wake of the Tiananmen Square massacre, Chung thought grimly. Most of them a single rifle bullet in the back of the neck, with the relatives of the victims being made to pay for the ammunition and the kidneys of the executed sold for transplants. The Chinese had a saying which went back centuries: Kill one, educate one hundred. The old men in Beijing had no qualms about killing as a warning. What was the population of China? One billion? So how many would have to be killed to warn them all? Ten million? Would the old men in Beijing do it? Chung snorted to himself. Without doubt, they would. They'd already killed more than one million Tibetans during their forty-year rule there. The only reason Zhong Ziming hadn't been put to death, he was sure, was because he still had friends at the top, friends who, while they weren't prepared to speak up for him, were able to wield enough influence to keep him alive.

The French had chosen the right time to overthrow their masters, Chung thought ruefully. The French aristocracy had no tanks to send into Place de la Concorde, no battalions of the People's Army to open fire on students and peasants, no media to manipulate to tell the masses of the population that what was happening was nothing more than a "counter-revolutionary rebellion". Chung wondered how the French Revolution would have fared in the twentieth century. Probably would have ended up the same as the Pro-Democracy Movement had at Tiananmen Square: mown down by submachine-guns, crushed by tanks, the bodies piled up by bulldozers and burnt in petrol-soaked pyres. Followed by secret trials without appeal and long prison sentences and executions. The French didn't appreciate how lucky they were. Or maybe they did, thought Chung. Why else would the French authorities be so keen to offer sanctuary to Chinese dissidents who feared to return to China? And it was an open secret that it was French diplomats who were responsible for getting many of the leaders of the dissident movement out of Beijing after the June 4 massacre in 1989. The French had proven themselves good friends to the Chinese dissidents, which is more than could be said for the British and Americans who paid lip service but little else.

He pushed open the door with his good arm and allowed a bow-tied waiter to lead him to a corner table where he chose a chair which allowed him to see the entrance. He ordered a chocolate. There was more than a touch of theatre about this, he knew, but he'd spent a good deal of the past six months playing one part or another and he figured that he deserved this one curtain call. He wondered how his father would look after almost six years in virtual solitary confinement. He would be over sixty now, though to be honest the old man had never really come clean about exactly how old he was. He'd been born in a small village in northern China, he claimed, but he'd been vague about most of the details of his early life, including the date of his birth. Zhong Ziming had survived as long as he had by bending with the political winds, and his lack of roots had been a valuable survival mechanism, even though it often drove Chung to distraction when all his searching questions went unanswered with a dismissive wave of a hand. Dates, names, specifics — at times it seemed as if it would be easier for Zhong Ziming to grasp mercury than to keep a firm grip on a single fact of his life.

Chung took a small tin from the pocket of his suit and winced as the movement sent a spasm of pain through his injured elbow. It was painted a glossy black with a pattern of red and gold flowers and dark green leaves. He rolled it in his hand. It contained jasmine tea, from China, and it was his father's favourite. He'd discovered it a week earlier in a gourmet food shop in the street where he lived. The chocolate arrived. Chung showed the tin to the waiter.

"I'm expecting a guest," he explained in fluent French. "An old man. When he arrives, would it be possible to bring him a pot of tea made from this? It's jasmine tea, his favourite."

The waiter, a greying man with a paunch and jowls like a bloodhound, sniffed and shrugged and began to protest that such a thing would not be possible, that if Chung would prefer a *thé citron* it could be easily provided but his eyes widened when Chung produced a 200 franc note.

"It would please an old man," Chung explained.

The waiter's protests vanished as quickly as the banknote and he took the tin box to the kitchen. That was one of the many things Chung liked about the French. Their flexibility.

He looked at his watch again and felt a tremble of anticipation in his stomach. Six years in solitary confinement. Could Anthony Chung himself have survived such an ordeal? Did he have the inner resources? He doubted it. But his father, he was different. His father had survived the upheavals of the Cultural Revolution, emerged unscathed from the purging of the Gang of Four and had thrived during the opening up of China during the early eighties. Anyone who could tread such a dangerous path should have been able to take imprisonment in his stride,

Chung told himself. His father's only mistake had been to align himself with Zhao Ziyang, the former Communist Party General Secretary who had led the students to think that China was ready for democracy. When Zhao was toppled, his father was put under house arrest. The apartment in Beijing was comfortable, and he had been allowed his own food and books, but six years without being able to talk to your friends? Could he have coped without losing his mind for six long years? And what of the last twelve months? His confinement had originally been in the relative comfort of his Beijing apartment, albeit guarded night and day by the Public Security Bureau, until Anthony Chung had approached a leading member of the Chinese government with his audacious plan. Once he'd persuaded the old men in Beijing that he was serious and he'd assured them that it would work, at no risk to themselves, then they decided to raise the stakes by moving his father to Beijing's Qincheng maximum security prison. There were no comforts there, Chung knew. Some of the cells had neither doors nor windows, just a trapdoor in a ceiling so low that standing upright was impossible, and he had often cursed himself for being responsible for his father's change in circumstances. There were times when he'd woken up in the middle of the night sweating and panting and wondering if in fact he would end up being the death of his father rather than his rescuer. All those fears were behind him now. He finished his chocolate and ordered another.

Chung was sure his father would like Paris. In many ways the French were similar to the Chinese, with their love of history, good food, and children. He'd feel at home in the crowds, too. The language was going to be a problem because his father's knowledge of French was patchy to say the least, but his English would be good enough for him to get by until he picked up the basics. Chung had made a room ready in his apartment and his father would live there until he felt settled in the city and then they'd decide together where he should live. There were many areas of the city where there were enclaves of Chinese, especially in the 13th arrondissement, where perhaps he'd feel more at home, but that was for the future. There was plenty of time.

The door opened and a waiter stepped to the side, obscuring Chung's view, then he moved and his father was there, slightly stooped, looking to the right and left like a child frightened to cross the road. Chung stood up and raised his right hand in greeting, but his father didn't seem to see him as he peered around. He wasn't wearing his glasses, Chung saw, and he wondered for how long the old man had been without them. Probably from the first day he was arrested. The Chinese authorities were like that, heaping every indignity they could upon those they wanted to break.

The old man screwed up his eyes and looked in Chung's direction. Chung moved towards his father, a smile breaking out as he got closer, then, when he was just six feet away, his father saw him and he smiled too and reached to hold him, not seeing the sling and pressing his son to his chest. The pain ripped through Chung's arm but he barely felt it. He held his father with his good arm and rested his forehead on the old man's shoulder, using the material of his jacket to wipe the tears from his cheeks. They stood together for many minutes, not speaking, and they attracted several glances from those sitting at the tables, but there were smiles, too, from those who guessed that something special was happening in the restaurant, that the meeting held some significance, the nature of which they'd never know but which none the less made them feel somehow warm. Chung kept wanting to say something but each time he tried to form words the tears flowed again and something swelled in his throat and all he could do was to swallow and hold his father.

It was Zhong Ziming who spoke first. "*Merci, mon fils*," he whispered. The accent was atrocious but Chung laughed and cried at the same time, knowing that the old man must have asked someone how to thank his son in French. It was a sign, too, that he had retained his sense of humour, despite all he'd been through.

"I never thought I'd see you again," whispered Chung, speaking in Mandarin Chinese.

Zhong Ziming took half a step back and put his hands on his son's shoulders. He looked up at his son. "I never had any doubt," he replied fiercely. "Never." For the first time he saw the sling and he frowned. "What happened?" he asked.

"A small accident," said Chung. "It's nothing. Really." He nodded towards the table. "Come sit with me," he said.

As the two men sat at the table the waiter came over and placed a small white teapot and a cup and saucer in front of Zhong Ziming. He slowly poured jasmine tea into the cup and Zhong Ziming looked at it, and then at his son, with obvious surprise.

"Jasmine tea!" he said, and again Chung felt the sting of tears. Zhong Ziming lifted the cup almost reverently to his lips, sniffed it, and then sipped, his eyes closed. When he opened them again it was with a smile of complete contentment on his face.

"Your flight was good?" Chung asked.

"Everything has been good," his father answered. "From the moment I left Beijing, everything has been perfect. The man Wong went to a lot of trouble for me. As did your friends in the French embassy. I cannot believe it. Yesterday I was Chinese. Today I am a Frenchman." He took the slim European-style passport from his jacket and put it on the table in front of him, by the side of the teapot. "I do not feel French," he said.

"You never will," said Chung. "We will always be Chinese. Always."

The old man nodded and sipped his hot tea again. "It is true," he said, almost to himself. "No matter what they do to us, we will always be Chinese. No matter how long we stay away, no matter what passport we carry or which language we speak, we can never be anything else." He shook himself as if waking from a dream, and then smiled at his son. "Still," he said, "I will become as French as is possible." The smile became a mischievous grin. "Though no matter how long I live here, my son, I doubt if I will ever get used to a tie such as that. Is that the fashion in France? Is that what the young men wear here?"

Chung shook his head and the two men laughed, though both still had damp eyes. When the laughter died down the two men sat in silence for a while. Occasionally Zhong Ziming would reach over and gently touch his son's arm, as if to prove to himself that he was really there. Chung drank his chocolate and the old man savoured his jasmine tea.

It was Chung who broke the silence first. "How much did they tell you of what I had planned?" he asked quietly.

Zhong Ziming shook his head slowly. "Almost nothing until I was freed. I knew something was happening when they came to take me from my home, but the guards refused to speak to me. A friend got a message to me in prison but it told me little more than that you were trying to secure my freedom. It was only when they allowed me to leave China that I found out exactly what you had done. Such an audacious plan. I still find it difficult to believe that you succeeded."

"I had help," said Chung.

"The man in Hong Kong, Michael Wong? He seems to be a good man. A good friend."

"No, not a friend," answered Chung. "He is a criminal, a leader of one of Hong Kong's triad organisations."

"So why did he help?"

"He got to keep a substantial portion of the money which we took from the Kowloon and Canton Bank. And he obtained certain — how should I describe them — guarantees from the Chinese government. It will not be an easy time for the triads after 1997, but Michael Wong's triad will, I believe, be finding it somewhat easier than the rest to adapt to life in the Special Administrative Region. He now has some friends in high places in Beijing."

"As do you, Juntao," said the old man.

Chung shook his head fiercely. "No," he said. "No father, you must never think that. They did not release you because I won their friendship. I gave them two things they have long coveted. I gave them control of a Western bank, and I showed the world that the British cannot maintain order in Hong Kong. As far as the world is concerned, it was only China's intervention which prevented the collapse of law and order in the colony. It will do much to wipe out the memory of what happened in Tiananmen Square in 1989. They become saviours rather than killers. It's part of the whitewash. But do not be fooled, Father. The cat might have changed colour, but it is still the same cat, and as Deng Xiaoping said, it can still catch mice. We have no friends in Beijing. None."

The old man reached over and put his hand on top of his son's. "I will not forget," he said.

Chung looked at him earnestly. "And, Father, do not think for one minute that you can continue the fight for democracy from here, that you can join the dissidents in Paris. You are in exile, but it must be a silent exile. My role in the events of the last six months must never be revealed, and your voice must never again be heard in criticism of the Chinese government. That is the deal I made. Do you understand?"

742

Zhong Ziming considered carefully what his son had said. It seemed to the old man that their roles had suddenly been reversed: that the son had become the father and the father, the son. He was being lectured by his own child, and it was not a pleasant experience. But he knew too that what his son said was the truth. The men in Beijing had a long reach, and even longer memories. He nodded slowly and squeezed his son's hand.

"I understand." He sighed. "I understand, and I agree." He looked around the crowded café and lifted the cup to his lips. "There are, I suppose, worse places to spend the winter."

The sound of laughing children echoed around the cobbled courtyard. A door was flung open and a line of youngsters filed out in pairs, little hands holding tight to other little hands, squinting in the beams of sunlight that streamed down into the corridor like spotlamps on a stage. The children skipped and ran down the stone stairs to the kitchen where they picked up large white plates and queued in front of an old wooden table where two nuns spooned fish stew and rice from steaming cauldrons. In the hospital wards other nuns in white habits wheeled trolleys and served lunch to the patients who were bedridden. Brand-new floor-mounted fans blew cooling breezes through the freshly painted wards and there was a lingering smell of disinfectant in the air.

The children in the refectory took their heaped-up plates and put them down on the long dining tables before sitting on wooden benches, their hands in their laps. When they were all seated an elderly nun led them in prayers, the children with their eyes tightly closed, mouths watering. The word "amen" had barely finished echoing around the large dining hall than the children were eating.

Sister Marie smiled at the happy children, and she was still smiling as she walked down the stone-flagged corridor to a section of the orphanage which the nuns used as administrative offices. There was more laughter coming from the main room there, deep-throated and hearty, the laughter of men.

Inside the room was a large, circular table, and on it a pile of money and cards. Around the table sat Lehman, Horvitz, Carmody and Doherty, cans of beer at their elbows as they studied their poker hands.

They looked up as they heard Sister Marie enter the room. "Can I be getting you gentlemen anything?" she asked in her soft Irish brogue.

"No, we're fine, Sister Marie," said Lehman. "How is lunch going?"

"The children have never seen so much food," said the nun. "And our larders have never been so well stocked. If I didn't know it was you gentlemen behind it, I'm sure I'd be thinking it was a miracle."

"Maybe it was," said Lehman.

"If you ask me, it was a miracle that Dan and Chuck managed to get our slick down on to that freighter," said Carmody. "I didn't even see it."

"I saw it," said Doherty, "but I never thought we'd reach it. It was an amazing piece of flying, Dan."

"It took two of us to land it," said Lehman.

"A slick?" said Sister Marie, frowning.

"A helicopter," explained Lehman. "We nearly crashed at sea. It was a close thing." He studied his cards, three tens and a pair of aces. It had been damned close, he'd never in his life been so close to death. The controls had fought and kicked all the way down, and the Huey was still spinning when it smashed into the crates on the deck of the freighter. Lehman had almost passed out, from the pain and from the loss of blood. The ship had a small crew of Filipino sailors and had been on its way to Thailand with a consignment of VCRs. They had more than enough money to bribe them to keep their mouths shut and to get ashore. The sailors had even helped to push the Huey overboard, once the vets had unloaded the gold and cash. Later, below decks, they'd counted out the loot. Five million dollars. "One million each," Lehman had said, and there had been no argument over Lewis's claim to a share. They'd travelled to Bangkok and Lehman had tracked down Josh and negotiated a new set of passports and papers for them all. Josh had heard about Tyler's grisly fate on the road to the coast, but he was prepared to work for anyone who could meet his prices. Lehman had told the rest of the vets that Lewis wanted his money to go to his son, and to help the orphanage in Ho Chi Minh City, and he'd been pleasantly surprised when they'd all agreed to go with him.

The Americans had decided that Vietnam was a good place to wait while the furore caused by the bank heist died down, and the nuns had been more than happy to

745

offer them a place to stay, partly as a gesture of thanks for the half a million dollars they'd given them, and partly because the men had been keen to offer their time, mending the leaking roof, replacing broken windows and painting the walls.

Carmody studied his hand, the cards clipped between the prongs of his claw. The eight, ten, jack, queen and king of hearts. He had told everyone he planned to go to California eventually and open a bar.

Doherty threw a hundred dollar bill into the centre of the table. He had decided to go back to Thailand, but was happy hanging around with the Americans for the time being.

Horvitz had a straight, and he saw Doherty and raised him another hundred dollars. He'd told Doherty he wanted to spend some time in Thailand, the Land of Smiles, but he'd been hatching several business plans with Carmody and it was looking increasingly like he'd be ending up in California.

It was Lehman's turn to bet, and he threw 200 dollars into the pot. Lehman wasn't sure yet what he intended to do. He knew one thing for sure: first he had to fly back to the States to talk to a small boy, and there was a college fund to be set up. Then he'd come back to Vietnam, for a while at least. He had things to do here, things that Bart would have wanted done if he'd been alive. He flicked the corners of his cards. He was looking forward to helping the nuns and their children. For the first time in a long while, he felt lucky.

746